MW00879047

Jon Christopher has written a masterpiece on many levels. It is so well written because of its simple style, done almost in a nineteenth century narrative. That is not easy to do! It is an incredibly thoughtful look at the noted warrior. Taken from one of the oldest existing poems, and one of my favorites, Jon has an in depth knowledge of the 6th century and the early history of Scandinavia and the Norsemen. His creative take on this amazing story is pure genius. This is a story that needs to be nurtured and relished: but because it is so entertaining I can't put it down! So it provides me a delightful dilemma. Being a retired Librarian, this is a book that I would highly recommend to anyone who enjoys reading excellent literature.

—D. Taylor (Author of "Bogata By Bus")

"Beowulf, The Bear's Son is a must-read. I picked up this book to read during the holidays, and just couldn't put it down.....I loved the rich and exciting descriptive narrative each chapter offered! NETFLIX would be wise to make this a series! This book's creativity from cover to cover is off the charts, and it's thought provoking moral was truly refreshing. It's like a hybrid of Don Quixote and Braveheart. Highly recommend to the young and old!"

—Navy Engineer, Silvia Faulstich

I am captivated by this book, so well written and I can't wait to get further into the story. I'm only on chapter 28....too bad I have to sleep and go to work! Even friend's that aren't into this genre are enjoying it! A must buy. I will be buying it for Christmas gifts.

—Cat Frank

"Magical!"

—Erik B., in the Sea of Cortes

"Want to know "the rest of the story?" Read this!"

—Christina

"Great reading, enjoyed the story, kept wanting it to continue..."

—Hector

A Novel
by
Jon Christopher, J.D.

SECOND EDITION

Published by Misty Bay Books ® Ojai, California

Beowulf: The Bear's Son
Collectors First Edition 2016
Second Edition 2017

Published by Misty Bay Books ®
Post Office Box 992
Ojai, California, 93024

Contact The Author
c/o
beowulfthebearsson@gmail.com

Graphic Design by Misty Bay Books®

Christopher, Jon (B. 1948---?)
BEOWULF: THE BEAR'S SON, Second Edition /
Written by Jon Christopher, J.D.
Ojai, CA: Misty Bay Books, 2017.
660 pages. Paperback; 2. 2 Lbs.

Includes Mao & 'Glossary of Names'
ISBN: 9781545145043

1. Sixth Century Norse Saga. 2. Epic Saga 3. Origin Story
4. Fiction / Fantasy. Title: BEOWULF: THE BEAR'S SON

Edition:10 9 8 7 6 5 4 3 2

AUTHOR'S INTRODUCTION TO THE SECOND EDITION

From the beginning, I have had but one goal in mind—to breathe new life into the character of Beowulf and the poem that has been his refuge for the last one-thousand years.

I attempted to do this by transforming the Work into an Origin Story while maintaining fidelity with the three essential elements of the poem: First: Beowulf's battle with the creature, Grendel on behalf of the Danish King, Hrothgar. Second: Beowulf's battle with Grendel's Dam, and Third: After fifty years as King of his tribe, Beowulf's final battle with a Fire Drake.

It is what the anonymous author of the poem does not explain or elucidate in detail that interests me. For example, the author tells us that Beowulf's father, Ecgtheow, marries King Hrethel's only daughter, but she is never named nor is there any mention of her relationship with her son. The poet tells us Beowulf possessed the strength of thirty men in each arm but never are we told how he acquired such superhuman strength. The preceding are but two of a score or more such omissions.

Hence, I provided answers to elements of the story that the poet ignored altogether; or were alluded to, but left to dangle for centuries with no explanation. I incorporated the answers that came to me into a novel which I based on; I repeat: based on, the poem, nothing more. Thus, having received permission from One-Eyed Odin and the gods of Asgard, I transformed the Work into an Origin Story with only my Muse guiding me.

Parenthetically, I stripped away references to the Christian Religion not because I am anti-Christian, but because the story is that of a Sixth Century Norse warrior, a Pagan living at a time in Scandia when the Old Gods held sway over Heaven and Earth.

So! To those who would quibble with this or that relating to what I have done, try to understand that I never set out to retell the poem in its entirety, down to every last detail of the poem's three-thousand-one-hundred-and-eighty-two lines.

"Beowulf The Bear's Son" is a retelling of a cherished work of art and was never intended to be a line by line recasting of the poem in prose narrative.

I hope the reader will feel I have given Beowulf new life while doing honor to the anonymous author of what may be the oldest extant poem in the English Language.

Jon Christopher, J.D.

CONTENTS

PART ONE

PART TWO

PART THREE

For
Seamus Heaney

1939-20

PART ONE

MIDGARD
LAPP LAND
BRONDINGS
TROLL'S NEST
FINN'S LAND
BEANSTANBÖRG
SCANDIA
SVEARLAND
MANNEN MÖRDARE
SVEAR
N
W
E
S
UPPSALA
LAKE VATTERN
GEATLAND
MÖRK SKOG
GEATS
WYLFINGS
VINDINSTEDT FOREST
FALCON'S NEST
VINDINSTEDT FARM
VÄRG SLÖTT
HELL'S GROVE
JUTES
BAY OF KRYL
MÖRK SAND
HEOROT
FRIHAMM
HARII VILLAGE
LAND'S END
DANES
FRANKS
ANGLES
POLANSKA
FRISIANS
HEATHOBARDS
GERMANIA
MAP OF THE NORTH

1

DEATH COMES CALLING

So. It was spring. Although vestiges of winter remained, the Whale Road was once more navigable. Northmen would go *aviking* in their dragon-prow boats while those who depended on the land turned their thoughts to planting and harvesting crops.

† † †

The village of Mörk Skog numbered eighty souls and was half a day's ride north of West Fall's Forest. A haze of blue smoke from a dozen cooking fires hung over huts made from stones and thatch. The smell of burning pine cones and sap permeated the air.

Inside his workshop, Uruk the metalsmith was first to see the warrior approach on a black stallion, one born and bred for war. Despite the extreme heat cast by the furnace that caused rivulets of perspiration to drip down his arms and face, the metalsmith felt a knot twist and pull at his innards, and he felt short of breath. Working the bellows the metalsmith's young son saw a look of dread spread across his father's face; then he, too, saw the warrior.

The rider sat tall in the saddle: a dark woolen cloak trailed past his shoulders. Concealing his face was a bronze helm embossed with silver, and he wore hand-forged chainmail armor that clung to broad shoulders and tapered to a narrow waist. As was the metalsmith's, the warrior's arms were thick with muscle. The boy felt a shiver travel the length of his spine. Atop the stallion, the warrior was what the boy imagined Death itself would appear when making its rounds, and he, too, became afraid. Resting the butt-end on the toe of his boot, the warrior held a spear fashioned from ash wood that had a long, iron point serrated on one edge for cutting bone. Uruk rested his hammer on the anvil and licked his dry lips.

"Keep the fire going," he said, as he started toward the rider.

"Yes, Poppa," said the boy.

The warrior saw the metalsmith approach and stopped his horse.

“I seek Uruk, the metalsmith.”

Before he glimpsed the sword strapped to the warrior’s saddle, the metalsmith felt rooted in place by the depth of the warrior’s blue eyes, visible on either side of the nose guard affixed to his bronze helm.

“I’m Uruk,” he said.

It was then that Uruk took careful note of the refined artistry that went into the creation of the spear and sword the warrior carried.

This is no ordinary man-killer, Uruk told himself.

"The plight of your village moved your King,” the warrior said. “He has granted your petition.”

Tears flooded the metalsmith’s eyes. Uruk dropped to his knees and clasped his hands together.

“Praise the gods! Thank you, my Lord! Thank you! Thank you!”

From atop the stallion, the warrior saw the contorted faces of the villagers staring at him from the relative safety of their huts. This village in the hinterland was the fifth he visited in the last twenty days. It was always the same—the looks of fear and suspicion on the faces of those he encountered while enforcing King Hygelac’s will. But the furtive stares and half-hidden glares, like the names, whispered behind his back, no longer annoyed him.

Far older than his age, Beowulf had embraced his fate twenty summers before, as a child in the wilds of Vindinstedt Forest.

He looked toward the stone well in the center of the village.

“My horse needs water.”

Inside their cave, Olf Olbermann and five of his six sons warmed themselves in front of the fire and picked at the carcasses of a hen and two rabbits. Behind Olf and his brood of thieves in the recesses of the cave, clutching each other for warmth, were two girls: one eleven, the other ten winters young. Near them were baskets of foodstuffs, the tribute from their father’s village. There was more booty as well, taken from the occasional hapless traveler passing-by on the wagon road. Shivering in the rags that their shifts had long since become, the girls were too cold and too hungry to make more than a whimper. They dared not speak; they knew to do so would invite a beating or something far worse.

Outside the cave, a light snow fell. The bandit Lord's sixth son kept vigil from inside a sturdy lean-to built to hold the elements at bay. Camouflaged with pine branches the lean-to was on an embankment inside the tree line. From that vantage point, they had an unobstructed view of the wagon road that snaked its way east and west across the frozen ground.

Olf belched; he stared past the flames of the fire at one of his sons. "Relieve Orm!"

"I'm eating," protested Bors, a stocky, full-bearded facsimile of his father.

Olf gave him a look sufficient to compel Bors to his feet. Wrapping himself in a blanket, he took an axe and a spear and left the cave.

† † †

Orm stamped his feet on the hard-packed snow. He was hungry and thought of warming himself beside the fire inside the cave. Orm heard the sound of feet crunching through the snow in his direction. He glanced over his shoulder and saw his brother, Bors. Returning his attention to the road, he saw a horse and rider come into view.

"Look," said Orm. He flicked his head toward the figure in the distance.

"I'll tell the others," said Bors.

"Don't bother, he's alone; he'll be easy pickings."

Bors thought a moment. "Let's get to it. I'm tired of eating rabbit."

They moved behind the trees that stood along the embankment parallel with the road. Both were eager to kill, warmed by the thought that soon they'd have horseflesh to devour.

The bandit Lord scratched his belly. Orm should have returned by now, he thought. He got to his feet. He was stiff, in need of stretching. Olf raised his arms and yawned. Two objects the size of melons rolled through the entrance of the cave and came to a stop at his boots—the severed heads of Bors and Orm, eyes open, mouths agape.

The bandit Lord stumbled backward.

"Get up you lazy bastards," he said. "Arm yourselves!"

His four remaining sons scrambled to their feet and in the firelight searched for their weapons. On their way outside, Olf's brood saw the heads of their brothers on the floor of the cave, and they shuddered.

As he searched for his sword and buckler, Olf could hear the sound of fierce fighting accompanied by death cries until all was again quiet. He grasped his sword and remained rooted in the center of the cave near the fire. Despite his proximity to the flames he began to shiver. For the first time in many a winter, Olf Olbermann felt dread.

There must be more than one, but how many, he wondered?

Facing the mouth of the cave, Olf felt his heart pound. The silhouette of a warrior appeared outside. As the warrior lifted back the hood of his cloak, the sunlight flashed off his polished helm. In one hand the stranger held a sword dripping blood that stained the snow crimson. Olf grabbed a knife from his waistband. Holding sword and knife poised to strike, he positioned himself near the fire and waited.

At the back of the cave, the two girls heard Olf cursing, and they crawled forward on hands and knees. They saw Olf beside the fire and the silhouette of a tall warrior as he entered the cave.

The girls held each other as the two men clashed. Olf swung his sword side to side igniting sparks in the air as blades clashed and made loud, clanging sounds in the confines of the cave. The girls cried out when Olf's right arm landed on the ground in front of them, sword in hand, fingers twitching. They clasped their hands over their ears to muffle the sound of the bandit Lord screaming until he screamed no more and there was silence.

† † †

It was midday when the metalsmith and his son saw the warrior return to the village. A strong wind swirled the snow at their feet. Sitting on the stranger's horse behind him, wrapped in his cloak, were Uruk's daughters.

"Elsa," said the metalsmith, "Our girls have returned to us."

His wife ran to the well where the warrior was lifting the girls to the ground. Hearing the metalsmith's family shouting, the villagers left their huts to see what had occurred. They could not believe their eyes, that one warrior had prevailed against the murderous Olf Olbermann and his six sons. Before Uruk's wife hastened away with her daughters, she took each of the stranger's blood-stained hands into her own and kissed them.

"How can we thank you?" said Uruk.

"Remain loyal to Hygelac, your king," the warrior said.

"By all the gods, we shall; I swear it," said Uruk, careful to look his King's assassin in the eyes.

The wind began to pick up. Impatient to leave, the warrior's stallion struck the ground with one of its hooves.

"A league from here you'll find a cave," said the stranger. "It's up an embankment just inside the tree line. Take your carts. Inside the cave, you'll find food, weapons, and booty. I suggest you go while my tracks remain visible."

"But what about—"

"They won't trouble you again," said the warrior.

The two girls came running from their parents' hut. Their mother had scrubbed their faces and replaced their rags with clean shifts. In their hands, the girls carried smoked salmon wrapped in dill weed and cheesecloth and a fresh loaf of rye bread. They stopped alongside the warrior and held up their gifts. The warrior looked at the girls and nodded. He took the food they offered and placed it inside a saddle bag; then he started away in the direction from which he first came.

"We don't know your name," said Uruk.

The warrior said something the metalsmith's ears could not make out in the howling wind. Uruk looked at his son.

"What did he say his name was?"

"Beowulf," said the metalsmith's son.

"Great Odin's beard! The bear's son—here!"

Seven words Uruk would repeat throughout the day, and for a long time to come.

2

TWENTY SUMMERS EARLIER

Twenty summers before Beowulf Waegmunding rode into the village of Mörk Skog; he stood with his mother outside the stake wall that surrounded Vindinstedt farm. Together they watched Beowulf's father, Ecgtheow, ride away in the direction of Falcon's Nest on the west coast of Väster, or Western Geatland. Seven winters young, Beowulf was tall for his age, with hair blacker than a raven, and he had Liv's eyes—"blue chips of ice" Ecgtheow called them.

When Ecgtheow turned, looked back and waved, Beowulf raised the wooden sword he held with both hands and waved it back and forth.

"When will Poppa come home?"

"As soon as he can," said Liv.

"Is he going to see Grandpoppa?"

"Yes."

"How come we can't go?"

Liv bent, kissed Beowulf on the cheek and smiled. "Because your father needs us here."

"Why?"

"To protect our farm."

"From who?"

Liv knew her son would not relent until he got answers to his questions. Beowulf lowered his wooden sword to his side. They would stand there just as they always did each time Ecgtheow went away until his receding silhouette was no longer visible.

"You're sad again, aren't you, Mamma?"

Liv swept several strands of Beowulf's hair away from his face. Looking into his eyes, she marveled at the way they probed her thoughts. *I've never lied to him before,* she told herself, *I won't begin now.* "Yes, my beautiful boy," said Liv, "I'm sad."

"Can we go to Frigga's shrine later?"

"Would you enjoy that?"

"Yes, Mamma," said Beowulf, "you're happy when you're there."

Liv smiled and took Beowulf by the hand.

"Come, little prince," she said, "I'll make your breakfast."

† † †

Beleaguered by the matter before him, with a loud sigh King Hrethel closed his eyes and slumped against the back of his throne. A servant added hot water and salt to the basin where the old King's feet rested. None of the news to reach Hrethel's ears that day was gladdening. Raiders prowling the unmarked border between Väster Götaland and Öster, or Eastern Götaland, had waylaid another ox train on its way to the port of Frihamm. Hrethel's weary eyes blinked open; he looked at his youngest son, Hygelac, a thoughtful, quick-witted young man devoted to his father.

"Where are your brothers?" said Hrethel. "Where's Herebeald and Haethcyn? They should be here."

"They left the Citadel this morning, my King," said Hygelac.

"For where?"

"They said they were going to hunt boar," said Hygelac.

"They're poking whores more likely," said Hrethel.

"I don't know," said Hygelac. *Yes,* Hygelac thought; *they're hunting young women, Father, but they'd come at me with fists flying were I to confirm your suspicions.*

Hrethel snapped his fingers.

Lord Magnus, Captain of the Kungens Vakter, the king's Personal Guard, approached with Naegling, the Sword of Kings. Magnus placed that storied heirloom in its sheath across Hrethel's legs. Holding the sword of his father, what the kings of Geatland each held before him. That cherished blade across his lap soothed old Hrethel's nerves during times of crisis.

Alongside Hygelac stood Hrethel's adviser in matters of commerce and diplomacy, a former slave, an Angle named Ragmund. While going abroad across the Whale Road, King Hrethel, much younger and robust then, led a raiding party into Germania. He found Ragmund left for dead with a severed Achilles tendon on the bank of the Elbe River near a village the Thunder-Geats had attacked and plundered.

Hrethel pitied the boy. He saw to it that Ragmund's wounds were healed, gave him sanctuary, a home, and his freedom, on condition that Ragmund remains at the Citadel as Hrethel's servant and confidante.

Ecgtheow Waegmunding stood to one side of the dais; aware

Hrethel was perplexed. Chief of Clan Waegmunding, Ecgtheow took immense pride being the warrior his king most relied on, much to the displeasure of Hrethel's oldest sons, Herebeald and Haethcyn. Ecgtheow's keen mind for strategy, and his skill, with spear, axe, and sword, was known throughout all Götaland—east and west. It was Ecgtheow who enforced Hrethel's will and did so with a penchant for ferocity that had made him notorious and served his tribe well when squeezed by their larger, more powerful neighbors.

Ecgtheow studied the look on Hygelac's face as the young prince watched his father grapple with the matter before him.

It's a pity Hygelac is Hrethel's last born, thought Ecgtheow. *As a man, he stands head and shoulders above his brothers.*

"Can anyone tell me who these outlaws are?" said Hrethel. His voice flat, void of energy.

Hygelac stepped forward.

"I cannot say with certainty, my King," said Hygelac, "but the raiders must be in the Dark Queen's employ. Why else would they act so close to Frihamm?"

"As you say, my son, you lack certainty," said Hrethel, "but what you suggest is plausible."

Hygelac bowed and stepped back.

"Tell me what these thieves took, Ragmund," said Hrethel. "

No matter that I told him but a short while ago thought Ragmund, *it goes into his one good ear and out the other.*

Dragging his bad leg behind, Ragmund shuffled forward. Holding a piece of parchment, he cleared his throat and recited from what he'd written:

"The raiders made off with two carts, each cart carrying ten bushels of barley."

"That's not so bad," said Hrethel.

Hearing what seemed was the good news, Hrethel relaxed his grip on Naegling.

"Hah! I hope the bastards choke on it," said the old king.

"There's more, your Grace," said Ragmund.

"Oh," said Hrethel; he slumped as before against his throne.

"Additionally," said Ragmund, "Clan Eriksson reported the loss of six carts, each loaded with six barrels of mead. In total, the loss stands at eight carts, plus the chattels therein, and sixteen oxen."

"Oxen?" said Hrethel.

"Yes, Great King," said Ragmund, "That pulled the carts."

"Of course, of course," said Hrethel, "I'd forgotten about them. Tell me again, Ragmund, whose goods the thieves took this time?"

Hrethel's memory grows worse with age thought Ecgtheow. *If my mind turns on me the way Hrethel's has against him, may the All Father grant me a quick death in battle.*

"Clan Eriksson's," said Ragmund.

"Is Stenn Eriksson here?" said Hrethel.

"No, Great King, he was murdered by the raiders."

"Too bad," said Hrethel, "How many others did they kill?"

"None," said Ragmund. "Stenn Eriksson's first born is here; he's waiting in the antechamber to see you. Shall I have him brought in?"

Before Hrethel could reply, Hrethel's sons, Herebeald and Haethcyn entered the Throne Room and did do so out of breath. They approached the dais, bowed to their father, then stood alongside Hygelac.

"We came as soon as we heard the news, Father," said Herebeald, the oldest son.

"Where were you hunting," said Hrethel, "when the news, as you say, reached you?"

Herebeald looked at Haethcyn.

"We decided to postpone hunting," said the middle son, Haethcyn.

"That's right, Father," said Herebeald, "we stayed in Falcon's Nest and priced horses from Land's End."

"Priced horses, you say?" said Hrethel.

"Yes, Father," said Herebeald.

Haethcyn turned toward Ragmund. "Why is Knut Eriksson outside?"

"He came to petition your king for relief," said Ragmund. "It was his father's chattels thieves stole outside Frihamm."

Herebeald snickered. "Iron Jaw's a worse pain in the arse than his father if you can believe it."

Hygelac remained quiet as his brothers laughed. Hrethel's hand signaled for silence.

"The father died protecting what belonged to Clan Eriksson," said Hrethel. "Show the son respect. Bring him in, Ragmund."

Ragmund bowed and shuffled off.

For pity's sake, Ragmund told himself, *why can't Hrethel send Lord Magnus to summon young Eriksson; he knows it pains me to walk this late in the day.*

The aged king gave Ecgtheow Waegmunding a look that needed no words behind it; Hrethel was beside himself for the lack of a solution.

Ragmund returned with a young man who, at eighteen, still had the blush of youth in his otherwise pale cheeks. He also had a square, protruding jaw, and a cleft chin. Knut Eriksson bowed to his king. As he straightened, Knut's eyes darted around the Throne Room. This visit was his first visit to the Citadel, the stone fortress on the heights overlooking the city, and as close as he'd ever come to his king. Knut licked his lips. He knew enough to bow to Herebeald, Haethcyn, and Hygelac.

"We're sorry for the loss of your father," said Hrethel. "Stenn was an able warrior."

"Thank you, my King," said Knut.

"Tell his Grace what happened," said Ragmund, "Just as you described it to me."

Knut drew a deep breath: "We came to Falcon's Nest six days ago, my King, and sold almost all our barley. When my father learned he could sell our mead for double, maybe triple the price in Frihamm, he decided to take it there."

Herebeald and Haethcyn each raised a hand to their mouth to stifle forced yawns at Knut Eriksson's expense. Hygelac elbowed Herebeald and cast an angry look at Haethcyn, urging them to stop.

"Continue," said Hrethel, none too pleased by the antics of his oldest sons.

"Yes, my King," said Knut. "We were maybe three leagues from the coast when raiders ambushed us. Their shields bore neither insignias or tribal markings. My father tried to bargain; he offered them half of what we had if they would let us pass. The one who led them just laughed; then he drove his sword through my father's throat. We were too few, and they were too many. It shames me to say it, my King, but we fled."

"I have a question for young Eriksson," said Ecgtheow."

"Ask," said Hrethel.

"Who told your father he could sell his mead for double or triple the price, by taking it to Frihamm?"

"A Bronding we sometimes see in the farmers' market at Land's End," said Knut. "He said the flooding in Öster Götaland and Germania has caused a scarcity of rye and barley leaving very little beer or mead in the east. When my father asked him how he knew this was true, the Bronding told us he was a buyer who sees and hears things while traveling the coast for the benefit of his employer, a Roman merchant named—"

"Gaius Aurelius," said Ecgtheow, interrupting.

"Yes," said Knut, "named... Gaius Aurelius."

Hrethel lifted his hands into the air. "By all the gods, what has any of this to do with a small band of thieves? Gaius Aurelius commands the Roman Emperor's Imperial Gold Ship."

"Forgive me, my King," said Knut, "I know nothing of the man Lord Waegmunding named, but it was no small band of thieves who attacked us. The raiders numbered between forty and fifty, maybe more; they wore armor, and their horses were well bred."

Herebeald stepped forward and faced Knut. "Were you and your kinsmen so bedazzled by their horses and armor that you couldn't let loose a single arrow at them?"

The blush in Knut's cheeks deepened to crimson.

"There were ten of us, my Prince," said Knut, "with no more than two swords between us."

Hot, angry tears pooled behind Knut's eyes.

"Once we reached Frihamm, my father intended to hire Berserkers, as many as he could afford, to prevent the very thing that happened to us."

So angry had Knut become, his body shook.

"Berserkers," said Hygelac, "are animals with names. Lunatics dressed in wolf skins if dressed at all!"

"Yes, Prince Hygelac," said Knut, "and I would part with my right hand had I ten Berserkers with us that day."

Ecgtheow stepped up to Knut; he placed both hands on the young man's shoulders, calming him where he stood.

"Braver men than you," said Ecgtheow, "have run from less a threat. Gather your breath. No one can fault you who wasn't there himself."

Ecgtheow cast a sharp glance at Hygelac's older brothers.

"Well put, Ecgtheow," said Hrethel. "You may go, son of Stenn."

"Thank you, my King," said Knut. He bowed and turned to leave.

"I've one more question," said Ecgtheow.

Hrethel nodded. Knut had already stopped and was looking at Ecgtheow.

"I know after such things happen," said Ecgtheow, "they can be difficult to recollect, but is there anything about the raiders' leader you can tell me?"

Knut thought a moment.

"He wore a hooded cloak over his armor, and his helm concealed his face. I'm sorry, Lord Waegmunding, but apart from that, I can't say I saw his person."

"Take a moment," said Ecgtheow; "and forget his face. Is there anything about him that stood out; something you noticed, above all else?"

"Yes," said Knut, "there is something else I remember. On the first finger of his sword-hand, he wore a blood-red stone, big and round as a baby's nose, that flashed when it caught the sunlight."

3

THE DIE IS CAST

Ecgtheow nodded. "I've no more questions."

Knut bowed and left Hrethel's Hall.

"Tell me, Ecgtheow, what am I to make of this? Three ox trains waylaid by these—whatever they are."

"I agree with young Eriksson," said Ecgtheow, "I don't believe the raiders are a ragtag band of thieves, my King."

"I agree," said Hrethel, "after hearing the way young Eriksson described them."

"Why should we trust what Iron Jaw says?" said Herebeald.

"Herebeald's right," said Haecythn, "who knows what Iron Jaw saw; he ran from the fray. He said so himself."

"I care nothing," said Hygelac, "for Knut Iron Jaw; he's a smuggler like his father was, and he shirks from paying taxes, but that doesn't mean he didn't see what he says he saw."

"If I may, Great King," said Ragmund.

"Yes," said Hrethel, "speak."

"What strikes me as significant, Great King," said Ragmund, "young Eriksson saw what the owners of the first two ox trains reported: well-armed riders, using harsh terrain to mask their numbers, and each time striking within two leagues of Frihamm."

"Are you suggesting the Dark Queen is behind this?" said Hrethel.

"Not at all, Great King," said Ragmund. "Modryth's Queendom depends on the Geatfolk, Väster Geats and Öster Geats alike. Her wealth derives from the taxes she levies on the sale of every pig, horse, a bolt of cloth or bushel of barley that changes hands and goes out across the Whale Road from Frihamm. I won't say she doesn't have a hand in this mischief, but I believe someone else directs it."

"What say you, Ecgtheow?" said Hrethel.

"I agree with Ragmund. Modryth is too smart, my King to risk fouling her nest, but I'll wager my grandfather's sword, Stenn

Eriksson's mead is being drunk in Frihamm this very moment.That, or…"

"That, or what?" said Hrethel.

"The Dark Queen knows that with rye and barley a scarcity in Eastern Götaland, the price of mead will leap skyward. That's when the thieves will unload the mead they stole—to whoever bids highest."

"How do you know they'll do that?" said Herebeald.

"Because, my Prince," it's what I'd do."

"Please tell us, Lord Waegmunding," said Ragmund, "why King Amunwolf would allow the Dark Queen to steal inside his domain? Wylfings, too, are Geatlanders; it makes no sense for them to take from their kind."

"No, Ragmund," said Ecgtheow, "it makes perfect sense. You've lived among us long enough to know Wylfings are not the same as us; neither in their customs nor what they value most. What's more, Amunwolf has no fewer than sixty Longships and can muster two-thousand men-at-arms in a fortnight."

"What are you saying?" said Hygelac.

"Yes," said King Hrethel; "what do you mean?"

Ecgtheow turned toward Hrethel. "Amunwolf doesn't fear the Thunder-Geats, my King; he tolerates us."

"Then you'll have to explain it better, Ecgtheow," said Hrethel, "because it makes no sense to me. It's true, the Wylfings are several times our number, but why risk war over such a thing as mead?"

"Young Eriksson suggested a likely answer, my King," said Ecgtheow, "when he mentioned the flooding in Germania, and Öster Götaland. Wylfings aren't farmers; they're warriors and herdsmen. When not going aviking to steal, they raise cattle to barter. To make beer, they need barley and to make mead they need honey bees. When was the last time you heard that King Amunwolf was husbanding honey bees, and brewing mead?"

Hrethel's sons erupted with laughter, so did Hrethel; he enjoyed a good joke as much as any conscientious king. Hrethel knew Amunwolf ruled his Kingdom with a cold heart and an iron fist. Over the course of three decades, Amunwolf had brought the bickering tribes in Eastern Götaland together with his unbending will, coupled with backstabbing and bloodletting. The image of

King Amunwolf husbanding bees or otherwise engaged in the non-lethal business of making mead was worthy of a good laugh and Hrethel needed something to lift his spirits. Nevertheless, laughter is a short lived thing, and the silence that filled Hrethel's ears when that moment of mirth died away was deafening. Moreover, it brought the King of the Thunder-Geats back to the problem staring him in the face; finding who was responsible for plundering his people and bringing them to justice. Hrethel was perplexed; it showed in the deep creases that appeared on his forehead.

"Think about it, my King," said Ecgtheow, "In Öster Götaland, the Wylfings are facing shortages of rye and barley. Much that was pasture is flooded or has turned to mud, making it unfit for their cattle to graze. They'll let tribes unaffected by the flooding grow and cultivate what they need; then they'll take it for themselves if they can."

The anger building in Hrethel brought color to his face. He slammed his fists on the armrests of the throne.

"To Helheim with Amunwolf," said Hrethel, "to Helheim with the Wylfings! I won't suffer any more of this! Ragmund—send word to the Clan Chiefs. Summon every man and boy old enough to fight; tell them to gather at Falcon's Nest!"

"At once, Great King," said Ragmund, "But—" Ragmund stopped himself.

"But, what?" said Hrethel.

Ragmund wilted. He slunk back and almost tripped over himself.

"Nothing, Great King," said Ragmund. "Forgive me; I'll have word sent at once."

"We need evidence," said Ecgtheow, drawing everyone's attention.

"Say, what?" said Hrethel.

"You've heard our suspicions, my King, but no one here can prove the matter. Before you commit us to a war we're unprepared for, allow me to gather evidence; something I can put before you to consider."

Hrethel sat on his throne and breathed a full breath.

"Very well, Ecgtheow," said Hrethel. "Find out what you can. Either way, I want these raiders sent to Hel. Let the Queen of the dead judge them."

"I understand," said Ecgtheow. "Before I take my leave, my King, I would ask a favor."

"Ask," said Hrethel.

† † †

Beowulf watched his mother light incense and candles. Inside the shrine, Liv had already cut and prepared the choicest parts of the meat she brought with her to place before the effigies of the gods of Asgard.

"You pray a lot to Frigga and Thor," said Beowulf.

Liv smiled at Beowulf as she washed her hands. "I pray to all the gods, little prince."

"Yes," said Beowulf. "I know you do, but you pray mostly to Frigga and Thor."

Liv stopped what she was doing. "You're right. I often pray to Frigga and Thor."

"Why?" said Beowulf.

"Your father is Geatland's greatest warrior. Thor, Lightning Bringer, and Hammer Bearer is the god of war, so I pray to him that he protect your poppa and help him vanquish our enemies."

"Vanquish?" said Beowulf. "What does that mean, Mamma?"

Liv took a moment before answering. "When I say vanquish, I mean, kill."

"Dead?" said Beowulf.

"Yes, my son—dead!"

"Dead as the goat we brought?"

"Yes."

"And who are our enemies?" said Beowulf.

"Those who would do harm to our tribe and us."

"One day I will be a warrior like Poppa."

Liv felt the breath go out of her. "Yes," she said. "One day you will serve our king as a warrior the way your father does."

"Tell me about Frigga, Mamma."

"Frigga is the All Father's wife and all-seeing warrior goddess of wisdom, and Magic. Frigga can see what is destined and although she cannot change Fate, her powers of Magic are such that she can change that shape of what is to come. I pray to Frigga to watch over you and your father and to bless our clan with healthy children and abundant harvests, so we do not go without, in winter."

"Then I will pray to Thor, Lightning Bringer, and Frigga, too."

"That pleases me," said Liv. She bent down and kissed Beowulf on the head.

† † †

Ecgtheow sat at the banquet table in what was the Main Lodge—his lodge. He sipped from a horn of ale and listened to his younger brothers, Einar and Elifr, talk in low voices with their cousin, Weohstan. The plan Ecgtheow put forward was something he wanted his kinsmen to deliberate without him looking on or otherwise influencing their decision.

"My father, as did yours," said Weohstan, "died at the Battle on the Ice, defending our tribe against the Svear. Today, the Svear are more powerful and a greater threat to us than before."

"True, said Ecgtheow, "King Ongentheow's desire to rule all Scandia remains unabated. But when we four became the sole defenders of our clan, even though we were mere boys, we did so for all of Gotaland—Väster and Öster Gotaland, both. But the Svear are not our king's present concern; it's these raiders and, simply put, he wants them dead."

"Then we may as well go to war with the Iron Wolf and be done with guessing who's behind it," said Einar.

"But we don't know," said Elifr, "if Amunwolf is behind these thefts."

"Our King's wishes aside," said Weohstan, "the Svear lay claim to all of Scandia. Their king even has his eyes set on Daneland, and Zealand, since they're but a day's sailing from our port at Land's End. It's Onegentheow we should concern ourselves with."

"You're right in what you say, Weohstan," said Ecgtheow, "and each time Onegentheow asserts his will to conquer all of Scandia, time and again, we Thunder-Geats, along with the Spear Danes, Sea Brondings and Wylfings have sent the Svear back to Uppsala with their tails between their legs. To thwart Onegentheow's ambition, we may need the Wylfings again, especially their horse warriors. But right now, we need to put king Hrethel's mind to rest, and deal with these thieves who menace commerce traveling through Hell's Grove."

Not one to put his kinsmen into harm's way, not without giving them the ultimate say in the matter, Ecgtheow got up, walked away from the table and stretched. When Ecgtheow heard the sound of children laughing in the distance, he set aside thoughts of impending war, went to the door, opened it and stepped outside into the fresh air.

He saw Weohstan's wife, Ursula, and his brothers' wives, Alfhildr and Bothilda. They were returning from a walk with several children. The oldest child was his cousin Weohstan's son, Handscio, seven winters young. The children charged through the Main Gate past the stake wall, followed by their mothers. At the sight of Ecgtheow, Handscio laughed and charged forward, fast as his little legs could carry him.

Strange, Ecgtheow told himself, not to see Beowulf and Handscio together.

"Cousin Ecgtheow," said Handscio, "make me fly."

Ecgtheow knelt and opened his arms. Handscio launched himself into the air. Ecgtheow lifted Handscio overhead and twirled him around before placing his feet on the ground; something he found himself doing for each of the other children who were jumping up and down, waiting their turn to "fly."

When the last of the children had flown, "Enough, enough," said Ecgtheow. "Inside, there are milk and honey cakes. Now, shoo, you beggars. Shoo!"

Squealing with pleasure at the thought of what awaited them, the children scampered toward the lodge. The mothers followed the children inside. Weohstan's wife, Ursula, stopped alongside Ecgtheow.

"Liv told me to tell you she'll be home soon. She's attending to Frigga's shrine."

"When is she not?" said Ecgtheow.

"Liv's devotion to the Gods doesn't make her less devoted to you, Ecgtheow Waegmunding."

Ecgtheow knew Ursula was right. Chastened, he nodded. Ursula continued inside as the other three Waegmunding men were on their way out. The sounds of children laughing and yelling as they pillaged honey cakes and a flagon of milk drove Weohstan, Einar, and Elifr to retreat to where they could hear themselves think. Last to exit from the lodge, Weohstan gave Ursula a swift pat on her buttocks as she passed; then he closed the door behind. Ecgtheow gave his cousin and brothers a look that mirrored the seriousness of the matter he left them to debate among themselves.

"You've not had much time to think it over," said Ecgtheow, "just the same; I want to hear your thoughts."

"We've talked it over, and we're with you," said Weohstan. "Just tell us what you want us to do."

† † †

The shrine was located deep within a grove of Linden trees. Liv placed additional offerings of food and drink on the altar and was about to leave when she saw Ecgtheow approach on horseback. Beowulf saw his father and ran to greet him. Close to his chest, Beowulf clutched a rag doll sewn in the floppy likeness of a long-eared rabbit.

Just as they had done many times before, Ecgtheow reached an arm down, scooped Beowulf off the ground, kissed him on both cheeks and placed him on the stallion. Beowulf craned his head around and looked at his father.

"Reins, Poppa," he said, and he thrust the doll against his father's chest.

Ecgtheow smiled as he took hold of the rabbit. "Ah," said Ecgtheow, "You steer Rain Dancer, and I carry Uncle Rabbit, is that it?"

"Yes, Poppa," said Beowulf.

Ecgtheow placed the reins into Beowulf's hands.

"Hold tight," he said, "but don't pull. Rain Dancer knows the way."

"Yes, Poppa. I know what to do."

Ecgtheow halted the stallion. He knew better than to walk on sacred ground unwashed and armed and, at that particular moment, he was both. As Liv left the environs of the shrine and walked toward him, Ecgtheow felt his chest swell with the love he felt for her, King Hrethel's daughter.

Liv stopped alongside the stallion; she caught sight of the doll in her husband's hand and laughed. He gave Uncle Rabbit to her.

"How long has my son played with dolls?" he said. "What happened to the wooden sword I made him?"

"He doesn't play with dolls," Liv said. "Handscio gave him Uncle Rabbit for saving Handscio from a Fire Drake yesterday while you were in Falcon's Nest. As for the sword you made him, I had to take it away."

"Why?" said Ecgtheow.

"Because he almost poked Handscio's eye out while they were playing kings and dragons."

"So?"

"So?" repeated Liv. "It happened right in front of Ursula."

"Oh," said Ecgtheow.

"You're leaving again, aren't you?" she said.

Ecgtheow extended his free hand. Liv took hold of his arm, and he pulled her up, onto the back of the stallion. Liv wrapped her arms around Ecgtheow's waist. Rain Dancer needed no urging; he turned and started away from the grove.

Beowulf laughed. 'Look, Mamma! I have the reins!"

"Yes, my love, I see you. Such a big boy you are."

Ecgtheow didn't need to see Liv's face to be aware of the sadness come upon her; he could feel it as she leaned forward against his back and clung to him.

† † †

While Liv and Ecgtheow sponged each other's body in the steaming hot spring, Beowulf sat near the pool fed by a waterfall and laughed each time a trout broke the surface to snatch a morsel from his fingers. He knew Liv and Ecgtheow were watching him and he could sense what they were feeling. They weren't happy—not the way Beowulf wanted them to be, and he knew it was because his father was leaving again—soon.

"When?" said Liv.

"Soon," said Ecgtheow.

"This is my father's doing, isn't it?" she said.

"I do what I do for our tribe, Liv, and for you and our son, not just for your father."

"I know that," said Liv. "But that doesn't mean I have to like it."

"I'm not asking you to like it; just don't make leaving more difficult than it already is."

Liv straddled Ecgtheow. When their lips parted, Liv opened her eyes and looked into his: "Just come back to us," she said.

They saw Beowulf watching them with a child's wise comprehension.

4.

HEL'S GROVE

Accompanied by Prince Hygelac, King Hrethel arrived at Vindinstedt farm with his Personal Guard a day after Ecgtheow departed. It thrilled Beowulf to see the KungensVakter atop their war horses, and the sound the pennants attachedto their spears made, flapping in the breeze.

Liv saw the weariness in her father's face as Lord Magnus, Captain of the Kungens Vakter, assisted his king to the ground.

"Grandpoppa," said Beowulf. He ran ahead of his mother to where his Grandfather stood with outstretched arms.

"Where is he?" said Hrethel. He winked at Liv. "Where's my grandson, Beowulf?"

"Here I am, Grandpoppa," said Beowulf. He threw his arms around the old king's legs.

"What?" said Hrethel. "You can't be my grandson, Beowulf."

"Yes, I am, Grandpoppa. See? It's me."

"Oh, no," said Hrethel. "My grandson is just a little fellow, no taller than King Salmon is long. You can't possibly be him."

"But it is me, Grandpoppa. I promise."

Liv stepped to her father's side and kissed Hrethel on both cheeks.

"Welcome, Father-King, to Vindinstedt Farm."

"Thank you, daughter," said Hrethel.

"Hello, brother," said Liv to Hygelac. "You look well."

"As do you, sister. You're even more beautiful than when you last visited Falcon's Nest."

"Mamma! Tell Grandpoppa and Uncle Hygelac it's me," said Beowulf.

Hrethel and Hygelac laughed. To the amazement of both Liv and her brother, Hrethel lifted Beowulf into his arms and kissed him.

"I know it's you, little Prince," said Hrethel. "And so big you are now."

"Yes," said Liv. And too heavy for you to be holding him."

She took Beowulf from her father's arms and put him on the ground. "You shouldn't be lifting him—not with your back the way, it is."

"Nonsense," said Hrethel. "I'm as strong as ever, and my back is fine."

Liv and Hygelac looked at each other and rolled their eyes.

"Of course, Father," said Liv. "Now come inside and rest. Then, you and Hygelac can tell me what brings you here."

"You wouldn't happen to have any honey cakes inside—would you?" said Hrethel.

"Perhaps," said Liv. She looked at Hygelac and grinned: "There may even be some Lingonberry jam and cold milk inside."

"Then what are we waiting for," said Prince Hygelac. "Would it make you happy to ride on my back, little Nephew?"

"Oh, yes," said Beowulf.

† † †

Wearing a gray woolen tunic beneath his cloak, Ecgtheow looked over his shoulder at the ox train that followed. The train numbered twenty carts, all from Clan Waegmunding's four farms, each with a driver, each pulled by a team of oxen, and each with its contents covered by a colored tarp made of woven wool, the same as sailcloth.

After three days traveling, Vindinstedt Farm was well behind them to the west. Another three, perhaps four more days, Frihamm, on the southeast coast of Öster Götaland, would be in sight. To reach it they had to follow a well-worn wagon road through a dense patch of woods known as Hell's Grove, so named in honor of Loki's daughter, Hel, Goddess of the Underworld.

Frihamm was a seedy port town ruled by the Dark Queen; a place where traders could strike bargains, purchase protection and move merchandise across the Whale Road with little to fear but Fate. Ecgtheow's face was somewhat familiar in Frihamm. His reputation preceded him, and no doubt helped keep him alive, no less than his considerable skill with spear, axe, and sword. Whispers of "assassin" no longer bothered Ecgtheow, no more than the muttering and sputtering of loose-lipped drunkards in brothels and taverns. Such was Ecgtheow Waegmunding's lot: to be hated by many, feared by most; reviled by his enemies; a man with few friends outside his clan—a man who cherished his wife and child and the heat of battle, above all else in life.

† † †

While Hygelac entertained Beowulf with swordplay outside in the Common Area near the well, Liv sat with Hrethel inside at the banquet table. After he had his fill of honey cakes smeared with Lingonberry jam washed down with fresh milk, Liv combed morsels of honey cake from her father's beard.

"Hygelac looks well, and so handsome he's become. I'm surprised he hasn't taken a wife."

"Ha," said Hrethel. "There'll be plenty of time for that. Right now I need your brother as he is—attentive to the needs of our tribe."

"What of Herebeald and Haethcyn?" said Liv. "How are they?"

"Worthless. You'll see that for yourself soon enough. Your brothers are the same dim-witted ne'er-do-wells they've always been."

Liv waited a moment.

"Why are you here, Father?"

"You're my daughter. Beowulf is my only grandson. Aren't you glad to see me?

"Of course I am," said Liv. "But I have never known you to do anything on a whim."

"True," said Hrethel. "Was not on a whim that I came, my daughter."

"Ecgtheow asked you to come—didn't he?"

"Yes," said Hrethel.

"Why?"

"Ecgtheow asked me to foster father Beowulf while he's away."

"What danger does my husband face, Father? For him to ask that of you, you must have sent him into Hell itself."

"There is always danger when Ecgtheow goes about my business, daughter. If there were a Thunder Geat who could better enforce my will, I would send them instead; but there isn't one.

Ecgtheow is Geatland's greatest warrior. He is feared, not just by a few, but by all who seek my ruin and an end to our tribe. I gave Ecgtheow my word that I would look after you and his son—my grandson. And that is what I intend to do."

† † †

As they neared Hell's Grove, Ecgtheow rested the palm of his right hand on the pommel of his sword and glanced skyward. The sun was overhead. Barring the unforeseen, the ox train would reach Frihamm before nightfall.

Ecgtheow looked side to side; he knew this stretch of woods:

Perfect for an ambush, he thought.

The ground on either side of the road sloped upward, dense with trees whose branches blocked the sunlight and left the ground steeped in perpetual shadow.

Ecgtheow had not ridden much further when a lone rider bolted from cover. Ecgtheow halted and raised his hand, signaling the drivers of the oxen to stop.

The stranger wore a cloak that covered his helm and upper body, but Ecgtheow could see it: a blood red stone on the forefinger of the rider's right hand, sparkling in the sunlight. The rider halted his horse less than ten paces from Ecgtheow.

"Leave the carts and depart," said the stranger.

Ecgtheow lifted back the hood of his cloak.

"Now why would I do that?"

The rider whistled. From places of concealment, forty raiders brandishing spears appeared on horseback and took positions on both sides of the ox train.

"I'll have to signal my drivers," said Ecgtheow.

"Then do it, fool!" said the raiders' leader, "Before I change my mind and kill you—all of you."

Ecgtheow reached down and took hold of a ram's horn tied to his saddle. He lifted the horn to his lips and blew. The shrill sound carried through the air, prompting the drivers to throw back the tarps that covered their carts.

The tarps came off. In each cart, three warriors holding bows, sixty warriors in all, stood as one and loosed their arrows at the raiders. At the same time from the rear of the train, Weohstan and Ecgtheow's brothers, Einar and Elifr rode their horses at a gallop to join the fight. Caught by surprise, the raiders, those who Ecgtheow's men didn't kill outright, had nowhere to go but back up the sides of the ravine for the shelter of the woods.

Ecgtheow drew his sword and urged Rain Dancer forward. Before the raiders' leader could react, Ecgtheow rested the point of his sword against the leader's throat, breaking the skin, causing blood to trickle down his neck. Their swords wet with blood, Weohstan, Einar, and Elifr rode to Ecgtheow's side.

"How many more men have you?" said Ecgtheow.

"Just those you saw escape," said the leader.

Ecgtheow lowered his sword.

"You plundered an ox train that came through here three weeks ago."

"What of it?" said the leader.

"The man whose chattels you stole was a man known to us and deserved a warrior's death. You deprived him of that honor."

"Such is Fate," said the leader. "It was his time to die. Besides, he was a Väster Geat."

"He was a Clan Chief," said Weohstan.

"And a father," said Einar.

"A plague on all Thunder-Geats," said the Leader. He spat toward the ground.

"The ring on your finger," said Ecgtheow. "Give it to me."

The raider removed the ring and handed it to Ecgtheow.

"Who are you and these others?" he said.

Ecgtheow swung his sword sideways. The edge of the blade caught the leader's neck below the helm and removed the head straight across. The stranger's horse wheeled and galloped away; the headless body fell to the ground.

"Thunder-Geats," said Ecgtheow. "We're Thunder-Geats."

"What are your orders, brother?" said Einar.

"Make haste," said Ecgtheow. "Gather the raiders' weapons and armor and turn the carts around. See that our men get home."

"What about you?" Weohstan said.

"I'm going to Frihamm and have a look around."

Ecgtheow looked at the ring in his hand; then handed it to Weohstan.

"Take this ring to our king. Tell him the raiders will no longer vex him. That should put a smile on Hrethel's face."

"As soon as we return," said Weohstan, "I'll make straight for Falcon's Nest."

Ecgtheow rode along the length of the ox train and thanked his men, all of whom volunteered to make that perilous journey with him. It would take three days for Weohstan and the Freemen to make their way back, not just to Vindinstedt, but to the other Waegmunding farms, from which three-fourths of the men and half the ox carts originated.

"Tell the men to keep a sharp watch and their bows at the ready," said Ecgtheow. "There may be more in Hel's Grove who wish us harm."

After the ox train had turned around and started west, Ecgtheow went among the corpses strewn over the ground until he found a large leather pouch that had come loose from a Wylfing's saddle. He emptied the contents of the bag on the ground; then he found the raider's head on the grass, eyes shut, mouth open as if to speak. Ecgtheow removed the raider's helm and put the head inside the leather pouch.

Ecgtheow ate a meal of cheese, and black bread then removed his peasant garb and replaced it with a clean white linen tunic. Putting on his cloak, he slung his sword crosswise over his back in the Wylfing manner, then urged Rain Dancer toward Frihamm. Weohstan pleaded with Ecgtheow to wear a chainmail shirt and helm, but Ecgtheow would hear none of it; besides, he had left his battle gear at home, on purpose.

"The less I stand out," said Ecgtheow to Weohstan, "the better I'll blend."

5

FRIHAMM

When striking a bargain in Frihamm, keep one hand in your purse, the other on your sword. So went the saying after Modryth arrived twenty springs earlier and claimed Frihamm as her Queendom. So it was that Modryth came to Öster Götaland—a refugee with three Longships and her Personal Guard, one-hundred Slavs, all swarthy men-at-arms. They were outcasts, forced to flee their homes on the coast of northern Russia when overwhelming numbers of Huns migrated through.

† † †

Fifteen winters young and beautiful to behold, Modryth stood with her Father and Mother and two older brothers outside the Main Gate to their village. Because her father was Chief of their tribe, they were there to make a peaceful showing and welcome a migrating horde of Huns traveling west along the coast of northern Russia. The Huns had been plundering and destroying everything in their path.

Modryth's father begged the Huns' bald, bow-legged leader, Bahba Bozza, to take what they wanted, but to spare the village and its inhabitants. While Modryth's father was pleading, Bahba Bozza had his dark eyes, what one sees on a pig, fixed on young Modryth.

"I will spare your village," said Bahba Bozza; "but I want assurances that once we pass you don't attack us from behind after we've made camp for the night."

"Assurances, great Lord?" said Modryth's father. "We have one-hundred men-at arms, and you have a thousand or more."

"Still," said Bahba Bozza. "I want assurances. Hostages."

"Hostages?" said Modryth's father.

"You and your family will come with us. If the night passes

peacefully and your people behave themselves, I'll release you in the morning, and we'll continue on our way."

Modryth's father looked at his family. The fear they felt showed in their eyes.

"Very well, great Lord; it will be as you say."

No sooner had the Huns made camp for the night, a festive mood prevailed. The invaders lighted cooking fires by the hundreds. They roasted sides of goats and whole pigs on spits and consumed kegs of fermented yaks' milk throughout the night.

After Bahba Bozza and his generals had finished feasting in private, guards ushered Modryth and her family into Bahba Bozza's tent. Spacious enough to accommodate forty or more guests and servants, he adorned his tent with beautiful carpets from Mongolia, Persia, and lands twixt the two, and with glazed vases from Cathay and gold and silver plates and drinking goblets—all of it plundered. Modryth and her family were given seats on cushions and served all manner of delicacies by slaves who, despite being from different lands, shared one physical characteristic in common: none had tongues.

After Modryth's family had eaten but little, they were made to stand to one side while servants rolled a section of carpet out of the way. Modryth, her father, mother, and brothers were seized, gagged and bound by Bahba Bozza's guards; then, beginning with the Father, one by one, Modryth's family was hung upside down, except for Modryth. Forced to watch, Modryth could feel her prolonged screaming bottled-up in her lungs by the gag stuffed into her mouth. She looked on as her Father, Mother, and two brothers had their clothes cut from their bodies; after which, female servants skinned them from the toes to the top of their heads.

When Modryth tried to close her eyes, Bahba Bozza stripped and beat her with his leather riding crop, until the physical pain from the beating proved greater than the mental anguish and horror at the sight of her family being flayed and disemboweled. The sound Modryth heard was Bahba Bozza and his generals laughing. When there were no more signs of life from Modryth's parents and brothers, Bahba Bozza turned his attention to her.

Still a virgin, he robbed her of that with a flick from the point of his dagger; then had his way with her until, exhausted, he passed out. His generals took turns raping her until they, too, were satiated and fell asleep. Then it was the guards who had at her until she blacked out.

When Modryth came to, she was outside the main gate of her village. She lay on the ground naked, covered with dirt and dried blood. How she got there, she couldn't remember, but it was near dawn.

Modryth wasted no time. She crawled and dragged herself to the sleeping quarters of a mercenary named Germanicus whom her father had hired and placed in charge of his Personal Guard.

"Alert the Guards, Germanicus; we're leaving."

"What about your father and family?"

"Dead," said Modryth.

"Will the Huns return?" said Germanicus.

"I don't care," said Modryth; "we're leaving."

"The whole village? Now?"

"No. Just me, you, and the entire Guard. We'll take the Longships."

"But what of the rest of your people?"

"What of them?" said Modryth, voice void of emotion.

† † †

So it was that Modryth came to Öster Götaland. A refugee with three Longships and her Personal Guard, one-hundred Slavs, all dedicated to their child-queen.

Modryth wasted no time convincing Amunwolf, King of the Wylfings, to forgo putting an immediate violent end to her trespass and ambition. Using her feminine wiles and considerable charms over the course of several warm summer nights, she convinced Amunwolf she was worth having around.

Nine months later, Modryth bore him a son—a bastard. When Amunwolf heard he had sired a child with Modryth—her first, his fifth, he defied his advisers' advice to the contrary and went to see his alleged progeny. Even at such a tender age, the baby's resemblance to Amunwolf and Modryth were undeniable; he had Modryth's pitch-black hair and eyes, and Amunwolf's cleft chin.

Rather than have the infant strangled and fed to his hunting dogs, Amunwolf let the child live, acknowledged him as a prince and gave Modryth a Queendom. In exchange, Modryth transformed Frihamm from a sleepy port nestled at the back of a fjord, into a major hub of trade. A settlement that soon numbered over four-hundred lodges, Frihamm was open to purveyors of goods throughout Scandia and far across the Whale Road. Of much greater importance to Amunwolf, Modryth kept his bed warm when it suited him, and his coffers filled with gold and silver.

† † †

"Father will be furious when he learns you've returned to Vindinstedt," said Hygelac.

"I need to go back for a few days, brother," said Liv. "And check on the farm. Ecgtheow would expect no less."

"No, Liv! Ecgtheow expects you to do your father king's bidding by staying here with Beowulf until he returns."

"Beowulf and I will come back to Falcon's Nest, brother," said Liv. "Soon. I promise."

"Very well," said Hygelac. "But I will send some of the Kungens Vakter to accompany you."

"That won't be necessary," said Liv. "The Freemen who accompanied us here are escort enough."

"Two old men and four beardless boys?" said Hygelac.

Liv laughed and kissed Hygelac's cheek. "You worry too much, brother."

† † †

On the outskirts of Frihamm, Ecgtheow stopped at the lodge of a metalsmith named Usul. Time had not been kind to the old man. He was almost blind, cataracts clouded his vision, and his hands had become so gnarled they were useless when it came to working with tong and hammer. The metalsmith lived alone with his granddaughter, Moira. Twelve winters young, she was a quiet girl devoted to the care of her grandfather. Usul now used his smithy as a stable where, for a wedge of silver, he would stable a wayfarer's horse for the night. Over time, Ecgtheow had often taken lodging in the metalsmith's barn and trusted him. He knew Usul was a man who could keep his mouth shut. At the same time, Usul never failed to provide Ecgtheow with the latest gossip concerning Frihamm and the Dark Queen.

Inviting Ecgtheow inside his lodge, Usul poured them each a horn of dark beer; his granddaughter set out sliced bread, honey, and sausage before going outside to feed the goats and chickens. Ecgtheow watched as Usul grasped his drinking horn twixt both hands and steered it to his lips with difficulty.

"Good to see you, old man," said Ecgtheow.

"At my age," said the metalsmith, "it's good to be seen. But tell me: what brings you here? Or shouldn't I ask?"

"I come in search of answers," said Ecgtheow.

"Answers, you say," said the metalsmith, "such as?"

"Traders bringing their wares overland to Frihamm must pass through Hel's Grove."

"Yes, of course," said the metalsmith. "The ox trains pass by my door, just as you must do, to get to town. But why is that important?"

"Have you noticed anything strange in their comings and goings since the last full moon?"

"Strange?" said the metalsmith.

"Yes," said Ecgtheow, "anything out of the ordinary?"

Usul wet his lips with a sip of beer.

"Aye," said the metalsmith, "now that you ask. Ox trains used to pass my door at all hours of the day but never at night. Of late, they come no sooner than dusk."

"Anything else?" said Ecgtheow.

"Moira told me she sees the same men driving the carts."

"That is strange, indeed," said Ecgtheow. "Tell me, Usul—any news of the Roman?"

"I hear he's back," said the metalsmith, "in that bloody big ship he commands."

"The Gold Ship?"

"Yes."

Gracing the metalsmith's palm with a gold ring and several wedges of silver, Ecgtheow left Rain Dancer in the granddaughter's care and went the rest of the way to town on foot. He took with him the dark leather bag containing the raiders' leader's head, drained of blood, tied to his belt.

After walking a half-league, Ecgtheow entered Frihamm. With nothing to do apart from keeping the peace, the guards at the Main Gate, and those behind the stake wall gave Ecgtheow nary a glance. To them, he looked no different from a hundred other strangers who came to Frihamm that day.

Ignoring the "come hither" looks and gestures from a colorful array of women occupying the main thoroughfare, all eager to give pleasure to a man with gold or silver in his purse, Ecgtheow continued to the center of town. Walking through the open marketplace, a blend of unusual smells, scents, odors, and aromas assaulted his nostrils, some pleasant, others sharp and pungent; they came from the tents of incense makers, and fishmongers' stalls, and from fire pits where a variety of meats simmered on spits. So farsighted was Modryth's vision for Frihamm she created a place outside of town for handling human waste. Collected morning, noon and night by slaves whose sole function was to keep Frihamm clean, they transferred the waste from chamber pots to barrels and transported it by ox cart to a landfill for final disposal by fire. In Frihamm, men and women died of natural causes, or from having their throats cut, or from lingering wounds that never healed, but to die by pestilence or plague was unheard.

Ecgtheow stopped in the center of the marketplace. He lifted back the hood of his cloak; then he removed the head from the bag at his side. He climbed onto an empty ox cart. Grasping the head by the hair, he held it up and said:

"Does anyone recognize this face? I killed the man who belonged to this head, and I'll reward anyone who can tell me who he is—or, rather, who he was."

Silence spread throughout the marketplace the way a ripple spreads across the surface of a lake, but faster. Those who saw the head were horrified. Holding the head as high as his arm would reach, Ecgtheow turned in a slow circle so all could see.

"I'll give a gold ring to anyone who can tell me who this is!"

said Ecgtheow. "My name is Ecgtheow Waegmunding. If anyone knows whose head this is and wants my gold; you'll find me aboard the Gold Ship."

Ecgtheow waited a moment; then, shunning the silence surrounding him, Ecgtheow put the head into the bag and resumed walking in the direction of the waterfront.

† † †

Twenty summers earlier, Amunwolf allowed Modryth to build a great dock along the shore. He did it to accommodate the trade Modryth had foreseen in her dreams.

"Build it, and they will come," she said. This boast from a girl fifteen winters young at the time.

Modryth was right. In time, from near and far, vessels crossed the Whale Road to Frihamm. For the first time in a long while the region knew an uneasy peace. The tribes in the north land flourished: Brondings; Finns; Svear; Wylfings, Thunder-Geats, Spear Danes, Frisians, Zealanders, Franks, Latvians, Estonians, Slavs; even the Romans of the Eastern Empire, and the Persians—all prospered.

Well before he reached the waterfront, Ecgtheow could see the Gold Ship anchored offshore. Even though he had seen that seagoing behemoth before, its size and structure still amazed him in a way few things made by the hand of man could, apart from a well-crafted sword. As Ecgtheow approached the dock, the ship's gold lacquered hull glistened in the waning light of day.

Ecgtheow wove his way among the ox carts and throng of workers unloading and loading vessels moored to the dock. He caught sight of a knarr taking on cargo: oak barrels such as Sven Eriksson used to convey his mead. Overseeing the loading was a Greek whose tunic bore the insignia of the Emperor Anastasius. Ecgtheow stopped alongside the knarr and waited until he caught the overseer's attention.

I have business with your master, Gaius Aurelius."

The overseer was an unpleasant fellow who looked down on Northmen. "What business would that be?" he said.

"That would be for your master's ears," said Ecgtheow.

"And who are you?"

"I'm an acquaintance of your master and no one to insult. Do as I ask and I'll tell Gaius Aurelius not to nail your head to the mast after he hears how you kept me waiting."

Ecgtheow stood at the prow of the knarr as it left the pier and made its way toward the Roman's Longship. Built of pine with a wider, deeper hull than a Longship built for battle, a knarr sixteen meters long could carry up to fifteen-tons of cargo. True, knarrs were slow as sea snails, but they were seaworthy, reliable even in a squall or thunderstorm. As the knarr closed the distance between itself and the Gold Ship, Ecgtheow recalled the first time he set eyes on it, several summers earlier, when that colossal floating palace with its two-tiered, gold lacquered hull and crimson sails dropped anchor in the Fjord of Kuurin, above which loomed the Citadel.

Sixty-yards in length and built to withstand the rough-and-tumble of the open sea, it had a crew of three-hundred men, including one-hundred-and-twenty rowers. The Greek shipbuilders who designed that Leviathan wanted to provoke awe in those who saw it. If it also struck fear into the hearts of would-be pirates, all the better.

The Emperor Anastasius tasked Gaius Aurelius with visiting the kings in the north to gain their goodwill and to pave the way for trade. King Hrethel cared little for the Roman Emperor in Constantinople, and he couldn't stand Gaius Aurelius; nor could Ecgtheow or any other Northman who came close to the Roman. The Roman's perfume repelled all but the most jaded nose and did little to mask the foul odor he exuded through every pore beneath the finery of his embroidered robes. Like many Romans, Gaius Aurelius was an unapologetic epicurean, a man with rare appetites such as sweet bread made from human hearts, and testicles, and so-called "blue wine" from grapes grown on the fertile plain of Tarragona, south of the Pyrenees' Mountains in Iberia. Aurelius's friends and detractors alike said his hawk-shaped nose could smell a profit at the bottom of a dung heap if there were a profit there worth having. Gaius Aurelius was in charge of matters related to the Eastern Roman Empire's commercial undertakings in the far north; which, of necessity, took him back and forth across the

Whale Road once, sometimes twice every spring.

This spring, Black Fox fur was the commodity the Roman sought for the enormous profits it generated among merchants catering to the stylish whims of aristocratic women in the affluent Mediterranean cities of Accra, Constantinople, Athens, and Miletus.

Once the knarr reached the Gold Ship, Ecgtheow wasted no time climbing aboard. The first sight to greet his eyes was the naked body of a boy, face-up, awash in a pool of blood. Slaves were stuffing the boy's corpse, minus the heart and genitals, into a linen bag, weighted with rocks which they were about to toss over the side to a watery grave.

While slaves transferred cargo from the knarr to the main deck of the Gold Ship, Ecgtheow presented himself to the Proreus, the Lookout in charge and asked to see Gaius Aurelius. The Proreus, with two spearmen, escorted Ecgtheow below decks to Aurelius' private cabin. Ecgtheow waited outside the door while the Proreus announced his presence.

"Of course, of course," said the Roman, "Show King Hrethel's emissary in."

Ecgtheow entered Aurelius' quarters. The air was thick with the smell of frankincense. He found the Roman dining at a table set with gold plates and goblets and crowded with a wide array of meats, cooked vegetables, and fruit. Lamps burning whale oil illuminated the room, and a thin cloud of blue smoke generated by the incense clung to the ceiling.

"Are you hungry?" said Aurelius. "My cook just finished grilling fresh sweetbreads. You're welcome to join me?"

"No thank you, my Lord," said Ecgtheow. "I'm not hungry."

"Really?" said the Roman. "Most enjoy this delicacy because it reminds them of bacon—for me, it's the smooth texture of the meat as it glides down my throat. Then something to drink perhaps?"

"Thank you, no," said Ecgtheow.

"My, my," said the Roman, "All business, are we?"

"Yes, my Lord," said Ecgtheow.

He wanted to shove the sweetbreads down the Roman's throat.

"Very well," said Aurelius. "How goes it with King Hrethel?"

"Well enough, my Lord, but of late he's vexed," said Ecgtheow.

"Vexed? Oh, dear me, how so?" said Aurelius.

“Since the last full moon, raiders have plundered no fewer than three of our tribe’s ox trains on their way to Frihamm. They also murdered one of our Clan Chiefs trying to bring his mead to market."

Aurelius gulped a long drink, and belched. "Mead, you say?"

"Yes," said Ecgtheow. "In oak barrels no different than are now being loaded aboard the Gold Ship."

Aurelius coughed and got to his feet. "Who are you," he said. "You look familiar to me."

"If I look familiar," said Ecgtheow, "It's because we met at Falcon's Nest, when you came to present your credentials to King Hrethel. My name is Ecgtheow Waegmunding."

The Roman's eyes widened. His mouth dropped open. "I know that name. You're Hrethel's assassin."

The Roman's bottom lip began to quiver.

"I'm here for answers, my Lord. Nothing more."

"What is it you want to know?" said the Roman.

"I want to know the identity of the raiders' leader."

"What makes you think I would know his identity?"

"It is a well known fact, my Lord; you have spies everywhere; almost as many as the Spear Danes across the Whale Road from Geatland. Perhaps if you were to see his face you might recognize him."

"You say that as though he was outside my cabin door."

Ecgtheow smiled. "In truth, my Lord, he's closer than that."

Gaius Aurelius looked perplexed. He drained the wine from his goblet; then wiped his mouth with the back of his hand.

"Is this some kind of joke," said the Roman.

"No, my Lord."

Ecgtheow reached into the leather pouch and pulled the head out by the hair. He placed the head facing the Roman, on top of a plate piled high with dried dates from the Euphrates Valley.

The Roman gasped.

"Ah!" said Ecgtheow, "You recognize him."

"Of course I recognize him," said the Roman. "It's Prince Heatholaf."

"The bastard son of the Iron Wolf and Queen Modryth?"

"Yes, yes, yes! It's him. You murdered a Wylfing Prince."

"Not murder. Justice was done."

"You have to leave. Now!" said the Roman. "I will restore the mead to King Hrethel, or give you gold for it. Right here. Right now! But you must leave, and leave quickly."

"As I came aboard I saw a boy's body on the deck. His privates had been cut off and his body sliced open from his throat to his arse."

"He was a slave. A petty thief. He was no one. A nobody."

The Roman pushed his chair back and stood.

Before Gaius Aurelius could cry out, Ecgtheow grabbed a bread knife from the table and sliced the Roman's throat from ear to ear. The Roman tried to speak but gurgling sounds were all he could make as his blood spurted out. Ecgtheow put the Roman back into his chair. A moment later, the Roman went face-down onto the plate filled with sweet breads.

6

FLIGHT

Ecgtheow left Aurelius' quarters and approached the two spearmen standing guard in the companionway.

"I've finished my business with your master," said Ecgtheow. The spearmen led Ecgtheow back to the main deck. Slaves had finished unloading the knarr, and its crew made ready to return to the docks. The waterfront was teeming with the denizens of Frihamm including a dozen of the Dark Queen's warriors. At the sight of Ecgtheow on the deck of the Gold Ship, those on shore began to shout and flail the air with their hands.

"There he is!" said a man among the crowd.

"He murdered our Prince!" said another.

"Kill him!" said a hundred voices in unison.

Ecgtheow leapt feet-first into the water and sank from sight. When his head next broke the surface, he was on the other side of the Longship. He surfaced long enough to fill his lungs with air and down again he went. Weighted by his sword and garments, he yanked his cloak off.

Kicking with his feet and pulling with his arms, Ecgtheow could feel his heart pound. Fighting against the tide, he swam underwater toward shore.

Seated on her throne in the darkened hall, Modryth sipped wine from a golden goblet and remained impassive as Gaius Aurelius's Second-in-Command, a Greek named Phaeton removed her son's head from a wicker basket. Phaeton had used it to convey the Prince from the Gold Ship to Modryth's three-tiered lodge. Craftsmen built it from oak and pine; this, her palatial dwelling on a hill from which she could look east and see over the town, past the waterfront, out to sea.

"Where's the rest of him?" she said.

"We haven't found his body yet, my Queen," said Germanicus, Captain of Modryth's Guard. A tall, broad-shouldered Frisian mercenary, fifty winters old, Germanicus was one of Modryth's two male lovers. "We're searching Hell's Grove for it even as I speak, my Queen."

"I want the body found, Germanicus, before the animals get to it, and have my physician sew Heatholaf's head back on when you've recovered the rest of him."

"Yes, my Queen," he said.

Modryth looked at the Greek, now in temporary command of the Gold Ship.

"Thank you, Phaeton. You may go."

"Yes, great Queen," he said, and he set the basket on the floor.

"When you reach Constantinople," said Modryth, "Tell Emperor Anastasius I am sad over the death of Gaius Aurelius. Tell him we will not rest until we hunt down his murderer and punish him."

"Yes, great Queen."

As was customary in the lodge of the Dark Queen, Phaeton kissed Modryth's feet and departed.

"Now," said Modryth, "I want to know who murdered Prince Heatholaf."

"The killer identified himself in the marketplace, my Queen," said Germanicus. "His name is Ecgtheow Waegmunding; a Thunder-Geat in the service of King Hrethel."

"I want him found," said Modryth. "Offer a reward for his whereabouts. Do whatever you have to do. But find him!"

Germanicus kissed Modryth's feet and departed.

"I'll find him, great Queen," spoke a full-throated voice from the back of the room.

"Come closer," said Modryth, "So I can see your face."

A Wylfing warrior approached the throne. Not tall, but muscular, he stopped a respectful distance away from Modryth and bowed.

"I'm Lars Ásmundr, great Queen, Chief of the Black Water Clan. King Amunwolf has ordered me to find Prince Heatholaf's killer and deliver him for justice. I have a hundred of my best riders outside the city gate, waiting."

Modryth took a moment to think on the matter.

"Bring Prince Heatholaf's killer to me; alive if you can. If not, his head will do. If he has a wife, kill her. If he has children, kill them and bring me their heads. Spare no one. Destroy everything in your path but do nothing, mind you, that will lead to all-out war with the Thunder-Geats. It would disrupt trade in Frihamm and make business difficult to manage."

"I understand, great Queen. King Amunwolf already made that clear to me."

"You may go now," said Modryth.

The Wylfing bowed and started away.

"You forget something," said Modryth, pointing to her feet.

The Wylfing chief turned and faced her. "I serve the Iron Wolf, great Queen—not you."

Modryth leashed her rage deep in her gut. Saying nothing, she watched the Wylfing Clan Chief smirk and leave her Hall.

Hurling the goblet in her hand to the floor, Modryth stood and hastened to her "Special Room." There, she wasted no time visiting her wrath upon the men, and women confined in filthy iron cages that ran the length of the room's back wall. Illuminated by torches, the room had one function beside storing her wealth: to facilitate the infliction of maximum pain. Not to be distracted by the cries and screams of her victims, Modryth ordered them gagged and their hands and feet bound; that way they could be hung upside down and eviscerated in ways that suited Modryth's momentary whims before she slit their throats—or not.

Up to his neck in the cold water, Ecgtheow waited until the sun went down before crawling onto shore and hid among tall reeds. He watched the Dark Queen's men-at-arms search the wharf with torches until they moved off to scour the shoreline. They came close to where Ecgtheow lay in the mud, a feast for flies, bugs, and mosquitoes; but, in the darkness, Modryth's men passed him. When they had gone elsewhere to continue their search, Ecgtheow crept along the shoreline. He avoided the search parties by keeping a short distance behind them until he had circumvented

Frihamm. Cold, weary and in need of rest, Ecgtheow made his way to the metalsmith's dwelling, but there was no light coming from within. He waited behind trees and watched a large column of riders pass by on the road with torches; they were riding in the direction of Hell's Grove. When all was again quiet, apart from the hooting of an owl, Ecgtheow saw Usul and his granddaughter step outside their dwelling. Moira held a torch overhead.

"Are you out there, Ecgtheow?" said the metalsmith.

Outside her bedchamber, Modryth's household slaves sang a lover's lament in her native tongue, a lament that evoked memories of wet grasslands and the dark, brooding sky of her former home on the coast of Northern Russia. While myrrh burned throughout Modryth's lodge, lamplight flickered inside the chamber where she lay in bed. She was alone, but for Prince Heatholaf. The Dark Queen's physician had sewn the prince's head to his bloodless body, and Modryth had seen to the washing of his corpse herself. Mother and son lie naked on their sides facing each other, their noses touching. Lulled by the singing outside her bedchamber, Modryth closed her eyes and let sleep overtake her.

† † †

While Moira dried his boots and garments in front of the hearth in her grandfather's lodge, Ecgtheow lay shaking, teeth chattering, his eyes closed, wrapped in a blanket on a bed of straw near Rain Dancer. He had spent a long time up to his neck in the water eluding the Dark Queen's patrols. The icy fingers of the Whale Road had penetrated him to his core.

"You're not well," said the metalsmith, kneeling beside Ecgtheow. Usul rested the back of one wrist against Ecgtheow's forehead.

"You're burning with fever."

Every now and again the sound of a horse galloping by alerted them to the ongoing presence of the Dark Queen's patrols.

"As soon my clothes are dry enough to put on, I'll leave," said Ecgtheow.

"You need to rest and get better," said Usul.

"It won't be long," said Ecgtheow, "before they stop to search your dwelling. If they find me here, it'll mean your death and the death of your granddaughter. I won't let that happen."

"If it is your wish to leave," said Usul, "be it so."

"It is," said Ecgtheow.

"I'll have Moira bring you more hot broth. Drink it all. In the meantime, I'll clean and oil your knife and sword lest they rust."

"Many thanks, old man."

Usul nodded and left the stable. Ecgtheow curled-up on his side and pulled the blanket around him. When Ecgtheow's boots and garments were dry, and his knife and sword polished with sand and vinegar, Moira and her grandfather brought his clothes and weapons to the stable.

Dressed, ready to depart, Ecgtheow filled Moira's hand with silver, thanked the old man and left under cover of night. The metal smith could not make out Ecgtheow as he climbed on his horse but Moira could. She, too, had felt Ecgtheow's fevered brow and wondered how long her grandfather's mysterious friend would be able to stay in the saddle.

7

WAGES OF GLORY

To make better time, Weohstan left Einar and Elifr in charge of getting the Freemen home and rode west at a canter.
Ecgtheow's right, Weohstan told himself, news of our victory will put a smile on Hrethel's face.

Although it would be dark soon, Weohstan wanted to cover as much ground as he could. He was pleased beyond measure that Ecgtheow's plan had worked so well. Weohstan laughed aloud—save for very few, the raiders were dead on the ground in less time than it took Weohstan to drain his bladder.

As the sun began to set Weohstan found a good place to camp for the night. There was a stream of water and sweet grass for his horse. Weohstan would sleep well. He would think of Ursula and the list of things around the farm she wanted him to do. He would also think of Handscio; how he would hold and bounce him on his knee, once they were together again.

† † †

Glad to be out from under the wool tarps they had used to conceal their presence in Hell's Grove, the sixty Freemen following Ecgtheow's brothers elected to shoulder their bows, stretch their legs and walk alongside the carts. They decided to walk rather than having their innards jostled a second time with every slow turn of the carts' iron-banded wheels. To accommodate the pace set by the oxen, Einar and Elifr rode their horses at a walk.

"I'm pretty sure I killed more than you, brother," said Einar.

"By the gods," said Elifr, "no, you didn't. Cutting the throats of those wounded bastards don't count. Besides, I killed just as many as you."

"Did not," said Einar.

"Did too," said Elifr.

The euphoric feeling that attends killing and emerging from a battle unscathed possessed them. Declaring an unspoken truce in their ongoing verbal war to outdo the other, the brothers agreed on how well Ecgtheow's plan had worked; then stopped talking. When the sun dropped low on the horizon, and a full moon began its ascent, Einar and Elifr called a halt and made camp for the night.

† † †

Liv sat at the long table in front of the hearth with three other women: Ursula, Alfhildr, and Bothilda. Playing nearby were their children. Beowulf and Handscio sat together with Uncle Rabbit and fed pine cones to the fire while the other toddlers chased one another around the room. Their mothers sipped ale and nibbled cheese melted over toasted dark bread.

The women kept each other amused with stories of their husbands. With their men gone, and with no way of knowing where they were, or when they'd return, sharing stories, and laughing at the things their men did in private, was one way the women could allay their fears. Alone at night was the worst; it was when there were no more chores to attend, and the children were asleep. Not knowing if they'd be widows or wives from one day to the next made for a fitful sleep, and sometimes no sleep at all. Ursula got Liv's attention and pointed to Beowulf and Handscio.

"Two peas in a pod, they are," said Ursula.

Liv smiled. "I know."

† † †

With a full moon overhead, Ecgtheow slumped forward in his saddle while Rain Dancer continued at a walk. Rather than take the shorter, direct route west to Väster Götaland, the same as used by the ox trains, Ecgtheow headed south-southwest toward the coast. Burning with fever, he rested his head on Rain Dancer's neck. How long he rode that way he didn't know, his thoughts tumbled over one another as he drifted in and out of consciousness. In his mind's eye, the one image that presented itself was of Liv and Beowulf at the hot spring. With the first faint light of dawn, the familiar sound of waves breaking reached Ecgtheow's ears. Cold salt air filled his nostrils. Ecgtheow fell from his saddle and darkness closed around him.

† † †

From his vantage point on the ridge, the Wylfing chief looked at the encampment a quarter-league away. It vexed him that he hadn't found Ecgtheow Waegmunding. For the time being, Lars would have to content himself with the men camped in the distance. After having spent most the night searching Frihamm and Hell's Grove, Lars felt vindicated; he had pushed his men and horses almost beyond endurance. The breeze that blew over the ridge carried with it the smell of wood smoke and food cooking. Lars felt himself salivate as he drew his sword. As for the men below, the tracks left by so many ox carts in Hell's Grove where the Dark Queen's men found Prince Heatholaf's headless body was proof enough for Lars that the men camped below were as much involved in the murder of the prince as was Ecgtheow Waegmunding. Just the one-hundred warriors riding with him, Lars was in an ill humor and eager for a fight, a hot meal, and some rest.

† † †

The sun rose above the hills. Einar and Elifr sat in front of their campfire with their cloaks pulled around their shoulders and warmed their hands in front of the fire and stared at the pot of beggar's' stew—leftovers from the day before. Around them, the Freemen, eighty in total, including those driving the ox carts, were doing the same.

Feeling the onset of a cramp in his right leg, Einar got to his feet and shook his leg as if something unwanted had crawled up his leggings.

"What ails you, brother," said Elifr.

"I got a cramp in my bloody leg," said Einar, hopping about in-place.

Einar was about to sit when he and Elifr felt the ground tremble; then they heard it: the sound of horse's' hooves churning the ground, and coming fast in their direction.

"Arm yourselves," said Einar.

The Wylfngs struck the encampment with the full force of a gale. The Geats found their bows, took cover behind carts and loosed what arrows they could. The defense the Freemen put up was fierce, but against so many mounted warriors, it was short-lived. Einar and Elifr were among the last to die—at about the same time their stew was simmering.

It was two days and one night before Ecgtheow's fever broke, but the sound coming from his lungs worried her. Inside the sweat lodge where Ecgtheow lie, Eydís withdrew her naked body from against his and placed a blanket over him. Ecgtheow was no longer shaking or shivering, but his raspy breathing and spasmodic coughing told her he was not out of death's reach, far from it. Eydís added more driftwood to the fire that was burning beneath a brazier lined with smooth stones she gathered off the beach. She ladled more cold water over the brazier. The steam that came off the stones added additional moisture to the confines of her hut. Whatever demon was residing in the handsome stranger's chest, she would have to burn it out of him if he was going to live. Eydís added more peppermint leaves to a pot of boiling water, then rubbed oil of peppermint into his chest. Straddling Ecgtheow's hips, Eydís placed her hands underneath him and lifted his rib cage with each inhalation. When he coughed, she turned his head to one side to drain the mucus that worked itself out of his lungs, up his throat, and out his nose and mouth. Day and night she stayed with Ecgtheow, never leaving his side.

King Hrethel imploded with joy when Weohstan placed the blood-red stone in the palm of his hand. Prince Hygelac stood with his brothers, Herebeald and Haethcyn, off to one side. Together, they watched their father's reaction.

"Have you ever seen him grin that way?" said Haethcyn.

"Never," said Herebeald.

"Thank you, Weohstan," said Hrethel. "You came far to bring this good news, and you deserve to rest. Later we'll feast and celebrate your victory."

"Had it not been for Ecgtheow, my King, and the Freemen who volunteered to go with us, there would be no victory. It was Ecgtheow's plan from the beginning; he put himself where the danger was greatest. Even now I fear for his safety. The ring in your hand, Ecgtheow took from the raiders' leader before he killed him. It's yours, my King; Ecgtheow wanted you to have it."

"When Ecgtheow returns," said Hrethel, "we'll honor him here; besides, I haven't seen Liv since she returned to Vindinstedt without telling me and I intend to scold her. Nevertheless, Weohstan, stay the night here."

"Aren't we company enough for him?" Herebeald said to Haethcyn and Hygelac.

"Softly, brother," said Hygelac. "Let father enjoy his time with Weohstan."

"I say we go into the city," said Haethcyn; "find three obliging young women and sheath our swords 'til the cock crows."

"I'm with you, brother," said Herebeald. "What say you, Hygelac?"

"Go ahead, brothers," Hygelac said. "I want to stay and hear Weohstan's account of the battle in Hell's Grove."

"Suit yourself, little brother," said Haethcyn. "But gathering crumbs at father's table won't gain you his throne."

"That's right, little brother," said Herebeald. "Sooner or later, I'll be the one on the throne and you two barn apples will be kissing my lily-white arse."

Hygelac looked at Haethcyn and grinned.

"Fate has played a cruel trick on us, brother," said Hygelac. "Me, the runt of the litter and, you—the fat one stuck in the middle."

† † †

Their losses had been light, eighteen men in all. Lars took his time torturing the prisoners, not because he wanted information, that was a small part of it. Lars enjoyed inflicting pain on the helpless when it came to slicing; even more so when it came to dicing and peeling the skin off Väster Geats. Before the last prisoner's screams died away, Lars was no closer to finding Ecgtheow Waegmunding than before, but now he knew the exact location of Ecgtheow's farm. Given the number of Väster Geats dead on the ground, Lars concluded Clan Waegmunding would have far fewer seasoned warriors to withstand an attack. With that in mind, Lars tasked twenty men to return to Öster Götaland with the ox train and the heads of the Väster Geats they killed. Of the men remaining, he ordered all but fourteen to fan out and double-back in search of Hrethel's assassin. If they still hadn't found him by the time they reached Hell's Grove, they were to return to the Iron Wolf's lair at Värg Slött. At the back of Lars's mind were thoughts of the glory that would come—the glory he would gain by killing so notorious a Thunder Geat—none other than Ecgtheow Waegmunding.

8

BLOOD FOR BLOOD

The day before Lars Ásmundr and his band of marauders attacked Vindinstedt farm, Weohstan's wife returned with Handscio to their farm. They did so over Beowulf's and Handscio's protestations since both boys wanted to spend the night on a bed of straw in the loft of the milking barn; something they did often, once they demonstrated to Ecgtheow's and Weohstan's satisfaction they could climb the loft-ladder without breaking their necks.

Liv and Beowulf had already broken fast and had started walking toward the shrine that Liv maintained to honor the gods.

† † †

Using grappling hooks and ropes, several Wylfings scaled the stake wall and opened the Main Gate to Lars and the others waiting on horseback. The Wylfings made short work of the boys and old men who tried to defend the palisade. Some of the women were killed outright fighting the Wylfings with pitchforks, carving knives and fists. The remainder were herded into the Main Lodge and questioned as to Ecgtheow's whereabouts and the location of his wife and son. Satisfied that Ecgtheow was not there, Lars mounted the wall-walk and looked in all directions. As he looked north toward Vindinstedt Forest, he saw a woman running with a child across a field planted with rye.

"You four," said Lars. "Get on your horses. Waegmunding's woman and child are trying to escape."

† † †

Liv felt her lungs on fire as she ran with Beowulf through fields of uncut rye away from Vindinstedt Farm. Clutching

Beowulf's hand, they ran toward the tree line. In his other hand, Beowulf held Uncle Rabbit. Behind them, pillars of smoke rose into the sky from the outbuildings the Wylfings torched. Worse, five Wylfing riders were in pursuit. Heart pounding, she heard the sound of horses approaching. Liv reached the outer edge of Vindinstedt Forest just as an arrow hissed past her ear and a Wylfing shouted:

"Silver for the one who brings me Ecgtheow's brat!"

"Run," screamed a voice inside her head! Liv zigzagged beneath spruce and pine trees. She knew the forest well—precious to her were the hours she and Ecgtheow spent in those woods. It was a lovers' ritual each time Ecgtheow returned after going aviking for Liv's father.

The closest Wylfing rider was twenty paces behind Liv when he hurled his spear. A she bear and her cub emerged from the bushes. Liv heard the bear growl but ran on without looking back. She tore her way through dense undergrowth that scratched her milk-white shoulders and tore the pleats of her linen shift. The spear intended for Liv fell short and struck the cub, killing it.

Seeing the bear, the lead rider's horse reared. Thrown from his saddle, the Wylfing landed on the ground with a bone-jarring thud. Within seconds the she bear was on him and tore out his throat with a single sweep of her claws. The she bear lunged toward a second Wylfing rider and broadsided his horse, knocking the rider to the ground. The Wylfing scrambled to his feet and tried to aim his bow. The bear seized him by the head and crushed his skull between her jaws. She tossed the corpse aside and went to her cub. She tried to coax it to its feet by nudging it with her snout. When her cub did not respond, the bear threw back her head and bellowed with rage.

"Leave those two!" said Lars. "And forget the bear! Find the woman and the boy!"

The Wylfings gave the maddened she bear a wide berth and continued after the woman and her child. When the undergrowth became denser, Lars and the two remaining Wylfings dismounted, spread out and cleaved the undergrowth with sword and axe—certain were they the woman and child were close.

Liv gasped for breath; she knew she and Beowulf couldn't run much further through the undergrowth. Beowulf was aware of his mother's fear; it was palpable to him, yet he remained quiet, calm and unafraid. As he ran the forest passed before his eyes in a blur, a patchwork of green, gold and tall, dark shapes that were the trunks of trees. Above him, filtered through the thick branches of trees, sunlight shone into his eyes as if the forest was raining sparkling beads of amber. The air felt soothing against his face, and the smell of pine needles and old wood filled his nostrils.

Liv entered a clearing. Her strength spent, she stopped and knelt in front of Beowulf. She kissed him on both cheeks and whispered, "I love you, Beowulf."

Liv heard the Wylfings; they were close. She left Beowulf concealed behind the trunk of a tall spruce tree and stepped back to the center of the clearing. She crouched low to the ground and prepared to spring.

"Frigga, Thor," Liv beseeched, "Have I not always honored you and those On High? Have I not been an attentive priestess, devoted to you both? I pray thee, protect my son. Give him the strength to vanquish our enemies. Let him fear no man and grow to be a warrior like his father. Steady my hand; give it purpose, Great goddess, and you, Thor, Lightning Bringer, I beg you."

The first Wylfing to enter the clearing did not expect to find the woman in front of him. His eyes widened with surprise as she leapt. The blade of Liv's knife entered his throat. Choking on the warm blood that filled his mouth, the Wylfing dropped to his knees and fell face-forward to the ground. Liv would not have the benefit of surprise a second time.

Lars and the other remaining Wylfing reached the clearing at the same time. Seeing their dead comrade and the woman standing over him, Lars stopped.

"Ecgtheow's son—where is he?" said Lars, his voice cold and menacing.

"Far away from here by now," Liv said.

Lars looked at the Wylfing alongside him and laughed: "I think not," said Lars, and a sinister grin formed on his lips. "We'll have him soon enough!"

"You'll have to slay me first," replied Liv, her voice calm and steady.

She tightened her grip on the knife and adjusted her stance the way her brother Hygelac taught her when she was a mere girl. The

Wylfings advanced with swords in hand. No match for either warrior Liv reversed her grip on the knife. Taking hold of the tip of the blade between her thumb and forefinger, Liv hurled her knife at the closest Wylfing. The blade cut through the air and sank deep into one eye, staggering him.

Liv tried to lure Lars away from the clearing, but she stumbled. In an instant, Lars was on her. He thrust the iron blade of his sword into Liv's back, piercing her heart. Lars wiped Liv's blood off his blade and glanced in all directions.

"No need to hide, little one. Come to Lars."

Beowulf dropped the floppy-eared rabbit Handscio had given him and stepped from behind the spruce tree. He looked at the body of his mother, motionless on the ground. Sensing eyes on him, Lars turned to see Beowulf in full view staring at him.

"Come here, boy. Say goodbye to your mother while she's still warm. Lars won't hurt you."

Lars had no sooner spoken than the she bear lurched from the undergrowth. Too late to run, Lars cried out as the bear dragged him to the ground. Lars screamed as she tore into his flesh and spilled his innards and then he screamed no more. Her vengeance complete, the bear started away.

Beowulf knelt beside his mother. Using both hands, he rolled Liv onto her back. Placing one hand on Liv's shoulder, Beowulf shook her, but she didn't move or look at him. Beowulf shook her again and again but to no avail.

The bear had not gone far when she heard a sound unlike any ever made in the forest before that day: a sound that caused birds to take flight from the branches of the trees, and other animals big and small to cower. The she bear's head whipped-around and she rose on her back legs. She saw it was from the Manlings's cub that the cry emanated. The sound died away, and the forest became quiet—a silent witness to what transpired there that day.

The she bear went to Beowulf's side. Hot tears stung his cheeks, but he returned her gaze unafraid. The bear sniffed Beowulf and licked the tears from his face.

Using her snout, she urged him to his feet. With his free hand, Beowulf grasped her fur, and he went with her—deep into the forest, away from the eyes of men.

† † †

Weohstan Waegmunding was in the barn saddling his stallion, Gray Bold, in preparation for riding to Vindinstedt Farm when one of his men, Axel, ran into the barn.

"What is it, Axel?" said Weohstan.

"Smoke, Lord Weohstan," said Axel. "Black as black can be, coming from the direction of Lord Ecgtheow's farm."

"Gather the men, Axel. Tell them to get their weapons and saddle their horses—all but six, who'll remain here to guard the women and children. Go!"

† † †

By the time Weohstan and his Freemen reached Vindinstedt Farm, they could hear shouting and laughter from inside the Main Lodge. Outside, all the other structures and outbuildings had been set afire and the farm animals, those not loose to graze in the pastures, had been slaughtered.

The Wylfings inside the Main Lodge were too drunk to put up much of a fight when Weohstan led his men inside. In short order the Wylfings were killed—none were left alive, and the floor of the Banquet Hall was awash with Wylfing blood. That, and the blood of the women the Wylfings sated their lust with before cutting their throats.

Weohstan wasted no time searching the forest for Liv and Beowulf. All they found were five dead Wylfings including a Clan Chief Weohstan recognized as Lars Ásmundr, despite the mutilated condition of his corpse. They continued to search that day and for days to come, but they found no trace of Ecgtheow's son.

† † †

Ecgtheow's eyes opened. He was alone on a bed of straw in the semi-dark confines of a hut. By the sound reaching his ears, he judged he was no more than a stone's throw from the seashore. Apart from sunlight that found its way through an open entryway and gaps in the thatched roof, the hut was dark. Built from driftwood lashed together with twine, someone made the roof from common reed and Heather, and Ecgtheow could hear the cry of seagulls and the sound of waves breaking on the shore. He knew he made it to the coast, but where he remained a mystery.

The tall silhouette of a man appeared in the entryway. When he entered, he was not alone. Following behind were two more men and a young woman who carried a wicker basket. Wearing the garb of men who traversed the Whale Road for a living, the three men stopped and stared at Ecgtheow. The woman stepped around them, knelt beside Ecgtheow and placed the basket to one side. She put her hand on Ecgtheow's brow. Her hand was light and cool to the touch, and for a brief moment, Ecgtheow thought of Liv. The woman withdrew her hand and turned to the men behind her.

"Will he live?" said the tall man.

The woman nodded and removed a bowl from the basket. Using a wooden spoon, she dipped into the bowl.

"Here," she said to Ecgtheow, "broth mixed with herbs; it will help you regain your strength."

The tall man and the two men with him left the hut. As Ecgtheow ate, he had never felt so weak. With considerable effort, he managed to prop himself up on his elbows. Even in the dim light, he could see she was pretty, with dark eyes, full lips and chestnut hair that hung past her shoulders. When he had eaten his fill, he lay flat on his back.

"Thank you," he said. "That was delicious."

The woman laughed. "Had I fed you boiled seaweed and sand crabs you would have found it delicious."

"Is this a Wylfing village?" said Ecgtheow.

"Wylfing?" said the woman. She turned her head and spat. "By the gods, no! We're Harii."

"You're a long way from home," said Ecgtheow.

"We Harii have no home—not anymore," she said, "except for this village, such as it is."

"I don't know your name," said Ecgtheow.

"My name is Eydís, and you are Ecgtheow Waegmunding," she said.

"How do you know my name?"

"The whole village knows your name. You're the Thunder-Geat

whom the Dark Queen and the Wylfings pursue."

"My horse," said Ecgtheow, "is he—"

"He's well," she said. "We haven't eaten him if that's what worries you. My little brother and sister are walking him on the beach."

"Good," said Ecgtheow, "that's good. I need to be going."

"You need to rest," she said. "You won't get half a league, not until your breathing sacks are clear."

"But—"

"But, nothing," said Eydís, interrupting again. "You need to rest to get your strength back. Don't worry, Ecgtheow Waegmunding, you're safe here; at least until my father decides what to do with you."

"That was your father I saw earlier?"

"Yes," she said, "the tall one."

A long moment passed in silence.

"I need to piss," said Ecgtheow.

† † †

When Weohstan left for Falcon's Nest to tell King Hrethel of the attack, Ecgtheow's brothers and the men with the ox train had not yet returned. Weohstan feared that Wylfings overtook the train and that Einar, Elifr, and the Freemen with them were now dead. The fact that the Wylfings had descended on his cousins' farms leaving no one alive reinforced Weohstan's fear that no help would be forthcoming.

Weohstan gave orders to his men to bring the families, those who survived the raiders' onslaught, to his farm; there they would have protection, for the time being. As he rode toward Falcon's Nest, he rehearsed what he would say, when it came time to stand in front of Hrethel and tell him Liv and his grandson were dead. It angered him: *I shouldn't be the one doing this* Weohstan thought as he rode across the causeway, and past the Main Gate into Falcon's Nest. *It should be Ecgtheow telling Hrethel—not me.*"

Ecgtheow slipped his tunic over his head. Eydís had washed that also and cleaned his breeches and mended them where he had torn them. Dressed, Ecgtheow pulled his boots on and cinched his leather belt around his hips. His knife and sword were missing, as was a leather pouch with several gold rings and silver wedges. Ecgtheow was not concerned. Had these people wanted me dead, he told himself, they would have killed me. Still feeling weak, Ecgtheow took slow, measured steps as he left the hut.

The first sight to greet him was a cove that sheltered the village and a weathered knarr. Villagers moored the cargo craft alongside a pier where they could load and unload cargo. Sunlight warmed his head and shoulders, and salt air filled his nostrils; both sensations gave Ecgtheow cause to pause. A seagull's cry made him look upward. How blue the sky appeared. At that moment he realized how long it had been since he'd taken notice of the clouds or the murmurings of the sea. It brightened his mood as waves lapped upon the shore.

The village comprised twenty lodges and huts and seven score men, women and children; many of whom paused to stare at him as he walked through the village to where Eydís's little brother and sister were grooming Rain Dancer. The children ceased brushing the stallion's mane when they saw Ecgtheow approach. Rain Dancer's ears perked and he whinnied.

"He missed you," said the girl.

"And I, him," said Ecgtheow. "But I'm glad Rain Dancer found capable hands to care for him. You're Eydís's brother and sister—yes?"

"Yes," said the boy. "I'm Ungur. My sister's name is Azril."

"Well, Ungur and Azril, my name is Ecgtheow. I'm in your debt."

"You owe them nothing," said Éydis.

Ecgtheow turned and saw Éydis behind him.

"My father wishes to speak with you," she said.

"May we walk Rain Dancer by the water?" said Ungur.

"I tell you what," said Ecgtheow. "You and Azril can ride him if your older sister says it's all right."

"Can we, Éydis, can we?" said the children.

Éydis nodded. "But just for a walk," she said.

"We know," said Ungur.

Ecgtheow helped Ungur onto Rain Dancer's back; then placed Azril behind her brother.

"Hold onto your brother's waist," he said.

Ecgtheow put the reins into Ungur's hands.

"You're just taking him for a walk, mind you, so keep the reins down and hold them as you would a baby bird. Whichever way you want Rain Dancer to turn, nudge him with your knee; he'll know what to do."

Ecgtheow and Éydis watched the children guide Rain Dancer along the water's edge. Éydis turned to Ecgtheow.

"Ready?" she said.

† † †

"Here, from Värg Slött," said Amunwolf, "I rule over seven petty tribes, and all seven are squabbling because of shortages."

The Iron Wolf's coastal fortress at Värg Slött was three leagues north of Frihamm; close enough for Modryth to travel there by land or water in half a day. To influence the Iron Wolf, she knew she must heat the iron before she could shape it. She would use Amunwolf's desire for her as both hammer and anvil.

The Wylfing King ordered the Throne Room cleared except for Lord Yngvarr, his trusted confidante, and Battle Lord. Amunwolf's oldest son, Prince Adalfuns, was also present. The product of the Iron Wolf's first marriage, Adalfuns loved ships and the ocean ever since he was a child. It was no great wonder that Amunwolf made Adalfuns Kommander of his fleet of sixty Longships, all fast, all battle-worthy. Each ship had twenty oars to a side and was capable of transporting forty men-at-arms to any place along Öster Götaland's coastline in less than a day.

Apart from asking Amunwolf for privacy, Modryth knew better than to demand anything of the Iron Wolf in the presence of others. Modryth would appeal to his vanity to get what she wanted. It was a well-practiced tactic that had worked countless times. She was confident it would work again. Modryth knew Lord Yngvarr, and Prince Adalfuns despised her, and in their presence, she would need to be cautious.

I must choose my words carefully; she told herself as she

entered the Iron Wolf's Throne Room.

"There," said Amunwolf, "but for the four of us, the Hall is empty. What do you want, Modryth?"

"News, my Lord," she said. "Many days have passed and still no word of our son's killer."

"Scandia is a vast place, Modryth," said Amunwolf, "much more than just Öster and Väster Götaland. Tell her, Yngvarr."

"It's true, great Queen," said Yngvarr. "Scandia stretches far north through the land of the Svear, all the way to Norwegan and the land of the Brondings. The places where one man can hide are countless."

"I didn't come for a lesson in geography, Lord Yngvarr," said Modryth. "With all your spies, why have we heard nothing about Ecgtheow Waegmunding?"

Before Yngvarr could reply, Amunwolf waved him back. "Be patient, Modryth, Heatholaf's killer will be found."

"Heatholaf was our son, my Lord, made of our flesh. Your thirst for revenge matches mine. You're the greatest king in all of Scandia. Exert your will, my Lord; I beg you—find our son's killer."

"Did you not get the heads I sent you packed in sea salt?" said Amunwolf. "There must be over eighty of them. That should have assuaged your grief a little—yes?"

"No, my Lord," said Modryth, "it lessened none of it. Eight, eighty, eight-hundred heads, it matters little if one of them isn't Ecgtheow Waegmunding's. Knowing he roams wherever he pleases is more than I can bear, my Lord. Please, I beg you—use your power and influence; find Ecgtheow Waegmunding and deliver him to me. I'll do the rest."

"In your Room of Rooms," said Prince Adalfuns, grinning.

"Yes, Prince," said Modryth, "if it pleases you to call it that."

She turned and faced Amunwolf. "If ever you cared for me, great Wolf, send riders to the four winds and across the Whale Road. Let the word go out that Modryth, Queen of Frihamm, will pay gold to whoever brings me Ecgtheow Waegmunding, chained and bound."

"Very well, Modryth," said Amunwolf, "you have my promise —the word will go out.

9

WORDS GO FORTH

Ecgtheow followed Eydís into her father's lodge where he and four men waited.

"I am, Haraldr," said the Harii. "These men are my kin." Haraldr turned to Eydís. "You may go, my daughter."

Eydís nodded and left the hut.

Ecgtheow stepped forward, "I am—"

"We know who you are, Ecgtheow Waegmunding," said Haraldr. "Bad news travels fast on the coast. The Dark Queen's offered your weight in gold to anyone who'll deliver you to her—alive."

"Had you wanted," said Ecgtheow, "you could've done that by now."

"True," said Haraldr, "we could have, but we despise the Wylfings almost as much as we hate the Dark Queen; moreover, we are neither Öster Geats nor Väster Geats. We are Harii. We care nothing about the quarrels that divide your two tribes.

"What do you want?" said Ecgtheow.

"To be left alone," said Haraldr. "But as long as you remain there's always the risk Wylfings will come searching for you. As is, we pay the Iron Wolf a tax; in turn, the Wylfings leave us alone."

"Something tells me you don't pay Amunwolf's tax with fish," said Ecgtheow.

The men with Haraldr laughed. Haraldr remained somber.

"If your trade is smuggling," said Ecgtheow; "that's your business, not mine. You took me in. You gave me shelter. No doubt, your daughter, Eydís, saved my life. Tell me how I can repay you?"

"By leaving," said Haraldr. "The sooner you go, the safer we'll be."

"Very well," said Ecgtheow, "I'll leave today."

After Modryth had departed by Longship for Frihamm, Yngvarr poured mead into three drinking horns for his king, Prince Adalfuns and himself. After the three had taken a long drink, Amunwolf belched and vented his exasperation.

"By the gods," he said, "that woman's an unbelievable pain in my arse."

"Would you have me kill her, my King?" said Lord Yngvarr.

Amunwolf laughed. "At least once every season for the last twenty winters you've asked me that same question."

"Yes, my King," said Yngvarr.

"Modryth is crazed," said Prince Adalfuns. "Give the order, Father—put the witch to death. Lord Yngvarr and I can do it together."

"When you both first told me Heatholaf was behind the raids on the ox trains, I should have reined him in and put a stop to it. But I didn't. Now I've myself to blame for his death, not Ecgtheow Waegmunding. Ecgtheow did what any loyal Thane would do for his king."

"That's true, Father," said Adalfuns, "but you can't blame yourself for Heatholaf's death."

"It's Heatholaf's damn fault, my King," said Yngvarr, "and his, alone. He was reckless and impulsive. You said it many times yourself. Besides, it was Heatholaf's time to die."

"Blame it on Fate, you say?" said Amunwolf.

"Yes, my King," said Adalfuns.

"But there's one thing we should consider," said Yngvarr.

"What?"

"Lars Asmundr has not sent us a word. Even if he didn't find Ecgtheow Waegmunding, he must at least have raided Clan Waegmunding's farms."

"Meaning?" said Amunwolf.

"I think Lars and his men are dead."

"I agree with Yngvarr," said Adalfuns. "We should have heard something by now."

Amunwolf appeared deep in thought.

"Tell me, Yngvarr, who do you place the most confidence in?"

"That would depend, my King, on whether it's a question of war or peace."

"Both," said Amunwolf.

"Ah," said Yngvarr, "in that case, I look to Prince Adalfuns. Who better to lead an attack or negotiate peace?"

† † †

Before Ecgtheow left the lodge, Haraldr returned Ecgtheow's sword and knife to him, along with Ecgtheow's pouch containing gold rings and silver wedges.

"Keep what's in the pouch," said Ecgtheow, "as a token of my gratitude."

"I took half," said Haraldr, "the rest is yours."

Ecgtheow accepted the pouch. Haraldr gestured to one of the five men who stepped forward with a hooded cloak and placed it into Ecgtheow's hands.

"Wear it in good stead," said Haraldr. "It's old and faded and won't make you invisible, but it hasn't any fleas, and it'll keep the rain off your head."

"Many thanks," said Ecgtheow.

† † †

Ecgtheow found Eydís near the water's edge. Ungur and Azril were with her; they held the stallion's reins.

"You're leaving," said Eydís.

"Yes," said Ecgtheow, "as soon as I've saddled Rain Dancer."

"I'll fix you something to eat," said Eydís; "you can take it with you for later."

"I owe you my life," said Ecgtheow.

"No," said Eydís.

She placed a hand on his forearm, "you fought with Death, and you won. It wasn't your time to die, Ecgtheow Waegmunding."

Hrethel stood on the western wall-walk of the Citadel which overlooked the harbor. With him were his counselor, Ragmund, and his three sons. Together they watched in silence as half of

Amunwolf's battle craft departed in the distance. Lord Yngvarr had delivered the Iron Wolf's cloaked message threatening war. There was no reason for a Wylfing of Yngvarr's stature to linger there, other than to vex the Väster Geats by reminding them how outnumbered they were, both in men-at-arms and ships.

"You did the right thing, Father," said Herebeald. "Ecgtheow brought this calamity on us. Were it not for him, Liv and our nephew would still be alive."

"Silence," said Hrethel. "Ecgtheow served me well and is loyal above all others. I owe him much. If you want to blame someone for your sister's death and the death of my grandson, blame the Dark Queen, since I sense Modryth's hand in this. Still, I want no war with her or the Wylfings."

"I agree with you, great king, said Ragmund. "War will cost you men and treasure, and you've little chance of defeating the Iron wolf."

"What if Ecgtheow is dead?" said Haethcyn.

"Then be it so," said the old king.

"But if," said Ragmund, "Ecgtheow's not dead, he'll return to his farm. I suggest you send word to his cousin, Weohstan, Great King. Tell him you've exiled Ecgtheow Waegmunding under pain of death. Let that be the end of it. You will placate Amunwolf; you will save face; peace and continued prosperity will be the victor for every tribe with a stake in the matter."

Hrethel put his hands on Hygelac's shoulders.

"Ride to Weohstan's farm, my son; tell him what transpired here. Tell Weohstan if Ecgtheow is alive, it's better he hears my decree from someone he trusts. Take men from the Kungens Vakter with you."

"No need to send men from your Personal Guard, Father. We'll accompany Hygelac to Vindinstedt," said Herebeald.

"No," said Hrethel. "You two idiots will remain here, where I can keep my eyes on you. Go, Hygelac. Deliver my message and return with the ashes of my daughter and grandson."

Tears formed in Hrethel's eyes.

Without looking at his brothers, Hygelac turned on his heel and hastened from the Throne Room.

10

HOMECOMING

Two days and nights had passed when Ecgtheow rode toward the entrance of his farm. The Main Gate was open and the grappling hooks the Wylfings used to scale the stake wall were still in place. Ecgtheow dismounted and led Rain Dancer past the gate.

The outside of Ecgtheow's lodge was intact. The Wylfings had burned the outbuildings and left nothing more than charred ruins and ashes on the ground. Carcasses of farm animals lie scattered and putrefying. Ecgtheow's farm was no longer a farm—it had become a place of death, and a wave of terror swept over him.

"Liv!" Ecgtheow said. "Beowulf!"

He shouted their names, but the reply that came to him was the wind as it blew past and stirred ashes into the air.

† † †

Weohstan stopped to vomit twice. Great was the anguish inside him. As he rode to Vindinstedt Farm his sorrow over the death of so many innocents gnawed at his innards, so much so he could not sit straight in his saddle. That changed when he entered the palisade and saw the stallion tethered outside Ecgtheow's Lodge. Gladdened by the sight of Rain Dancer, Weohstan's heart raced. He dismounted and ran to the entrance, pushed the door open and stepped inside the darkened lodge.

Before he could call out, Weohstan felt a hand grasp his hair and yank his head back, exposing his throat to the cold iron of a knife blade.

"It's me, Cousin," said Weohstan.

Weohstan felt the pressure of the blade lifted from his throat. Ecgtheow stepped in front of him.

"Forgive me, Cousin; I didn't know it was you."

Weohstan saw the look in Ecgtheow's face—he was a man

devastated.

"Where are they, Weohstan—Liv and Beowulf? I've found nothing but dried blood on the floor."

"The blood you saw," said Weohstan "is Wylfing blood mixed with the blood of our women. Still, my heart breaks to tell you—Liv is dead. We found her body in Vindinstedt Forest with five dead Wylfings, including the Clan Chief who led the raid."

Ecgtheow's mind reeled. He grasped Weohstan by the shoulders. "What about my son? Is he alive?"

"I'm sorry, Ecgtheow; we couldn't find Beowulf. We searched every day but found no trace of him."

Ecgtheow released his hold on Weohstan and staggered outside. Weohstan followed him to the well. There, Ecgtheow raised a bucket on a rope and splashed water over his face.

"I'm sorry, Ecgtheow," said Weohstan. "But better you heard it from me than a stranger."

Ecgtheow nodded. He slid into a sitting position with his back against the stone well. He wore the look of a man for whom life no longer held meaning.

"My brothers are dead," said Ecgtheow, "as are the Freemen who accompanied us to Hell's Grove."

"I feared as much," said Weohstan.

Ecgtheow buried his face in his hands and wept. Not knowing what else to do, Weohstan looked away until Ecgtheow got to his feet. Ecgtheow wiped his eyes and cheeks dry.

"The blame is on me," said Ecgtheow, "on me alone!"

"Don't blame yourself," said Weohstan. "You had no way to know the raiders' leader was Prince Heatholaf."

"Prince Heatholaf? How do you know it was Heatholaf I killed?"

"Hygelac came to see me with a message from our king."

"What message?"

"Hrethel has ordered you into exile, under pain of death should you return."

"What? Why?" said Ecgtheow. "Hrethel wouldn't have done it willingly. He has no reason to."

"To placate Modryth, the Iron Wolf sent half his fleet to Falcon's Nest along with his Battle Lord, Yngvarr, to present Hrethel with an ultimatum. The Dark Queen wants you dead. If you're in exile Modryth's assassins can hunt you without interference from Clan Waegmunding or the Geatfolk—or so she thinks."

A long moment had passed in silence before Weohstan spoke.

"What will you do?"

"Do?" said Ecgtheow. "I'll leave Väster Götaland."

"For where?"

"I don't know," said Ecgtheow. "I think it's better if no one knows. What did you do with Liv's remains?"

"Cremated—Hygelac demanded her ashes, so I surrendered them. I'm sorry, Cousin."

Ecgtheow nodded. "No need to be sorry, Cousin. You did what's right."

Ecgtheow held Weohstan close.

"I leave Vindinstedt farm and the farms of my brothers in your care, Weohstan. Bring them back to life if you can."

Weohstan removed Liv's knife from where he kept it tucked inside his belt. He held it out.

"Liv's knife," said Ecgtheow; he took it from Weohstan's hand.

"Yes," said Weohstan. "I found it in the forest where she died. She acquitted herself well, Ecgtheow. She made the Wylfings pay."

"Not nearly enough," said Ecgtheow. "Not nearly enough."

They remained at Ecgtheow's estate long enough for Ecgtheow to collect his battle gear: a shirt of hand-ringed chainmail and his bronze helm embossed with gold and silver—both were gifts from King Hrethel the day Ecgtheow took Hrethel's daughter, Liv, for his wife.

They rode together in silence until it came time to go different directions: Weohstan to his farm and family, Ecgtheow south toward Land's End.

"Die well, Cousin," said Weohstan.

"Die well," said Ecgtheow.

Eydís sat alone on the sand and watched the sunset. She thought about the man whose life she saved. With Ecgtheow gone, Eydís knew her life in the village would go on as before except she felt different now, forever changed. The days and nights Eydís spent holding Ecgtheow, sharing her naked warmth, infusing him with her life force as he lay at death's door, had worked some inexplicable alchemy on them both. There was something of each inside the other now that would always be there—of that Eydís was certain.

Whether or not Ecgtheow would recognize that "something" for what it was, was a matter of a different sort.

One-eyed Odin, the All Father, sat on his throne in Gladsheim, the Great Hall in Asgard situated on the Golden Plain of Ida. Nine Valkyries stood guard on either side of his throne. On his shoulders sat two ravens: Hugin and Munin; or, to use the Common Tongue of Midgard where humankind dwells, "Thought" and "Memory." They were gifts from his adopted daughter, Hel, and served the All Father by bringing him news and tidings from the Nine Worlds encompassed by Yggdrasil, the World Tree that binds the Cosmos together. Curled at Odin's feet were two, giant white wolves: Geri, the Ravenous, and Freki, the Greedy One.

Odin fixed his one good eye on the three gods standing before him. They were his wife, Frigga, the Vanir warrior goddess of love and beauty, unrivaled in wisdom and magic. The Aesir god, Thor, Lightning Bringer and god of thunder, bearer of the hammer Mjöllnir, the Destroyer. And Loki's daughter, Hel, Judge of the souls of the dead, Ruler of Helheim, was present.

It was plain by the All Father's expression he was weary from adjudicating the matter before him.

"Tell me again, Hel," said Odin, "why I should spare the child."

"Because he's no different," said Hel, "than any one of the hundreds of children who die each day in Midgard. As matters stand, he's lost in the wilds of Vindinstedt Forest; his mother is dead, and his father cannot protect him; meanwhile, a powerful tribe has marked the child for death. If the creatures of the forest do not soon kill him, starvation or the elements will. It's just a matter of time, All Father."

Odin ran his fingers through the gray locks of his hair. Frigga stepped forward.

"Neither Thor nor I am here to deny what our Vanir sister goddess says. Hel puts forth the matter accurately, and we will not take issue with any of it; yet—" Frigga paused. She looked at Thor.

Thor smiled and nodded.

"Go on, Frigga, tell him."

"In all of Midgard," said Frigga, "there was never a human more devoted to us than Hrethel's daughter. Since Liv was a child, she served us, did honor to our names and made sure the Geatfolk respected our shrines. She kept them open to those who sought comfort, no matter their rank or station. She always offered the choicest cuts of meat to us during our Name Days. For spring's eve, she brought Geatfolk together to honor the All Mother and us with games and celebration. Liv was the daughter of a king; she was a conscientious priestess, devoted to Asgard, a faithful wife and the best of mothers who possessed the heart of a Valkyrie. Liv died a warrior's death protecting her son. For that alone, we should honor her last wish."

"An impossible task," said Hel; "we cannot grant the endless stream of wishes humankind casts toward Asgard!"

Thor looked at Hel. "Are you saying there's something the All Father cannot do, O daughter of Loki?"

"Do not twist my words, Lightning Bringer," said Hel. "That's not what I meant, All Father."

Thor dropped to one knee with arms outstretched and looked at Odin.

"At the very least," said Thor, "allow this one prayer from Midgard; Liv's dying wish. Do this, All Father or the day will come when humankind no longer honors or fears us; rather, they will curse our names. Or worse still, they will forget us entirely if they believe we no longer care about them."

As the All Father pondered his options, so, too, did the ravens, Hugin and Munin, whisper into his ears, things about the child and his mother and father.

"Very well, said Odin. "I've made up my mind. Thor, Frigga, do what you think is in the best interests of Asgard. But hear me well; I forbid you from taking sides in a blood feud twixt Clan Waegmunding and the Wylfings. Do you understand?"

"We do," they said.

"Then, go," said Odin, "and grant the mother's prayer."

Frigga and Thor bowed to the All Father and departed for their chariots that would take them across the Bifrost, the Rainbow Bridge that connects Asgard with Midgard.

Odin opened his arms and welcomed Hel upon his lap:

"Are you going to scold me now, my adopted daughter?"

"No," said Hel; she kissed Odin on his cheek. "As in all things under the World Tree, I defer to your judgment, All Father. But for good or ill, who can say what fate awaits Midgard if you let the child live?"

† † †

Hel left Gladsheim undaunted by the All Father's decision to allow Thor and Frigga to grant the dead human's prayer.

Right or wrong, she thought, this child warrants watching.

With a snap of the reins, two Asgardian Forest Cats hissed and started home to Helheim. No sooner did her chariot arrive at her icy realm, Hel sent word straight away to Death, requesting he attend her.

When Death appeared, it was after a battle in Svartalfheim, one of the Nine Worlds, and home to the Dark Elves. She was furious that Death should take so long to come, but Hel kept her anger restrained.

Death came clad in dark armor—armor fashioned by dwarf Lords in Nidavellir, another realm bound by the World Tree. Beneath a spiked helm, Death's deep sunken eyes shone like two, large, pale yellow moons:

"What do you want, daughter of Loki?"

11

FROM ON HIGH

A Aware of the fur-less man cub clutching her side, Lüma shortened her stride to accommodate legs that in length and girth resembled white sticks; sticks she would break should she step on them.

Without me, the man cub will not live through the day, she told herself.

After walking the remainder of the morning, and watched by more eyes than she was accustomed, Lüma rested beside a stream. Beowulf stretched out on his belly. He formed his small hands into cups and drank from the cold water.

Putting the forest on notice, Lüma stood on her hind legs and roared. When she was satisfied that they were once again alone and unwatched, Lüma drank her fill from the stream, then reclined against a rock. Beowulf sat beside her. When by happenstance he saw a drop of milk trickle from one of her teats, he didn't hesitate; he suckled.

Grateful to be unburdened of milk she carried, Lüma bore the loss of her cub in silence. She draped a foreleg over Beowulf as he fell asleep beside her.

That night the she bear kept a close watch on the entrance to what was no longer her cave—but their cave. She did this for many nights to follow.

† † †

Those first days together Lüma taught Beowulf to urinate and defecate outside the cave. Moreover, he learned to drag and carry pine branches and gather leaves that his fur mother would rake into the cave for bedding. Anticipating he might go off by himself and become lost, Lüma led Beowulf back and forth along a trail she made from her cave to the nearest fresh-water stream and thicket of wild berries.

On their seventh day together, after Beowulf's first bath, they found representatives of the Forest Folk waiting for them outside Lüma's cave.

There was the Boar Lord, Jägare Bane, feared by hunters throughout Scandia. Prince of Reindeer, Flotta Av Mul, fleetest among the cloven foot was present; so, too, was Ratatosk Lang Svans, the cunning, self-appointed Empress of weasels, marmots, foxes, and gossips. Tysta Mördaran was there, along with her consort, Mjuka Tassar, representing the lynx and their Sabre Tooth cousins, the Forest Cats of Midgard.

Representing the packs that composed the Gray Brethren was the Wolf Lord, Långa Klor and his life mate, Vitt Hår. Representing the bear clans was Botten Skakapparat, known as Earth Shaker. Watching from the branch of a pine tree was the far seeing Eagle Lord, Kungörn, the Bold. But what the she bear and Forest Folk didn't see; what Beowulf alone saw, was the silent arrival of the goddess Frigga. She arrived in her chariot pulled by two immense Forest Cats: Vlad, the Ghost, and her sister, Mörkret, the Darkness.

Frigga wasted no time. Seeing Beowulf and the she bear, Frigga cast a mood spell on them to alleviate their grief and to cast off those twin hobgoblins—Fear and Doubt. Thor arrived in his chariot pulled by the giant goats of Asgard, Tanngrisnir, and Tanngnjóstr, or, in the Common Tongue, Teeth Barer, and Teeth Grinder.

Frigga smiled at Beowulf and raised a finger to her lips, signing him to be quiet. Beowulf smiled at her; then he looked at the giant muscular man with red hair and beard accompanying Frigga. Thor didn't smile, but he gave Beowulf a reassuring nod.

Lüma directed Beowulf to one side; then turned and faced the Forest Folk.

"*What's the meaning of this*?" Lüma said using the Silent Tongue.

The weasel was first to speak. It was to the Bear Lord, Botten Skakapparat:

"*Listen to her, as if she didn't know. Tell her, Earth shaker; tell Lüma why we've come.*"

As much as the Bear Lord detested the little weasel, he knew she was right; someone had to present the concerns that brought them all to Lüma's cave. Botten Skakapparat looked at Beowulf; then turned to face the she bear.

"*Greetings, Lüma; do you know who I am*?"

"*Yes, Earth shaker; I know who you are. But that doesn't tell me why you're here—you, and these others.*"

The Bear Lord flicked his head toward Beowulf. "*The man cub, Lüma—is the reason for our visit.*"

"*He's no longer a man cub, Earth shaker; he suckled at my teat and drank of my milk; that makes him mine.*"

"*She can't be serious,*" said the weasel, "*anyone can see she's not in her right mind; it's grief speaking through her.*"

"*You've lost your cub,*" said the Bear Lord. "*And we mourn with you, Lüma, but—*"

"*But, what,*" she growled. "*Without me to care for him he will die.*"

"*Too bad,*" said the weasel, "*but that's how things are, Lüma; it's how they've always been. Some live, some die. The All Mother wills it so; but as long as the man cub remains among us, we're all in danger.*"

"*Ratatosk Lang Svans is right,*" said the Bear Lord. "*The man cub isn't in the forest by accident; he's being hunted by others of his kind—here, where we dwell. Soon, more Manlings will follow.*"

"*And that,*" said the Forest Cat, Tysta Mördaran, "*means more Forest Folk will die.*"

Jägare Bane, long-tusked lord of boars, came forward and added his voice: "*I do not fear the Manlings because I can fight them, as can some of you; but when they come on horses and in large numbers, it always goes badly for us—all of us.*"

"*Jägare Bane speaks the truth,*" said Tysta Mördaran's consort and half-brother, Mjuka Tasssar, "*We aren't organized to fight them in large numbers.*"

Flotta Av Mul, the reindeer prince, snorted, shook his sharp pointed antlers and asserted his presence:

"*Who can dispute that it's my kind Manlings favor hunting. Not only as food but for sport; therefore, I speak out loudly against allowing the man cub to remain. I'm sorry, Lüma; but who knows —if allowed to stay, one day he may hunt me and my brethren.*"

Without waiting for a reply, "*Good hunting, all,*" said Flotta Av Mul as he departed deep into the forest.

The Bear Lord looked up at Kungörn on the branch above the gathering.

"*What say you, Sky Lord? Because you range far and wide and have seen much, we Forest Folk respect you. What are your thoughts on the matter of the man-cub*?"

Kungörn spread his wings and adjusted his stance, one set of talons at a time.

"*One might not think Sky Folk have a stake in this matter, but they'd be wrong—we do. The Manlings kill us in vast numbers. Not so much to eat, they kill us for our feathers to use as fletching for their arrows, and to stuff into cloth sacks for bedding. It doesn't matter if the man-cub remains with Lüma; the Manlings will continue hunting Sky Folk. They will go on making war on all of us. Like it or not, that is the way of this world.*"

The silver-backed wolf lord, Långa Klor, and his life mate, Vitt Hår came forward: "*When I first set eyes on the man cub,*" *said Långa Klor,* "*I saw no more than one meal, one that would scarcely feed my pups. But in the short time we've been here we've seen something more.*"

He turned to his life mate: "*Tell them, Vitt Hår.*"

"*We have seen how Lüma looks at the man-cub*," said Vitt Hår, "*and how he looks at her. It's as Lüma said; she and the man cub are bonding.*"

Vitt Hår turned away from Lüma and faced the others.

"*The man cub belongs with Lüma; we won't object to him staying in the forest.*"

"*Have you all eaten tainted meat,*" said the weasel. "*I don't believe my ears. Tell them Earth Shaker; you're closest to Lüma in mind and body. Tell the others it is madness to let the man cub live among us!*"

"*No,*" said the Bear Lord. "*I won't. Kungörn has persuaded me, so have Långa Klor and Vitt Hår. The more I think about it, the more I believe it should be Lüma's choice and hers alone.*"

"*Good hunting, Forest Folk,*" said Kungörn, the Eagle Lord. With a great flapping of his mighty wings, he flew away.

"*We agree,*" said Långa Klor and Vitt Hår with one voice. "*We've decided the matter; the man-cub will live another day.*"

"*Very well,*" said Jägare bane, the Boar Lord. "*The man-cub stays with Lüma. I see no good coming from it, but I won't interfere.*"

"*Nor will we,*" said Tysta Mördaran.

"*Good hunting one and all,*" said Mjuka Tasssar.

Without further deliberation the Forest Folk went separate ways, ready to resume the All Mother's dance of Life and Death. The Bear Lord, however, stayed. Furious, Ratatosk, Empress of weasels, foxes, marmots, and gossips, slithered off through the undergrowth.

"*Madness,*" she hissed; "*but for that pompous reindeer they're all as stupid as mud turtles.*"

"*I ask you, Lüma,*" said Botten Skakapparat, "*reflect a moment, for soon the leaves will drop from the trees and snow will settle on the All Mother's breast. Our kind needs to rest through the whole of winter and into spring. What will the man cub do while you sleep the Deep Sleep?*"

It was apparent to the Bear Lord: Lüma had no answer, and Botten Skakapparat saw no reason to press the matter.

"*Good hunting Lüma,*" he said and ambled away.

"*Good hunting, Earth Shaker.*"

Lüma went to where Beowulf stood. "*It's been a sad, bad day, little cub... but together... we'll get through this—I promise.*"

† † †

Just when she thought they were alone, Lüma saw the leaves at their feet begin to stir and blow across the ground; then, as in the face of a strong, north wind, branches of nearby trees began to pitch and sway. Above, gray-black clouds appeared where no clouds had been a moment before.

Beowulf raised his finger and pointed toward Thor and Frigga. Lüma saw nothing but trees and brush. Then, because the two gods allowed it, Lüma sensed others watching them.

"*Who's out there?*" said Lüma.

Thor and Frigga materialized in a golden light so bright it cast Lüma backward on her haunches. Bewildered though she was, it strengthened her that the man cub showed no sign of fear in the presence of such wondrous beings.

"*You needn't be afraid, Lüma,*" said Frigga, using the Silent

Tongue. "*I'm Frigga. With me is Thor, Hammer Bearer, and Lightning Bringer.*"

"*Did the All Father send you*?" said Lüma

"*Yes*," said Thor. "*We're here to help the child.*"

"*Help*?" said Lüma.

"*Show her*," said Frigga.

Thor knelt beside Beowulf. "*Fear not, little prince.*"

Thor scooped Beowulf into one arm and held him against his chest. Beowulf tugged once on Thor's beard but otherwise remained calm.

Thor raised his iron hammer, Mjolnir upward. There came a sound of rolling thunder. Sky fire penetrated Thor's hammer and traveled the length of his arm into his heart before passing through his chest into Beowulf.

Helpless, Lüma watched the man-cub's body convulse until the blue-white fire that enveloped him subsided. Beowulf's eyes rolled back; his body went limp. Thor placed Beowulf in front of the she bear's cave.

"*He needs to sleep now,*" said Thor. "*When he awakens he'll be different.*"

"*What did you do, Hammer Bearer*?" said Lüma.

"*I gave him strength,*" said Thor, "*and the will to overcome his enemies. He will be fast afoot—fast as the fastest of the Forest Folk; his eyes will see farther than the far seeing lords of the sky. Though unable to dwell there, he will be at home underwater, and Water Folk will know and respect him. In all of Midgard, there will be none like Beowulf, the bear's son.*"

"*From your milk,*" said Frigga, "*Beowulf can speak the Silent Tongue, the same as we are doing now.*"

"*We're done here, Frigga,*" said Thor, "*and have other places to be.*"

"*Wait,*" said Lüma. "*My kind must sleep through winter. How will the man cub survive*?"

"*Before the first snowfall,*" said Frigga, "*a trusted servant of the All Mother will come for the child and care for him until spring.*"

"*Shouldn't he be with his kind*?" Lüma said.

"*Yes—but his kind are also trying to kill him,*" said Thor.

"*Goodbye, and good hunting, noble Lüma,*" said Frigga.

Proceeding to their chariots, Frigga and Thor disappeared in another flash of golden light.

Lüma looked at Beowulf. She breathed a full breath and gazed at the forest around her. She took hold of this strange new cub and carried him into her cave. Outside, a light rain began to fall.

† † †

In the weeks that followed, Lüma walked through the forest with Beowulf beside her. She resolved not to let the Manlings surprise her in the way they had that fateful day when she and her cub foraged for berries.

She marveled at how Beowulf learned which trails were safe and which trails to avoid. She taught him that just as he got hungry and needed to feed, so also did the Forest Folk, and some of them would be inclined to eat him if they had the chance, while others would not.

Lüma showed Beowulf where to find the sweetest berries, the fattest termites, and crunchiest crickets. She showed him how to locate honeycombs, and she taught him how to ask the Bee Folk for their amber nectar without being stung.

Toward the end of each day, they would bathe in the stream where she taught him to be patient and wait for the fattest fish to show before seizing one from its watery abode.

If there was any sadness in the man-cub Lüma couldn't sense it, and in her way she marveled at the changes, she could see taking place: he was growing beyond belief and although in obvious pain he never whimpered or cried. At night, however, she could hear him moan as, half-asleep, he rubbed his hands over his arms and legs to ease the aching.

On cold nights they would go to the warmest part of their cave to sleep. Beowulf would lie beside her, his back against Lüma's warm belly. She let him use one of her forelegs for a pillow, and when he had settled-in, she would drape her other foreleg over him. There, beside her, where he could feel her heart beating against his back, Beowulf felt safe and protected.

Lüma sat on one of the many flat rocks surrounding a large natural pool. A waterfall fed the pool and was close to a hot spring. The flat rocks soaked-up what heat there was from the sun and warmed her haunches. She could sense the subtle change in temperature, a slight chill in the air, the harbinger of a cold winter to come. She tilted her head toward the waterfall where Beowulf stood waiting for her to watch.

On moss-covered rocks at the very edge of the falls, Beowulf waited for Lüma to look. When she did he waved to her and laughed; then he leapt into the water below. When he came to the surface, he held a trout between his teeth. He pulled himself out of the pool and went to where she sat.

She took the wriggling fish straight from his mouth and swallowed it whole.

"*I'll get more, Fur Mother,*" said Beowulf.

"*No, little cub; I've had all I need. One more fish and I'll burst.*"

As a breeze passed over them, Beowulf shivered, and his teeth began to chatter. He sat on Lüma's lap where it was warm. She wrapped her powerful forelegs around him and held Beowulf close.

"*Is it time*?" said Beowulf.

"*Yes.*"

"*How do you know*?"

"*I just know,*" she said.

"*How long will you sleep*?"

"*Until spring,*" she said. "*when the snow melts*."

"*Why*?"

"*It's the way of my kind, Beowulf.*"

"*Why*?"

"*That is something the All Mother can answer—not I.*"

Beowulf took a moment to think. "*Won't you be hungry*?" he said.

"*No,*" she said. "*I'll survive, and so will you.*"

"*How do you know? You won't be able to see me when you're sleeping.*"

"*That's true; I won't, but someone will take care of you until spring; then we'll be together again if Fate should will it so.*"

"*Who will take care of me*?"

"*A servant of the All Mother,*" she said. "*Now no more questions, little cub; they're like the fish you fed me. One more, and I'll burst.*"

Beowulf turned, threw his arms around Lüma's neck and hugged her.

"*Don't leave me.*"

"Careful, little cub, or you'll break my neck. You don't know your power."

Beowulf relaxed his hold so she could draw her breath.

"*I'll be here in the forest with you,*" *said Lüma,* "*I'll just be asleep for a while. I promise—I won't leave you.*"

While Lüma snored, Beowulf rubbed his arms and legs. He was aware of his increasing strength, but his limbs remained sore where they joined the trunk of his body. Something beyond his control stretched him day and night in all directions. There were other changes: his hair was fast growing longer; so, too, were his finger and toe nails. Beowulf found himself biting his nails when they got in his way. Moreover, his baby teeth had fallen out, and his gums ached as new teeth emerged.

Beowulf no longer possessed the vocabulary of innocence available to little children. His kind had ripped that from his consciousness. Fate evicted him from the comfortable home he was born in, the place that once succored and sheltered him from the world. The sense Beowulf made of what was happening to him, what was occurring around him, he deduced from the range of emotions he now experienced; those, and the painful physical sensations which accompanied his every waking breath.

Forest sounds, such as the wind murmuring through the branches of tall trees. Or thunder, heralding a storm. Even Lüma, snoring as she slept; or rain pelting the roof of their cave or the cry of an eagle high above the forest floor—these sounds became a significant part of Beowulf's new vocabulary. The sounds he used to interpret the feral, primal reality that enveloped him.

12

CAME AN ANDÉ HERRÉ

In his memory's orb, the once indelible image of his mother receded a little more with each passing day; her face sometimes hazy, or surrounded in a golden mist. He could see but two faces as though they were in front of him: his father, and his cousin Handscio. When Beowulf recalled Handscio giving him Uncle Rabbit for saving him from the dragon, it made Beowulf smile. Try as he might, Beowulf could not feel sadness recollecting the loss what once caused him joy but was now beyond his reach, so powerful was the spell Frigga cast over him.

Beowulf watched Lüma snore. It was midday, plenty of time to grab for fish but he didn't want to leave the cave. It was then a voice deep and resonant called to him. The words were full-throated, spoken in the Common Tongue of Midgard.

"Come, young Lord. It's time to go."

Outside the cave, Beowulf saw a tall, barrel-chested man. He was well over six-feet in height with a bushy white beard that hung to his chest. Berry juice had stained his beard dark blue down the middle. Leaning on a staff, he dressed in furs and sealskin breeches. His furs exuded the smell of wood smoke, and he carried a backpack. Over one shoulder, he carried a double-bladed battle axe.

"No need for us to use the Silent Tongue," he said, "we can sound our words. But now we have a good deal of walking to do." Rain began to fall. The stranger held out his hand. For a moment Beowulf looked at the leaden gray sky before casting a backward look at the cave.

"She sleeps the Deep Sleep," said the stranger.

"I know," said Beowulf.

Disregarding the man's hand, he looked straight into the stranger's eyes.

"I can walk by myself," said Beowulf.

The stranger looked Beowulf up and down, noting his torn linen shirt and tattered breeches; those, and the worn, sheepskin booties that no longer contained Beowulf's feet.

"We'll make you some proper clothes once we're settled," said the stranger. He glanced skyward.

"Are you cold?"

Beowulf moved his head side to side.

"Good," said the stranger, "because I'm not here to coddle you. I expect you to keep up. Understand?"

He didn't know why, but as Beowulf looked back toward the she bear's cave, he felt angry. Beowulf glanced at the stranger and nodded. As it began to pour rain, side by side they started north toward the lake country.

For the first two leagues, the stranger whistled and sang a tune that was neither familiar to Beowulf nor pleasant to his ears. When the stranger caught sight of the disapproving looks Beowulf cast in his direction he stopped.

"What?" said the stranger. "You frown like you swallowed a mouthful of bugs?"

"Lüma would disapprove," said Beowulf.

"Disapprove would she?"

"Yes," said Beowulf. "Of the loud noises you're making."

"I don't fault your fur mother for that; one must be careful in the forest to survive, but I make this noise for a good reason. I'm announcing our presence over the sound of the rain so that the Forest Folk will take notice. Understand?"

"No," said Beowulf.

"You will," said the stranger. "Now then, young Lord, with your permission, we'll be on our way."

Nonsense, Beowulf told himself; *nothing this white-beard says makes sense.*

"*I heard that*," said the stranger, using the Silent Tongue.

It was no longer raining when the stranger stopped alongside a stream. He removed his axe and backpack and placed them on a rock.

"We'll pass the night here young Lord," said the stranger.

"Here?" said Beowulf. "Out in the open? What will I sleep on?"

"You'll sleep on the All Mother's breast and be grateful for it," said the stranger.

"I'm hungry," said Beowulf. "And my legs hurt."

The stranger reached into his backpack and pulled out a half-loaf of rye bread.

"Here," said the stranger. He held out the bread.

Beowulf snatched the food from the stranger's hand, sat, and devoured every crumb.

"Not so fast, young Lord," said the stranger, "chew each bite ten times, or you'll throw it up, and that'll be the end of supper."

Beowulf paused. "Where are we going?" he said.

"To the Lake in the Clouds," said the stranger.

"Where's that?" said Beowulf.

"The land of lakes," said the stranger, "high country."

"When will we get there?"

"Three, maybe four more days. If you can make it, that is—what with your legs being sore and all."

"I don't think I like you," said Beowulf.

"That's all right, little Lord," said the stranger. "I'm not sure I like you either."

After the stranger had gathered enough dry kindling and had a fire burning, he gave Beowulf a woolen blanket to wrap around him.

Beowulf's nose wrinkled.

"This blanket smells of smoke," he said.

"I know," said the stranger. "I love the smell of wood smoke."

That night, Beowulf stretched out beside the warmth of the fire and stared at the stars. The sound of an owl hooting nearby lulled him into a dreamless sleep.

The next morning after breaking fast by eating a handful of rye bread, with some water to wash it down, Beowulf looked at the stranger.

"I'm still hungry," said Beowulf.

"Me, too," said the stranger. He shouldered his backpack and axe and started away. Beowulf stood in place. The stranger turned and faced him.

"You won't find any food standing there, young Lord," said the stranger.

"I don't like you," said Beowulf.

"So you said," said the stranger without looking back.

Beowulf took a deep breath and followed.

At midday, they came upon what appeared to be a trapper's

lodge and stopped. Skins of wolf, beaver, fox, rabbit, and elk hung on scaffolding, curing in the sunlight. Near the lodge was an enclosure; home to two pigs and a half-dozen chickens. Inside a pen nearby was a female goat and her two kids. A male goat roamed loose outside the lodge.

"Wait here behind these bushes," said the stranger. "And keep out of sight."

"Why can't I come with you?" said Beowulf.

"Because I said so," said the stranger.

"That's not a reason," said Beowulf.

The stranger stopped. A moment had passed before he turned around.

"When they told me you'd no longer think childish thoughts, they were right. Telling you to wait, just because I said so, isn't a reason. It was me being lazy. But hear me: the fewer people who know you're alive, the better off we'll be—when it comes to keeping you that way. Now, do you understand?"

Beowulf nodded.

Three, barking Jämthunds—elk hounds to use the Common Tongue, came bounding out of the woods, straight toward Beowulf and the stranger.

The stranger gave Beowulf his walking staff to hold; then stepped forward and spoke in the Silent Tongue.

"Have you three beauties forgotten me so soon?"

The stranger knelt on one knee. The hounds ceased barking and began licking the stranger's face and hands. The stranger patted each of the hounds, scratched behind their ears and called them by name before he got to his feet. Escorted by the hounds, the stranger continued to the door of the lodge and knocked. A moment later the door opened; a stocky man with long, thinning gray hair appeared. Behind him, looking over his shoulder was a woman with hair just as gray with a face no less full of creases and wrinkles. Upon seeing the stranger, the trapper lowered the axe he held. He and the woman smiled and opened their door wide. The dogs and the stranger went inside. The woodsman looked in all directions before closing the door. As he waited behind the bushes, Beowulf looked at his feet. They were red and swollen and hurt the way the rest of him did. When at last the stranger emerged from the lodge he was laughing and held a rough-spun burlap bag in one hand. The stranger joined Beowulf behind the bushes.

"Here," he said, "I'll trade you the bag for my walking stick."

Beowulf gave the stranger the staff and took hold of the bag. It was heavy, at first unwieldy, and he could tell by the smells that reached his nose that the bag held food. As the stranger started away, Beowulf looked inside the bag. He saw three wheels of goats-milk cheese wrapped in cheesecloth, each half as big as his walking companion's head. There were six round loaves of rye bread, forty or more rutabaga, a slab of bacon, and one of pork jerky, a bundle of deer jerky and six, foot-long summer sausage. Beowulf smiled, slung the bag over his shoulder and trudged off after the stranger.

"Who are they?" Beowulf said.

"Friends," said the stranger.

That night, Beowulf and the stranger sat beside their campfire and feasted on summer sausage and toasted rye bread topped with pine seeds and melted goats milk cheese. As he chewed his food, Beowulf could feel his anger toward the stranger diminish.

† † †

Three more days passed, three days of walking from sunup to sunset. With each passing day, Beowulf felt the air become crisper, colder as it stretched his lungs. His steps quickened, and Beowulf knew that he was getting stronger. However, Beowulf longed for something more than human food, something more than bread, cheese and sausage to eat. He missed Lüma; he missed the warmth of her soft round belly against his back and the sweetness of her fresh warm milk.

Eight days had passed since Beowulf left Lüma's cave. Upon waking the stranger gave Beowulf more bread and cheese to nibble on before they headed north. They walked a short distance when the stranger began talking to himself. He was speaking in a loud voice about matters and things in a language Beowulf couldn't fathom. When from the corner of his eye the stranger saw Beowulf drop the bag of provisions and hold his hands over his ears the stranger laughed. He didn't speak another word until the sun was low in the sky and they arrived at the shore of a lake. Straight ahead, three-hundred paces offshore was an island thick with conifer trees and shrouded in mist. On the near shore was a skiff that contained a single pair of oars. The stranger dragged the skiff into the water.

"Get in," he said.

Beowulf climbed inside the small boat and sat at the bow. His eyes widened when the stranger stepped aboard. The skiff rocked side to side while the stranger positioned his ponderous self on a plank and took up the oars. In a gruff voice, he muttered some unintelligible phrase similar to an incantation and began rowing toward the island. Other than the noise of the oars twisting in their locks and the splashing of the paddles in the water, an eerie silence hung over the lake. Beowulf peered into murky, deep green water. Try as he did, Beowulf could not see to the bottom nor could he glimpse any fish; nothing stirred, as though nothing lived beneath the surface.

"Where are the fish?" Beowulf said.

"Hiding from you, no doubt," said the stranger.

Clouds gathered overhead, and a gentle rain began to fall by the time the skiff touched shore on the island. Undaunted by the cold and the wet, Beowulf removed the tattered remains of the boots he had outgrown and left them in the skiff.

"Good," said the stranger. "Give your feet a chance to stretch and breathe. You'll have another pair of boots soon enough."

Beowulf nodded and followed the stranger through a thick grove of pine, fir and spruce trees. They came to a clearing where there were furs of wolves, wolverines, and mink, along with hides of elk, caribous, and reindeer stretched and hung on poles.

A short distance further was a lodge. It was twenty-paces by twenty-paces square, built of timbers hewn from the abundance of trees on the island.

"Is this your cave?" said Beowulf.

The stranger looked at the lodge and chuckled. "I suppose it is," he said.

As they approached the entrance to the lodge, the stranger called out in the Silent Tongue. "Hear me well you marmots, rodents, and weasels; time for you to leave, for I bring the bear's son with me and he doesn't much care what he eats for his supper tonight."

Beowulf looked at the stranger. "I didn't say that."

"Yes, but they don't know it," said the stranger as he opened the door.

None too pleased, a marmot and his consort hissed as they raced past Beowulf and the stranger and scampered up the trunk of the closest tree.

"It wasn't my idea for you to leave," said Beowulf. He turned to the stranger. "Now they won't want to be friends."

"Forget them," said the stranger, "there no way to make friends with marmots and weasels. They must have come down the smoke vent."

"Why not?" said Beowulf.

"Why not what," said the stranger.

"Why can't I be friends with marmots and weasels?"

"Because," said the stranger, "they don't have it in them to be friends, not with their kind, not with forest folk, not with anyone."

"Why?" said Beowulf.

"Because they haven't any conscience, any sense of honor, that's why. Now forget about them. We need to get a fire going."

The stranger looked at the sky, at the shroud of gray clouds that had settled high above the forest. He turned to Beowulf, "winter's coming," he said.

Upon entering the lodge, the stranger unslung his axe and put it down; he removed his backpack and leaned it against a wall.

"After I've caught my breath, I'll make us a nice fire so you can get warm. Would you enjoy that?"

Beowulf looked at the fireplace with its stone hearth and nodded.

"Go around back. You'll find firewood stacked in cords. Bring some wood inside, and we'll get a fire going. But you better hurry; it'll be dark soon."

"What will you be doing?" said Beowulf.

"Me," said the stranger; "I'm going to rest awhile; then I'm going out front and bring those hides inside. One more thing, boy, there's an outhouse to your right as you go out the door. Piss anywhere you want outside, but when you empty your bowels, do it sitting on the throne in the outhouse, and beware that spiders hiding in the dark don't bite your privates. You know what your privates are, don't you boy?"

Beowulf nodded; he felt himself becoming angry again; he didn't know why, but he was. He went outside and welcomed the breeze; it tempered the heat coming off his brow. Behind the lodge he found where the wood was stacked; from that, he deduced what a "cord" was. Not far from the wood was a shed enclosed on three sides, half the size of the lodge. Inside the shed, Beowulf could see an anvil, a furnace, a forge and a bellows—what his father also had on their farm. There was a rack against one wall with an array of tools hanging on it, secured by leather straps.

Turning away from the shed and finding a foothold, Beowulf climbed atop a cord. Using his bare feet, he rolled logs off the top. Done, Beowulf jumped to the ground. He clutched several pieces at a time to his chest and carried them inside the cabin, dropped them on the floor and went back outside. It was dark when Beowulf returned with a fourth armload of wood. The stranger had a fire blazing in the fireplace and food cooking in a pot.

"That's plenty of wood for tonight," said the stranger. "You'll find a water jug somewhere around here and cloth you can wet and use to wash with."

"I'll bathe in the lake," said Beowulf.

"Oh, will you now," said the stranger.

Ignoring the stranger's skeptical tone, Beowulf made no reply. He walked outside and ran back through the grove the way they'd come. When he reached the shore, he took off his tattered shirt and breeches and waded into the water. So powerful was Frigga's magic, and the powers Thor infused into Beowulf's being, Beowulf had already grown to the size of a boy twelve winters young and, as the stranger soon discovered, no longer thought or spoke as would a child of tender age.

Beowulf waded deeper into the lake until the water reached over his head; then he swam back to the island. Once ashore he looked across the lake, through the gathering gloom of the forest beyond. He felt someone or something watching him from beyond the tree line.

Then he saw it—a giant shadow. It had passed between the trees before it turned toward him with eyes large and round and pale yellow like two full moons. Beowulf waited a moment before he gathered his garments and walked a short distance before running to the lodge, fast as he could.

13

A COLD NORTH WIND

Once inside, Beowulf tossed his clothes into the fire. The stranger watched but said nothing. Beowulf sat on a wolf skin spread over the hearth, clasped his arms around his knees and stared at the flames.

"There's something out there," he said. "It was watching me from across the lake."

"I know," said the stranger.

"You knew it was out there?"

"Yes," said the stranger; "but now that he knows where you are, he'll leave us be."

"Who is he?"

"Pay no mind to what you saw," said the stranger.

He wrapped a blanket over Beowulf's shoulder and handed him a bowl of beggar's' stew with a large wedge of cheese and rye bread. The stranger prepared some stew for himself and sat near the fire. Both ate without speaking while a cold north wind howled. The wind blew across the lake, rattled the door and pushed against the lodge's shuttered windows.

Beowulf eyed the entrance.

"Don't worry," said the stranger. "nothing's coming past that door tonight."

"How can you be sure?" said Beowulf.

"Because I won't allow it, that's why," said the stranger. "It's when the chill in the air turns bitter cold, and the surface of the lake freezes over that you need concern yourself with what's out there."

"Why?" said Beowulf.

"Because, young Prince, when the ice is thick enough, things will be able to walk across the lake—that's why," said the stranger.

"What kind of things?"

"Ha! Anything with feet, I suppose. Now finish your stew."

"It tastes good," said Beowulf. "What is it?"

"A little bit of this, and a little bit of that, all thrown together," said the stranger.

"Is there meat in it?" said Beowulf.

The stranger's brow furled: "Yes, there's meat—if it tastes different to what you're accustomed, it's because it's cooked. Anything is bound to taste better than raw fish, bugs and bears' milk—ay, boy?"

"I like Lüma's milk," said Beowulf. "It's good, but so is this."

"It's the herbs I use to cook with," said the stranger. "They bring out the flavor of the meat."

The stranger refilled Beowulf's bowl.

"Eat up, Beowulf, your body needs to be fed often, and fed well. I can see that now."

"What's happening to me?" said Beowulf. "I hurt all the time—all over,"

"Since you've been with your fur mother you're growing leaps and bounds. That's what's happening."

Beowulf lowered his bowl.

"Is that why I hurt so much?"

A moment passed. The stranger's expression became somber.

"You're not growing the way an ordinary child grows, Bear's Son. The bones that hold your flesh in place are growing quickly. As they lengthen they stretch your muscles and strain your joints where your arms connect to your shoulders, and your legs greet your hips, and so on—do you understand?"

"No."

"Well," said the stranger, "you will."

"When?" said Beowulf.

"Sooner than later, I suspect," said the stranger.

"What are joints and muscles," said Beowulf, "and the other things you spoke of?"

"Ha!" said the stranger, "they're half the glue that makes you, you."

Beowulf thought a moment; then he looked himself over.

"Where's the other half?" he said.

The stranger touched a finger to Beowulf's chest—over Beowulf's heart.

"In there," he said.

Then the stranger touched Beowulf's forehead: "And there,

Bear's Son. You cannot see what I speak of, but it's what makes each of us who we are. Without it, we're no more than bags of meat. I'm going to make some tea now, and I want you to drink it while it's hot."

"Why?" Beowulf said.

"Because it will help ease your pain and let you sleep."

The stranger got up, poured hot water into a small wooden bowl, added crushed herbs and handed it to Beowulf.

"Let it sit awhile before you drink."

"Sometimes you call me, Beowulf. A moment ago you called me Bear's Son. Why, both?"

"Because you are both," said the stranger. "Among your kind you're Beowulf, just as your mother and father named you. Here, in the Silent Tongue, the Forest Folk call you the bear's son. You need to remember that, and never forget—you're both now."

"Are you my kind?" Beowulf said.

"Hmm," said the stranger, "I suppose I am… more or less."

"The men who chased me and killed my mother, are they my kind?"

The stranger had taken his time before he spoke:

"Those men are no more—Lüma and your blood-mother killed them. But if by, 'your kind,' you're asking are they human, then, yes—it pains me to say they are."

"Why did they kill my mother?"

"They killed your mother to get to you."

"Why do they want to kill me?"

"It's complicated," said the stranger.

"Tell me," said Beowulf. "I want to know."

"Very well—because of something your father did."

"To them?" said Beowulf.

"No," said the stranger, "to someone they knew."

"Do they want my father dead?"

"Yes, that's why you're safer in the forest with your fur mother and me."

"Do Forest Folk hunt and kill their kind, the way those men did my mother?"

"Forest folk are of two kinds, Beowulf: some are the hunters, others are the hunted. It's part of the All Mother's Dance."

"Am I part of the All Mother's Dance?" said Beowulf.

"Oh, yes," said the stranger, "as was your mother and Lüma's cub a part. Just remember—seldom do Forest Folk kill their kind; but when it happens, it's usually by accident, as when two males fight over a female."

"I don't understand," said Beowulf.

"Ha! Come next spring, you will."

"I saw a three-sided shed behind the lodge," said Beowulf, "where the wood is stacked. I recognized some of the tools and other things inside. They're the same as my father has at our farm."

"Oh, you saw them, did you?"

"I just told you I did," said Beowulf.

"Well, that would be the smithy where I work with metal."

A long moment passed.

"What should I call you?"

"Beorn," said the stranger.

"What are you, Beorn?" said Beowulf. "I have never seen anyone like you before."

Beorn laughed. "Is it the colors in my beard?"

"No," said Beowulf. "It's something I feel coming from inside you—but I don't know what to call it.

"Ah," said Beorn. "Good for you, young Prince. That tells me you're both sensitive and intelligent beyond your years. I'm called an *Andé Herré*, a servant of the All Mother—which, in the Common Tongue means a healer and mystic, or Schaman, as is used throughout Midgard."

"You are many things, Beorn."

"Yes," said the Schaman. "Now eat."

They continued to eat in silence while the wood in the fireplace crackled and hissed. Beowulf sipped the tea the Schaman made, and as he listened to the wind, he thought of Lüma, asleep in her cave.

† † †

Seated on her throne in Helheim, Hel, Goddess of the Underworld nodded to Death as he materialized from the surrounding mist and stood before her cloaked in shadows.

"Hail, Lord of Shadows," said Hel. "What have you learned

about the boy child?"

"The boy is alive and well, goddess. Frigga cast magic to dispel his grief and quell his fears, and through the she bear's milk, he's acquired the ability to speak the Silent Tongue. A servant of the All Mother cares for him now while his fur mother sleeps the Deep Sleep."

"What about Thor?" Hel said. "It would be unlike him not to add his heavy hand to the mix."

"Thor, Hammer Bearer, gave the bear's son enormous strength, along with speed, agility, and farsightedness. With each passing day, the boy grows beyond his age and no longer thinks as a child thinks."

"Let me ask a question of a different sort."

"Ask," said Death.

"Do you feel cheated that the bear's son is alive?"

"No, Goddess."

"Why?" said Hel. "I feel cheated. How is it you don't feel as I do?"

"I have my reasons," said Death.

"Will you share them?"

"No," said Death.

† † †

It wasn't long after Death departed from Helheim that Hel had other visitors—the Valkyries, the vaunted emissaries of the warrior goddess, Frigga. They wore shining armor and bronze helms embossed with silver eagles. Each of the Valkyries wielded a gold-tipped spear.

"For what purpose did Frigga send you here?" said Hel. "I have no souls to release from here."

One of the Valkyries stepped forward.

"We've come to escort the woman known as Liv, to Valhalla."

"On whose authority?" said Hel. "It's for me to decide the final fate of the dead."

"It is Frigga who sends us, goddess, but the All Father commands it thus."

† † †

Autumn had reached its end and the days had grown colder. Frost, the harbinger of winter returned and left its mark wherever dew had settled the night before. The sun also acknowledged the approach of winter; it was rising later and retiring earlier.

Those first days on the island Beowulf familiarized himself with his immediate surroundings. He went about barefoot, clad in a loincloth. The Schaman fashioned it from the same wolf skin Beowulf favored sitting on when inside the lodge in front of the fire.

The Schaman watched him climb among the branches of tall trees where he would greet the occasional squirrel foraging for nuts or the eagles that put down to rest before scouring the surface of the lake for fish.

Heeding the Schaman's advice, Beowulf gave the marmots little mind. There were some trees the marmots favored, such as the white pines, and though Beowulf always greeted these members of the Forest Folk, he ignored their hisses and left them alone, just as he ignored the blisters that formed on his hands and feet that healed into callouses. In time, Beowulf was able to grasp and lift most pieces of firewood with one hand, and although the Schaman marveled inside at Beowulf's increasing strength, he said nothing about it.

Not yet dawn, the Schaman had a fire started. He was heating water for their ablutions later when he saw that Beowulf had one eye open and was watching him. The Schaman paused from feeding sticks to the fire.

"Hungry?" Beorn said.

"Yes," said Beowulf.

Beowulf pushed himself into a sitting position. He held his hands out toward the warmth of the fire.

"What do we have to eat?" said Beowulf.

"Beggar's' stew," said Beorn.

"Again?" said Beowulf.

"Yes—again!" said Beorn, "You won't be getting any milk out of me, Bear's Son."

Beowulf laughed; so did the Schaman.

"It's good to know you can laugh," said Beorn.

"My mother loved to laugh," said Beowulf.

Beowulf became quiet. He stayed that way a long time before speaking:

"I miss her laughter," he said. "It's the one thing I remember most about my mother."

"Then laugh often—for you and your mother," said Beorn. "She would want that. Yes?"

A moment passed.

"Yes," said Beowulf. "She would want that."

"When you think of your mother," said Beorn, "do you feel any aching in your chest, or pain behind your eyes?"

Beowulf took a moment to consider the Schaman's question.

"No," said Beowulf. "The beautiful lady in the Forest took the pain away."

"That was the All Father's wife, the goddess, Frigga, who did that," said Beorn.

"I know," said Beowulf. "At the shrine near our farm my mother prayed to Frigga every day and to Thor, Hammer-Bearer. She also prayed to the All Father, and many of the other gods."

"Yes," said Beorn. "I know."

After they had eaten, Beorn piled a stack of animal hides on the floor near the fire. He rummaged around the lodge until he found an awl for punching holes through leather along with a large, hook-shaped needle, an iron thimble, and long thin strips of dried squirrel gut for the thread.

"Did you kill the animals that wore those?" said Beowulf, pointing at the hides.

"Yes," said Beorn, "all of them, but you must never forget, Bear's Son: the Forest Folk that wore those hides were part of the All Mother's Dance, just as we are. When you take the life of an animal for its hide, or as food, thank it for enabling you to survive one more day."

"What if the animal is trying to eat me?"

"Then kill it," said Beorn, and give thanks to almighty Thor that you survived."

"One day, you and I are going to die—aren't we, Beorn?"

"Yes," the Schaman said. "One day."

"When you're dead, Beorn, is someone going to skin you?"

"By the gods," said Beorn, "I hope not."

The Schaman leaned close to Beowulf. "You're joking me—yes?"

Beowulf grinned.

"After breakfast," said Beorn, "We'll start."

"Start what?" said Beowulf.

"I'm going to show you how to forge a knife from iron; then I'll teach you how to use it and keep an edge on it. You'll learn how to use a knife to make a bow and arrows, and you'll learn where to hunt for the black rocks—what the Romans call obsidian, the ones that shine on the inside when you break them open. You'll learn how to shape the black rocks into arrowheads and cutting stones to peel the flesh off hides and to make them smooth as your skin. But for now, Bear's Son, we need to clothe you; so I'm going to teach you how to work with hides."

Beowulf nodded.

"Good," said Beorn. "We'll start by making some boots for those not so little feet of yours."

† † †

Beowulf sat on the floor in front of the fire and worked with strips of cured leather laces, furs, and hides; while the Schaman looked on.

"Tell me about my people, Beorn."

"Hmm? Your mother and father?"

"No," said Beowulf. "My people. My tribe. Where do we come from?"

"Ah!" said the Schaman. "Interested in your history, are you?"

"I wouldn't be asking if I wasn't," said Beowulf.

The Schaman laughed, but it was more of a bark than a laugh.

"Very well," said the Schaman. "Your people, the Thunder-Geats, came to Scandia long, long ago.

"How long ago?" said Beowulf.

"Hah!" said the Schaman. "So you want to know your people's history from the very, very, very beginning—Is that it?"

"Yes," said Beowulf, annoyed that he should have to repeat himself.

"Then listen well, for there are very few who know what I am about to tell you."

Beowulf sensed the serious tone in the Schaman's voice and nodded.

"Long ago—"

"How long ago?" said Beowulf, interrupting.

"Many, many, many winters ago, perhaps two-thousand, or—"

"How many is that?" said Beowulf.

The Schaman paused to take note of the earnestness of Beowulf's inquiry. Then his eyes sparkled.

"More than either of us can count on our fingers, young Prince," said the Schaman. "Now, do you want to hear the story, or not?"

Beowulf nodded.

"Two-thousand winters ago, a war was fought between two great peoples—the Greeks, and the Thracians. The Greeks launched a thousand ships to fight in the Thracian city of Troy, a place far to the south of where we are now. After ten winters of battle, and with help from some of the gods, the Greeks proved victorious, and the once proud city of Troy was no more. Thracians, by the tens of thousands, fled their homeland and took with them as much of the city's wealth as they could. Thousands of these early people—"

"Thracians?" said Beowulf.

"Yes," said the Schaman. "Thracians. They fled by the thousands in ships while thousands took flight overland. Those who went by land used the great rivers to guide and sustain their migration north. In time, those who went overland reached the coast of what is now Germania. They built ships and continued north across the Whale Road to Scandia. The vast treasure they had brought with them, they placed in a cavern where the Tern River empties into the sea. The warrior who led these Thracians north, overland from Troy, was Chirodamas, one of the sons of King Priam. His half brother, Aeneas, led the Thracians who fled west in ships over the Whale Road to a place called Carthage. Great misfortune once again befell the Thracians, those led by Chirodamas—who are the ancestors of your people—the Thunder-Geats."

"What happened?" said Beowulf.

"Fire Drakes. They came out of the desert lands in the east.

They felt nothing but loathing for humankind, these creatures, and they claimed the fertile green Northland for themselves. The Thracians managed to kill some of them but not before many hundreds of their people died by the winged worms, including King Chirodamas. The Thracians built a funeral barrow for him above the cavern where they placed the wealth of Troy."

"What of the winged worms that lived?" said Beowulf. "What became of them?"

"That, I do not know," said the Schaman.

"And the Thracians who survived?" said Beowulf.

"I am getting to that, young Prince," said the Schaman, pleased that Beowulf absorbed the story and yet was able to concentrate on working with the needle and leather.

"The Thracians who survived the battle with the Drakes could not agree among themselves as to who should be their next king. But, of one thing, they were certain—the treasure brought with them from Troy was now cursed by the Fire Drakes; so, they left it be."

"And then what happened, Beorn?"

"Some families banded together; others went separate ways. In time these families grew to be clans; then became tribes. Long ago, one such group split into two tribes: Thunder-Geats and Wylfings. Other clans that had grouped would in time divide. They became Kelts, Franks, Frisians, Spear Danes, Sea Brondings, Svear, Jutes, Angles, Saxons, Teutons, Cimbrii, Goths, Harii and so on. And there you have it, young Prince: the history of the people of Westernesse. So, having heard all that, what do you think?"

Beowulf held up a finished pair of knee-high boots for the Schaman to inspect:

"You tell me," Beowulf said.

14

HARD HEART, COLD IRON

The moon was overhead when Ecgtheow smelled smoke from their cooking fire and heard their laughter. Wylfings—he was certain of it. Removing his cloak, chainmail shirt, and helm, he left Rain Dancer tethered to a tree and crept toward their camp. His sword remained in its sheath, slung crosswise over his back. He held Liv's knife by the blade, clenched between his teeth. When he was no more than fifteen paces away from their fire, he stopped. He was close enough to count them—twelve. Nearby, the Wylfings had tethered their horses in a line upwind.

Ecgtheow waited until the Wylfings bedded-down wrapped in their cloaks near the fire. They posted one man to keep watch. Ecgtheow waited until the guard gathered his cloak around his shoulders, sat and nodded off, chin on his chest. He was the first throat Ecgtheow slit from ear to ear. Ecgtheow moved from one to the next, until all twelve were dead. Done, he left the head of each Wylfing on the chest of the body to which it belonged, a greeting to those Wylfings who might come looking for him. He gathered whatever food he could find in the Wyflings' saddlebags along with the gold rings and silver wedges he found in their pockets.

With the moon low in the sky and taking the Wylfings' horses with him, Ecgtheow mounted Rain Dancer and continued south in the direction of Land's End. The congestion in his lungs told him he needed more rest or risk a relapse from which he might not recover. He thought about the Harii village, about their kindness to him, and he thought about Eydís.

† † †

At dawn, Ecgtheow arrived at the farm of a Freeman named Arne Konr, a widower who had fought alongside Ecgtheow's father in the Battle on the Ice, many winters before. Arne Konr was

one of the few Thunder-Geats who survived to tell of that battle and the fell deeds done that day. Ecgtheow looked around—the lodge, the barn, and all the outbuildings were dark.
Something's wrong, he thought. *There's not a sound coming from inside or a light burning anywhere. Why aren't Arne and his sons working? And where are the girls? Where're Arne's daughters?*

The answers to Ecgtheow's questions greeted him when he stepped inside the lodge. The Wylfings had gotten there first and spared no one. The bodies of Arne Konr, his sons, Rolf and Vidar, and his daughters Sigrid and Svan, lie where their murderers butchered them. Ecgtheow led Rain Dancer and the Wylfing horses to the barn. He put hay down for them to eat before he returned to the lodge house.

For how many more deaths am I responsible Ecgtheow said to himself as, one by one, he dragged the bodies outside into the turnip garden where he spent the remainder of the day stripped to the waist, burying them. It was where the soil was loose which made it easier for Ecgtheow to dig graves and as he dug, Ecgtheow wondered why the Wylfings hadn't torched the Konr farm; then, it occurred to him:

They want Väster Geats to see their handiwork and not soon forget it.

When Ecgtheow finished burying the dead, he dumped buckets of water over his head to wash the dirt and sweat off his body. Done washing he sat in the sun and savored its warmth while he sharpened the blade of Liv's knife.
Later Ecgtheow rummaged through the lodge for food and blankets which he took to the barn. Resolved to stay at the Konr farm until he healed, Ecgtheow made himself a bed in the hayloft and slept for a day and night without waking; then he slept some more.

† † †

In Frihamm, the Dark Queen put off disposing of her son's remains. The smell of his putrefying corpse was so rank that, despite the clouds of incense that filled the air, her servants loathed to enter her bed chamber to empty the chamber pots and change the linens stained with the corpse's body fluids. Even after

Modryth had cremated Prince Heatholaf's body, the fetid smell of death lingered throughout the upper tier of her palace. The odor comforted Modryth. Having something to remind her of Heatholaf was better than nothing.

Germanicus knew better than to look the Dark Queen in the eyes when she was in one of her moods. Not before Prince Heatholaf's death had he seen Modryth so distraught.

"How many times," said Modryth, "must the moon wax and wane before you bring me Ecgtheow Waegmunding? If he's no longer hiding in Frihamm, where is he? And don't tell me the Wylfings have searched everywhere, Germanicus. If they had, we'd know where he is."

"No doubt, great Queen," said Germanicus.

"Have you any good news?"

"Yes, great Queen. Our spies say Lars Ásmundr's men killed Waegmunding's wife. It will please you to know she was King Hrethel's daughter; moreover, there was a child, Hrethel's grandson."

"The wife's death does please me," said Modryth, "but does little to assuage my grief. But what's this you say about a child?"

"The child is, or was, a male-child, great Queen, six, maybe seven winters young, but they never found his body. Some say the Wylfings killed him and beasts devoured his body. Some say he lives. Others say there's magic afoot in the forest where searchers found the mother's body; some even say an unseen force bore the child to safety."

"Magic?" repeated Modryth. "If the child is alive, magic might account for his disappearance. But if so what do I do about it? That's the question?"

"I may have the answer, great Queen," said Germanicus, "with your permission?"

Modryth nodded.

Germanicus turned to a hall steward.

"Bring in the Ostrogoth," said Germanicus.

Hathus, the Ostrogoth, was head and shoulders taller than Germanicus. In one hand, the Ostrogoth held a chain attached to the collar of a Torvemosehunden—a Swamp Dog. The Ostrogoth snapped his fingers; the dog sat. Hathus wore a sleeveless bearskin vest, suede boots and sealskin breeches held in place by a wide leather belt. His armor was nothing more than a circular iron chest plate large enough to cover his heart and engraved with tribal runes. Hand-linked iron chains hung over his shoulders and around his ribs securing the plate to his chest. He had no helm; few Ostrogoths wore them; since going into battle bareheaded was a symbol of defiance, an insult to would-be conquerors like the Romans that dated back two centuries. He wore his long red hair tied back in a horsetail that reached to his buttocks. His face was smooth but for a wiry red mustache, the ends of which hung past his chin. Tattoos covered the backs of his massive hands, his bare arms, chest, and forehead. His weapon of choice was a spear made from dark ash topped with barbed iron. For close combat, Hathus carried a long-handled battle axe slung crosswise over his back, and a knife with an elk horn handle that hung from his belt. Germanicus didn't know what to make of the lascivious expression on Modryth's face as she eyed the Ostrogoth up and down.

"This is Hathus, great Queen," said Germanicus, "once paid by the Romans to hunt deserters from their legions in Iberia and Gaul."

"Impressive," said Modryth. "Greetings, Hathus."

The Ostrogoth nodded. "The rumors of your beauty hardly do you justice, great Queen."

Modryth smiled.

"Are you as good with your spear as you are with your tongue?"

"Maybe better, great Queen," he said.

"Hmm," said Modryth, "perhaps, later, you can give me a demonstration."

A sly smile appeared on the Ostrogoth's face.

"Of course, great Queen."

The blood drained from Germanicus' cheeks.

"Did the Captain of my Guard tell you what I want to do?" said Modryth.

The Ostrogoth gave Germanicus a nod.

"Your Captain said I would be hunting an assassin; a Väster Geat named Ecgtheow Waegmunding."

"There's more to it now than just that," said Modryth.

"There usually is," said Hathus.

"Waegmunding has a boy child, six, maybe seven winters young. I want you to bring them both to me—alive. The problem is, they may not be together. Tell him, Germanicus."

"My men searched every lodge and outhouse in Frihamm," said Germanicus, "but they didn't find Ecgtheow Waegmunding. King Amunwolf's men hunted overland, throughout Öster Götaland and Väster Götaland both; still, Waegmunding eluded them. The Iron Wolf's men succeeded in killing the men Waegmunding came to Hell's Grove with and later they found and killed Waegmunding's wife in a forest near his farm. But the child may have survived."

"The child could have been carried off by beasts, great Queen," said Hathus.

"True," said Modryth; "but there's also talk of magic and an unseen force that protects the child. Does the thought of magic frighten you, Hathus?"

"No, great Queen," said Hathus. "I fear neither man nor magic. Neither does the Swamp Dog at my feet. A Master Metalsmith forged the tip of my spear in Gaul. He tempered the iron with blood from throats I cut—buckets of it from every man, woman, and child in the metalsmith's village. There's nothing alive that I cannot kill with that spear."

"The Captain of my Guard was right to send for you, Hathus. You're just the man I need to see this through."

"I do what I do for pay, great Queen. I want a hundred gold rings for the child, provided he's still alive, and twice that for the father—agreed?"

"I'll give you twenty gold rings now," said Modryth, "and the rest when you've brought me what I want. Agreed?"

"You needn't give me anything now, apart from food and drink and a place to sleep before I leave. Pay me in full when I return to them both. In the meantime, it would help if I knew what this assassin looks like."

Germanicus looked at Hathus.

"I'll round up vendors and merchants who were in the marketplace when Waegmunding appeared with Prince Heatholaf's head. You can speak with them."

"Rest assured, Hathus," said Modryth, "we'll find witnesses who can describe the assassin. Meanwhile, Germanicus, select four of your best men to accompany Hathus. I want the father and child brought to me alive. I don't care if it takes all winter to find them."

"I travel faster when I travel alone, great Queen," said Hathus.

"I've no need of your Captain of Guards or his warriors."

"Just the same," said Modryth, "If you want my gold you'll do as I say—agreed?"

The Ostrogoth took a long moment before answering.

"Of course, great Queen."

"One more thing, Hathus," said Modryth. "I don't handle disappointment well."

† † †

To avoid the smoke coming off the pile of dead animals they set on fire, Weohstan and the Freemen climbed ladders to the wall-walk inside the palisade near the Main Gate. The stench of the animals had prompted the men to tie strips of cloth doused with peppermint oil over their mouths and noses.

Weohstan looked around and noted what else there was to do. Apart from the Main Lodge, not one outbuilding remained standing: not the hay barn, or the milking barn, not the shed where Ecgtheow and his Freemen once did metalwork, not the sauna or bathhouses, not even an outhouse remained standing. Weohstan's Second-in-Command, a Freeman, named Leif, stepped to Weohstan's side.

"Once these carcasses are dealt with," said Leif, "what would you have us do, my Lord?"

"Ursula and the women can clean the Main Lodge. At the same time, Leif, I want trees cut, lots of them, enough to rebuild the outbuildings. We're going to relocate and strengthen the Main Gate, and we'll expand the stake wall making the grounds bigger. Ecgtheow's farm is the hub of the wheel, the other farms, mine included, are the spokes. Without the hub to hold us together, our farms will crumble. In the meantime, Leif, since Knut Iron Jaw reneged on his offer to assist us, I want outriders scouting in every direction for Wylfing patrols."

"Yes, my Lord," said Leif, "I'll do what I can, but we're short on men."

"Then send word from Falcon's Nest to Land's End; say Weohstan Waegmunding is looking for warriors who want to better themselves. It matters not if they're married or single, but mind you, I want no thieves, shirkers, ne'er-do-wells or Berserkers. I want men who aren't afraid of hard work and who know how to fight—understand?"

"Yes, my Lord," said Leif. "I'll send my cousins to spread the word. In the meantime, I'll gather our Freemen and as many teams of oxen as I can buy or borrow and start harvesting timber."

Weohstan continued to stare at the flames and smoke coming from the dead animals. What the fire didn't consume the Freemen would bury outside the palisade. The rage Weohstan felt, the rage he struggled to contain and conceal from Ursula, and Handscio seared his very core. He wanted vengeance, yet he knew in his heart revenge could best be gotten not with a sword or a spear but by Clan Waegmunding rebuilding what Wylfings had destroyed and he would make it better than it was before. Besides, Weohstan knew his cousin, Ecgtheow, all too well: *If he isn't already dead, Ecgtheow will spill Wylfing blood enough for us both.*

Weohstan returned to the Main Lodge for another look around. Without cooking fires burning or lamps illuminating the interior, shadows darkened the lodge. Large patches of dried blood stained the floor of the Banquet Hall.

It will take more than scrubbing to cleanse this place, Weohstan told himself.

15

LAND'S END

Land's End was unremarkable but for the fact that, on a rare clear day Hrethel's coast guards could look south and see ships approaching from seven leagues away. This fact allowed time to discern friend from foe and, if necessary, send the 'alarm' along the coast to the king in Falcon's Nest. The fog was a constant hindrance, but when the sun prevailed, Hrethel's Coastguards could look west and see the coast of Daneland where Hrothgar, son of Halfdane, ruled from the fabled gold-gilded Hall known as Heorot.

Further west beyond the island that was Daneland, was the peninsula of Jutland, a wild place claimed by Frisians, Angles, Franks, Euburones, and Saxons. It was also a place for sea raiders to roost during the winter when most others dared not risk going aviking on the Whale Road.

Once a small fishing community beneath the heights of Land's End, the village had grown eightfold over time and had become a major port-of-call. Ships coming and going from Modryth's domain in Frihamm could drop anchor at Land's End, trade and take on supplies for the next leg of their trip. Once a cluster of huts and fishing boats, as it expanded the village took the name of Land's End for itself. Over time it became for Hrethel what Frihamm was for Amunwolf—an ongoing source of revenue that made peace among the tribes a lucrative business in itself. From the heights of Land's End, where Hrethel's coast guards were quartered and maintained their lookout, the terrain sloped toward the sea below; which made the port accessible to buyers and sellers, cowherds and shepherds, all eager to trade their wares and chattels. However, there were others drawn there, like Ecgtheow, whose business was to commission a vessel for hire.

"Poppa, look," said Mikla. He pointed at the rider approaching with a string of horses. "It's Lord Ecgtheow and Rain Dancer!"

Nine winters young, Mikla was the son of Trygve, a Captain of coastguards posted at Land's End. Trygve and Ecgtheow were well acquainted and on favorable terms. Ecgtheow's comings and goings for King Hrethel had made it so. Ever since Trygve's son Mikla was old enough to ride, Ecgtheow let him care for Rain Dancer whenever he came to Land's End.

"Yes, boy," said Trygve, "I see them."

Trygve motioned to several of his men sitting around a cooking fire.

"Get off your arses and look sharp!"

Mikla saw a look of tension cross his father's face.

"What's wrong, Poppa?"

Trygve looked at his son and patted Mikla on the head.

"Nothing's wrong, Mikla. Ask Lord Ecgtheow's permission before you give Rain Dancer anything from your hand."

"Yes, Poppa," said Mikla.

"Hail, Lord Ecgtheow," said Trygve.

"Hail, Trygve," said Ecgtheow. "Hail, Mikla. Look at you—you've grown!"

"Yes, Lord Ecgtheow. "I'm nine winters young now."

"It shows," said Ecgtheow. "I'm sure Rain Dancer and these others could do with something good to eat."

He looked at Trygve and winked.

"And maybe later your father will allow you to ride Rain Dancer a half-league and back."

"Oh, yes," said Mikla. "May I Poppa?"

"Of course," said Trygve.

Trygve looked at his men.

"Help Mikla stable those horses!"

Two of Trygve's men, Geir and Ivar, hastened to the string of horses standing idle.

"These are Wylfing horses, Captain," said Geir, running a hand over one of the saddles.

"What of it?" said Trygve. "Take them to the stables and feed them—now!"

"Yes, Captain," said Geir.

Ecgtheow dismounted and handed the reins to Mikla. Grinning from ear to ear, Mikla kissed Rain Dancer on the nose and led him away.

Ecgtheow and Trygve became serious.

"Do you know why I'm here, old friend?" said Ecgtheow.

"Sad to say, I do, my Lord. The word from Falcon's Nest reached us several days ago."

Ecgtheow nodded: "Mu business travels fast on the coast."

"Bad news always does," said Trygve. "I'm sorry, my Lord, for your loss. Our king should be going to war with the Wylfings, not sending you into exile."

Ecgtheow cast a hurried glance side-to-side.

"Speak softly, Trygve, lest others use your words against you."

"If it pleases you, my Lord, let's talk in my lodge; there'll be no one there but us, to hear what's said."

Ecgtheow went with Trygve to his lodge where Trygve poured them both a horn of ale and set out bread and cheese. After Ecgtheow had eaten enough to quiet the rumblings of his stomach, he looked at Trygve.

"If others come asking, tell them you saw me board a ship bound for Frisia. Will you do that?"

"Frisia, my Lord?"

"Yes," said Ecgtheow, "Let them think I've gone to Frisia to sell my sword to the Frisians."

"Winter's coming," said Trygve, "there'll be fewer ships putting out to sea until next spring. Best you get some place safe, while the getting's still good."

"True enough," said Ecgtheow. "All the better I leave today, or tomorrow, at the latest."

"Very well, my Lord, as soon as you're gone I'll let word slip that Ecgtheow Waegmunding left Väster Götaland bound for Frisia."

"Good," said Ecgtheow. "As for the Wylfing war horses, sell them; distribute what you get to you and your men, but give the best horse to Mikla, if you think he's ready."

Trygve followed Ecgtheow from the lodge where Mikla waited with Rain Dancer. Ecgtheow and Trygve clasped forearms.

"Die well, Trygve."

"Die well, my Lord."

† † †

Built to carry cargo across the open sea, a knarr bound for Jutland by way of Daneland had room enough to accommodate Ecgtheow and the stallion. It was late autumn and crossing the Whale Road would soon be unthinkable for all but the most foolhardy traveler in the best of ships; even then, it was folly to contemplate going aviking so close to winter.

The mere thought of exile left a bitter taste in Ecgtheow's mouth, but without Liv and Beowulf, it no longer mattered where he called home. Amidst barrels carrying barley, casks of beer and mead and a diverse assortment of iron tools and weapons, Ecgtheow made a place for himself next to Rain Dancer. Uncomfortable as it might be, one or two days sailing to Daneland was nothing insurmountable.

Ecgtheow rubbed the palm of his hand over the tight skin of his shaven face. From a vendor at Land's End, Ecgtheow bought a sharp iron blade, long as his forefinger, with a walrus tusk handle. In the privacy of a sauna, he shaved his face raw. How strange his skin felt after wearing a beard that covered all but his nose and lips. The recollection of how Liv once shivered with pleasure when he brushed her skin with his beard, now caused him pain—pain from a wound so deep no fire, no hot iron could cauterize. Ecgtheow put aside recalling the past; he took comfort in the warmth Rain Dancer provided as the stallion nuzzled Ecgtheow's new face.

† † †

After coupling with Ursula for most of the night, Weohstan lay spent in bed, staring at the fire while Ursula nodded off. Weohstan knew the look of contentment on her face was a good thing since Ursula and the other women had not yet seen the condition of Ecgtheow's lodge which Weohstan would soon ask them to clean. Weohstan rehearsed what he would say, what he would tell Ursula what he wanted her and the other women to do. Then the door to their bedchamber opened.

Handscio tiptoed to the edge of his parents' bed.

"Poppa," he said. "Are you awake?"

"What is it?" said Weohstan. "Why aren't you in bed asleep?"

"I was having bad dreams."

"Hand me my robe," said Weohstan. "It's on the floor."

Handscio found Weohstan's robe and gave it to him. Weohstan slipped his robe on and got out of bed. He lifted Handscio into his arms.

Together in the dining hall they drank milk and ate honey cakes spread with lingonberry jam. When they had both eaten enough to suit them, Weohstan smoothed Handscio's hair back out of his face.

"Time for you to go to bed, little bug," said Weohstan.

"I miss him, Poppa," said Handscio.

"Who?" said Weohstan.

"Beowulf. I miss him, Poppa."

Tears spilled from Handscio's eyes. Handscio threw himself into his father's arms.

"I know you do," said Weohstan.

He kissed the tears off Handscio's cheeks and held him close.

"I know you do. We all do."

† † †

It was well after dawn, two days out from Land's End when the knarr approached Daneland and the port of Mörk Sand. Close to shore, past the breakwater, the fog lifted. The first sight to greet Ecgtheow's blurry eyes was Hrothgar's fleet of Longships, eighty in all, lashed together in preparation for waiting-out the winter. The Danes had furled the sails and lashed the hulls together in four rows of twenty battle craft each. A skeleton crew, six men per each row, was all that maintained watch on Hrothgar's fleet. As the knarr sailed into port, Ecgtheow saw the familiar iron stanchions and the torches they held that lined the length of the waterfront; they aided ships coming and going by facilitating the loading and unloading of cargoes. Once mooring lines had secured the knarr, fore, and aft, and workers unloaded its cargo, Ecgtheow led Rain Dancer up a ramp and onto the dock through a throng of men, seafarers, and merchants, toward the wharf beyond.

He walked Rain Dancer through the busy streets so the stallion could accustom his powerful legs to being on land again—

Ecgtheow, too. Uppermost on his mind was getting something decent to eat, fresh water to drink and obtaining grain for the stallion. After they ate they could both do with some sleep, real sleep, on a surface that wasn't out in the open, rolling and pitching beneath them while salt water stung their eyes each time the wind shifted—a barn would do just fine.

† † †

They were on the road to Hell's Grove, less than a league from Frihamm when Hathus signaled for Germanicus and the four warriors to halt. Just ahead was the metalsmith's lodge and barn.

"Why are we stopped here?" said Germanicus.

"Is this the last dwelling outside town?" said Hathus.

Germanicus nodded.

"Was it searched?"

"The Wylfings searched it," said Germanicus, "while my men searched for Waegmunding in Frihamm."

"Who lives there?" said Hathus

"An old man—a metalsmith by trade; at least he was before his eyes failed. His granddaughter lives with him."

"Ah!" said Hathus. "I have a fondness for such men. Shaping metal is a high art among my people; some even say it's a gift from the gods. I want to have words with him."

Bad as his eyes were, there was nothing amiss with Usul's ears. Hearing the riders approach, he and Moira went outside to greet them. Her eyes grew large with fear when she saw the Swamp Dog waiting alongside the giant, red-haired warrior staring at her.

"Greetings, metalsmith," said Hathus.

"Forgive me, good sirs," said Usul, "but I don't see so well. Who are they, Moira?"

"They're Queen Modryth's men, Grandfather," said Moira, "with an Outlander… and a dog, I think."

"There's nothing wrong with your eyes, girl," said Hathus. "I'm Hathus, an Ostrogoth. We search for Prince Heatholaf's assassin, a Väster Geat named Ecgtheow Waegmunding. You wouldn't happen to be hiding him inside your lodge, would you?"

"The Iron Wolf's riders searched this road," said Usul. "They didn't tell us why or who or what they were searching for, but now we know—don't we, Granddaughter?"

"Yes, Grandfather."

Hathus looked at Germanicus. "Have your men search the lodge and outbuildings," said Hathus.

"Why?"

"They know more than they're letting on," said Hathus. "I can sense it."

Germanicus motioned to his men; the four dismounted and drew their swords. Two warriors hastened toward the lodge, the other two headed for the metalsmith's barn. Several moments had passed before the four returned to their horses.

"There's no one else here nor any sign of Waegmunding," said one of the four.

"Very well," said Germanicus, "mount up."

"Waegmunding was here, wasn't he, old man," said Hathus.

"Better for you and the girl if you speak the truth," said Germanicus.

"A lone rider did stop here," said Usul. "But that was some time ago."

"Where was he headed?" said Germanicus.

"He didn't say," said Usul, "and I didn't ask."

Usul put an arm around Moira's shoulders.

"I sharpened the blade of his knife and sword, that's all; then he paid me and left. That's all I know."

Hathus got down from his horse and stood in front of Usul.

"Maybe," said Hathus, "maybe not."

Before Usul could reply, Hathus unsheathed his knife and cut Moira's throat. The girl collapsed into her grandfather's arms. Maintaining his hold on Moira, Usul sagged to his knees. With gnarled hands, he tried to stem the flow of blood spilling from Moira's throat.

The Ostrogoth kicked the metalsmith in the chest; the force of the kick propelled the old man into the dirt. While Usul struggled to catch his breath, Hathus looked at his dog and pointed at Moira.

"Drink," said the Ostrogoth.

The Swamp Dog lapped-up the warm blood flowing from her throat.

Hathus mounted his horse. "Let's go!"

Snapping the reins, Hathus started away. The others followed.

"Where now?" said Germanicus.

"Since the Wylfings went searching over land," said Hathus, "we'll head for the coast."

"Tell me something," said Germanicus.

"What?"

"You killed the girl, but not the old man."

"Yes," said Hathus.

"Why?"

"I told you," said Hathus, "I have a fondness for metalsmiths; besides, my dog was thirsty."

16

FOREST FOLK

In place of the rags he consigned to the fireplace three weeks before, Beowulf had new clothes to wear including knee-high boots. The Schaman grooved the soles of the boots for better traction and Beowulf waterproofed each boot with oil made from deer brains; which he rubbed into the leather, day and night. He wore deerskin pants that reached to his waist, with round buttons in the front which the Schaman helped him fashion from caribou horn and sew into the leather. The buttons made his pants easy to put on, take off and access the crotch when his bladder called. A wide leather belt made from several layers of caribou hide, glued together with pine sap helped keep his pants in place. For a belt buckle, the Schaman gave Beowulf one of his buckles made from bronze and a knife that the Schaman helped Beowulf shape and forge. Beowulf carried it in a tooled leather sheath that he wore on his belt along with a pouch made from elk skin. The Schaman put a whetstone for sharpening the edge of Beowulf's knife into the pouch, along with a flint and striking-stone for making fire. He included a piece of shaped obsidian, jagged on one edge for cutting through wood or bone and a needle, thread and a thimble.

Cured and brushed doeskin provided Beowulf with a loose-fitting tunic that hung past his thighs. To keep his head, ears, and neck warm when the days ahead turned bitter cold, the Schaman helped Beowulf fashion a hat from Black Beaver pelts. To further ward off the cold outdoors, Beowulf made himself a knee-length cloak out of wolf skins.

"Good job," said Beorn, "your new clothes will keep you warmer than not through winter. Now gather your bow and the quiver of arrows you made. We'll see if your aiming is any good."

"You already know it is," said Beowulf.

"Ha," said Beorn, "skewering a mark painted on a tree is one thing, Bear's Son; the real test of a weapon comes when life is in the balance—yours."

Beowulf did as told; then he followed the Schaman out of the lodge.

"The time may come when you find yourself alone in the forest," said Beorn, "with little to rely on but your wits."

"But I'm getting stronger every day, Beorn."

"Strength means little without a good head on your shoulders, Beowulf. Your father would tell you the same thing if he was here."

"Do you think he's still alive?"

The Schaman thought for a moment.

"Yes, I believe Ecgtheow's alive; but he's not here, so listen carefully to what I tell you—what I teach you might just save your life one day."

"Tell me," said Beowulf. "I'll listen."

"It's time you learned how to fend for yourself. I'll row you to the far shore. Once we're there, I want you to go into the forest and catch a rabbit. After you've killed it, I'll teach you how to skin an animal, so you won't spoil the meat or damage the hide; then, later, we'll roast it for supper."

Beowulf hesitated, his jaws tightened.

"What?" said Beorn. "You look as if you just swallowed a stink bug."

"I know I can catch a rabbit; I just don't think I can kill one."

"Why not?" said the Schaman. "As strong as you are you could break my neck if you wanted. Snap its neck quickly, and the rabbit won't feel a thing, believe me."

"Why don't I catch it… and you kill it?" said Beowulf.

"Listen," said Beorn; "When you were with Lüma, you killed bugs and ate them—yes?"

Beowulf frowned. "Sometimes," he said, "Mostly I ate berries and honey, or I fed on Lüma's milk."

"What about fish?" Beorn said. "Did you kill fish?"

"Yes," said Beowulf.

"And did you eat them?"

"Sometimes," Beowulf said. "Most of the time, I just caught them for Lüma."

"But sometimes you ate them?"

"Yes, part of them," said Beowulf. "I already told you I did."

"And why did you eat them?"

"Because I was hungry," said Beowulf, "and there was nothing else to eat."

"Ha," said Beorn. "You were hungry, so it didn't matter if you killed and ate them—did it?"

"No," said Beowulf.

"Listen, Bear's Son; we are hunters; it's why our eyes are in front; they face forward so we can see our prey. It's the same for every creature that hunts to survive."

"I just don't think I can kill a rabbit," said Beowulf, "not when I'm holding it in my hands, feeling its heart beating, watching it look into my eyes and knowing it wants to live."

Several moments had passed before the Schaman spoke.

"When I first laid eyes on you I said I wasn't going to coddle you—remember?"

"Yes," said Beowulf. "I remember."

"Good," said Beorn. "Now, listen! As long as men are hunting you, whether you live or die depends on you. Maybe not today, maybe not tomorrow, but one day you'll find this out for yourself. Your father, Ecgtheow is a warrior—a killer of men; so, too, will you become a slayer of men. The sooner you make peace with your fate, the better. The choice is yours, Bear's Son. Kill, or be killed."

Several moments passed. The Schaman sensed the anger building inside Beowulf.

"Did you give your knife a proper name?" said Beorn.

"It doesn't have a name yet," said Beowulf.

"Well, I'm sure you'll think of one," said Beorn. "Are you ready to go?"

"You needn't row me," said Beowulf. "I'll do it myself."

"Good hunting, Bear's Son," said the Schaman.

The Schaman waited on the shore and watched Beowulf launch the skiff into the water. Beowulf struggled for a moment with the oars before he got the doing of it. He rowed across the lake and disappeared into the forest.

Beowulf didn't know why he was angry with the Schaman; he just was, and the fact that his joints were sore and his muscles ached didn't help matters. The Schaman's herbal tea dulled Beowulf's pain but didn't cure it; there was no cure. His body had grown at an accelerated rate, pulled by an unseen force in all directions for weeks on end. The growth slowed, but every few days the Schaman found himself trimming Beowulf's finger and toenails. Beowulf's baby teeth had come out, replaced by other teeth suitable for gnashing and grinding and ripping flesh apart. Beowulf shouldered his bow and quiver of arrows. Before he disappeared into the tree line, he looked back toward the island and saw the Schaman on the far shore, watching him. Beowulf had taken no more than twenty paces when he turned around and went back.

He emerged from the tree line and stood beside the skiff. Just as Beowulf suspected, the Schaman was standing in the same place, staring in his direction.

"*I won't do it*," said Beowulf, using the Silent Tongue.

"*Fair enough*," said Beorn, "*and when you're starving—because you've killed nothing and have nothing to eat, who's going to feed you*?"

The Schaman turned and walked toward the lodge.

"I'll feed me," Beowulf said with a shout. "Do you hear, Beorn? I'll feed me!"

Beowulf watched the Schaman disappear from view before returning to the forest. He walked north and noted that the sun was on his right-hand-side.

The great star is in the east he told himself; *which means it's still morning. I'll walk until midday; then make camp.*

Beowulf did just that; he walked until the sun was overhead. It wasn't long before he found a clearing beside a stream. *This place feels right,* he told himself. *I'll make camp here.*

As best he could reckon, he had walked two leagues north of the little lake, far enough away the Schaman couldn't hear his thoughts; yet not so far he couldn't return to the lake in less than a day. That was when he realized that without the skiff the Schaman would have to remain on the island.

He'll have to stay there unless he has another skiff. Or maybe he can swim? Hah! Big as Beorn is he would sink to the bottom of the lake before he reached the shore.

Beowulf amused himself picturing the Schaman alone, not having Beowulf to order around. He conjured scenes in his head, each more elaborate than the one before, each at the Schaman's expense; he did this while he cut branches to make a lean-to if it rained. When he finished making a lean-to, he cut other branches thick with pine needles for bed.

After Beowulf had collected enough wood suitable for a campfire, he crushed dried leaves into a small pile and with his flint and striking-stone soon had a fire burning. Beowulf squatted and fed twigs and sticks to the flames while his thoughts returned to the island and the Schaman.

Maybe I'll keep walking tomorrow. It would serve Beorn right if I left him on the island with the marmots.

Beowulf was getting hungry. When the fire was burning well enough of its own accord, he removed his boots and tunic and rolled up the legs of his breeches before stepping into the stream. While his eyes searched the water, Beowulf thought about the rift between him and the Schaman:

If Lüma were here, we'd be hunting fish together, or I'd be hunting for her. But she's not here; I'm here, and I'm hungry. I've killed and eaten fish before. I'm going to kill and eat a fish again, and I'm going to roast it over the fire the way Beorn does squirrels.

A fat young trout came downstream close to the surface and was about to pass through Beowulf's legs when Beowulf snatched it from its cold water world.

"*Forgive me, little fish,*" said Beowulf, "*and know that I'm grateful to you and the All Mother for your sacrifice so that I might live another day.*"

"*Kill me quickly, Bear's Son,*" said the trout, "*I cannot breathe in your world.*"

Beowulf drew his knife from its sheath and knelt. He put the fish on a moss covered rock where he could sever the head with one quick cut then he stopped. Beowulf placed the trout in the water.

"*Go, little fish,*" said Beowulf. "*Swim home, but first tell me how you know my name.*"

"*All the forest knows who you are,*" said the trout. "*I won't forget your kindness, Bear's Son; but if it was me, I don't think I could catch a big juicy bug for dinner, then spit it out and send it on its way.*"

"*Celebrate your freedom, little fish,*" said Beowulf, "*if I catch you again I'll probably eat you.*"

"*Good hunting, Bear's Son,*" said the trout.

"*Good hunting, little fish.*"

Resting on hands and knees, Beowulf watched the trout swim downstream out of sight. He became aware of his reflection looking back at him. In the mirror the water provided, he saw how he had changed: his face was not the face that once looked back when he gazed into the pool beneath the waterfall near the hot spring. His hair hung well past his shoulders now; his face was thinner, accentuated by high cheekbones, thin lips, and a straight nose that, had his mother been there, she would have said was the 'Waegmunding' nose.' Beowulf's age had become inconsequential. His arms were firm and muscular; so, too, his chest and shoulders had broadened beyond what a boy of eighteen winters might have —had he grown up a slave in the coal mines of Norrland.

Who are you? Beowulf said to his reflection. "*What are you*?"

Beowulf returned to his campfire, put his tunic and boots on and sat. He placed several more sticks on the fire, feeding the flames. *Why* he wondered *does the wood not complain when I feed it to the fire? Fire devours everything it touches; even the hardest steel in the Schaman's shed cannot defeat it. I saw the proof of that working with Beorn on my knife. The fish did not complain when I pulled it from the water; it wanted a quick death, but that's all it asked of me. The fish didn't ask me to put it back. I did that because I wanted to do it. And now I'm still hungry.*

Running for its life, a rabbit sprinted into the clearing, saw Beowulf and stopped in its tracks. Beowulf was just as surprised as the rabbit but he made no effort to stand or reach for his bow and arrows.

"*You're welcome to pass through in peace,*" said Beowulf, "*I won't harm you—not this day.*"

"*And for that I'm grateful,*" said the rabbit, "*but if you want to live, Manlings, you better flee, or what follows will have you for its supper.*"

Beowulf could hear twigs breaking underfoot as something large came fast in their direction. Beowulf stood and raised his bow.

"*Get behind me, rabbit,*" said Beowulf.

The rabbit did more than that; it ran for the cover of the brush.

Beowulf fitted his bow with an obsidian-tipped arrow, jagged on both edges for ripping through flesh. His eyes widened with alarm, and his heart beat faster when a Sabre Tooth Forest Cat leapt into the clearing.

Seeing the Manlings with his upraised bow aimed in its direction, the Forest Cat stopped. Beowulf pulled back on the bowstring. In his haste and excitement, he used too much force; the bow broke in two. A cry of dismay escaped his throat; he tossed his broken bow aside and drew his knife. The cat threw back its head and roared.

"*Are you the Manlings they call the bear's son*?"

"*Yes*," said Beowulf.

"*Good. My pack will honor me all the more when it becomes known that my första döda, my first kill, was no rabbit, but the bear's son himself.*"

"*Your first kill*?" Beowulf said.

"*Yes*," said the Forest Cat, "*today I am one winter young; this is my Första Solo Jakt, my first hunt alone. To prove I am deserving of a place among my clan, I must bring back something worthy to eat.*"

"*And a rabbit would do that*?" said Beowulf.

"*It's customary for Yearlings to start with rabbits*," said the Forest Cat. "*After that, we hunt whatever we want; but mostly we hunt deer without antlers. It's always been that way with our kind.*"

"*Rabbits and deer without antlers won't fight back, Sabre Cat. I will. It will be better for us both if you hunt something else today.*"

"*Aren't you afraid of me, Bear's Son*?"

Beowulf took a moment to think. There was no simple answer to the Forest Cat's question, and it confused him.

"*Yes—and, no*," said Beowulf.

"*I don't understand*," said the cat. "*Either you're afraid of me, or you're not.*"

"*Well*," said Beowulf, "*There are voices in my head saying I should feel afraid. And I admit; I do feel fear as I look at your size and your long sharp teeth; yet, there's another voice inside my head that tells me 'I'm Beowulf, the bear's son—afraid of no one, or anything.*"

"*Is that so*?" said the cat.

"*It is*," said Beowulf.

"*The rabbit I was chasing is far away by now*," said the Forest Cat. "*The smoke from your fire covers its scent, but now you are here in front of me. No hard feelings, but I prefer to kill you instead.*"

The Forest Cat crouched, ready to spring. Beowulf adjusted his stance and his grip on his knife, just as Beorn had taught him.

"*You can try,*" said Beowulf, "*but I won't become a meal for you and your clan; not today, not tomorrow, not ever.*"

17

TOOTH

The Forest Cat sprang. Its weight knocked Beowulf onto his back. At the same time, the cat sunk its teeth into his shoulder. Beowulf screamed and drove his knife once, twice, three times into the cat's throat. The Forest Cat roared with pain and rolled to one side, away from the bear's son's knife. Beowulf leapt on top of it. He stabbed the cat over and over in the chest until blood trickled from its nose, mouth, and wounds in its throat. Then the young Sabre Tooth Cat lie still. Beowulf continued sitting beside his kill. He could feel the warmth of his blood flowing from the wounds beneath his tunic. As he sat there, the rabbit left the cover of the brush and approached.

"*You, again,*" said Beowulf.

"*I've never seen anything like that, Bear's Son,*" said the rabbit. "You could have killed me, but you didn't."

"*Don't be too grateful,*" said Beowulf. He got to his feet. His hand was shaking as he sheathed his knife. "*If we meet again it might end differently. Go home now, Uncle Rabbit.*"

The rabbit hopped out of sight. Beowulf recalled what the Schaman told him:

"*If ever you're bleeding badly, slap hot iron on the wound and be sure to bite down on a stick when you do, or you'll grind your new teeth to mush.*"

Beowulf sat beside his campfire and placed the blade of his knife among the fiery coals. He added a few more sticks to the flames. While he waited for the blade to get hot, he looked at the dead Forest Cat. *It looks so much smaller dead* he thought.

As Beowulf's breathing evened-out, he placed a stick between his teeth, grasped the handle of his knife and placed the tip of the blade over the puncture wounds one at a time. Never before had he felt such concentrated pain, and he bit down on the stick until it cracked and pieces of bark fell from his mouth. As his knife slipped from his hand, his head whirled, and his vision grew blurry while the smell of cooked blood, seared flesh, and singed leather flooded his nostrils.

As darkness fell upon him, Beowulf saw two, pale yellow moons looking down at him. Beowulf's eyes closed and he felt himself floating through darkness—weightless, numb to all sensation except a cold wind on his face.

† † †

When Beowulf's eyes next opened he was in the lodge on his pallet near the fire. The Schaman appeared and knelt beside him. In his hands, the Schaman held a cup and a bowl.

"Here's broth mixed with herbs," said Beorn. "It will cleanse your wounds from the inside, and I made more—"

"Beggars' stew," said Beowulf.

"Yes," said Beorn, "to give you strength. Drink first, then eat."

Beowulf sat up. His left arm rested in a sling. The Schaman handed the cup to him and put the bowl of stew in Beowulf's lap. Beowulf drank the cup dry then began to eat.

"This is good," he said. "but the meat's a little chewy."

The Schaman noted how much Beowulf's voice had changed. He no longer spoke with the voice of a child seven winters' young; rather, his voice projected the tone and tenor of a boy much older.

Beowulf moved his right hand to his left shoulder and winced.

"It will heal in time," said Beorn. "You did a fitting job sealing the wounds."

Beowulf had eaten several more bites of stew before he put the bowl aside.

"How long have I slept?"

"Two days and nights."

Beowulf looked around.

"How did I get here?"

"It was near sunset," said Beorn. "I went outside to see if perhaps you were on your way back. I found the skiff resting on our side of the shore. You were inside it, unconscious."

"Someone must have brought me to the island, Beorn—but, who?"

"What does it matter? You're here, you're alive, and made your first, real kill—one you can be proud of."

"It matters to me," said Beowulf. "If you think you know who brought me here, tell me!"

"How should I know who it was?" said Beorn.

"You know who it was, Beorn; I know you know because I can see it in your face, so tell me!"

"He has many names," said Beorn.

"Then give me one of them," said Beowulf.

"The Shadow Lord," said Beorn.

"Stop it, Beorn; give me a name I know!"

"Death! Death brought you here."

Several moments passed.

"But why?" said Beowulf. "Why would Death do that?"

"I can't answer that," said Beorn. "Truly, Beowulf, I don't know."

"It was the Shadow Lord, wasn't it, watching me from the treeline when I first came here?"

"Yes," said Beorn.

"Why didn't you tell me then?" said Beowulf.

"I saw no point to it," said Beorn. "You had enough to deal with."

Several more moments passed in silence.

"Where's Tooth," said Beowulf.

"Tooth?" Beorn said, puzzled.

"My knife," said Beowulf. "I need to go back and find it."

"I found your knife where you killed the Forest Cat," said Beorn. "When your shoulder's better you can use Tooth to make another bow."

"When I first saw the Forest Cat," said Beowulf; "I was excited. I pulled back hard on the bowstring—too hard."

"I doubt if you'll make the same mistake a second time, Bear's Son; but there's more to it than that."

"What?"

"Sooner or later the bow was bound to break. I'm surprised it didn't break while you were practicing with it."

"I don't understand," said Beowulf.

"The wood we used hadn't cured and was the wrong kind of wood to start. White pine is suitable for building a stake wall, lodge or an outhouse but not for making a bow—at least not one you can depend on—it's too brittle, just as you discovered. Yew is among the hardest of the softwoods and easy to work with; it will bend more than pine, but without breaking."

The Schaman's voice seemed to drone on and on and crowded Beowulf's head until it hurt.

"Birch and ash are hard woods," said the Schaman, "good for the shaft of a spear or an axe handle. They're good for making bows but need to be thicker and wider than a bow made from yew. Whichever wood we use, whether yew, ash or birch, we need to keep the timber dry for a full four moons to cure it."

"Stop!" said Beowulf. "All this talk of wood is making my head hurt."

Beowulf thought a moment.

"You sent me into the forest with a bow you knew would break."

"Yes," said Beorn.

"Why?"

"To test whether you can think fast on your feet, and survive. You proved that you could."

"Part of me is very angry with you, Beorn," said Beowulf.

"I know," said Beorn. "Listen, Beowulf—any fool with a bow can kill. However, a warrior has to be able to slay an enemy up close. You proved you can do that. I'm proud of you, Bear's Son. Remember, what doesn't kill us makes us stronger."

A moment passed in silence.

"Tell me, Beorn, what it's like to kill a man?"

Beorn thought long and hard before answering.

"Do you ask because of what happened with the Forest Cat?"

"Yes," said Beowulf. "I watched it die. I saw the life go out of the cat's eyes. It made me feel empty... more like sad."

"Good," said Beorn.

"Why?"

"Killing is part of the All Mother's dance. You have the scars now to prove it. Most creatures kill to survive, and you've proven you can do that. But killing a man? At first, you'll find it hard. And killing should be hard—every time a warrior takes a life it should be in self-defense, or in defense of his clan and tribe; otherwise, he's no warrior at all; just a killer—a brute unworthy of a seat in the Halls of Valhalla. A righteous man kills when he must; monsters kill because they like it. The first time you kill a man,

Bear's Son, you may feel sick. That's all right. It's understandable. But, later, when you're cleaning your weapons and armor after a fight, you'll feel a glow about you. A certain... something that leaves you feeling alive, more than you've ever felt before."

A moment passed in silence.

"What did you do with the Forest Cat?" said Beowulf.

The Schaman grinned. "You're eating him."

18

FATHERS & SONS

Weohstan was pleased with the pace Leif and the Freemen set for themselves rebuilding Vindenstedt Farm. The workers extended the triangular stake wall on all three sides a hundred feet and added a watchtower over the Main Gate and additional towers where the three sections of the stake wall came together. The enlarged space inside the palisade allowed for the construction of nine more lodges to quarter Freemen, their wives, and children, along with household servants and a separate barracks for warriors without wives, whose sole function was to stand guard on the wall-walk at night and patrol the fields and pastures by day. The workers built new bathhouses, one for men, another for women, along with a sauna, new outhouses, a milking barn, a grain barn and stable, a tannery, and a metal shop for making and repairing farm tools and weapons. Weohstan set aside a practice field where the inhabitants, including women, and children who were old enough, could hone their skills with bow, spear, sword and axe. Weohstan expected them all to fight for Clan Waegmunding should the need for fighting occur.

"More heat, Ragmund," said Hrethel.

"Of course, Great King," said Ragmund.

Ragmund got up from the polishes cedar bench where he sat opposite Hrethel. Dragging his leg behind he proceeded to the large iron brazier in the center of the sauna.

The brazier stood upright and contained lava rocks suitable for heating and reheating. In the fireplace beneath the brazier were coals. Ragmund needed to add a few more sticks to the fire to bring up the heat. He did this while Hrethel flogged himself across his sagging chest and bony shoulders with birch twigs laden with fresh leaves bundled together. On the floor nearby was a water bucket and ladle. Finished attending the fire, Ragmund limped back to the bench. With a good deal of discomfort and no small effort he sat.

"Ah," sighed Hrethel, "that's much better. This old body of mine needed a good sweat."

"I'm glad you find the conditions in the sauna favorable, Great King," said Ragmund.

"As matters stand, I fear for my people's future, Ragmund. I
relied on Ecgtheow for his advice, just as I rely on your keen ability to assess the good and bad of a situation. Still, I miss Ecgtheow."

"Gods willing, the future will usher-in better times for Geatland, Great King."

"The future," said Hrethel, "looms darkly in my mind, Ragmund, when I think of my sons and how ill-suited they are to rule. Hygelac shows the most promise, except he's the youngest and last in line for the throne. Do you know why I gave my daughter to Ecgtheow Waegmunding?"

"No, Great King," said Ragmund, "I do not presume to know your thoughts."

"Because Ecgtheow is the man I most wanted my sons to become—strong, courageous, uncompromising in matters of right and wrong and loyal to a fault. Ecgtheow was not just my Battle Lord and son-in-law; he was my friend. It broke my heart exiling him. With Liv and my grandson gone, haven't I suffered enough?"

"I will pray to the gods," said Ragmund, "and implore them to ease your pain, Great King."

"Be a good boy, Ragmund," said Hrethel, "and fetch me water. My throat is parched."

"Of course, Great King."

Ragmund got up from the bench and limped toward the water bucket and ladle. *I am the same age as Herebeald,* he thought, *yet he calls me "boy." How can he not know it pains me to get up and down. I'm no different than a gelded hound with Hrethel as my master.*

Ragmund bent down over the water bucket and filled the drinking ladle. With his back facing Hrethel he spat into the ladle and limped to where his king sat waiting.

Hrethel took the curved wooden spoon from Ragmund's hand. "Good boy—thank you."

Ragmund looked into Hrethel's tired eyes and smiled. "You're welcome, Great King."

† † †

Seven leagues east of Falcon's Nest, Hrethel's sons spent the morning in Dark Lake Forest hunting deer and wild boar with an entourage of sycophants and bodyguards. At midday, they retired to their father's hunting lodge. Leaving their entourage in the Banquet Hall to drink while cooks prepared a feast for later, Herebeald, Haethcyn, and Hygelac bathed in a large hot tub outside the lodge, well beyond earshot of their guests.

"What troubles you, Hygelac?" said Herebeald. "You don't seem your usual carefree self."

"That's right," said Haecythn, "Come to think of it, Hygelac, I've not heard you laugh once all day."

"Because I still mourn the loss of Liv and Beowulf?"

"Gnashing your teeth will not bring them back," said Herebeald.

"Them?" said Hygelac. "Can you not even speak their names?"

The three brothers sat in silence. Steam from the hot tub rose around them, and perspiration dripped from their foreheads.

"Well," said Herebeald, "if neither of you two is going to say it, I will."

"Say what?" said Hygelac.

"What we've all been thinking," said Herebeald.

"And what would that be, brother?" said Haethcyn.

"That the sooner he dies, the better for Väster Geatland."

"You mean the better for you," said Hygelac.

"Of course it's what he means," said Haethcyn.

"No, the better for the three of us," said Herebeald. "Of late, all Father does is sit in his sauna with that Angle cripple, and flog himself with birch leaves; who knows, maybe he and Ragmund flog each other."

Haethcyn laughed. Hygelac cast Herebeald a disapproving look.

"What," said Herebeald, "you don't approve of what I said?"

"No," said Hygelac, "I don't approve. Father's old. His body's suffered much. He almost died during the Battle on the Ice. Mother is long gone; his sauna is the one thing that gives Father pleasure."

"Maybe it does," said Herebeald, "but it sickens me to think of what he might be doing in there with the cripple."

"Ragmund is merely a glorified servant," said Hygelac. "He is devoted to our father, and he's harmless."

"Maybe so," said Haethcyn, "but Father listens to Ragmund far more than us, little brother."

"Despite Hygelac kissing father's arse all the time, it's Ragmund's counsel father pays attention to," said Herebeald.

Hygelac got out of the tub and wrapped himself in a towel.

"We hurt his feelings," said Herebeald. "Hygelac's going off to have a good boo hoo."

"Try not to drown," said Hygelac. "It would break father's heart to lose such devoted sons."

19

UNDER A DARKENING SKY

While a light snow fell, Beowulf followed the Schaman through the forest and listened as Beorn identified the different trees they saw.

"Remember, Beowulf, whichever wood you choose; you want a tree or sapling at least six feet in length and—"

"I know," said Beowulf, interrupting. "And thick as my middle finger is long, maybe a little longer.

"Right," said Beorn, "but before you cut, make sure the wood is straight and without disfigurements. And remember, it comes to us as a gift from the All Mother, so when you cut, do so with respect. More than just alive, Beowulf, trees are the All Mother's lungs."

When Beowulf came upon a small yew tree, he ran a hand over its feathery branches.

"This is the one I want," said Beowulf.

"Ah," said Beorn. "A yew—good choice; cut her cleanly near the base, and we'll take her home."

"Home?" said Beowulf. "I don't have a home, do I, Beorn?"

"Nonsense, Bear's Son," said Beorn. "All Midgard is your home! Never forget it! No matter the king nor the size of his kingdom, one day you will stand head and shoulders above them all. Trust me. I've seen it."

"I do trust you," said Beowulf.

"But now it's getting cold, and I crave a warm fire and a mug of hot lingonberry wine. Sound like a good thing?"

Beowulf nodded.

The Schaman leaned close to Beowulf until their noses almost touched.

"Careful, Bear's Son," said Beorn, "you just might smile."

Beowulf stared at the Schaman a moment before they both laughed. Beowulf knelt beside the yew tree and began cutting. He used the piece of obsidian he carried in his pouch. The Schaman watched Beowulf use firm even strokes to cut the tree, and he marveled at Beowulf's strength. Although Beowulf's body had stopped growing, for the most part, his body was lean and hard and stood over six-feet in height. With each passing day, he grew stronger and agiler.

"Winter's coming," said Beowulf.

The Schaman looked through the canopy of the forest at the leaden gray sky above.

"Yes. Winter is coming."

† † †

When Ecgtheow went abroad it was always as his king's eyes and ears; yet, despite the number of times he ventured to Daneland to count Longships, and note where the Spear Danes garrisoned their warriors, he never attempted to enter Heorot Fort, let alone Heorot Hall. This time he would access both without pretense or disguise. After sleeping for a day and a night in the barn, Ecgtheow polished his chainmail shirt with sand and vinegar, courtesy of the stable's proprietor.

When the stable boy finished grooming the stallion, he watched the mysterious warrior polish his armor until it began to glint in the daylight.

"May I help you, my Lord?" said the boy.

Ecgtheow looked over at his helm; picked it up and tossed it to the boy.

"Yes," said Ecgtheow, "you may."

Ecgtheow and the stable boy sat on the straw near Rain Dancer and worked side-by-side polishing Ecgtheow's battle gear. From somewhere outside they could hear a young girl sing. Ecgtheow noted how the boy's ears perked up.

"What's your name?" said Ecgtheow.

"Turin, my Lord."

"She has a pleasant voice, doesn't she, Turin?" said Ecgtheow.

Turin smiled. "Yes, my Lord."

"Do you know her?"

"Yes, my Lord. Her name is Freydis."

"Are you sweet on her?"

Turin blushed. He looked at the helm in his hands.

"Yes, my Lord," he said, and kept working.

"Is she sweet on you?"

Turin looked at Ecgtheow. "Perhaps, my Lord; I don't know."

"Perhaps you should just come out and ask her."

"I wouldn't know how to ask her that, my Lord."

"It's called, 'talking,'" said Ecgtheow.

Sensing the boy's discomfort, Ecgtheow smiled.

"Courting a woman, Turin, is the same as going to war."

"My Lord?"

"Well," said Ecgtheow, "think about it. You could lay siege to Freydis; then, while you're waiting for the walls to come down and her to make up her mind, a courageous interloper could steal her away. Or, you could try to win her heart with sweet talk, flowers, and honey cakes. Then, after days, weeks, perhaps even months have gone by, and if her father approves, he'll allow you to take Freydis for a walk in the moonlight; while her mother and grandmother and sisters follow behind. However, the danger with a long siege, Turin, is that conditions change; they always do."

Ecgtheow stopped talking.

"Meaning, my Lord?"

"Meaning you could attack full force with flowers, honey cakes and sweet talk—all at the same time. Tell her father that you want to marry his daughter, but you mustn't try to buy her love. Flowers and honey cakes are best at first. But don't give her too much of value. She'll think you want something special in return; which you do, of course, but don't be obvious about it. Don't offer her 'this' and expect 'that,' if you take my meaning. Besides, if all goes right, her father will pay you handsomely to take her off his hands —do you understand?"

"I'm beginning to my Lord," said the boy. "But I've nothing to give Freydis. At least, not yet."

"Oh, but you do," said Ecgtheow. "You have something no one else in all the world can give her."

"I do?"

"Yes—Yourself, Turin. Either she'll see your worth or she won't. If she doesn't see it, let Helheim have her. Let her make some other man miserable while you find yourself a woman deserving of you and all that you have to offer."

"What would you do, my Lord—if the choice was yours?"

"Me?" said Ecgtheow. "If it was me, and I knew she was the one girl in the whole of Daneland I wanted, I'd attack full force with honey cakes, flowers, and sweet talk and I wouldn't stop until I made her mine."

"Thank you, my Lord," said the boy. "Now I just need to work up the courage to do it."

"What will she do—bite and kick you if you say 'hello'? I think not," said Ecgtheow. "Show some courage, Turin; you can't stay a boy forever. Victory in the war I speak of depends on how much you want her."

Turin nodded. A moment passed. Ecgtheow rested his right hand on the handle of Liv's knife.

"Do you know who I am?" Ecgtheow said.

"No, my Lord," said Turin.

"Are you sure, boy? Look closely at my face."

"I'm sorry, my Lord," said Turin.

A look of fear came over the stable boy.

"I've never seen you before."

"You wouldn't be lying to me, would you?"

"No, my Lord."

"What about the stallion?" Ecgtheow said. "Do you recognize him?"

"No, my Lord, I do not."

"Good," said Ecgtheow. "Your honesty has served you well, Turin."

Before he left the barn, Ecgtheow put his armor and helm on; then he pressed a gold ring into the boy's hand.

"You do good work," he said, then he patted Turin on the head.

The stable boy gasped to see the gold ring in his hand. He bowed as the tall, clean-shaven warrior walked past him with the stallion. Turin followed Ecgtheow outside. While Freydis sang from somewhere nearby, Turin watched the warrior ride out of view. He looked again at the gold ring in his hand and grinned.

Ecgtheow stopped at the edge of the village. His first instinct was to return to the stable and silence the boy.

Then, what? Ecgtheow said to himself. *Am I to cut the throat of the stable keeper, too, and every other Dane, young or old, man or woman who stares at me? You're here to court the friendship of the Danes, Ecgtheow, not cut throats—remember that! If your enemies follow you here—be it so.*

† † †

Two leagues inland from Mörk Sand and one league south of the village of Hleiðra, King Hrothgar built a fortified military camp built on high ground surrounded by farmland. If need be Heorot Fort was large enough to garrison a thousand men-at-arms plus the king's counselors and advisers, armorers, metalsmiths, surgeons, cooks, and servants. The Fort was circular, surrounded by a ditch, four yards wide and three yards deep. Because of frequent rains, the bottom of the trench was thick with mud which made walking or standing difficult and running impossible. Were an enemy to avoid almost certain death at the hands of the defenders by attempting to scale the ditch, the first of two stake walls would confront them—one, six yards high, supporting the outer face of the earthworks. A second stake wall, three yards high, bolstered the inside wall.

Between the two stake walls, on top of the earthworks, was the wall-walk, four yards wide. The wall-walk allowed the Spear Danes to stand four deep if need be with ample room to loose their arrows, hurl stones and spears and fight off attackers with the sword, knife and axe should the enemy reach the wall-walk itself. A rock causeway over the ditch, five yards wide and ten yards long provided access to the camp's northern entrance, a gate three yards wide, four yards high, built from oak timbers reinforced with iron bands. From the gate, a tunnel four yards in height, illuminated with torches and lined with wooden beams continued for ten yards through the earthworks allowing access to the heart of the camp.

Hrothgar's gold-gilded Hall was three leagues southwest of Heorot Fort. Heorot Hall was five stories high. On sunny days, the Hall was visible for several leagues in all directions.

To attack the Hall, an enemy would have to occupy Mörk Sand first, where the Danes stationed the entirety of Hrothgar's battle craft; then they would have to fight their way inland on foot to Heorot Fort. If that same enemy conquered Heorot Fort, the way to Heorot Hall would be clear. There was one approach an enemy could risk taking, but it was a route that could prove disastrous. It was the one way to avoid Mörk Sand and Heorot Fort but required an enemy to land further south on Daneland's coast and risk moving in-force across treacherous fog-bound moors that acted as natural barriers east and west of Hrothgar's Great Hall.

Unknown to the Spear Danes, Ecgtheow knew a shortcut across the moors to Heorot Hall, and that was the way he rode after leaving Mörk Sand. It was his business to find such secret paths.

The entrance to the Great Hall was a door two-yards wide and four-yards high made from oak beams bolted together. Just as with the gate to the fort, the Danes had reinforced the door with iron bands that attached it to the door frame on hinges. A crossbeam of oak thick as a grown man's thigh secured the door from the inside when so desired.

Wulfgar gestured to a groom waiting nearby. The groom approached to take the reins from Ecgtheow's hand.

"The stallion will be in good hands while you're inside," said Wulfgar. "Now, before you enter I must ask for your weapons."

Ecgtheow nodded. He gave Rain Dancer's reins to the groom and his spear, sword, and knife to Wulfgar. A moment passed before a tall warrior with noble bearing appeared from inside the Hall accompanied by two warriors.

"This," said Wulfgar "is Lord Aeschere, Chief Adviser to our king. He will accompany you to the Throne Room."

Wulfgar handed Ecgtheow's weapons to a guard. Ecgtheow bowed first to the Gate Warden, then to Aeschere.

"Your reputation precedes you," said Aeschere. "You're well known to us, Ecgtheow Waegmunding."

"I make no apologies, Lord Aeschere. All my life, I've striven to serve my clan and king faithfully."

"Nor should you apologize," said Aeschere. "King Hrothgar has eyes and ears throughout Götaland. We heard what passed twixt you and the Dark Queen and how dearly it cost you."

Ecgtheow followed Aeschere through the doorway. They entered a wide corridor that torches attached to the walls illuminated. Ecgtheow saw wooden racks where those who sought an audience with the King checked their weapons, his included. The corridor extended fifteen yards before it reached the Mead Hall and further still—the heart of Heorot, the Throne Room, wherein sat Hrothgar, son of Halfdane.

20

SHIFTING WINDS

The Ostrogoth halted within sight of the village.

"Who are they?" said Hathus.

"Harii," said Germanicus. "They pay a yearly tribute to the Iron Wolf, so he leaves them alone to smuggle mead across the Whale Road to Polanska. Mostly they return with weapons and armor to trade with merchants bound for Land's End. That way, they avoid paying taxes to the Dark Queen.

"The Harii are formidable warriors," said Hathus.

"I know," said Germanicus. "My tribe fought the Harii many winters ago—at the mouth of the Elbe River. They painted their bodies and shields black and attacked at night. We had lost many a shield brother before the sun rose the next day. Those you see yonder are quarrelsome beyond belief. It's better if we leave them be. We have a long ride ahead. We should push on."

"First let me find out what I can," said Hathus. "Waegmunding may have come this way; if so, perhaps the Harii know what direction he's going. Wait for me here; I won't be long."

There was a conciliatory tone in the Ostrogoth's voice, and it took Germanicus by surprise. A conciliatory tone, however, was not enough to overcome Germanicus' dislike of the Ostrogoth. Germanicus nodded and signaled to his men to stay put as Hathus rode toward the village.

"I come as a friend of the Harii," said Hathus. "Like yours, my tribe has also suffered at the hands of the Wylfings. Even now they're holding my wife and sons hostage and will surely kill them if I don't do their bidding and track the man they're hunting."

"What man would that be?" said Haraldr.

"A Väster Geat who killed the Dark Queen's son. Too bad for me he didn't kill the Dark Queen, too."

"Hmm," said Haraldr. "By the sound of it, you're between a rock and a hard place, Outlander, but that has nothing to do with our village."

"Perhaps," said Hathus, "but they're well armed and spoiling for a fight and will come for your food and women just the same."

"Will they now?" said Haraldr.

"They will," said Hathus.

He removed a small leather pouch tucked under his belt and held it up.

"There are five gold rings inside. They're yours if you see to it that when I depart those five Wylfing pigs don't follow me."

"What about your wife and sons if those five should happen to go missing?" said Haraldr.

"I know where my family is," said Hathus. "Two men guard them. I can kill those two, steal their horses and make good my family's escape, north to the land of the Svear."

Haraldr thought for a moment before holding out his hand. Hathus tossed him the pouch.

"Give us a moment to prepare the Wylfings a proper welcome," said Haraldr, "then send them here."

Hathus nodded and rode off. One of Haraldr's brothers, a Harii warrior, named Avagis, leaned close to Haraldr.

"Do you believe what the Ostrogoth said, brother?"

"Not a word," said Haraldr.

Hathus returned to where Germanicus and his men waited.

"They have him!" said Hathus. "They're holding the Waegmunding prisoner in one of their lodges. They'll turn him over if the price is right—in gold."

"Good enough," said Germanicus. "I've gold to give them. Let's go!"

Germanicus dug his boots into his horse's flanks and galloped toward the village followed by his men. Hathus let them ride a distance ahead before he and his dog started west.

Haraldr stood with his brothers in the center of the village. Germanicus and his men halted in front of them.

"We're here for the Geat," said Germanicus. He took a pouch from his belt and held it up. "I've gold rings to give you in return for Ecgtheow Waegmunding—twenty rings in all."

"Not nearly enough for a man worth a hundred times as much," said Haraldr.

From the surrounding lodges stepped twenty Harii, their bows raised, primed with arrows. Before Germanicus and his men could turn and flee, the arrows of the Harii found their marks. The first arrow found Germanicus' throat and passed clean through; two more arrows lodged in his chest, knocking him out of his saddle. The other four riders went down just as hard. Haraldr slit the throats of three who, despite the arrows in them, were still alive. Haraldr turned to his brothers.

"We'll dump the bodies and saddles at sea and eat the horses later," said Haraldr.

Hathus and the Swamp Dog continued along the coast. Hathus would wait until the sun was close to setting before making camp.

† † †

Ecgtheow removed his helm and held it tucked under one arm as he followed Aeschere into the Throne Room. Hrothgar was a king with no queen. A man of fifty winters, Hrothgar possessed a healthy man's appetite for women but had never taken a wife—war had been his mistress many seasons while he increased the lands and holdings of the Spear Danes. A few of Hrothgar's Lords and advisers attended him that day, along with the Järngardet or "Iron Guard," warriors handpicked to protect the Spear Danes' king.

"Wait here," Aeschere told Ecgtheow.

While Ecgtheow waited, Aeschere walked forward, stopped before the dais and bowed.

"My King, I bring before you a Thunder Geat, Ecgtheow Waegmunding by name, once Chief of Clan Waegmunding, and now an outcast in his land, condemned to live in exile by King Hrethel."

Hrothgar gestured for Ecgtheow to approach.

"Come closer, Ecgtheow."

"Yes, Great King," said Ecgtheow.

He stepped forward alongside Aeschere and bowed. The formal introduction completed, Aeschere bowed and stepped back.

"Tell me if Aeschere heard rightly, Lord Waegmunding—you came here to offer your sword to my service."

"That's true, Great King," said Ecgtheow. "I'm no longer welcome among the Thunder-Geats."

"I've heard rumors," said Hrothgar, "but I'd sooner hear it from your lips why King Hrethel banished you under pain of death from the land of your birth."

"King Hrethel did what a prudent shepherd of his people should do, Great King; he put the welfare of many before one. What I did in Öster Götaland, in Hell's Grove, I did under King Hrethel's orders. Neither he nor I knew at the time that the murderer and thief we sought to punish would turn out to be the bastard son of the Dark Queen and Iron wolf. King Amunwolf threatened to go to war unless Hrethel turned me over to Amunwolf's emissary. I was beyond Hrethel's reach at the time, so he ordered me into exile under pain of death. I lost my wife, Liv, and perhaps my son, Beowulf, slain by Wylfings in the service of the Dark Queen. Hrethel lost his daughter, and his grandson, whose whereabouts remain a mystery. Many more Thunder-Geats died because of what I did, including my two brothers, their wives, and children. I have lost everything I cherished. My hatred for the Wylfings and the Dark Queen remains alive inside me. There is no more to tell, Great King."

Several moments passed in silence.

"Every word you've spoken rings true," said Hrothgar. "Moreover, it speaks well of you that even in exile your loyalty to your king shines through the darkness surrounding you. We heard about you long before now, Ecgtheow Waegmunding. It matters not that you have often spied on us in the past. I, too, have eyes and ears that range everywhere across the Whale Road. Little of importance takes place in Götaland that I'm not aware of; besides, you're a warrior of considerable renown. The question is—how to make the best use of you?"

Hrothgar's counselor, Aeschere, stepped forward.

"May I speak, my King?"

Hrothgar nodded.

"Thirty of the Iron Wolf's Longships recently rounded Land's End," said Aeschere. "Twenty-nine of those ships commanded by Amunwolf's Battle Lord visited King Hrethel. One ship, however, carrying Prince Adalfuns, turned south at Land's End and headed for Germania. We concluded that the premise of Amunwolf's Battle Lord's visit to Falcon's Nest concerned you, Lord Waegmunding. However, why so many ships—why so many battle craft? And what might be Adalfuns' errand in Germania?"

"It sounds to me," said Ecgtheow, "by sending Yngvarr and half his fleet, the Iron Wolf has more in mind than intimidating my king."

"We agree," said Aeschere, "but, what—that's the question."

"Has the Wylfing fleet not returned to Öster Götaland?" said Ecgtheow.

"No," said Aeschere, "our spies at Land's End would have seen them between dawn and dusk. That, or they would have heard the sound of the Wylfing's oars at night, close to shore where they could use the lights from Land's End to help navigate the way east along your shoreline."

"And they've not been sighted elsewhere?" said Ecgtheow.

"No," said Aeschere.

Ecgtheow stared at the ceiling of the Throne Room and for a moment studied the matter before he looked at Hrothgar.

"Have you thought of something?" said the King of the Spear Danes.

"I have, Great King. When I arrived at Mörk Sand I saw your fleet at rest, sails furled, hulls lashed together."

"Just as we always do at autumn's end," said Aeschere, "this close to winter."

"And what a perfect way to destroy your fleet, Great King, without a fight—without you even putting out to sea," said Ecgtheow.

Ecgtheow heard a chorus of murmurs go up from Hrothgar's counselors standing behind him, scoffing at such a simple notion. Hrothgar raised a hand, signaling for "Silence."

"Tell me more, "Lord Waegmunding."

"What better way to defeat the Spear Danes, Great King, then with your fleet anchored at Mörk Sand?"

"Perhaps Lord Waegmunding can tell his Grace precisely what he's getting at," said Aeschere.

"Just this, my Lords," said Ecgtheow; "I now believe the Iron Wolf has no intention of bringing his ships home—not immediately. Yngvarr needs only sail south-southwest to Jutland, find a place to hide, and wait."

"Wait for what?" said Hrothgar.

"For an opportune time to strike the Danes, Great King."

"Even if there's merit to what you suggest, Lord Waegmunding," said Aeschere, "what constitutes an 'opportune' time for the Wylfing Kommandar to attack?"

"Surprise! Lord Yngvarr commands thirty ships, probably the Wylfings best battle craft, but he's not stupid; he knows he'll have one chance to destroy your fleet. And he'll try to keep the odds in his favor."

"How so?" said Hrothgar.

"My guess is King Amunwolf sent Prince Adalfuns to enlist the help of an ally."

Aeschere leaned close to Hrothgar's ear and spoke so no one else could hear. Finished speaking, Aeschere looked at Ecgtheow. "And who do you think is a likely ally of the Iron Wolf, Lord Waegmunding?"

"My guess would be the Franks," said Ecgtheow. "King Botheric has many ships and not far to sail to join forces with Lord Yngvarr if, as I suspect, Yngvarr is in Jutland by now."

"If, you say; if Yngvarr's hiding there," said Aeschere.

"Yes," said Ecgtheow. "It's true; I'm guessing, but it's what I would do."

"By all the gods," said Hrothgar, "Jutland is a big place with plenty of inlets, and coves to conceal ships by the hundreds."

"Kryl Bay, Great King," said Ecgtheow.

"Say again," said Hrothgar.

"Kryl Bay," said Ecgtheow, "on the northeast coast of Jutland, is deep enough to conceal a fleet—it's out of the wind and well situated to launch a surprise attack on Mörk Sand."

"What about the weather?" said Aeschere.

"The weather won't be kind to anyone going abroad at this time," said Ecgtheow, "but coming from Jutland your enemies would have the north wind to their backs; it will speed their ships here in less than a day and night. It will be different for the Franks. For Botheric's ships to get to Jutland to join the Wylfing fleet, the Franks will have to use their sails and oars against the wind. Even if they're on the way north right now, it will take their Longships a week to reach Jutland."

A silence hung in the Throne Room.

"Were we to find merit in what you assert," said Hrothgar, "what would you advise we do."

"Strike first, Great King," said Ecgtheow, "and hit hard!"

"After many winters of peace among the tribes, do you realize what you're asking King Hrothgar to commit to?" said Aeschere.

"I do, Lord Aeschere," said Ecgtheow.

"Then let us hear it from your mouth," said Aeschere.

Ecgtheow turned to Hrothgar.

"Great King—war is upon you."

21

SHORT DAYS, ROUGH SEAS & COLD WEATHER

At dawn, the Ostrogoth rode the mare west along the coast until her heart burst and she collapsed. Hathus slit the horse's throat; then looked at his four-legged canine friend.

"Eat!"

While the Swamp Dog ate and drank its fill, Hathus shouldered his saddle and saddlebags and went his way on foot. He wasn't worried about leaving the dog behind; it would catch-up soon enough.

† † †

The day was growing dark when Hathus reached Land's End and went to the wharf; which, for the most part, was quiet with little activity. There was one knarr tied at the dock, loading cargo for its next destination.

"Tell me, friend," said Hathus to one of the knarr's crew. "Where are you bound for?"

"We sail for Frihamm tomorrow," said the crewman.

"Have any ships gone west recently?"

"None that I've seen," said the crewman.

"Can you tell me," said Hathus, "where's the best place to get a cup of honey wine and some information without getting my skull split?"

The seafarer laughed.

"That'll be the Bloody Boar in the village, a stone's throw from here. And if you're itching for a woman or some ink, you'll want to visit Thor's Hammer, around the corner from The Bloody Boar."

"Thank you, friend," said Hathus.

Except for the Mead-House keeper and several seafarers who were eating and drinking at a table in front of the hearth, The Bloody Boar was empty. Hathus approached the Mead-House keeper. He dropped his saddle and saddlebags on the floor in front of the counter.

"What'll you have?" said the Mead-House keeper while eying the Swamp Dog.

"Information," said Hathus. "And don't stare at the dog. He doesn't take to being stared at."

"Information, mead or beggars' stew," said the Mead-House keeper, "it'll cost you a silver wedge."

Hathus placed a silver wedge on the counter.

"I'm looking for Ecgtheow Waegmunding."

"Gone," said the Mead-House keeper.

His fingers had no sooner touched Hathus' silver when the Ostrogoth slapped his palm over the Mead-House keeper's hand and held it there.

"Gone, where?" said Hathus.

The hair on the back of the dog crept upward. What the Mead-House keeper saw in the Ostrogoth's eyes convinced him to speak.

"Word is, Ecgtheow Waegmunding sailed southwest to Frisia."

"When?" said Hathus.

"A week ago, more or less," said the Mead-House keeper.

"Well," said Hathus, tightening his grip on the Mead-House keeper's hand, "was it more, or less?"

"Less, I think," said the Mead-House keeper. "Yes—less than a week ago, a few days maybe."

"One more question," said Hathus.

"There won't be any ships sailing west from Land's End until spring," said the Mead-House keeper, "if that's what you want to know."

"No," said Hathus, "that isn't what I want to know. Tell me where I can buy a horse—a strong one."

"On top of the bluff at the Coastguards' camp," said the Mead-House keeper; "I heard they have Wylfing warhorses to sell."

The Ostrogoth freed the Mead-House keeper's hand; lifted his saddle and saddlebags and left The Bloody Boar. The Swamp Dog raised a leg, urinated on the floor and followed his master outside.

It was dusk. Mikla couldn't take his eyes off the Swamp Dog while he stood with his father outside the barn where the coastguards quartered their horses. The boy had never before seen a dog larger than a wolf, until that day.

Finished securing his saddle and saddlebags the Ostrogoth mounted a bay mare.

"Someone at the wharf told me Clan Waegmunding is hiring warriors," said Hathus, "to replace those they lost in their feud with the Dark Queen. I want to offer myself to their service, but I don't know where to find them. Can you give me directions?"

"Ride north, northeast," said Trygve. "Tell the Geatfolk you meet along the way that you seek Weohstan Waegmunding; they'll direct you to his farm, or they'll kill you—one, or the other."

The Ostrogoth smirked and urged the bay mare away at a canter.

"Was that a Swamp Dog?" said Mikla.

"Yes," said Trygve.

"Is it true the dead breed them in Helheim?"

"No, Mikla, that's just silly talk."

"Is the Outlander a Goth, Poppa? Like the ones who defeated the Romans?"

"Yes," said Trygve.

"Who do you think he is?"

"A dangerous man, my son," said Trygve, "a very, dangerous, man."

† † †

Weohstan walked the length of the new wall-walk on each of its three sides. He found it firm and capable of supporting the weight of many full grown men-at-arms. Weohstan was pleased with the work the Freemen had done. He returned to the Watch Tower over the Main Gate to keep an eye on the construction taking place around him. Was then he espied four riders approaching from the south. Weohstan climbed down from the Watch Tower.

Outside the gate, Weohstan's Second-in-Command, Leif, approached.

"Three of the riders are my cousins," said Leif, "I tasked them with patrolling."

The riders halted their horses in front of the Main Gate.

"We found this Ostrogoth on his way here, my Lord," said Leif's cousin, Magnus. "He said he has business with you."

Weohstan looked at the Ostrogoth. "What business would that be?" Weohstan looked at the dog. As he did, he felt a chill down his spine.

"I ask permission to cross your land, my Lord," said Hathus, "to enter the forest north of here."

"Vindinstedt Forest?" said Weohstan.

"If that's its name—yes," said Hathus.

"What is it you want there?"

"I was told the son of Ecgtheow Waegmunding went missing there, my Lord, and has yet to be found."

Weohstan stiffened.

"Whether the boy's dead or alive, what's that to you?"

"When it comes to tracking, my Lord, I and my dog have no equal. If the child—"

"My nephew," said Weohstan.

"If your... nephew is alive, somewhere in that forest I'll find him."

"You're very sure of yourself," said Weohstan. "Have you a name?"

"I am Hathus, son of Bugg, my Lord."

"Well, Hathus, son of Bugg, if you were to find my nephew, what would you want in return?"

"For a child of so few winters," said Hathus, "I ask only for his weight in silver."

"Winter's on its way," said Weohstan.

"All the more reason I start to search soon, my Lord—with your permission, that is."

Several moments had passed before Weohstan spoke.

"Very well," said Weohstan. "You have permission to proceed north. My Second-in-Command will see that you have food to take with you."

"I bought the horse from a captain of coastguards at Land's End," said Hathus. "With your permission, my Lord, I'll leave the horse here. As for food, I'll find what I need in the forest."

"Very well," said Weohstan, "pass in peace, Hathus, son of Bugg."

† † †

The Schaman opened his eyes and yawned. Apart from the glow of embers in the hearth, the lodge was dark. He rested on one elbow and looked around—Beowulf was gone. After the Schaman had dressed he added wood to the fire, then went outside.

"Beowulf," said Beorn.

There was no reply.

"Beowulf!"

Again there was no reply—nothing but the sound of the wind blowing across the lake, rustling the branches of trees surrounding the lodge. The Schaman found Beowulf standing at the water's edge, staring at the stars still visible in the morning sky.

"Who am I, Beorn?" said Beowulf. "What am I? Over and over I chase these questions, but I never catch the answers."

"You need to be patient. Winter is coming for a visit. Days will be short, Nights long. I'm going to teach you the power of words. When I'm not teaching you that, I'll teach you sword play, and how to wield a spear. After that, I'll teach you more of what you'll need to know. Sound all right?"

Beowulf nodded.

"Good," said Beorn. "Now—Let's go back to the lodge, put more wood on the fire and eat. After that, we can light the furnace."

"What are we going to make?" said Beowulf.

"We're going to melt iron, and while I'm pouring it into molds for spear tips, you're going to take my axe, row across the lake and find some fine young trees to chop down."

"For spear shafts," said Beowulf.

"Yes," said Beorn, "for the spear shafts you're going to make."

"When can I make a sword?"

"I can't answer that," said Beorn.

"Why?"

"Because it is tradition—the father that bestows a sword on his son; but whether or not that happens, first you need to learn to dance with iron. To be any good with a sword, you need to practice, practice, practice, and then practice some more. Until then—"

"Until then, you want me to be patient."

"Yes, Bear's Son," said Beorn. "And trust Tooth."

Beowulf drew his knife from its sheath; he ran his thumb along the cutting edge, testing its sharpness—blood appeared. Beowulf sheathed Tooth and looked the Schaman straight in the eyes.

"I do trust Tooth," he said.

† † †

While Hrothgar conferred with Aeschere and his counselors in the Throne Room, Wulfgar took Ecgtheow on a tour of nearby Heorot Fort.

"What do you think of the fort's defenses?" said Wulfgar.

"I think an enemy would be hard-pressed to overcome them," said Ecgtheow. "Traversing the ditch alone would cost an enemy several hundreds of warriors and several hundred more to scale the earthworks."

"Your assessment rings true, my Lord," said Wulfgar. "You have a good eye for details."

"Your willingness to show me around tells me the odds of me leaving Dane Land alive are slim, Lord Gate Warden."

Wulfgar laughed.

"Not at all, Lord Waegmunding, when the word goes out that Heorot Fort is impregnable, we Danes will be the better for it."

A messenger rode at a gallop into the fort.

"Lord Wulfgar!"

"Here!" said Wulfgar.

"The King wants Lord Waegmunding back at Heorot Hall," said the guard.

Ecgtheow stood before the dais. Aeschere spoke into Hrothgar's ear before stepping away.

"I've weighed your words, Lord Waegmunding," said Hrothgar,

"against those of my advisers—"

At the sound of footsteps approaching on the run, Hrothgar stopped talking. Wulfgar entered in haste. He went first to Aeschere and spoke in a hushed voice. Done, Wulfgar stepped to Ecgtheow's side and nodded as he would to a good friend.

Aeschere went again to the Throne. He relayed Wulfgar's message to Hrothgar. The King of the Spear Danes face paled; his expression turned grim.

"King Botheric's fleet was sighted leaving the mouth of the River Spree in Germania at dawn. Our spies say his ships put out to sea and head north. A Wylfing ship with Prince Adalfuns aboard leads them. It would seem my advisers judged you hastily, Lord Waegmunding, as did I."

Hrothgar cast a look around his Throne Room.

"I won't make that same mistake again. Now then, Lord Waegmunding, what do you suggest?"

Despite the time that passed since the Wylfing raid the Ostrogoth had little difficulty finding the trail left by the Wylfings' horses when they trampled the bracken in pursuit of the woman and her child. Moreover, the Swamp Dog found what Weohstan and the Freemen missed—Handscio's gift to Beowulf, his stuffed doll, Uncle Rabbit.

The trail left by the Wylfings led to a clearing and the discovery of the remains of Lars Ásmundr and two of his men, their headless corpses putrefying after being torn apart by forest animals. Throughout the clearing, their scattered bones lie moldering on the damp, dark earth. The Ostrogoth took the doll from the dog's mouth, raised it to his nose and inhaled the scent—once, twice, three times. The Ostrogoth then held it close to the dog's nose.

"Search!" said Hathus.

The Swamp Dog zigzagged back and forth in the clearing, distinguishing the odors that the corpses gave off from the latent scent of the she bear and the scent of the man child which permeated the doll. The dog stopped; barked once, and set off running.

The Ostrogoth tucked the doll under his belt and followed.

When Beowulf finished chopping down a third young ash tree, he stripped the trunks of their lateral branches. Done, he bound the three pieces together with leather ties at both ends. Each piece measured ten-feet in length and was as wide across as his thigh. With careful cutting, shaping, those three pieces would furnish all twelve shafts. Beowulf slung the Schaman's axe across his back; then he lifted the bundled trees over his shoulder. He paused and looked around. The forest was quiet, the air still. The snow on that blanketed the ground sparkled in the sunlight. Bouncing the saplings on his shoulder, Beowulf knew he could carry five-times the weight, and more. Exhilarated, he looked skyward.

Thank you, Beautiful Goddess. Thank you, Hammer Bearer. From the branches of a tree, a large clump of snow landed on Beowulf's head. He sat on the snow-covered ground and laughed.

"Thank you, All Mother!"

22

A DEBT FOR THE OFFERING

The wind whipped the pennants attached to the spears of the Iron Guards and made loud snapping sounds as Lord Hakon, Kommandar of Hrothgar's fleet, approached his king and bowed.

"Your orders, my King?" said Hakon.

"Ask Lord Waegmunding," said Hrothgar.

"Your Grace?" said Hakon, not certain he heard what he heard.

"Do it," said Hrothgar.

Lord Hakon bowed and turned to Ecgtheow.

"Lord Waegmunding?"

"King Botheric's Kommandar will bring his ships north," said Ecgtheow. "When he—"

"How can you be sure?" said Hakon.

"Because it's what I'd do," said Ecgtheow. He looked at Hrothgar.

"If I were hurrying to join forces with the Wylfings in the Bay of Kryl, the fastest way there is north between the islands of Langeland and Lolland, your Grace."

"Through the Langelandbælt," said Hrothgar.

"Yes, Great King," said Ecgtheow, "which will lead them to the Storebælt—the Great Belt.

Hrothgar looked at Hakon. "You have your orders, Lord Hakon. Gods willing, you'll return to Daneland victorious. Or not at all."

"Gods willing, my King," said Hakon. "I would rather perish than fail you."

"I would rather you die than fail me, also, my Lord. But you won't fail, Hakon; you're too fine a warrior; one in whom I have complete confidence."

Hakon's chest swelled; he bowed and hurried off. A short while later, Ecgtheow stood with Hrothgar on the jetty at Mörk Sand. They watched forty of Hrothgar's battle craft set sail south toward Germania under Lord Hakon's command.

"Lord Hakon has a good head on his shoulders," said Hrothgar, "and the best of my ships; he'll not fail me."

"The Franks'Longships serve them best in the inland waterways," said Ecgtheow. "They don't handle worth spit in the open sea, especially in rough waters. When Prince Adalfuns and Botheric's Kommandar see what's coming, they'll piss themselves."

Hrothgar ran his tongue over his lips.

"Let's hope the battle goes as you think it will, Lord Waegmunding. Now then, the forty ships I've given you to command, how do you intend to use them?"

"I know these waters well, great King," said Ecgtheow. "I'll sail under cover of darkness. Come dawn tomorrow; I'll lead your ships into the Bay of Kryl and, gods willing, return with a victory."

"If you're victorious," said Hrothgar, "Tell me what you want in return—gold, silver, land—I leave it to you to name it."

† † †

The Swamp Dog stopped and waited for his master. When the Ostrogoth arrived, the dog was sitting in front of the entrance to a cave. Hathus leaned on his spear. While he caught his breath, he studied the place where the child's scent had led the dog.

I'm too late, thought the Ostrogoth. A bear or some other cave dweller found the child. Even so, perhaps the bones remain inside. If I gather and bag them, I' may get some silver for my trouble; then I can go after the father. No sense in going inside to kill what's in there, not when I can smoke it out.

The Ostrogoth was about to place his spear on the ground and gather firewood when the dog began to growl.

The Ostrogoth went to where his dog was pawing at the earth. Hathus knelt and studied the ground. Though faint, the Ostrogoth could make out the clear leather-booted tracks of a large, heavy-set man walking with a staff. Alongside those tracks were other tracks, tracks of a child. The two had walked from the cave during rain and had imprinted their tracks in the mud; mud that had long since hardened.

Strange, Hathus thought; *the one set of tracks belongs to a child, but what sense am I to make of the heavy-set man accompanying him? Could it be the bloody father? Could I be so bloody lucky to have both the father and son in my grasp?*

The Ostrogoth looked at his dog.

"Search!"

† † †

Beowulf rowed the skiff across the lake to the island. Each exhalation turned to steam in front of his eyes. He enjoyed feeling his muscles stretch and contract as he rowed; just as he enjoyed feeling the power that flowed through his upper body and arms when he cut firewood. Cutting trees was a task Beorn relinquished when it became apparent Beowulf's strength far surpassed his own.

After crossing the lake to the island and securing the skiff to the shore, Beowulf shouldered his bundle of timber and headed for the lodge. As he walked, the sounds he heard came from his boots as they crunched the snow.

Entering the lodge a blast of warmth from the fire greeted the bear's son's cold nose, cheeks, and lips. He closed the door behind and placed the timber on the floor. Beowulf removed his Black Beaver hat and wolf skin cloak and left them to dry where the Schaman wouldn't complain.

He knelt in front of the fire and warmed his hands. He could hear the sound of the Schaman's boots trudging through the snow. The door burst open. Beorn entered holding a half-dozen iron spear tips.

"Get the door," said Beorn. "There's a blizzard coming.

"How can you tell?"

"Ha!" said Beorn. "I've lived through enough of them to know when one's on its way. Trust me, Bear's Son, the next time you cross the lake you'll be doing it on your feet. One more thing, you'll want to line the throne with evergreen."

"Why?" said Beowulf.

"So your arse doesn't freeze to the wood when you have a sit-down—understand?"

Beowulf nodded and closed the door.

The Schaman placed the spear tips on the floor then stretched his upper body side-to-side.

"I must be getting old," said Beorn. "My back hurts. What's for supper?"

"You already know," said Beowulf.

"Beggars' stew," said Beorn.

Beowulf nodded.

The Schaman went over to the bundle of trees on the floor.

"These should do nicely."

Beowulf ran his hands over the iron spear tips. "They're still hot," he said.

"Aye," said Beorn. "The other six are hardening in the molds and still too hot to carry. I'll bring them in later."

"I can do it," said Beowulf. "You should rest your back."

The Schaman looked at Beowulf for a long moment; then smiled.

"Very well, Bear's Son. I will. Now then, do you remember what to do with these logs?"

"I'm going to cut them straight across, top and bottom,"

"And how long should they be?" said Beorn.

"Eight-feet," said Beowulf.

"Then what are you going to do?"

"I'm going to split each log down the middle."

"How are you going to accomplish that?"

"With great care," said Beowulf.

"Yes. Then, what?" said Beorn.

"I'll cut each half down its middle. When I've done the same to the other two logs, I'll have twelve pieces in all, enough for twelve spear tips."

"But before that?" said Beorn.

"We cure the wood."

"And how do we strengthen the shafts?" said Beorn.

"We keep them dry until the moisture's gone out of them."

"And then?"

"We'll know the wood's ready to shape," said Beowulf.

The Schaman nodded. "Let's eat."

Ecgtheow looked into the faces of Lord Berenson and the forty warriors gathered before him, each a battle tested warrior, hand picked to command the forty Longships Ecgtheow would lead into battle. Behind Ecgtheow stood King Hrothgar flanked by the Iron Guard.

"My name is Ecgtheow Waegmunding," he said. "For killing the son of the Dark Queen, my King exiled me from the land of my forefathers. My king did this to prevent a war with the Iron Wolf. I do not fault him. We Thunder-Geats are a small tribe with few battle craft to launch against our enemies. However, war has come upon you. Franks and Wylfings have joined forces against your noble king and are preparing to attack Daneland. But before they can join their fleets together, we will sail west to the Bay of Kryl, and strike the Wylfing fleet. We are forty ships in number. Five of you will anchor your ships north of the Bay and disembark. Another five will do the same to the south. Come dawn tomorrow we'll attack the Wylfing camp from three sides, on land, and from the sea. When my ram's horn blows three times, we will descend on the Wylfings as would a storm—an iron storm!"

† † †

The Ostrogoth knelt in the snow beside the Swamp Dog. Concealed by bushes, he stared at the lodge twenty-yards away. A thin wisp of smoke rose from the chimney, enough to tell the Ostrogoth someone was inside; but not who, or how many. He took note of a pen suitable for pigs and an enclosure for other animals, perhaps goats. Close to winter, he knew the owner probably put his animals inside the lodge to protect them from predators and the full force of the elements.

The Ostrogoth looked skyward: *There's a blizzard on the way* Hathus told himself. *"What do you think, Dog—Is this a good place to spend the night?"*

The door to the lodge opened. Outside ran the trapper's three Elk hounds.

Using his spear, the Ostrogoth struck the lead dog in its chest, piercing its heart. The Swamp Dog sank its fangs into a second Elk-Hound and tore out its throat. The third guard dog bit into one of the Swamp Dog's hind legs; the Ostrogoth plunged his spear through the Hound's ribcage. When the three hounds lie dead on the ground, a silence fell over the place.

It was then the trapper emerged from his lodge wielding a woodcutter's axe. A boy followed him, fifteen winters young, armed with a spear. The dog owner's eyes widened at the sight of his dead hounds and the wild eyed warrior accompanied by a Swamp Dog.

"Get back inside," said the trapper. "Bar the door and protect your mother!"

The boy retreated into the lodge.

"You've killed my hounds!"

"You ought not to have set them on me," said Hathus. "But never mind that. A tall man with a walking staff passed this way some time ago. He had a boy child with him. Have you seen them?"

"You'll be getting nothing from me, you Goth bastard," said the trapper. "Leave! Or by the gods, I'll bury this axe in your head!"

The Ostrogoth's spear impaled the trapper to the lodge door. The settlor screamed, his axe fell from his hands. With what strength he had left, he tried to free himself, but the spear wouldn't budge. The Ostrogoth brought his axe down on the man's neck, removing the head. The Goth pulled his spear out, and the corpse collapsed to the ground. Blood poured onto the snow and pooled around the Ostrogoth's boots. The Swamp Dog ceased licking its hind leg, faced the lodge and growled.

"Yes," said Hakus, "we'll leave what's inside on four legs alone —until we want to eat it."

The Ostrogoth kicked the door open. A spear sailed through the air and grazed the Ostrogoth's cheek, drawing blood. The Ostrogoth looked at the Swamp Dog: "Kill!"

† † †

Buffeted by a strong north wind, and hard-hitting waves that slammed against their prows, the Longships under Ecgtheow's command with their waterproofed hulls and sails painted blue and white sped over the surface of the water—low-flying birds of prey.

Feet planted with knees bent and with both hands gripping the tiller, Ecgtheow guided his ship north-northwest along the coast of Daneland; then west across the Strait of Samso toward Jutland and the Bay of Kryl.

On either side of Ecgtheow stood two warriors; they held torches aloft for the ships behind them to follow. The thought of killing Wylfings raced through Ecgtheow's mind, exciting him, and he steeled himself for what was coming.

Death will have his hands full tomorrow thought Ecgtheow. The thought of sending so many souls to Helheim warmed Ecgtheow where he stood, even as the cold wind licked his face and blew through his hair.

I'll have my vengeance, Ecgtheow told himself. *And I'll go on having it until Hel, herself, has had enough.*

23

WIDOW MAKER

Sheltered by the bay from the wind, Lord Yngvarr and the thousand warriors with him pitched tents on shore. Glad they were to bed down on land, build campfires, dry their garments and clean their armor after six days and nights at sea. Yngvarr did not expect Prince Adalfuns and King Botheric's fleet to arrive for another two, perhaps three days because they would be sailing into the wind.

Inside his pavilion, lulled to sleep by the sound of waves lapping on the shore, Yngvarr slept content with the knowledge the Spear Danes had lashed their fleet together and left it unmanned and idle for the winter in Mörk Sand. Even if the Franks wanted no part of a war with the Danes and kept to themselves, cruising the rivers of Germania for plunder, Hrothgar's fleet would remain a tempting target, too tempting for the Wylfing Battle Lord to ignore.

His dreamless sleep ended at dawn when three blasts from a ram's horn shattered the silence over the Bay of Kryl. Yngvarr gasped. Arrows pierced his pavilion, one stuck in the sand between his feet. The excited shouts of his men ushered him outside into the dim blue twilight.

While rams' horns continued to blare, Yngvarr saw a brilliant, blood red sun rise above the ocean appearing like the eye of a terrible sea monster. Arrows by the hundreds rained on the Wylfing camp as the Spear Danes attacked from land and sea.

The full-throated war cries of the Spear Danes wrought havoc in the hearts of the Wylfings. A mind numbing panic spread among Yngvarr's warriors, most of whom had not had time to gather their weapons and their battle gear. Even as Yngvarr donned his helm and unsheathed his sword, the Spear Danes had entered the camp.

Unable to organize a defense, Wylfings fled the fighting in large numbers. It wasn't long before Yngvarr found himself alone, surrounded by Spear Danes. Defiant to the end, he yelled and swung his sword in a wide arc. The next moment he lay dead on the ground, his blood forming a dark patch, what the next high tide would erase.

By the time the sun had risen the Wylfings had thrown down their weapons, dropped to their knees and raised their hands in surrender.

Prince Adalfuns commanded the lead ship. Behind him were King Botheric's fifty Longships, the entirety of Botheric's fleet. Standing near the prow, holding the folds of his cloak together to ward off the chill, the Iron Wolf's first-born son was in an ill humor and unprepared for what his eyes beheld: the silhouettes of forty Longships approaching from the north with full sails and the wind at their backs.

Always the pragmatist, Prince Adalfuns wasted no time shouting to the two Tillermen to steer east and make haste, away from the area. Adalfuns urged his men to forget to arm themselves and row faster. With the sail billowing full, Adalfun's battle craft initiated an attempt to escape due east, for home.

The Wylfing prince looked over his shoulder to see if the Danes were pursuing him—they weren't. Unable to look away, he watched the Spear Danes' ships descend on the outmatched battle craft of the Franks.

The fire arrows of the Danes streaked through the sky by the hundreds and rained flames upon Botheric's battle craft.

Prince Adalfuns wanted no part of it. It would take a week, maybe longer for him to reach Värg Slött, his father's fortress, provided that the Danes didn't catch him first. While Adalfuns' ship continued east, the muffled sounds of battle followed across the water. As ancient enemies collided there was the sound of oars snapping, wood planks cracking and splintering apart as hulls caved-in, along with the high-pitched ringing of iron against iron. Above the din, above it all, the screams and cries of the wounded and dying prevailed—sounds that would haunt Prince Adalfuns for many days and nights to come.

After the fighting in the Bay of Kryl had concluded, the Danes stripped the Wylfings of their weapons and armor and set fire to what remained of the Wylfing camp. Lord Berenson searched for Ecgtheow. Berenson found him at the water's edge, his helm on the sand beside him as he washed the blood and gore from his face, arms and hands.

"You've given us a great victory, Lord Waegmunding," said Berenson.

"The gods favored us today," said Ecgtheow, "and you and your men fought well."

"What are your orders?" said Berenson.

"Put the Wylfings' weapons and armor aboard the ships we captured, with enough of your men to crew them, and we'll return to Daneland."

"What about the Wylfings?" said Berenson.

"Leave them," said Ecgtheow.

"Leave them, my Lord?" said Berenson, dumbstruck.

"What would you have me do?" said Ecgtheow. "Send them home so their king can continue to threaten Geats and Danes alike? Tell me, Lord Berenson—what would you do?"

A moment passed. Berenson said nothing. Ecgtheow stood and put his helm on his head.

"One ship," said Ecgtheow. "I will leave them one ship."

"One ship," said Berenson, "for eight, maybe nine-hundred men?"

"Give the order, Lord Berenson, before I change my mind and leave them with nothing."

Following Ecgtheow's orders, skeleton crews boarded the Wylfing ships for the return trip to Daneland. The rest of the Danes returned to their ships with the captured weapons and armor.

Ecgtheow's ship was the last to shove-off from the beach. The Wylfings crowded the shore to watch the Danes depart. One Wylfing Longship remained anchored with its sail furled, thirty-yards offshore. A Wylfing Clan Chief waded into the water: "What of us?" he said. "Are we not your prisoners?"

"Not any longer," said Ecgtheow. "You're free to return to Öster Götaland. You have my word on it."

"How?" said the Wylfing, "you've left us one ship, and we are hundreds!"

Ecgtheow shouted so the Wylfings who crowded the water's edge might hear: "Those of you who want to see your homes again, your wives and children, will find a way. Or you can remain where you are and die of cold and starvation. The choice is yours."

"Who are you?" said the Wylfing chief.

"Ecgtheow Waegmunding!"

"May the gods curse you, Ecgtheow Waegmunding, now and forever," said the Wylfing chief.

Ecgtheow turned his back on the Wylfings. They already have, he told himself.

Had Ecgtheow looked he would have seen Wylfings clawing each other, gouging eyes and biting ears; fighting with bare hands; drowning and trampling each other as they swarmed the water the way maddened animals desperate to survive would do.

† † †

Ecgtheow stood alongside Lord Berenson at the prow of their Longship. As their battle craft drew near the rest of the fleet, Ecgtheow heard sixteen-hundred victorious Spear Danes shouting in his direction.

"Why are they shouting?" Ecgtheow said.

"They're honoring you," said Lord Berenson.

"I can't make out what they're saying," said Ecgtheow.

"They're calling you, Änka tillverkare," said Berenson.

"Widow Maker," said Ecgtheow.

"Yes," said Berenson. "Widow Maker."

Ecgtheow drew his sword and raised it high. *Whether to honor me or not,* he thought, *it's what I'm going to call you, my cold iron friend.*

For the first time in a long while, Ecgtheow smiled while he continued to gaze at his sword's nicked blade and the blood that dried there.

Outside, the wind howled and pushed against the door of the

lodge. Beowulf sat cross-legged near the hearth. Using the firelight to see by, in his left hand he grasped an eight-foot length of ash and held it steady. With his right hand, he kept the sharp edge of his knife straight up-and-down, perpendicular to the shaft so as not to cut into the grain. He moved the blade away from his body, back-and-forth, several inches at a time. Turning the shaft in his hand, little by little, Beowulf gave the wood more of the smooth cylindrical shape vital for wielding a spear. The Schaman sat nearby and rubbed Libden oil into one of the ten shafts that Beowulf finished sculpting.

"How long will the snowstorm last?" said Beowulf.

"Until it's over," said Beorn.

"It's been almost three days, Beorn."

"Yes," said Beorn, "but we're warm and dry. We've got wood for the fire and food to eat."

"We've no more goat cheese," said Beowulf, "and no more bread or sausage and very few turnips left. Apart from that, we've nothing to eat except jerky."

"That may be," said Beorn, "but look at what you've accomplished these last few days: a dozen spear shafts finished, top to bottom. Believe me, Bear's Son, the blizzard will be over sooner or later; then you can go outside and stretch your legs. Maybe you can even catch a rabbit if you have a mind to."

"That's not funny," said Beowulf.

"No," said Beorn, "I suppose not." A wide grin spread across the Schaman's face.

Beowulf paused from what he was doing.

"When the blizzard's over, can we go to the trapper's lodge to get more cheese?"

The Schaman looked at Beowulf: "Have you forgotten? The settlor's lodge is three days from here. In the snow it would take four, maybe five days to get there and another four or five days to return. That's a long way to go for cheese."

"I suppose you're right," said Beowulf.

Beowulf and the Schaman resumed working. Again, Beowulf paused and looked at the Schaman.

"The trapper," said Beowulf, "does he have a family?"

"Yes," said Beorn, "Dag has a wife, Ermin, and a son, Gild."

"I would like to have someone to talk to," said Beowulf.

"Ha," said Beorn, "you have me to talk to."

Beowulf raised one eyebrow and gave the Schaman a questioning look.

"Trust me, Bear's Son, they're decent enough folks, but settlers, especially Svearlanders, aren't much for talking, especially to strangers."

"Who are the Svear?" said Beowulf.

"A powerful tribe," said Beorn. "It's the stubborn resolve of Geats and Wylfings both, that's kept the Svear from realizing their king's ambition to rule all Scandia."

Beowulf studied the Schaman's words for a moment.

"If, as you say, the trapper is a Svearlander, why did he give you food?"

"Because Dag knows and trusts me," said Beorn, "and he felt he owed me for saving the life of his son when Gild fell ill last spring. Not all Svear think as their king does, Beowulf. There are many such as Dag and Ermin who want the freedom to live their lives in peace. So they come here, to settle and make do for themselves in the wilderness."

"As we do."

"Yes," said Beorn, "as we do."

"Why can't the Svear King be content with what he has?" said Beowulf. "Why must he try to take what doesn't belong to him?"

"For the same reason the Wylfing King wants the land of the Thunder-Geats," said Beorn, "and I dare say, that of the Spear Danes' King, too, if he can get it. For a tribe to flourish, Beowulf, it needs to grow in number, and for that to happen, there must be land for raising families, crops and livestock, a place with access to the Whale Road."

"I've never seen the Whale Road," said Beowulf.

"Gods willing," said Beorn, "you will have one day."

"I'd like that," said Beowulf.

Finished with the shaft, he was working on; he held it out to the Schaman. The Schaman took hold of the shaft and held it before his eyes.

"Straight enough," said Beorn. The Schaman ran his fingers back and forth over the length of the shaft.

"Smooth as a baby's bottom," said Beorn.

"One more left to make," said Beowulf.

24

A SETTLING

"Now we can put the tips on. When we finish, and the blizzard quits, I'll take some spears to a Svear settlement north of here and barter for food and supplies."

"Take me with you."

"Too risky, Bear's Son. No telling how far the Dark Queen's reach extends."

"I'm strong enough to take care of myself, Beorn; you know I am."

"Yes, which is why I want you to stay and guard the throne—lest the marmots try to claim it."

A moment had passed before Beowulf laughed.

"That's a good boy," said Beorn.

"I'm tired of being patient," said Beowulf.

"I know you are, Bear's Son, but it won't always be this way, I promise. Will you do it—will you wait here while I'm gone?"

† † †

The news that poisoned King Amunwolf's mood and put him in a humorless state of mind had come three days ahead of Prince Adalfuns' ignominious return. For three days the Iron Wolf's fury festered.

"Where are they?" thundered Amunwolf. "Where's my Battle Lord? Where's Lord Yngvarr? And where are my bloody ships?"

Adalfuns stood with his head bent and stared at his feet. The Throne Room was empty, but for the Iron Wolf's twelve-man Bodyguard and the six Clan Chiefs, Amunwolf summoned to Värg Slött after the news of Lord Yngvarr's defeat in Jutland arrived.

"Well?" said Amunwolf.

When no words were forthcoming, Amunwolf shook Adalfuns by the shoulders. "Did you lose your tongue while sneaking back here?"

"No, Father," said Adalfuns. "But you already know of our defeat."

"Not our defeat," said Amunwolf, "your defeat! Never forget that."

Amunwolf turned to one of his guards.

"Bring Argrim in!"

The guard hastened away. Adalfuns' eyes darted around the Throne Room in hopes he would find a friend—there was none. The guard soon returned with the same Clan Chief who stood on the shore and cursed Ecgtheow Waegmunding as the Danes departed from the Bay of Kryl. Argrim bowed to his King.

"Tell him, Lord Argrim," said Amunwolf. "Tell my son what happened there."

"Yes, my King," said Argrim. He turned and faced Prince Adalfuns. "After reaching Jutland, we anchored our ships in the Bay of Kryl. So certain was our Battle Lord that we arrived there unseen, Lord Yngvarr ordered us to make camp on the shore where there was a freshwater stream and ample firewood nearby. We waited for you, my Prince, to join us with King Botheric's fleet but the Spear Danes got there first. They came with the dawn and rained havoc on our heads. Lord Yngvarr died on the beach. We tried to mount a defense but were overwhelmed on three sides with a black-water marsh to fall back. It shames me to say it, but we surrendered—nine-hundreds of us. Certain were we that the Spear Danes would treat us with honor."

"And did they?" said Adalfuns.

"After stripping us of our weapons and armor, they set torches to our tents and stores of provisions."

"But they obviously left you ships to return with," said Adalfuns.

"One ship, my Prince," said Argrim. "Their Fleet Kommandar left one ship anchored offshore. We crowded into the water and fought our way toward it. All I could think of was getting home to my wife and children. No longer shield brothers, we tore each other to pieces as we struggled to keep from drowning. Out of nine-hundred men who went into the water that day, thirty of us made it aboard that ship. Then, while some of us used the oars for clubs to crush the heads of those who tried to board, we dropped sail and departed for home."

"Tell him, Argrim," said Amunwolf, "tell Prince Adalfuns the name of the Spear Danes' Fleet Kommandar."

"Ecgtheow Waegmunding," said Argrim.

Adalfuns jaws went slack; his mouth dropped open.

"What do you think King Hrothgar will do now, Father?" he said.

"Gods willing," said Amunwolf, "nothing. As for what Ecgtheow Waegmunding did as Hrothgar's Kommandar, I don't fault him. I would've done as he did to keep from fighting the same men again some other day."

"I don't understand," said Adalfuns. "Why would Hrothgar do nothing? We tried to destroy his fleet."

"Hrothgar decimated half my army in the Bay of Kryl, you idiot. Now he has twenty-eight of my ships—Wylfing ships! The Franks almost lost their entire fleet. Trust me; I know King Botheric. He hasn't the stones to send more ships out on the Whale Road anytime soon. Ecgtheow Waegmunding handed Hrothgar a victory beyond his wildest dreams. Curse me for a fool; I handed Hrothgar, Ecgtheow Waegmunding! No, Hrothgar needn't do anything—he's already won!"

† † †

After removing their genitals and major organs, the Ostrogoth cut off the heads, hands, and feet of the trapper, his wife, and their son. He buried those parts before fastening the flayed bodies to meat hooks. He hoisted the carcasses into the branches of the closest tree, high enough from the ground to prevent animals from getting at them. The cold would preserve the meat; Hathus could cut and thaw what pieces he wanted when he wanted. The pigs and goats had died of sheer terror in the presence of the Swamp Dog. Hathus wasted no time skinning and cleaning them; then he hung their carcasses in the branches, alongside those of the trapper.

The Ostrogoth could feel it in the air: a blizzard was on its way. As he sat near the hearth and warmed his feet by the fire, the dog lay curled beside him. Hathus marveled at their fortuitous fortune. No matter how long the wind blew or how cold it got outside, no matter how long the snowstorm lasted, Hathus knew he and the dog could wait it out in comfort.

"We'll find them," said Hathus. "Soon as the weather permits we'll pick up their trail. Until then, Dog, we have a warm place to sleep, and food aplenty."

The Ostrogoth leaned forward; in one hand he held the floppy rabbit to his nose and inhaled the scent that lingered there—Beowulf's scent. With his other hand, he rubbed the Swamp Dog behind the ears.

"Life is good—ay, Dog?"

Hrothgar's counselors, along with Daneland's preeminent warriors and Clan Chiefs, crowded the Throne Room in Heorot Hall. Most of those present had participated in the battle at the Bay of Kryl, or in the sea battle with the Franks near the Isle of Langeland.

After Hrothgar had praised Lords Berenson and Hakon, he gave them each given a large purse of gold rings and, for every warrior, the promise of gold rings and a commemorative silver torque. Berenson and Hakon bowed and stepped away from the dais. Hrothgar motioned for Ecgtheow to approach.

"Never in my wildest dreams," said Hrothgar, "could I have foreseen such a victory. When I asked what you wanted if you returned victoriously, you told me, 'ships.' Well, you shall have them, all twenty-eight of the Svear battle craft you captured, if that's your desire. Where you'll find the men to crew them remains a mystery."

The Danes in attendance laughed. Hrothgar signed for "silence."

"Which is why, Great King," said Ecgtheow; "at the risk of seeming ungrateful I ask for something more."

"Ask," said Hrothgar.

"I pray you send all but one of the Wylfing ships north as a gift to King Hrethel and I will keep one for myself. With those ships and the ships Hrethel already possesses, my tribe can withstand the Iron Wolf's ambition to destroy the Thunder-Geats just as he wants to ruin the Spear Danes. Moreover, I ask you, Great King, to think of the Thunder-Geats as your ally in the north. Let our two tribes enjoy lasting peace and friendship. Let our tribes pledge mutual defense in times of war. The Thunder-Geats will become stronger. The bond between our tribes will grow strong. Together, we can control the Whale Road; tribes who desire peace can enjoy peace, and all of us will prosper."

Several moments passed in silence. Hrothgar's counselor, Lord Aeschere stepped forward.

"My King," said Aeschere, "Hrethel could use those ships against us."

Hrothgar looked at Ecgtheow for clarification.

"I give you my word, Great King," said Ecgtheow. "Hrethel is an honorable man and an able shepherd to his people. He would not sully his name by doing what Lord Aeschere suggests."

"I believe you," said Hrothgar. "I'll take up the matter later with my counselors and hear what they have to say. But tonight we'll feast in celebration of our victory."

Ecgtheow bowed and stepped away from the dais. What he wanted was one thing, what he needed was another—and now he needed to ride Rain Dancer in the open air. With luck and a long bath, he would rid himself of the stench of death that followed him from the Bay of Kryl.

25

ICE

Greetings, *Blåskägg*," said Hermengild, a one-armed man sixty-winters old. Once a Svear warrior, in Ongentheow's service, the fact Hermengild had lost an arm during the Battle on the Ice didn't prevent him from swinging a cudgel if and when a visitor forgot to behave.

At the moment the Schaman entered, Hermengild was butchering the carcass of a pig.

Beorn stepped inside and closed the heavy door behind, shutting-out the cold wind that accompanied him to the small settlement on the fringe of Svearland. Beorn acquired the name 'Bluebeard' by the blue stain that ran the length of his otherwise snow-white beard, straight down the center from his chin to his chest. Some said the stain bespoke the Schaman's fondness for berries: blue, black and red. Others said the Schaman was an agent of the gods, and they had marked him as such. A few said the stain was an old man's attempt to garner the attention of young women, though no one would say it to his face. More than a few folks thought Beorn a forest spirit, perhaps even a demon. In any case, the Schaman's size and the double bladed battle axe he carried were sufficient to deter insults.

"Greetings, Hermengild," said Beorn.

The Schaman looked around; there were perhaps a dozen men present, some sitting near the hearth drinking beer and eating goat's' milk cheese melted on toasted rye bread; others were bartering for tools or weapons or dried venison. The looks they cast the Schaman as he entered were benign. They gazed with interest, however, when the Schaman revealed three spears made of polished ash and iron bundled together.

"I've come to trade," said Beorn.

It had been four days since the blizzard ended. During that time the extreme cold froze the surface of the lake making it possible to cross from shore to shore in most places.

To keep busy and to keep his mind occupied, Beowulf cut trees down. He would drag or carry the timber back across the ice to the lodge; there he would chop logs into manageable pieces of firewood. When Beowulf exerted himself, his muscles sang, and his whole body would rejoice, his lungs fueled sounds that forced their escape by way of his throat—feral, guttural sounds mixed with laughter. Unaffected by the cold, the more work he did, the better he felt and the better he slept. At night indoors, relaxing, Beowulf would sharpen Tooth and the edge of a woodcutter's axe. Other times he would sit by the fire and stitch new things to wear, from the assortment of skins stacked in the corner of the lodge.

At midday, while it was still light, and the air cold, crisp and clean, Beowulf gathered several logs and carried them to the lodge. He had left the door ajar and, with arms full, he pushed it open with his foot.

He stacked the logs, walked back to the door and was about to shut it when he saw them—a tall man and a dog, on the far shore looking straight at him. Motionless, as though Nature carved them from the side of the mountain, it was the steam that issued from their mouths which suggested the two were indeed alive. Beowulf felt the tiny hairs on the back of his neck rise, and fear raced down his spine. The man was tall and broad as the Schaman and carried a double bladed battle axe slung over one shoulder. He had blood-red hair and leaned on a spear that was longer than a common warrior' spear, longer even than those used by the Spear Danes.

The dog was sitting and it, too, frightened Beowulf. It was larger than the largest wolf he had ever seen. He took two spears from the rack on the wall and walked outside. Neither the man nor the dog had moved.

"What is it you want?" said Beowulf, his voice loud enough to reach the far shore.

"A man with a heavy foot," said Hathus, "and a boy child, seven, maybe eight winters young."

"There's no one here like that," said Beowulf in as firm a voice as he could muster.

He dropped one of the spears aside.

"Strange," said Hathus, "Dog tracked them to this very place."

The Swamp Dog rose and growled. The Goth pulled the floppy-eared rabbit doll from his belt and tossed it onto the ice.

At that moment Beowulf recalled something the Schaman told him:

"As long as men hunt you, whether you live or die depends entirely on you, Beowulf. Maybe not today, maybe not tomorrow, but one day you'll find this out for yourself. Your father, Ecgtheow is a warrior—a killer of men; so, too, will you become a slayer of men. The sooner you make peace with your fate, the better. The choice is yours, Bear's Son. Kill, or be killed."

"What's wrong, boy—lose your tongue?" said Hathus. "I don't know what magic is afoot here, but Dog seems to think you're the child I seek; although, to look at you, you can't be less than seventeen, maybe eighteen winters old. Now how can that be?"

"Move on," said Beowulf, "you and your dog. You're not welcome here."

"We've come too far to turn around and go back," said Hathus. "By the gods, you're him, aren't you, boy? You're Beowulf Waegmunding, son of Ecgtheow Waegmunding."

"I'm not afraid of you, or your dog," said Beowulf. It was less than the truth, but not entirely a lie.

"Well, boy," said Hathus, "you should be. If Dog doesn't tear your throat out, I'm going to hang you by your ankles and carve the skin from your bones—while you're still alive."

Beowulf made no reply; rather, he tightened his right-hand grip on the shaft of his spear and stepped several paces forward. He positioned his left foot just ahead of his body and relaxed his weight on the ice--it held.

"Your silence betrays you, boy; you're the one I seek. Tell me: is it your father who accompanied you here? I ask because the Dark Queen has offered a pretty sum for both your heads."

"I know no Dark Queen," Beowulf said.

"No Matter," said Hathus. "That changes nothing. Alive, you're worth nothing to me, boy, and I mean to cut your father's heart out and feed it to Dog."

A sudden rage took hold of Beowulf—with all his might he hurled his spear. It cut through the air faster than a falcon flies. The

Ostrogoth had no time to duck. The point of the spear cut through his bearskin vest, pierced his left shoulder beneath the collarbone, and exited out his back. The impact of the spear spun the Ostrogoth in a complete circle and dropped him to one knee. He clasped a hand over the wound; then he took it away. Blood spewed from the hole—his blood. The Ostrogoth struggled to his feet and looked at the dog.

"Kill!"

The Swamp Dog dug his claws into the ice-bound surface of the lake and charged forward. Beowulf retrieved the other spear near his feet and waited. As the dog approached, it lost its footing, tumbled headfirst and slid several yards before righting itself.

Snarling, desirous of ripping-out Beowulf's throat and drinking his blood, the dog came forward in the manner of a long-tusked boar, head tilted upward. Five yards from Beowulf, the dog launched itself into the air; Beowulf dropped to one knee with the spear angled upward. The point penetrated the dog's chest, continued through its heart and out its back, severing the spine. Without a sound, the Swamp Dog collapsed in a heap at Beowulf's feet.

The Ostrogoth screamed with rage. Grasping his spear in his right hand, he hurled it at the killer of his beloved companion.

Beowulf watched the spear come toward him. At the last moment, he stepped aside and snatched it in mid-air. While the Ostrogoth looked on, Beowulf broke the shaft of the Ostrogoth's spear across his knee.

Again the Ostrogoth screamed, so consumed was he with pain and rage. He removed his axe from across his back and started toward Beowulf. The Ostrogoth had not gotten far when a deep, menacing voice halted him.

"Walk no further, Goth!"

The Ostrogoth whirled around and saw the Schaman. The Schaman dropped a burlap bag on the ground and took-up his battle axe in both hands.

"Are you Ecgtheow Waegmunding?" said Hathus.

"I'm the one who's going to kill you. That's all you need to know. I'd let the boy do it, but that would be too easy."

The Ostrogoth spat.

"Are you going to talk me to death Bluebeard, or fight?"

"Ha!" said Beorn

The Schaman stepped forward, axe poised to strike.
The Schaman and the Ostrogoth shortened the distance between them and squared off, eyes locked on one another.

The Ostrogoth bellowed, lurched forward and swung his axe sideways. The blade hissed through the air and cut through the Schaman's wolf skin coat, grazing his chest, drawing first blood. The Schaman swung his axe with both hands, striking the Ostrogoth alongside his head with the heavy, butt-end of the handle. The Ostrogoth's head snapped to one side. As Hathus staggered backward, he spat a mouthful of blood and teeth.

The Ostrogoth charged forward; he swung his axe high and low, and each time the Schaman ducked or stepped to one side. When an opening presented itself, the Schaman raised his axe and brought it down. His blade sunk into the Ostrogoth's soft flesh between neck and shoulder.

The axe dropped from Hathus's hands, and he collapsed to his knees. Blood spilled from his torso and puddled on the ice. Using his foot, the Schaman pushed the Ostrogoth onto his back. As he lay there, blood bubbled out of his mouth. Hathus tried to speak but he couldn't because of the gurgling sound that issued from his throat.

Beowulf approached and stood beside the Schaman.

"Will he live, Beorn?"

"For a while, perhaps."

"Good," said Beowulf. He knelt on the ice beside the Ostrogoth.

"I want you to live, Goth," said Beowulf, "long enough for me to hoist you by your heels and flay you head to toe. When I've carved the flesh from your bones, then will I let you die."

26

OLD SCARS, NEW WOUNDS

Wearing boots and breeches the Schaman lay on his pallet near the hearth and watched Beowulf alternate the flat of his knife blade side-to-side over the flames.

"Tooth needs to be red hot," said Beorn.

"I know. I've done this before—remember?"

"Too well, young prince," said the Schaman.

The blade of the Ostrogoth's axe had sliced the Schaman's belly the length of a man's hand, but not so penetrating as to sever intestines or spleen. Still, the wound needed to be cauterized to stop the bleeding.

"Tell me something," said Beorn.

"Tell you what?"

"Had the Goth lived would you have skinned him as you said?"

Beowulf looked straight at the Schaman: "Yes. And why shouldn't I? He meant to flay me. Besides, who knows how many people he killed doing the Dark Queen's business. Yes, I would have skinned him and taken my time doing it. Now, why is that wrong, Beorn? Tell me."

"You aren't wrong to feel what you're feeling right now, Bear's Son."

"Just answer my question, Beorn."

"Very well," said Beorn. "I will answer your question—by asking a question. But before I do, I want you to calm yourself."

Beowulf breathed several times until he felt his anger subside.

"Very well," said Beowulf; "ask."

"I helped you kill a man today. You will kill more. I have seen it in my visions. But you must ask yourself—would you be a warrior, such as your father? Or do you want to be the same as him—a wanton killer of men, women, and children?"

Beowulf got to his feet and crossed the room to a table. When he returned, Beowulf handed the Schaman a thick piece of leather.

"Bite on this."

The Schaman placed the leather strap in his mouth. Beowulf resumed holding his knife over the flames until the iron began to glow.

"Tooth's ready."

The Schaman nodded, placed his hands on the floor and braced for what was coming. Beowulf removed his knife from the flames. The Schaman stiffened as his flesh sizzled and cooked.

In twelve blinks of the eye, it was over. Beowulf put Tooth aside and gave the Schaman a drink of water.

"How does it look?" said Beorn.

"Ugly," said Beowulf, "but the bleeding's stopped."

When the Schaman's eyes next opened it was nighttime. The fire in the hearth and several candles on the table provided light, such as it was. After his eyes had focused, the Schaman saw Beowulf kneeling beside him holding a bowl.

"You need to eat," said Beowulf.

The Schaman raised himself on his elbows and looked at his belly. Where the Goth cut him, there appeared an angry red mass of seared flesh—the harbinger of a scar forming.

"Did you wash it first with vinegar and salt the way I told you?"

"Yes," said Beowulf, "then I put on pine tar. Just as you instructed before you passed-out."

The Schaman drew a full breath.

"Good job, lad. Help me sit, so I can get a taste of what you've made. It smells good."

"Beggars' stew," said Beowulf; "I used some of your herbs to give it more flavor."

Beowulf dipped a spoon into the bowl and held it up to Beorn's mouth. The Schaman hesitated.

"Promise me something," said the Schaman.

"Promise you what?"

"Promise me I'm not eating Goth."

Beowulf grinned.

Hrothgar looked around the crowded Throne Room. His advisers were there along with Daneland's Clan Chiefs; so, too, was Ecgtheow Waegmunding.

"If our brief war with the Wylfings and Franks taught me anything," said Hrothgar, "it's this: we must always remain vigilant. Had Lord Waegmunding not come seeking sanctuary our fleet would be in ruins at Mörk Sand.

Lord Aeschere stepped forward.

"It will be a long while before the Wylfings or Franks contemplate attacking us again. By destroying half the Wylfing fleet and a thousand of their finest warriors you cut the balls off the Iron Wolf and have rendered him impotent, my King."

"Perhaps, Aeschere," said Hrothgar, "nevertheless, I want you to double, even treble, the number of spies we have. Let them spread the word: the Spear Danes are mobilizing to attack Öster Götaland. Let's give Amunwolf something to fret over late at night while he's grieving the loss of his ships and men. Is Lord Ulthur here?"

"I am, my King," said Ulthur.

"I promised Lord Waegmunding I'd deliver the captured Wylfing battle craft to King Hrethel. See that it gets done."

"At once, my King," said Ulthur. He turned on his heel and hurried away.

"I realize ships will not recompense you, Lord Waegmunding, for what you've lost, but you've proven yourself worthy of my trust."

Shouts of approval issued from among the Danes. Ecgtheow looked at Hrothgar.

"From this day forward, Great King, my sword is yours to command.

† † †

"From Daneland to Frihamm," said Adalfuns, "our spies say the same thing: the Spear Danes will attack in the spring."

"By all the gods above and below, I knew it," said Amunwolf. "Here I sit with fewer than thirty seaworthy battle craft and less than half the number of warriors I had before while Hrothgar now has a hundred Longships to bring against us."

"Father," said Adalfuns, he has no more ships now than before."

"What's that you say?" said Amunwolf.

"Our spies in Daneland report that Hrothgar has the same number, eighty in all. The ships we lost at the Bay of Kryl Hrothgar sent to Geatland—Hrothgar's gift to King Hrethel."

The Iron Wolf hurled his drinking horn across the room.

"Truly the gods have cursed me," said Amunwolf. "Now I have Hrethel and the Thunder-Geats to vex me. I should never have allowed Modryth to avenge herself on Heatholaf's killer."

"I'll mobilize the army," said Adalfuns.

"Do that, but do it quietly," said Amunwolf. "I have something in mind other than another war."

"What, father?" said Adalfuns.

"Leave that to me," said Amunwolf.

Prince Adalfuns' jaw tightened. Stung by his father's rebuke he bit his lower lip, bowed and left the room.

† † †

For two days and nights, the Schaman did little more than rest on his pallet, allowing the salve made from pine tar and herbs to do its work. His wound was healing, and he would have wanted to be outside in his smithy, hammering on steel, but he dared not risk opening his wound anew.

"Tell me again what you've learned." said Beorn, "Who is the Wylfings' king?"

Beowulf lowered the bowl he held near his mouth.

"The name of the Wylfing king is Amunwolf, also called the Iron Wolf."

"Good," said Beorn, "and what does the Iron Wolf rule over?"

"He rules over all of Öster Götaland and the tribes therein."

"Good," said Beorn. "And where is Öster Götaland?"

"East of my father's farm—east of Väster Götaland."

"And who is Amunwolf to you?"

"My enemy," said Beowulf. "As are all Wylfings."

"Good," said Beorn, "and who is the Dark Queen?"

"The Dark Queen is Amunwolf's consort," said Beowulf.

"Have I told you yet what a consort is?" said Beorn.

"No," said Beowulf.

"Well," said Beorn, "one day I will. And who is the Dark Queen, besides being the Iron Wolf's consort?"

"Her name is Modryth. She ordered my mother and father killed. She ordered the Ostrogoth to hunt me. It is she who wants me dead."

"Yes," said Beorn, "and you must never forget that."

27

BY ANY OTHER NAME

"What kind of men do such things, Beorn?"

Beowulf and the Schaman stood looking at the frozen flayed remains of the trapper, his wife and son, hanging from the branches of the Libden tree outside their lodge.

"The same kind of men," said Beorn, "who killed your mother —men who would put suckling babes to the sword if there was gold or silver to be gotten. Some do it just for pleasure. Think of them not as men, Bears Son, but as something twixt animal and man: in a word—monsters."

"Should we bury your friends?"

"Yes, and deep," said Beorn. "So the Forest Cats can't get at them."

After burying the remains of the trapper and his family, Beowulf and the Schaman made camp for the night. They erected a sturdy lean-to that would shelter them from the wind. They did this rather than sleep in the trapper's lodge because the lodge still reeked of Ostrogoth and Swamp Dog.

† † †

The Wylfing King let the news go forth that his oldest son Adalfuns would soon set sail for Daneland on a mission of peace. This did not go unnoticed by Hrothgar's network of spies. Word of Adalfuns' intended visit reached King Hrothgar well before the prince's Longship reached the port of Mörk Sand. Spear Danes were massed on the dock. Void of all subtlety, it was Hrothgar's way of reminding the Wylfing King, through the eyes of the prince that the Spear Danes were a force to be reckoned with on or off their island.

From Mörk Sand, Adalfuns was taken on horseback around Heorot Fort; since Hrothgar's advisers found it imprudent to allow the Wylfing prince to assess that mighty fortification from the inside. Once they passed the fort, Lords Aeschere, Berenson and Hakon escorted Prince Adalfuns the remaining distance to Heorot itself, where King Hrothgar waited to receive him.

Adalfuns bowed: “Hail, Great King.”

“Welcome to Daneland, Prince Adalfuns,” said Hrothgar. “The news of your coming reached us some time ago. Tell me, has the Iron Wolf come to his senses?”

Adlafuns’ face flushed crimson.

“He was ill advised, Great King, or he never would have sanctioned Lord Yngvarr's mad adventure against you.”

“Ah!” said Hrothgar, “it was Lord Yngvarr's doing?”

“Yes,” said Adalfuns, “but Yngvarr died in Jutland and our fleet has been diminished by half, which your spies already told you. Great King, my father seeks a lasting peace with the Spear Danes

“I don’t suppose you’ve met Ecgtheow Waegmunding,” said Hrothgar.

“No, Great King,” said Adalfuns, “I haven't.”

Adalfuns nodded to Ecgtheow.

Ecgtheow neither spoke nor in any way acknowledged the presence of the Wylfing prince.

“My people call Lord Waegmunding the 'Widow Maker'—did you know that?” said Hrothgar.

“Yes, Great King,” Adalfuns said. “We heard as much.”

“Ecgtheow thinks it's easier to make a war,” said Hrothgar, “than a ‘lasting peace’. Would you agree?”

“Of course,” said Adalfuns. “Which is why my father sends me with an offer he thinks worthy of your consideration, Great King.”

“Gold?” said Hrothgar. “Silver, perhaps? More ships?”

The Danes laughed; they knew their king already had gold, silver and ships aplenty.

“No, Great King,” said Adalfuns, “You already have much of that. What I offer is something far more precious to the Iron Wolf than gold, silver or ships.”

† † †

The journey from the trapper's lodge to the Lake in the Clouds took three days; during which time little was spoken. In his mind, Beowulf replayed his fight on the ice with the Ostrogoth and what followed. Beowulf stopped and looked at the Schaman.

"I want a sword, Beorn."

"That is something your father must give you," said the Schaman. "Be patient, Bear's Son. It will happen."

"But when, Beorn? We don't even know if he's alive or where in Midgard he could be."

"Trust me, Beowulf; your father is alive. I feel it in my bones."

"But where? And why isn't he trying to find me?"

"He is trying to find you. But who knows what obstacles remain twixt him and you."

Beowulf proceeded toward the lodge. Beorn watched him walk away. Though he didn't speak of it, the Schaman was astonished how far-thinking the goddess Frigga had been. The spell she cast had accelerated Beowulf's physical growth commensurate with the tremendous strength that Thor, Hammer Bearer and Lightning Bringer imbued him with. So, too, had Beowulf's mind developed far beyond his age. He was eager to learn and devoured everything the Schaman had to teach without complaint.

† † †

The two Spear Danes King Hrothgar entrusted to return with Prince Adalfuns to the Iron Wolf's lair, Lords Aeschere and Berenson, bowed before the Wylfing King.

"Lord Aeschere, Lord Berenson, welcome to my domain," said King Amunwolf. "I'm overjoyed that at last we'll have peace between our two great tribes."

"As is Hrothgar, King of the Spear Danes," said Aeschere.

Lord Berenson snapped his fingers and a Spear Dane stepped forward holding a spear, sword and shield.

"As is customary among our tribes, King Amunwolf, we bring you *Brud Beltalning*—the Bride Payment: a sword, shield and spear once wielded by the father of our people, Half-Dane, himself."

It was an outright lie, one Lord Berenson delivered with a straight face, but it was enough to cause the Iron Wolf's eyes to brighten. A smile crossed his face, which of late was something unheard of.

"There is more to our coming, Great King," said Lord Aeschere, "something of the utmost urgency."

Amunwolf took note of the grave look his son Adalfuns gave him.

"Everyone, out," said Amunwolf.

When the room had cleared, Lord Berenson snapped his fingers a second time and four muscular Spear Danes stepped forward bearing a chest.

"I don't understand," said Amunwolf. "The Bride Payment has been made, and it does me honor."

"Silver, my King," said Adalfuns; "the chest you see before you is filled to the top with silver wedges, coins and rings."

"By the gods," said Amunwolf, "tell me, Lord Aeschere, for what reason does Hrothgar send me such treasure?"

"*Weregild*, Great King—blood money. My king and ring-giver seeks to put an end to the blood feud twixt you and Ecgtheow Waegmunding by making restitution for Prince Heatholaf's death."

"Ha!" said Amunwolf. "If Ecgtheow Waegmunding hadn't killed that little bastard, I would've. Give Hrothgar my greatest thanks. Tell him the feud twixt Wylfings and Ecgtheow Waegmunding is over and done with."

"There is one more thing, Great King," said Lord Berenson.

"Speak," said Amunwolf.

"Prince Adalfuns tells us the Dark Queen is not of a mind to put aside her thoughts of revenge, not now, not ever."

"And what did King Hrothgar say to that?"

"Nothing," said Lord Aeschere; "but Ecgtheow Waegmunding was there when the Prince mentioned it."

"That's true, my King," said Adalfuns. "He stood as close to me as I am to you now and said: 'Out of gratitude to King Hrothgar, I will quit my feud with the Iron Wolf."

"Clever," said Amunwolf." Notice how Waegmunding said nothing concerning Modryth."

"Our King," said Lord Aeschere,"told Ecgtheow Waegmunding

his business was his own and didn't concern the Spear Danes; that is, as long as our shared interests in the Port of Frihamm weren't threatened."

"And Waegmunding's response?" said Amunwolf.

"He just looked at me with hatred in his eyes," said Adalfuns.

† † †

Wealtheow sat at a loom under the watchful eye of a lady-in-waiting tasked with teaching the Iron Wolf's daughter what was expected as she approached womanhood. Adalfuns entered the chamber, dismissed Wealtheow's teacher; then held his little sister close.

"When did you get back from Daneland, brother?" said Wealtheow. "I've missed you."

"Just today, baby bird," he said.

"Did you bring me a present?" she said.

Adalfuns laughed. "Now why would you ask me that?"

Wealtheow giggled, and her cheeks blushed. "Because you always bring me presents after going aviking," she said.

"Hmm," said Adalfuns, "you're right; I do, don't I?"

"Yes, you do," said Wealtheow.

"Very well," said Adalfuns, "now close your eyes, keep them shut, hold out your hand and no peeking."

From a leather pocket sewn into his tunic, Adalfuns withdrew a silver ring set with a large square piece of polished amber. He placed the ring on the palm of his sister's outstretched hand.

"It's heavy," said Wealtheow, eyes still closed.

"Go on," said Adalfuns, "look."

Wealtheow's eyes opened. Her face brightened. She cried aloud..

"It's beautiful," she said.

She slipped Adalfun's gift over the forefinger of her right hand. "It fits."

"Of course it fits. It was made to fit that finger, little sister."

Wealtheow hugged her brother.

"I love you," she said.

Tears of joy streamed down her cheeks. Adalfuns looked into

his sister's large brown eyes:

How can I possibly tell her, he asked himself, *and not break her heart?*

Ecgtheow found Turin, the stable boy, where they first set eyes on one another—in the barn at the stables near the port of Mörk Sand. Turin was busy working and had his back to Ecgtheow.

"Still here, I see," said Ecgtheow; his voice resonated with strength and purpose.

Turin spun around. Upon seeing who it was, he dropped a bucket from his hand.

"Lord Ecgtheow," he said. The color drained from Turin's face.

"What's wrong, boy—you look ill?"

"Forgive me, my Lord; but I thought you might be here to kill me."

Ecgtheow laughed.

"Nonsense. Don't take the name your people gave me seriously. So—are you still in love?"

"Yes, my Lord. But she's in love with another."

"Then forget her. I've something better to offer."

PART TWO

28

THE SUBLIME ART

The Night Watch had little trouble seizing a handful of Frihamm's homeless, who inhabited the back streets, near the dock—a dozen more souls to fill the dark cages beneath Modryth's three story lodge.

Each dank cell was without a slop bucket which forced her captives to relieve themselves on the straw beneath their feet. Modryth ordered the so-called "bedding" changed each day but over the passage of time there developed a foul odor of putrefaction and human waste that clung to every board and beam of her dungeon.

Modryth had no reason to believe Germanicus was dead or, for that matter, that Hathus, the Ostrogoth, had also met his demise. If Ecgtheow Waegmunding's child was indeed alive, Modryth wanted his son in her grasp, however long it took to find him. Of course, if her minions found Ecgtheow Waegmunding, so much the better. Winter had given way to spring, but still, no word had reached Modryth apprising her of Germanicus' progress. Patience not being one of Modryth's strengths, she sent several of her ships south across the Whale Road. The men she sent she instructed to search the ports of Polanska, Estonia, Latvia, Belarus and Northern Russia to gather a band of assassins, the most bloodthirsty and vicious ever enlisted with but a single purpose—to find and kill Ecgtheow Waegmunding and his son.

To pacify herself while waiting for this vaunted band of cutthroats, Modryth spent more time than usual tormenting those she imprisoned: men, women, children—it didn't matter. The one thing in all the world that gave Modryth the greatest pleasure in life had been her son, Heatholaf, dead by the hand of Ecgtheow Waegmunding.

Now, her one delight came from inflicting pain on the weak and the helpless. For Modryth, torture was a sublime art—one she excelled.

Ecgtheow faced Turin and the ten boys with him: none older than sixteen, or younger than fifteen and, like Turin, they, too, were orphans.

They stood shoulder-to-shoulder aboard Ecgtheow's ship. He moored it in Mörk Sand. Its hull still lacquered black, and black sail furled.

"It's a brave thing you've all chosen to do. It won't be easy. You will think me hard, perhaps even cruel. I am hard. And I can be cruel, But that is the way of the warrior. Choose to stay, and I will make men of you—warriors even, for that is what I need. Men I can trust. Men I can depend on; even when things look their worst. Stay with me, and I will teach you how to sail and how to row. I will teach you how to gauge the wind and set a course over the Whale Road. You'll learn how to fight. Because you're young, I'll teach you first how to use a bow. You'll learn how to loose arrows fast and straight as any Bowman twice your age. I'll teach you how to fight at close quarters with spear, sword, and axe. Choose to stay aboard the Black Ship, and I promise you: you'll have adventures beyond your wildest imaginings. But remember—death will never be far from you, for that, too, is the fate of a warrior. Can I promise you a long life? No. I cannot. But I promise you this: should you choose to remain with me, to sail and fight at my side; I'll die, if need be, to defend and protect you—all of you, as though you were my sons."

Ecgtheow had use of an abandoned farmhouse on the outskirts of Mörk Sand. The main lodge was large enough to accommodate Ecgtheow and the boys under his wing, with plenty of room to spare. They took meals together, and each boy took his turn standing watch. Caught napping while on-watch and Ecgtheow would slap the offender alongside the head to wake them.

The first week they spent exercising—lifting rocks after breaking fast each morning around dawn. The rocks were from a crumbled wall that surrounded the farmhouse. The boys carried these rocks from one pile to another and back, over and over and over again. Later, after a short rest and a mid-morning bowl of gruel and sausage, Ecgtheow had them run in pairs, each pair carrying a thick oak beam overhead. Toward the end of the day, Ecgtheow had the boys pull a rope, hand over hand. The free end was attached to an ox cart in which Ecgtheow stood. He had them do this to condition and strengthen them for the rowing that would come later. Their reward after a hard day's work was dinner—roasted pork or goat, dill weed soup and toasted rye bread with a mug of pale ale to wash it all down.

† † †

After the seventh day of training, Ecgtheow stood in the open doorway of the lodge at dawn and watched three of the boys hasten away, each with their bedroll and few possessions; while the others slept.

Ecgtheow, Turin, and the six other lads who chose to stay broke fast in silence. Toward the end of their meal, Ecgtheow stood and addressed them.

"It's true," he said, "three of your comrades have chosen to leave us. The training was too much for them. Still, I won't begrudge them for leaving. I want warriors at my side. Warriors! Men who won't complain of blisters on their hands when they're rowing or whine when the work is hard or when it's hot, or if it's cold. I want warriors at my side. Hear? Warriors who have a fire in their bellies, and ice in their veins."

"When will you teach us how to fight, Lord Ecgtheow?" said Turin.

"Soon enough, Turin," said Ecgtheow. "When you are strong and have learned to sail and know how to pull together in a storm. As to the three who abandoned us, I say 'good riddance.' And to you who remain, I promise you: your training will get easier because each day you're growing stronger."

"What's it feel like to kill a man, Lord Ecgtheow." said one of the seven who remained.

Ecgtheow took his time; he looked each of the boys in the face before he answered:

"Killing is the hardest thing you'll ever do. It's no easy thing killing a man in combat, not when you're eyeball to eyeball, and you can smell his breath and the sweat and fear coming from him. But that's just part of it: when you kill a man you're killing someone's father or son, brother, cousin, or uncle. You're killing a man same as you, who has hopes and dreams of his own. But he's also a man who, if you let him, will kill you without hesitation and brag about it later. In time, I promise you; killing will get easier. It's learning to live with it, that requires some accommodation."

Ecgtheow saw the seven listening as if spellbound—eyes wide open, each holding his breath.

"Now go clean your teeth," he said."Throw water on your faces and meet me outside. We've training to do."

Those who had remained trained day-in and out. Under Ecgtheow's watchful gaze, each of these young men, or so they were becoming, trained as though his life and the lives of his ship mates depended on it—and they did. They learned this as the summer made its presence known.

† † †

It was then that Ecgtheow let them row the Avenger beyond the harbor of Mörk Sand into the open sea. When they had cleared the harbor, Ecgtheow ordered the boys to make fast their oars and unfurl the sail. That done, a strong east wind filled the huge sail. Not minding the salt spray that blew in their faces while the ship gained speed, it enthralled them—the sensation of speeding over the waves. Seeing them react so, brought a smile to Ecgtheow's face.

For one boy, Lando, the pitch side-to-side of the Black Ship made him sick to his stomach and unsteady on his feet. Knowing he was about to vomit, Lando gripped the railing with both hands and leaned over the side.

Turin was with Ecgtheow manning the tiller. They heard the other boys laughing despite the sound of the wind and the waves that slapped the hull. They saw Lando at the other end of the ship, near the bow, leaning over the side, heaving his guts out.

"Pull Lando back aboard," said Ecgtheow, in as loud a voice as he could muster.

Two of the boys stopped laughing and went to do just that when a monster the Sea Brondings call a Vit Haj; or, in the Common Tongue: a White Shark, broke the surface and seized Lando's head and torso with its gaping mouth and rows of triangular shaped teeth. In the time it takes to blink, the Vit Haj pulled Lando over the side, into the depths, out of sight.

† † †

After the Black Ship returned to Mörk Sand Ecgtheow ordered the boys to make fast the oars and furl the sail. It wasn't until that night after their supper, while the lads sat at the long table with their heads down, ashamed for having laughed at Lando when Ecgtheow spoke:

"Lift your heads," said Ecgtheow, "and straighten your spines." There was no tenderness in Ecgtheow's voice: "Lando was a good lad. He was your friend and shipmate. Had he lived he would have become an able warrior and seaman. But Lando's dead, and there's no getting him back. What happened to him could have happened to any one of you. Lando was seasick. I realize that. But he broke one of the three most important rules I've been trying to impress on you. Can anyone tell me what order Lando broke? Anyone?"

Turin raised his hand.

"Speak, Turin," said Ecgtheow.

"You want us to respect ourselves. Everyone else. And everything that surrounds us. It was the last rule that Lando failed to remember."

"Good, Turin," said Ecgtheow. "You're right. Lando failed to respect what surrounded him; in this case—the sea. Go to your beds now. You probably won't sleep but little, but try; because tomorrow we go out on the Whale Road again."

† † †

The Summer was mild on the coast of southern-most Geatland. Eydís was in her hut crushing herbs, creating another healing potion. Gifts from the All Mother, she called them.

That's when she heard the trumpeting sound of a conch shell

three times. Deep, resonant and loud, the sound was more than enough to rouse the Harii from their lodges.

The men armed themselves and were ready for battle; at the same time, the Harii women took up knives and spears and gathered the children behind them.

Eydís grabbed her bow and quiver of arrows and ran to where the men were assembling on the beach. That's when they saw it: the black hull and black sail of a Longship, sleek and battle worthy, capable of carrying forty men and more. What struck Haraldr and the Harii as odd, however, was that the vessel appeared empty save for a tall man alone at the tiller, with a wild mane of dark hair and a beard to match and six beardless youths who stood amidships, furling the sail.

It was Eydís who recognized the Tillerman in an instant, and her heart beat faster. She looked over her shoulder at her father; he fitted his bow with an arrow.

"Put aside your weapons—all of you," she said. "It's Ecgtheow Waegmunding."

Aboard the Black Ship, Ecgtheow stood before Turin and the others.

"Before we go ashore," said Ecgtheow, "there's something I want to do. You know I have a son. I believe he's still alive and one day I intend to find him, even if I have to search all Midgard. And yet, in the time we've been together I've come to feel for you what a father feels for his children."

Turin and the others exchanged looks; their chests swelled with pride and love for the man who had taken them—castaways, all—and had made them into men. No longer, boys, they conducted themselves under Ecgtheow's keen eye as young men knowledgeable of sailing and skilled with a bow and the other weapons Ecgtheow trained them to use.

"Turin," said Ecgtheow. "Put your right hand out in front of you, palm down."

Once Turin did as Ecgtheow said, Ecgtheow looked at the others, each in turn:

"Erna," said Ecgtheow. "Place your right-hand palm down on top of Turin's. Eel, Dagh, Claus, and Broder will do the same."

When the boys did as ordered, Ecgtheow drew his knife and cut the palm of his left hand.

"Tell me," said Ecgtheow, "the creed I've taught you; the creed you've sworn to live by."

"Respect ourselves," they said in unison. "Everyone else. And Everything that surrounds us. Honor the gods, and live without fear."

Ecgtheow positioned his hand above their outstretched hands so his blood could trickle over them.

"In the time we've been together you've shown me you have what it takes to be shield brothers. From this day forward, I, Ecgtheow Waegmunding, accept you as my foster sons, as members of Clan Waegmunding. Tell me! Will you have it so?"

"We will, Foster Father," said Turin and the others. Their voices trembled with emotion.

Ecgtheow could feel what they were feeling and his eyes, too, became moist.

† † †

The men from the south who signed-on to do the Dark Queen's bidding numbered forty when Modryth met with them on the beach of an uninhabited, windblown island several leagues east of Svearland.

Sitting on a makeshift throne beneath a pavilion, she gave them each a down-payment: five silver bars, as promised by her agents.

"There—" said Modryth; "you've been paid as promised, just by coming here. I need twenty of you, no more than that. Those twenty I will pay half a hog's head filled with gold when you return with the head of Beowulf Waegmunding. Bring me the head of his father, Ecgtheow, and I'll double your reward."

A swarthy warrior named Kiev, from Belorussia, stepped forward and bowed.

"My name is Kiev. Five bars of silver is indeed a worthy prize, Great Queen; but I also want the gold. Tell us, if you hire twenty, how will you decide which twenty you want and which twenty must return home?"

"One of the ships that brought you here will take those of you home who want to leave. I've gold enough for twenty—not forty. If everyone feels as you do, Kiev, and it's the gold you're after, you must pair-off and fight—those who are the better fighters are the twenty I'll hire. Fair enough?"

All forty assassins were in a foul mood after being buffeted by squalls during the trip across the Whale Road. Modryth knew they would relish an opportunity to pair-off and fight. Not one of the forty chose to return—all were in it for the gold and if they had to kill the man standing next to them, or die trying, then be it so.

"How do you know it's not a rumor?" said the Iron Wolf.

"Because, my King," said Adalfuns; "Modryth made no attempt to deny it—but she refuses to speak to me in detail about the matter."

"How many?"

"We don't know the exact number, my King."

"Then, guess," said Amunwolf.

"Less than a hundred, I've heard, give or take a few," said Adalfuns.

"When will they arrive?"

"Our spies don't know. It's possible they're in Scandia already; still, it's doubtful Modryth would have them come to Frihamm to meet with her. She'll likely meet with them elsewhere, if at all."

"Why would she do that?" said the Iron Wolf while stroking his beard.

"She knows we expect them to come to Frihamm, my King. Besides, if her plan should cause you trouble with the Thunder-Geats and Danes, she'll deny bringing assassins to Scandia; then, she'll rely on the tender spot you have in your heart, the part that wants to believe everything she says."

"That tender spot in my heart, as you call it, boy, fell off like an old scab many winters ago."

King Hrethel waved Herebeald and Haecythn back, away from the dais, where he sat slumped against his throne.

"Idiots," he said. "I send you wide and far for news of Ecgtheow, and all you bring me are rumors of a ghost ship prowling the Whale Road with Ecgtheow at the tiller. Bah!"

With the look of two sheep that Hrethel badly sheared, Herebeald and Haecythn stepped back, away from the dais, with their heads lowered.

"Perhaps Prince Hygelac learned something useful while he was away, my Lord," said Ragmund.

"Come forward, son," said Hrethel. "Tell us what you've learned—but, please, no more rumors or wild stories of a phantom ship on the Whale Road."

Hygelac stepped forward.

"My spies in Land's End and Frihamm confirm that over the course of the last three full moons, the Dark Queen has assembled a band of mercenaries from across the Whale Road with one purpose—"

"To kill my grandson and Ecgtheow," said Hrethel.

"Yes, Father-King. Most likely they are already in Scandia."

"That whore of whores," said Hrethel. "Will no one kill her for me?"

"We can do it," said Herebeald, Hrethel's eldest son. "Me and Haethcyn—Hygelac, too, if he's up for an adventure."

"Nonsense!" said Hrethel. "I forbid you three to do anything of the kind. But why would Amunwolf not stop her? Ragmund?"

"It's possible," said Ragmund, "the Dark Queen carried out her plan in secret, my King. Amunwolf wouldn't jeopardize his peace accord with the Spear Danes. Since King Hrothgar paid the blood debt for Prince Heatholaf's death, why would the Iron Wolf risk war with you now, or a war with the Danes by betraying his pledge to Hrothgar? It doesn't make sense, Great King."

† † †

Beowulf was on his way back from the Svear trading post with supplies when the Schaman intercepted him on the trail. Beowulf could sense the alarm behind the look in Beorn's face. Even more curious, the Schaman carried a bundle of spears under one arm.

"What is it, Beorn?"

"We're leaving," said the Schaman, in as foul a mood as Beowulf had ever seen Beorn embrace.

"Leaving?" said Beowulf. "For where?"

The Schaman took a moment to catch his breath; as he did, his face began to relax.

"Further north," said the Schaman."

"Why now," said Beowulf; "when we've not even packed for a trek?"

"No time for that," he said. "And no more questions. There's no time for that either.

"No. I won't budge until you tell me why we're leaving," said Beowulf.

"Very well," said the Schaman.

Beorn took a deep breath:

"The Dark Queen hired assassins—to kill you and your father. They chose to avoid Frihamm and Öster Götaland by putting ashore in Svearland; then they came west, first by boat, using the Vättern River, and they did it with the Svear King's blessing. Now, they're coming here."

"How did you learn of this?"

"The goddess, Frigga, told Kungörn, Lord of the Eagles, of the Dark Queen's scheme. She told him to bring word to me."

"Are these men the same as the Ostrogoth we killed?"

"Yes," said Beorn. He handed Beowulf the floppy-eared rabbit doll. Beowulf looked at it a moment then dropped it on the ground.

"You don't want it as a keepsake?" said the Schaman.

"No," said Beowulf. "Because of it, the Goth and his dog were able to track us here. I won't make that mistake again. So, Beorn—when will these monsters reach the Lake in the Clouds?"

The Schaman noted the tone of anticipation in Beowulf's voice.

"Better for us if we stay well ahead," said the Schaman.

"Why not make a stand at our lodge? I can pick them off with my bow before they cross the lake."

"You seem eager for a fight," said the Schaman.

"I am. You say these men are monsters like the Ostrogoth. Why should I not want to kill them? You told me it was my fate to become a killer of men, Beorn, like my father."

"We're wasting time, young Prince. If need be, we'll make a stand elsewhere. But not here on the trail."

29

THE CHASE

Three brothers from Estonia: Kuldar, Kustav, and Paavo used a metalsmith's hammer to crush the skull of their first victim. They were six, nine, and ten winters young at the time and did what they did for what they could find in an old woman's pockets. So it was, these same three brothers were first to arrive at the lake, and first to launch the Schaman's skiff into the water.

The other seventeen arrived soon after and peered into the mist from the shoreline. It wasn't long before the cut-throats heard a commotion: arms and legs thrashing the surface of the lake.

"What's going on out there?" said Jukk, a Latvian warrior who received his training while living among the Tartars.

"There's a hole in the skiff—it's sinking," said Kuldar from a distance of thirty yards.

"So swim back to shore you fools," said a red-headed Frisian mercenary named Alari.

"We can't swim," said Kustav.

"Why not?" said a Frank named Andres—master with the three-bladed spear.

"We don't know how," said the oldest brother, Paavo.

Splashing and thrashing in the lake grew louder than before. The men on shore exchanged looks among themselves and laughed until the thrashing and splashing and cry for help ended and all was quiet.

A tall, broad-shouldered Angle named Eedu looked at the others.

"There's a lesson to be had from what just happened to those fools," said Eedu. "Whoever is protecting the child knows we're coming."

"So let's get across the lake and kill them both," said a Frisian named Aster.

"You miss my point," said Eedu. "They may have set more traps."

"Traps?" said Andres, the Frank.

"Balls!" said Jukk. "While we stand here wringing our hands, doing nothing, the sun climbs higher."

"Very well," said Eedu; "then I suggest we make rafts and cross the lake immediately."

"Build rafts?" said Kardo, a Gaul with thick brown hair braided to his waist, and was missing an ear. "That'll take 'til midday."

"Yes," said Eedu; "but if you'd rather swim across the lake to whatever awaits you—go! No one will stop you."

"No—by Odin's eye, they won't," said Kardo.

Kardo stripped to his boots and breeches. He took with him his two-bladed battle axe slung across his back, and a knife with a handle made of deer antler that he gripped between the few rotting teeth he possessed.

The others watched the Gaul wade into the lake and swam until the mist enveloped him and all they heard was the sound of his arms and legs slapping the water, propelling him toward the island.

It wasn't long before those waiting on shore heard the Gaul shout.

"I made it, you bunch of lily arses. I'm across."

"What do you see?" said Eedu.

"Trees," said the Gaul, "and a lodge set back among the pines."

"Mind yourself over there," said the Slav, Peetrus.

"What can a child do? I'm Kardo, remember—from Gaul!"

The sixteen on shore could hear the Gaul laughing to himself, so pleased was he that he and he alone was first to reach the island.

Then there came the sound of screaming that soon grew fainter, followed by a low, moaning sound, until silence descended over the lake.

Eedu looked at the others:

"Let's start on the rafts."

"Who made you the leader?" said Jukk, the Latvian.

"No one—but have you a better idea?"

While Ecgtheow's adopted foster sons waited aboard the Avenger, Ecgtheow waded through the surf to Eydís' side.

"I knew you'd come back to me, Ecgtheow Waegmunding."

"So did I," he said.

Eydís' father, Haraldr, like the rest of the Harii on the beach that day, was in no mood to cheer Ecgtheow's return. However, seeing Ecgtheow with his daughter and watching them embrace, Haraldr's anger dissipated, replaced by a feeling that Fate brought Ecgtheow back—Fate, and the love his daughter felt for this Thunder Geat who the Wylfings called the 'Widow Maker.'

† † †

Beowulf and Beorn made fast time to the trading post. Hermengild, the one-armed proprietor, raised his eyebrows at the sight of Beowulf and the Schaman.

"What brings you here, Bluebeard? Did the lad forget something?"

"Yes," said the Schaman. "A few things for a trek."

"Very well—so where might you be headed?" Hermengild said.

"Better you don't know, old friend," said the Schaman.

"Those spears bundled under your arm," said Hermengild. "for barter, are they?"

"No," said Beowulf.

"What my young companion meant to say," said the Schaman, "is that they're not for barter just now."

"I sense trouble at the back of your throat," said Hermengild.

"Men will come here asking about the lad and me," said the Schaman.

"Which men?" said Hermengild.

"Mongrels from across the Whale Road, far south of here—perhaps twenty, although I suspect they'll be fewer in number by the time they get here."

"What would you have me do?" said Hermengild.

"If they ask, tell them we were here but that you don't know where we are or which direction we went. Which is true, Hermengild—you don't know. But beware—these men will plunder your village if they think you're lying."

Hermengild raised the stump of what was once an arm.

"I didn't lose this arm at the Battle on the Ice to be bullied by a ragtag band of Southlanders in my lodge. Now tell me what you and the lad need; then get yourselves gone. And may the gods watch over you."

When Beowulf and the Schaman had traveled a league from Hermengild's trading post, Beowulf stopped and looked at Beorn.

"I think it's true." said Beowulf.

"What?" said the Schaman.

"That the gods watch over us."

Beorn laughed. "You're living proof that they do, Bear's Son."

† † †

With Eydís at his side, Ecgtheow stood before Haraldr and the Council of Elders inside the Common Lodge. It was a lodge where the entire village could assemble when events warranted a communal gathering. Ecgtheow's unexpected arrival on the Black Ship was such an event.

"My people want to know why you've returned, Widow Maker," said Haraldr.

"For two reasons," said Ecgtheow. "First, Haraldr, to ask your permission to marry Eydís."

A loud murmur rippled through the lodge. Haraldr motioned for 'silence.'

"And the second reason?" said Haraldr.

"Together we can acquire more wealth than you can imagine."

"First, Ecgtheow: if I assent to a marriage between you and my daughter, what do you offer as payment for the Bride?"

"You all saw my Longship, Avenger," said Ecgtheow. "A battle craft I painted black, because that is the Harii way, and that is my Bride Payment. With my ship, we can make the Harii feared again."

† † †

While Haraldr performed the marriage rite, Turin and his brothers stood by, witnesses. The Harii community formed a circle and sang *Hochzeitslied*—the Marriage Song, for that was the Harii way. After the wedding feast had ended, Ecgtheow's foster sons spent the night aboard the Avenger. They kept vigil through the night while their foster father and his bride retired to her hut.

30

TRAIL OF BLOOD

Around mid-day Modryth's group of assassins stepped aboard two rafts. Using paddles fashioned from tree cuttings, and up to their shins in water, they cursed as they paddled toward the island.

After reaching the shore, they disembarked and readied themselves for an assault on the Schaman's lodge.

The assassins hadn't gone far when they found Kardo, the Gaul. He had walked on leaves and branches concealing a pit and had fallen face-down on a half-dozen sharpened stakes.

"I suggest we all take a good look at Kardo," said Eedu. "And remember—something or someone protects the child we seek, so expect more traps."

"But who's protecting him?" said a Slav called Valdeko.

"Who cares," said one of the Frisians. "We'll kill him, too."

"But what if it's more than a man guarding the boy?" said a Finn with half a nose, named Priidu.

"What if. What if. What if," said Alari. "Forget all that. Let's storm the lodge and get it done."

"Lead the way, Alari," said Eedu. "We'll be right behind you."

"Hah! Good joke, Eedu; I feel safe already," said Alari.

He gripped his spear and strode forward toward the lodge.

The others fanned-out behind Alari and followed the Frisian toward the door of the lodge. Someone shuttered the windows; there was no smoke coming from the roof. Alari stopped short of the door and looked back at the others with a wide grin. When Alari kicked the door open he triggered a spear the Schaman rigged to launch from inside the lodge. The spear struck the Frisian in the heart with so much force it passed through Alari and landed at the feet of Priidu, the Finn. Priidu stumbled backward and landed on his buttocks—much worse than that, considering his present company, Priidu soiled himself.

"How can we be sure the boy's in there?" said Aster, a Frisian who favored a spiked cudgel for close-in fighting.

“We go inside and find out,” said Eedu. “Any volunteers?”
No one stepped forward.

When Eedu emerged from the lodge, he was brushing soot off his hands.

“What did you find?” said Valdeko.

“Some of the embers in the hearth are warm,” said Eedu. “They can't be too far ahead.”

† † †

Jukk led the way into the Svear settlement, but they saw no villagers and the villagers had shuttered the windows of the lodges they passed. Seeing smoke rising from inside the trading post the assassins trudged to Hermengild's door and filed inside. But for the one-armed proprietor behind the counter, the lodge appeared deserted.

“Where is everyone?” said Eedu.

“Minding their own business,” said Hermengild.

“Are they, now, old man?” said Jukk.

“We're tracking a boy,” said Eedu. “His name is Beowulf. He's the son of Ecgtheow Waegmunding. Have you seen him?”

“Yes,” said Hermengild. “a couple of days ago.”

“Really,” said Eedu. The old man's lying—I can hear it in his voice Eedu told himself.

Hermengild nodded.

“And the man with him—did he say where he was taking the boy?” said Eedu.

“No,” said Hermengild, “and I didn't ask.

“Very well, old man,” said Eedu. “We'll be going. But first, we need supplies.”

“You won't find any here,” said Hermengild.

“You're lying, old man,” said a Belorussian named Ivan.

Ivan stepped forward toward the counter: “Look around, old man!” he said. “There's smoked meats and sausage hanging from every beam.”

"They're not for trade," said Hermengild.

As Hermengild spoke, he reached with his good arm under the counter and grasped the cudgel he kept there.

"You one-armed fool," said the Belorussian. "Then we'll take what we—"

The Belorussian never finished his sentence. Hermengild's cudgel split his skull down the middle, and he dropped in a heap. At the same time from the back room, Svear villagers rushed into the Mead-House. They swung hand scythes and wood axes and caught Modryth's assassins unaware.

"Get out," said Eedu to his companions. "It's a trap!"

Juri, the Estonian, was next to die when a villager's axe took his head off. The remaining assassins fought their way outside. There they found themselves confronted by the rest of the men of the village. A storm of arrows brought down six more of Modryth's assassins.

Eedu and the others ran to safety beyond the confines of the village. Now they numbered seven. There was Eedu, the Angle; Jukk, the Latvian, Andres, a Frank; Aster, a Frisian; Peetrus, a Slav; Valdeko, another Slav; and Priidu, the Finn with half a nose.

"Anyone for turning back," said Jukk, after they had made camp for the night and partook of their meager rations by the warmth of a fire.

"After what we've already survived," said Priidu, "I want to push on until we have the little bastard's head in a sack."

"I'm with Priidu," said Andres. "Besides, we have our reputations to uphold. If we go back with our tails between our legs—"

"The Dark Queen will have our balls for dinner," said Aster.

"Then it's agreed," said Eedu. "We push on before first light."

31

MANNEN MÖRDARE

Two days after leaving Hermengild's trading post, Beowulf stared at the snow covered mountain in the distance. The sun had just risen, and the mountain sparkled and shimmered with salmon pink and golden light.

"It's beautiful, Beorn."

"Yes," said the Schaman. "Beautiful... and treacherous."

"Has it a name?"

"Of course it has a name," said the Schaman: "the Brondings call it, "Mannen Mördare."

"Man Killer," said Beowulf in the Common Tongue.

Beorn nodded.

"Once we're over the top, young Prince, we'll be in Norwegan—land of the Sea Brondings."

† † †

Modryth's band of assassins—what remained of them—stood at the base of Mannen Mördare. They were catching their breath when Priidu the Finn spotted two shapes moving toward the summit.

"Look there," said Priidu. "It's them."

"Where?" said Valdeko. "I see boulders and snow."

"There," said Priidu. He pointed toward two dark figures trudging up the mountain.

"Priidu's right," said Eedu; "but they appear to be men."

"Balls! Who else could it be?" said Valdeko.

The other Slav, Peetrus, agreed. "So the boy isn't a child—so what? The Dark Queen got his age wrong."

"Not likely," said Aster.

"Who cares," said Eedu. "Let's stop this yammering and get after them."

"I count seven if these old eyes see right," said the Schaman.

"You see just fine," said Beowulf. "There are seven. Six have spears, and at least two carry double-bladed broad axes like yours."

"There are no axes like mine," said the Schaman, "not in all Midgard."

"Four have swords and bucklers," said Beowulf, "and one wields a spiked cudgel. What do you want to do?"

"I think we should get to the other side of Mannen Mördare and let the Brondings deal with them," said the Schaman.

"They'll be on us before we reach the top, Beorn."

Beorn took a moment before replying.

"You're right," said the Schaman; "I'm slowing us down."

"No, you're not," said Beowulf. "Don't think like that."

"Lies don't become you, Bear's Son."

"I say we wait here, Beorn. Here where we have the high ground. They'll be weary after coming uphill, while we rest. Plus we have the spears you brought."

"Very well," said the Schaman. "We'll make our stand here."

That said, the Schaman let fall the bundle of spears he carried. Beowulf counted them. There were five.

"Too bad you left my bow and arrows behind," said Beowulf.

"Pardon me all the way to Helheim," said the Schaman. "I was in a hurry."

"No matter. I'll make each spear count."

"That would be helpful," said the Schaman.

"That was a joke—yes?"

"Yes, Bear's Son, I was making a joke."

Modryth's assassins were fifty yards below Beowulf and the Schaman when the first spear impaled Priidu, the Finn. As Priidu's blood began to stain the snow crimson, the others stopped, save for Eedu.

"What are you stopping for," said Eedu.

The second spear struck Peetrus, and he crumpled face-down. Valdeko bellowed with rage and hurled his spear. It had traveled all of thirty yards before it fell to the snow-covered ground.

"Forget that," said Eedu. "They have the high ground. Your spears won't reach them from here."

"Fight us man to man, you cowards," said Valdeko.

Valdeko charged up the slope.

"We intend to," said the Schaman.

Beowulf's third spear struck Valdeko in the throat with such force his head came off; it landed near the Latvian, Jukk. Those assassins who had spears hurled them with all the force they could muster, and still, they fell far short. Beowulf's remaining two spears didn't miss: Jukk and Andres went down, leaving Eedu with his sword and the Frisian named Aster wielding a spiked cudgel. Beowulf squared off against Eedu. Beorn faced Aster.

As Beowulf drew Tooth from its scabbard, Eedu stopped and gave him a look—part scorn, part disbelief.

"You intend to tickle me with that?" said the Angle.

"No," said Beowulf.

Beowulf changed his grip on Tooth and hurled it. Tooth entered Eedu's chest. The Angle dropped to his knees, eyes wide with amazement.

"Who are you?" said Eedu.

"Beowulf—son of Ecgtheow Waegmunding."

"You can't be Beowulf Waegmunding," said Eedu, spitting blood. "He's a child."

"Yes," said Beowulf. "So they say."

When Beowulf pulled Tooth from Eedu's chest, the Angle toppled face forward in the snow—dead. Beowulf turned in time to see the Schaman's axe cleave Aster the Frisian, straight down the middle, head to belly.

"What you did here today, Bear's Son, is the stuff of legend—too bad no one will hear the bards tell of it."

"We're alive," said Beowulf. "That's good enough for me."

The Schaman grinned. Those were the words he hoped to hear.

Ecgtheow's plan was simple: with the Black Ship, Avenger, crewed by Ecgtheow's "boys" and seasoned Harii warriors, they would eliminate the competition smuggling goods and wares to Land's End and Frihamm. Smuggling had never been the enterprise of any one particular group or tribe. Many tried their hand at it. What was needed to smuggle was a fast, seaworthy vessel, and a crew willing to risk their lives and fortunes on the Whale Road. Seafarers who took a liking to the inherent dangers of sailing under the noses of Wylfings, Thunder-Geats, Finns, Spears Danes, Sea Brondings, Franks, and Svearlanders, all of whom had a vested interest in keeping the Whale Road open—free of Berserkers and other renegades. Ecgtheow was no fool. He and the Harii would not stop or hinder any vessel that wasn't itself a purveyor of contraband they could resell to merchants in Land's End, or Frihamm—no questions asked.

Later that night, as Eydís and Ecgtheow lie in each other's arms, they could hear the gentle lapping of waves on the shore.

Eydís saw a faraway look in Ecgtheow's eyes.

"Don't I please you, husband?" she said. "You look far away."

"Forgive me," he said. "My son came to mind as if he was calling me."

"Perhaps he is," said Eydís.

"I wish I could be certain," said Ecgtheow.

Eydís put a finger to his lips and kissed his chest.

"What's meant to be will be, my love," she said; "even if it never happens."

A moment passed in silence.

"Tell me, Eydís," said Ecgtheow; "do I please you?"

Eydís smiled as she guided his hand to where it had been:

"Beyond measure."

"By all the gods, Wealtheow, you're more beautiful than I

imagined," said Hrothgar.

Wealtheow stood before the Throne with her brother Prince Adalfuns. Behind them were three ladies-in-waiting, Wylfing women handpicked by Adalfuns and dedicated to the care and protection of his younger sister.

"Thank you, Great King," said Wealtheow.

"Please, Wealtheow, we've no need for formality—address me as 'Hrothgar,' or 'My Lord.' Either will do."

"If you insist, Great—" Wealtheow caught herself: "If you say so... Hrothgar."

"There," said Hrothgar, "That wasn't so hard—was it?"

"No, my Lord," said Wealtheow. "It was not."

Prince Adalfuns made no outward expression of it, but he was pleased beyond measure by Hrothgar's initial, outward reaction to his sister. He was even more pleased by the ease with which she related to the King of the Spear Danes.

This may be easier than I thought, Adalfuns told himself. Already she has him twisted around her little finger.

"You must be tired from your journey," said Hrothgar.

"I am, my Lord," said Wealtheow.

"Lord Aeschere will show you and your servants to your chamber in the Keep above. While you refresh yourself, there are matters your brother, and I need to discuss."

After Wealtheow had departed, Hrothgar had the Hall cleared, apart from his Personal Guard, so he and Adalfuns could talk and not have others hear.

"As long as Modryth is sending assassins after Ecgtheow Waegmunding and his son," said Hrothgar, "the accord I have with your father hangs by a thread the Dark Queen might easily cut."

"I agree, Great King," said Adalfuns. "Much is at stake. But be assured, my father had no part in her recent scheme to hire assassins to track Ecgtheow. It is Modryth, and she alone, who conceived the plan."

"Does the Iron Wolf not understand it makes him look weak, not keeping a leash on that creature?"

"He does, Great King," said Adalfuns.

"Then by the gods, why doesn't he get rid of her and let someone else govern Frihamm. You, for instance, Prince Adalfuns."

A look of surprise crossed Adalfuns' face.

"Great King," said Adalfuns. "You honor me."

"Two things are clear," said Hrothgar. "The Dark Queen's reign must end."

"I agree. And the second, Great King?"

"It should be obvious what else needs doing—sooner, rather than later," said Hrothgar.

A moment had passed before Adalfuns spoke: "Yes, Great King and the timing is almost right."

"Then I'll leave both matters in your capable hands, Prince Adalfuns."

"Thank you, Great King, but as to the Dark Queen, for me to put myself in the mix could cause unrest among those who favor her presence in Frihamm."

"Then let me suggest someone," said Hrothgar.

"Of course, Great King—name him and I'll seek him out."

In Asgard the All Father confronted Thor and Frigga where they stood before his throne.

"You're angry with us, Husband," said Frigga.

"Yes," said Odin, "if what Hel tells me is true, you're still meddling in the life of the Manling, Beowulf. After what my ravens, Hugin and Munin found out, it would seem Hel is right—you're bending outcomes in Midgard to your liking and shaping Fate in the process."

"No, All Father," said Frigga. "You gave me and Thor permission to save the child, and we did. Now it's the All Mother's servant; a Schaman named Beorn who guides the boy. We have not interfered beyond that, despite what Loki's daughter tells you. For some reason, it irks her, my husband, that the boy didn't die that first day in the forest—as though Thor and I cheated Hel of a soul. Now she has this insatiable need to know the boy's every move. Ask Death; he will tell you what I say is so."

"Take care," said Odin; "lest Hel's father, Loki, involve himself in this nonsense."

"It seems the rumors about the Black Ship are true," said Hygelac.

They sat alone in a shaded garden where King Hrethel sometimes retired to think. But it was his youngest son, Hygelac, whose company he sought that morning.

"So it's truly Ecgtheow who commands this Black Ship," said Hrethel.

"Yes, father, it seems so."

"I miss him, my son, and owe him much. I always trusted his advice, and I could use it now."

"I'm not Ecgtheow, Father, but if you ask for my help, I will give it."

"I know, my son, I know."

"Let me seek out Ecgtheow and encourage him to return home," said Hygelac, now that the Iron Wolf has quit his feud."

"Do it," said the old king. "And find out what you can about these persistent rumors that my grandson's still alive."

"If it's true," said Hygelac, "that the Dark Queen sent assassins north, then west, then north again, across the breadth of Svearland, it's more than a rumor, Father. Beowulf is alive."

32

THE BLACK SHIP

Modryth preferred to keep her chests of gold and silver below her palace in her "special room" where she kept her captives; that is, for the short time she kept them caged. Every day she counted her riches. Modryth knew, to the last gold ring, coin and silver wedge, what she possessed.

Soon, she thought, *I'll need a larger room.*

Haber, appointed as the new Captain of Modryth's Palace Guard entered, dropped to his knees and kissed the Dark Queen's feet.

"What is it, Haber?"

"News of the Black Ship, Your Worship."

"Tell me," she said.

"The one who commands the Black Ship is none other than Ecgtheow Waegmunding."

"Are you certain?"

"I am, great Queen—unless you're spies are mistaken."

"My spies are never wrong, Haber. If they say the outlaw commanding the Black Ship is the assassin, Ecgtheow Waegmunding, believe it—it's him."

"Your orders, great Queen?"

"Send out my fleet. Find the Black Ship, and sink it. But take Ecgtheow Waegmunding alive!"

† † †

Charged by the King of the Spear Danes with finding Ecgtheow Waegmunding, Prince Adalfun's plan was simple. The knarr was well-lit, anchored three leagues offshore from Land's End when the Black Ship came out of the fog and made straight for it.

Adalfuns instructed his men to stay calm and remain seated on their benches. Adalfuns held one hand on the hilt of his sword, the other on the flat of the blade; then he raised his arms—a sign of surrender among Northmen.

From the Black Ship no arrows or spears were loosed; rather, the Black Ship came abreast of the knarr. Grappling hooks were tossed over the side securing the vessels together. A moment later Ecgtheow, Turin, and the other lads leapt aboard the knarr.

"Welcome aboard this humble craft, Lord Waegmunding," said Prince Adalfuns. "I've been waiting for you."

"What is it you want, Wylfing?" said Ecgtheow.

"I have news," said Adalfuns.

"Speak," said Ecgtheow.

"The Dark Queen has mercenaries—assassins to find you—you and your son."

Ecgtheow felt his throat constrict:

"My son?"

What Modryth didn't realize until the Captain of her Guard explained the situation to her three times: she had men sufficient to crew four of her ten Longships; the rest being needed in Frihamm to act as the Night Watch, and her Personal Guard inside her lodge.

"I don't care how few men I have," she said. "I want you to put out to sea today!"

"Yes, your Worship," said Haber.

He kissed her feet and hurried off.

Haber put a warrior named Bulgar in charge of the four battle craft tasked with finding the Black Ship. After outfitting them with water and provisions, Bulgar departed with his small fleet of ships for the Whale Road. He didn't relish the orders Modryth gave him, nor did the men who went with him. Every Longship Modryth possessed was over twenty-five winters old. Each had benches to seat fifteen oarsmen to a side, two men at the tiller and one man standing lookout at the prow to guide the ship.

Before the sun went down and dusk gave way to night, Lord Bulgar ordered the four battle craft lashed together. That way, if attacked, each could help defend the ship alongside. It was a sound defense for ships at sea; except—it was Ecgtheow Waegmunding, the Widow Maker, they were chasing.

† † †

In the darkness preceding a blood red dawn, from the sky came a fiery storm—what seemed an unending shower of arrows from the Black Ship; while it circled the Dark Queen's four battle craft. The shouts and screams of Bulgar's men shattered the calm that otherwise blanketed the Whale Road that night. Modryth's men struggled to put out the fires aboard their vessels, but more flaming arrows descended.

Lord Bulgar raised his sword overhead: "We surrender," he said to the tall, dark figure at the prow of the Black Ship.

"A wise decision," said Ecgtheow. "Throw your weapons down and put out the fires aboard your ships. Do it, and I'll see that you and your men reach Land's End—alive."

"Thank you, Lord Waegmunding," said Bulgar. "A hundred times—thank you!"

What Ecgtheow told Bulgar was a lie. Once Modryth's men had disarmed and then extinguished the fires that threatened to consume their battle craft, Ecgtheow ordered the Dark Queen's men overboard; they could try swimming to shore, or take an arrow where they stood.

"I understand now why Wylfings call you 'Widow Maker,'" said Haraldr.

"Does it bother you?" said Ecgtheow.

Haraldr laughed.

"Not in the least, my friend. Besides, now we have four more ships to call our own."

33

THE SEA BRONDINGS

Frigga, the Vanir Witch-Queen of Magic, and Thor, Hammer Bearer and Lightning Bringer, warrior god of the Aesir, had already rendered Beowulf's age meaningless. Now, his physique more than matched that of a grown warrior. Beowulf's mind had also expanded, much to Beorn's delight. The Schaman could now converse with Beowulf about the mysteries of Life, and the Great Truth that embraced the Nine Worlds and those who inhabited them.

"So," said the Schaman, during their last night together before leaving the Lake in the Clouds, "name the Nine Worlds beneath the branches of Yggdrasil, the Tree of Trees that binds the Cosmos together."

"First," said Beowulf, there is Midgard, where we dwell along with the Forest Folk, Sky Dwellers and the All Mother's creatures beneath the Whale Road."

"Good," said the Schaman. "Continue."

"There is Asgard, home of the Aesir gods and goddesses and the great Hall of Heroes—Valhalla. There is Vanaheim, home to the Vanir gods and goddesses; Jotunheim, the world of the giants, where Odin's nemesis, Loki, hails from; then there is Alfheim, wherein dwell the Elven folk; and Svartalfheim, home to the Dwarfs."

Beowulf hesitated.

"What else, Bear's Son," said the Schaman. "You've three more to name."

"I remember now," said Beowulf. "There's Niflheim, that commands the forces of cold, mist, ice, and darkness. Niflheim is at war here on Midgard with the forces of Muspelheim, the world of fire and heat. It is because the All Mother divided the seasons between them that they haven't destroyed one another and all of Midgard as well."

"Very well done, Bear's Son, and the last of the Nine?"

"The one I care for not at all," said Beowulf. "Helheim, where Loki's daughter, Hel, judges the dead."

The Nine Worlds aside, it was the war between the Vanir and the Aesir long before that Beowulf delighted hearing over and over again.

"And how did the Great War end?" said the Schaman.

"Badly for the Vanir, since the Aesir were victorious," said Beowulf, "and to seal the peace, the Vanir goddess, Frigga became the All Father's wife; although you say she has no love for him."

"Ha!" said the Schaman. "Right you are, young Prince, and right you've been. You know how to listen, and that's good. Now let's see if you understand what's to be until the time of Ragnarök."

"The All Father," said Beowulf, "is the unchallenged Ruler of the Cosmos and will remain so until the time of Ragnarök; or, in the Common Tongue: the Doom of the Gods."

"Which is?" said the Schaman.

"The Doom of the Gods will be the Great Struggle; the Mother of all Battles that destroys the Cosmos. It will overthrow the Old Gods, Vanir, and Aesir alike; then, Ragarnok will birth a new cycle, a new Cosmos, reborn."

From the time he was a child, Beowulf could sense what others were thinking, but with a little prodding from the Schaman and the friends he made among the Forest Folk, he also proved himself quick-witted and discerning when it came to making choices.

Beorn's purpose in taking Beowulf to the Svear trading post from time-to-time had been to socialize him, first with villagers—simple folk, around whom Beowulf could listen and observe. Beorn had forbidden Beowulf to do anything in public that might reveal his actual strength or identity.

Beowulf became a quick thinker; he was adept at grasping the nuances and subtleties of irony, and although Beowulf did not laugh much, Beorn often struck at Beowulf's sense of humor; or, rather, the lack of it.

Those who saw Beowulf and Breca together that first day assumed they were the same age. Breca had a shorter, stockier physique, typical of Scandia's northernmost tribes. Beowulf was head-and-shoulders taller than Breca, had a smaller waist, and measured wider from shoulder to shoulder.

Soon, Beorn thought, Beowulf will grow a beard. Or perhaps he'll start shaving—like a damn Roman!

“Can neither little bird speak,” said a girl's voice.

The voice belonged to a tall, gray-eyed girl with honey colored hair. She was Breca's cousin, Elin. Sixteen winters' young, she lived under the protection of King Beanstan’s roof. Elin stood alongside Beorn in the company of the King, six swarthy bodyguards, and several Clan Chiefs.

Beorn looked at Elin and grinned. “I assure you, Lady Elin—they will speak.”

“More likely, Magister Beorn, I'll be old and gray before one of them so much as peeps,” she said, louder than before.

Beowulf and Breca turned toward the source of the insults that came at them straight as arrows. Breca scowled, his face turned crimson. Beowulf's face showed no emotion at all. At that moment he could have been made from stone, except for what he felt inside when he saw who was insulting him.

To Beowulf, Elin was a vision of unsurpassed beauty—the most beautiful girl he'd ever seen; more beautiful than his mother, Liv, whose face he often had difficulty picturing.

“*Careful, Bear's Son*,” said Beorn, using the Silent Tongue; “*I can hear your heart beating from over here.*”

“*She's beautiful*,” Beowulf said.

“You see,” said Elin; “Not so much as a sparrow's peep from either of them.”

No sooner had the last word escaped her mouth, Beowulf let loose a full-throated cry—a Golden Eagle's ear-piercing screech, straight at Breca.

Shaken as were they all in King Beanstan's Hall, Breca recoiled. In an instant though, this Prince of Sea Brondings composed himself and shouted a crow's' call three times: Caw! Caw! Caw—straight into Beowulf's face.

Beowulf and Breca stared a moment at each other and then laughed; they stepped forward and clasped forearms—two reluctant comrades-in-arms, each one wary of the other.

“Welcome to my father's keep, Prince Beowulf,” said Breca, his voice sincere, without reservation.

"Thank you, Prince Breca, son of Beanstan, King of the Sea Brondings."

Beowulf looked at Elin, then again at Breca:

"I know my time among you will be well-spent, for I'm eager to learn the ways and customs of your great tribe."

"Well spoken, Beowulf," said King Beanstan. "Listen all! Tonight we feast in honor of Beowulf's arrival, along with my old friend and teacher, Magister Beorn—for no truer friend or ally have we Brondings had."

"Thank you, Great King," said Beorn. "As always your hospitality is offered when needed most."

† † †

Hel, Queen of Helheim, greeted Death, the Lord of Shadows, from atop her throne as he stepped from the mist.

"You sent for me," said Death.

"That was long ago," said Hel.

"I've been busy," said Death.

"It's not the never-ending stupid feud twixt Elves and Dwarfs that has me disconcerted, Lord of Shadows; nor the countless souls you've sent me because of it. It's the man-child in Midgard whom some call the bear's son that I'm eager to hear. Tell me how he fares, you who sew fear and loathing in the hearts of men."

"Why, Goddess?"

"Because," said Hel, "the soul of an Ostrogoth arrived here—a great warrior killed by the bear's son and the Schaman who watches over him."

"I know," said Death. "I was there. I saw the Ostrogoth die."

"It rankles that, because of Frigga and Thor, this man-child can bend the will of Fate. I tell you this because it wasn't the Ostrogoth's time to die; although he deserved the death, he got. Now his innards will be eaten for eternity by the dog he raised to kill others. Tell me, Dark Lord, you who can see the future: had the Schaman not intervened, would Beowulf have triumphed over the Goth?"

"Yes, Goddess. He's no longer the helpless child you thought he was."

"What is his Fate, Lord of Shadows? Tell me—I want to know."

"I can shape Fate," said Death; "but I do not control it, nor may I reveal it; not even to the All Father. You see, Goddess, even I have limitations."

"At least tell me where he is," said Hel.

"Very well," said Death; "The Schaman took Beowulf north to the land of the Sea Brondings. He now enjoys the protection of King Beanstan."

"And what of his father? What news of Ecgtheow Waegmunding?"

"The father lives in Daneland and serves Hrothgar, King of the Spear Danes. So—is there something else you wish, Goddess? If not, I've work to do... elsewhere."

"No, Lord of Shadows, I've no more questions."

Death turned and vanished into the bleak, frozen mists of Helheim.

Hel had lied. She still had many persistent questions crowding her thoughts, questions regarding Beowulf's father, the Schaman, and others. But they were questions that would go unanswered. Death answers to no one, not even to the gods.

† † †

After enjoying a long sit in the dry heat of a sauna, Beowulf and Beorn retired to the comfortable lodge King Beanstan maintained for dignitaries and other special guests. There, Beowulf and Beorn could rest on pallets piled high with soft furs and spoke their minds in private before the feast commenced.

"I feel happy here, Beorn," Beowulf said.

Beorn chuckled.

"Hah! Because of the girl."

"Maybe," said Beowulf.

"No maybe's about it, Bear's son; you're happy here because of Elin. Those gray eyes of hers have your head spinning."

"And what if they do? Is there something wrong with that?"

"Not a thing, young Prince, but you need to be cautious while living among the Brondings. Their women are precious to them, and Elin is under King Beanstan's protection."

"I would never hurt her," said Beowulf.

"I know that Bear's Son, but if you and she become close—I mean very, very close, things could happen that might prove awkward for us... and impossible to undo."

"Are you talking about sheathing my sword, and what can come from it?"

"Yes," said Beorn. "That's what I'm talking about."

"Well, you needn't worry," said Beowulf; "I haven't been getting those feelings you've been talking about—at least... not often."

"You mean until now," said Beorn.

"Yes," said Beowulf; "until now."

"Which is why I'm warning you, young Prince."

"Warning me against what, Beorn? Against looking at the most beautiful girl I've ever seen?"

"No," said Beorn," "against sheathing your sword in her. At least not until—"

The Schaman became quiet.

"Tell me, Beorn—not until when?"

"Not until the time is right," said the Schaman.

"How will I know when the time comes?" said Beowulf.

"You won't," said the Schaman. "Then, again, maybe you will. It's hard to know. The sword may be hard as steel, ready and eager for battle. The sheathing, however, may not be so accommodating. It's hard to predict these things. Now get some rest. But before you do, drink this."

The Schaman mixed a combination of herbs into a gourd filled with goat's milk.

"What is it?" said Beowulf.

"Trust me. Breca will test you tonight, and for many days to come. Now drink!"

"Will he challenge me to fight?" Beowulf said.

"No, of course not," said the Schaman. "That would be considered bad manners since this is your first night under King Beanstan's roof. Just the same, Breca will try in some way to humiliate you in front of Elin. But never mind that now. You don't want to be late for your party, do you?"

"No," said Beowulf; "but—"

"But nothing," said the Schaman: "Drink! And trust me—you'll feel better for it tomorrow."

† † †

In his Throne Room, Beanstan conferred with his Clan Chiefs. The question on their minds was what to make of Beorn's sudden unexpected arrival with the tall, broad-shouldered boy the Schaman claimed was the son of Ecgtheow Waegmunding.

"What if what the Schaman says is true?" said a Clan Chief named Aksel, King Beanstan's closest adviser. "What if the lad truly is the son of Ecgtheow Waegmunding? Ecgtheow is King Hrethel's spy, assassin, and Battle Lord."

"He was those things," said Beanstan. "But no longer—now he's in exile."

"Still, my King," said Aksel, "the Dark Queen has placed a bounty on both their heads. Won't we be inviting trouble by giving Ecgtheow's son sanctuary?"

"Yes," said Beanstan. "But have you forgotten how many times Beorn came to our aid in the past?"

"No, my King, we haven't forgotten. We don't dispute the good deeds Magister Beorn has done for us, but what if—"

"What if, be damned," said Beanstan. "Beorn has never expected, nor asked us, for anything—until now."

34

A DISH BEST SERVED COLD

Before Beowulf and Beorn entered the Throne Room they placed their weapons just as they had before, on a bench in the antechamber reserved for that purpose—Beorn left, Sanning, Truth in the Common Tongue, his legendary, two-bladed battle axe; Beowulf left Tand, Tooth, his knife in its tooled leather scabbard.

Walking with a noticeable limp after the fight on the slopes of Mannen Mördare, the Schaman maintained a tight grip on his walking staff.

† † †

In Daneland, Prince Adalfuns put on a happy face as he entered the uppermost chamber at the top of Hrothgar's Keep. There he found Wealtheow attended by her ladies-in-waiting. Wealtheow dressed in a traditional Wylfing wedding gown made of plain white linen that hung to her ankles, with hand embroidered runes of different colors—one for each of the gods of Asgard. Around her slender waist, she wore a belt embossed with gold and silver and a necklace made from beads of polished, moss-colored agates.

"What a beautiful bride you'll make," said Adalfuns.

His voice was as cheerful as he could muster. Wealtheow turned away from her reflection and looked at her brother:

"Why am I not dressed as the bride of a Spear Dane?"

"Because you look like Freya, goddess of the night and because, little sister, you're a Wylfing, and this way you do honor to our tribe. Think about it, little bird: the most powerful tribes in Scandia are about to be united, and you're the link in the chain that made it happen."

"Our people say Ecgtheow Waegmunding made it happen when he destroyed our father's fleet."

"People say, people say—it's rubbish—all of it," said Adalfuns.

"But isn't Hrothgar the most powerful king in Scandia now—not father?"

Adalfuns dismissed the ladies-in-waiting with a flick of his head. When he was certain he and Wealtheow were alone, he held her by her shoulders.

"True—King Hrothgar controls the Whale Road now. If the Iron Wolf wants to remain, king of the Wylfings, he may need Hrothgar's ships and warriors one day. Do you understand what I'm saying?"

"Perfectly," Wealtheow said. "Father bartered me in exchange for peace with the Spear Danes. I'm not a bride, Adalfuns; I'm Hrothgar's hostage, and you're the one who delivered me to him."

Adalfuns kissed his sister on both cheeks.

"Don't hate me, Wealtheow. I did what I had to do. You're wise beyond your age, little sister. Forget about Hrothgar and forget about father—forget him, just as I did, long ago. He's our king; that's all. He cared nothing for us as children and cares nothing for us now. All the Iron Wolf wants is for us to do his bidding outside the walls of Värg Slött. Trust me, sister, once you've become Queen of the Spear Danes, your power will grow beyond your wildest dreams."

"What power, Adalfuns? Look at me; I'm a girl—just a girl."

"The Dark Queen was just a girl once—now look at her," he said, "she's the most powerful woman in Scandia."

"Modryth is a witch," said Wealtheow. "I hate her. I hate everything about her. I don't want the kind of power she has."

"The power I speak of," Adalfuns said, "is the power you'll have one day to influence Hrothgar's thinking and his decisions—never forget that."

The sky was cloudless, and the moon waxed full when, sail furled, oars slack, the black painted hull of Ecgtheow's battle craft glided over the surface of the water.

The Black Ship soon entered the Fjord where, a short distance ahead, Frihamm lie nestled in darkness. The town was asleep but for three sentries posted at the dock and another three guards in the watchtower over the Main Gate that allowed access to Frihamm by land.

Modryth was also awake that night. Intoxicated by the pain she inflicted, Modryth inflicted more pain on one of her recent acquisitions. A young girl, whom the Night Watch found begging in a back alley near a brothel visited by Modryth's warriors, was near death.

Outside the Palace, Modryth's men had become lazy and complacent. They had little to do apart from living a well-fed, comfortable life in Frihamm, under the protection of the Iron Wolf.

The King of the Sea Brondings was without a queen at the moment, and Beowulf couldn't help but notice the Laplander standing behind Beanstan. No older than Elin, she had large green eyes and black hair that hung past her waist.

Beowulf watched the girl eat some of everything on Beanstan's plate; since Beanstan, being a cautious man, with many enemies, used the girl as his food taster.

Easy enough to become a king by succession; not so with Beanstan. He became King of the Sea Brondings by killing everyone who stood in his path. However, he soon realized many of his tribe wished him dead because it was their kin he had murdered during his ascension to power. In that respect, Beanstan was not too dissimilar from Amunwolf, the Wylfing King.

The Laplander, whose name was Ell, neither spoke nor smiled, but met Beowulf's gaze when he looked at her. He sensed a deep sadness that reached to her core. Beowulf glanced at the Schaman seated in a place of honor on Beanstan's right-hand-side.

“Don't stare too long at the Laplander,” said Beorn, using the Silent Tongue; “lest our host catch sight of it.”

“I've no feelings for her, Beorn; apart from the sadness I feel behind her eyes.”

“Well, let her sadness lurk there—it's no business of yours. Surviving your stay in the land of the Brondings is the one thing you must concern yourself with.”

Beowulf looked away.

Unlike the Bronding King, Beorn required no official "taster" to sample his food before eating it; rather, he devoured what servants put in front of him with ravenous contempt for any poison it might contain. It pleased Beowulf to hear Beorn and Beanstan laugh as they recounted old times.

Seated opposite Beowulf at the King's table were Breca and Elin. At the other tables in the Hall were several Bronding Clan Chiefs and their women, along with a select group of warriors—Beanstan's Personal Guard.

"Tell us, Beowulf," said Breca, "Tell us about life at Falcons Nest?"

"Yes," said Elin, "Tell us. We've never been there."

Beowulf became aware of Beorn looking in his direction.

"Be careful what you say," said Beorn in the Silent Tongue.

Beowulf looked at Breca and Elin:

"I don't remember," said Beowulf, "I was a child when I last visited my grandfather at Falcon's Nest."

"How odd," said Breca.

"Breca thinks everything that happens beyond our borders is strange," said Elin, quick to come to Beowulf's defense.

"Is it because King Hrethel exiled your father for starting a feud with the Dark Queen that cost your mother her life?" said Breca. "Is that why you're not welcome at Falcon's Nest any longer?

"Breca," said Elin.

"What—" said Breca. "It's a fair question, isn't it?"

"Yes," Beowulf said. "It is a fair question, and it's true. King Hrethel exiled my father. To this day, I don't know where he is, or whether or not he's alive."

"How sad," said Elin. "We'll do what we can to make you feel welcome here, Prince Beowulf—won't we, Breca."

Breca smiled: "Of course we will. Let's have some mead and toast Prince Beowulf's arrival."

"No mead for me, cousin," said Elin; "it gives me a headache the next morning. I'll stay with ginger beer."

"Very well, cousin," said Breca. "You drink ginger beer and our guest, and I will drink a cup or two or three of mead—sound all right to you, Prince Beowulf?"

"I don't know," Beowulf said; "I've never tasted mead."

Breca slapped a hand down hard on the table which garnered

the Schaman's attention.

"What?" said Breca. "Are you saying you've never tasted the nectar of the gods? By Odin's one eye you must be the same age as me, yet you say you've never tasted mead."

"It's true," said Beowulf. "I have not."

Breca glanced at Elin; then he winked and said: "What else haven't you tried."

Elin's face flushed red.

"You can be such a pig, Breca," she said.

"I was just making a joke, Elin. Don't be angry."

"Seafood," said Beowulf. "I've never eaten seafood."

So loud was the laughter that erupted from Elin's mouth she used both hands to stifle it.

Breca cast a harsh look at Elin. Beyond that, he didn't know what to make of Beowulf's remark.

"So," said Breca; "you've never tasted seafood?"

"True," said Beowulf.

"That means you've never speared a fish?"

"I didn't say that," said Beowulf. "The fish I've caught I caught with my bare hands—in the streams and rivers of Vindinstedt Forest—where Wylfings killed my mother."

"Beware what you say, Bear's Son," said Beorn in the Silent Tongue from across the table.

"So, Prince Beowulf, you've never harpooned a whale, I suppose."

"No," said Beowulf. "I haven't."

"Or even seen a whale?" said Breca.

"No."

"That means you've never speared a hag," said Breca; or, in the Common Tongue, a shark. "One with a mouth wide enough to swallow a man whole. Nor have you fought the Ondskas—the black and white assassins of the Whale Road."

"That's true, Breca; I haven't," said Beowulf. "I've never seen any of the creatures who dwell in the cold, dark depths of the All Mother's womb."

Seeing the flash of blue fire in his eyes, coupled with the sincerity in Beowulf's voice and the calm and steady tone that accompanied it, Elin found herself wanting to hear more from the handsome young stranger from Väster Götaland.

How unlike Breca and the other men around here he is, thought Elin. Perhaps there's more to this Thunder Geat than his beautiful eyes.

Beowulf looked at Elin. There was a trace of a smile on his lips. A wave of panic passed through her.

Beowulf looks at me as if he heard my thoughts she told herself, then averted her eyes.

"Well," said Breca; "I'm sure while you're here you'll learn many things, as I had to. You'll do much that you've never done before—manly things, mind you—so prepare yourself, Prince Beowulf."

"I'll do my part, Prince Breca," said Beowulf; "I'll do my share of hunting, and I'll do it with gratitude to the All Mother for what she provides, but let me ask you this—"

"Ask away," said Breca.

Beowulf could feel Beorn's eyes on him, Elin's also:

"Have you ever sucked the teat of a she bear?"

"What—" said Breca.

Elin's eyes opened wide. Intent on hearing Beowulf's every word, she leaned forward and pushed her plate aside. She rested her elbows on the table and cupped her chin in her hands.

"Careful what you say, Bear's Son," said the Schaman.

"Stay out of this, Beorn. I know what I'm doing," said Beowulf in kind.

"Never mind that," said Beowulf. "Tell me, Breca; have you ever killed a Sabre Tooth Forest Cat using just your hands and a knife?"

"No," said Breca, following a burst of laughter: "Have you?"

"Yes," said Beowulf, "when I was eight winters young."

"Bollocks! I don't believe it," said Breca.

"I do," said Elin. "I believe every word Beowulf says."

"Bollocks," said Breca a second time.

When Beowulf met Elin's gaze she felt the fire from his eyes; it traveled the length of her spine and took her breath away.

"What about a man?" Breca said, not bothering to mask the sudden enmity in his voice. "Have you ever killed a man in battle?"

"Yes," said Beowulf. "Several. How many of your enemies have you killed?"

"None," said Elin before Breca could answer. "Breca has no enemies and has never fought in a battle. Isn't that right, Cousin?"

Breca stood and glared at Elin; then at Beowulf:

"Bollocks," said Breca. I don't believe you did any of that—not a word of it. Besides, I have to piss."

That said, Breca left his father's Hall.

Elin stood.

"Come, Beowulf; let's get some fresh air."

35

THE WORM TURNS

The guards in the Watchtower were the first of Modryth's men to die that night. Six Harii warriors were wearing dark, sealskin boots and breeches, and using grappling hooks, scaled the stake wall unseen. The same as the other Harii accompanying Ecgtheow, their faces, and upper bodies were painted black. In the moonlight nothing but the whites of the Hariis' eyes was visible. In less time than it takes a starving dog to gnaw scraps off a bone, the guards lie in a heap, their throats cut.

Ecgtheow, too, was indistinguishable from "his boys," and the forty Harii with him. They all had charcoal painted faces, dark boots, and breeches; even the buckler Ecgtheow carried in his left hand was painted black; it was the Harii's preferred mode of attack—at night, invisible, surprising their enemies with their speed and ferocity.

As the Black Ship neared the dock, a hail of arrows took out the three guards warming their hands beside a large circular brazier. Modryth ordered a fire be kept burning from dusk to dawn to guide ships through the darkness and fog to Frihamm.

After the arrows had done their work, Haraldr looked at Ecgtheow and grinned.

"Good of them to light the way for us," said Haraldr.

Ecgtheow nodded. Once the Longship reached the dock, the crew tossed ropes ashore. The Harii, along with Ecgtheow's boys, disembarked. They left spears behind: this night's work they would do in close quarters with axe, knife, and sword.

Haraldr took twenty men to join the six he knew would be waiting at the Main Gate. From there they would proceed to the barracks where, given the hour, most of Modryth's men would be drunk or asleep.

Ecgtheow took his boys and the rest of the Harii, twenty in number, and stormed the Dark Queen's lodge using an iron, hand-held battering ram to access the Main Door.

† † †

Outside King Beanstan's Hall, Elin looked at the night sky. The Aurora Borealis burned with emerald green fire across the horizon.

"It's beautiful, isn't it," she said.

"Yes," said Beowulf; "but not more than you are."

"What did you say?"

"I think you're beautiful," said Beowulf, savoring Elin's scent.

"Do you mean that?" she said. Flattered though she was, Elin was taken aback by his directness.

"Didn't you tell Breca you believe every word I speak?"

Elin laughed. "You're right; I did say that—didn't I."

"Yes," said Beowulf. "Were you lying?"

"No... Well... To be truthful, I said it because I knew it would make Breca angry. He was rude, and I didn't care for it. After all, you're our guest."

"Ah," said Beowulf. "You were protecting me from Prince Breca's tongue."

"More or less," she said and laughed.

They walked for a moment in silence, staring at the green fire on the horizon. Elin stopped and looked at Beowulf:

"Is it true you killed a Sabre Tooth Forest Cat when you were seven winters' young?"

"I think I was eight at the time," he said.

"And you caught fish with your bare hands?"

"Yes," he said.

"And you killed men in battle?"

"Yes. Is there anything else you want to know, Lady Elin?"

"Yes," said Elin. "Many things."

"I'm afraid I'm not much good at that," said Beowulf.

"Good at what?"

"Talking about myself," he said.

Elin Laughed. "The way you handled Breca? Believe me, Prince Beowulf, you speak quite well for a Väster Geat."

"What does that mean?" said Beowulf.

Elin smiled: "I was making a joke."

Beowulf's head whipped to one side.

"What is it?" said Elin.

"We're not alone."

"Ah," said Elin. "Now you are joking."

The next moment the Schaman stepped out of the shadows.

"Beowulf has answered enough questions for tonight, Lady Elin," said the Schaman. "Now he must return to your uncle's Hall. Prince Breca has been bragging how he can out-drink any Thunder Geat no matter who sired him. Do you hear me, Bear's Son? Return to King Beanstan's Hall and enjoy yourself. When you drink, match Breca cup for cup and don't stop drinking 'til he passes out."

"Why did you call Prince Beowulf 'Bear's Son' just now, Magister Beorn?"

"Yes," said Beowulf. "Why did you call me that in front of Lady Elin?"

"Because she's the one."

"The one what?" said Beowulf.

"Well..." said the Schaman, then he hesitated. "You know! The one!"

When he realized neither Beowulf nor Elin were going to respond to his cryptic pronouncement, the Schaman coughed and mumbled something unintelligible.

"You said I'm the one for Beowulf—the one, what?" said Elin.

"King Beanstan and I have seen the way you look at each other," said the Schaman. "Two, perhaps three winters hence, you'll wed."

"Isn't that something for me to decide?" said Elin.

"And me?" said Beowulf.

"Yes, yes, of course—you're both right," said the Schaman.

He stepped between them.

"But for now, Beowulf should return to King Beanstan's Hall. There's much Lady Elin deserves to hear, and often the truth can be messy; so it's best she hears it first from me."

"Hear, what?" said Elin.

"What I must tell you about Beowulf," said the Schaman.

† † †

The fighting was over in less time than it took a butcher to eviscerate a hog. Ecgtheow and the Harii let Modryth's servants leave her lodge unharmed past the bodies of Modryth's palace guards. Taking one servant with them, one who volunteered the whereabouts of the Dark Queen, Ecgtheow and Haraldr made their way through a hidden passage to the dungeon that served as Modryth's “Special Room” and Treasury.

Ecgtheow and Haraldr had done much killing in their lifetimes, and they were all too familiar with the horror and brutality of war, but nothing could have prepared them for what their eyes beheld when they entered that chamber.

The floor of Modryth's Special Room was awash with the blood and gore that accumulated from the men, women, and children—what remained of them—who were thrust upon meat hooks and hung from the ceiling—butchered slabs of meat. There were others still alive in cages, waiting for Modryth to slaughter them like pigs.

“How dare you enter this place without my permission,” said Modryth, naked, deranged and covered with blood—none one of it was her own.

“Silence, hag!” said Haraldr.

He turned to Ecgtheow. “Tell me what you want, Ecgtheow.”

“Unlock the cages and let them out.”

“This black painted demon called you, 'Ecgtheow,'” said Modryth. “You are him? Ecgtheow Waegmunding? The Thunder Geat who murdered my beautiful son?”

“If you mean: am I the one who cut his head off, the answer's yes.”

“I'll kill you!” said Modryth.

Modryth charged forward waving a curved butcher's knife.

Ecgtheow struck the Dark Queen on the mouth with his fist. The force of the blow knocked Modryth to the ground spitting blood and teeth. Haraldr returned to Ecgtheow's side.

“It's done, Ecgtheow. What now?”

“Now we hang Modryth by her ankles and leave. Let these others do with her as they see fit.”

“And these chests of gold and silver?” said Haraldr.

Ecgtheow smiled. “We take it—all of it.”

Ecgtheow looked into the frightened faces of the men and women Haraldr freed.

“I'm Ecgtheow Waegmunding. You're free now. The Dark Queen's reign of terror is over. Do you understand?”

"And what of the Dark Queen?" said an emaciated young girl with dark sunken eyes.

"Do to her as she would do to you," said Haraldr.

The former captives' eyes lit up. They would exact their revenge, pure and simple, not just for themselves but for every citizen of Frihamm who had died at the hands of the Dark Queen.

Those who were there said Modryth's screams went on throughout the night and well into the next morning before there was silence.

Not long after, the people of Frihamm cremated the Dark Queen's mutilated corpse. They spread her ashes in the sewer. Ashamed for their obedience to Modryth, the residents of Frihamm wanted no reminder of the evil they endured for so long.

† † †

The Iron Wolf was alone in his private sauna except for two young Wylfing women massaging him.

Prince Adalfuns entered unannounced.

"I didn't send for you," said Amunwolf.

"No, father. You didn't."

"So, close the bloody door—you're letting the heat out."

Prince Adalfuns gave the two women a look. Not bothering to cover their nakedness they hurried from the room.

"Well, get on with it, boy," said Amunwolf. "Tell me what you mean by coming here in the middle of the night?"

"I mean to take your throne, old man."

Before Amunwolf could get to his feet, Adalfuns thrust a dagger into the soft spot beneath his father's chin. He buried the eight-inch blade to the hilt, piercing the Iron Wolf's brain. With his free hand, Adalfuns covered his father's eyes so he wouldn't see them staring at him. The Iron Wolf's body convulsed several times and then went limp.

† † †

The Schaman shook Beowulf awake. Beowulf pushed himself up on his elbow and stared at Beorn.

"How do you feel, young Prince?"

"Terrible," said Beowulf. "I thought the potion you made would prevent any ill effects from the mead."

"No, no, no," said Beorn. "The potion I gave you was to keep your ardor for Elin in-check."

"That's why you had me return to Beanstan's Hall? So I'd get drunk and pass out?"

"Exactly," said the Schaman. "I'm told you out drank Prince Breca, if that's any consolation."

"It's not," said Beowulf.

Beowulf grabbed one of his boots and hurled it at the Schaman. Beorn ducked, the boot sailed over his head. The Schaman held out a bowl filled with goat's milk and herbs.

"Drink this," said the Schaman. "You'll feel better soon after."

"Bollocks," said Beowulf. "I don't believe you."

"Ha!" said the Schaman. "You're even cursing like a true Northman now!"

"Probably," said Beowulf, "because it's the one word I recall hearing last night. Here, give me the remedy."

"That's a good lad," said the Schaman.

Beowulf drank the contents of the bowl and frowned: "It tastes terrible."

"You'll think better of me soon—trust me. Now get dressed and throw some water on your face."

"Why? What's going on?"

"What's going on is—I'm leaving."

"When?"

"Now, soon as you dress."

"Where are you going?" said Beowulf.

"South," said the Schaman.

"South? But, why?"

"I'm going to find your father."

"What?"

"You heard right," said the Schaman. "And as long as you remain here, among the Brondings, you'll be safe."

"But I want to come with you."

"I know you do, young Prince. But they could still be hunting us. Better we part company for awhile. Besides, you'll be safer here with people you can learn from—such as Elin, who can teach you things—things you'll need to know when it comes time to return to Geatland."

The Schaman looked long and hard into Beowulf's eyes.

"Don't be angry, young Prince. You have my word on it—I'll find your father."

"I'm going to miss you, Beorn."

"And I'll miss you," said the Schaman. "One more thing, Bear's Son: give Lady Elin time to embrace what sounded strange, perhaps even frightening to her."

"That I'm eleven winters' young—walking about in a man's body? Killing men, and drinking mead?"

The Schaman shrugged. "Yes—more or less."

"Does anyone else know?"

"No. And she swore she wouldn't tell anyone: not King Beanstan; not Prince Breca; not her friends; no one."

"How much time do I give Elin before I dare look her in the face?"

Again the Schaman shrugged:

"That's something Elin must decide. You'll need to be patient."

"But, now, when I need your advice most, you leave."

"Focus your thoughts on me, Bear's Son, and no matter where I am, chances are I'll feel you reaching out."

Beowulf stepped forward and hugged the Schaman.

"Die well, Beorn."

"Die well, young Prince."

36

AS ABOVE, SO BELOW

When at dawn, the Harii loaded the last chests of gold and silver aboard the Black Ship, Haraldr approached Ecgtheow.

"That's the rest of it," said the Harii Chieftain; then he laughed. "I doubt Amunwolf will be any too pleased to find his consort in pieces, and her Treasure Chamber empty."

"Amunwolf is dead," said Ecgtheow. "Adalfuns rules Öster Götaland now."

"Adalfuns usurped the throne?"

Ecgtheow nodded.

"By all the gods, Ecgtheow—Adalfuns murdered his father?"

"If I've learned anything about Wylfings," said Ecgtheow: "blood matters little to them, and betrayal comes easy."

"True—we Harii know them for the treacherous dogs they are," said Haraldr; "but now the question is—will Adalfuns try to reclaim Modryth's treasure?"

"I think not," said Ecgtheow. "Adalfuns won't risk war with the Thunder-Geats or Spear Danes, unless—"

"Unless?"

"Unless he has an ally—one that can tip the balance of power in his favor."

"The Svear King, Onegentheow, could prove such an ally," said Haraldr. "Besides, the Svear are always greedy for more land."

"I agree," said Ecgtheow. "Onegentheow has ships and warriors aplenty—enough over time to make Adalfuns his puppet."

"If that happens," added Haraldr, "the Svear King will control the Wylfings and Frihamm, both."

"Not if it happens, Haraldr; but when it happens," said Ecgtheow. "Then name me one tribe willing to risk war with the Svear?"

"What of us, Ecgtheow? What should the Harii do—our numbers are too few to matter?"

"Are you asking me as your friend or as your son-in-law?"

"Both," said Haraldr.

"Other tribes have always feared your people," said Ecgtheow, "and now you have wealth and ships—enough to rebuild your army. Reclaim the land of your fathers and their fathers before them. Unite the Cimbrii and Teutons. Believe me, Haraldr; your people—scattered though they are, trust you. Gather them together, and when your numbers are sufficient—return to Germania. The Franks and Frisians will scatter when they hear the Harii, Cimbrii, and Teutons have returned in force to reclaim their homeland."

"What of you and Eydís? Will you join us?"

"No, my friend. My son is alive somewhere—I feel it in my bones, and I intend to find him. Eydís is free to decide for herself, whether to go with me or stay with you—that is the Harii way. The choice is hers, but the path will be perilous, no matter what direction we take."

† † †

Beorn set sail aboard King Beanstan's personal Longship, Wave Rider. Beanstan's ship had a large, blue woolen sail that had Beanstan' s schedule—a rendering of Thor's Hammer in black, crossed by a white streak of lighting.

With the wind at its back, Wave Rider glided over the waves while the Schaman stood at the prow and looked back toward shore.

† † †

On the beach, Beowulf stood alongside King Beanstan. They watched in silence as the Schaman departed south, away from the land of the Sea Brondings.

Beorn did not try to shout over the sound of the waves; instead, he knew Beowulf could hear him using the Silent Tongue.

"*Remember, Bear's Son, ask the Forest Folk or Sky Dwellers to send word to me, and they will. And remember—though the distance between us be great, we won't be far apart—not in spirit. You have my word on that.*"

Beowulf raised his hand.

"*I won't forget what you've taught me.*"

"*It's what I haven't taught you that worries me, young Prince*," said the Schaman.

Beowulf and the Schaman held each other's gaze until the ship entered a patch of fog and passed from sight.

It was then Beowulf sensed eyes on him coming from the heights overlooking the shoreline. As he turned, he glimpsed Elin standing there looking down at him. She, too, wanted to be present when the Schaman departed.

What did Beorn tell her, Beowulf wondered. *And how could it make sense to her? How will Elin understand what I am; what I've become... when I don't understand myself*? Those were the thoughts that hammered Beowulf's mind with the force of iron striking iron for the rest of that morning and far into the night.

Beowulf's eyes captured Elin's gaze from the bluff, and he sensed neither sadness nor joy, just incomprehension. Beowulf raised his hand to greet her. As he did, she turned and vanished.

"She'll come around to the idea, young Prince," said King Beanstan. "You'll see."

"Your Grace?" said Beowulf.

"To being married."

"Ah!" said Beowulf. "Elin needs time to think about marriage, or about marrying me?"

"Marrying you, of course. Besides, what's to consider? A wedding-bond twixt you and Elin will unite our tribes—Thunder-Geats and Sea Brondings. That in itself is a serious matter, young Prince, worthy of your consideration. Beorn and I stayed up all night drinking and thinking the matter through. We concluded that you and Elin are a perfect match."

"With all respect, Great King," said Beowulf, "Elin and I just met. We don't know one another, other than by name."

"Ha!" said Beanstan, "there'll be plenty of time for that. You may not know this, but Beorn was my teacher, but that was long ago when I was a boy, Prince Beowulf. Or should I call you, Bear's Son?"

One-Eyed Odin could stand no more of it—the vitriol had elevated to screaming between Hel and Frigga. Even Thor and the other gods and goddesses present, were weary of listening to the two goddesses insult one another; so much so, they left the All Father's Great Hall.

From Odin's Hall, most went to visit and drink with the most courageous warriors from the other worlds, male and female, who had died in battle, thus earning a place in the sacred Halls of Valhalla.

"Enough," said Odin, in a voice so loud it made the marble floor tremble beneath the goddesses' feet.

In obedience to the All Father's command, Frigga and Hel became silent. They turned away from one another to meet the All Father's gaze.

"No more arguing," said Odin. "I have listened to you both to the point of exhaustion. My head aches because of it. I have weighed the merits of Hel's demands, with Frigga's reasoned arguments. On the one hand, Hel feels cheated. I understand that. It was not Hathus the Ostrogoth's time to die, or so Hel argues, and certainly not at the hand of the bear's son, a mere child, who eluded Death when Thor and Frigga bestowed him with special powers. Now there is no mortal in Midgard such as him. I understand that. But who else will be killed by this man-child, Hel asks, before their allotted time? It's a reasonable question, but one with no answer since Fate is Fate and, like Death, answers to no one. Hel's greatest worry, however, concerns a matter far more important. I have listened to both of you and have considered your arguments carefully. Now listen well—for here is my decision; then I will hear no more about it from either of you."

Wanting to be alone with the strange new feeling possessing her, Elin sought the solitude of a secluded place not far from the fortified village by the sea that served as Beanstan's seat of power. She, too, had tasks, same as any Bronding girl or boy, and it mattered not that her uncle was King. But when her time was her own, Elin preferred her refuge in the woods. The animals were accustomed to her coming and going. They accepted Elin, not as one of them, but as a kindred spirit to the Forest Folk.

There was a small grassy clearing. At its center was a large rock made flat on top over the passage of time. It was there, surrounded by fir trees where Elin preferred to sit and sometimes recline to feel the warmth of the sun on her skin.

She had not been sitting long when the branches of the trees began to pitch and sway. What at first seemed to be the wind was followed by a flash of light. Elin covered her eyes with her hands until the brilliance of the light subsided.

In front of Elin appeared a woman, tall and beautiful with thick chestnut-colored hair that hung in braids past her waist.

Elin got to her feet: "Mamma?"

"Yes, darling daughter. But don't be frightened."

"I'm not," said Elin."Truly, I'm not."

Elin ran to her mother's outstretched arms. In silence, they held each other.

"How can this be?"

"First," said Elin's mother, "let me stand here a moment and feel the warmth of the sun once more. Ten winters since the avalanche claimed your father and me."

"I know," said Elin, "Not a day goes by I do not cry for missing you so."

"Yes, daughter, but now you must move beyond your sadness and live the life you were meant to have. Even in Helheim, your thoughts and prayers reach us. But I must hurry, Elin, for I cannot stay long. It was Hel who brought this about, but was the goddess Frigga who persuaded the All Father to allow me to carry his message to you."

"Message? My head is awhirl, Mamma, but if you cannot stay long, tell me what I must know."

"Not even the All Father can see your future, my daughter. But this much he does know. If you decide to give yourself to the man-child known as Beowulf, the bear's son, your love for each other will be strong—strong as any love you could ever wish. But you will birth no children—that, the All Father will not allow."

"Not allow?" said Elin.

"Yes. To placate the goddess, Hel and, more importantly, to prevent her father, Loki, from making mischief throughout

Midgard if Hel does not get her way. Therefore, the All Father must deny you children—you and Beowulf."

"I don't even know if I could love Beowulf Waegmunding, not when he's—"

"Unlike any other in all Midgard?"

"That's not what I was going to say, Mamma."

"Don't judge him by the few winters he's seen, Elin; rather, trust your heart."

"Is there any way the All Father will change his mind?" said Elin.

"Yes—if you marry someone other than Beowulf Waegmunding. That way you can have as many children as you desire. Trust me when I tell you: Great Odin said: 'Beowulf Waegmunding will not be allowed to sire children; not Elin's; not anyone's.'"

There was a flash of light.

"No," said Elin's mother. "Please. Not yet."

"Mamma?"

Surrounded by a golden mist, Elin's mother vanished.

37

TOGA HÖNK

The worst had come and gone. The great winter storms spawned by the long-standing domestic quarrel between Aegir, god of the ocean depths, and his consort, Rán, goddess of the Seven Seas, were replaced with the tolerable lashings of less violent squalls. Still, even these minor storms commanded the incoming tides further inland, sparing little and no one in their path.

† † †

Prince Breca found Beowulf at the Guest Lodge which, following the Schaman's departure, became Beowulf's private dwelling.

"You want to learn what it means to be a true Sea Bronding—yes?" said Breca.

Beowulf had dressed, but for his boots.

"Yes," said Beowulf.

Breca had a look of mischief about him.

"That's very, very good," he said. "Soon as you've put your boots on, meet me down by the waterfront."

† † †

Beowulf found Prince Breca and thirty warrior-whalers waiting. They stood alongside the pier where Breca's battle craft, the Sea Raven, was moored.

"Up for a game, Prince Beowulf," said Breca.

"Game?"

"Yes," said Breca. "You've been keeping so much to yourself, now that winter's near its end, you really should focus on getting ready."

"Ready for what?" said Beowulf.

"So you'll be in shape. The Whale Road's calling. Soon we'll be putting our ships out to sea. To make up for the men I lost last season I need to replace them with the best oarsmen I can find. My father seems to think you'll make a competent warrior-whaler. Even Elin said so."

"Elin said that?"

Breca grinned. "No. I was joking you. I haven't heard Elin mention your name since father's smelly old friend departed."

"Smelly old friend?" said Beowulf.

"Why, yes—the Schaman who brought you here."

Beowulf felt his face flush with anger. His hands tightened into fists.

"Did something offend you, Prince Beowulf?"

From someplace afar Beowulf could hear Beorn whisper in his ear as though the Schaman was standing beside him.

"Calm yourself, Bear's Son. Pay Breca no mind. I told you—he will do all he can to provoke you."

Beowulf took a slow deep breath and counted in his head to ten. His hands relaxed, and the tension in his face disappeared.

"Tell me about the men you lost," said Beowulf.

"Some fell overboard and drowned. Others died after returning with broken arms or shattered legs that later turned rotten. Others were snatched off the ice by Ondskas while we hunted for seals. Sometimes a hag, or what some call a shark, will grab a man from over the side of the ship and devour him whole. The Whale road is full of such creatures, Prince Beowulf—all of them man-killers."

"That's good to know, Prince Breca—so tell me about this game. I wouldn't want it said I broke the rules.... after I've won."

Prince Breca's jaws tightened when the warriors behind him laughed. Breca silenced them with an angry look. He turned toward Beowulf.

"It's called:"Toga Hönk," said Breca.

"Tug-of-War," said Beowulf, using the Common Tongue.

"Good," said Breca; "you've heard of it.

"Of course," said Beowulf. "That 'smelly old friend of your father' who brought me here, said it's a warriors' game—a game of strength that tests the will and conditioning of a man. He said the rope used is as thick as a large man's wrist."

"By any chance," said Breca, "did old Bluebeard tell you the particulars of the game?"

Ignoring yet another insult to his friend and mentor, Beowulf nodded:

"Two men face each other with several yards of rope between them," said Beowulf. "Many men can play, but whether two men, twenty, or two-hundred, there's always an unpleasant outcome that awaits the loser."

"It's more than just a game," said Breca, "for we Sea Brondings, Toga Hönk is an excellent way Clan Chiefs can decide which men will make capable oarsmen aboard their vessels. The strongest most capable rowers are assigned to our Longships, whether for battle or when we go whaling. The least strong, the less capable, sail our fishing skiffs or one of those knarrs you see over there, used for hauling cargo. To be sure, rowing is not for weak kneed, limp-wristed weaklings. Now you know all there is to know."

"Am I mistaken—thinking you brought me here to play Toga Hönk," said Beowulf, "and not just talk about it?"

This time it was Breca's face that flushed crimson with anger. He stepped toward Beowulf but stopped an arm's length away when Beowulf neither flinched nor retreated. Breca pointed toward a pit six-feet in diameter the Bronding men filled with mud that smelled of pig shite.

"If you want to test yourself, Prince Beowulf, stand there, ten feet away from the pit."

"Ah," said Beowulf, "and you'll stand on the other side with the rope between us?"

"Actually," said Breca, "the first man to test himself against you is the first you see in line over there. Brun is a veteran warrior-whaler and as good an oarsman as any under my command. If for some impossible reason you should manage to defeat him, into the pit he'll go. Then you can face the next man. Defeat all thirty, and you will have earned the right to test your strength against mine."

Beowulf laughed.

"Do you find that amusing?" said Breca, "or does your laughter mask your fear?"

"Yes, to the first part," said Beowulf; "and, no, to what followed."

"Meaning?" said Breca.

"I see no reason to test myself against these mighty warriors one at a time. I'll stay on this side of the pit with my end of the rope. Your men can take a position on the other side—agreed?"

Breca's mouth fell open. "Balls!" he said. "You alone—against thirty of my best oarsmen?"

"No," said Beowulf. "Thirty-one if you include yourself."

"Balls!" said Breca.

"Do it Breca," spoke a familiar voice from among the gathering that had formed.

The voice belonged to Elin. "Accept Prince Beowulf's challenge," she said.

"Yes! Yes!" said the crowd, in unison. "Do it, Prince Breca! Do it!"

Without saying a word, Beowulf removed his belt and tunic. Elin stepped to his side.

"Here," she said; "I'll hold them."

Beowulf placed his belt and tunic into her hands. As their finger tips connected, she felt a surge of energy flow into her, down her spine to her feet.

Breca had been watching: "How very sweet, and so, so touching," he said, loud enough that the crowd would hear.

"Do it, Prince Breca! Do it!" said the crowd, unamused by Breca's taunt.

"Very well," said Breca. "I'll give this boastful Thunder Geat a lesson he'll never forget."

"Nor will you forget it, Cousin," said Elin.

"What?" said Breca, uncertain of the meaning behind Elin's few words.

The look Elin gave Beowulf made the beating of his heart quicken. He could feel his blood on fire for her, commingled with a lust for battle—not to kill, but to humiliate the Prince of the Sea Brondings.

Breca cast a perplexed look at Elin; then he got about the business of forming his men into a straight line with his best oarsman, Brun, in front. Breca placed himself last in line to serve as an anchor. Beowulf wrapped his end of the rope twice around his waist; then grasped it in a way that suited him. What remained of Beowulf's half of the line lay the way a docile serpent might, coiled at his feet. The remainder of the rope was stretched taut across the pit almost three feet above the filth that filled it.

Brun looked over his shoulder and shouted to the men behind: “Let's show this foul-weather Geat what Sea Brondings are!”

From the back of the line, Prince Breca looked at Elin and smirked.

“Give the word, Cousin, and we'll start,” he said

Elin looked at Beowulf and nodded. Beowulf nodded and tightened his grip on the rope. The crowd became silent.

“Begin,” said Elin.

“Pull!” said Breca.

With much shouting, cursing and grunting, the Sea Brondings pulled their half of the rope. They pulled the way they rowed when struggling against the wind and waves, or when going into battle on the Whale Road.

Despite the Brondings' best efforts it soon became apparent something inexplicable was taking place. The crowd gasped and cried-out when what they saw confounded their eyes. Even Breca's cursing and wild exhortations lapsed into silence, for Beowulf stood in the same position as when the contest began. Breca's men gasped for breath and dripped sweat as they strained to pull Beowulf toward the pit.

As with so many women in the crowd who were watching, for a moment Elin felt unsteady on her feet when she saw Beowulf's torso, rippled with muscle. There wasn't a feather-weight of fat on him. His muscles bulged and his veins expanded well beyond normal. The muscles in his legs swelled, defined by the confinement his sealskin breeches imposed.

From the front of the line, Brun cast a look of dismay at Prince Breca.

“Pull harder, damn you,” said Breca. “All of you! Pull harder!”

The Brondings continued to struggle; they pulled as if their very lives depended on dragging Beowulf into the pit. Beowulf remained steadfast. Then, all at once, he leaned back, dug the heels of his boots in the ground, and pulled on the rope, reaching one hand over the other, taking-up the slack. Foot by foot, hand over hand, he pulled the Brondings closer to the pit.

Speechless, the crowd watched Brun topple face-first into the mire; then, while all three-hundred pounds of him struggled to climb from the pit reeking of pig shite, a second, third and fourth Bronding warrior followed him into the hole. So it went, until

Breca, alone, was left unsullied.

While Breca pulled, Beowulf released the rope from his grip. Breca lurched backward and landed on his buttocks.

"Enough," said Beowulf. "The game's over."

Humiliated, Breca leapt to his feet. "No! It's not over. You still have me to beat."

"Be grateful, Cousin," said Elin, "that Prince Beowulf stopped when he did. Otherwise, you'd be standing there smelling of pig shite, just the way Brun and the others do."

"Stay out of this Elin," said Breca. "Beowulf quit before the contest ended. Therefore, I declare myself the winner, unless he dares face me."

"Very well, Prince Breca," said Beowulf, "if you wish to continue, pick up the rope and put distance between us, as much as you dare."

"Stop this nonsense now," said King Beanstan emerging through the crowd surrounded by his Personal Guard. "Stop now, I say."

"But, father?" said Breca.

"But, nothing," said King Beanstan. "Prince Beowulf has shown you the strength of his arms, but also his strength of character. Despite your bluster, my son, Beowulf spared you further humiliation however deserved."

† † †

All day King Beanstan questioned his eyes regarding what he saw that morning at the waterfront: a boy no older than his son who possessed the strength of over thirty men in each arm.

By all the gods, how is such a thing possible? he asked himself.

That was the same question on the minds of Aksel and the other Clan Chiefs seated in King Beanstan's Hall.

"I was there also, my King," said Lord Aksel. "I saw what everyone else in this room saw—but how is such a thing possible?"

The other Clan Chiefs shouted similar sentiments to one another until Beanstan raised a hand and signaled for "silence!"

"We saw what we saw," said Beanstan. "A mere boy on the edge of manhood proved himself stronger than thirty of my best warriors."

"But how?" said Aksel.

"The Schaman, Beorn, must know the how and why of it," said Logan, a Clan Chief and adviser to Beanstan."

"Yes, Logan," said Aksel, "but the Schaman's not here to tell us."

"Sorcery," said a Clan Chief named Lurdonson. "How else can we explain it?"

A murmur of agreement went up from many of the chiefs.

"No mere boy," said Lurdonson, "could do what Beowulf Waegmunding did without witchcraft behind it. I'm telling you there's dark magic come to Brondingland."

"Careful what words you use, Lord Lurdonson," said King Beanstan. "For any of us know, Beowulf was born with the strength he has. And whose to say the gods themselves don't have a hand in this. None of us know how Beowulf came to be the way he is; although his father, Ecgtheow, is himself a mighty warrior."

Murmurs of agreement issued from the Clan Chiefs.

"The question," said Lord Aksel, "is what are we to do with him?"

King Beanstan took a moment to think.

"Beowulf has shown us what kind of warrior he will make. Besides, we have Beorn's own words confirming the boy's character and good sense. I will give this young Thunder Geat his Longship and thirty capable oarsmen."

"Why thirty," said Lord Aksel, "when he could row a Longship by his lonesome."

King Beanstan and the others laughed.

"That's true," said Beanstan. "In which case, he can tiller the ship."

"But he's never gone whaling before," said Lunderson.

"Something tells me he'll do fine," said Beanstan.

38

THE WHALE ROAD

Ragmund made his way to the dais where King Hrethel sat on his throne, soaking his feet in a tub of warm salt-water.

"Yes, Ragmund," said Hrethel. "What is it?"

"An old man reeking of wood smoke, Great King, requests an immediate audience."

"Reeking of wood smoke, you say?" said Hrethel.

Lord Magnus, the Captain of the Kungens Vakter, stepped forward toward the dais.

"A beggar most likely, my King. I'll have him ejected."

"He's no beggar, Lord Magnus," said Ragmund.

"Then who is he?" said Hrethel.

"He says he came here to heal what ails you, Great King."

Princes Herebeald and Haethcyn laughed. Prince Hygelac maintained a straight face. He had learned from Ecgtheow Waegmunding long before; there's more to a man than his outward appearance.

"Did he now?" said Hrethel.

"He's obviously a charlatan," said Herebeald. "Have Lord Magnus throw him out on his ear."

"Or perhaps he's a conjurer of spells, Father," said Haethcyn. "In which case, we should burn him in the Great Square outside the Citadel."

"Burn him?" said Hrethel.

"To reassure our people we're watching over them," said Haethcyn.

"He's no charlatan," said Ragmund; "nor is he a conjurer as Prince Haethcyn suggests. My instincts tell me, Great King, the old man, has great powers despite his strange appearance."

"What makes you say that, Ragmund?" said Hygelac.

"Something about him—a quality you can hear in his voice and see in his eyes," said Ragmund. "Besides, Great King, he arrived here by way of King Beanstan's Longship."

"Lord Magnus?" said Hrethel. "Did you not know of this?"

"Forgive me, my King; I did not."

"How do you know this, Ragmund?" said Hrethel.

"The Harbor Master felt certain you would want to know, Great King, so he sent a message directly to me."

"He should have come to me first," said Lord Magnus, irritated that the Harbor Master circumvented protocol at his expense.

"Calm yourself, Lord Magnus," said Hrethel. "It matters little at this point."

"Very well, my King," said Magnus.

"Where's the harm, Father?" said Hygelac. "I say we give the old man man an audience."

"We?" said Herebeald.

"Enough," said Hrethel. "I agree with Hygelac. Show him in. I want to see this old man who smells of wood smoke."

† † †

Beowulf stood at the tiller and guided the Longship over the waves. The wind was behind him and filled the sail. Handpicked by the King, the thirty oarsmen with him were devoted to their king; they felt honored to be chosen to row for the young Thunder Geat whose strength was already the stuff of legend. Fifty yards away, sailing parallel with Beowulf's vessel, was Breca's Longship, the Sea Raven.

While two of his men worked the tiller, Breca stood at the bow where the prow resembled a raven's head. Breca held a harpoon. He looked to one side and saw Beowulf across from him, manning the tiller alone, enjoying himself as he guided the Longship over the waves. Beowulf's incredible strength, his effortless mastery of rowing, sailing and piloting a Longship—all of that caused Breca to brood and over time would leave worry-lines carved on his brow.

Beowulf saw Breca looking at him across the distance that separated their two ships. Beowulf raised his hand. Breca looked away.

At the sight of the Schaman's height, girth, furs, long white hair and snow-white beard stained blue down the center, Princes Herebeald and Haecythn could not keep from laughing; however, a stern look from their father sufficed to keep them quiet.

This strange old man has seen many winters thought Hygelac; far more than my father; yet, aged as he is, he carries himself with a straight back, and there's a singleness of purpose with each step he takes. But what does he want?

The Schaman stopped short of the dais and bowed.

"Hail, Hrethel, son of Swerting, King of the Thunder-Geats."

"Who are you," said Hrethel, "and how are you called?"

"I serve the All Mother," said the Schaman. "Others call me, Beorn."

"A true servant of the All Mother is always a welcome guest, Magister Beorn," said Hrethel.

"Thank you, Great King."

The Schaman turned to Prince Hygelac and smiled.

"You would be right to think I've seen many winters, Young Prince. And where I go, there's always purpose to it."

Hygelac's mouth dropped open. By all the gods, he thought; this old man can hear my thoughts.

"Have you met my son before?" said Hrethel.

"Once," said the Schaman. "In a vision."

"Bollocks!" said Herebeald. "I told you he was a charlatan."

"Silence!" said Hrethel. He turned his attention to Beorn.

"In a vision say you?" said Hrethel.

"Yes, Great King," said the Schaman. "I have them—often."

Hrethel took a moment before speaking.

"When asked what brings you here, you told my adviser you could heal what ails me?"

† † †

A warrior-whaler standing watch at the bow turned and shouted in Beowulf's direction:

"Two Blues! Just ahead! A mother and her calf."

"You two," said Beowulf to the oarsmen seated on the benches closest to him. "How are you called?"

"Ansgar," said the Bronding seated to the left of the tiller.
"Alfhild," said the Bronding seated to Beowulf's right.
"Can you see any other whales?" said Beowulf.
"No, Prince Beowulf," said Alfhild. "Just the two of them."
"They're coming in our direction, Prince Beowulf," said Ansgar.
"All the easier to kill them," said Alfhild.
"No," said Beowulf. "I won't hunt a calf, or make an orphan of one," said Beowulf.
"Even if we don't kill the calf," said Alfhild; "Prince Breca will still want the mother."
"Then let Prince Breca kill them both if that's what he wants," said Beowulf.
"But we're closest to her, young Lord," said Ansgar. "The kill is ours, for the doing."
"The herd can't be far off—we're sure to find males we can hunt," said Beowulf.
"Maybe yes, maybe no, Prince Beowulf," said Ansgar. "But right now the herd's not staring us in the face, like these two."
"They're beautiful," said Beowulf.
Ansgar and Alfhild exchanged looks mirroring their bewilderment over Beowulf's reluctance to kill the sea creatures.

† † †

Aboard the Sea Raven Breca watched Beowulf re-assume his position at the tiller and steer away from the whale and her calf.
"Kill them!" said Breca in as loud a voice as he could muster. "Kill them both you fool! It's what we're here to do."
Breca saw Beowulf look at him across the distance that separated their Longships. Beowulf cupped one hand to his ear and shook his head, suggesting he couldn't hear above the sound of wind and waves.
Balls, Breca told himself. *He hears but pretends otherwise. What it is, I can't say; but something's not right about this Thunder Geat. He may have Elin and my father fooled—but not me.*
Breca watched as Beowulf changed course. Breca signaled his Tillermen to follow.
"Are we to go back empty-handed, Prince Breca," said Brun.

"Just because this Thunder-Geat has no appetite for the hunt?"

Breca looked at Brun's puzzled face and the faces of his men staring at him.

"No," said Breca. "We won't go back empty-handed; not while I'm in a mood to kill something."

† † †

"*Go in peace with your calf, Mother Whale. I will not harm you,*" said Beowulf in the Silent Tongue.

"*And who would you be, Land Swimmer—who speaks the Silent Tongue*?" said the mother whale.

"*I am called Beowulf by my kind. To the Forest Folk and Sky Dwellers, I am known as the bear's son.*"

"*I will tell those like me, Bear's Son,*" said the mother whale, *"that you chose to let me and my calf go our way in peace."*

"I cannot promise you it will always be so," said Beowulf.

"Of course not, Bear's Son; we have our parts to play in the All Mother's Dance."

With that, the whale and her calf dropped below the surface out of sight.

† † †

Inside Hrethel's sauna, servant girls massaged the old King's feet with a special blend of herbs and honey that when heated transformed into a thick salve. Had it not been for the lavender and mint the Schaman added the salve would have reeked of something best unmentioned.

"I cannot tell you enough, Magister Beorn, how comforting that tar feels on these old feet of mine. Ordinarily, they would be aching beyond belief this time of the day."

"The 'tar' as you call it will ease the pain, Great King. I'll leave you enough to last for some time but the one remedy, Great King, the remedy that will have a lasting effect, calls on you to make changes. Changes that will rid you of the pain altogether."

"What changes?"

"Your diet, Great King; what you eat and drink."

"I eat very well, Magister Beorn," said Hrethel. "Perhaps too much of some things, but I eat well."

"You eat too well, Great King."

"I don't understand," said Hrethel.

"To rid yourself of the pain in your feet, you must first stop eating red meat, and drinking mead, or drinking other fermented brews."

"Give up red meat, you say?" said Hrethel. "And mead?"

"Yes. Eat more fish, fresh vegetables and fruit. Instead of red meat, eat chicken, pheasant, pork or rabbit. Drink mint tea. You'll find it soothing when times are difficult."

"For a king, Magister Beorn, times are always difficult."

"Precisely why you should drink tea. It will help clear your mind of the clutter that gets in the way of sound judgment."

"All at once..." Hrethel snapped his fingers. "Quit red meat and mead?"

"You must, Great King, if you want to cure your body of what ails you."

Hrethel motioned for the two servant girls to leave. When Hrethel and the Schaman were alone, the old king leaned toward the Schaman and whispered: "My gut tells me it isn't my feet that brought you here, Magister Beorn, and that the change you speak of includes more than my diet."

† † †

Ecgtheow and Eydís stood together on the shore after the last of the Harii, their possessions, and the plunder from Frihamm was aboard the Longships they had taken from the Dark Queen. The time to leave the southern coast of Gotaland had arrived. They were ready and eager to set sail for their ancestral lands in Germania.

"You're not angry with me for choosing to stay with my people?" said Eydís.

"No, dearest Eydís," said Ecgtheow. "Your tribe will face many perils in Germania. Your healing skills will be much needed there."

"I will continue to pray to the gods that you find Beowulf, my love."

Eydís looked into the faces of Ecgtheow's foster-sons.

"I will pray for all of you. Take care of yourselves, for you're a family now. Just as Ecgtheow will foster father you, he is also my husband, and I ask you to watch over him, as would blood sons."

"We shall, Lady Eydís," said Turin.

That said, Ecgtheow lifted Eydís into his arms and carried her into the surf toward the Longship her father commanded.

"Maybe one day, my love," said Eydís.

"For me, there's now—today. Do you understand?"

Eydís nodded.

It was then Haraldr lifted his daughter from Ecgtheow's arms.

† † †

It was Glan, Beowulf's spotter at the bow, who counted thirty black triangular fins slicing the surface of the water. They were on a course straight for the Sea Raven. Glan looked back toward the tiller, filled his lungs with air and shouted: "Orcas!"

Aboard Beowulf's ship, the oarsmen waited for Beowulf's orders.

"Ansgar! Alfhild!" said Beowulf. "Have these creatures ever attacked your ships?"

"Never, Prince Beowulf."

"By Odin's one eye," said Alfhild, "these Ondskas mean to fight."

"But, why?" asked Beowulf.

"Perhaps, young Lord," said Alfhild, "They think we're after the two whales we just passed."

"Maybe," said Ansgar. "Or maybe these nasty brutes just don't want us here."

† † †

Breca saw them also, and well he should have since the Ondskas were coming toward the Sea Raven while in pursuit of the Blue whale and her calf.

"Make fast the oars, lads," said Breca. "Take up spears and bows. These bastards mean to sink us."

39

BLOOD & WATER

The Schaman passed the ladle to Hrethel so that the old king might wet his parched throat. Hrethel drank, then wiped the perspiration from his forehead. The heat drained the weariness from Hrethel's bones.

"What is it, Magister Beorn," said Hrethel, "that brings you to the Citadel?"

"A quest, great king."

"A quest?"

"Yes," said the Schaman. "To find Ecgtheow Waegmunding."

"But, why? For what reason? Tell me, Magister Beorn—does it concern my grandson, Beowulf?"

The Schaman's eyes sparkled.

"Tell me he's alive. Tell me my grandson lives!"

"Yes, Great King. Beowulf is very much alive. When last we spoke I promised I would find his father."

"You have indeed cured what ailed me most, Magister Beorn: not knowing if my grandson was dead or alive has left me feeling numb and cold inside."

"Because you failed to keep your promise to Ecgtheow."

"You know of that?" said Hrethel.

"That you would foster father, Beowulf?"

"Yes," said Hrethel. "But how could you possibly know I made such a promise?"

"Because asking you to foster father his son is what I would've done in Ecgtheow's boots, Great King."

"I want to hear everything, Magister Beorn. But not here. Not now. These joyful tidings leave me light-headed. I need to rest. Tell me tonight over supper. My sons will also want to hear."

"Can they be trusted?" said the Schaman.

Beorn got to his feet and looked into the old King's eyes.

"I ask you again, Great King: can your sons be trusted?"

† † †

"Steer into them!" said Breca to his Tillermen with the full force of his lungs. "Don't let the brutes broadside us."

Too late, the Ondskas at the front of the pack rammed Breca's Longship amidships where the mast was. Again and again, in sets of five, the "brutes," as Breca called them, struck the left side of his Longship splintering oars and cracking the hull.

Breca's warriors hurled harpoons but to no avail and when they were out of harpoons they turned to spears, bows, and arrows. Nothing turned the Ondskas back. Meanwhile, as half his crew tried to fight-off the beasts, the others used buckets to scoop-up the water accumulating from the holes the Ondskas made in the Sea Raven's hull.

As one warrior emptied a bucket, an Ondska struck the ship. The concussion sent the man sprawling. As he tried to regain his feet, an Ondska came out of the water and yanked him over the side. The Ondska dragged him in a wide arc until a second Ondska took hold of the warrior and, together, they tore him in half.

† † †

Beowulf ordered his men to resume rowing; then he watched the Ondskas descend on Breca's Longship the way a wolf pack would on a wounded Elk struggling to escape in the snow.

"Ansgar. Alfhild," said Beowulf. Take the tiller."

"What are your orders, Prince Beowulf?" said Ansgar.

"We're changing course," said Beowulf. "Steer left."

"What?" said Ansgar. "We must go to the aid of our Prince and the Sea Raven."

"Are you giving the orders now, Ansgar?"

"No, my Lord," said Ansgar. "It's just that—"

"I thought not," said Beowulf. "Now steer left."

Their harpoons and spears gone, Breca and his men continued to fight using the bows they kept aboard should they encounter Berserkers or other pirates. Now they had few arrows left and were ankles deep in salt water. In waves of five, the Ondskas continued to broadside the Sea Raven.

Brum stood alongside Breca and pointed at Beowulf's Longship: "Look there, my Prince. The Thunder Geat is changing course."

"By all the gods!" said Breca, "He's running. May Hel judge that Geat bastard for the coward he truly is."

† † †

Beowulf's Longship turned out of the wind while his oarsmen rowed with all their strength.

"Make straight for the Ondskas," said Beowulf.

"Are you serious," said Alfhild.

Beowulf looked into Alfhild's eyes. "Do it!"

"And where will you be?" said Ansgar.

"In the front, at the bow," said Beowulf.

As Beowulf made his way forward toward the mast, between the rows of oarsmen, he shouted:

"If it's a fight the Black-and-Whites want, we'll give them one. Right now your prince and kinsmen need us. So take up oars and row."

"And when we make contact," said a warrior; "what then, young Prince?"

"That is for Fate to decide," said Beowulf.

"Prince Breca," said Brum.

Breca grabbed hold of the mast to steady himself as the Sea Raven tilted hard to the left.

"We're sinking, my Prince," said Brum.

"We're not going to sink, damn you. Now take up a bow and get back in the fight."

"Look," said Brum. He raised a hand and pointed.

When Prince Breca looked, he saw Beowulf's Longship make its way around the Sea Raven's stern, straight into the pod of

Ondskas. In front, at the bow, harpoon in hand, stood Beowulf.

Beowulf stood on the right side of his Longship and saw Breca watching him. Then, as a dark shape crossed the bow of Beowulf's ship, Beowulf hurled the harpoon with all his might. It struck the Ondska on the side of the head. The creature screeched in pain, turned on its side and floated on the surface while its blood formed a red slick on the water.

"Bring me more harpoons! Ansgar! Alfhild—steer closer to the Sea Raven."

As Beowulf's Longship closed the distance between it and the Sea Raven, the Ondskas focused their rage on Beowulf. They came in waves of five, just as they had against Breca. Five more times Beowulf hurled harpoons, and each found its mark. Now, six dead Ondskas floated on their sides on the surface of the water. Overhead, a flock of seagulls circled, eager for the free meal that was coming.

With a harpoon in hand, Beowulf climbed onto the prow sculpted in the shape of a sea serpent's head.

"Hear me," said Beowulf, "Hear me, whoever leads your pack and listen well; for it is I, Beowulf Waegmunding, the bear's son, who calls on you to break off your attack. In exchange, our ships will turn around and head back to land. There need be no more killing this day."

An Ondska of great size came toward the prow. It lifted its head and looked Beowulf in the eyes. Its snout was nicked and bleeding from the many times it struck the Sea Raven's hull.

"In all my days," said the Ondska, "never have I heard a Land Swimmer speak the Silent Tongue. Why would I call off our attack when we can sink your wooden wave rider? Besides, six of my brothers and sisters lie dead around me, and I must avenge them.

"Yes," said Beowulf, "six of your family is dead, and seagulls will feast on their flesh; as will other creatures. But what if I were to kill you—what then?"

"If I were to die," said the Ondska, "the others would return to the depths to choose a new leader, for that is our way."

"Once more," said Beowulf, "I ask you to let us depart in peace. Seek your vengeance another time, for the Sea Brondings are certain to return to hunt the blue giants."

"No, Bear's Son," said the Ondska. "I intend to kill you—this very day."

"I'm sorry," said Beowulf.

"Sorry for what?" said the Ondska.

Beowulf hurled the harpoon. It entered the Ondska's mouth and came out the top of its head. At the sight of their leader impaled, the remaining Ondskas let loose high-pitched cries and withdrew.

While the Brondings cheered and slapped one another on the back, the Ondskas submerged. A warrior approached as Beowulf climbed down from the prow.

"Your orders, Prince Beowulf?"

"We gather the dead Ondskas and lash them to our ship. When that's done, we take Prince Breca's crew aboard before the Sea Raven sinks."

Beowulf looked across the short distance that separated the two Longships. He saw Breca staring at him.

Breca made a fist of one hand and paid tribute to Beowulf the Bronding way: he beat on his chest three times, then raised his arm overhead.

Beowulf nodded. As he looked away, he thought: I have withstood your insults since first arriving here, and now you salute me as if to say I've earned your friendship. Well, Breca, I don't need it.

Again the Brondings cheered and chanted the young Thunder Geat's name: "Beo—wulf! Beo—wulf!"

I salute the Thunder Geat as a gesture of goodwill thought Breca, yet he spurns me with a simple nod and looks away. Very well, Beowulf Waegmunding. If that's how it's to be between us—be it so.

† † †

"Our guest has glad tidings to share," said King Hrethel. "Tell them, Magister Beorn."

They were seated at the King's table in the Mead Hall: Hrethel,

Beorn, Ragmund, Herebeald, Haethcyn, and Hygelac. Mead had been poured, except for Hrethel who waved the servant away and drank water. Servants set the table with roasted pig, toasted rye bread topped with melted goats' cheese and steamed dill weed smothered in a mustard sauce.

"Yes," said Hrethel's oldest son, Herebeald. "Share these glad tidings."

"Let me guess," said the middle son, Haethcyn; "Magister Beorn has convinced our father-king to quit drinking spirits and no longer eat red meat."

"How would you know that?" said Herebeald.

"I have spies in the kitchen," said Haethcyn.

King Hrethel brought his fist down hard on the table.

"I'll not allow either of you to diminish the significance of this night with buffoonery. Forgive them, Magister Beorn. I have been lax raising my sons after the passing of their mother—except for my youngest."

"I take no affront," said the Schaman. "The news I bring is this: Beowulf Waegmunding is alive, living under the protection of Beanstan, King of the Sea Brondings."

"No better news have I heard then this, Magister Beorn," said Hygelac. "Tell us—how is he? Is my nephew in good health?"

"He's well, young Prince. So well that none of you would recognize him."

"Not so, Magister Beorn," said King Hrethel. "I'd know my grandson anywhere."

"Can you tell us how he escaped the Wylfings?" said Hygelac.

"I can indeed," said the Schaman. "Beowulf would have died had a she bear not interceded."

"What?" said Herebeald.

"A she bear?" said Haethcyn. "By all the gods—you can't be serious."

"He isn't," said Herebeald. "He's joking us."

"And a sick joke it is," said Haethcyn. "How dare you raise our father's hopes with such a terrible lie."

"Silence!" said Hrethel. "Both of you! Better still, I want you out of my presence. Now!"

Herebeald and Haethcyn slammed their cups on the table and left.

"Please forgive my brothers, Magister Beorn," said Hygelac, "for judging you falsely."

"No!" said Hrethel. "Don't forgive them, Magister Beorn. I won't. They think of nothing but drinking and whoring while waiting for me to die."

† † †

"Father's right about that," said Herebeald from where he and Haethcyn eavesdropped outside the arched entrance to the Mead Hall.

"Quiet brother," said Haethcyn. "Let's hear what else the old charlatan has to say."

† † †

"I must admit, Magister Beorn," said King Hrethel, "as much as I want to believe you I find your story hard to embrace. A she bear interceding in Vindinstedt Forest to save my grandson? Such a thing defies all reason."

"I understand, Great King but what's real can be stranger than our wildest imaginings."

"And after the she bear interceded, Magister Beorn," said Hygelac; "what then?"

"She taught Beowulf how to survive among the Forest Folk. Nursing on her milk, Beowulf acquired the ability to speak the Silent Tongue."

"The 'Silent Tongue'?" said Hrethel.

"It's how creatures on land and sea communicate—not just with their kind but with other creatures also."

"Tell us more, Magister Beorn," said Hygelac.

"As that summer passed and winter came, the she bear retired to her cave to sleep the Deep Sleep. It was then the All Mother sent me to take Beowulf north and look after him. Killing your daughter, Great King, was but a small taste to quench the Dark Queen's larger thirst for vengeance. To that end, Modryth hired assassins, the best her gold could buy. The first to find us was an Ostrogoth named Hathus. His Swamp Dog tracked Beowulf and me to my lodge at the Lake in the Clouds. Beowulf killed the Swamp Dog and mortally wounded the Goth. But others eventually came—Southlanders. Twenty of them. All but seven died to chase me and your grandson north. Those seven met their doom on the eastern slope of Mannen Mördare. I killed one, Beowulf killed six."

"My grandson is a child," said Hrethel, "no more than eleven winters young now—how could he possibly kill a Swamp Dog, let alone a Goth and six other capable warriors?"

"Beowulf is no longer a child, Great King, despite his tender age," said the Schaman.

"These tidings are beyond belief, Magister Beorn," said Hrethel.

"Truly they are," said Hygelac.

"I understand your reluctance to believe a word of what I've told you, but it's true—all of it."

"So tell us, Magister," said Hygelac; "how Beowulf came to become—my tongue can hardly say it—this thing you describe?"

"Do you believe in the gods, Great King?" said the Schaman.

"Yes. Of course."

"And you, Prince Hygelac—do you believe in the gods?"

"I don't know," he said. "I want to believe, but deep down... I cannot say if I believe, or not."

"Then, listen," said the Schaman, "and I'll tell you how the All Father's wife, Frigga, and Thor, Lightning Bringer, changed Beowulf from a child into what he has become."

"And what would that be, Magister Beorn?" said Hrethel.

"The greatest warrior in all of Midgard," said the Schaman.

40

WHERE VIPERS LIE

Still standing where they had secreted themselves outside the entrance to their father's Mead Hall, Haethcyn leaned close to Herebeald and whispered: "We need to talk, brother, but alone—without Hygelac present."

"I agree," said Herebeald.

They left the Citadel and walked to a Mead-House in the center of Falcon's Nest. They went there often to amuse themselves. For a small price, they could buy the privacy they wanted out of earshot of the servants and guards who reported to Ragmund for a wedge or two of silver or if the information was truly significant—a gold ring. It was how Ragmund kept his finger on the pulse of the Citadel and, for that matter, Falcon's Nest itself.

"Do you believe the Schaman, brother?" said Haethcyn. He kept his voice just above a whisper.

"Not a word of it," said Herebeald. "But this, I believe."

"What?" said Haethcyn.

"Father means to put Hygelac on the throne ahead of me—and you, too, for that matter."

"Can he do that?"

Herebeald cuffed Haethcyn alongside the head. "Of course he can you idiot. He's the bloody king. He can do whatever he wants."

"But you're the oldest," said Haethcyn. By right of succession the crown should go to you when he dies."

"Mark my words, Haethcyn, Hrethel will turn the throne over to Hygelac before he passes."

"Certain are you?" said Haethcyn.

"I'm bloody certain," said Herebeald. "I can see it in father's face. Think about it: when he wants something important done, he tells Hygelac to do it. And at night, when he can't sleep, does he send for one of us? No! He sends for Hygelac to keep him company."

"What are we to do?"

"I'll tell you what we can do," said Herebeald. "We can kill them. With the Wylfing ships, we now possess, added to what we already have, we can expand our borders and who's to stop us? With me as King, the Thunder-Geats can become the most powerful tribe in all Scandia."

"But killing them both—our flesh and blood?"

"Listen," said Herebeald. "It's them or us, brother. Either we act now, or we stay at the bottom of this dung heap."

"But how? We don't have a plan."

"I have a plan," said Herebeald. "It's in here." He tapped his head. "It's been in here for some time. Now, brother, what say we get a girl and have some fun?"

Prince Breca would not abandon his Longship, nor did he allow his men to board Beowulf's ship for the trip back to Beanstanbörg. He did allow the two ships to be tied together, which enabled Beowulf's vessel to tow the Sea Raven. Of help was the wind—it would be at their backs. All the while, Breca's men rowed and bailed water to keep the Sea Raven afloat.

After the two ships had reached the harbor and men secured the tie-lines to the dock, Breca supervised the job of getting the Sea Raven out of the water to make repairs. He and his men along with Beowulf's crew shook their heads as they examined the damage the Ondskas had inflicted.

Meanwhile, Beowulf told his men to do with the dead Ondskas whatever was called for, since he knew nothing about whaling, or what to do with the carcasses.

That done, Beowulf went to his lodge. He found a tub filled with hot water waiting.

Elin he told himself. *This bath is Elin's doing.*

Soaking in the water pleased and relaxed him and helped him gather his thoughts. So much had happened that day, Beowulf struggled to think through all that had taken place. Of one thing he was certain: he and Breca would remain at odds with each other as long as Breca thought himself the better man; which, given Beowulf's real age, caused Beowulf to laugh out loud.

As Beowulf ladled hot water over his head, he told himself: Breca is no better than me, though he thinks he is. The time is soon coming when I'll prove to him and everyone else who is stronger.

After his bath, Beowulf retired to his bed and fell into a deep sleep, so much so he never heard the door to his lodge open nor did he see Elin enter. When she knelt beside him and touched his arm, he opened his eyes and saw her looking at him.

"King Beanstan is honoring you with a feast tonight," said Elin. "He sent me to tell you."

"Honoring me for what?" said Beowulf.

"For what you did today on the Whale Road," said Elin. "It's the thing people are talking about."

"For killing the Ondskas?"

"Yes, and for saving Prince Breca and his men."

"Oh. That."

"Do you not want to go?" said Elin.

"Lady Elin, I'd rather sleep."

"Is that what you want me to tell King Beanstan? That you'd rather sleep?"

† † †

"To my amazement, Magister Beorn," said King Hrethel, "I don't miss red meat as much as I thought I would."

"Good," said the Schaman. "You just need to stay with this new diet. Remember two spoonfuls of vinegar, mixed with a cup of warm water, at bedtime. In no time at all your joints will feel better."

"I can't stop thinking about my nephew, Magister Beorn," said Hygelac. He looked at his father: "I can be on a ship to Bronding Land tomorrow and bring Beowulf home."

"I think it better he remains awhile with King Beanstan," said the Schaman. "There's no telling how many more assassins might be searching for him."

"But the Dark Queen is dead, Magister Beorn," said Hygelac. "So, too, is Amunwolf."

"Even so," said the Schaman; "we still don't know what pieces of Modryth's plan are still in play."

"I agree with Magister Beorn," said King Hrethel; "pains me though it does, now that we know my grandson is alive."

"I understand the pain it causes you, Great King," said the Schaman. "But better Beowulf remain there while I search for his father."

"When last we heard," said Hrethel, "Ecgtheow had left the land of the Spear Danes following his victory at the Bay of Kryl. He gifted me with twenty-four Wylfing Longships—"

"Twenty-seven Wylfing ships," said Hygelac, correcting his father.

"Oh, yes," said Hrethel; "twenty-seven Wylfing ships. Now he commands a Black Ship called the Avenger. Our spies tell us Ecgtheow preys on smugglers, Berserkers, and pirates, scuttling their ships and taking their chattels to sell at Land's End or in Frihamm."

"And the Whale road is a much safer place because of it," said Hygelac.

"My son-in-law will not be easy to find, Magister," said Hrethel.

"Tell us how we can assist you in your search," said Hygelac.

"Have your spies put the word out that I know the whereabouts of Ecgtheow Waegmunding's son. I will make my way south toward Land's End. Should Ecgtheow hear that he will come looking for me."

"When do you intend to resume your quest, Magister Beorn?" said Hrethel.

"At first light tomorrow, Great King," said the Schaman.

"My son will make certain you have a horse for your journey, Magister Beorn. May the All Father watch over you and speed you on your way."

"Many thanks, Great King," said the Schaman.

"Now, if you will excuse me," said the King. I need to rest my eyes."

† † †

After King Hrethel had retired for the night, Prince Hygelac took the Schaman aside: "How can we reward you for everything you've done, Magister?"

"You owe me nothing, young Prince. But guard your father well, for there are those who would do you both harm."

"What? How do you know this?" said Hygelac.

"I've seen it in a vision, Prince Hygelac. One more thing."

"Yes," said Hygelac.

"Soon you'll be King. So prepare yourself."

"What's that?" said Hygelac.

Hygelac felt the air go out of him, as though struck by a giant iron fist. The Schaman placed a hand on Hygelac's shoulder.

"We'll see each other again, young Prince."

† † †

Elin sat beside Beowulf at King Beanstan's table, across from the king and Breca.

"By the gods, Beowulf," said King Beanstan, "you have the whole city talking. What you did out there today is the stuff of legend."

Beowulf saw Breca staring at him the way the Sabre Tooth Forest Cat had, just before it sprang at him that day in the forest near the Lake in the Clouds. Breca averted his eyes.

"Thank you, Great King," said Beowulf. "Prince Breca and his warriors bore the brunt of the fight. They fought valiantly against the beasts. It was a sight to behold. It was because Prince Breca and his crew stood off the beasts that I had time to bring my ship around and take the Ondskas by surprise."

Breca's cheeks flushed crimson.

"Well, Breca?" said King Beanstan. "What say you?"

"Yes, Father King," said Breca. He took a quick sip of mead. "Beowulf tells it right."

Later, as the night wore on, and after jugglers finished juggling and drunken warriors wrestled to the amusement of all, a scop, or bard, to use the Common Tongue, entertained the throng in Beanstan's Hall. The bard sang of the fall of the House of Finn, a Frisian King who, while hosting guests from far off Daneland, was slaughtered by those self-same Spear Danes, along with his clansmen. His jewels and wife the Danes spirited across the Whale Road to Daneland.

Beowulf turned to Elin. "Strange, don't you think, to hear such a sad song sung during a time of celebration?"

Elin placed a hand on Beowulf's wrist and leaned close.

"The song of the fall of the House of Finn," said Elin, "is my uncle's sly way of reminding his Clan Chiefs that he knows his undoing could come at any time. And that it could be from any direction, at the hands of anyone—be they friends or enemies."

"Elin," said Beowulf; then he hesitated. He felt a lump at the back of his throat.

"Let's go outside," said Elin. "We need to talk, but not here."

† † †

They had walked but a short distance from King Beanstan's Mead Hall when Beowulf saw Elin tremble. He took his wolf cloak from his shoulders and wrapped it around her:

"Better?"

"Yes," she said. "Thank you for the kind words you spoke on Breca's behalf, deserved or not."

Breca stepped out of the shadows. "Oh, I deserved them, all right, and Beowulf knows I did."

"Is that why you followed us outside?" said Elin. "To remind us?"

"No," said Beowulf. "Breca followed us outside so he could tell me he's stronger and faster and in all ways a better man than me. Isn't that right, Prince Breca? In fact, there's a part of you that wishes you'd died today—rather that than have me save you and the Sea Raven."

"So, why not settle our differences once and for all," said Breca. "Agreed?"

"Agreed," said Beowulf.

"Tomorrow, then," said Breca. "Meet me at the waterfront at dawn."

They watched Breca walk off. When he was no longer in sight, Elin took hold of Beowulf and stood on her tip-toes. She kissed him hard on the lips. No sooner did she kiss him, she stepped back.

"I'm sorry," she said. "I shouldn't have done that."

"I'm sorry you're sorry," said Beowulf. "I enjoyed it."

"You did?"

"Yes."

"Have you never been kissed before?" said Elin.

"Not that way."

"No, of course not," Elin said. "I need to remind myself that—"

"That what?" said Beowulf. That I'm truly just a little boy?"

"No," said Elin. "That's not at all what I meant?"

"It isn't?"

"Well... perhaps. in part, it is, but I was thinking something else."

"What?" he said.

"I'm not sure Magister Beorn would approve of us—kissing."

"Beorn isn't here, and as long as I don't sheath my sword in you, I don't think he'd mind."

Stunned by Beowulf's directness, albeit softened by the innocent way in which he spoke, Elin's mouth dropped open.

"What?" said Beowulf. "Have I offended you?"

Elin laughed. "No," she said. "You haven't offended me—at least I don't think you have. It is what you said—about sheathing your sword inside me."

"Beorn warned me against doing it until the time is right," said Beowulf.

"I understand," said Elin. Again she laughed: "I've just never heard it said that way."

"It?" said Beowulf.

"Yes." she said. "It. Doing what you said!"

"Sword sheathing?"

"No, Beowulf. Love making."

"How do you make it?" he said.

"Me?" she said.

"Yes. You. I know how to make fire. I can make a bow, and

arrows to go with it. But how do you make love, when love is something you're supposed to feel—"

Beowulf placed the palm of one hand over Elin's heart. "Here," he said. "When you care for someone more than you care for yourself."

Elin was no longer laughing.

"Close your eyes," she said.

When he closed his eyes, Elin stood once more on her tip toes so she could reach his lips. As their lips met Beowulf enfolded her in his arms. He could feel her heart beating against his chest. When at last their mouths parted, and Elin's feet were flat on the ground, she said: "You can open your eyes now."

He looked at her and smiled.

"Before you think about sheathing your sword in me, Beowulf Waegmunding, we really, really, need to talk."

† † †

It was just after dawn, a half-league from King Hrethel's hunting lodge. While Prince Hygelac and a score of retainers made a commotion beating the brush to flush deer and boars from cover, Prince Haethcyn stared at his older brother, Herebeald, a few yards distant. While they waited for Hygelac they drank mead and traded insults; it was a game they relished and had since boyhood.

"When you were born," said Herebeald, "Father said if your pathetic little cock had been any smaller he would have named you, Hilda!"

Haethcyn belched. "Maybe, Haethcyn, but the best thing about you..."

"What, fat man, tell me," said Herebeald.

"Father said the best thing about you ran down our mother's leg."

"Ah! Good one, Haethcyn."

"It was," said Haethcyn.

"Guess what I'm going to do first, once I'm king?" said Herebeald.

"Why," said Haethcyn, "I doubt if you know, you bottomless piss pot."

"Soon as I'm king," said Herebeald, "I'll have you sent to the stables to shovel horse shite for the rest of your life."

"I believe you," said Haethcyn.

"Yes, believe it," said Herebeald, "now shut up before you scare the game away."

A moment passed in silence. The brothers could hear the retainers' drums beating closer while here and there small animals darted past in search of cover.

"Brother," said Haethcyn.

"Be quiet," said Herebeald. "Lest you scare the game away and Hygelac with them."

"But you're going to want to see this," said Haethcyn.

Herebeald turned around in time to see his brother draw his bow.

"What are you doing?" said Herebeald.

"This," said Haethcyn.

He let fly an arrow that entered Herebeald's left eye and passed through the back of his skull.

† † †

Hygelac found Haethcyn sitting on the ground, sobbing beside Herebeald's body.

"What have you done?" said Hygelac.

Haethcyn looked at Hygelac through bloodshot eyes. His cheeks were puffy, red, and stained with tears.

"It was an accident, brother," said Haethcyn. "By all the gods, I swear it was an accident."

† † †

After the news of Herebeald's death had reached the Citadel, Hrethel spent long hours alone throughout the day pacing on the wall-walk that ran the length of the Citadel's perimeter. Otherwise, the old king remained in his private chamber on his pallet, unable to sleep. After Herebeald's death, Hrethel seldom ate, and he drank water—nothing else.

No one other than Hygelac, Ragmund and Lord Magnus of the Guard were allowed into Hrethel's bed chamber, apart from the servants who came twice each day to empty his chamber pots and to bring food that, for the most part, went uneaten.

Ragmund entered the king's chamber just as Hygelac was leaving. He bowed to Hrethel's youngest son and received a curt nod in return. Ragmund went to the chair placed at Hrethel's bedside, sat, and took hold of the king's hand. He noted how frail it felt; not at all the hand that once wielded the Sword of Kings in battle.

"I'm here, Great King," said Ragmund.

Hrethel opened his eyes.

"Good," said the old king, "there's something I want you to do—but I want you to do it quietly."

"Of course," said Ragmund.

"One more thing," said Hrethel.

"Great King?"

"My son, Hygelac, is not to know—not ever!"

Not able to look his father in the eye, Haethcyn had remained at the hunting lodge. He was alone except for six female servants, all of them eager to please the new heir to the throne. Now his father stood between him and the Crown of Geatland—no one else. The thought of it made Haethcyn giddy.

Poison thought Haethcyn. Poison should do the trick. And who'll be the wiser? It 'll appear as though father died of a broken heart.

Ragmund arrived at the hunting lodge on horseback accompanied by three men he found in a back-alley Mead-House in Falcon's Nest. Before they left the city, Ragmund gave each of the three a leather purse filled with wedges of silver.

"You'll each get a second payment equal to the first," said Ragmund, "once you complete the task."

"Your orders, my Lord?" said one of the three.

"Be quick and be quiet about it," said Ragmund.

While Ragmund's three hirelings moved toward the front of the lodge, Ragmund dragged his crippled leg to the back yard. There he found Prince Haethcyn up to his neck in the hot tub, drunk.

Hearing the sound of feet shuffling Haethcyn turned and looked. He lowered a drinking horn from his mouth.

"Oh, it's just you, Ragmund," said Haethcyn, slurring his words. "I thought it might be Clotilda with more mead."

"No, great Prince," said Ragmund, "as you said, it's just me."

Haethcyn belched and looked away. "Did father send you?"

"Yes," said Ragmund.

"Well," said Haethcyn, "get on with it. What does the old man have to say?"

From one sleeve of his over-shirt, Ragmund let slip a butcher knife he borrowed from the king's kitchen. Pulling back on Haethcyn's head by the hair, Ragmund drew the edge of the blade from ear to ear, almost severing the prince's head from his shoulders. Soon after, Ragmund heard the short-lived screams of the women inside the lodge.

Ragmund invited his hirelings to help themselves to as much food and drink as they wanted.

"I know where there's a keg of very special mead," Ragmund said. "Go ahead, enjoy yourselves, I'll be right back with it."

"You do that, my Lord," said one of his hirelings.

The poison Ragmund mixed with the mead did its work in less time than he anticipated. Task completed, Ragmund remained at the lodge overnight, eating, drinking and relishing his time away from Hrethel and his duties at the Citadel.

The sight of the lodge going up in flames warmed Ragmund's heart as he returned to Falcon's Nest the next morning.

41

LASHING OF THE TIDES

"Are you mad?" said Elin. "A storm is brewing. What does it prove if you both drown? Look! The clouds should convince you —Aegir and Rán are arguing again. See for yourselves, you halfwits! Besides, those two rowboats you plan to use are laughable; they'll break apart before you reach the mouth of the breakwater."

"Those two laughable boats will be perfect for a rowing contest," said Breca.

Breca clapped his hands. Brum stepped forward holding a long-sleeve shirt of forged, hand-ringed chainmail armor. Brum gave Beowulf that piece of battle gear.

"My Grandfather on my mother's side was a great warrior," said Breca. "He was a tall man like you, Beowulf. It should fit you perfectly."

"Thank you. But why are we wearing armor?"

"In case we're attacked by Ondskas," said Breca. "Or Great Whites. It doesn't hurt to prepare. Or don't you agree?"

Beowulf tested the weight of the shirt: "If you go into the water, the weight of your body armor will drag you to the bottom."

"Most definitely," said Breca, with a wide grin. "So I suggest neither of us falls out of our boats."

"It wasn't me I was talking about when I said it would drag you to the bottom. I can wear it and still swim."

"Balls!" said Breca. "You're strong; I'll give you that, but not stronger than me."

"Are you trying to frighten me, Prince Breca? Or maybe you think I'll be so terrified by the thought of being out there in these tiny boats among man-killers I won't want to go?"

Breca shrugged his shoulders but didn't reply.

"Do you hear yourselves?" said Elin. "Two silly boys having a spat over nothing, rather than two young men bonding as friends—as equals."

"Enough, Elin," said Breca. "Beowulf's been warned. He knows the risks. If he wants, he can withdraw from the contest."

"If your father knew about this he'd be furious—with both of you."

"Which is why I gave the Laplander girl a gold ring to keep him occupied throughout the morning." said Breca.

"If the two of you think I'm going to wait here," said Elin, "wringing my hands with worry, you're wrong. I'm going inside where it's warm and wait-out the storm."

"So, go!" said Breca. "No one's forcing you to stay and watch me win."

Elin looked at Beowulf with eyes that implored him to stay ashore.

"I'll be fine, Elin," said Beowulf. "I promise."

"What good's a promise if you're dead?" she said.

Beowulf saw tears forming in her eyes before she turned and with several of her girlfriends departed.

"Now you've done it," said Breca. He grinned. "You've made my cousin cry."

"Let's get this over with," said Beowulf. He breathed a full breath and exhaled as if by doing so he could dispel his anger.

† † †

The chainmail armor fitted him well and hung to mid-thigh. Beowulf cinched his leather belt and positioned his knife, Tooth, in its tooled leather sheath on his left hip. He watched one of Breca's men place a sword and spear into Breca's boat.

"I thought this was to be a rowing contest?" said Beowulf, so that Breca would hear.

Breca looked at him, and shrugged: "Hope for the best but prepare for the worst."

"I did," said Beowulf. He patted the sheath containing Tooth.

Breca laughed. "So you have. Anything else you want to take?"

Beowulf looked around. "Yes," he said and walked to where there was an empty wooden bucket. He picked it up and handed it to Brum.

"Put the bucket in my boat, Brum."

Brum looked at the bucket; then at Prince Breca. Breca nodded. Brum laughed and put the bucket into Beowulf's boat.

"Anything else?" said Breca.

"Yes," said Beowulf. "What must I do to win?"

"Quite a sense of humor you have, Prince Beowulf."

"Not really. That 'smelly old man' who brought me here says I need to work on it."

"Well," said Breca; "be that as it may, the winner must row past the breakwater and out of the bay," said Breca; "then he must be the first to return. Understand?"

"Understood," said Beowulf.

"Then let's get to it," said Breca.

† † †

Breca and Beowulf descended stairs leading down off the waterfront to a landing where Brum tethered two rowboats. Brum and several Bronding warriors were there to help steady the boats as Beowulf, and Breca climbed aboard.

Beowulf and Breca centered themselves and took-up oars.

"Ready, Prince Beowulf," said Breca.

Beowulf nodded.

"All right, lads," said Breca. "Push us off, and we'll be on our way."

Brum and the men with him untied the tethers and gave each boat a shove. Without hesitation, Breca rowed toward the breakwater. Beowulf sat still and watched the way Breca worked his oars.

His right arm is the stronger, Beowulf told himself. *To stay on course, Breca will have to work his left arm harder.*

Breca was twenty yards ahead when Beowulf first dipped oars in the water.

Standing on the landing, Brum watched the wind banners flapping toward shore. He turned to the men standing with him: "Bad enough the current's against them; they'll have the wind pushing them back, from here to the breakwater."

The breakwater at the mouth of the bay was a league away. The Sea Brondings had built it over a span of ten summers after Beanstan had become king and renamed the capital to Beanstanbörg. He did this to honor himself and efface the memory of the previous king.

One, two, three, pull! Beowulf told himself. It was a slow cadence, and he rowed with deep, deliberate strokes.

They had traveled about a quarter-league when the water became choppy. Beowulf looked at the horizon, at the billowing black mass of clouds moving inland, accompanied by intermittent streaks of lightning and rolling thunder.

There's no way Beowulf told himself Breca can beat the storm.

Breca was thirty yards ahead of Beowulf when he stopped, looked back and grinned.

"Had enough yet?"

"No," said Beowulf. "Have you?"

"Hah!" said Breca. "You wish it was so."

"Not at all, said Beowulf. "I'm enjoying this."

"Are you now?" said Breca.

"I am. Feels good to stretch my arms."

Breca resumed rowing, but it was toward Beowulf.

"Listen, Breca. See the storm coming? We can go on with this game of yours, but I'm telling you, we should both turn back—now."

Breca laughed. "You're a Thunder Geat. You should feel at home in the middle of a storm."

Breca rowed around Beowulf.

"I could do this all day," said Breca.

"Listen," said Beowulf. "Your left arm is tiring. I can tell by the way your boat pulls to the right. You have overworked it. There's no shame if we turn around now. We can have this stupid contest another day—when the weather's right for it. What say you?"

"I say you're afraid to go on. That's what I say, Beowulf Waegmunding."

"Very well. You leave me no choice," said Beowulf.

"Hah," said Breca. "So you're going back, are you?" *Yes, Beowulf. By all the gods, turn around* thought Breca. *Go back! You were right. My left arm is tiring. And the storm's coming faster than I guessed it would. Elin was right. But I'll not quit, not unless you do.*

One, two, three pull! Beowulf repeated to himself while increasing the cadence, rowing faster and faster until his arms and oars were a blur.

When Breca looked over his shoulder and saw Beowulf but a few yards away, his mouth dropped in disbelief. As Beowulf drew abreast of Breca, he looked Breca in the eye and said: “Don’t say I didn’t warn you.”

Wait!” said Breca.

Beowulf passed Breca. Faster and faster he rowed; doubling, trebling, ever increasing the distance twixt him and the Prince of the Sea Brondings. Beowulf heard Breca call out loud as he could muster:

“Who are you?” said Breca. “What are you?”

Beowulf turned his face out of the wind so Breca would hear him: “I don’t know,” said Beowulf.

Breca stopped rowing and watched as Beowulf continued toward the breakwater leaving Breca further and further behind.

“You’re not a man,” said Breca, straining his voice. “I don’t know what you are—but you’re not a man.”

Breca’s words were carried off by the wind. Beowulf heard not a sound but the slapping of the waves against his boat.

† † †

By the time Breca reached the breakwater Beowulf was there, waiting, rowing against the current to maintain a static position; but now the storm was on them, darkening the sky, pelting the ocean with rain. Lightning streaked above them accompanied by successive peels of thunder. Conjured by the tempest, waves began to smash against the breakwater, rocking and lifting both boats.

Breca rowed alongside Beowulf. “By all the gods,” said Breca; “what are you doing waiting here? Why didn’t you return to shore?”

“I wasn’t going to leave you out here alone, Breca.”

Though the distance between their boats was small, they needed to shout to make themselves heard.

“Well, that was stupid.” Breca glanced skyward. “You could’ve

beaten the storm to shore the way you were rowing."
"I know."
Breca lowered his head and took several deep breaths and looked at Beowulf.
"We're in it now," he said.
"Yes."
"What do you suggest we do?"
"Lash our boats together and try to row back," said Beowulf.
"And if we can't row back?"
"Try to ride out the storm until it passes."
Breca laughed.
"Why are you laughing," said Beowulf.
"That's some argument, Agar and Rán are having—ay?"
"Yes."
"I've no rope with me. Have you?"
"No."
Beowulf extended an oar.
"Grab it, Breca. I'll pull you over. That way we can stay together. We just need to outlast the storm—remember?"
"Right," said Breca.
Breca grabbed the oar with both hands. Beowulf pulled the boats together while waves jostled and pummeled them.

† † †

There was no reckoning whether it was day or night. There was the darkness of the storm and nothing more.
For the longest time, Beowulf and Breca sat in their boats without speaking; until Breca laughed and looked at Beowulf: "At least we won't die of thirst," said Breca.
"We're not going to die. Just hold on. Talk to me."
"About what?" said Breca.
"About anything."
"I don't know if I can hold on much longer," said Breca.
"Don't talk that way, and don't let go—we can beat the storm!"
"I'm sorry, Beowulf."
"Sorry for what?"
"For treating you as I have."

"Save your breath—for my part, it's done and over with."

"Listen," said Breca. "Save yourself. It may be my fate to drown. Not yours. I don't believe there's anyone or anything that can kill you."

"Listen, Breca. We're going to get through this. The two of us—together."

Breca laughed. "My boat's taking on more water."

"So is mine," said Beowulf. "I've got a bucket. I'll toss it over."

"Why didn't I think of that?" said Breca. "I have a spear. I have a sword. I have armor that'll sink me to the bottom. And what do you bring? A knife and a bucket."

Beowulf tossed the bucket into Breca's boat.

"I'll have to let go of the oar."

"Do it," said Beowulf. "I'll grip the side of your boat while you bail."

"What about the water in your boat?"

"Just bail!"

Beowulf got on his knees and gripped the side of Breca's boat. The wood was slippery. He tightened his grip and watched Breca bail bucket after bucket of water from his tiny vessel. Breca tossed the bucket into Beowulf's boat.

"Now you do the same," said Breca.

Gripping the side of Breca's boat with one hand, Beowulf bailed water from his vessel.

† † †

For five days and nights, the storm tossed Beowulf and Breca on the waves, assailing them with all its fury. And for those five days, they never saw nor felt the warmth of the sun. There was just the wet, freezing darkness illuminated by lightning, and followed by the deafening sound of thunder.

"I can't do this anymore, Beowulf," said Breca. "My strength is spent. All I want to do is close my eyes and sleep."

"Don't quit on me, Breca. We'll get through this."

It was then that Breca's vessel came apart and water poured in.

"Beowulf!"

"I see it. Toss the bucket over; then give me your hand."

Breca flung the bucket into Beowulf's boat then extended his arm. Beowulf released his grip on the side of Breca's vessel as it sank underwater. He grabbed Breca's forearm and dragged him into his boat.

The exposure to the salt water made their eyes sting as they both sat there staring at each other.

"Forgive me, Beowulf."

"For what?"

"I shat and pissed myself."

"So did I," said Beowulf.

"Good," said Breca.

"What's good about it?"

"I was beginning to think you're some thing that neither shat nor pissed."

"Whatever our differences, Breca, I'm the same as you. I shite and piss the same. I bleed the same, and one day I'll die the same as you—but not today."

"Look, Beowulf," said Breca. "With me in your boat, we're taking on more water. I'm sinking us."

"No, Breca. The storm is drowning us. Listen. If I get out, can you summon the strength to bail?"

"Get out? Are you crazed?"

"Can you bail?"

"Yes, by the gods, I can bail."

Beowulf slipped over the side, into the water. He gripped the boat until the force of the wind and waves wrenched it from his grip, and carried it, along with Prince Breca, away.

"Beowulf!" said Breca, over and over.

Breca shouting his name was the last thing Beowulf heard as the boat and Breca disappeared into the darkness.

42

FINNS & TROLLS

Beowulf tread water and watched as the waves carried away the boat with Breca aboard. Breca was shouting Beowulf's name with all the strength he could muster. Soon, there was nothing more than the sound of the sea and the storm that filled Beowulf's ears.

† † †

Beorn's eyes opened wide. His vision of Beowulf in a dark, perilous place left him shaken. He pushed himself into a sitting position beside his campfire. Nearby, the horse Prince Hygelac provided him snorted.

"You'll have your breakfast when it's light, my friend," said the Schaman. *"But right now I've got to clear my head and think."*

As he was thinking Beorn heard an owl hooting in the branches of the tree above him.

"Friend Owl," said the Schaman. *"Forgive me for interrupting your song. I am Beorn, servant of the All Mother, and I ask a great favor of you—one I cannot repay except with a word of thanks."*

"You need but ask, servant of the All Mother. We Forest Folk and Sky Dwellers know you well."

"I seek knowledge of the Manling, the bear's son. I believe he is lost and in great peril. I must find out where he is."

"I will do my best to spread the word," said the owl. *And with that, it flew away.*

† † †

It was his sixth day adrift when the storm continued past on its way inland. As the twilight gave way to dawn, Beowulf rejoiced when his eyes beheld the sun rising over the sea. The screech of a seagull circling above drew Beowulf's swollen burning eyes upward, and he called to it:

"Greetings, sea bird."

"Are you a seal. If so, you have a funny head."

"No, I'm not a seal."

"Are you some other kind of water creature?" said the gull.

"No, sea bird. I'm a Land Swimmer. My name is Beowulf."

"Well, why aren't you on land? Why are you here?"

"The storm carried me here. I'm trying to reach land."

"Well, you have a distance to go, but if you travel in the direction from which the great fire rises each day, you might reach land."

"Thank you, friend sea bird. It would be of great help to me if you would spread the word to your brethren on land that I'm here."

"What would you have me tell them?" said the gull.

"Tell them the bear's son asks that they send word to the All Mother's servant, a Schaman known as, Beorn. Ask them to tell him where you last saw me. Would you do that?"

"What do I get in return?" said the gull.

"I'm sorry, sea bird. I don't know what I can give you."

"Your head," said the gull.

"My head?"

"I've been a long time out at sea and must rest. Let me rest on your head."

"Very well," said Beowulf.

"You won't try to eat me, will you?" said the gull.

"No. You have my promise: I won't try to eat you."

The sea gull alighted on Beowulf's head with a loud screech and sat.

† † †

The sun was well above the horizon when the seagull screeched and flew upward.

"I will pass along your message, bear's son, but I don't think it will do much good."

"Why not?" said Beowulf.

"Because I fear a hag will soon eat you," said the gull.

"What?"

"Turn around," said the gull, *"Look!"*

Beowulf turned and saw it: a large, dark, triangular shaped dorsal fin slicing through the water in his direction.

"I think I'll wait," said the gull.

"If you're thinking about eating what's left of me, forget it," said Beowulf. "I haven't come this far to be food for sea wolves or sea birds."

"What's coming for you is more than an ordinary fish," said the gull. *"And there will be others coming once they smell your blood in the water."*

Beowulf felt his heart quicken its beat. The exhaustion he felt moments before vanished. His eyes stung, but his vision was keen. He drew Tooth from its sheath and waited as the creature came for him.

Closer it came until it was almost on him. Beowulf could see its dark, lifeless eyes stare at him and its mouth open wide as it rolled to one side to make its bite. Was then that Beowulf pushed himself down into the water. As the hag, or shark in the Common Tongue, passed over, Beowulf thrust his knife into its belly. The creature's momentum propelled it forward against the blade allowing Beowulf's knife to make a long deep gash, spilling the hag's blood, exposing its entrails.

† † †

It wasn't long before others came, more black-finned sharp toothed creatures drawn by the blood Beowulf spilled. They tore the carcass of the dead sea wolf into shreds, devouring great chunks of flesh with each bite. The seagull did indeed make a meal from the fleshy morsels that rose to the surface and lingered there. The blood in the water drove the creatures into a feeding frenzy, and their attention fixed on Beowulf.

"I am Beowulf Waegmunding, son of Ecgtheow, known by the forest folk as the bear's son. Do not think I will be so easy to kill. I am at home in water, just as on land."

They circled Beowulf until one bit at his arm. The chainmail shirt he wore would not permit the creature to sink its teeth deep into his arm and rip away his flesh. Again and again, Beowulf stabbed and each time Tooth found its mark—this time in the creature's eyes and gills. Beowulf watched it sink from sight before he surfaced for air.

Six more creatures came at Beowulf. Tooth dealt each a similar fate.

"I wouldn't believe had I not seen it, bear's son," said the gull.

"Can you see any more of them?" said Beowulf.

From on high the seagull searched the surface of the water but saw no fins approaching.

"I see nothing—nothing but water," said the gull. *"I'll be leaving now."*

"And the favor I seek from you?"

"Don't worry, Bear's Son, I'll fulfill my part of the bargain."

"Good hunting," said Beowulf.

"Good hunting," said the gull.

† † †

The sun was straight overhead. Beowulf continued to tread water. Now and then he would rest his swollen red eyes. And yet, even though they stung from the salt water his vision remained intact.

Beowulf felt something glide past below him, just under his boots. He ducked underwater. Was then that he saw the great black and white patches of an Ondska far larger than the seven he killed. This assassin of the Whale Road circled Beowulf, then lifted its head out of the water.

"Would you be the land swimmer who killed my seven brothers and sisters?" said the Ondska.

"Yes," said Beowulf.

"Then know I am going to eat you, Land Swimmer, bite by bite; one for each of my brothers and sisters you killed. But I will wait a short while. I want you to feel the dread—knowing your fate in advance. I want you to feel terror before I slowly tear you apart."

"Great Ondska," said Beowulf, *"I am too weary and too hungry to feel anything more than anger. Anger that I'm here. I am angry that I didn't listen to Elin, who warned me against leaving the land in the face of the storm. Angry that I was forced to kill more ocean folk to survive. Angry that my kind is trying to kill me. So no more talk. But know this, Great Ondska, I have not suffered all I have suffered, to die here."*

"You have quite a mouth, Land Swimmer, but not like mine. You have no teeth like me. You lack my size, my strength."

"No more talk," said Beowulf, *"Come!"*

The Ondska came straight on. Beowulf took a deep breath and submerged. The creature rolled to one side and seized Beowulf around his torso. Once more his chainmail shirt proved its worth and kept the Ondska's teeth—each a small dagger—from penetrating Beowulf's flesh. The force and power of its jaws clamping down on him was violent, the pain intense. The beast dragged Beowulf down deep into the water. The sea creatures that lived there, those that were not frightened off, watched the spectacle. Beowulf drove Tooth into the Ondska's snout and one of its eyes. It was that final strike that allowed the bear's son to prevail.

† † †

It was still daylight when Beowulf felt something scoop him onto its back. It was the mother Blue Whale, accompanied by her calf.

"Do not fear, Land Swimmer. I will see you safely to shore."

Beowulf sheathed Tooth and extended his arms. He felt carried by the wind, lulled by songs the mother whale and her calf sung. Beowulf soon fell into unconsciousness on that creature's back and slept, a long, dreamless sleep.

Numb with cold and fatigue Beowulf woke to the sound of waves lapping on the shore and sea birds screeching. As his eyes opened and began to focus, he found himself on a wide expanse of beach at low tide with the sun overhead, burning its way through a layer of fog. Tangled around Beowulf's arms and legs were long slimy tendrils of brown and green kelp—what fishing folk call sea weed. From nearby he heard the sound of children giggling and whispering. Once he had untangled several strands of kelp from his arms and pushed himself to his knees, he saw a cluster of children —twelve in all, their ages ranging from five to ten winters young.

Beowulf struggled to his knees. As he did, the children ceased giggling and whispering. They stepped back several yards for they saw Tooth in its sheath, where it rested off Beowulf's left hip.

"Please," said Beowulf, "Don't be afraid. I won't hurt you. I have been adrift at sea. Tell me—what land is this?"

"Finn's land," said a boy who appeared to be the oldest.

"Then I have drifted north. I come from the land of the Sea Brondings," said Beowulf.

"We see their ships from time to time when they come to hunt seals."

"That's good to hear," said Beowulf. "Is your village close? I'm hungry and thirsty."

"It's not far from here," said the boy.

The sound of someone blowing a ram's horn in the distance reached out and grabbed the children's attention. The children's eyes widened; fear showed on their faces.

"We have to go," said the boy.

The children ran toward dunes that marked the end of the beach.

"Wait," said Beowulf. "What's happening? Why must you leave?"

"Troggolls," said the boy.

Beowulf stood there and watched the children climb the dunes to the other side and vanish from sight.

Beowulf started walking in the same direction as the children.

"How strange it feels he thought*, to be walking on land again.*

Beowulf soon came to a village. Twenty huts formed a circle; in the center of which was the common area, and a well for drawing-water. There was one other structure round in shape but much larger than any of the huts. The villagers had built it of stone, and it had no windows. The entrance to it was a door of solid oak banded with iron. Tethered to an iron stake near the well was a goat. The village appeared deserted as Beowulf entered. He saw neither man, woman nor any of the children he had seen on the beach, just the goat that stared at him and munched straw.

"Tell me, friend goat," said Beowulf, *"where are the villagers?"*

"In there," said the goat. The goat turned toward the stone building.

"All of them?" said Beowulf.

"All of them," said the goat.

"But, why? What are they doing?"

"Hiding," said the goat.

"From me?"

"No."

"So tell me why they're hiding."

"Troggolls," said the goat.

"Troggolls?"

"Yes," said the goat. *"Which is why I'm here and not in my pen."*

"I don't understand," said Beowulf.

"The Troggolls spare your kind as long as the village people give them something else to eat. Today it's me."

"You appear to be handling it well," said Beowulf.

"I won't be handling it well," said the goat, *"when a Troggoll gets here."*

"Why don't the villagers fight them?"

"Fight the Troggolls?"

"Yes—fight the Troggolls."

"That would be madness. Have you ever seen one?"

"Never," said Beowulf.

"Well," said the goat, *"they're bigger than you, with pond-scum skin, long sharp teeth and one eye in the middle of their head."*

"I want to meet one," said Beowulf.

"You're joking," said the goat.

"Not at all. Mind if I wait here with you?"

"You would do that?"

"Yes," said Beowulf. "But I'm hungry."

"The villagers left me some grass to eat." said the goat. *"I'll share it with you."*

"They left the grass for you to eat while you wait for a Troggoll to eat you?"

"Yes," said the goat. *"It was thoughtful of the villagers to do that, don't you think?"*

"No, friend goat, that's not what I think."

† † †

While he waited, Beowulf decided to look in the huts of the villagers for something to eat.

He returned to where the goat waited. In his hands, he held a wheel of salted goat's cheese, a loaf of rye bread, boiled turnips, and a roasted chicken. Beowulf sat beside the goat.

"*I'll share this with you,"* said Beowulf.

"Gladly will I partake," said the goat, *"of all but the hen; I knew her when she still had feathers."*

"I understand," said Beowulf.

When he finished eating, Beowulf drew a bucket of water from the well and poured half of it over his head and drank the rest.

The goat bleated: *"It's coming."*

The Troggoll was just as the goat described; he stood two heads taller than Beowulf and was broad around the middle, like an old oak. With each ponderous step it took, the ground beneath its feet shook.

Beowulf stood in front of the goat and held his hands out to his sides as a showing of peace.

"Why are you not hiding in the stone house with the others?" said the Troggoll.

"Because," said Beowulf; *"I have never seen a Troggoll before."*

"Is that so?"

"It is."

"We prefer the name: Trolls," said the Troggoll.

"No matter," said Beowulf. *"Whatever name you go by you're the ugliest creature I've ever seen."*

Taken by surprise the Troggoll's mouth fell open.

"You're nothing special to look at Manlings—your kind is ugly to us, you're puny, weak and hideous with your two beady little eyes. And now I'm in the mood to kill you."

"That is most unfortunate," said Beowulf.

"You're not from this village, are you Manlings?"

"No," said Beowulf, *"I'm a Thunder-Geat. My home is far to the south."*

"Well, Thunder-Geat, you're standing between me and my family's supper. Prepare to die."

"If you mean to eat the goat, you can't have him."

"Why not?"

"Because he and I have become friends."

"Then I'm going to kill you both," said the Troggoll. *"And tonight my family will gnaw the flesh from your bones, same as the goat."*

"I'm sorry," said Beowulf, *"but I won't let that happen."*

"Stop me," said the Troggoll.

"I will."

The words had no sooner left Beowulf's mouth when he drew his knife and hurled it full-force at the Troggoll. Tooth found its mark in the creature's eye. The Troggoll bellowed and started to reach for the knife; then its hand dropped to its side. It teetered on its thick legs before its knees buckled and it fell over, onto its back —dead. Beowulf untied the goat.

"Go back to your pen, friend goat."

"Gladly," said the goat. *"But first tell me how others call you."*

"I'm Beowulf Waegmunding—the bear's son."

43

TRICKS & SPIRITS

Beowulf retrieved his knife from the eye of the Troggoll just as villagers filed out of the stone house. Their mouths were agape with amazement at the sight that greeted them.

"What have you done, stranger?" said one of the villagers, horrified by the sight of the dead creature.

"I've rid your village of one of the monsters who afflict you."

"That's terrible," said another villager. "Now they'll come looking for him when he fails to return with our offering."

"Terrible," said a villager.

"We're doomed," said another. "The stranger has brought ruin upon our heads."

"Why do you not fight them?" said Beowulf.

"We are peaceful folk, stranger—farmers, not warriors. We will have to abandon our village now because of what you've done."

"I'm sorry," said Beowulf.

"Sorry won't change a thing," said a villager.

"No," said another, "it won't change a thing—you have doomed us!"

"And if I were to rid you of the Troggolls, altogether—what then?"

The villagers exchanged looks among themselves as they pondered Beowulf's question.

"Well," said one of the villagers. "I suppose we wouldn't be doomed."

"And we wouldn't have to abandon our homes," said another.

"Very well," said Beowulf; "tell me where they live and I will do my best to put things right."

"The Troggolls have a nest underground. Inside a barrow that holds the body of a great warrior, along with treasure buried with him. But that was long ago."

"Have you any beer or mead?" said Beowulf.

† † †

Following directions provided by the villagers, and with a barrel of mead over one shoulder, Beowulf arrived at the barrow. From a distance, it resembled a mound of dirt covered with winter grass. The bleached bones of many creatures lie scattered around. An unpleasant smell rose with smoke through a hole on top of the mound, a hole by which the Troggolls ventilated their nest.

Beowulf placed the barrel on the ground and climbed on top of the barrow. He gathered a bunch of winter grass and placed it over the smoke-hole, sealing it, trapping the smoke inside. That done, he climbed down and seated himself on top of the barrel and waited.

Six male and female Troggolls came out of the barrow coughing and choking, each rubbing their one eye, red and moist with tears. When they stopped coughing and recovered their breath, they took notice of Beowulf sitting on the barrel near the entrance to the barrow.

"*Who are you*?" said one of the Troggolls.

"*No one of consequence*," said Beowulf.

"*That's a strange name*," said one of the Troggolls.

"*Why are you here*?" said another Troggoll.

"*I was asked by one of your kind to bring you this,*" said Beowulf. He stood and pointed to the barrel.

"*That would be Grogg*," said another Troggoll. "*Why did he not bring it himself*?"

"*I don't know,*" said Beowulf. *"He's still drinking the same stuff as what's in this barrel. He didn't want you to have to wait, so he sent me on ahead with more of the same. He should be here shortly with a fattened goat for your supper.*"

"*What is it called*?" said a Troggoll. "*The stuff you bring*."

"*Mead*," said Beowulf, as he punched a hole in the top of the barrel.

"*Mead?*" said a Troggoll.

"Yes," said Beowulf. *"also known as the nectar of the gods. Please, great Troggolls—try some.*"

"Some?" said a Troggoll. "We'll have all of it, and we prefer to be called 'Trolls,' not Troggolls."

"*And then*," said another, "*We might just eat you, Manling, if Grogg doesn't return soon.*"

"*I take it you want me to stay and wait*?" said Beowulf.

"*Of course*," said a Troggoll.

One after another the Troggolls lifted the barrel and filled their mouths with mead. Soon they were belching and laughing and knocking their heads together. It was a Troggoll custom when showing affection. They drank and drank until the barrel was dry; then, one by one they fell asleep.

Beowulf returned to the barrel and sat there as the sun dropped low in the sky. When all there was to hear was snoring and farting, Beowulf unsheathed Tooth and cut their throats. Without waiting for the Troggolls to bleed-out, Beowulf entered the barrow.

Torch in hand, Beowulf walked into the far recesses of the barrow, beyond what the Troggolls used as their dwelling. There, on a slab of granite, was a skeleton housed in dusty armor—a warrior-Lord who passed in fierce battle with Lapp Landers many winters before. As Beowulf stood looking at the warrior's remains, two objects caught his eye: the first was a well-made helm of bronze, with a silver eagle above the nose guard; the second was a spear made of ash and iron. The spear was long and tapered—one side was serrated for cutting through bone, and smooth and sharp on the other for deep penetration. Beowulf cleaned the dust and cobwebs from both helm and spear.

"I claim this helm and spear as my own, and I pledge to the spirit of the warrior who wore this gear, that I will honor it always."

By the time Beowulf returned to the village the sun was setting. When the villagers saw him, they cheered and ran to greet him.

"The Troggolls?" asked a villager.

"Dead," replied Beowulf. "And now I want to bathe."

"Of course," said a villager. "And why you bathe we'll prepare a feast, young Lord. You have freed us forever from the Troggolls."

Village folk prepared a bath in one of the huts. Beowulf was left alone there to luxuriate in the tub filled with hot water.

When he reemerged from the hut to join the villagers in the common area, he found tables and benches placed around, and a fire pit dug for roasting the main course. Beowulf felt relaxed and pleased with his accomplishments that day. He looked forward to the feast the villagers prepared. He looked around for his four-legged friend.

"The goat I freed from its tether—where is he?"

A villager pointed to the animal on the spit.

"We're cooking it."

44

JOURNEY TO THE HEART

Ecgtheow anchored the Avenger in a cove sheltered from the wind; the water was waist-high and calm.

When Turin and the other boys returned with fresh water and small game for their supper they found Ecgtheow standing near the mast looking into the sky. The lads' eyes turned skyward, and they saw a seabird circling above their foster father, a scarce few feet from the top of the Avenger's mast.

"Is all well, Foster Father?" said Turin.

"I'm not sure, Turin," said Ecgtheow. "The Seabird you see above us has been circling overhead since you lads went ashore. It circles, then it starts away west, then returns and circles and, there! Watch!"

The boys watched the seabird start away west, then return and resume circling.

"What does it mean, Foster Father?"

"Maybe something. Maybe nothing. But my gut tells me someone or something summons me into the west."

Ecgtheow looked at the boys: "Pull up the anchor and make ready to leave. We're going to follow the bird."

† † †

Beowulf awoke at dawn on a comfortable bed of grass. Forsaking the villagers' celebration the night before he helped himself to a water-bag, made from a cured sheep's stomach, a loaf of rye bread, and a container of lingonberry jam. Beowulf sat there watching the sun rise. As he ate, he thought of Handscio, for that had been one of their favorite past-times: sitting together in front of a fire, watching the flames dance while munching bread spread with Lingonberry jam.

I miss you, Handscio. I miss the fun we had together. So much has happened and it seems so long since last we played or sat eating bread and jam. I do not know if you would recognize me now. I hardly know myself. I have been living with others much older than me who think me older than I am. The funny part is, I do feel older than my age by far. Oh, Handscio, I miss you, cousin. I miss us.

Once he finished breakfast, such as it was, Beowulf walked south, following the coastline. On his head, he wore the helm he took from the barrow, and in one hand he carried the spear made from ash-wood and iron.

† † †

"*I bring news from Kungörn, Lord of Eagles*," said the Falcon.

"*You have my thanks*," said the Schaman.

"*The Manlings whose whereabouts you seek, the one Forest Folk call the bear's son, has been seen alive and unharmed in Finn's Land.*"

"*Praise to the All Mother*," said the Schaman. "*This is good news you bring, Friend Falcon. Give the Eagle Lord my thanks when next you see him.*"

"*I will*," said the Falcon. "*Good hunting.*"

"*Good Hunting*," said the Schaman.

The Schaman took up his staff and began walking south. "This is indeed a glorious day."

Prince Hygelac entered his father's Throne Room accompanied by a beautiful young woman, wise beyond her age, slender in form, with kind eyes, and goodwill in her heart. Her name was Hygd.

Hrethel looked away from Ragmund with whom he'd been conversing.

"Who is this beautiful flower you bring before me, my son?" said Hrethel.

"Father King," said Hygelac, "this is Hygd. I wish to make her my wife."

While Turin and his brothers outfitted the Avenger and scrubbed the ship's planks clean, Ecgtheow made his way from the dock at Land's End to town. For a reason he could not fathom, he felt his feet guided through the streets and twisting alleys until he arrived at a Mead-House called the Whale's Tale.

The area looked deserted, and there was no one waiting outside the entrance. Ecgtheow paused. No sounds came from inside the tavern. Ecgtheow gripped the hilt of his sword, brushed the curtain aside and entered. The Mead-House was dark, and deserted, but for the house keeper behind the counter, and a large, bearded man. He was sitting by himself at a table in a darkened corner.

"I've been waiting for you, Ecgtheow Waegmunding," said the man in the shadows.

† † †

For twenty-one days and nights, Beowulf walked south along the coast. He passed from village to village unmolested, and unchallenged. All that came his way were curious stares from the strangers Beowulf encountered. He saw his reflection in the water of a stream. He looked long and hard at it—wearing, as he was, his chainmail and the bronze helm, and holding the spear he took from the barrow.

I look like a warrior now he thought. *I wonder if Beorn would approve of me taking the helm and spear from the barrow? Why am I asking myself that? Beorn isn't here to approve or disapprove. And did he not tell me: my fate is to be as my father—a killer of men. Well, I am. And now, with this armor, helm, and spear, I look the part.*

While Turin and the other boys went ashore to fill the water bags and acquire provisions, Ecgtheow and Beorn remained aboard.

"You're troubled," said the Schaman.

"Yes," said Ecgtheow. "My mind stills reels with all that you've told me. I can barely grasp it. The last time I saw him, he was a little boy, standing alongside his mother, waving the toy sword I made him. You tell me he was saved and suckled by a she bear in Vindinstedt Forest, and that he is tall and lean and possesses the strength of thirty men in each arm and has the mind of a full-grown man who can talk with animals. Don't you see, Magister Beorn—how such news plays havoc with my head? What's more, you tell me he's killed no fewer than seven men, a Sabre Tooth Forest Cat and a Swamp Dog—and him—all of what: twelve winters young now?"

"You must forget that, Ecgtheow Waegmunding. Beowulf's age is no longer relevant; although, I do believe he'll remain the same as he is now until his true age catches-up with the rest of him."

"Will I recognize my son, Magister Beorn?"

"Your eyes are green. What color were Beowulf's mother's eyes?"

"Blue," said Ecgtheow. "Like blue chips of ice."

"Ah! You'll recognize him," said the Schaman. "And, gods willing, you'll come to know each other anew, in the present, as father and son—but as your fully grown, son—not the child you last laid eyes on."

† † †

Before returning to the Avenger with the water they obtained, Turin and the others: Erna, Eel, Dagh, Claus, and Broder rested themselves on the shore and soaked-up the sun.

"Which one of us is going to say it?" said Dagh. He waited. "Well?"

"Well what, Dagh?" said Turin.

"This quest we're on. To find our foster father's blood-son, Beowulf."

"What of it?" said Turin. "I would do the same if I were Ecgtheow. It's his right."

"Yes," said Broder. "But haven't you been listening to foster father and Magister Beorn talking these last twenty-one days and nights? His son has changed into something strange, as if by magic, or sorcery, even. Foster father may not even recognize Beowulf. It's been a while since they were separated and Beowulf was just a child at the time. And what about us—? Foster father trained us. We have fought at his side, no matter the odds against us. I don't think there's one of us who wouldn't give his life for Ecgtheow."

"Yes," said Turin. "Which is why we must support him every way we can. I don't think he loves or cares for us less because his blood son is alive."

"I agree with Turin," said Adolf. "In Dane Land we were orphans. Cared for by none. Wanted by none. Now we are Thunder-Geats, part of a clan—Ecgtheow Waegmunding's clan. If called on to give my life, I will do so happily, and die as a warrior. Because that is what foster father has made us—warriors."

"I will embrace his son," said Claus, "I owe Ecgtheow that—and more."

"Then we are of one mind?" said Turin. He scanned the faces of his foster brothers. "We do everything to aid our father in his quest."

"How are we to aid him, Turin?" asked Erna.

"By accepting his son as one of us," said Turin.

"Very well," said Dagh; "but—?"

"But, what?" said Turin.

"Will his blood-son accept us?"

† † †

As Beowulf knelt beside the stream and filled his water-bag, he sensed eyes watching him, not from one creature but several. Beowulf tied the spout closed and put the water bag to one side. He took his helm off. Leaving his spear on the ground, he stood and opened his arms in a welcoming gesture.

"*I am Beowulf, the bear's son,*" he said. *"I come this way in peace. Now show yourselves, or be gone from here.*"

Out of the bushes came three bears of equal size. They were young but full grown. They stopped on the other side of the stream.

"*Greetings, Bear's Son,*" said the bear in the middle. "*I am Gupp. With me is my sister Awp and our brother Grupp.*"

"*Greetings, Bear's Son*," said Awp and Grupp.

"*Greetings to you all*," said Beowulf. "*Is this where you dwell?*"

"*No*," said Gupp. "*Our home is far south of here, in Vindinstedt Forest. Our mother, Lüma, sent us to find you. The All Mother's servant, Beorn, sent word that you were missing, somewhere in the north. We've been searching for you with help from Lord Kungörn and the Sky Folk*."

Beowulf sank to his knees. Tears filled his eyes. "*Tell me, please,*" said Beowulf. "*How is my fur mother?*"

"*She's well, Bear's Son*," said Gupp.

"*She misses her hairless cub*," said Awp.

"*The All Mother's servant waits for you*," said Grupp, "*at a place not far from here. We will guide you.*"

"*And when you return to your home, tell my fur mother I love her,*" said Beowulf.

"*We will*," said Awp. "*She asked us to tell you the same*."

Beowulf nodded and wiped his eyes and cheeks dry.

† † †

When at last Beowulf saw the Schaman, Beorn was sitting on a large rock that rose up out of a field of grass. To one side, Beowulf could see the ocean and a Black Ship at anchor. There were seven men aboard. A tall man and six others of lesser age and size. The tall man was pacing back and forth while the six remained seated at their rowing stations.

"Praise to the All Mother, and to the gods above," said Beorn.

Beowulf stepped into the Schaman's open arms.

"Not too tightly," said the Schaman. "you'll break my back."

Beowulf laughed. "I've been waiting for this moment, Beorn. I feared it might never come."

"Well it has," said the Schaman.

Beowulf went to where Gupp, Grupp, and Awp waited. He touched each with a loving hand on the head.

"*Many thanks, fur brothers and sister. My heart is at peace now. Tell Lüma I will see her again one day*."

"*Good hunting,*" said the bears.

"*Good hunting*," said Beowulf.

Beowulf watched his fur brothers and sister amble off until they were out of view. Again he wiped his tear-stained cheeks before he turned and faced the Schaman.

Beorn looked Beowulf up and down, noting his bronze helm and spear of ash-wood and iron.

"Look at the young warrior," said Beorn. "That's a noble helm you wear, Bear's Son, and a well-made spear you wield."

"I took it from a barrow," said Beowulf. "A nest of Troggolls was using it as their home."

"They prefer to be called, Trolls," said the Schaman.

"It doesn't matter now, Beorn—they're all dead."

"By your hand?" said the Schaman.

"Yes, by my hand alone. Do you not approve?"

"I don't disapprove, young Prince. My task is to prepare you for what Fate has in store for you."

"A tall order?" said Beowulf.

The Schaman laughed. "By all the gods, you've acquired a sense of humor after all."

"Such as it is," said Beowulf. He pointed toward the Black Ship offshore. "Friends of yours?"

"See the tall man? There, near the mast, looking in our direction."

"Yes," said Beowulf.

"That's your father, Beowulf. Ecgtheow Waegmunding."

Beowulf's eyes widened. He dropped that fine ash and iron spear from his hand and walked toward the water.

"Beowulf," said the Schaman. "Wait. We should talk first."

Beowulf continued. As he drew closer to the water, he tossed his bronze helm aside then pulled off his shirt of hand-forged chainmail armor and let it fall in a heap on the ground. Beowulf stepped into the water and began to swim with powerful strokes toward the Avenger.

Aboard the Avenger, Ecgtheow saw Beowulf approaching the ship. Without hesitation, he leapt over the side and swam toward his son.

They stopped just short of each other where they were able to stand in waist-deep water.

How long father and son gazed on one another there was no way to measure. Tears flooded Ecgtheow's eyes, Beowulf's also. Without speaking, they embraced.

Ashore, Beorn collected Beowulf's war gear and watched son and father reunite.

So, too, did Beowulf's brothers aboard the Black Ship.

What words passed twixt father and son were never shared by either—the moment was theirs, and theirs, alone, to savor.

Beorn returned to the Avenger with Beowulf's war gear then set about the business of preparing a hot meal for Beowulf's brothers—Beggars' Stew. He did this while Beowulf and Ecgtheow remained on shore, basking in the warmth of the sun while their clothes dried.

"Do you remember the waterfall and Hot Spring, Beowulf? Do you remember being there with your mother and me?"

"Yes, Father. I remember. Do you still have Rain Dancer?"

"I do, yes; stabled at Land's End with Trygve, Captain of the Coast Guard."

"It'll be wonderful to see him again. And Handscio."

"And so you shall, my son. So you shall."

Ecgtheow placed a hand on Beowulf's shoulder. "Look at you! Look at us! I'm not ashamed to say it, Beowulf—you've grown well beyond my understanding. But I thank the gods for it, and that we're together. 'Tis a bitter cup we've drank. The Dark Queen took your mother, and stole your childhood."

"I'll honor mother's memory always. As for my childhood—I don't miss what I didn't have. I accept what I've become; what I am this very moment. And so should you, father."

Tears pooled in Ecgtheow's eyes. "You're right, my son. By Odin's one good eye, you're right."

Once more aboard the Avenger, Ecgtheow had his boys gather around that he might introduce them to Beowulf.

"Beowulf, these six fine lads are your foster brothers: the tall one there is Turin. Beside him is Erna, then Eel, Dagh, Claus, and Broder. They, too, are now part of Clan Waegmunding. They have been with me through thick and thin while we searched for you. They've become capable warriors and are loyal beyond measure—to one another and me. It is my greatest wish that you will accept, honor, and respect each other. That has always been the Waegmunding way, and I would have it so again."

"Then brothers we are! Ay Turin?" said Beowulf.

"Aye, Bear's Son," said Turin.

"Erna?"

"Aye, brother Beowulf."

"Eel?"

"Aye, Beowulf."

"Dagh?"

"Be it so, Beowulf."

"Claus?"

"Aye, Beowulf."

"Broder?"

"Be it so, Bear's Son."

One by one, Beowulf embraced his brothers in a manner befitting shield-brothers.

"Good!" said Beorn. "Now, my lovelies—let's eat."

"What's for supper?" said Ecgtheow.

Beorn looked at Beowulf and winked.

45

BEOWULF TAKES A BRIDE

The trip to the land of the Spear Danes was carefree and joyous. During the days, Beowulf and his father spent much of the time together at the tiller, guiding the Avenger toward Mörk Sand. The Schaman enthralled Beowulf's brothers by the stories he told about his time with the bear's son. Beowulf did not speak about the things those things. When he did talk, the other boys listened, and they believed his every word. They could see Beowulf was much like their foster father, reserved but sincere—a warrior first and foremost.

To the amusement of all, sometimes Beowulf would row on one side of the Avenger while Ecgtheow worked the tiller and Beowulf's brothers took-up oars opposite him. Turin and the others were amazed by his strength, at the effortless way Beowulf rowed and how he could do so, long after they reached the point of exhaustion.

Once, when they had dropped anchor for the night, Turin and the other boys challenged Beowulf to wrestle, one at a time.

Was then that Ecgtheow stepped in: "I want no broken bones," he said to his "sons."

"*Don't hurt your brothers, Bear's Son,*" said the Schaman, using the Silent Tongue. "*They know you can row better than them, but your brothers are still boys at heart, and they want to test you.*"

One by one, beginning with Turin, Beowulf proceeded to toss each of his brothers a long distance overboard. Turin's head popped-up out of the water:

"By Thor's hammer, that was just like flying," he said spitting salt water. "Come, Beowulf; let's do it again!"

Standing inside the Great Hall of Heorot, Beowulf and his brothers stood behind Ecgtheow and Beorn and took-in the feel of the place.

"Welcome back, Ecgtheow," said Hrothgar, King of the Spear Danes. "Now, then—who are these others who accompany you?"

"Beside me, Great King is Magister Beorn—a faithful servant of the All Mother who reunited me with my son, Beowulf."

"You are most welcome here," Magister Beorn."

"Thank you, Great King," said the Schaman. "I am honored to stand inside the Great Hall of Heorot."

"Which of the lads behind you, Ecgtheow, is your son Beowulf?"

"The tallest one, Great King," said Ecgtheow.

"And the others?" said Hrothgar.

"My foster-sons: Turin, Broder, Erna, Dagh, Claus, and Eel."

"You are all most welcome," said Hrothgar.

Beowulf and his brothers bowed the way Beorn had instructed them in advance of their arrival at Hrothgar's Keep.

"Come forward, Beowulf," said Hrothgar, "and let me get a good look at you."

Beowulf stepped forward. His chainmail shirt, helm and spear he left on the Avenger as his father wished.

"From time to time we've heard stories about you, Beowulf; but we knew not what to make of them."

Beowulf bowed. "I don't know what to say, Great King."

"You needn't say a word, Beowulf. I can see much of your father in your face, except for your eyes."

"I'm told I have my mother's eyes, Great King."

"Forgive me. I would introduce you all to Wealtheow, my wife, and queen, but she returned to Öster Geatland to visit her brother, King Adalfuns."

"Another time, perhaps, Great King," said Ecgtheow.

"Where from here will you go next, Ecgtheow?" said Hrothgar.

"North, Great King. To the land of the Sea Brondings."

"Ah," said Hrothgar. "Give King Beanstan greetings from the Spear Danes, Ecgtheow."

"I shall, Great King."

"And might we ask what business you have there?" said Aeschere, Hrothgar's chief adviser.

"Of course, Lord Aeschere. I owe King Beanstan my thanks. He gave refuge to Beowulf when he and Magister Beorn arrived there after fleeing the minions of the Dark Queen."

"Whose name shall not be spoken here," said Hrothgar.

"We have another reason to go there, Great King," said Ecgtheow. He looked at Beowulf. "My son tells me there is a Bronding girl, for whom he has strong feelings."

"Ha!" said Hrothgar. "Happy is the man with a Bronding woman for a wife. Good for you, Beowulf. Good for you. I wish you both every happiness."

King Hrethel wept at the wedding of his son, Hygelac, to the Lady Hygd. At the feast that followed, he went from bench to bench greeting all his guests—his Clan Chiefs and their wives, those who he invited, even those he had not invited, like Knut Eriksson.

Following the death of his father in Hell's Grove, Knut had become Chief of his clan and had prospered as a brewer of mead. That, and as a smuggler of same to avoid paying taxes. More important to Hrethel that night, his feet no longer bothered him. The Schaman's advice had proven sound.

As the Avenger passed the breakwater and entered the bay, it was met by three Bronding battle-craft.

When they saw Beowulf aboard manning the tiller, and the tall man and youths with him, they put up their bows and lay aside their spears, cheered and blew on rams' horns.

Escorted by the Brondings, the Avenger tied up at the dock. A crowd had formed, and they cheered the sight of the Bear's Son.

Entering Beanstan's Mead Hall with his father and brothers and the Schaman, Beowulf saw what his heart had hoped against all hope of ever seeing Elin again.

With a broad smile on his face, King Beanstan looked at Elin.

"Well, girl," said Beanstan, "why are you waiting? Go to him."

Tears in her eyes, Elin ran to Beowulf's arms, and long was their embrace.

"If it pleases you, Great King," said Beowulf, "allow me to introduce those who accompanied me here."

"Wait a moment, Prince Beowulf," said a familiar voice.

Beowulf saw Prince Breca enter the Hall with a smile on his face that was heartfelt. Breca went to Beowulf, and they clasped forearms as befits shield-brothers.

"You made it home," said Beowulf.

"Thanks to you, my friend," said Breca. "Thanks to you."

"Ecgtheow Waegmunding," said King Beanstan. "By all the gods, after all these winters past, it is you."

"It is, Great King," said Ecgtheow. "Good, it is, to see you again."

"We've much to talk about, my old friend," said Beanstan. "And you, Beorn—good to have you back among us. Tonight the mead will flow. Now introduce these others, with you, Ecgtheow."

"My foster-sons, Great King: Turin, Broder, Eel, Erna, Dagh, and Claus."

† † †

In the garden, Beowulf held Elin close. They said not a word at first, but held each other and kissed.

"I thought I lost you, Beowulf."

"I won't let that happen, Elin. No matter where I go, I will always come back to you."

"Swear it," she said.

"I swear."

"I don't want to wait, Beowulf. I'll tell my uncle we want to marry. Today! Now!"

"Beorn can marry us. Your uncle can give you away, and Breca shall be my Best Man. My brothers and father shall be witnesses to our marriage."

"We ask that you marry us tonight, Great King," said Beowulf to King Beanstan. "But I have no Bride Payment to offer you."

"You sacrificed yourself to save my son's life, young Prince. That is Bride Payment and more."

"Gladly will I marry them in your Hall, Great King," said Beorn.

"I ask Breca to be my Best Man," said Beowulf, "and that my father and brothers be present to witness my marriage."

"Of course," said Beanstan, his eyes moist with tears. "It will be as you wish, young Prince. Yours will be a marriage blest by the gods."

"I will take my leave, Uncle," said Elin, "for there is much to do before I wed this Prince of Geatland. But before I go, I ask Beowulf's father to give me his blessing."

Ecgtheow stepped to Elin's side: "You have it, Lady Elin. Now and always."

46

HALCYON DAYS

Following the marriage of Beowulf to Elin, Beowulf, his father, brothers and the Schaman remained in Beanstanbörg another ten days. Little was seen of Beowulf and Elin since they seldom left the lodge they shared as husband and wife.

When Beowulf and his Bride departed on the Avenger for Geatland, it was a bittersweet moment, for great was the bond twixt Beowulf and Breca. Knowing his niece would soon leave, King Beanstan could not disguise the sadness he felt.

"Where will you go next, Ecgtheow?" said Beanstan.

"It's time we returned to Geatland, Great King. To my farm near Vindinstedt Forest. I want to give my sons a normal life. A life lived in peace, gods willing, nurturing the land as the All Mother sees fit."

"Will it be that easy, my old friend?" asked Beanstan. "To leave behind the life, you've lived. You were the enforcer of King Hrethel's will among the Thunder-Geats, his Battle Lord, too, when called on."

"Easy or not, Great King," said Ecgtheow, "a life of peace is what I want for Clan Waegmunding."

"Then, by the gods, Ecgtheow," said Beanstan, "may it be as you desire. Die well, old friend."

"Die well, Great King."

Beowulf and Elin walked side by side. Turin and Beowulf's other brothers walked behind. Ahead of them all, leading the way, walked Ecgtheow and the Schaman. They had left the Avenger anchored in the harbor below the cliffs that buttressed the Citadel.

They had to walk the long way around, but they did so without reservation, for great was the feeling they shared—that good tidings had followed them home.
Through the morning mist appeared the earthworks surrounding Falcon's Nest. Above Falcon's Nest, the Citadel's stone walls and towers loomed dark and ominous.

"It seems so long ago," said Ecgtheow; "since I last put a foot in Hrethel's stronghold."

"The color of Hrethel's hair has changed," said the Schaman. "From white to whiter. Apart from that, it's the same snakes' nest. No matter where it's played, the game of power remains the same."

† † †

Escorted by Ragmund and several of the King's Guard, Beowulf and the others entered the Throne Room. To one side of the dais, flanking King Hrethel, stood Prince Hygelac and Lord Magnus, Captain of Hrethel's Guard.

"Hail, Hrethel—King!" said Ecgtheow and the others in unison.

"Beorn!" said Hrethel. "Welcome back. Share my sweat lodge with me tonight. There are matters I want to speak to you about—in private."

"As you wish, great king," said the Schaman.
Hrethel's eyes turned to Ecgtheow.

"It seems such a long time, Ecgtheow. Now I can thank you for the gift you made of the Wylfing ships you captured at the Bay of Kryl. Because of you, we Thunder-Geats have a fleet of our own to send aviking when and where we want. My heart soars to see you, old friend."

"Thank you, my King. As does mine."
Ecgtheow bowed and stepped aside.

"Tell me, Ecgtheow," said Hrethel, "who are the young Falcons behind you, and who, by all the gods, is the beautiful young woman who accompanies you here?"

Ecgtheow pointed to Beowulf: "That one there is your grandson, my King, my first-born: Beowulf, With him, is his wife, Elin, and my foster sons: "Turin, Broder, Erna, Dagh, Claus, and Eel."

"Welcome to my Hall, you sons of Ecgtheow," said Hrethel.

Beowulf and his brothers bowed in the manner Beorn had taught them.

Hrethel looked at Beowulf and smiled.

"Come closer, Grandson; let these old eyes of mine get a better look at you. And bring the young lady with you."

Whispers of 'the bear's son' raced through the Hall.

Beowulf took Elin's hand and escorted her forward. They stopped in front of the dais and bowed:

"My King," said Beowulf.

Hrethel studied Beowulf's face: "I see my daughter, Liv, on your face, especially your eyes."

Old Hrethel took a moment to wipe his eyes dry before looking at Elin. "And who would you be?"

Elin bowed: "Elin, daughter of Gunner and Britta, Great King."

"My King," said Beowulf. "She is King Beanstan's niece and cousin to Prince Breca."

"By all the gods, Grandson, lucky is the man with a Bronding woman for a wife."

"That is how I feel," said Beowulf. "Lucky."

"This is indeed a joyful day," said Hrethel. Once more his eyes were moist with tears.

"You and Elin should bow," said Beorn, using the Silent Tongue; "then step back alongside your father and brothers."

Elin took her cues from Beowulf as he bowed and stepped back, away from the Throne.

"Being reunited with my grandson is cause for great celebration. Hygelac, my son. Welcome your nephew home."

Prince Hygelac stepped forward and embraced Beowulf:

"I would not believe it, Nephew, were you not standing here before me in the flesh. To see you stand there plays havoc with my head, but it is you, I know it. In my heart of hearts, I know it. Now let me introduce my wife to all of you—Lady Hygd, my future queen."

They rode horses given to them by Beowulf's grandfather, the King. Beowulf and Elin took in the many fragrances borne by the wind as they neared Vindinstedt Forest. He remembered each of a hundred different scents. The thought of seeing his fur-mother, Lüma, caused his heart to sing. He didn't know it was possible to feel such happiness as he did that day, upon returning to his ancestral home. Elin could see it in Beowulf's face—the happiness he felt, but his greatest joy was when he looked into Elin's eyes and face and felt her caress his skin.

† † †

Waiting for them just inside the stake wall, in the common area near the water well, was Weohstan and his son, Handscio. Handscio had grown, too, over the last five winters. For a boy of twelve, he was robust and smart and fast on foot.

Handscio searched the faces of the riders. He recognized none of them save for Ecgtheow.

"I don't see Beowulf," said Handscio to his father.

Weohstan could feel the trepidation in Handscio's voice.

"Where's Beowulf?" said Handscio.

"Patience, my son," said Weohstan.

Beowulf recognized Handscio straight-away. He got down off his horse and lifted Elin from hers. Ecgtheow, Beorn, and the others also dismounted.

"Welcome home, Cousin," said Weohstan to Ecgtheow. "Welcome to you all."

Ecgtheow and Weohstan embraced.

"It's good to be home," said Ecgtheow. "Handscio, do you recognize your cousin among these fine-looking lads? Do you see Beowulf?"

Beowulf approached. "Handscio! It's me—Beowulf!"

Handscio looked long and hard at Beowulf. His eyes filled with tears. "You're not him," he said. "You're not Beowulf!"

Handscio turned and fled in the direction of the milking barn which is where Beowulf found him. He was sobbing on a heap of straw. Beowulf sat beside him.

"Not a day passed, Handscio, when I have not thought of us."

"You're not him," said Handscio. "You're not my cousin, Beowulf."

"But it is me," said Beowulf. "And I can prove it."

Elin stopped at the entrance to the milking barn and watched without making her presence known.

"How? How can you prove it?" said Handscio.

Beowulf could feel Elin's eyes on him.

"I'll tell you how I can prove it," said Beowulf. "Kings and Dragons, and do you remember what you gave me when I saved you from being eaten by the dragon?"

Handscio wiped the tears from his cheeks. "I remember what I gave Beowulf. He had it with him when—"

Handscio stopped talking. He looked into Beowulf's eyes.

"Yes," said Beowulf, "I had Uncle Rabbit with me when the Wylfings came and killed my mother. I dropped Uncle Rabbit in the forest. I'm sorry, Handscio, but I'm afraid I lost him."

"Beowulf?"

Beowulf put an arm around Handscio's shoulders. "Yes, Handscio—it's me."

Elin could not keep the tears away as she watched Beowulf and Handscio sit together, Handscio's head on Beowulf's shoulder, saying nothing.

† † †

It was a matter of several days before Ecgtheow sent Turin to summon Beowulf and Elin to the stables. There, saddled and waiting, was a beautiful black stallion, sired from Frisian stock, that Ecgtheow had traveled to Land's End to find.

"What do you think?" said Ecgtheow to Beowulf.

"He's beautiful," said Beowulf. "*Yes you are beautiful, my dark friend*," said Beowulf in the Silent Tongue.

Beowulf stroked the stallion's neck and kissed his forehead.

"Then ride him," said Ecgtheow, and he walked off.

"*Am I to be yours*?" said the stallion.

"*I could no more possess you than I could the wind. Let us be equals and friends. For my part, I will care for you as though we are of the same blood*."

"Then," said the stallion, *"for my part, I will carry you wherever you desire—even though it be into harm's way, for I was bred to abide the chaos of battle."*

"Storm Bringer," said Beowulf. *"I will call you, Storm Bringer, for the mere sight of you on the battlefield will bring fear to the enemies of my people."*

"And what shall I call you?" said the stallion.

"I am called Beowulf—and sometimes the bear's son. Either will do."

"Very well," said the stallion. *"I will call you, Bear's Son."*

"You're talking to him, aren't you?" said Elin.

"Yes," said Beowulf. "His name is Storm Bringer."

"He's beautiful," said Elin.

Beowulf leapt into the saddle and held his arm outstretched for Elin to take hold.

Elin took hold of Beowulf's arm, and he pulled her up behind him.

"Where are we going?" said Elin.

"For a ride. There's someone I want you to meet."

† † †

Beowulf let the stallion set his own pace as he and Elin rode toward Vindinstedt Forest.

From behind, Elin gripped Beowulf around the middle and squeezed.

"I love you, husband."

"I love you also—if I could just remember your name?"

"What a terrible thing to say," said Elin, and they both laughed.

"Say it," she said.

"Say, what?"

"My name, you terrible man, or you'll find yourself sleeping in the barn with Storm Bringer tonight."

"Elin. There. I said it."

"You'll need to do more than that," said Elin. "Much more."

"Very well," said Beowulf. "You're my love, my lady, my wife. There is no other in all of Midgard who compares to you. Am I forgiven now?"

"Perhaps."

"And tonight?"

"You'll just have to wait and see, Bear's Son."

Deep into Vindinstedt Forest, they arrived at a Blue Spruce that rose tall and straight, whose branches extended wide and far to the sides, providing shade to the ground where there grew an abundance of sweet grass.

Beowulf lifted Elin down, and as he held her, she pressed herself close to him and sought his lips with her own. How long they kissed can't be reckoned, but the sound of Storm Bringer neighing caused them to cease.

"*Wait for us here, Storm Bringer, where there's shade and sweet grass to eat. We'll return soon.*"

"*As you wish, Bear's Son.*"

"So," said Elin, "where is this someone you want me to meet?"

"Not far from here. Come. Give me your hand, and do not be frightened."

"Well, I am a bit frightened, Beowulf; now that you've said that."

Beowulf laughed and took Elin's hand. "Come, and whatever you see, be not afraid."

"Stop it, Beowulf! You're making me afraid."

Beowulf kissed her. "I'm sorry, my love. Come. You'll see you have nothing to fear soon enough."

They had walked but a short distance when they came to the entrance to Lüma's cave. Elin stopped.

"I'm not going in there," she said.

"You won't have to," Beowulf said. "I'll tell Lüma we're here; although I suspect she already knows."

"Lüma?"

"My fur mother."

The blood drained from Elin' cheeks as out of the cave came Lüma. Elin placed herself behind Beowulf.

"*Fur Mother, this is my life mate, Elin. I wanted her to meet you.*"

"*She's frightened,*" said Lüma.

"*Yes, Fur Mother, but she will get over her fear of you.*"

"*Ask her to approach,*" said Lüma.

"Lüma wants you to come closer," said Beowulf.

"You can't be serious? What if your fur mother decides she doesn't like me and bites my head off?"

"Then I will ask her to give me your head back, and we will go home."

"How can you talk so lightly, Beowulf?"

"Elin, listen—but for Lüma I wouldn't be alive today. And we would never have met, nor become husband and wife. Do you not trust me?"

Elin breathed a full breath and exhaled.

"I trust you," she said.

Elin walked forward, each step shorter than the one preceding it; until, at last, she stood within reach of Lüma. Elin looked back at Beowulf.

"What is it she wants me to do?"

"Stop shaking and embrace her, Elin. That's all she asks."

Elin stepped forward and took Lüma's head in her hands. Lüma placed her forelegs around Elin and licked Elin once before she released her hold. Elin stepped back, alongside Beowulf, and with the back of her hand wiped her face dry.

"Is that all?" she asked.

Beowulf laughed. "Yes," he said. "That's all."

Beowulf looked at Lüma and then at Elin.

"Lüma wants to know how many cubs you'll give me."

"As many as I can," said Elin.

"*As many as she can, fur mother.*"

"*That's good. You chose well, my son. Bring your mate back soon to visit.*"

"*I will, fur mother. I will.*"

47

VALLEY OF SHADOWS

For seven winters, Ecgtheow and Clan Waegmunding knew peace and contentment. Although it was a time of peace, Ecgtheow and Weohstan were not fools nor in any way naive. They knew peace was no more than a prelude to war. Thus, for Beowulf. his brothers and Handscio, every day they spent training. While Ecgtheow and Weohstan trained the young men for war, Beorn, trained their minds.

† † †

News of the attack on Geatland was slow to reach Vindinstedt Farm. An old enemy from the north, the Svear king, was once again trying to over-run Väster Götaland. Their king had paid Adalfuns in silver, and in secret, to stay his hand and not join the Thunder-Geats as the Wylfings had done before when faced with their common enemy—the Svear.

Some tricks, the tricks he learned from his father, Amunwolf, proved impossible for Adulfuns to unlearn—treachery being foremost among them.

† † †

The Geats, eleven hundreds of them, horse and foot combined, occupied the high ground to the south that overlooked the Valley of Shadows—land that had once belonged to Geatland, what a Svear King had taken as his own, long before when King Hrethel was a mere boy. Rather than wait for the Svear to assail Falcon's Nest, Hrethel marshaled his army and took it north to meet the Svear.

A quarter-league away, the Svear army waited. They, too, were on high ground, numbering eighteen-hundred warriors on foot and two-hundred on horseback.

The two armies would meet below on the valley floor where the ground flattened for several leagues in breadth and length.

The sun burned away the mist; both armies became visible to each other. That was cause sufficient to provoke the warriors on both sides to trade insults and hurl words of abuse and scorn. Banter soon gave way to shouting.

Svear bowmen rattled their arrows in their quivers as was their custom. In kind, the Thunder-Geats beat on their Linden shields.

Hrethel's battle-plan was a simple one: attack the Svear straight on! King Hrethel rode out in front of his army, accompanied by Prince Hygelac.

"Hear me, men of Geatland. From this day forward, no longer will we pay tribute to the tyrant, Onegentheow. From this day forward, we take back the land the Svear took from us. From this day forward, never forget—you are Thunder-Geats!"

Hrethel's army shouted his name and beat on their shields. Hrethel returned to the center of the formation where surrounded by his personal Guard, he would direct the battle. The shrill sound of a hundred rams' horns signaled the attack.

The Geat horse warriors urged their horses forward at a steady clip. Behind them came the bulk of Hrethel's army on foot.

† † †

It was well after dawn when Clan Waegmunding halted their horses atop a ridge overlooking the valley. They exchanged grim looks among themselves as they watched Hrethel's army surrounded on three sides, giving ground, and near defeat.

"Listen, all of you," said Ecgtheow, "Stay close to Weohstan and me, and watch each other's back—Do you understand?"

Beowulf and his brothers, along with Handscio, nodded.

"Die well, my sons," said Ecgtheow. "But not today."

Ecgtheow returned with his foster-sons, except for Turin, to his place alongside Weohstan.

"Die well, my brother," said Beowulf.

"Die well, brother," said Turin.

"You too, Handscio," said Beowulf. "Die well."

"Die well, Cousin," said Handscio. He licked his dry lips.

Beowulf removed his battle helm and tied it to the saddle.

"Your helm does no good off of your head, brother," said Turin.

"True, but I'm too hot with it on," said Beowulf.

Turin looked at Handscio and shrugged. Beowulf adjusted his hold on Death Stalker, the name he had given his spear; then he stroked the neck of his young stallion. Through his chain-mail armor, Beowulf could feel his heart pounding. The sounds of combat and the sight of hundreds of warriors locked in a desperate battle sent a shiver of excitement down the length of his spine.

"Now's the time," they heard Ecgtheow say. "Ride on to glory, my sons!"

"*Now's the time, Storm Bringer—run! Run like the wind*," said Beowulf.

A Svear Clan Chief saw the Thunder-Geats on horseback riding full speed toward the battle from the ridge. He signaled to one of his lieutenants to ride out with forty horse warriors to meet the Thunder-Geats coming late to the fray.

When the two groups of riders met there was a great commotion: horses collided, Svear riders went down. The sounds of shouting, the clashing of weapons, and shields breaking was deafening.

"Beowulf—behind you!" said Handscio.

As Beowulf turned, a Svear rider struck at him with a sword. Too late to block the blade with his shield, Beowulf flinched. As he leaned back, the tip of the Svearlander's blade struck flesh beneath Beowulf's right eye and cut a deep gash that reached to Beowulf's chin.

Ecgtheow appeared from the side and killed the warrior who had almost killed his son.

"Both of you—wake up!" said Ecgtheow. "And put your helmet on, Beowulf. Next time you may not be so lucky."

Ecgtheow winced at the sight of Beowulf's wound, then he rode off, back into the thick of the fray.

"Are you alright?" said Handscio, sickened by the sight of blood that poured from Beowulf's wound.

Beowulf wiped his hand on the right side of his face. He felt the deep gash and exposed cheek bone and saw his blood dripping through his fingers.

Handscio and Turin saw Beowulf's eyes harden into a look they had never seen before.

For the second time in his life, from the center of Beowulf's being, came a sound, loud and terrifying—a war cry that filled the air and carried over the entire battlefield.

Beowulf put his helm on; then he urged Storm-Bringer forward. He cast his shield aside and with his spear, Death Stalker, and his knife, Tooth, struck at every Svear who came at him. Unable to keep pace, Handscio and Turin rode behind Beowulf, guarding his back.

A short distance away, Handscio spied Ecgtheow. He had been thrown from his horse and was fighting on foot with five of Beowulf's brothers alongside him. Svear on horse and foot had the Waegmunding men surrounded.

"Beowulf! Turin!" said Handscio.

Beowulf and Turin looked to where Handscio was pointing and saw their foster brothers and Ecgtheow hard-pressed on all sides.

"To me! To me, my sons!" said Ecgtheow.

They stood shoulder to shoulder and with axe and spear drove back the Svear that came at them. A Svear chief waved his footmen back; Svear archers rushed forward.

The first to fall to the arrows of the Svear was Claus; then Broder, Erna, and Eel.

Beowulf and Turin rode into the Svear, dispersing them. Handscio joined the melee. Beowulf dismounted and fought alongside Ecgtheow on-foot. Dagh was next to fall, with an axe blow to the back of his head. Beowulf, Turin, Handscio, and Ecgtheow stood shoulder to shoulder as more Svear closed-in around them.

Beowulf stepped forward and swung Death Stalker. With every thrust, his spear's heavy iron blade splintered shields and cleaved helms. Beowulf heard his father cry out. He turned and saw Ecgtheow drop to his knees, the point of a spear protruding from his father's chest.

Beowulf knelt beside Ecgtheow and lowered him to one side. Using his hands, Beowulf snapped the shaft in two, then pulled the spear-tip free of Ecgtheow's torso. With blood bubbling out his mouth, Ecgtheow struggled to speak. While Handscio and Turin stood guard over them, Beowulf held his father in his arms.

"Never forget you're a Thunder Geat," said Ecgtheow. "Your King and people will need your strength, Beowulf—serve them well."

Ecgtheow's eyes closed. A death-rattle escaped his body. Beowulf saw several Svear coming toward him, and he picked up his father's sword, Widow Maker. Wielding spear and sword, Beowulf charged forward. He struck right and left and dodged and ducked the blades that sought his flesh. He whirled in a circle and lunged in every direction, and he killed those foolish enough to face him. It didn't matter how many Svear came at him or whether they did so on horseback or foot. No one could stop this young death-dealer who wielded sword and spear as would a farmer, cutting barley with his scythe. With Handscio and Turin beside him, Beowulf roamed the length and breadth of the battlefield as though he was Thor, the god of war himself, incarnate, killing with savage abandon.

† † †

High above the battlefield, the Lord of Eagles, Kungörn, circled and watched. Below, he saw the bear's son and his companions drive a wedge through the ranks of their enemies, breaking shield wall after shield wall.

Kungörn soared low over Beowulf's head: "*Good hunting, Bear's Son*," said Kungörn.

Beowulf looked up at the Lord of Eagles. "*Good hunting, Kungörn.*"

Kungörn circled the battlefield once more and noted in detail the killing ground below. He then flew north and disappeared.

† † †

Surrounded by the Kungens Vakter commanded by Lord Magnus, and with Prince Hygelac alongside, Hrethel drew

Naegling, the Sword of Kings, and with a loud voice encouraged his warriors to "Fight on!" as he rode out to join them.

"No retreat," said the King of the Thunder-Geats, in as loud a voice as he could muster, "No retreat! No surrender."

His armor and horse smeared with blood, the blood of the men he'd killed, Hygelac rode to his father's side.

"Look there, my King," he said and pointed with his spear at where the Svear were giving ground.

"Beowulf?" said Hrethel.

The sigh of relief in Hrethel's voice was palpable.

"Yes, Father," said Hygelac. "Beowulf."

On and on the battle raged. Then, at midday, from the north, with the sun overhead, Beorn appeared on horseback accompanied by Prince Breca leading two-hundred Bronding horse warriors.

The appearance of the Brondings caused panic among the Svear Clan Chiefs. They tried to rally their men. They screamed at them to form two shield walls: one facing south, toward the center of Hrethel's army. The other facing north toward the Brondings—a defensive maneuver that proved too little, too late.

The Schaman and Prince Breca fought their way past the Svear until they reached King Hrethel and Prince Hygelac.

"Let them through," said Hygelac to Magnus, Captain of the King's Guard.

"What joy it brings us," said Hrethel, "to see you, Prince Breca, and you, Magister Beorn."

"You can thank, Beorn, Great King," said Breca, "for the Brondings being here."

"We do, indeed, thank you, Magister Beorn," said Hrethel.

"How did you find us, Prince Breca?" said Hygelac.

Breca looked at the Schaman.

"It was Kungörn, Lord of the Eagles," said Beorn, "who found Beowulf and led us to this place."

King Hrethel and Beorn, along with Princes Hygelac, and Breca, watched Beowulf's onslaught continue. With the arrival of the Brondings, they soon realized the battle had tipped in their favor. The Bronding horse warriors proved too much for the Svear to overcome. Pressured front and back, the shield walls of the Svear crumbled, leaving small pockets of Svear warriors scattered about the battlefield, desperate to survive.

"By Thor's Hammer," said Hygelac, "Beowulf's gone berserk."

"No, my Prince," said the Schaman. "He's what Fate always meant him to be—the greatest warrior in Midgard."

Disheartened by the unstoppable ferocity of the Geat warrior opposing them, and with most of their Clan Chiefs dead among the piles of corpses that blanketed the battlefield, the Svear broke ranks and fled east in the direction of Uppsala.

The last to die by Beowulf's hand that day was the Kommandar of Onegentheow's army, Sven Olson.

Exhausted, his armor nicked and shredded and himself bleeding from numerous wounds, Sven Olson tossed his bronze helm aside and gasped for air. He leaned forward, feet wide apart, and held his sword with a loose grip pointed at the ground.

"Who are you," said Olson.

The deep cut on the right side of Beowulf's face was still bleeding. He could feel his blood dripping from his chin onto the ground between his boots. He looked at Onegentheow's Kommandar.

"Who am I?" said Beowulf.

"Yes," said Sven Olson, "by all the gods, who are you?"

"The one who killed you," said Beowulf.

Days later, when they returned to Vindinstedt Farm, Elin was able to count five riders: Beowulf, Weohstan, Beorn, Handscio, and Turin. Her eyes filled with tears as she ran from the fields to greet them.

Was then Elin saw Beowulf's bloodied face, disfigured by the crude pattern of stitches that held his wound closed. Beowulf's wound troubled her, but nowhere near as much as the fierce, cold look hardened behind Beowulf's eyes—so much so, he might well have been a stranger whom Elin was encountering as for the first time.

The look in his eyes sent a chill through Elin, and she trembled, for she knew not what to say. She knew no words would comfort Beowulf—not then, not the next day—perhaps not ever.

That night, Elin lie in bed waiting to hear the sound of Beowulf's boots ascending the stairs to join her, but the sound she heard was Beowulf sharpening the blades of his spear and sword on a wet-stone downstairs in the Banquet Room.

He was still there, sitting in front of the fire when Elin came down to prepare his breakfast. For the next night and the night after, Beowulf sat alone before the fire, saying nothing as he honed the blade of his father's sword ever sharper. As she had before, Elin paced in their room until, overcome with anguish, she cried herself to sleep.

After ten days had passed, Beowulf sat on a bench in the Banquet Hall, and while Beorn looked on, Elin snipped the stitches that bound the flaps of skin together, from his right eye to his chin. The wound had healed well but left a long red scar that in time would turn wax white.

"If you ask me," said the Schaman. "That scar is one of the best I've seen on a Northman."

"That isn't funny, Magister Beorn," said Elin.

Beowulf said nothing as he stood.

"No," said the Schaman, "I suppose it's not."

"I have something to do," Beowulf said and turned toward Elin. "Don't wait up for me."

Elin was about to question Beowulf, but she held back. He no longer seemed to be the man she once thought she knew; at the same time, Elin told herself to be patient: I have to give him time she told herself, over and over and over.

† † †

Leaving Storm Bringer behind, Beowulf left Vindinstedt Farm on foot and headed north toward Vindinstedt Forest.

Standing on the wall-walk, Beorn, Elin, and Turin watched Beowulf depart.

"What's he doing, Beorn?" said Elin.

"What he must, Lady Elin. Be assured; he'll come back when he's ready."

"But as what?" said Elin. "Which Beowulf will he return? The Beowulf I wed, or the man he is now—cold and distant?"

"That I cannot say," said the Schaman. "His father was the last remaining root that connected him to his past. Now, with Ecgtheow gone, that root, too, has been severed."

"Then we must give him new roots—a new sense of family," said Turin.

Elin smiled and touched Turin on the arm "You're right, Turin. We three are his family, his roots now."

† † †

Beowulf found Lüma near the waterfall that fed the great pool where Beowulf and Elin often went swimming. Lüma was eating blackberries when Beowulf approached. Her joy upon seeing her man-cub was tempered by the sight of the angry red gash down the side of his face.

"*Come, my son,*" she said, "*Come closer and let me look at your wound.*"

Beowulf knelt and looked into her eyes.

"*There was a great battle, fur mother. My Father and all but one of my foster brothers are dead. Something inside me has changed. I don't know what it is—but I feel it, a coldness deep within me that wasn't there before.*"

"*Hold still,*" said Lüma.

She began to lick the length of Beowulf's facial scar.

"*This will help cleanse and heal what remains of your wound,*" said Lüma. "*But you're right, my son—you've changed. I can see it in your eyes. Before the great battle that marked you, your eyes shined brightly. Now they burn as when sky fire strikes a great tree and sets it ablaze, but it's a cold fire that I see. You've suffered a great loss, Beowulf, and there's no getting it back. You must live with that loss—just as we did long ago.*"

That night, inside the cave, Beowulf stretched out alongside Lüma the way he had as a small boy. And just as before, Lüma provided him a pillow with one of her forelegs and wrapped the other around him. Her warmth soothed Beowulf in a way he hadn't felt since the Battle at the Valley of Shadows.

Elin had tried to comfort Beowulf in every way she knew, but he had withdrawn far into himself. Good that she heeded the Schaman's advice to be patient, no matter the pain, no matter the sadness it caused her. Whatever Beowulf's state of mind, Elin had Beorn's, Turin's and Weohstan's strength to draw from; they, too, felt the change in Beowulf and were pained by it; although they bore their suffering in silence. Like Weohstan, Turin, also, was grieving—grieving the loss of his foster father and his brothers. The Schaman's herbs helped, but great was the emptiness they all felt.

"*What about your mate?. Does Elin know you're here*?" said Lüma.

"*No, fur mother. I told no one where I was going.*"

"*Does she no longer please you, my son*?"

"*Yes, fur mother and my love for her is strong, but ever since the battle that marked me this way, a dark cloud hangs over me. Wherever I go, it follows.*"

"*In time the cloud you speak of will pass, just as it did the day our paths crossed. You need time, my son. The loss you feel will always be there, but it won't gnaw at you, not the way it does now.*"

"*I want to believe you, fur mother.*"

"*Believe me, my son. Now rest your mind, and sleep.*"

The last thing Beowulf had felt before he fell into a dreamless sleep was the steady beating of Lüma's heart against his back.

When Beowulf entered the Main Lodge the next morning he found Elin, Beorn, Weohstan, and Turin sitting at the banquet table; they were talking in low voices while servants cleared the table.

Elin and Turin stood at the sight of Beowulf.

"I have been selfish," said Beowulf. "I let my feelings cloud my vision. I forgot what I still had. I have only to look at the four of you to know how rich I am. I love you all and always will. I ask for your forgiveness, for the pain my brooding has caused while you yourselves are grieving."

Elin was first to rush into Beowulf's arms while the others looked on and wiped their cheeks dry.

Beowulf had come home, and each, in turn, embraced him. Sweet is the feeling that's never forgotten.

PART THREE

48

BACK TO THE BEGINNING

As Beowulf rode south, away from the village of Mörk Skog, he stroked the stallion's neck and spoke in the Silent Tongue: *"Soon, Storm Bringer, we'll rest."*

Storm Bringer neighed.

Beowulf recalled an abandoned farmstead they passed that morning on their way north. It was there he intended to spend the night. A fire had gutted the dwelling, and there was no roof; the barn, however, such as it was, would shield them from the elements.

Beowulf caught their scent in the wind even before the stallion. Beowulf slowed Storm Bringer to a walk. *"We have company, my friend."*

The wolves were twelve in number and blocked the way forward; eyes riveted on the horse and rider. Beowulf lifted-back the hood of his cloak.

"Hail, sons of Ulf, we come in peace."

The largest of the twelve, a male with gray fur, a scarred muzzle, who looked older than the others, answered Beowulf in kind:

"How is it you know the language of the Forest Folk, Manling?"

"I learned it from my fur-mother as a child," said Beowulf.

"We know the story of a man cub raised by one of the Forest Folk in Vindinstedt Forest, but that was before my time. If you'd have us believe that cub was you, tell us by what name the Forest Folk knows you—and be quick about it! My comrades and I are hungry!"

Beowulf removed his helm; his long, black hair spilled past his shoulders.

"My tribe knows me as Beowulf, son of Ecgtheow, but among the Forest Folk I was, and always will be—the 'bear's son.'"

The pack leader, whose name was Adalwolf, spoke:

"We know your reputation as a slayer of men, Bear's Son. Ride

on. I, Adalwolf, guarantee you safe passage."

"You have my thanks, Adalwolf. Good hunting, sons of Ulf."

"Good hunting, Bear's Son!"

That said, the wolf pack howled in one loud voice. It carried through the depth of the forest, announcing Beowulf's presence there that cold, and moonless night.

† † †

Upon reaching the farmhouse, Beowulf and Storm Bringer took refuge in the barn. Although in disrepair, it would keep the wind and snow at bay. Beowulf got a fire going. After feeding Storm Bringer, he assuaged his hunger with the food the metalsmith's daughters gave him before departing from their village.

Aside from the crackling and hissing of the fire, the forest was silent—its inhabitants called a truce for the night knowing the bear's son was among them.

The Forest Folk was content to wait until the morrow to resume the All Mother's Dance of Life and Death.

After eating, Beowulf made a place by the fire to sleep. He held his hands palms-out toward the flames, warming them.

Strange, he thought; *it feels like many winters since I used the Silent Tongue, other than with Storm Bringer. And longer still since I last heard someone call me, Bear's Son.*

Beowulf continued staring at the fire, allowing it to work its magic. The flames danced before his eyes and lulled him into a familiar dream-state.

† † †

At dawn, Beowulf rode south. By midday, he reached Vindinstedt Forest. The hot spring was not far off; he would stop there to cleanse himself and wash his armor, cleaning it off, removing the gore he'd accrued doing Hygelac's bidding over the previous three weeks.

As the hot spring and waterfall came into view, Beowulf felt heaviness weigh upon him, a mixture of emotions that clawed his heart. Beowulf tethered Storm Bringer where there was sweet-grass to graze on.

Walking the short distance to the falls, Beowulf removed his helm and chainmail shirt. Stripped of his boots, breeches, and undershirt, Beowulf dove naked into the clear water of the pool. Swimming underwater was most to his liking, and he went three times around the circumference of the pool playing catch-and-release with a school of trout before surfacing.

Leaving the cleansing cold water of the pool, he immersed himself in the hot spring. In a short time, Beowulf felt his weariness depart through every pore of his body. He sighed and tilted his head up to feel the air on his face. As far as looks go, women found Beowulf easy on the eyes—except for the pale, wax-colored scar that ran deep from the corner of his right eye to his chin. Still, scars gained in battle were to Northmen what amber and tortoise shell were to their women—things prized for their sake.

It was the depth of Beowulf's gaze, however, that left farm girls and well-born maidens weak-kneed, for they still burned with an intensity that pierced straight to the heart of things.

Clean, refreshed, Beowulf left the hot spring. Soon after, he rode past the cave that had been his home with Lüma. She was long dead, and Beowulf rode on without stopping. He knew the she bear would not want him to linger there.

"Be not sad on my account," she would have told him. *"I died a good death."*

Beowulf did stop, however, when he reached the clearing where the Wylfings murdered his mother. He let the reins go slack and extended his hands to his sides.

Mother, Father, I know you are both in Valhalla; perhaps you even see and hear me. You'd be pleased, Mother, to know Elin maintains Frigga's shrine, but it would sadden you both knowing we have no children. The All Mother has blest us with much, but not yet with offspring.

Beowulf gathered the reins in his hands and urged Storm Bringer away. A short while later, as the last slice of the sun was retiring for the night, Beowulf halted Storm Bringer atop a knoll overlooking fields ready for plowing.

Visible in the distance, a league away was the stake wall that enclosed the lodges and outbuildings.

Thin columns of smoke rose into the sky from the lodge fires and beckoned—gray-blue fingers saying:

"Come, Bear's son! Come home!"

Each time he returned home it was the same—the instant recollection of the battle in the Valley of Shadows those many summers past that took the lives of his father and all but one of his brothers and left him scarred.

"If the thought of a scar bothers you, grow a beard!" the Schaman told him after sewing the wound shut on the battlefield. It was while they stood among the dead when there was a stillness over the valley, but for the ravenous cawing of crows and ravens.

† † †

Elin sat on the bed clad in a night shift while Handscio's young wife, Asa, brushed Elin's honey-colored hair down the length of her back. The flames from the fire licked the air while shadows danced on the walls and ceiling of the chamber.

Elin raised a hand; Asa ceased brushing.

"What is it, Elin?"

"Beowulf's coming," she said. "I can feel him. Get me my prettiest ribbons, Asa—the ones Beowulf brought me from the Tin Isles."

Several moments passed. Elin's heart quickened its beat at the sound of boots plodding upstairs toward her room.

Handscio entered the chamber with an armload of wood. Tossing the wood down, he placed two logs on the fire.

"These should keep you warm through the night," he said.

"Thank you, Handscio," said Elin; she spoke in a whisper lest her voice betrays her disappointment.

"If you've no more need of Asa," said Handscio, "we'll bid you good night and pleasant sleeping."

"Of course," said Elin. *There's never a good night, she told herself, nor do I sleep without Beowulf beside me.*

Handscio and Asa left the chamber. Elin raised a hand to her head to untie the ribbons in her hair.

"No," said a voice that reached to her core, "Leave them in."

In the days following his return, Beowulf busied himself with matters on which the farm depended: the growing of barley and rye and the raising of sheep, goats and dairy cows.

Beowulf was now the last of his line, apart from his distant cousins, Weohstan, and Weohstan's son, Handscio. They were all that remained of Clan Waegmunding but for Turin, Beowulf's foster brother.

The families who lived outside the stake wall under Beowulf's protection were Freemen who shared in Vindinstedt's prosperity and no family suffered. Indeed, it was on the labor of these Freemen, their wives, and children, that the farm depended. Moreover, the small village that Vindinstedt Farm had become looked after the women and families whose men had died in Beowulf's service.

The bear's son would not have it otherwise.

At midday on spring's Eve, Beowulf led the men to the fields. The women and children followed and wore colorful ribbons and flowers in their hair. Ox-drawn wagons carried wood for a bonfire and baskets filled with baked bread, smoked pheasant, venison, pickled herring and vegetables, a portable altar, ritual banners and a cask of mead.

Close to nightfall, after the Blessing of the Fields, torches would set the wood ablaze. The ensuing bonfire would be visible for many leagues and burn so bright it would chase away any malevolent spirits lurking about—or so the Geatfolk believed.

Near sunset, the Freemen would slaughter several sheep and roast them on spits. Thus the Thunder-Geats celebrated the advent of spring by feasting and drinking. They took comfort from the warmth the great fire would provide, a portent of the warmer days of summer to come.

It was cause for much laughter among the Geatfolk that the biggest number of babies birthed during any given season was traceable to Walpurgisnacht and the spring's Eve celebration nine moons prior.

"I'll wager that smelly old conjurer forgot what day it is," said Handscio.

"Take care what you say, Handscio."

"I was joking, Beowulf. I know how much you care for that old man."

"No, you don't," said Beowulf. "None of you do."

49

HONOR TO THE ALL MOTHER

It wasn't long before Beowulf saw the Schaman's silhouette. Staff in hand, he was a quarter-league off, making his way on foot in their direction. A pack-horse followed behind him loaded with bags of herbs, roots, and trinkets. The herbs and roots were to heal, flavor meat, and invite the Schaman's visions, just as before. Nothing about the Schaman had changed—nothing.

While the women set out foodstuffs, the Freemen unloaded the wood and began to stack it in the form of a pyramid for the bonfire. The women placed the altar facing north and bedecked it with flowers: Bluebells, Buttercups, Forget-Me-Nots and delicate White Anemones.

Beowulf put a ceremonial knife and a drinking horn embossed with gold and silver on the altar. There were five ritual banners, each attached to a pole. Beowulf placed them upright on the ground in front of the altar. Each banner was made from a different colored cloth and sewn onto each was a rune: each rune a symbol for one of the gods the Geats at Vindinstedt Farm would honor that day.

There was a banner for One-eyed Odin, Chief of the gods, another for mighty Thor, Hammer-Bearer. A third to honor Frigga, Chief of the Valkyries, the demigods who transported the bravest and noblest warriors to Valhalla. The fourth banner honored Freyr, patron of fields and crops. A fifth honored Idun of the Golden Apples, the Goddess of Spring.

As the men finished stacking the last of the wood, Beorn arrived. The Schaman stood before the assemblage blowing steam from his mouth with each exhalation. The Schaman's legendary battle axe, Sanning, or, in the Common Tongue, Truth, hung over his back. From his belt, Beorn wore a modest leather pouch containing a few gold rings and a striking-stone for making fire.

"Greetings, Beorn," said Beowulf.

Beorn pulled Beowulf close in an embrace.

"Hail, Prince of Geatland," said the bristled old Schaman.

Bespeaking the Schaman's fondness for wild berries and fermented grapes, Beorn's otherwise white beard was still blue, almost purple down the middle, all the way to his chest, and he still reeked of wood-smoke. Beorn embraced Elin, also Handscio's wife, Asa, then Turin.

When Handscio stepped forward to greet the Schaman, Beorn spun him around and kicked him in the buttocks.

"What was that for?" said Handscio, rubbing his backside.

"For calling me a 'smelly old conjurer,'" said Beorn.

Handscio was dumbstruck. How in the name of all that's possible, he wondered, could Beorn have heard me?

"I may be old, son of Weohstan, but there's nothing wrong with my ears," said the Schaman.

The color drained from Handscio's face.

"Well then," said Beorn; "Let's begin."

Standing before the altar, Beowulf handed the drinking-horn to the Schaman. Into the horn, Elin poured a full portion of mead. Beorn stepped in front of the altar and held the drinking-horn up before the ritual poles:

"Hear us who gather on spring's eve to honor you, O' gods on high: Odin, oldest and wisest, whose one eye sees all things, we gather in your name to honor you. We pray you bless this land and give it your protection."

Beorn poured mead on the ground before Odin's banner.

"Mighty Thor," resumed the Schaman; "Lord of Thunder, Shaker of Mountains, in your name we gather to honor you. We pray you bless this land and give it your protection."

Again, Beorn poured mead on the ground.

Moving to the next banner, Beorn repeated the same invocation: to Frigga, Freyr, and Idun. When Beorn had made the last offering, he turned and faced those in attendance.

"Who," said Beorn, "comes forth this day to give his blood to the All Mother, that she allows her breast to be cleaved by the iron claws of your plowshares?"

Beowulf stepped forward: "I, Beowulf, son of Ecgtheow and Liv, Chief of Clan Waegmunding, offer my blood to the All Mother, that we may partake of her bounty."

Beorn took the ceremonial knife from the altar and stood before

Beowulf. Beowulf raised one arm, already scarred in many places. The Schaman drew the blade across the fleshy part of Beowulf's forearm, making there a cut. Beowulf's blood dripped on the ground and blended with the soil. When several moments passed, Beorn raised his arms and addressed the assemblage.

"Done!" said Beorn.

A joyful shout went up from the Geatfolk. They lit several cooking-fires to roast the meats they prepared: sheep, chicken, rabbit, and deer. Handscio poured cup after cup of mead to all but the children not yet eighteen winters old.

As the Geatfolk celebrated, Elin went to Beowulf's side with a threaded needle shaped into a hook. She began to stitch the cut on his arm closed. Beorn placed a healing poultice on the wound and Elin bound the poultice in place with a clean strip of cloth.

When the light began to fail, Handscio and Turin ignited the bonfire. The Geatfolk cheered as flames leapt high into the air.

Beowulf held Elin close as they watched the fire's growing ferocity.

"How long do I have you for this time?" said Elin.

"Until I'm called away again," said Beowulf.

"Then kiss me," she said.

"Here?" said Beowulf, "Now—in front of everyone?"

"Yes," said Elin. "Here and now! Or you can sleep in the barn tonight with Storm Bringer."

"What—?"

"You heard me," said Elin, laughing. "On a bed of straw, with nothing more supple to squeeze than the rear-end of the nearest cow."

Suppressing a smile, he kissed Elin long on the lips, and savored the scent of her, while the bonfire roared and cast its warmth on them.

"I want your child," said Elin. "I want to bear you a son."

"What's wrong with a daughter?" said Beowulf. "I would be happy with either."

"Then we should have one of each," said Elin. "A son and a daughter."

"You'll get no argument from me," said Beowulf.

"Good," said Elin. "I want you to remember that tonight when we take to our bed."

"You're a harsh taskmaster," said Beowulf, as he held Elin close.

† † †

Just before dawn Beowulf's eyes opened. In the twilight, he looked at Elin's face as she slept. Without making a sound, Beowulf left their bed and dressed.

Outside he joined Weohstan, Handscio, Turin and the Freemen. Freemen loaded plowshares into the back of carts hitched to oxen. Led by Beowulf, the men went to the fields to plow the ground in preparation for planting. Smoke from the bonfire wafted into the morning sky, a large mound of embers glowed red with flame.

Around mid morning Beowulf and the Freemen broke fast to eat the food the women brought to the fields. They were still eating when Beowulf saw a rider coming toward them from the west, riding at a gallop.

It wasn't long before Mikla, now a Captain of coastguards, as was his father before him, halted his horse.

"Hail, Prince Beowulf."

"Greetings, Mikla. What news?"

"Not good, I warrant," said Turin.

"It seldom is," said Handscio.

"Let's hear it, Mikla," said Beowulf.

"Two Longships anchored off our shore this morning."

"Where?" said Beowulf.

"Otters'Bay," said Mikla. "A raiding party, I fear."

"How many?" said Handscio.

"I counted eighty men, well-armed, but no horses."

"Were you able to determine their tribe?" said Handscio.

"Their shields have no markings, and the sails of their boats are without insignia, but—and this will seem odd: by the look of them, the ships Ibelong to the Svear."

"Marauders have come to our shore," said Beowulf; "For now, that's all we need to know."

"Your orders?" said Turin.

"Pick twenty men to accompany us, and bring Mikla, a fresh horse."

† † †

Dressed for battle, Beowulf mounted Storm Bringer. Standing alongside, Elin held Beowulf's helm.

"Come back to me," she said.

Beowulf took his headgear from Elin's hands and smiled.

"When have I not?"

Beorn approached and stood before Beowulf and the riders.

"Remember whose land this is," said the Schaman. "May mighty Thor grant you strength this day, and if it's your time to die—die well, you Sons of Geatland! You Thunder-Geats!"

Beowulf urged Storm Bringer away. Twenty warriors followed him out the Main Gate, Handscio, Turin and Mikla among them.

Elin hurried to the wall-walk and watched until the riders receded from view.

50

OTTERS'BAY

Otters'Bay was a half-day's ride from Vindinstedt Farm. Beowulf and the Freemen halted their horses on the crest of a high dune that sloped toward the beach. Behind them, a short ride inland, little remained of a small farming community apart from the smoldering ruins of huts and barns and the mangled corpses of those who had lived there. From the dune, the Geats watched in silence as the marauders hurried on foot through the fog that blanketed the beach. The marauders were making their way to their Longships—two, sleek battle craft anchored in the bay.

Impatient for action, Storm Bringer neighed and stamped his hooves. The Geat warriors adjusted themselves in their saddles and looked at Beowulf, awaiting his command.

Holding his spear, Death Stalker, he removed Widow Maker from its sheath. Beowulf looked left and right at the grim faces of his men. In a voice colder than the briny sea, colder even than the blue eyes beneath the visor of his bronze helm:

"No prisoners," he said.

The Thunder-Geats urged their horses forward.

A score of marauders trudged along the beach far behind their companions. They were weighted-down by the plunder they took from the village and were the first to hear the thudding of horses' hooves. In less time than it took these stragglers to drop their plunder, the Geats were upon them, trampling some under their horses' hooves and killing others with spear, sword, and axe. With the force of waves crashing on the beach the Geat riders charged along the edge of the water, their gray woolen cloaks trailing from their shoulders. The remaining marauders heard sounds of battle and saw the riders descending on them. Most began to flee while others formed a shield-wall.

The bristled one-eyed chief commanding the raiding party was a Frisian named Brum, a distant cousin of Day Raven, King and Battle Lord of Frisland. Brum roared at his men, commanding them to stand their ground. Some did, many more did not, and chose instead to run. Some of the marauders were wading into the surf, trying to reach the relative safety of the closest Longship. As the Thunder-Geats bore down on them the marauders' shield-wall faltered; then they broke ranks and fled.

Beowulf signaled to his men to pursue the invaders before he leapt from his saddle and advanced toward Brum, their chief.

Brum looked long and hard at the tall, broad-shouldered Geat striding across the sand in his direction. A splendid bronze helm, embossed with silver, concealed all but his eyes and chin, and he armed himself with spear and sword, both dripping blood. Abandoned by his men, Brum licked his lips and spat.

"I recognize you," said Brum. "You're Beowulf—Hygelac's lapdog."

"I'm the one who's going to kill you," said Beowulf. "That is who I am."

Raising his broad axe, Brum gave a desperate shout and rushed forward. He struck at Beowulf and each time Beowulf sidestepped. Arm-weary and drenched with sweat beneath his chainmail shirt, Brum lowered his shield and gasped for breath.

"If you don't fight me, say so, and I'll be off. To Helheim with you and this cursed shore!"

Beowulf split the Frisian's shield from top-to-bottom with a single downward blow that took Brum's arm off at the elbow. Brum hollered and looked in disbelief at the blood gushing from the stump that remained. At his feet, he saw his severed forearm attached to the splintered wreckage of his shield. He attempted to fight, but as he lifted his axe, Beowulf struck a second blow that took Brum's right arm off at the shoulder. Brum sank to his knees. As his one eye began to close, Brum felt Death coming for him, and he looked into the eyes of his killer.

"I'm Brum, kinsman to Day Raven. He'll pay good ransom for my body."

In his heart, Brum knew it was a lie. Day Raven would no more ransom Brum's remains than he would the corpse of a dog. Still, seeing his life pouring out of him, it was a lie Brum clung to in the hope he'd receive a burial befitting his status as a Clan Chief.

"No," said Beowulf; "You came with one purpose—to kill and steal. Your body will remain here with those of your men to slake the hunger of crabs and carrion birds. But first, tell me how a Frisian happens on two Svear battle craft?"

Brum could not answer; his armless trunk fell forward on his face. No longer would he sully the air of Geatland.

Meanwhile, Handscio, Turin and the Thunder-Geats killed the remaining marauders except for ten who managed to wade to the closest Longship and were climbing aboard. Beowulf arrived on foot and stood among his men. They watched the last few marauders preparing to make their escape. Handscio and Turin, their shields and armor awash with blood, went to Beowulf's side.

"Our losses?" said Beowulf.

"Two dead: Dolph and Gundur," said Handscio.

"We have six wounded," said Turin.

Beowulf nodded and sheathed Widow Maker. He handed his spear to Turin, then he strode past Handscio and grabbed a shield from the ground. He slung the shield over his back and continued into the water in the direction of the closest Longship.

"Beowulf, wait!" said Handscio.

Handscio and Turin grabbed shields and followed Beowulf into the water.

The last of the marauders were hurrying to drop sail and lift the anchor when they saw Beowulf wade through the surf in their direction. Some of the marauders took up bows, but before they could let their arrows fly or recover the anchor, Beowulf lifted that heavy iron hook from beneath the water. The marauders looked-on in amazement as Beowulf pu the anchor on his shoulder and pulled their ship toward shore. Handscio and Turin held their shields high, deflecting the arrows that sought their flesh.

"Get back to shore, both of you!" said Beowulf.

"No!" said Turin. "Elin will feed our manhood to the pigs if we let anything happen to you."

Beowulf made a low growling sound. Handscio and Turin might have laughed but for the arrows striking their shields. It wasn't long before Beowulf had beached the marauders' ship. While Beowulf, Turin, and Handscio sat catching their breath, the Geats swarmed the vessel and made quick work of the raiders left on-board.

While the Geat warriors stripped the marauders of their weapons and armor and gathered the plunder strewn over the beach, Beowulf walked alone along the water's edge. Overall he was satisfied with the outcome. He removed his helm and dropped it on the sand. The tide was beginning to ebb. Kneeling, Beowulf cupped his hands and filled them with seawater which he splashed on his face. He looked up, eyes searching the tops of the waves.

There was something out there, watching him, and his right hand fastened on his spear. Beowulf stood. He thought he heard his name called, but by whom, or by what, he couldn't tell. Beowulf peered through the fog, and again the voice called. Then he saw it —a dark, all too familiar specter rising out of the waves.

Beowulf felt a chill crawl up the length of his spine. It was Death clad head-to-toe in gleaming black armor, emerging from the sea.

The iron-spiked helm Death wore obscured his face, save for his eyes that shone through the fog—the same pale yellow moons Beowulf had too often seen. Beowulf raised Death Stalker in one continuous motion and held it poised to throw.

"You, again!" said Beowulf."What do you want?"

"All things by turns, and nothing long."

"You're, Death," said Beowulf.

"Yes."

"And now you've come for me—Is that it?"

"No, Bear's Son, you're much too strong yet."

"So tell me," said Beowulf. "Why have you shown yourself?"

"Over these many winters, I've taken a liking to you."

Handscio and Turin appeared out of the fog and Death vanished. Beowulf continued to stare out to sea. A long moment passed before Beowulf turned and faced his cousin and brother.

"Did you see it?"

Handscio and Turin glanced side-to-side.

"See what?" said Turin.

Beowulf looked; he saw the mist and nothing else.

"Nothing," said Beowulf. He lowered Death Stalker.

Handscio held out his hand. In his palm was a leather pouch.

"I took this off the marauders'Chief."

Beowulf held his hand palm-open. Into it, Handscio poured gold rings, each with a distinct mark.

"This is Hygelac's gold," said Handscio. "Look—our king's mark on them!"

Beowulf looked long and hard at the rings before returning them to the pouch and Handscio's hand.

"Do any of the others know of this?"

"No one," said Turin.

"Good—let's keep this matter to ourselves. Break each ring into eight pieces and give the men equal shares, and you…"

"What?"said Turin.

"Both you and Handscio pocket some for yourself."

Handscio smiled. "The marauders brought many fine swords. What would you have me do with them?"

Beowulf looked out to sea as far as the fog allowed. He saw nothing but the waves, curling and breaking on the shore.

"Distribute the best of them to the men. What's left, we'll give to our king."

† † †

The Geats beat on their shields, as was their custom, and made a sound of thunder in honor of their dead. They did this that the fallen might hear and know they would always be Thunder-Geats, even in the blessed Halls of Valhalla. Later, the Geats loaded the Longships with the weapons and armor they stripped from the marauders.

Turin found Beowulf off by himself, combing Storm Bringer's mane.

"The men wish to make camp here and burn our dead," said Turin.

Beowulf stopped what he was doing.

"Hygelac needs to hear of this attack, Turin—sooner than later. I want you and Handscio to sail the marauders'Longships to Falcon's Nest. Until then, remind the men that the best way to honor our shield-brothers is to avenge them in battle."

"Truly, Beowulf—is that all you want me to say?"

Beowulf thought on it. "No," he said. "I'll talk to them."

Turin gathered the men.

"You fought well," said Beowulf, "against a desperate enemy. Remember—to live as a Freeman, to live as a Thunder Geat, means reckoning with death. Let each of us strive for glory, that the bards may sing of us when we're gone. But now, my friends, there's work to be done, and I need your help."

Mikla departed south to resume watching the coastline from his post at Land's End. Beowulf ordered Handscio, Turin and all but four of the Freemen to sail the captured Longships north along the coast to the Fjord of Kuurin and the harbor below Falcon's Nest.

After the Longships had departed, Beowulf and the four men he picked to ride with him buried their two shield-brothers.

Done, they returned to the village and labored past sunset burying the dead—every man, woman, and child.

51

ON THE WAY NORTH

The next day Beowulf spoke not at all as he and the four rode north toward Falcon's Nest. The men accompanying him didn't question Beowulf's silence; they knew he lacked a glad tongue. For that matter, none of them could say they'd ever heard Beowulf laugh. The four Freemen sensed a dark cloud over Beowulf, and it made them uneasy. Still, just as with Turin and Handscio and the others aboard the Longships, they would follow Beowulf anywhere, even into the Great Abyss beyond the Whale Road if he asked it of them.

Sunlight began to quit the day, and Beowulf and his men camped by a river. Taking off his armor and undergarments, Beowulf felt the eyes of his men on him. He heard them talk in hushed voices about the action on the beach. They were in awe how Beowulf beached the marauders' battle craft with nothing more than the strength of his arms.

Beowulf waded into the river and began to shave with the same sharp blade his father had bought in Land's End over twenty winters before. That Beowulf shunned wearing a beard made him the subject of curiosity among the Northmen, but not so much among his people. Many a young Geat emulated this killer of men whom some still called the bear's son. But carving the hair from one's face with a sharpened shell or iron blade was both puzzling and troubling to many an older Geat warrior; although it was not so contentious a topic as to provoke a quarrel over, not with Beowulf Waegmunding.

Beowulf looked at the four Geats staring at him, and they looked away. When he had finished, Beowulf threw the shaving-blade onto the bank and dove underwater. When the bear's son came to the surface, Beowulf held a large Salmon in one hand. He tossed that prince of fishes in the direction of his men.

"Since you've no better thing to do than yawp and gawk—cook this!"

Later, while his men slept wrapped in their cloaks beside the campfire, Beowulf sat looking into the star-filled sky. An owl hooting nearby relaxed him—somewhat. That Death had stared Beowulf in the eyes weighed on his thoughts; things rooted in this life, not the next. Marauders had attacked Geatland:

The marauders' boats are Svear by design, Beowulf told himself, *yet the chief leading them claimed kinship with Day Raven. Frisians or not, how did Brum come by Hygelac's gold?* Weary of thinking about things for which he had no answers, Beowulf threw the last stick on the fire and gave himself over to thoughts of a much different sort. Beowulf closed his eyes to everything but the image of Elin's face and gray eyes—cat's eyes, he called them.

Through the mist, the sun poured its light down on Beowulf and his men, warming them in their saddles as they rode across rugged valleys and verdant hills. Every so often they passed a village or farm whose inhabitants, those brave enough to show themselves, cheered and waved to Beowulf. The Schaman, Beorn, had warned Beowulf long before that most Geatfolk would fear him. The fact he possessed the power of thirty men in each arm played a role as to their fear of him. But, and moreso, they saw in Beowulf a creature straddling two worlds: one, the world of men, brutish, vicious, recognizable because they were part of it; the other—a dark, murky world—a feral, untamed place—a place humans dreaded but dared not contemplate.

† † †

Farther north, not far from the border separating Gotaland from the land of the Svear, a cloaked rider waited upon his horse in a grove of birch trees. He wore the hood of his cloak pulled low, obscuring his features. He had not waited long when two riders arrived to meet him. They, too, wore the hoods of their cloaks pulled down and with good reason—men hunted them: Eanmund and his younger brother, Eadgils, sons of the dead Svear king,

Ohthere.

The Spear Danes had killed their father and much of his army on the shore of Daneland three months earlier. It was then that their uncle, Onela, usurped the crown when, by right of succession, it belonged to Eanmund since he was Ohthere's oldest son. Although some among the Svear supported Eanmund as the rightful heir to the crown, they were too few to matter, and Onela went unopposed. Ohthere wasted the Svear army in Daneland, and it would take time for Onela to rebuild it; hence, Onela sent crafted words of peace to Hrothgar, King of the Danes, reminding him that it was to Hrothgar's sister, Astrid, that Onela was married. It was also true that Onela had refused to accompany Ohthere to Daneland since he wanted no part of a conflict pitting his tribe against the tribe of his wife. Besides, Astrid was still young, and she warmed their bed to his liking.

"Hail, sons of Ohthere," said the rider.

"Hail, Prince Heardred," said Eanmund.

"What news?" said Eanmund's younger brother, Eadgils.

"The Frisians have the Longships you provided," said Heardred, "and half the gold I promised them."

"You mean your father's gold," said Eadgils.

Quick to perceive a slight, Heardred moved his hand to the hilt of his sword.

"I apologize for my brother," said Eanmund. "Your gold or your father's gold, it matters not. We're in this together."

"Truly, I meant no offense," said Eadgils.

"Good," said Heardred; "since we're three princes of like mind, cheated by fate and desirous of what is rightfully ours! Alone we can do little, but together—together, we'll attain our due!

"You paint a pretty picture," said Eanmund.

"What must we do now?" said Eadgils.

"For now, we wait," said Heardred. "For the war that will come when Hygelac learns of the raid on Geatland."

"Are you certain your father will believe the marauders were Svear—ordered there by our uncle?" said Eadgils.

"I am," said Heardred. "Besides, it was my father who killed your grandfather, and he has no great liking for Onela. But there's still one obstacle in our way."

"Your cousin," said Eanmund.

"Yes," said Heardred, "the bear's son."

On the third day following the battle at Otters'Bay, Beowulf reached the outskirts of Falcon's Nest. On the heights beyond the earthworks that surrounded the city, the Citadel loomed through the mist. Hygelac's father, Hrethel, finished building the Citadel. Geat kings built that fortress out of stone high upon cliffs that were impossible to scale from the west—the side facing seaward. The Citadel overlooked the harbor where the Geats anchored their fleet of fifty Longships including the two battle craft that arrived earlier with Handscio and Turin. It was from that well-positioned fortress that Hygelac ruled Geatland, just as his father had and Hrethel's father's father before him.

While the four who accompanied Beowulf followed, Beowulf rode over the stone causeway that spanned the ditch encircling the perimeter of Falcon's Nest. He rode past the Main Gate into the city. The Geatfolk shouted for they recognized Beowulf as he rode astride his warhorse looking like the God of War, sunlight flashing off his helm and hand-ringed, chainmail armor.

The news of Beowulf's coming had already reached the city, and crowds formed shouting his name. A woman lifted her infant son to see Geatland's Battle Lord, but at the sight of Beowulf's helm, the boy recoiled.

"Forgive him, my Prince," said the child's mother.

Beowulf stopped Storm Bringer. Looking at the mother and her son, Beowulf removed the battle gear from his head.

"Let me hold him," said Beowulf.

Without hesitation, the boy's mother lifted the child into Beowulf's outstretched arm. Beowulf sat the infant on his thigh.

"You see, little Thunder Geat," he said, "there's nothing to fear."

Beowulf shook his helm and held it so the boy could see inside and know that without a head to give it purpose, it was little more than an empty vessel. Beowulf returned the boy to his mother's arms.

"He'll grow into a strong warrior one day."

"Thank you, my Prince," the woman said. She took her son and stepped back into the crowd.

Beowulf rode until he reached a large, iron-banded door that guarded the single means of egress and ingress to the Citadel. The warriors standing guard on the wall-walk above saw Beowulf coming and they called-out to those below to open the door.

Beowulf found Handscio and Turin waiting for him in the passageway that connected the entrance to the Citadel's interior.

The Door Warden and several guards approached. Greetings made, Beowulf, Handscio, and Turin walked shoulder-to-shoulder toward an arched entrance at the end of the passageway that led to the Mead Hall.

Beowulf gave Handscio a sidelong glance. Handscio's brow had furled and his jaws clenched, bone biting down on bone.

"Something troubles you," said Beowulf. "I see it in your face."

"Don't you feel the intrigue in the air?" said Handscio. "The stench of bargains struck in secret. I tell you—this place reeks of it!"

"Softly, Handscio," said Beowulf; "lest unfriendly ears hear your words and misconstrue their meaning."

"Haven't you seen the faces of the chieftains, Beowulf," said Turin. "The way their expressions change when they see you? How the vinegar in their voices vanishes and honey spouts from their arses."

Beowulf stopped and grasped Turin by the shoulders.

"Don't you two understand the meaning of 'softly'?"

Turin let out a deep breath: "I'm sorry, Beowulf; my anger bested me. Like Handscio, I don't like it here."

"You'll both feel better once we're home," said Beowulf

"I'm counting on it," said Handscio. "The air is cleaner there."

"Agreed," said Turin.

They continued through the Mead Hall and proceeded along a torch-lit corridor until they reached the Throne Room.

Ragmund, now Hygelac's adviser in matters of diplomacy and commerce, greeted Beowulf, Turin, and Handscio with a courteous bow.

"Welcome back, Prince Beowulf."

Prince Heardred rode south at a gallop toward Falcon's Nest. His mind raced as fast as his steed, and he could feel his heart pound in his chest. There was much in flux; still, he had bested his fears and taken the first step—initiating a war between Geats and Svear, or so he believed.

My father thinks Beowulf's mere presence on the battlefield can determine the outcome even before iron strikes iron or blood wets the ground. The bear's son mustn't be here when war breaks out, but how do I make that happen?

52

THE TRUTH OF THE MATTER

It was no secret: Hygelac trusted no one more than Beowulf Waegmunding—not Hygd, his young queen, nor his son, Heardred. As Hygelac watched Beowulf, Turin, and Handscio approach the dais, he recollected that day in the Valley of Shadows.

So many times, Nephew, have I revisited that battle. You killed a hundred of Ongentheow's warriors that day! I remember it as vividly as when I first bedded Hygd. A Svear blade sliced your face when all was noise and confusion, and you took your father's sword off the ground and wielded sword and spear like scythes! That scar on your face is a tribute to your courage, Bear's Son. Do you remember the bodies we had to walk over when we quit the field?

Ragmund stopped a measured distance from the dais.

"Your Battle Lord, Great King—Beowulf, Chief of Clan Waegmunding, Prince of Geatland."

Ragmund's introduction complete, he stepped to one side. Handscio and Turin stepped away from the dais. All the Clan Chiefs were present at Falcon's Nest that day. Hygelac had sent for them after Handscio brought news of the raid at Otters'Bay.

Both Hygelac and Beowulf understood one simple fact: the clans composed the soul of Geatland, but it was of the people, and the people, alone, that Geatland's strength resided.

"Welcome back to Falcon's Nest, Nephew," said Hygelac.

"Thank you, Uncle. It pleases me to be back." It was a lie Beowulf told, but harmless.

"Yes," added Hygd. Her voice was warm and welcoming, "We've missed you, Beowulf."

"Handscio and Turin brought news of your victory at Otters'Bay two days ago," said Hygelac. "They arrived here with two ships piled high with weapons and armor."

"I'm glad, my King. Still, I'm duty-bound to tell you if Handscio and Turin did not: the marauders destroyed a village and left none alive—not even the newborns."

"Handscio mentioned as much," said Hygelac. "Still, hearing the news a second time is no less difficult to bear. Good, you got to Otters'Bay when you did, or the marauders would've killed more of our people."

"I can't speak to that, my King. But perhaps, had I pushed my men harder, I could've saved that village."

"Don't trouble yourself with dark thoughts, Beowulf," said Hygelac. "You can't take responsibility for the death of the villagers at Otters'Bay. It was Fate, and Fate works its will where it will and spares no one in the doing!"

"Then I'll leave the matter at that, my King."

"Good! Now tell us if Handscio's account is accurate, or was it the mead talking."

Beowulf looked over his shoulder at Handscio. Handscio raised his hands to his sides to protest his innocence. Turin put a hand over his mouth to keep from laughing.

"I remember little about that night, my Prince," said Handscio.

Beowulf looked at his uncle.

"And what story would that be, my King?Handscio is a master storyteller, especially when mead soaks his tongue."

"Handscio told us how you prevented the marauders from escaping," said Hygelac, "by dragging their battle craft onto the beach."

"Handscio was not far wrong in the telling, my King; some of the marauders sought to make good their escape, but I was lucky to catch hold of the anchor. With the tide in my favor, and with Handscio and Turin guarding my back, I managed to pull their battle craft to shore. The rest was butcher's work."

From the side entrance, Prince Heardred entered the Throne Room; he bowed to his father and mother.

"Good of you to favor us with your presence," said Hygelac, annoyed by Heardred's timing; or rather the lack of it.

"I'm sorry, Father," said Heardred, and he turned his eyes toward Beowulf.

Beowulf nodded. "Prince Heardred."

Heardred nodded but made no reply.

Hygelac's eyes flashed: "Is that how you greet my Battle Lord, with a curt nod and silence?"

"My apology, Father—and to you, Cousin Beowulf; I apologize."

To those within earshot, Heardred's voice sounded civil, but it was a voice cloaked with malice and Beowulf sensed it.

Standing in the shadows at the back of the Throne Room, Knut Iron-Jaw, Chief of Clan Eriksson shifted from foot to foot. Eager was Eriksson to leave Falcon's Nest for the nearest brothel. It rankled him to be anywhere near the Citadel, so strong had his hatred for Hygelac become. No different than many other Clan Chiefs, Knut Iron-Jaw was indebted to Beowulf's father for past services rendered; yet, as did many, they feared the bear's son; for they knew his first allegiance was to King Hygelac. They knew he would kill without hesitation should Hygelac order it.

"As I passed through the marketplace," said Heardred, "I heard the people speak of a raid. Is it true, Father, that the Svear attacked our shore? If Geatfolk died, we must act, and act now! Geat honor demands—"

"Honor!" said Hygelac, interrupting. "What do you know about honor? Despite your age, Heardred, you still talk like a boy! You know nothing about honor—or battle! The foes I've seen you kill were deer and an occasional pig! Now then, Beowulf—where were we?"

"Prince Heardred is right," said Beowulf, "to suggest the need for a response, my King; but the question is—against whom?"

"The boats belong to the Svear," said Hygelac. "Both built in the Svear manner, and each has Onela's clan mark carved on the tiller."

"There's more to it than that, my King," said Beowulf.

"More? What more is there? You killed the Svear who murdered our people and captured two battle craft! What more do we need to know?"

"I would rather we speak in private, my King."

"Very well," said Hygelac, "Everyone out, except for Hygd. And you, Heardred—you may stay. You might even learn something."

When the Throne Room was otherwise empty, Hygelac turned to Beowulf.

"Now then, what more is there to know?"

"The marauders were not Svearlanders, but Frisians," said

Beowulf. "I say this because the chief leading them was a Frisian and a cousin of Day Raven. What's more, he had a bag of gold rings, stamped with your mark on his person."

Heardred knew nothing about this. His mind reeled to hear of Brum's defeat and the loss of the ships and gold. The blood drained from Heardred's face. According to his plan, the Frisians were supposed to make a brief showing in Geatland, sack a defenseless village, or two, and depart! The Svear Longships were to be Heardred's gift to the Frisian King, Day Raven, for supplying men for the mission.

"Svear Longships, Frisian marauders, and a bag of my gold," said Hygelac; "Speaking of which—where is it?"

"I distributed it to the men who went with me to Otters'Bay," said Beowulf, "including the two Freemen who died there: Dolph Eckhart, and Gundur Johansson—for their families."

Hygelac nodded in the affirmative. "Fair enough," he said. "You did a good thing; your men deserve the gold. Now, let's get back to the crux of the matter. Give me the long and short of it, Nephew."

"We were attacked by Frisians in Svear boats paid for with gold —your gold, Uncle."

"I say it was the Svear, plain and straightforward!" said Heardred.

"You may be right, Cousin," said Beowulf, "and yet—" Beowulf stopped mid-sentence.

"And yet?" said Hygelac.

"And yet I can't answer the one question that needs answering. Perhaps Prince Heardred can."

"Answer what?" said Heardred.

"Why raid Geatland?" said Beowulf. "Why now, when our tribe is stronger than ever before?"

Heardred was swift to reply. "The Usurper, Onela, would have us pay tribute, just as we did when Ongentheow was king. Besides, now that Onela is on the Throne he'll want to avenge his father. After all, it was you, Father, who slew Ongentheow."

"It was Eofor, your brother-in-law, who slew Ongentheow," said Hygelac; "Somehow the credit passed to me. Still, I rewarded Eofor with your sister, Ingrid. What difference does it make who killed him? Onela plays a dangerous game if he thinks he can test me—and now he must answer for it!"

Six winters a king, Hygelac was not comfortable delving deep into matters of conjecture, not when the possibility of war loomed.

"Geat honor at stake," continued Hygelac, "which means my honor's at stake! I dare not sit on my arse and twiddle my hands!"

"After Ohthere's defeat in Daneland, Onela needs time to build an army," said Beowulf; "which is another reason I don't think he'd provoke war—at least, not now."

Heardred swallowed over the lump forming in his throat.

My father accepts the lie like a bloated codfish choking on a hook, but not Beowulf— he senses something afoot!

"Mounting a war against the Svear could prove unwise and costly in men, ships, and treasure," said Beowulf. "As matters stand, Uncle, I can't say a war with Onela will gain us much, aside from the satisfaction you'll feel by killing him. Nevertheless, appeasing Geat honor will cost our tribe dearly if we look toward war as a means of settling this business. One more thing: Svear ships can be bought, pirated, or copied, same as any other, no matter the design, or the clan-mark on the tiller."

Queen Hygd saw her husband tap the flats of his fingers on the armrests of his throne and sensed his discomfort.

"What do you think your king should do?" said Hygd.

"Yes," said Heardred; "You're father's Battle Lord. What do you propose?"

"Order the Clan Chiefs to prepare for war."

"And—?" said Hygelac.

"Nothing," said Beowulf. "Let whoever planned this raid wonder long and hard what became of his men and ships. Meanwhile, I'll try to discover who's behind this."

Hygd placed her hand on Hygelac's arm:

"Beowulf rode long and hard to get here, my husband; let us celebrate his return before you send him on another of your errands."

Heardred stepped back unnoticed, into the shadows. *Fate plays a trick on me. I'm next in line, for the throne, yet I feel the crown slipping away; moving in Beowulf's direction. Why do the people not shout my name when I pass? It's bad enough my father prefers Beowulf's company to mine, but why do the people love the bear's son, and not me?*

While he watched his father and Beowulf talking, Heardred wished himself elsewhere, far from Falcon's Nest and the Citadel, away from his father's critical eye, away from his mother's doting, away from those who mocked him. Hygd's love gave her son no solace. The solace Heardred found was in fornicating—and in the plans, he contrived, the plans he now conspired to carry out.

I need you dead, Beowulf, Heardred told himself. *As dead as I can make you, but I'll need help for that.*

Beowulf looked in Heardred's direction. Heardred tried but couldn't look away.

Beowulf looks at me as though he hears my thoughts.

† † †

That night in Beowulf's honor, Hygelac and Hygd hosted a feast in the Mead Hall. A bard played upon his lyre and sang of heroes and ancient battles while cooks served roasted pig and deer, along with warm loaves of honey-baked bread, and biscuits. There were dried fruits and dried vegetables, fresh salmon, herring, sprigs of dill, and leaves of boiled pigweed.

Servants poured mead from many a barrel of Hygelac's home brew. The servants were mindful to pour that potent honey-wine into the cups of the Clan Chiefs and their women. However, the chieftains attending the feast were fewer in number now, Hygelac's invitation notwithstanding. Knut Iron-Jaw was absent; so, too, was Prince Heardred.

Beowulf's plan was to leave for Vindinstedt Farm at dawn and return his men to their families.

I'll miss you, Beowulf, Queen Hygd told herself while watching Beowulf and Hygelac talking in hushed voices. Noting Heardred's absence, Hygd decided to make no mention of it to Hygelac.

It will put him in a foul mood when we take to our bed later. Besides, he has eyes of his own to see who's here and who's not.

"A splendid feast—ay, Nephew?"

"Indeed, Uncle," said Beowulf.

Beowulf scanned the Mead Hall and saw that Heardred and Knut Iron-Jaw were absent. Beowulf ate and drank but little once he and Hygelac finished speaking. There was much on Beowulf's mind, matters he needed to sort out, some having to do with his cousin, Heardred.

Beowulf hoped Hygelac's heir might take him aside and voice his grievance, to clean the air between them. Beowulf sensed Heardred's resentment before, but of late Heardred's unspoken maledictions had become palpable.

† † †

A short ride from the earthworks surrounding Falcon's Nest, the Mead-House was little more than a renovated barn with several large rooms and an upstairs loft. The dining room featured a fire-pit for warmth and straw on the floor to soak-up spilled beer, mead and vomit. The Mead-House keeper and his wife were in bed upstairs. Their two daughters were still up, scrubbing mead horns and utensils for the morrow. Unaware of the identities of the two men talking in whispers in the back room, the girls judged them, warriors of importance, maybe even highborn. Beyond that, the girls knew the young, handsome one had given their father a pouch filled with silver wedges and was not to be disturbed.

"That's your idea," said Eriksson, "provoke a war with the Svear and hope Onela kills Hygelac?"

"More or less," said Heardred.

"Well," said Eriksson; "Is it more, or less? I won't commit my Berserkers to a conspiracy birthed by a fool with an ill-formed plan."

Eriksson disliked Heardred; he thought him weak and useless. Still, he hated the father more and had from the first day he exchanged words with Hygelac and his two brothers in the Citadel, over twenty summers before.

The son is a fool, to be sure, thought Eriksson, but far better with Heardred on the throne than Hygelac.

"I need your Berserkers, Eriksson, not your insults," said Heardred. "My father is all but convinced the Svear sacked the village at Otters'Bay, but now Beowulf has cast doubts as to that. He's the one obstacle to my plan. I thought he would hear the news that the Svear attacked Geatland and that would be that. I didn't count on his catching the Frisians bloody-handed. That was just bad luck."

"So," said Eriksson, "you want my Berserkers to kill him."

"Yes," said Heardred. "I believe your Berserkers are capable of defeating Beowulf Waegmunding, but to do so, they must take him by surprise using all their stealth. Moreover, they must attack in a pack. No man alive can defeat the bear's son in single combat; except, perhaps, the Frisian giant, Day Raven."

A contemptuous look appeared on Eriksson's face.

"So, you believe that bull dung, do you—Beowulf, the bear's son, suckled by a she bear in Vindinstedt Forest, living on bugs and honey and leaving the land of the Brondings with the strength of thirty men in each arm?"

"Yes," said Heardred. "I believe the stories; besides, it is well-known there's magic in Vindinstedt Forest. Listen, Eriksson, I need an ally I can count on, one who will go the full measure. That's why I chose you from among the other chiefs. Perhaps, when my plan succeeds, you'll think better before insulting me to my face. Who knows, maybe you'll even respect me when I become king!"

Heardred watched Knut Iron-Jaw think-through the long and short of Heardred's strategy.

"If you're going to be the next King of Geatland," said Eriksson, "You'll need a thicker skin, young Prince; yours bruises too easily. Still, your idea has merit. In exchange for my help, I want my land to be free from taxation. Also, what I gather in plunder from going aviking will remain mine and mine alone. That's my price for killing Beowulf Waegmunding."

"When?" said Heardred. "Where?"

"That's for me alone to know," said Eriksson. "But take comfort, young Prince—it will be sooner than later. I promise you that."

"What about Eanmund and Eadgils—will you help them?"

"Yes, I'll give them sanctuary, but it'll cost them silver—a lot of it."

"I understand," said Heardred. "You'll have what you want."

"Swear to it," said Eriksson.

"I swear it!"

"Then, young Prince, we have a bargain. Let's shake."

Knut and Heardred each spit onto the palm of one hand; then clasped their hands together, sealing the bargain. Business concluded, the two men left the Mead-House and rode off in opposite directions.

Heardred rode his horse at a canter toward Falcon's Nest. His mind was a whirl as he planned his next move. However, something else vied for his attention that night, something unrelated to war or the theft of a kingdom. Rather, the sweet faces of the two young sisters back at the Mead-House revisited his mind, beckoning him. As the moon passed in and out from behind clouds, Heardred felt giddy for having secured an alliance with Knut Iron-Jaw. Eriksson had become a renowned warrior, and his twenty Berserkers were worth a hundred ordinary men; although Eriksson was cautious not to use them—not in Geatland, under pain of death, for Hygelac would not allow it.

Heardred recalled how he once saw a Berserker enter Berserkergang—the fury state. It happened when Heardred accompanied his father and Beowulf on a journey, one that brought them to Knut Iron-Jaw's estate. Hygelac had learned from Beowulf that Knut had returned with Berserkers from Germania. Hygelac, being a conscientious king, wasted no time warning Eriksson against using those "lunatics," as he called them, to work Knut's will in Geatland. The Berserker Heardred saw was laboring in a field trying to separate the massive stump of a severed oak from its resting place in the ground. As often was the case, the Berserker wore no more than a loincloth. Heardred saw the Berserker's exertions arrive at a fever pitch: his body began to shiver, and he growled—a mixture of man and beast. The Berserker's teeth began to chatter when he stepped away from the trunk. His face swelled and changed color to bright red. The Berserker howled, seized an axe and attacked the thick roots that held the stump in place. Sweat poured from the Berserker's body as he brought the axe down until the last of the roots relented. Other men secured ropes around the base of the stump and with a team of oxen they dragged the stump from the dark earth. The Berserker dropped to his knees, drained of his strength and exhausted. Moreover, the Berserker would remain weak as a newborn until rested, for that was the other face of Berserkergang.

The Berserkers' strength is their weakness, it's true, but that changes nothing Heardred told himself. *My plan is a simple one, yes; but it's a sound plan—Eriksson's Berserkers will kill Beowulf for me.*

Weary of thinking, Heardred wheeled his horse about and rode at a gallop, back toward the Mead-House—back to the girls he knew would welcome him and his silver.

The feast concluded, the king and queen retired to their bedchamber; so, too, did the chieftains depart to rooms prepared for them in Hygelac's Keep. Beowulf passed the night in the Mead Hall with Handscio and Turin and the Freemen of Vindinstedt Farm. Hygelac made better quarters available, but Beowulf wouldn't have it. He lay on one of the tables the servants cleared for just that purpose. Using one arm as a pillow, and his cloak for a blanket, Beowulf slept despite the loud snoring of some of his men and the occasional, gaseous smell, that wafted past his nostrils in the semidarkness.

The following morning after sunrise, Beowulf departed from Falcon's Nest with Handscio, Turin and eighteen others for Vindinstedt Farm.

They had ridden a short distance when, from behind, came the sound of shouting. Beowulf and his men wheeled their horses about and saw a rider approaching. The rider was Sigmund, Captain of the Kungens Vakter, the King's guard. He had earned the position after distinguishing himself in battle, at the Valley of Shadows; where Lord Magnus, the Guards' Captain, perished from a Svear arrow meant for King Hrethel.

"Stay your swords!" said Beowulf. "A friend approaches."

"Prince Beowulf!" said Sigmund. "Hygelac bids you return with all haste. An emissary from the Spear Danes has arrived, and the news he brings is dire!"

Beowulf looked at the faces of his men.

"All of you, save for Handscio, return to your families. Turin, you are in charge of Vindinstedt Farm in my absence."

† † †

Beowulf and Handscio went to the Throne Room. The king and queen were waiting there with Ragmund and King Hrothgar's emissary, Ulthur, the Danish Lord who had brokered the peace between Clan Waegmunding and the Wylfings. A peace bought by the death of King Amunwolf, a chest of Hrothgar's silver and the youngest of Amunwolf's daughters, Wealtheow, now Hrothgar's wife and Queen. Ulthur was knowledgeable of the northern tribes and was himself a warrior of note who doubled as one of Hrothgar's spies. Beowulf was no different; he served as Hygelac's eyes and ears and the enforcer of Hygelac's will, just as Ecgtheow had done for King Hrethel, before him.

"There you are, Cousin!" said Hygelac. "There's much you need to hear."

"Greetings, Prince Beowulf," said Ulthur.

"Hail, Ulthur," said Beowulf. "What news?"

"Tell him, Ulthur," said Hygelac.

"Fiends lay waste to Hrothgar's Kingdom."

"Fiends," said Beowulf, "what manner of fiends? Do you mean Trolls?"

"No, these are far worse. Two misshapen beings, the larger of which we call Grendel. Much taller than men, both have scales for skin—skin that can turn the points of our spears and best iron blades."

"Is it possible such creatures exist?" said Handscio. His voice did not rise above a whisper.

"Apparently," said Beowulf.

He turned again to Ulthur. "And your king—how goes it with Hrothgar?"

"It weighs on him," said Ulthur. "He's a proud man but feels he can no longer protect his people. That's how it goes with Hrothgar."

"My father said Heorot Fort was impregnable," said Beowulf, "no matter the size of the army assailing its gate."

Ulthur stifled a nervous cough: "That's something we hope our enemies continue to believe, Prince Beowulf. These fiends—Grendel and his dam, by-pass Heorot Fort by traversing the moors at night. Together, they possess the power of mighty Thor Himself. They smashed through the Main Gate of Heorot Hall the night of their first attack; then fought their way past a hundred warriors, killing many before dragging others away, no doubt to devour."

"By all the gods," said Handscio, "how can that possibly be?"

"Yes, Lord Ulthur," added Beowulf, "how is that possible?"

"The scales that cover their hides are like no armor in all of Midgard, great Prince," said Ulthur. "No matter how many we let loose, our arrows bounce off them, as did the points of our spears. Not one of our warriors was able to get close enough to lay a sword blade on them. The reach of their arms and the sharpness of their talons are like scythes. They mowed our warriors down the way a farmer does a field of barley."

"What of Heorot Hall?" said Beowulf.

"They destroyed the Main Gate, then they battered down the entry door of the Hall," said Ulthur. "They splintered an oak crossbeam, thick as your thigh to do it. The next day, while we cleaned the Hall of blood, our warriors rebuilt the Main Gate and replaced the door. It was to no avail. The second night of the full moon, Grendel and his dam came again, and again they smashed the crossbeam barring the Main Gate. They entered the palisade and once more we tried to stop them. More brave warriors died, and the monsters ripped the new door from its hinges. They butchered what remained of Hrothgar's Iron Guard and left. The reason King Hrothgar survived the fiend's wrath is that Grendel and his dam are too large, too massive to fit through the winding, stone passageway leading to Heorot's highest tower where our king and queen retire at day's end. The next day, our king disbanded the army into the hills, out of harm's way, and ordered that the Main Gate left open, as it is now, smashed and splintered off its hinges; so, too, with the door leading into the Hall."

While Ulthur was speaking, Heardred entered the Throne Room unnoticed. He remained standing in the shadows, listening to Ulthur's strange tale. Beowulf sensed Heardred's presence but made no show of it.

"Truly," said Hygelac, "calamity rules the land of the Spear Danes, and it saddens us to hear it. Hrothgar has been a loyal friend to the Geatfolk."

"I pray it will always be so," said Ulthur, "that Danes and Geats greet each other as friends."

"How is it," said Beowulf, "that these two creatures came to Daneland?"

"That's my question as well," said Heardred, stepping forward, "for it's well known your king maintains an extensive ring of spies, here and around Daneland."

"A fair question, Prince Heardred," said Ulthur. "These... things did not come from outside our borders; they came from within."

"How so," said Hygelac, "how could such creatures you've described go about unnoticed?"

"Several days before the waxing of this past full moon, there was a tremendous convulsing throughout Daneland. The earth shook beneath our feet—a shuddering, so long and forceful that Heorot Hall trembled. People felt the shaking across the length and breadth of Jutland. When the shaking quit and the earth at rest, fishermen living near Lake Neff came to Heorot to tell Hrothgar what they'd seen. They felt a great commotion beneath their feet, as did we all. They thought the All-Mother's heart was breaking, so terrible was the shaking. The waters of the lake rippled toward the shore in waves as tall as small trees. They said it was like the sky itself dropped into the lake. They fled to higher ground, leaving their nets and fishing spears behind. Terrified as they were, they continued to watch as the water began to bubble and froth and a waterspout burst upward. What issued from the waterspout was brackish and foul smelling. Before the eyes of those fisher folks, across the breadth of the lake, fish began to float to the surface by the thousands—dead. Even now, animals that drink from the lake die on the shoreline. No, these fiends didn't come to Daneland from abroad. Nor did they slip past our spies. It is from some great abyss, deep beneath the lake itself, that Grendel and his dam sprang forth."

"That's quite a tale," said Heardred.

"Every word," said Ulthur, "I spoke honestly."

"Even so," said Heardred, looking at the faces around him, "it's Hrothgar's problem. It concerns the Geatfolk not at all."

"Enough!" said Hygelac. "Don't interrupt!"

Humiliated by his father, yet again, Heardred would not interrupt; he could not, so thick was the anger caught-up in a ball at the back of his throat.

"That is the extent of my report, Great King," said Ulthur. "Soon, there'll be another full moon and, I fear, the slaughter will continue."

"What can the Geatfolk do for the Spear Danes?" said Hygelac.

"Hrothgar seeks nothing, Great King," said Ulthur. "He sent me here to warn you."

"To warn me?"

"Yes," said Ulthur. "We Danes can no longer guarantee you early warning should your enemies move against you. The word is, Day Raven and the Frisians are restless to gain a chokehold on the trade routes our tribes share."

"This is grave, indeed," said Hygelac.

"Long have the Frisians wanted war with us," said Ragmund. "And so, too, have the Svear. It's our alliance with the Spear Danes that keeps them at-bay."

"That, and the strength that resides in my Battle Lord's arms," said Hygelac.

Heardred turned pale hearing his father praise Beowulf.

I'll see you dead, Father—you and the bear's son both!

"What if I went to the land of the Spear Danes," said Beowulf, "and offered Hrothgar our assistance. I can leave today—with Ulthur."

"Not without me, you won't," said Handscio.

"Alas, Prince Beowulf," said Ulthur, "I have another stop to make in Hrothgar's stead; one that will take me further north to the land of the Brondings where Breca is king."

"That matters not," said Beowulf, and he turned to Hygelac. "Soon the moon will wax full. I can do what must be done and return to Geatland in a fortnight."

"But what if you're needed here?" said Ragmund. "Otters' Bay was a warning. If Onela attacks from the north and the Frisians from the south—what are we to do? The fiends Ulthur speaks of have rendered our alliance with Hrothgar meaningless!"

"What say you to that?" said Hygelac.

"What Ragmund says is true," said Beowulf. "It's possible the Svear and Frisians will attack. So, too, might the Franks, Hugas and Gifths, even the Wylfings, once they learn Geatland stands alone. However, if I can be the remedy to Hrothgar's affliction, our alliance with the Danes will stand. Once more united, our combined armies can put an end to the ambitions of Onela and Day Raven—once and for all if that is your choice, my King."

"I can't bring myself to order you to do it, Nephew—not after what Ulthur has told us."

"Then I'll leave of my own accord, while the tide's up and the water calm. And I'll take Handscio with me."

"You'll take more than Handscio, or you won't go at all," said Hygelac.

"Very well, Uncle. Give me Sigmund and thirteen handpicked warriors from among your Guard, the Kungens Vakter."

Hygelac left his throne and placed his hands on Beowulf's shoulders. "Come back to us, Nephew."

53

BEOWULF RETURNS TO HEOROT

Elin was in the fields when Turin and the riders returned. That Beowulf and Handscio were not among them, filled her with dread.

As Turin came through the Main Gate and halted his horse near the well, Elin took hold of Beorn's hand.

"Fear not," said the Schaman, "If something bad happened to either of them, I'd feel it in my bones."

Turin got down from his saddle.

"Turin," said Elin. "What of my husband and Handscio?"

"Both Beowulf and Handscio were safe when last I saw them, Lady Elin. We were on our way back to Vindinstedt when Sigmund, Captain of the King's Guard, found us and summoned Beowulf to Falcon's Nest."

"And of course Handscio went with him," said Elin.

"Of course, Lady Elin."

"Freemen of Vindinstedt," said Elin. "I welcome you home, though I do not see Dolph or Gundur among you. Tonight, in Beowulf's name, we will honor you and those we lost."

Turin gave Elin the gold coins Beowulf set aside for the dead men's families.

"Dolph and Gundur's share of the spoils, Lady Elin."

"Thank you, Turin," said Elin. She turned to the other riders.

"Go to your families now, brave men of Vindinstedt."

Glad to be home, the riders did as Elin commanded and rode off.

† † †

From among the Longships that were beached or anchored in the harbor, Beowulf chose The Avenger, with its black hull and sail.

The Avenger glided over the water on its way to Daneland with the wind behind it, straining the mainsail to its fullest. There would be no need for oars during that crossing until it came time to furl the sail, drop anchor and disembark on Daneland's shore. Beowulf and Handscio stood at the prow. Behind them, at the stern, two Geat warriors worked the tiller and steered the Longship south-southwest. The other eleven warriors sat idle wrapped in their cloaks, Sigmund among them. Excluding Beowulf, they were fourteen in number, all battle-tested.

With Beowulf leading them they were a killing force twenty times their number would be hard-pressed to overcome.

"What do you think awaits us there?" said Handscio; he had to shout over the sound of the waves that slammed against the prow.

"Death," said Beowulf. "Death waits for us!"

"Leave it to you, Cousin, to cheer me up," said Handscio.

In the privacy of his bedchamber, Heardred was beside himself with joy over the fortuitous turn of events: Beowulf left; which was almost as good as having Beowulf dead:

With Beowulf gone he won't be able to find the answer he seeks regarding the attack at Otters'Bay. Better yet, he may even die in Daneland. To hear Ulthur tell it, the creatures that haunt Hrothgar's Hall surpass even Beowulf's strength.

Heardred decided to return to the Mead-House that very night and revisit the Mead-House keeper's daughters. After that he would ride to Knut iron jaw's stronghold, to apprise Eriksson and the Svear Princes of recent goings-on in Falcon's Nest and the Citadel.

That night, at Vindinstedt Farm, the Geatfolk feasted. Elin and the Schaman listened as Turin, and the Freemen told all there was to tell about the Battle at Otters'Bay. As Turin recounted the battle, servants set out food and poured mead. Long into the night, good cheer and laughter abounded.

Later, after the Freemen and their families had departed, Elin, Turin, and Beorn sat before the fire and talked.

"Do not despair, my friends," said Beorn, "there must be a good reason why Hygelac recalled Beowulf and Handscio to the Citadel."

† † †

Not long after sunrise, Beowulf saw the shore of Daneland appear out of the fog. The Geats raised sail and took to the oars as they neared the coastline.

"Why do we not disembark at Mörk Sand?" Handscio said.

"The fewer eyes that see us, the better I like it," said Beowulf.

When a location presented itself to Beowulf's satisfaction, the Geats dropped anchor. Donning their battle gear, they leapt into the water and waded to shore. The sun burned through the fog as Beowulf and his men assembled on the beach.

"Look, my Prince!" said Sigmund.

Twenty Spear Danes on horseback approached at a gallop—Hrothgar's coastguards.

"Don't draw your weapons—any of you!" said Beowulf.

Beowulf raised his right hand, palm-out in front of him, as a gesture of peace. Beowulf stood in front of his men, feet planted in the sand, his armor gleaming. The Danes halted their horses just short of the strangers on their shore. Their spears pointed toward the chests of the Geat warriors.

The Captain of the coastguards moved closer:

"You hail us in peace," he said, "but you dress for war. What's your business here? I urge you to speak and be quick about it!"

"We're Geats, come on an errand of friendship," said Beowulf. "I'm Beowulf Waegmunding, son of Ecgtheow. My father knew your king well and visited Daneland often. We seek an audience with King Hrothgar."

"I've heard of Beowulf Waegmunding. He came here once with his father, the Widow Maker. He was a strapping young boy then, but just so I know you're Beowulf Waegmunding, by what other name do Northmen call you?"

"The Bear's Son," said Beowulf.

The Captain of coastguards signaled to his men; the Danes raised their spears.

"Welcome to Daneland, Prince Beowulf," said the Captain.

"Come—we'll escort you to Heorot, but we must hurry and make good use of the daylight. It'll be faster going once we're clear of the beach."

"And our ship?" said Handscio.

"None will molest your ship," the Captain said.

"Then, lead," said Beowulf. "We'll follow."

Beowulf and his men walked in a column flanked by the Danes on horseback. Wasting little time to rest, after a quarter day's march, Beowulf and his men caught sight of Hrothgar's fabled Hall—Heorot. Even as the light began to quit, and gloom settled over the land, Heorot's Keep, that gold-gilded tower, shimmered on the horizon.

"We must hurry while there's still light," said the Captain.

Both riders and Geats quickened the pace. Handscio leaned close to Beowulf.

"What kind of warriors fear the darkness?"

"Don't judge them, Handscio. The answer to your question awaits us at Heorot."

Three long blasts of a ram's horn signaled the arrival of the coastguards. Waiting outside the Main Gate of Hrothgar's once mighty Keep was a shield-wall of thirty Spear Danes led by the Gate Warden, Lord Wulfgar. The terror wrought by Grendel and Grendel's dam had done more to age him than the previous twenty winters; it showed on his face, where dark circles underscored both eyes.

"Hail Wulfgar," said the coastguard: "These warriors are Geats led by Beowulf Waegmunding, Battle Lord of Geatland come to see our king."

Wulfgar's eyes fixed on Beowulf: It truly is the bear's son! But, why is he here—why now?

"When first we met I was with my father, Ecgtheow Waegmunding," said Beowulf. "It's no secret why we come to Daneland, Lord Wulfgar."

It was as though Wulfgar had aired his thoughts aloud.

"Lord Ulthur brought news of the creatures afflicting Daneland. We come to offer your noble king our help—if he'll have it?"

It's true! Beowulf has the gift, Wulfgar told himself.

"Follow me, Prince Beowulf," said Wulfgar, "you and your men."

The Danes rebuilt the Main Gate, but left it open; for no matter how they reinforced it, Gates proved no obstacle to Grendel.

"This place is cursed, Beowulf," said Handscio. "I feel evil in the air."

"You're not alone, Handscio. I sense it too."

They followed Wulfgar past the entry door; it, too, had been rebuilt but now was left open. Inside the dim corridor where the weapons of visitors were stacked, Wulfgar stopped.

"You and your men will have to leave your weapons here, Prince Beowulf. I will announce your presence and be back."

While the Geats stacked their weapons and shields against the walls of the long corridor, Beowulf watched Wulfgar proceed past the torches toward the Mead Hall and the Throne Room beyond.

† † †

Wulfgar stopped in front of the dais on which sat Hrothgar's Throne. As in happier times, a great fire burned in the circular pit to one side of the dais where Hrothgar and his young queen, Wealtheow, sat. After three unspeakable nights of terror during the last full moon, Hrothgar's once proud Hall had become a cheerless cavern of shapes and shadows where the living mingle with the unavenged spirits of the warriors who died defending their king.

"The bear's son comes to our shore, my King. He brings men-at-arms, all handpicked by the looks of them."

"Beowulf Waegmunding," said that old gray-hair king. "Here—at Heorot?"

"Yes, my King."

"Bring him to me."

Wulfgar hurried away. Wealtheow, Hrothgar's beautiful Wylfing queen, took hold of her husband's hand. "Perhaps the son returns to pay the father's debt."

"I'd welcome Beowulf under any circumstance, wife."

They heard the sound of men approaching. Wulfgar approached the dais with Beowulf and the Geats behind.

"Beowulf Waegmunding, my King," said Wulfgar, "Battle Lord

and Prince of Geatland."

Wulfgar stepped to one side and stood among Hrothgar's chiefs, all of them eager to set eyes on the son of Ecgtheow Waegmunding, the 'widow maker.'

Beowulf stepped forward and bowed to Hrothgar and his queen.

"Hail, Great King."

"We welcome you, Beowulf," said Hrothgar. "My queen and I have little reason to be glad of late—but your presence here gives us a reason to smile. What brings you to Daneland?"

"I come to convey King Hygelac's gratitude for having sent your emissary, Ulthur, to tell us of the goings-on affecting our two tribes—Geats and Danes alike."

"Hygelac's been a good friend to the Danes," said Hrothgar; "sending Lord Ulthur to warn him was only right. But you've come a long way over the Whale Road just to say 'thank you.'"

"Lord Ulthur told us how the creatures, Grendel, and his dam, lay waste to Daneland, Great King. I came here to offer our swords in defense of Heorot. You once helped my father by ending his blood feud with the Wylfings. I come here now to pay his debt."

Queen Wealtheow gave her husband a self-satisfied look.

"Beowulf mocks the Danes!" said a warrior standing to one side.

It was one of Hrothgar's advisers, a Clan Chief of some renown named Unferth who strode forward, intent on challenging the bear's son.

"Beowulf mocks us by coming here, my King," said Unferth, "as if to say, 'Poor, pathetic Danes—I'll fight your battle for you.' Could it be he didn't hear how we defeated the Svear three months ago when they came to our shore? Doesn't he know we returned Ohthere's head to Uppsala in a basket?"

"You heard Beowulf state his reason for coming," said Hrothgar. "I sense no mockery in his voice. Besides, it was Beowulf who sent word to us that Ohthere meant to attack. Take care, Unferth, I'll not hear Prince Beowulf insulted in my Hall."

Unferth bowed to Hrothgar. "I intended no insult, my King, but Daneland's honor is at stake by his coming here with men-at-arms. And remember, my King, the Geatlander who stands before you —"

"Prince!" said Hrothgar. "You mean, the prince standing before me—Hygelac's Battle Lord! By the gods, Unferth, you're beginning to vex me!"

"I take no offense over Unferth's words, Great King," said Beowulf; "I'm not here to mock the Spear Danes. When I learned that Ohthere's fleet set sail for Daneland, I was honor-bound to warn you. Your troubles are our troubles, Great King. Should we Thunder-Geats be hard-pressed, I believe the Spear-Danes would do the same."

"I won't break my pledge to Hygelac," said Hrothgar, "the same oath as I made to Hrethel when Hrethel was king. Our two peoples have enjoyed a long peace, and I want the goodwill between our tribes to continue. However, great is our affliction now. I put my younger brother, Halga, and my nephew, Hrothulf, in charge of my army at Heorot Fort, and in Mork Sand, to safeguard my people, and my fleet. There are few Spear Danes in Heorot Hall now, save for the warriors and Dane Folk you see around you. Should trouble come to Geatland, I'll be hard-pressed to come to your aid. That's why I sent Ulthur to warn Hygelac—Day Raven's lust to control the Whale Road grows unchecked."

"Beowulf and his companions came a long way, husband," said Wealtheow, "we should celebrate their arrival."

"And so we shall," said Hrothgar.

"The moon will be full tonight, my King," said Wulfgar, "sooner than later."

Hrothgar looked at Beowulf: "Tonight, when we retire upstairs, you and your men are welcome to join us."

"Thank you, Great King," said Beowulf. "I prefer to sleep in this Great Hall with my men. Should Grendel make the mistake of coming here again, he'll find Thunder-Geats waiting.

54

WAITING ON THE MOON

Before the sun quit the sky the Danes lit a fire in the circular fire-pit of Heorot Hall. Over the flames, they roasted a fattened sheep and pig while servants poured mead. Hrothgar gave Beowulf and his men their table near the dais.

Hrothgar's two young sons, Hrethric, the oldest, and Hrothmund, stared in fascination at Beowulf until Wealtheow diverted their attention with honey cakes and milk.

As Wealtheow and her daughter, Freawaru, helped pour mead, Freawaru's eyes fixed on Beowulf in the hope he'd take notice of her. He did and was pleased by what he saw.

The singing of a young Scop, or bard, to use the Common Tongue, elevated the mood in the Hall. His voice wove its way through the air like a sweet unseen aroma of incense. The bard sang of Shield Sheafson who began life as a foundling but by sheer strength of arms subdued the tribes across the Whale Road and became Founder of the ruling House of Daneland.

"Tell us, Beowulf," said Unferth, "your plan for later tonight."

"Don't spoil the mood, Unferth," said Hrothgar.

"I don't mind, Great King," said Beowulf. "My plan, Unferth, is a simple one: Meet Grendel in combat and defeat him by the strength of my arms alone."

Overcome with anger for the supreme self-confidence Beowulf's words evinced, Unferth jumped to his feet and shouted:

"Have you any notion, Storm-Geat, as to what you'll be facing?"

"No, Unferth, I don't," said Beowulf, his voice calm.

Beowulf stood and faced that Danish chieftain. As he did, he motioned to his men to remain calm in their seats.

"What Unferth struggles to convey," said Hrothgar, "is Grendel's power. For three nights straight, Grendel smashed his way into my Hall. What followed was slaughter—as though a Berserker fell upon a flock of sheep with a scythe. Grendel stays as long as there are men to tear apart and devour. In their comings and goings, the fiends remain unfazed by our spears and arrows. When the moon began to wane they ceased their visits, he and his dam. We've rebuilt the Main Gate and entry door to the Hall, but neither will shut Grendel out so now we leave them open. I bid you reconsider, Beowulf—when we've finished feasting retire with us to the Keep along with your men. You'll be safe there."

"To hear you tell it, Great King, I don't doubt Grendel's power; nor will you ever see me assail a stronghold with nothing more than my fists. In fairness to myself, I'll just come out and say it: I, too, possess exceptional strength. In single combat, no man in all of Midgard can stand against me."

Beowulf looked at Unferth. "No man," he said.

He turned to Hrothgar and his queen.

"I once battled Ondskas on the Whale Road. Intent they were on breaking my battle craft into splinters with their gaping mouths and rows of ivory teeth. I defeated them all and towed them back to Bronding Land. On my way home on foot from Finn's Land, I cleaned-out a Troll nest. I freed the people of those foul inhabitants after they befriended me with food and lodging. I've bested monsters at sea and on land. I protect my tribe, enforce Geatland's laws, and take vengeance on the enemies of King Hygelac. I'll meet Grendel here—in Heorot Hall. And I'll kill him."

Freawaru, Hrothgar's daughter, appeared at Beowulf's side. Trembling with excitement, she refilled his mead cup. Beowulf nodded to Freawaru and drank.

Unferth stepped to the front of the assembly:

"This is the same braggart who challenged Breca, the Sea Brondings' king, to compete on the Whale Road. No one could save them from it, insane a wager as it was. Beowulf and Breca rowed in freezing waters for seven nights, until Breca out-did Beowulf and reached the shore of the Heathoreams first. Breca returned to the land of the Brondings no worse for the wear—the winner. It matters not, Beowulf, how you've fared, heretofore. No man can last the night against Grendel. You'll die tonight, and so will your companions."

"Enough, Unferth," said Hrothgar. "You've had too much to drink."

"It's all right, Great King," said Beowulf. "I take no offense at

Unferth's words, but he tells the story wrong. Each of us armed, Breca and I rowed five days and nights, our boats lashed together, the two us shoulder-to-shoulder, with the sea doing its worst. Breca's boat came apart and, exhausted as he was, he would have drowned had I not pulled him inside my boat and taken his place in the sea. A creature pulled me below, and I dealt it a quick death. Other sea-monsters attacked. My armor came between them and my undoing. I had killed nine of those hags before a Blue Whale left me on the coast of Finn's Land. Tell us, Unferth—recount even one struggle, one fierce battle you emerged victorious from, that measures up to the battles I've fought. All I've heard about you is that you murdered your kin for personal gain. If you're as courageous as you'd have us believe, remain in the Hall tonight with my men and me."

"It grows late, my husband," said Wealtheow; "the moon will soon be up."

"Very well," said Hrothgar, "it's time we Danes retire to the Keep."

"May Great Odin watch over you and your men, Prince Beowulf," said Wealtheow.

Beowulf bowed to the king and queen as they started toward the winding spiral stairway leading to the highest part of Hrothgar's Keep. The other Danes followed, including servants and cooks. Freawaru, Hrothgar's daughter, was last to leave the Hall. She wasn't able to stop staring at Beowulf. Beowulf saw her and smiled. Her heart racing, Freawaru spun around and dashed upstairs. Handscio and Sigmund went to Beowulf's side.

"What are your orders?" said Handscio.

"Have the men gather their shields and weapons; then push the benches to the sides of the Hall. They can use them to sleep. I'll wait for Grendel there." Beowulf pointed to the dais on which sat Hrothgar's Throne.

"Handscio, take Sigmund with you and secure the entry door to the Hall. Grendel will enter the Palisade unopposed, but when he reaches the door to the Hall, we'll give him reason to announce his presence."

"That won't improve the demon's mood," said Sigmund.

"No, Sigmund, it won't... and that's to my liking."

"But Hrothgar ordered both the Main Gate and the entry door

kept open," said Handscio.

"True," said Beowulf, "he did. I promise you: come morning the door to the Hall will be open—albeit in need of repair."

Quick to sense the humor in Beowulf's words, dark as it was, Handscio and Sigmund laughed and hastened away.

In their bedchamber, Hrothgar and his Queen prepared to retire. They went through the same motions as on any other night. It was one way of coping with the dread they felt since the arrival of the fiends. Hrothgar's two sons were already under the covers, curled-up asleep. Hrothgar sat on the side of the bed. He watched his young wife brush her copper-color hair.

"When Ecgtheow returned here with his son," said Hrothgar, "Beowulf appeared to be no more than seventeen winters' young, and quite tall for his age, as a young Linden tree. Nevertheless, he was a quiet boy and looked as if he meant to get at the meaning of everything and everyone around him."

"I remember hearing his eyes are what others first notice about him," said Wealtheow. "That they burn with blue fire."

"Yes—even as a boy, Beowulf's gaze was far-reaching."

"Your daughter's beside herself with joy since his arrival," said Wealtheow.

"Freawaru is merely acting her age."

"I'm just saying, husband; no better match could a king make than to pair his daughter with a prince like Beowulf."

Hrothgar laughed. "Like Beowulf? There are no others like Beowulf. Besides, Freawaru will marry Prince Ingeld, and put an end to this stupid feud between Ingeld and me."

"King, or not, Ingeld is a treacherous pig," said Wealtheow.

"I know what he is, Wealtheow, but what our people need is one fewer enemy south of us, and making peace with the Heathobards is key."

"Strange, don't you think," said Wealtheow, "the way Fate weaves us together like so many threads."

"How do you mean?"

Wealtheow ceased brushing her hair and looked at her husband.

"The history our three tribes share in common: Wylfings, Geats, and Danes. Think about it, husband—had Ecgtheow Waegmunding not assassinated my kinsman there would've been no blood feud for you to end when Hrethel dared not intervene on Ecgtheow's behalf."

"I've not forgotten," said Hrothgar; "it's how you came to be my wife. As you said, Wealtheow, the son returns to pay the father's debt."

Wealtheow put her hairbrush down, removed her under-gown and stepped to the edge of the bed. She placed her hands on Hrothgar's shoulders and smiled:

"I'm ready for bed, my King."

Looking at Wealtheow, his eyes drank her beauty. Hrothgar's back straightened. With renewed energy, Hrothgar placed his hands on her hips. He looked into Wealtheow's face.

"So am I," he said.

† † †

The Geats who went with Beowulf to Daneland endured two days' hard sailing and a forced march inland to Heorot. Add to that the cups of mead they'd consumed, and it was no wonder they soon fell asleep. The Geats wrapped themselves in their cloaks with their weapons close. The flames from the fire pit cast shadows that danced over the walls, and ceiling of the Hall.

Handscio rested with one eye open and stared in the direction of the dais where Beowulf sat cross-legged, stripped of armor. Beowulf's sword and shield were on the floor in front of him, and his eyes were wide open, fixed on the entry door beyond the antechamber at the far end of the darkened Hall.

You *frighten me, Cousin,* thought Handscio. *Without sword and shield, you give the creature too great an advantage. What do I tell Elin? That I sat idly on my arse, while you battled the monster alone? I cannot do that, Bear's Son. I won't do it.*

55

THE HORROR COMES TO HEOROT

To assuage their loneliness Elin and Asa slept together. Neither woman spoke of the fear she felt, the fear of not knowing when their husbands would come back, if at all. Doubting that Beowulf and Handscio would return was unthinkable; yet doubt lurked at the back of their minds, prowling like a malevolent spirit seeking its way inside their dreams. No matter how they tried, Elin and Asa could not shut their fears out.

Elin had heard the disturbing news from Beorn during the Schaman's coming and going from the Citadel; the rumor that Handscio's father, Weohstan, had offered his sword for hire to King Onela. If the rumor proved to be true, Elin knew it wouldn't sit well with King Hygelac, now that the likelihood of war loomed over Geatland. Weohstan had told no one where he was going, or what compelled him away. After Ohthere's disastrous raid on Daneland Onela needed time to rebuild the Svear army—hiring mercenaries and outcasts from other tribes would suffice. Weohstan was old, but he was still sound of body, and he wielded a sword better than most warriors half his age; moreover, Weohstan's skill as a tactician was well known and lauded by friends and foes alike. Onela would indeed be pleased to have a warrior like Weohstan Waegmunding among the many battle-tested mercenaries and renegades who flocked to his banner, for the silver Onela promised them, to fill the ranks of his new army.

Beorn sat alone, warming his feet in front of the fire in the Banquet Hall. He stared into the flames while he crushed and mixed herbs together with mortar and pestle. When done, Beorn added the potion to a cup of mead; drank it down and invited what visions as might come—to come.

Outside Heorot the moon waxed full and slipped in and out behind silver clouds. Fog settled on the land, and there was stillness in the air. Every living thing stayed hidden that night and crouched in terror.

Creatures great and small attuned their senses to Grendel's comings and goings, and they trembled. Through the great rift that the earthquake created at the bottom of the lake, Grendel and his dam had escaped from their subterranean world to the world of men. The world below the lake was a terrifying place where chaos and cannibalism reigned. Grendel and his Dam were the last; the last of their kind, and there was precious little to eat in their shadowy domain. They counted it their great luck that the rift in the earth sucked them upward, for it brought them to a new world, a world containing all manner of living things to slake their fiendish appetites.

Pulled upward into the lake, Grendel and his mother discovered a large underwater grotto. Inside there was life-sustaining air to breathe, dank and moldy as it was, that entered the cavern through an aperture in the rock overhead.

The grotto was once the armory of an ancient race of warriors who contested against giants for glory and riches. However, it was not riches that littered the floor of the cavern—but the bones of Hrothgar's warriors.

As he loped through the fog, with the moon to light his way, Grendel was beside himself with glee. Soon, he and his mother would feast again on the flesh of men.

Puny and weak are these Manlings, Grendel thought. They cannot match my power, nor can their weapons hurt me. In time, I, and she who birthed me will rule this world of plenty.

Grendel knew nothing about happiness, joy, or love. Grendel knew that he and his mother were free from that dark dominion beneath the lake and on the threshold of conquering a new world, one where they would never lack flesh to eat or blood to drink. As Grendel continued on his way toward Heorot, something strange happened that caused him to stop.

It was a voice he heard call him from far off, but the voice was clear as though it was inside his head, as real sounding to him as were his thoughts.

"*Come! Come to me, Grendel, if that be your name. I am here, waiting to slay you, foul, disgusting thing.*"

Grendel looked around. There was nothing, save for the fog. Even the frogs had ceased croaking as news spread that Grendel was afoot.

"*Who's there*?" said Grendel. "*Show yourself*!"

"*I'm here, fiend, inside your head—waiting for you. Do not waste my time, Grendel. Get yourself here, to Hrothgar's Hall, for tonight will be your last night in Midgard.*"

Grendel clutched his head in his hands and shook his head side-to-side.

"*Get out*!" said Grendel. "Get out of my head, whoever you are!"

"*No! I'm in your head to stay. Death alone can release you from my voice.*"

Grendel bellowed and struck his head over and over with his clenched hands.

"*Out! Get out of my head*!" said Grendel. "*I'm going to tear you apart and devour every morsel of flesh on your bones*!"

"*Then, come, hell-hound!*" said Beowulf. *"While the moon waxes full. Come! I am waiting for you."*

† † †

Beowulf sat motionless as the time passed. He continued to stare into the darkness that cloaked the far end of the Hall. Just a few torches lit the way past the entry door while flames from the fire-pit illuminated the Hall. The tiny hair on the nape of Beowulf's neck stood-up, the same as at Otters Bay when Death sought him out at the water's edge.

"*You're close, aren't you, Grendel. The breeze carries your stench on its breath. Come, death-dealer! Come to Heorot! You'll find a Thunder Geat waiting. It's me, Beowulf, the 'bear's son,' who calls you out!"*

"Know this, Beowulf, bear's son—that means nothing to me. Just know that I will take my time killing you."

Grendel entered the deserted palisade. He stopped and sniffed the air. Wood-smoke from inside the Hall greeted his flared nostrils. Eager to rip apart and devour any Manlings he found, he strode toward the entry door and found the way inside blocked.

Just the mere thought that the Manlings would try to hinder him enraged the fiend. Grendel formed his claws into fists and hammered the door. Deafening was the noise inside the Hall as the monster rained blow upon blow with his fists.

Beowulf ignored the shouting of his men as they roused themselves from their sleep. Handscio and the others took up arms and made a shield-wall in front of the fire-pit. Beowulf stood upon the dais, ready to receive Grendel's fury. Out of the darkness came the sound of the crossbeam breaking as Grendel smashed the door from its iron hinges.

From the corridor the monster strode inside the Hall, bellowed with rage and started for the dais. On it, Grendel saw a Manling facing him. For Grendel it seemed all too easy. Dragging his talons over the stone floor of the Hall he stopped thirty paces short of the dais. Looking in the direction of the fire-pit Grendel saw fourteen warriors arrayed for battle. The fiend stuck his chest out, lifted his arms high, threw back his massive head and roared.

† † †

Hearing the terrible sounds announcing Grendel's return, King Hrothgar and his queen gathered their sons to their bed.

"May One-Eyed Odin be with you, Bear's Son," said Hrothgar.

The King of the Danes placed his hands over the ears of one of his sons while Wealtheow covered the ears of the other.

Their daughter, Freawaru, kept to her own bed. She buried her face in her pillow to extinguish the sounds from below. Trembling,

Freawaru curled herself into a ball and sobbed.

Elsewhere in the Keep, Unferth and the Danes heard Grendel's roar and their blood ran cold. The Danes averted their eyes from one-another knowing that fifteen men from Geatland were facing the monster in their stead. In every chamber of the Keep, Danes cowered and listened to the din below.

† † †

Grendel turned his gaze toward Beowulf. The full-measure of the fiend's malice coalesced behind his eyes.

"*It's you, isn't it?*" said Grendel, using the Silent Tongue. *"The voice inside my head. Well, Manling—I'm here! So, come, if you dare! Face me*!"

Beowulf's jaw dropped in disbelief at what he saw: Grendel towered over him and with each foul breath exuded untold power. The hardened scales of Grendel's skin flashed with the reflected firelight, and saliva dripped like rain from his fangs. The talons on Grendel's hands were sharper than any blade fashioned by man and could cut through armor with ease—a lesson the Spear Danes had learned too well.

Holding his shield and spear in hand, Handscio saw Beowulf hesitate as if in the grip of some unseen force. Beowulf was in the grip of a hidden force—the force of panic.

"Take up your sword, Beowulf!" said Handscio from across the Hall.

Beowulf's shield and sword were within arm's reach yet he ignored them and remained standing on the dais, paralyzed by the sight of the monster. Grendel stepped closer and looked at Beowulf the way a fox looks at a cornered rabbit. At that, Handscio didn't hesitate. He strode toward the fiend and hurled his spear. The spear struck Grendel on the right side of his neck but didn't penetrate. The monster bellowed and whirled to face the Manling who dared resist him.

"Die well, Beowulf!" said Handscio with a shout.

Shaken awake, as from some terrible dream, Beowulf saw Grendel lurch toward Handscio. Sigmund and the Geats hurled their spears. Those well-crafted spears struck the fiend yet drew no blood—not so much as a drop.

"Get back, Handscio!" said Beowulf, in command of himself. "All of you! Get back!"

Handscio's heart beat with joy to see Beowulf take up the fight. Handscio stood his ground while the Geats behind him withdrew. Beowulf picked a spear off the floor and hurled it at Grendel, striking the shadow-stalker between his shoulder blades. Grendel turned toward Beowulf and snarled. Beowulf retrieved his sword from the floor and strode forward:

"*I'm the one you want*!" said Beowulf. "*Fight me*!"

Seeing the monster look away, Handscio rushed forward and struck Grendel with his sword. That steel blade Weohstan gave Handscio on the eve of his first battle hit Grendel on the forearm but bounced off.

With a swipe of one arm, Grendel tore the shield from Handscio's grasp. Grendel's talons raked across Handscio's chainmail shirt and opened four deep wounds in his chest. Handscio's sword fell from his hand.

Grendel grabbed Handscio by the hair and lifted him off the ground. While Beowulf looked on in horror, Grendel bit down on Handscio's throat, snapping his neck like a twig. Grendel bit through flesh, bone and sinew, severing Handscio's head from his shoulders while his headless body dropped in a heap.

Holding Handscio's face between his fangs, the shadow-stalker looked at Beowulf. He spat Handscio's head to the floor. It rolled to a stop at Beowulf's feet.

"*Now, Manling, now it's your turn to die,*" said Grendel.

Beowulf tossed his sword aside just as Grendel leapt. Beowulf planted his feet and seized Grendel's left wrist with his right hand. Assured of the grip, Beowulf clamped down and began to squeeze.

"*No*!" said Beowulf. "*I think not*."

Grendel flailed the air with his right arm trying to free himself but it was no use. Beowulf ducked each time Grendel swung his talons. Beowulf continued to increase the pressure on Grendel's wrist even after he heard the sound of bones breaking. Grendel bellowed with pain and for the first time in his life felt fear. Never before had the monster encountered anything that matched his power until now.

In his panic and thinking to escape, Grendel tried to pull away.

He dragged Beowulf with him down the corridor toward the shattered door. It was then that Beowulf took hold of Grendel's arm with both hands and pulled him back into the Throne Room.

Using all his waning strength, Grendel struggled to flee but Beowulf's grip was unrelenting. That tug-of-war ended when Grendel's left arm tore loose from the shoulder socket.

Beowulf stumbled backward with Grendel's arm still in his grip. The talons of Grendel's left hand continued to twitch. Numb with fear, and seeing his life's blood spewing, Grendel screamed and ran off into the night, back the way he came.

From where he sat staring at the flames, in his mind's eye Beorn saw a great Hall cast in darkness. Inside the Hall, a monstrous form draped in shadows seized a man between its teeth. The death dealer lifted the hapless person into the air and Beorn saw the warrior's face—it was Handscio. All at once the unspeakable evil bit through Handscio's neck. From a chamber above the Banquet Hall a woman screamed.

Beorn's eyes opened, the vision gone.

Woken by the sound of screaming, Elin found Asa sitting in bed, shaking.

"Asa, what is it?"

"Handscio—I saw him! He's dead!"

"You had a nightmare, that's all."

"No, Elin! I saw him. I saw Handscio, just as if I was there—he's dead!"

There came a soft tapping on the door of the chamber. Elin found Beorn standing there.

"Asa had a dream," said Elin in a whisper, "that's all."

Beorn held out a cup.

"Have Asa drink some of this; it'll help her sleep."

"Thank you, Beorn," said Elin, taking the cup from the Schaman's hand. "I'll drink some myself."

"You'll find it soothing," said Beorn, and he turned to leave.

"Beorn?" said Elin.

The Schaman stopped.

"It was a terrible dream. Nothing more—yes?" said Elin, her voice trembling.

Without looking at the women, Beorn nodded and walked away.

In the Keep high above the Mead Hall King Hrothgar held his queen and children close. The Hall below was quiet. Tears formed in the eyes of that proud king. He was positive that Beowulf and the Geats had perished.

Unferth and the Danes were on their feet, listening to the fighting. Now, a silence cold to the bones ruled Hrothgar's Keep.

"If no one else is willing to say it," said Unferth; "I will—Beowulf Waegmunding is dead!

56

BITTER CAME THE DAWN

The next morning when Hrothgar and his Chiefs returned to the Throne Room unprepared for what they saw—Grendel's left arm dangling from a rope tied to one of the overhead beams. Beowulf and his men were nowhere in sight.

Hrothgar and the Danes found the Geats outside; they were burning Handscio's remains using wood from the shattered entry door. The flames of the pyre roared, hissed and climbed into the air. Out of respect, the Danes held back.

While the pyre burned, Beowulf looked on, tormented by the thought that one moment of fear, one moment of hesitation had cost the life of his shield brother and lifelong friend.

Tell me, Handscio, how am I to tell Weohstan and Elin you're dead because of me?

Such were the thoughts that crowded Beowulf's head.

After the fire had consumed Handscio's remains, King Hrothgar stepped to Beowulf's side. The old king placed his hands on Beowulf's shoulders.

"It saddens me," he said, "the loss of your shield brother."

"His name was Handscio," said Beowulf, "he was my cousin, shield brother, and best friend."

"Tonight we'll feast in Handscio's honor," said Hrothgar, "and celebrate your victory over the fiend."

"If there's to be feasting tonight, Great King, let it be in Handscio's honor, and his alone. I earned no glory here last night."

Sigmund and the Geats exchanged looks. To a man, none of the Geats faulted Beowulf for Handscio's death—none except for Beowulf himself.

"Great King," said Beowulf, "I ask for horses for myself and my men; I intend to follow Grendel's tracks."

"Horses you'll have, and we Danes will ride with you."

† † †

For two hours Danes and Geats followed the monster's blood spatter to where it ended at the shore of the lake. There was no other sign of Grendel or his mother.

"The monsters must have their lair nearby," said Hrothgar, "but without his arm, Grendel is surely dead."

Hrothgar turned to his men and proclaimed, "Grendel is dead! The time of our affliction is over!"

The Danes cheered and shouted. Beowulf kept silent as they turned their horses around and returned to Heorot.

† † †

That night, Danes and Geats celebrated the death of Grendel in Hrothgar's Hall. Again there would be a full moon but the thought of it no longer struck fear in the hearts and minds of the Danes. Grendel's reign of terror was over. Mead flowed, and the young bard sang, and everyone rejoiced; everyone, that is, except Beowulf and his men. Handscio's death oppressed them. Nevertheless, the Geats ate and drank with healthy appetites—careful not to insult that good and generous king in whose Hall they found themselves.

As the night grew, late Queen Wealtheow went among the Geats accompanied by her daughter, who carried with her a willow basket filled with gifts. The Geats stood and bowed. To each man, Wealtheow gave a gold ring and arm bracelet of silver.

Wealtheow and Freawaru came to Beowulf last. From the basket, Freawaru handed her mother a torque of twisted gold and silver, in the shape of a serpent devouring its tail.

"This torque belonged to Halfdane, my husband's father," said Wealtheow. "We want you to have it, Prince Beowulf."

Beowulf lowered his head; Wealtheow placed the torque around his neck.

"Thank you, noble Queen." He looked at Hrothgar. "Thank you, Great King."

"A token of our gratitude for what you've done," said Hrothgar, beaming.

When the queen and her daughter returned to their place on the dais, Unferth approached Beowulf.

"I was wrong," said Unferth, "to have spoken ill of you."

"And I was wrong to have brought up the killing of your brothers, Unferth. You had your reasons. Let us clasp arms and forget the matter."

Beowulf and Unferth clasped forearms in friendship, and a tremendous shout of approval came from Danes and Geats alike.

As the evening wore on Beowulf left the Hall to be alone with his thoughts. He ascended steps that led upward to the wall-walk near the Main Gate. It was a clear night, and the moon was not yet visible. A breeze cooled Beowulf's face as he stared at the stars.

Sensing a presence, Beowulf turned and saw Death standing near him on the wall-walk, staring at him.

"You, again," said Beowulf.

"Yes," said Death.

"What do you want from me?"

"Nothing, just keep doing what you do so well."

"Why don't you leave me alone?"

"I choose to go where you go, Beowulf—Do you think because you can't see me, I'm not with you?"

"Prince Beowulf?"

Beowulf turned to see Princess Freawaru ascending steps to the wall-walk.

"Who are you talking to?" she said.

"No one," said Beowulf.

"I like looking at the stars, too," said Freawaru, "Especially when I feel alone."

"You should go back inside, Princess."

"Why? You've made Heorot safe."

"Does your father know you're out here?"

Freawaru laughed. "I'm almost fifteen, Prince Beowulf; I'm not a little girl."

"That's true," said Beowulf, "and you will soon be a beautiful, young woman, Freawaru, but you're also the daughter of the king. It wouldn't be right for you to be seen alone with me."

"Please Prince Beowulf, just a little while longer, please-please-please?"

"Very well," said Beowulf; "a little while—no more."

"Do you have a woman waiting for you in Geatland?"
"Yes."
"She must be very special."
There was no small disappointment in Freawaru's voice.
"She is to me," said Beowulf.
"Among us Danes, it's permissible for a man to have more than one wife."
Beowulf could not help himself; he laughed.
"Are you mocking me?"
"No, sweet Princess. I was thinking how difficult it is to satisfy the needs of one woman."
"Father says I am soon to wed Prince Ingeld."
"The son of Froda, the Heathobards' King?"
"Yes, to bring an end to the long-standing feud between the Froda and my father."
"Your father is a good and wise king, Freawaru. I'm sure he's doing what he thinks best for you and the Spear Danes. And now, Princess, it's time for you to say good night."
"I'll go," said Freawaru. She started down the steps, then turned and looked back. "My heart breaks for you over the death of your friend."

† † †

Beowulf and his men bedded-down in one of the barracks left empty after Hrothgar dispersed his army. Once more Hrothgar's Iron Guard would take their place as guardians of Hrothgar's Throne Room. The Danes moved benches aside and spread bedding across the floor. With their polished shields at their heads, weapons and armor they stacked where they could be gotten to should the need arise.

Over the Danes hung Grendel's arm, a stark reminder of the past terror.

In the underwater grotto beneath the waters of the lake, Grendel was stretched-out upon a slab of polished granite—dead.

Moonlight entered that dark foreboding place from an aperture in the rock above the grotto. In that ancient armory, the she-demon wept as she cleaned her son's body. She was alone, and she despaired, yet the thought of exacting revenge on the Danes comforted her. As she washed her son's lifeless body, she hissed into his ear, promising to kill every living thing that crossed her path that night, and every full-moon night after that.

Two torches lit the barracks where the Geats slept. Unable to sleep, Beowulf stared past the torchlight into the darkness. He thought of Vindinstedt and all that awaited him there. A presence interrupted his thoughts: something beyond the stake wall surrounding Heorot, something dark and malevolent was approaching.

Beowulf sat up. Sigmund was asleep on the pallet next to him. Beowulf shook Sigmund awake.

"What is it, my Prince?"

"Wake the men!"

The she-fiend entered the palisade. Now that Grendel was dead no one thought to close the Main Gate nor had Hrothgar ordered it closed. There were no lookouts on the wall-walk to shout the alarm, and she entered the Hall unchallenged. The Danes did not replace the door for the same reason they left the Main Gate open —Grendel no longer threatened them.

The Danes slept, lulled into slumber by the mead they consumed. The she-fiend peered through the dim light and shadows cast by the fire-pit.

At the sight of her son's arm hanging by a rope from the ceiling, she shrieked and awoke the Spear Danes.

One warrior, Aeschere, leapt to his feet and shouted: "Awake! Grendel's dam has come to Heorot!"

The she-fiend jumped on a bench and pulled her son's arm free from the hook where it hung. She snarled at the Danes as they took up their shields and weapons.

As she started to leave the Hall, Aeschere barred her way. He hurled his spear with as much force as he could muster. His spear struck her chest but bounced off. She leapt. When her feet touched the floor, she yanked Aeschere's shield from his arm and raked him with her talons. Aeschere dropped to his knees, clutched his face and tried in vain to stem the flow of blood. The she-fiend grabbed him by his hair and dragged him screaming, from the Hall, into the fog-filled night.

Hearing screaming, Beowulf took up arms and went to the Hall to see what was amiss. Once inside, Beowulf and his men found Unferth and the Danes talking among themselves. On the floor in front of them was a pool of blood—Aeschere's blood. Beowulf saw Grendel's arm was missing.

"What happened, Unferth?" said Beowulf.

"The she-fiend came to retrieve Grendel's arm. She took it along with Aeschere, a chief much loved by my King."

"What did you say about Aeschere?" said Hrothgar, descending the stairs and entering the Hall. "What of Aeschere? Speak, Unferth!"

"Taken, my King," said Unferth, "by the she-fiend after she claimed Grendel's arm. It happened too fast to stop her."

"What can you tell me about this hag?" said Beowulf.

"She seems not as powerful as Grendel," said Unferth, "but she's faster and agiler."

"Tell me, Beowulf," said Hrothgar, "What do you propose we do?"

"Find her and kill her," he said.

"Find her where?" said Hrothgar.

"The lake, Great King; I sense her lair is there, beneath the surface of the water."

57

IN THE SHE-FIEND'S LAIR

Riding beneath the full moon, Danes and Geats rode with hatred in their hearts. At dawn, they reached the shoreline of the lake and stopped at the foot of the cliff.

There they found Aeschere's head on the ground, mouth agape, eyes were frozen in terror. Distressed beyond measure, Hrothgar acted without delay. He ordered Aeschere's head placed in a saddle bag and kept out of sight, lest it cast dread on all who saw it.

"How can the she-fiend survive," said Hrothgar, "when no living thing can taste those waters and live?"

"There has to be an underwater grotto, Great King," said Beowulf, "that affords her air to breathe."

"What do you suggest, Beowulf?" said Hrothgar, "Wait for her to show?"

"No," replied Beowulf. "I'll seek her out."

"That's madness, Beowulf," protested Sigmund. "Let's wait for the hag to surface."

"That could be days," replied Beowulf. "The she-fiend may not feel the need to return to Heorot for some time. I mean to find her lair and settle accounts today."

"As before, Beowulf," said Hrothgar; "I can't ask you to risk your life that way."

"The choice is mine, Great King, and I mean to end the terror here and now."

When Beowulf dismounted, so also did his men. Hrothgar nodded to his chieftains; the Danes, too, dismounted. Beowulf removed his helm and placed it on the ground. Beowulf kept his chainmail on, Breca's gift to him, since there was no finer armor to turn the point of a blade or the bite of an Ondska.

Unferth went to where Beowulf stood. In his hands, he held a sword.

"It would honor me if you took my sword, Hrunting, with you. A master metalsmith forged it long ago for my grandfather's father and tempered the blade in blood. It's never failed in battle."

Beowulf took his sword from its scabbard and handed it to Unferth.

"If it's my fate to die today you'll have my father's sword, Widow Maker, to recompense you for the loss of Hrunting."

"I'll keep your sword safe for your return," said Unferth. He bowed and stepped back.

"Noble King," said Beowulf, "If I don't return, I ask you to see my men safely away from Daneland's shore."

"I will," said Hrothgar, "you have my word."

Beowulf handed Sigmund his helm.

"If I don't return," said Beowulf, "tell Elin my last thoughts were of her."

"Die well, my Prince," said Sigmund.

Beowulf waded into the water until he disappeared beneath the surface of the lake. The weight of his armor helped him descend until his feet touched the ground.

Through the dim light at the bottom of the lake, Beowulf saw what could be the entrance to an underwater grotto. He took no more than a few strides when, out of the reeds, sprang Grendel's dam. The she-fiend seized Beowulf by his ankles, upending him.

The hag proceeded to drag Beowulf into the underwater grotto and up steps into her lair. She released her grip on his ankles,; the she-fiend leapt on Beowulf's back.

"*You are the Manling who murdered my son*!" said the she-demon. "*I smell my child's scent on you*."

She flailed Beowulf with her talons, but his armor won out. Pushing himself to his knees, Beowulf reached behind and grabbed hold of the monster's hair. Beowulf tossed the she-demon against one of the walls of that ancient armory. He got to his feet with Hrunting, poised to strike. The she-fiend hit the wall with a great thud and fell to the floor.

"Yes," said Beowulf. "It was I, Beowulf, the bear's son, who killed the thing you spawned from your worm-infested womb. And now I mean to kill you."

Beowulf glimpsed many splendid weapons hanging on the walls of the grotto—swords and battle-axes, fashioned during the

Age of Giants, and all of them too hefty for any ordinary warrior to wield.

The she-fiend leapt to her feet and sprang. Ready for her, Beowulf swung Hrunting and brought the blade down on her head. Unferth's family's heirloom did not bite nor even bruise her skin. Beowulf rained powerful blows upon her to no avail—Hrunting had failed to do its work, and Beowulf tossed Unferth's sword aside.

The she-fiend snatched a broad-bladed knife from the wall and attacked. Beowulf grappled with her, and they fell to the ground, a tangle of arms and legs. Beowulf's armor turned the tip of the she-demon's blade, saving his life again.

Beowulf broke loose and rushed to the wall. He took a sword no ordinary man could wield from its mounts and faced her. The she-fiend hissed and threw her knife. The tip of the blade struck Beowulf square in the chest, knocking the breath from his lungs, forcing him back. The knife fell to the floor.

Believing her skin impervious to any blade wrought by man, the she-fiend threw herself full-force at Beowulf. Holding the hilt of that ancient sword with both hands, he struck the she-fiend on the neck. The force of the blow severed the monster's head, and it rolled down the steps of her lair, into the water, where it bobbed up-and-down. Her body crumpled to the ground spewing blood as brackish as the water of the lake.

Looking around, Beowulf saw Grendel's corpse on the slab of granite.

Unferth went to Hrothgar's side.

"I fear the worst, my King."

"As do I," said Hrothgar. "Very well, we'll return to Heorot."

Hrothgar went to where Beowulf's men stood to watch the surface of the lake.

"Brave Geats," said Hrothgar. "I'm returning to Heorot while it's still light. I invite you to come with us."

"Thank you, Great King," said Sigmund, "but we'll stay here to await our prince's return."

"How long will you wait?" said Unferth.
"As long as it takes, my Lord," said Sigmund.

Beowulf stared at Grendel's face. It was as hideous in death as when the monster lived. Beowulf severed the hag's head. The blade of that ancient sword began to melt. Beowulf found Hrunting on the floor and returned Unferth's sword to his scabbard.

He took Grendel's head with him along with the remains of that ancient sword for its maker had inlaid the hilt with gold and jewels that flashed in the dim light.

Before he left that gloomy place, Beowulf threw back his head and let loose his war cry. The sound of it shook rocks loose from the ceiling and echoed throughout the grotto.

When Beowulf burst upward out of the water, his men cheered and clapped one another on the back. Once more on dry ground, Beowulf let loose of Grendel's head.

"Hrothgar and the Danes feared you were dead," said Sigmund.

"They were almost right," said Beowulf. "I can't fault them for leaving, but here I am—alive."

It took the strength of four warriors to mount Grendel's head on a spear to transport it to Heorot. The Main Gate was open, but now there were guards posted on the wall-walk. It was a sign of a return to normalcy—the mere act of posting sentries. The Danes stared in awe as Beowulf and his men entered the Palisade bearing Grendel's head and made straightaway for Hrothgar's Hall.

Struggling under the weight of it, four warriors lowered the head to the floor. While Beowulf led the way, another four warriors, fresh and rested, proceeded to drag the monster's head by the hair across the floor toward the dais. Hrothgar and his Queen watched in silence, stunned by the spectacle the head provided.

"By all the gods, Beowulf," said Hrothgar, "we thought you dead."

"No matter, Great King, but as you can see, I'm quite alive."

Down the steps of the Keep ran Freawaru, her eyes were red and swollen from crying since the Princess also thought Beowulf dead. When she saw Beowulf, her head grew light. She rubbed her eyes to make sure they saw right:

"Prince Beowulf!" she said. "You're alive!"

"Yes, noble Princess."

Freawaru ran to Beowulf and hugged him. "I prayed to the Goddess Frigga to send the Valkyries to protect you."

"Daughter!" said Hrothgar. "I can't have you squeezing the life out of Prince Beowulf, now that he's returned to us alive."

Aware that all eyes in the Hall were looking at her, she relaxed her hold on Beowulf and stepped back. Freawaru blushed and went to the dais and sat near her mother's feet.

"The Danes will suffer no more at the hands of Grendel or his dam," said Beowulf. "I swear it—"

"Unferth," said Hrothgar, "remove that foul-smelling thing from the Hall. Take it outside and burn it!"

"Allow me a word with Unferth first," said Beowulf.

"Of course," replied Hrothgar.

Beowulf and Unferth exchanged swords and even-tempered words; then Unferth summoned several Danes.

They grasped that gruesome trophy by the hair, dragged it outside, and doused it with oil. The Danes wasted no time lighting the head on-fire, and it took the remainder of the day and night before the flames reduced the head to ashes and pieces of bone. The Danes gathered the ashes and buried them deep in the earth in an unmarked grave far outside the palisade.

"Words fall short to express Daneland's gratitude, Beowulf," said Hrothgar. "You've freed us from the curse we lived under these past two moons."

Beowulf bowed; then he held up the remains of that ancient sword that bested Grendel's dam. The gold and jewels embossed on the hilt gleamed.

"Unferth's sword, Hrunting, failed to penetrate the she-fiend's hide. I found this blade in her lair, and with it, I severed her head and did the same to Grendel. Their blood was hot and black; it melted the blade of this once great sword, like an ice sickle when spring comes. I give it to you, Great King."

Hrothgar took that wondrous shard with its jewel-encrusted hilt from Beowulf's hands, and his eyes beamed.

"Tonight, we'll feast and drink in Heorot like never before," Hrothgar said.

"Then let the celebration commence!" said his joyful queen.

True to Hrothgar's words, Danes and Geats celebrated long into the night. Killing the she-fiend assuaged little of the grief Beowulf felt, and of Hrothgar's mead, he drank but little. As the night wore on, Hrothgar called for silence while he could still speak without slurring his words.

"Beowulf, you've been a good friend to the Danes, and your fame reaches in all directions across the Whale Road. Once more I pledge my friendship. The Spear Danes stand ready to fight at your side. Send the word, and we'll come."

"Thank you, Great King. In turn, I renew our pledge in the name of King Hygelac that, should you Danes be hard-pressed, we Geats stand ready to return, with a thousand warriors, happy to go into action alongside the Spear Danes. Now, Great King, my men and I are eager to return to Geatland. With your permission, we'll retire for the night and tomorrow get an early start for home."

"This time," said Hrothgar, "you'll have horses to take you to the coast, and I'll accompany you."

† † †

The next morning Beowulf and his men rode from Heorot accompanied by King Hrothgar, his two advisers, Wulfgar and Unferth, and an escort of warriors. An ox cart went with them; it carried Hrothgar's gifts: a shirt of hand-ringed chainmail, a steel sword, and towering helm, a crimson standard, emblazoned with a horse's head, and seven fine warhorses bred to endure the chaos of battle. When Geats and Dane loaded the gifts aboard the Avenger, Beowulf and Hrothgar clasped arms on the beach and bid one another farewell.

Tears formed in the eyes of that old King as he watched Beowulf's battle craft head out to sea.

58

DARK PLANS, BROKEN HEARTS

After three days sailing against fierce currents and crosswinds, Beowulf and his men saw Geatland's shore, and they shouted with joy. Hugging the coastline, they continued to sail their battle craft North toward Falcon's Nest while Coast Guards under orders from Mikla raced ahead on horseback to alert their king of Beowulf's return.

Soon after their Longship entered the harbor, Beowulf and his men unloaded Hrothgar's gifts and went straight away to the Citadel.

Hygelac stood when Beowulf came into the Throne Room accompanied by Sigmund and the warriors chosen from Kungens Vakter. The smiles Hygelac and Hygd wore vanished, however, when they saw Handscio was not among those who returned.

"Welcome back, Nephew," said Hygelac, "but I don't see Handscio, and now I fear the worst."

"Handscio's dead, my King, slain by the monster, Grendel."

"He died well?" said Hygelac.

"Yes."

"And the monsters, what became of them?"

"Dead, my King—killed by my hand," said Beowulf.

Hygelac's eyes inventoried the many gifts arrayed before him: "By the looks of what you've brought you left Daneland in Hrothgar's good graces."

"King Hrothgar sent us off with the gifts you see before you, including seven war steeds being exercised as I speak, in your stables—all of which I give to you. The torque you see around my neck belonged to Hrothgar's father, Halfdane. I give it to you, my Queen."

Beowulf removed the torque and presented it to Hygd.

"You honor me, Beowulf," she said.

"You overwhelm us, Nephew," said Hygelac. "Will you keep nothing for yourself?"

"I want nothing, Uncle. I did what I set out to do. That is payment enough. Sigmund and the other men of your Guard acquitted themselves bravely in Hrothgar's Hall."

"And they'll be rewarded," said Hygelac. "Tell me, Nephew, how goes it with old Hrothgar, now that the Danes are free of the terror?"

"His heart is lighter, to be sure, Uncle, but I sense Daneland's days of peace may be fewer than Hrothgar would like."

"Because of the feud twixt him and Ingeld, King of the Heathobards?"

"Yes, although he intends to make a gift of his daughter, Freawaru, to Ingeld to ensure future peace."

"Hah!" said Hygelac. "Were it only that easy."

"With your permission," said Beowulf, "I'll leave for Vindinstedt Farm immediately—sooner the better."

"Very well, Nephew, but return as soon as you can. Matters of war and peace loom large."

"Before I depart we should speak in private, my King," said Beowulf.

"Very well—everyone out!" Hygelac turned to Hygd. "You, too, wife, I need to be alone with Beowulf."

"Of course, husband."

Hygd hugged Beowulf close: "My heart breaks for the loss of Handscio."

Hygd left the Hall with the others.

"Tell me, Nephew, will Hrothgar stand with us?" said Hygelac.

"Yes," said Beowulf. "The Spear Danes will come should we need them. I made the same pledge to Hrothgar in your name."

"Good—you've done well. Now we must find out what the Usurper, Onela, is plotting. I sent your cousin, Weohstan north to get answers but he hasn't returned. I told him to offer his sword for hire to gain Onela's confidence. But, for all I know, Weohstan could be dead."

"I'll look for him, Uncle; but the more I study on it, the more I believe the Marauders at Otters'Bay were Frisians. We need to find out who paid them. Hrothgar's spies convince me Day Raven is preparing to invade us. We need to learn when and where their attack will occur."

"Then go, Beowulf," said Hygelac. "Bring me answers!"

† † †

It was near sunset when Prince Heardred entered past the stake wall that encircled Knut iron jaw's estate. Heardred dismounted and went straight away to the Main Lodge. He passed a group of Berserkers sitting idle near the well. He felt their eyes bore a hole in the back of his head as he entered Knut's lodge.

"You're late, Prince Heardred," said Knut, from where he sat with the Svear princes, Eadgils and Eanmund.

"I had a feeling someone followed me," said Heardred, "so I changed direction several times, just to be safe."

Heardred nodded to Eanmund and Eadgils, and they to him.

"Better safe than sorry, I suppose," said Knut. "Sit down and have some mead."

"What news do you bring?" said Eanmund.

Heardred sat down beside Knut, across from the two brothers.

"Beowulf Waegmunding has returned from Daneland. I'm sure he creates doubt in Hygelac's mind as to whether the Svear attacked our shore. I'm afraid Beowulf's suspicions have become my father's."

"No matter if Hygelac thinks the Marauders were Frisians," said Knut; "it's getting Hygelac to go to war that matters—with whom is a paltry concern."

"But if Hygelac doesn't topple Onela from his perch, how will I obtain my throne?" said Eanmund.

"When the time is right, we'll kill Hygelac," said Knut. "His fondness for hunting is common knowledge. My spies will watch and wait for him to leave the Citadel. When he does my Berserkers will ambush him and his entourage. With Hygelac dead—"

"I will assume the throne," said Heardred.

"Yes," said Knut; "then you can have your war against Onela. And when Onela's defeated—"

Knut looked at Eanmund. "Eanmund will have his throne. How's that for a plan, my three young hounds?"

"I like it," said Heardred.

"As do I," said Eanmund.

Prince Eadgils averted his eyes and said nothing.

"What's not to like," Knut said. "Let's drink on it."

"And Beowulf Waegmunding?" said Eadgils.

"If my Berserkers haven't killed him Heardred can order Beowulf into exile once he's king."

"Banish him?" said Eanmund.

"Of course," said Heardred, flush with excitement at the mere thought of ordering Beowulf away. "How perfect! I'll send him into exile and proclaim his farm forfeit; Beowulf's lands and chattels will be mine!"

"No," said Knut, slamming both fists on the table. "Beowulf's land and chattels will be mine, young Prince—and why not? You'll have all Geatland to Lord over."

"Very well," said Heardred, "it'll be as you say, Eriksson. However, in the off chance, someone did follow me, I'll take Eanmund and Eadgils to my hunting lodge tomorrow. It's empty now, and their presence won't raise any eyebrows—agreed?"

"All right," said Knut, "let's drink!"

The four conspirators raised their drinking vessels and drank their cups dry.

"Are your daughters here?" Heardred said, not bothering to disguise his appetite for young flesh.

"They are," said Knut.

"Perhaps they'd like to join us, now that we've concluded our business," said Heardred.

"Can't," said Knut; "I've got them locked away in the barn for your protection."

Heardred shot Knut a questioning look. Knut iron jaw's eyes twinkled with licentious merriment.

"I set your imaginations on fire, didn't I," said Knut. "Don't worry; my girls can entertain you later after we've eaten."

† † †

Ragmund sat at his usual table which provided the greatest amount of privacy in the Mead House. As he filled his mouth with roasted chicken and washed it down with ale, he listened to what his spy had to say:

"I followed Prince Heardred all the way to Clan Eriksson's estate. He was there a long time, and when he departed, he had with him two others."

"Do you know where they went?" said Ragmund?"

"No, Lord Ragmund. It was almost sundown when they left Eriksson's Palisade. I thought it best to tell you right away."

Ragmund dropped several gold coins into the spy's hand.

"You did well. Now, go!"

† † †

It was ten days since Beowulf and Handscio set sail for Daneland. Handscio's wife, Asa, became depressed; so much so, she would neither eat nor leave her bed. Beorn left a potion to induce a good night's sleep, but Asa would have none of it.

Elin coped with her fears by staying busy.

Riding Storm Bringer through the better part of the night, Beowulf arrived at Vindinstedt Farm just after dawn.

Elin came running from the lodge as Beowulf dismounted.

"Beowulf!" said Elin.

She threw herself into Beowulf's arms and sobbed. Elin had seen Beowulf return alone; it was enough to tell her Handscio was dead. After they had withdrawn to their bedchamber, Elin watched in silence as Beowulf removed his battle gear and donned clean garments.

† † †

Beowulf sat with Elin in the Banquet Hall. In a soft but steady voice, he recounted Handscio's death at the hands of Grendel, absent the gruesome details. Sensing a presence, he looked to one side and saw Asa.

Still clad in her nightgown, Asa's eyes were red and swollen and her face pale. Beowulf stood. Elin got up, went to Asa and held her. When Beowulf went to embrace her, Asa hissed and backed away.

"Don't touch me," she said. "Handscio's dead because of you!"

Beowulf stopped.

"That's not fair, Asa," said Elin. "You don't know what you're saying. Handscio was a warrior; he understood the risks of battle."

"I saw Handscio die in my dream," said Asa, tears streaming down her face. "Beowulf just stood there with feet made of stone —and did nothing!"

Asa looked at Beowulf. "Don't tell me he died for glory or honor or any of the lies men tell, to justify their lust for glory. I hate you, Beowulf Waegmunding! I hate you!"

Asa turned and ran from the lodge.

"Asa shouldn't be alone," said Beowulf.

"I know," said Elin. "I'll go to her."

Beowulf sat in front of the fire. Elin sat beside him.

"Tell me what happened," said Elin. "I don't believe you would allow Handscio to die—not willingly."

"I told Handscio and the others to stay back," said Beowulf. "I wanted to confront the monster alone. I even bragged that I'd use my arms and nothing else to fight him. Nevertheless, when I came eye to eye with Grendel, I couldn't believe what I was facing. For a moment, fear rooted my feet to the floor. Fearing for my safety, Handscio rushed the monster, and Grendel killed him. When I came to my senses, I caught hold of the monster's arm, and my strength proved greater."

"You're wrong to blame yourself for Handscio's death, my love, and Asa shouldn't blame you. I'll tell her what you said; but later, when she's more herself."

Elin kissed Beowulf and left the lodge. Leaning forward, elbows on his knees, Beowulf held his cold hands palms-out in front of the fire.

Forgive me, Handscio—forgive me.

The sound of Elin screaming brought Beowulf to his feet. Running out of the lodge, Beowulf saw Elin inside the milking barn.

Others came running and gathered around.

Entering the barn, Beowulf saw Asa's lifeless body hanging from a rope tied to the rafters.

After Asa's burial, Elin and Beowulf rode to Vindinstedt Forest. They arrived at the hot spring just as a light rain began to fall.

They left their horses beneath the sprawling branches of a blue spruce tree and walked the rest of the way in silence. Without speaking, they undressed each other and stepped into the mineral water. Steam rose from the surface, enveloping them in a cloud. They sat side by side on the same bench of rock where Ecgtheow and Liv had sat so many times before.

Elin rested the side of her face against his shoulder. Tears fell from her eyes and mixed with droplets of rain.

Beowulf turned his head toward the sky.

Hear me Frigga, he prayed. *Handscio died well; he died with no thought of holding back or saving himself. He died a warrior's death. I beseech you, great goddess, send the Valkyries; let them guide his soul out of Helheim to Valhalla. He was my friend. He was my shield brother, and I will miss him, as I miss the sun in winter.*

59

THE GATHERING STORM

Elin rose at dawn, nauseated and inclined to vomit. Beowulf was not in bed beside her. She found him downstairs in the cooking chamber sitting on a bench in front of the fire polishing his war gear with sand and vinegar. Beowulf needed to find Beorn. If anyone could pass a message to Weohstan, Beorn could.

"Must you leave again so soon?" she said.

"Yes."

"But, why?" said Elin, unable to disguise the disappointment in her voice.

"Geatland's enemies are plotting our ruin, Elin."

"It isn't fair, Beowulf. Why must it always be you?"

Beowulf stopped what he was doing. "I know it's hard for you when I go. Just as it is for me to leave."

Elin sat on the bench beside Beowulf. "Can you at least tell me where you're going?"

"No, sweet wife; I can't. But I'll return when I can."

"What we have together, Beowulf; I don't want it to end. Promise me it won't end."

"It won't end, Elin—not even death can do that. I won't let it."

With her forefinger, Elin traced the length of Beowulf's scar, from beneath his right eye to his chin. She kissed him.

"I'll make you something to eat."

† † †

Although born to the Race of Giants, Loki became Odin's blood-brother when Loki proved himself a good friend and ally to the All Father. It was during the first war between giants and gods.

Now, as a god with special powers of his own, Loki could assume any form he desired; which, in no small way, helped him maintain the names he soon became best known by Strife Bringer and Mischief Maker. Hot tempered, it was Loki's nature to be impulsive, short-sighted and often cruel; qualities that, in time, made Loki despised by the gods of Asgard, and feared throughout Midgard by all humankind.

None but he Queen of the Underworld, Hel, Judge of the Dead, one of Loki's three children, loved him without reservation and often sought his help, as she did that day.

Rather than appear in his natural state, as a giant monster from Utgard, home of Giants, Loki presented himself to his daughter as a tall, handsome male from Midgard, clean shaven, with long black hair, and deep green eyes that were cold, and translucent, like polished emeralds.

No sooner did Loki arrive at Helheim, Hel rushed from her throne, knelt at her father's feet, and clasped her arms around him.

"I would have been here sooner, daughter, but I was in Midgard among the Kelts—you might even say I was their guest of honor."

"Thank you, for coming Father. Odin gave me his promise that a Manling called the bear's son would never sire children, lest his progeny acquires the powers Frigga and Thor bestowed on him when he was fated to die as a child."

Loki lifted Hel to her feet.

"I've heard the stories about this Manling," he said, "and I admit, daughter, I'm a trifle curious about him. But what makes you think the All Father would dishonor his promise to you?"

"Because the wife of the bear's son carries his child inside her, even as we speak."

"And what is being said about this in Asgard?"

"Nothing, Father. That's just it. No one says a word. Not the All Father, or Frigga, or even that drunken braggart, Thor. Everyone carries on as if they've forgotten the matter; so they say nothing."

"And you're sure they know the woman carries the bear's son's child.?"

"Oh, yes, Father. They all know."

Loki took a moment to think, then he smiled and said: "Well, daughter—a promise is a promise."

Turin was next in line to have his petition heard. He stood among a throng of Geatfolk, all of them seeking remedies from their king. When finished with the petitioner in front of him, Hygelac's eyes fell upon Ecgtheow's adopted son, and he beckoned to him. Turin stepped forward and bowed.

"What's your name, lad?" said Hygelac.

"Turin Waegmunding, the adopted son of Ecgtheow Waegmunding, my King."

"Ecgtheow's foster son?"

"Yes, my King."

"I remember now—you rode with Clan Waegmunding, and though you were but a few, you swooped down on the Svear like Falcons. You helped turn the tide of battle to our favor. Never will I forget that day, Turin. Adopted though you be, I know you made Ecgtheow proud that day."

"Nor shall I forget that day, my King."

"Your accent is that of a Dane—True?"

"It is, my King—I ask for a place among your warriors."

Before Hygelac could speak, Ragmund entered the Throne Room in haste, dragging his crippled foot.

"What is it, Ragmund?" said Hygelac.

"King Hrothgar's emissary, Ulthur is here and requests an audience, my King. He says it's urgent."

"Clear the Hall!" said Hygelac. "I'll see Hrothgar's emissary in private."

Sigmund cleared the Hall.

Accompanied by Ragmund, Ulthur stopped before the dais and bowed.

"Hail, Great King."

"What news, Ulthur?"

"Day Raven is assembling men and ships to invade."

"He plans to invade Daneland," said Hygelac.

"No, Great King," said Ulthur, "He plans to invade Geatland."

Hygelac's mouth sagged open.

"When?" said Ragmund.

"Sooner than later. Even now, Day Raven seeks alliances with the Wylfings and Svear. His plan is to attack Geatland together, at the same time—Frisians from the south, Wylfings from the east and Svear from the north."

"If that occurs, they will outnumber us in men and ships, my King," said Ragmund.

"King Hrothgar and the Spear Danes stand ready to join you," said Ulthur, "for good or ill, Great King, but it will take us time to gather our army."

"How much time do you need?" said Ragmund.

"I can't say, Lord Ragmund," said Ulthur.

Hygelac stood. He began to pace back and forth in front of the dais. He stopped and looked at Ulthur.

"I'll attack the Frisians first before they can join forces with the Wylfings and the Svear."

"Beowulf is your Battle Lord, my King," said Ragmund. "Shouldn't you consult with him first?"

"Ordinarily, yes, I would; but I sent Beowulf on an errand days ago. I dare not delay, Ragmund; I need to act, and act fast."

"I implore you, my King," Sigmund said, "Summon Beowulf to Falcon's Nest."

Hygelac thought a moment. "Beowulf's foster-brother, Turin Waegmunding, waits in the Mead Hall. Bring him to me."

Sigmund hurried off. A moment later, he returned to the Throne Room with Turin at his side.

"You've already proven yourself in battle and ready to join the ranks of my warriors," said Hygelac.

"Yes, my king. I want to fight. I'm more than ready," said Turin.

"You're young," Turin, but you have the heart! Does Beowulf know you're here?"

"No, my King."

"I've not seen Beowulf for some time, my King; nor am I certain of his whereabouts."

"Very well, Turin, I'll give you another chance to test your mettle."

"Anything, my King—command me," said Turin.

"I want you to ride north immediately. Take two extra horses from my stable. Ride hard and fast. Find Beowulf and tell him his king and people need him. The Frisians are preparing to attack us. There's little time, Turin—do you understand? Much depends on you."

"Yes, my King; I'll find Beowulf, or die, trying."

"That's the spirit," said Hygelac. "Geatland's existence depends on you. Now go!"

"Thank you, my King."

Sigmund presented himself in front of Turin; together, they hastened from the Throne Room.

Hygelac looked around: "Has anyone seen my son?" he said. "Has anyone seen Prince Heardred?"

"No, my King," said Ragmund. "Not for several days."

There was no disguising the look of contempt on Hygelac's face.

† † †

Near sunset the Schaman sat in front of his campfire roasting rabbit on a spit; he turned his gaze toward the dense woods immersed in darkness.

"I'm over here, Bear's Son, waiting for you."

Beowulf appeared on Storm Bringer.

"You're just in time for dinner," said Beorn.

"Sorry, Beorn, but assassins followed me," Beowulf said.

"Too bad for them," said Beorn. "There's just enough for us."

Beowulf laughed and dismounted. He removed the saddle from Storm Bringer and tethered the stallion beside the Schaman's pack horse. Beowulf placed his sword and spear on the ground and sat beside Beorn near the campfire.

"What are these assassins who followed you, Beowulf—men or beasts?"

"Something of both," said Beowulf as he removed his helm.

"Berserkers," said Beorn.

"Twenty of them; they've been shadowing me since I left the Farm."

"At whose bidding?"

"I'm not sure, Beorn, but if I were to guess, I'd say Knut Iron-Jaw."

"The Berserkers are close. I can smell them," said the Schaman.

"They're holding back a hundred paces from here," said Beowulf.

Before Beorn could reply, out of the distance came the long, high-pitched howl of a wolf. A moment passed, followed by more howling, each time close, but from a different location.

"These Berserkers even sound like wolves, don't they," said Beorn with a chuckle. "It must be the skins they wear."

"Those weren't Berserkers," said Beowulf. "Is that poor rabbit ready to eat?"

"Most definitely," said Beorn.

The Schaman retrieved the rabbit from over the fire and with one violent motion ripped the carcass in two. Beorn handed half to Beowulf. Beowulf took a bite and nodded.

"This is good; hot, but good."

"It's the herbs, remember?" said the Schaman.

"Just promise me I won't be having visions."

Beorn laughed.

The Berserkers were careful to maintain a distance. Concealed by the forest, they could see the flickering flames of a campfire no more than one-hundred paces away. It would be enough to guide them to their prey. The Berserkers wore naught other than a wolf skin hanging from their hips. In their hands, each Berserker carried a buckler and battle-axe.

From a pouch held by their leader, each Berserker received a large dose of crushed root and herbs that they gnashed and swallowed. The Berserkers began to shiver and shake, and their teeth chattered. Some gnawed on the edge of their wooden bucklers. When they heard the sound of wolves howling in the distance, they too began to do so, since the herbs were taking full effect. With their lust for blood inflamed, and their bodies growing numb, the Berserkers advanced in a line, toward the flames in the distance.

Beowulf and Beorn got to their feet.

"By the gods," said Beorn; "they're coming!"

Beowulf threw more wood on the fire; then he put on his helm and collected his weapons from the ground.

Beorn grasped his battle axe with both hands.

"I can hear their thoughts, Beowulf—and they're not pretty."

"Remain behind me, Beorn."

"I'll do no such thing," said the Schaman. "I've chosen my ground, and here I'll stand."

Knowing it was no use to argue, Beowulf looked into the darkness beyond the campfire: "Die well."

"And you, Bear's Son—die well."

Beowulf hurled his spear full force. There came a loud scream as the spear pierced flesh and bone. The sound of Berserkers crashing through the brush grew close; then, at the same time, snarling, gray-black shapes darted in and out of the firelight.

These four-legged phantoms of the night ran past Beowulf and straight toward the Berserkers.

The sound of death screams erupted in the darkness. Amazed by what he saw and heard, Beorn wet his lips with his tongue and looked at Beowulf.

"You knew the Gray Brethren would be here, didn't you," said the Schaman, shouting over the sound of the killing underway in the darkness.

"Yes," said Beowulf.

It wasn't long before the wolves tore apart the outnumbered Berserkers. Except for the crackling of the fire, the forest became silent.

The leader of the Gray Brethren, Adalwolf, stepped into the firelight.

"*All are dead, Bear's Son; none of the painted Manlings escaped.*"

"*You have my thanks, Adalwolf. I'll see that your pack has fattened sheep to feast on during the winter. Your pups won't hunger, nor will I forget what happened here this night.*"

"Good hunting, Bear's Son."

"Good hunting, Adalwolf."

The wolf Lord turned and disappeared into the night.

"By Odin's beard," said Beorn, "I thought I'd seen everything until now."

"Do you have anything to drink besides water?" said Beowulf.

"I do," said the Schaman. "I'll get it.

Beowulf and Beorn sat by the fire and drank in silence. After a while, Beowulf looked at Beorn.

"Handscio's dead."

"I know," said Beorn; "I saw his death in a vision."

"So did Asa," said Beowulf. "In a dream. Now she is dead."

"You can't let that gnaw at you, Beowulf. It was their time;

besides, Handscio died in battle. It was a warrior's death."

"Had I not hesitated, Beorn, he would be alive today."

"You're not like other men, Beowulf, but when all's said and done, you're still a man! Don't hold yourself to some impossible standard. If you need to feel guilty over Handscio's passing feel guilty, then drop it. To do otherwise will invite madness. Besides, you have much to live for now."

Beowulf gave Beorn a puzzled look.

"Didn't Elin tell you?" said Beorn.

"Tell me what?"

Beorn stared at his feet.

"Now I've done it. Fool that I am, I should have my tongue cut out."

"Tell me what, Beorn?"

"Elin carries your child," he said.

60

SETTLING DEBTS

Beowulf awoke to the sound of Beorn striking his flint to start a cooking-fire.

"I need to get a message to Weohstan," said Beowulf. "He needs to know Handscio's dead."

"He knows," said Beorn. "I told him of my vision when I was at Uppsala."

"How did he take it?"

"As any father would the loss of his first-born. But I can tell you this—he bears you no grudge." Having started a fire, Beorn placed a pot of water over the flames; into it, he added a pinch of crushed root. "This will help us stay alert," said Beorn. "I want you to drink it."

Beowulf nodded. "What did you learn from Weohstan?"

"He's heard nothing to suggest it was the Svear who came ashore at Otters'Bay. But listen to this: messengers and emissaries from the Wylfings and Frisians come and go from Uppsala every few days."

"Things are beginning to make sense," said Beowulf. "If Hygelac strikes north against the Svear, it will leave Geatland defenseless against the Frisians, in the south, and the Wylfings to the east."

"Do you think this has anything to do with why Knut Eriksson sent his Berserkers to kill you?"

"No, Knut wants me dead because he probably thinks he has something to gain from it."

"But, what?"

"Clan Waegmunding's land and chattels if Hygelac is no longer king. Someone must have given Knut reason to believe that with me dead, and Hygelac out of the way, Clan Waegmunding's wealth would be his."

"Do you know what you're saying? There's but one person who stands to gain with Hygelac gone."

"Yes, my cousin, Heardred. I'm sure of it: he conspires with Knut Iron-Jaw in order to seize his father's Throne. He wants Hygelac to go to war, because he wants Hygelac dead. He knows that alive, I'm too much of an obstacle twixt him and the throne."

"This all makes sense, as you say, Beowulf, but where's our proof? We've dead Berserkers to support what you say; although I doubt the wolves left much uneaten. In short, we lack evidence as to who commanded them."

"I know," said Beowulf.

"Then what should we do?"

"I need to return to Falcon's Nest and warn my uncle, but first I'll pay Knut Iron-Jaw a visit."

"I'm going with you, Bear's Son."

It was mid-afternoon when two warriors in the watchtower saw the Schaman approaching on foot. Beorn led Storm-Bringer and his own horse. Hanging from both sides of the saddle, Storm-Bringer carried Beowulf's sword and the battle-axes taken from the dead Berserkers. The Schaman stopped in front of the closed gate and smiled at the guards looking down at him.

"What do you want, old man?" said the guard in-charge.

"I'm a purveyor of herbs and potions," said Beorn, "and well-made weaponry. I also have trinkets for your women—fine combs and amber jewelry and a reflecting-plate of polished copper for the master of this fine place."

It was evident by the looks on their faces—the two guards were hesitant to admit the odd-looking old man with the stained beard.

"Wait there while I tell our chief!"

The guard in-charge climbed down from the watchtower. He wasted no time getting to Knut Iron-Jaw's lodge. Inside he found Knut in the Banquet Room eating and drinking with fifteen of his clansmen. Also present were Knut's daughters: Ansa, Arla and Alva, ages fourteen, thirteen and twelve. The girls were amusing themselves with a rat they trapped in a dark corner of the room.

"What is it?" said Knut, seeing the warrior enter in haste.

"An odd looking old merchant waits outside the gate, my Lord.

He wants to trade his wares: he has potions, weapons and trinkets and such."

"He comes to trade, does he? Well, open the gate and let him in; then kill him and bring his wares here!"

The warrior hastened back to the Main Gate and shouted to his companion in the watchtower:

"Come down and help me open the gate!"

The warrior in the watchtower descended the ladder.

"Are we letting that old fool inside?"

"Yes," said the guard in-charge, talking in a whisper. "Iron-Jaw wants us to kill him and take his wares."

"For ourselves?" said the second guard.

"No!" said the guard-in-charge, "for Iron-Jaw, you idiot!"

Together the guards lifted the massive crossbeam from the iron brackets that held the gate shut.

The guards gestured for the Schaman to enter. Beorn led the horses inside the palisade and stopped. The guard in-charge drew a knife from his belt and moved toward the Schaman's blind side. At the same time, the other guard pretended to examine the broad axes and swords hanging from Storm Bringer's saddle.

"These are some fine weapons you have, old man," said the guard.

"Thank you, my son," said the Schaman. "I can make you a good bargain for anything you take a fancy to."

"What's this," said the guard, "there's dried blood on the handles of these axes."

"Yes," said Beorn, "Berserker blood."

Beorn whirled around. He swang Truth in a wide arc and sank its cutting-edge deep into the chest of the guard in-charge. In almost the same instant, Beowulf appeared inside the Main Gate. He threw his spear at the remaining guard, killing him. Beowulf retrieved Widow Maker from Storm Bringer's saddle. Together he and Beorn went to the front door of Knut iron jaw's lodge.

"No prisoners," said Beowulf.

"Understood," said the Schaman.

Beorn kicked the door open. Beowulf led the way inside, hacking and hewing every warrior that crossed his path in the dim light of the lodge. Beorn's axe fell upon Knut's men, slicing them to pieces until one remained—Knut Iron-Jaw.

Seeing his clansmen dead, Knut threw his sword at Beowulf's feet and fell to his knees. Knut raised his hands over his head:

"Don't kill me. I'll give you all the gold and silver I have—spare me, my Prince."

"Tell me about Heardred's plan to topple the king!" said Beowulf.

"Heardred wants his father's throne," said Knut. "He thinks if he can provoke a war, it'll prove Hygelac's undoing if you're no longer a threat to him."

"So Heardred paid you to unleash your Berserkers on me?"

"Yes," said Knut.

Knut looked around the room, at the dismembered bodies of his clansmen strewn about the floor. Knut licked his lips when Beorn stepped behind him.

"I have more to tell."

"So, speak!" said Beorn.

"Ohthere's son, Eanmund, is in-league with Heardred. He seeks to overturn Onela and regain his father's throne."

"And the younger one?" said Beowulf.

"Eadgils has no stake in the matter, other than the fact his uncle wants him dead. He follows his brother's lead, like a lost puppy."

Knut watched Beowulf start to leave. "Aren't you going to kill me?"

"No," said Beowulf, with his back to Knut. "I'm not going to kill you."

"I am," said Beorn.

Before Knut could cry out the Schaman brought his axe down, cleaving Knut's skull in two.

Beowulf was at the well washing blood from his hands and the blades of his sword and spear when Beorn exited from Knut's lodge. Beorn held Knut's three daughters by their hair and dragged them kicking and screaming behind him.

"Look, Beowulf, at what I found hiding in a corner—three little mice! What should we do with them?"

"You're Knut's daughters?" said Beowulf.

The girls' heads bobbed up and down.

Beowulf studied their faces: "Gather food," he said, "and whatever else you need; you can no longer stay here."

"I curse you, Beowulf Waegmunding," said the oldest girl,

Ansa, "You, and your foul-smelling friend!"

She spat on the ground at Beorn's feet.

"Go," said Beowulf to the girls. "Leave while you can!"

Beowulf and Beorn torched every lodge inside the palisade; then they saddled one of the horses from the barn for Beorn to ride. They rode from the conflagration without looking back.

† † †

At the hunting lodge in the forest, where they secreted themselves, Heardred, Eanmund and Eadgils saw a great plume of smoke rising into the sky, two leagues away. Curious, they rode in the direction of Knut Iron-Jaw's estate. Soon they saw the unmanned ramparts of the stake wall. Deciding to have a closer look they found charred bodies scattered among the smoldering ruins of Knut's lodge.

"How could this happen?" said Ohthere's oldest son, Eanmund.

"I can tell you in three words how it happened," said Heardred.

"The bear's son," said Eadgils.

"Yes," said Heardred, "the bear's son."

"What do we do now?" said Eanmund.

"Beowulf will find and kill us."

"No," said Heardred. "I think Knut Iron-Jaw sent his Berserkers after Beowulf and they failed. What we saw back there is Beowulf's wrath. For now, you both should return to the hunting lodge. You'll be safe there while I return to Falcon's Nest and see where matters stand."

"And while you're gone, what are we to do?" said Eanmund.

"Try not to piss yourselves," said Heardred, "and wait for me to send for you."

† † †

Heardred wasted no time returning to Falcon's Nest. Arriving just after sunset, he found the city bustling with warriors. They came from the clans in response to Hygelac's call-to-arms.

Soon, eight-hundred warriors would crowd the harbor below the Citadel in anticipation of sailing with Hygelac to Frisia.

Heardred went straight away to the Throne Room where Hygelac was consulting with his advisers and Clan Chiefs. All the chieftains were present, but for Knut Eriksson and Beowulf Waegmunding.

Heardred's mother saw her son enter. When Heardred looked at her, Hygd placed a finger over her lips, signing him to b silent. When Hygelac had finished speaking, Heardred strode forward.

"Are we at war, father?"

"Where have you been?" said Hygelac.

"I've been traveling throughout Geatland, assessing the mood of the Geatfolk, that I might apprise you of their will."

"Come closer," said Hygelac.

Heardred stepped closer to the dais. Hygelac stood and without hesitating backhanded his son across the mouth. The force of the blow sent Heardred sprawling onto his back.

"Husband," said Hygd, "Heardred's your son!"

"Silence, Hygd!" said Hygelac. "He's the heir to my throne, and it's time he behaved like it! Get up, damn you!"

Heardred wiped the blood from his lips and stood trembling before his father.

"Day after tomorrow I'll sail with two-thirds of my army to Frisia. I mean to end Day Raven's ambition to rule the Whale Road. I've made it known—your mother will act as my regent and rule in my absence. Do you understand?"

"Yes," said Heardred without bothering to disguise the bitterness inside him.

Hygelac raised an eyebrow: "Yes, what?" he said

"Yes, my King," said Heardred.

"While I'm gone, learn from your mother; learn what it means to rule. Don't think because you're my son, my throne will be yours one day. When I return you'll have to prove yourself deserving of the Crown of Geatland. Do you understand?"

"Yes, my King."

"Good—now get out of my sight!"

Biting down on his anger, Heardred turned on his heel and left the Throne Room. Heardred felt himself on fire. He went outside to feel the cool damp air on his face. He walked along the eastern wall-walk and smiled: *Father going to fight in Frisia is more than I hoped. Now, gods willing, he needs to die there*!

† † †

Three days passed since Turin rode northeast by east with the hope of finding Beowulf's trail. Each day, he rode from dawn to dusk, careful to take the less traveled trails thinking Beowulf would do the same.

When the sun began to drop behind hills veiled with shadows, Turin made camp. He got a fire started then fed and watered his horse. From his saddlebags he removed what meager provisions remained: half a loaf of rye bread, some honey and smoked salmon. He sat down by the fire and ate.

What made Hygelac think I could find him? Beowulf could be anywhere! I've failed my king, my people and worst of all, Beowulf.

"Do you always make so much noise when you think?" said Beorn, stepping from the shadows.

Startled, Turin leapt to his feet, sword in hand.

"Beorn—how did you find me?"

"Dumb luck," said Beowulf, following behind, leading two mounts and a pack-horse.

"Good," said Beorn; "now that that's settled—let's eat."

"I haven't much but you're welcome to it," said Turin.

"Well it just so happens we have food aplenty, Master Turin," said Beorn, "and in a pig-bladder tied over my pack-horse, there's mead to drink, courtesy of Clan Eriksson!"

"It's not as good as Beorn's special brew," said Beowulf, "but it's potent!"

After seeing to their horses, Beowulf, Beorn and Turin sat down in front of the campfire.

"What news?" said Beowulf.

"Our king sent me to find you," said Turin. "Hygelac's preparing to sail to Frisia."

"What?" said Beorn. "He goes to war against Day Raven?"

"Yes," said Turin; "that's Hygelac's plan."

"How long before he departs?" said Beowulf.

"Anytime, now," said Turin.

"Tomorrow I must return to Falcon's Nest," said Beowulf.

"What would you have me and Turin do?" said Beorn.

"Return to Vindinstedt. Bring the Freemen and their families inside the palisade. See that the men go about armed lest our enemies take them by surprise."

"You can count on me, Beowulf," said Turin.

"I know I can, Turin. As sure as Handscio and Ecgtheow are in Valhalla drinking mead, and looking down at us."

Turin's chest swelled with pride and his eyes became moist. Turin got to his feet and walked off:

"The horses need grooming," he said.

"Anything you want me to tell Elin in your stead?" said Beorn.

"No, old friend," said Beowulf; "there's nothing you can tell her she doesn't already know."

† † †

When Beowulf arrived the next day at Falcon's Nest, he found the city quiet and diminished in warriors wandering the streets. Except for old men, women, and children, the city appeared deserted.

Proceeding to the Citadel, he took Storm Bringer to Hygelac's stable. There, Beowulf charged the grooms to take care of his stallion. Ragmund hurried off to alert the queen of Beowulf's presence.

It wasn't long before Hygd arrived in the Throne Room escorted by Sigmund.

"Beowulf, I give thanks to the gods you're here," said Hygd.

"I came as fast as I could, my Queen, but I come too late."

"Not by long. Your uncle sailed with the army this morning."

"Then perhaps I'm not too late," said Beowulf. "If you'll allow it, my Queen, I'll sail for Frisia today."

"Alone?" said Sigmund.

"Yes, but I must leave now."

"Then go, Beowulf," said the queen, "and may the gods speed you on your way."

Heardred entered the Throne Room. Beowulf stopped in front of Heardred and stared him straight in the eye. Heardred's lips began to twitch. Averting his eyes from Beowulf's gaze, he hastened in the direction of his mother.

61

DEATH OF A KING

In the Harbor Beowulf found the Avenger where Turin had left it anchored. Without a crew there would be no sailing it to Frisland; instead, he found three fishermen: a father and his two oldest sons who put themselves and their boat at Beowulf's disposal. They did this without fear of traversing the Whale Road despite the fact that Frisian Longships might be ranging far and wide, ready to contest the will of the Danes and Geats.

With few words spoken, Beowulf and the fishermen set sail. Before long, after leaving the Fjord of Kuurin, the current and less than obliging winds buffeted that small craft. The hours passed like days for Beowulf. Once or twice he thought he saw Death sitting at the prow, staring at him but each time he closed his eyes and looked again, the apparition vanished.

Beowulf thought of Elin and the child growing inside her—his child, and he wondered if it were a son or daughter they would soon welcome to the world.

When he sensed they were nearing Frisian' waters, he set all tender thoughts aside and steeled himself for what would come. Beowulf no longer doubted that where he went, Death went with him.

† † †

On the morning of the fifth day, the fishing boat arrived at the coast of Frisland. The fishermen brought their vessel close to the fogbound shore. Breaking through the mist, into view, was most of Hygelac's fleet, some beached, others anchored in shallow water.

A skirmish with Frisian coastguards had taken place, and corpses littered the beach. Coming from further inland, was the sound of battle: the clashing of swords on helms and shields, iron against iron, and the full-throated screams of the wounded and dying.

"I'll get out here," said Beowulf.

"Should you need us," said the fisherman, "we'll drop anchor offshore, my Prince, over there, beneath yonder cliffs."

"The choice is yours," said Beowulf, putting on his helm and taking up his spear. "Come what may, you and your sons have my thanks."

Beowulf leapt feet first into the surf. He carried no shield; his spear he held; his knife, and sword he sheathed across his back. He waded ashore and began to make his way across the sand.

Beowulf approached several riderless horses on the beach. *"It is I, Beowulf, the bear's son, who calls. I ask the strongest and fastest among you to speed me to the battle.*"

A roan stallion trotted to where Beowulf waited: *"I'll carry you into battle, Bear's Son."*

Beowulf took no mind of the blood that stained the saddle. Taking hold of the reins, Beowulf urged the stallion inland.

† † †

On a grass-covered plain, inland from the coast, two-hundred Frisian warriors surrounded Hygelac and his men: thirty warriors of his Guard. They were all that remained of the eight-hundred men-at-arms who had sailed from Geatland. The corpses of the Thunder-Geats mingled with the Frisian dead for half a league in an almost perfect circle.

Beowulf rode to the top of a hill and halted his mount. Bitter the taste in his mouth when he saw what had become of Hygelac and his army.

† † †

Hygelac swung Naegling, the Sword of Kings, killing the Frisians who rushed at him until, all at once, silence descended over the battlefield. The Frisians backed away from the King of the Geats. Their ranks parted as their king and Battle Lord, Day Raven, strode forward. He clad himself with armor from head to foot and wielded a broadsword.

Day Raven was head and shoulders taller than a horse, and as he stepped closer to Hygelac, his shadow fell upon the Geats' king, covering Hygelac in darkness. Hygelac took several, deep breaths before lifting his shield. As he raised his sword, he accepted as the fact he'd soon be dead.

"Look well upon your killer, Hygelac, and know it is I, Day Raven, who'll bed your queen, while your corpse lies here rotting."

Beowulf's battle cry shattered the calm over the battlefield and drew the eyes of every Frisian, including Day Raven, toward the hilltop. Hygelac also looked, and his heart leapt for joy.

"Beowulf," said Hygelac. He felt his strength renewed by the battle cry of his most loyal Thane and nephew.

Beowulf sat astride the stallion, his arms outstretched, his spear, Death Stalker in one hand, and his sword, Widow Maker, in the other. The horse was obedient to Beowulf's wishes; he charged forward off the hill and made straight for the battle.

"Beowulf won't save you," said Day Raven as he advanced. He swung his sword against Hygelac's Linden shield, shattering it. Dropping the wreckage of his splintered shield to the ground, Hygelac struck sideways at Day Raven's legs. The Frisian king laughed and blocked Hygelac's blow with his shield. In almost the same instant, Day Raven swung his sword with the force of an avalanche, severing Hygelac's sword arm at the elbow. Hygelac cried out and dropped to his knees. Without hesitation, Day Raven brought his sword down, cleaving Hygelac's Crown and helm in two. The cheering that followed turned into a chorus of confusion, as Beowulf rode into the Frisians' ranks dealing death with sword and spear. Looking over the heads of his warriors, Day Raven watched as Beowulf smashed through shield wall after shield wall, scattering his enemies. Beowulf rode straight for Day Raven.

"Yes! Come fight me, Bear's Son!"

Beowulf leapt from the saddle, and the stallion galloped off.

As Frisians began to close in Day Raven waved them back. "Get away from him!" he said. "This Geatlander is mine alone to kill."

Beowulf hurled Death Stalker from thirty paces away just as Day Raven raised his shield. Beowulf's spear struck dead center, broke through the bronze boss and double-thickness of Linden wood and pierced the back of Day Raven's hand.

Day Raven bellowed with pain. Enraged, he dropped his sword to the ground. With his free hand, he pulled Beowulf's spear from his shield.

Beowulf strode toward the Frisian Battle Lord.

His hand no longer impaled by Beowulf's spear, Day Raven retrieved his sword and stretched to his full height:

"Since first-hearing stories about you, Bear's Son, I've lived with a single purpose—that one day we'd meet in battle. As for the stories of what you did in Daneland, I don't believe them."

"Then today's your lucky day," said Beowulf.

As they clashed, sparks flew from the blades of their swords. After trading blows, Beowulf sidestepped and struck Day Raven's sword from his hand. Day Raven's self-assured expression turned to one of dread. As Day Raven stepped back, a Frisian warrior tossed him a battle axe. In one single motion, Day Raven snatched the axe from the air and swung it. Beowulf ducked, and the axe passed over. In the time it takes to blink, Beowulf drove his fist full-force through Day Raven's breastplate. The Frisian Battle Lord gasped as the force of the blow collapsed his lungs. That gasp turned into a high-pitched scream when Beowulf yanked his hand free, clutching Day Raven's beating heart. With a look of total disbelief frozen on his face, the Frisian King crumpled to the ground.

"Believe it," said Beowulf, then he spat on Day Raven's corpse.

Too stunned to speak, the Frisians watched in silence as Beowulf sheathed his sword and went to where Hygelac's body lay on the ground. He pried Naegling from his uncle's hand, then gathered the two halves of Hygelac's crown and stuffed them under his belt. Holding Naegling, Beowulf returned to Day Raven's corpse. With one cut Beowulf severed Day Raven's head and skewered it to the point of Naegling. He held the head aloft for every Frisian to see.

"See it and believe it," said Beowulf, "and know it is I, Beowulf Waegmunding, the bear's son, who fought here this day."

Holding Day Raven's head high, Beowulf retrieved his spear and walked in the direction of the cliff.

The Frisians parted ranks and let him pass. Like reluctant hounds after an enraged boar, the Frisians followed Beowulf. They knew he couldn't escape; yet, not one warrior relished the idea of crossing swords with Beowulf, not after what they saw him do to their king and Battle Lord.

When Beowulf reached the edge of the cliff and could go no further, he turned and faced the Frisians closing in on him. Beowulf hurled Day Raven's head like a melon from the tip of Naegling.

The Frisians dispersed as their Battle Lord's head fell among them, and rolled to a stop. In the instant that followed Beowulf leapt feet first, into the water.

As the Frisian crowded around each other at the edge of the cliff, some threw spears toward the surface of the water. A moment later the Frisians saw Beowulf's head appear a good distance away from where he had landed.

Beowulf raised Naegling high out of the water. Later in their lodges and around their campfires, the Frisians on the cliff that day would swear they heard the bear's son laughing as the mist swirled around him, concealing him from sight.

The fishermen appeared out of the fog. They were coming for Hygelac's Battle Lord in that best of small boats.

† † †

Seven days and six nights had passed before Beowulf reached Falcon's Nest. From the Harbor, he went on foot to the city.

Recognized by the Geatfolk, they followed him as he proceeded toward the Citadel.

"Where's our king," said a woman in the crowd.

"And our army?" said an old man, his trembling voice filled with fear.

"What news from Frisland?" said a metalsmith standing outside his workshop.

Beowulf said nothing but continued to walk in silence.

The guards at the High Door of the Citadel turned back the crowd as Beowulf entered. Ragmund greeted Beowulf in the Mead Hall.

"What news?" said Ragmund.

"Take me to the queen."

Queen Hygd sat on her throne in the company of several young servant women. Sigmund stood to one side, arms folded across his chest. The color drained from Hygd's face when she saw Beowulf enter.

"Tell us, Beowulf," said the queen, her voice quivering, "what news of the king? What news from Frisland?"

At that moment Heardred burst into the Throne Room heedless of Beowulf's presence.

"Is it true, Mother?" said Heardred. "The word is that our army was defeated!"

"Is that true, Prince Beowulf?" said Hygd, tears welling in her eyes.

"Yes, my Queen."

Feeling Beowulf skewer him with his gaze, Hygelac's heir approached the dais. Heardred took a long way around to his father's throne; then, without hesitation, plopped himself down on the throne, and smirked.

Sigmund's arms dropped to his sides and his jaws clenched.

"That means I'm king," said Heardred. He glared at Beowulf.

"Yes, my son," said Hygd, choking back her grief, "you are king now."

"Everyone—do you hear!" said Heardred to those few in attendance. "I'm now your king!"

The servants looked at one another, bewildered by what they were hearing. Beowulf and Sigmund exchanged grim looks; both knew with Heardred on the throne, great was Geatland's peril.

"Tell me, Beowulf, where's my father's crown? He wore it atop his helm when he set out for Frisland."

Beowulf removed the halves of Hygelac's crown from his belt and tossed them on the dais, at Heardred's feet.

"Your father's killer sundered the crown," said Beowulf, "cleaved in two by Day Raven's sword."

"You were there?" said Heardred.

"Yes."

"And what of Day Raven?" said Heardred. "Does my father go unavenged?"

"Day Raven is dead."

"Shouldn't you be answering: 'Day Raven is dead, my King'?"

"You're not my King," said Beowulf, "until you convince me you're not complicit in the evil that's befallen our king and tribe."

"Ragmund!" said Heardred. "Did you hear what he said? That's treason!"

"Prince Beowulf has come far after doing much," said Ragmund. "He's weary, my King, and means no disrespect."

"I meant every word," said Beowulf.

"Is that the Sword of Kings sheathed at your side?"

"Yes," said Beowulf.

"By right, it belongs to me," said Heardred. "Sigmund—take Naegling from this traitor!"

"Remain where you are, Sigmund," said Beowulf. "If Heardred wants the Sword of Kings, he needs to win it!"

"Please, Beowulf," said Queen Hygd, "leave Falcon's Nest. Keep Naegling for the time-being and let us mourn the passing of my husband in peace."

"Yes, Beowulf," said Heardred. "Go! I banish you from Geatland! Your land and chattels are now forfeit!"

Beowulf turned on his heel and started from the Throne Room. He went to the stable where he left Storm Bringer. As he was adjusting the saddle straps, Sigmund approached.

"What is it, Sigmund?" said Beowulf. "Did Heardred send you to kill me?"

"No, my Prince. I want to affirm my loyalty to you and Clan Waegmunding."

Beowulf looked Sigmund in the eyes. "Our queen will need a man by her side she can trust. You're that man, my friend. But, take care, Sigmund—Ragmund will play both sides against the middle, now that Hygelac's gone."

62

BABIES, SPIES & WAR

Beowulf let Storm Bringer set the pace. As the time passed, Beowulf released his hold on the reins. Knowing there would be fresh oats waiting, Storm Bringer snorted and stretched his powerful legs for home. The stallion's joy was apparent, but there was no joy in Beowulf when he beheld the stake wall on the horizon; what he felt was a deep resolve to safeguard his people from Heardred's malice, now that Hygelac's heir was King.

Seeing Beowulf approach, the warriors on guard at the Main Gate shouted words of his return. Elin, Turin, and Beorn exited from the Main Lodge. Beowulf dismounted and handed Storm Bringer's reins to a groom. Elin ran to Beowulf and embraced him. Turin and Beorn joined them, and together the four returned to the lodge.

Turin stoked the fire, and after they had eaten, Beowulf told them about the battle in Frisland, and how he fared at Heardred's hands upon his return to Falcon's Nest.

"What will we do, husband?" said Elin.

"We fight!"

"Heardred will use the army to enforce his will," said Turin.

"He might," said Beowulf, "albeit he has far fewer warriors to bring against us."

"Gods willing," said Elin, "Heardred will work his malice elsewhere."

† † †

Later that night as they lie in bed, Elin rested her head on Beowulf's chest. With his arms around her, she felt safe, protected.

"There's something I need to tell you, Beowulf."

"Tell me."

"We're going to—" Elin stopped.

"Tell me what you want," said Beowulf, in as gentle a voice as he could muster. Beowulf knew what Elin wanted to reveal, but he wanted to hear her say it.

"We're going to have a baby," said Elin, looking into his eyes. "Does the news please you, husband?"

Beowulf smiled and kissed her. "Yes, sweet wife, above all else —the news pleases me."

"I think it will be winter when our baby opens its eyes on the world."

"Be it so," said Beowulf. "Until then, I don't want you to work in the fields, Elin. I want you out of harm's way."

"Will you still love me when I grow fat as a cow?"

"Why wouldn't I—there'll be so much more to love."

Feigning displeasure with Beowulf's response, Elin reached up and pinched his nose:

"I won't let myself become fat as a cow! You should be ashamed for lying to me, Beowulf Waegmunding."

Elin lay enfolded in Beowulf's arms while outside a cold north wind began to howl.

† † †

In Uppsala, King Onela summoned the Thunder Geat to the Throne Room. Weohstan entered the torch-lit chamber under escort and proceeded to where Onela sat with his wife, Astrid.

In one hand Onela held a drinking-horn, which a servant took great care to keep filled. Weohstan stopped a respectful distance from the dais and bowed. Already present in the Throne Room were those Clan Chiefs who had survived the disastrous raid into Daneland over four months earlier when Ohthere ruled Svearland.

"You sent for me, Great King," said Weohstan.

"Your son, Handscio, I'm told a monster killed him in Daneland."

"Yes, Great King."

"Too bad," Onela said, "a father shouldn't outlive his son. Did he die well?"

"I'm told he did, Great King."

"I have other news, Weohstan: news of a happier sort—Hygelac is dead, and his army destroyed in Frisland."

"How do you know this?" said Weohstan, displaying no telltale sign of emotion.

"Aren't you the least bit curious as to what befell your cousin?"

"Yes," said Weohstan. "I am."

"Heardred has banished Beowulf. He's no longer Geatland's Battle Lord."

"And you're confident the news is reliable, Great King?"

"My spy in Falcon's Nest is not mistaken. He was there when Heardred ordered Beowulf into exile—weren't you, Ragmund?"

Ragmund stepped from the shadows and faced Weohstan: "I was, indeed, Great King."

Onela was pleased to see the Geatlander and the Angle appraise one another with such disdain.

So—I am not the only traitor here Ragmund told himself, I'd never have thought it of Weohstan Waegmunding. Still, I will tell Onela of my doubts about Beowulf's cousin's intentions here.

"Ragmund tells me that Heardred gives sanctuary to my brother's two brats, my nephews: Eanmund and Eadgils. What do you think of that, Weohstan?"

"There's a saying among the common folk, Great King," said Weohstan: "birds of a feather fly together. Fortune smiles on you since now your enemies are gathered in one place."

"Fortune is smiling on me," said Onela. "Within a fortnight I'll march south into Geatland, take Heardred's throne and cut my nephews' balls off."

"A brilliant plan, Great King," said Ragmund.

Queen Astrid stood and hurried away. Onela belched; he motioned to a servant to fill his drinking-horn.

"Don't mind her," said Onela; "Astrid is fond of my two nephews, especially the youngest one, Eadgils."

"What role would you have me play?" said Weohstan.

"What role, indeed," said Onela. "You'll accompany my army south and fight alongside me. Once I'm victorious, Weohstan, I'll give you Beowulf's lands and chattels. In exchange, you will enforce my will in Geatland; that is, once I've withdrawn my army —agreed?"

"You're too generous, my King," said Weohstan.

"Exceedingly so," said Ragmund.

"And you, Ragmund, you'll sit on the throne of Geatland and rule as my regent. Those who serve me well will find me generous;

those who don't will soon be dead."

"One thing concerns me, Great King," said Weohstan.

"Speak," said Onela.

"While Beowulf was in Daneland, no doubt he and King Hrothgar renewed pledges of peace and mutual defense. If you invade Geatland, I fear the Spear Danes will oppose you."

"When I married Halfdane's daughter, Weohstan, I was not king, but now that I am, and Hrothgar's little sister my queen, I don't think Hrothgar will want to sunder the ties that bind our tribes together. Why would he risk his army and his entire fleet coming to Geatland's defense now?"

"Especially," said Ragmund, "when he learns that Heardred conspired against his father to obtain the crown."

Weohstan bowed. "No doubt you're right, Great King. Forgive my doubts and concerns; they're misplaced."

† † †

Two weeks had passed since Sigmund returned to Falcon's Nest with the Svear Princes. Late into the night, Heardred would confer with Eanmund and Eadgils when no others were present. Heardred would not risk anyone overhearing his plans of conquest.

"Right now Onela is rebuilding his army," said Heardred. "It won't be long before he invades Geatland."

"Then we should strike first," said Eanmund. "Attack while Onela is still weak."

"Patience, Prince Eanmund. I also need time to rebuild my army. As matters stand, I have no more than four-hundred men-at-arms, foot and horse combined."

"Then you must do so, Heardred," said Eadgils.

"King Heardred, you mean," said Heardred.

Eadgils stood and bowed.

"Forgive me… King Heardred."

"You're forgiven! Now, then; let's drink some more, my friends, and celebrate the end of your days in exile! Besides, I've arranged companionship for us later."

Sigmund entered the Mead Hall in great haste. He went to where Heardred was sitting and bowed.

"I told you, Sigmund—no interruptions!"

"Forgive me, my King, but I convey a message that cannot wait."

"Very well—what is it?"

"The Svear army has crossed the northern divide into Geatland."

The blood drained from Heardred's face. Sheer terror revealed itself on his face.

"Sigmund—tell my mother to join me."

"Yes, my King."

Heardred hurried off and didn't stop until he reached the Throne Room; the Svear princes followed.

"What will you do?" said Eanmund.

"Quiet—I need time to think," said Heardred. His voice trembled.

Queen Hygd entered the Throne Room escorted by Sigmund.

"Sigmund gave me the news, my son. You'll need to decide on a course of action and follow through with it."

"Yes, yes, yes—I know that Mother; but what course of action —that's the question!"

"Send for Beowulf," said the Queen, "Tell him you were wrong to banish him. Ask him for guidance."

"Never," said Heardred. "I won't beg Beowulf for help." Heardred looked at Sigmund: "Sigmund, summon the Clan Chiefs!"

"Even if the new ones exist, my King, by the time we've sent word to them, the Svear could be at the city gate."

Shaken by the prospect of having to act, Heardred looked into his drinking-horn and ran his tongue between his lips. A moment had passed before he looked at Sigmund:

"My father trusted you, Sigmund; you fought many battles together—I'm naming you my Battle Lord. Tell me what we should do."

"Send for Beowulf," said Sigmund without hesitation. "The sight of him on the battlefield is worth a thousand men alone."

"Don't speak his name again—any of you!" said Heardred. "Suggest something else, and be quick about it!"

"March out with your army to meet Onela, my King; or—"

"Or, what?" said Heardred.

"Or you must sue for peace," Sigmund said.

"Sue for peace? You want me to subjugate myself to Onela?"

"No, my King," said Sigmund. "You asked me to recommend a course of action. You must fight or give up your crown."

Heardred leapt to his feet. "That is the talk of a traitor!" he said.

"No, my son," said Hygd, "Sigmund is advising you as a Battle Lord should advise his king—by telling him what needs saying, however pleasant or unpleasant it may be."

"Silence, Mother! And you, Sigmund; make yourself useful—find me an army!"

Sigmund bowed and started away. At the same time, Ragmund entered the Throne Room.

"Ragmund," said Heardred. "Where have you been? Have you heard the news?"

Ragmund shuffled forward in his slow, deliberate manner; he glanced at Sigmund as Sigmund passed.

"Yes, my King. I came as soon as I could," said Ragmund. "The Svear are marching toward Falcon's Nest."

Ragmund stopped before the dais and bowed; he nodded to Eanmund and Eadgils.

"There are so few here I can trust, Ragmund," said Heardred, unable to disguise the fear in his voice. "Tell me what I must do!"

"You have two options, my King," said Ragmund: "March north with the army and fight, or sue for peace. There's no other choice."

"You're telling me nothing I haven't heard already," said Heardred, his face red and contorted.

"I'm sorry, my King, but I see no other choices available, not with Onela's army as near as it is."

Heardred deliberated with himself at lightning speed in the dark beleaguered confines of his mind.

"I won't sue for peace," said Heardred, sounding like someone who'd shed a great weight from his shoulders.

"Of course not, my King," said Ragmund. "Since your mind on the matter is made, with your permission, I'll send word to the clans to assemble their men-at-arms."

Ragmund bowed and left.

Outside the Throne Room, Sigmund stepped from the shadows and confronted Ragmund.

"What is it?" said Ragmund. "Why do you detain me?"

"The king is determined to fight."

"Yes, of course, he is," said Ragmund.

"That is a grave mistake," said Sigmund. "The Svear outnumber us."

"Perhaps," said Ragmund; "but our warriors are seasoned and battle-hardened. They'll match up well against the conscripts and mercenaries Onela fields."

"How do you know Onela is fielding mercenaries?" said Sigmund.

"It stands to reason," said Ragmund, shaken by Sigmund's challenge.

"You seem eager for this war—why?"

"Don't be stupid, Sigmund. Now stand aside and let me pass!"

Sigmund reined-in his anger, and stepped aside, allowing Ragmund the right of way.

† † †

Hearing Turin shout the alarm from the watchtower over the Main Gate, Beowulf and Beorn hastened to the wall-walk to see who was approaching. Beowulf looked side to side to see how fast his warriors responded. The speed with which Beowulf's men took up their positions on the wall-walk pleased him.

"It looks like Ingmar," said Beorn. "Let's hope he learned something useful at Falcon's Nest."

"It is Ingmar," said Beowulf. "Open the Gate!"

It took three guards to remove the thick, solid oak cross-beam holding the Main Gate shut.

Ingmar entered at a gallop and pulled up on the reins. Bringing his horse to a halt, Ingmar leapt from the saddle. Beowulf, Turin, and Beorn were there to greet him.

"What news, Ingmar?" said Beowulf.

"Heardred marches northeast with the army, my Prince," said Ingmar.

"Who leads them?" said Beorn.

"Sigmund," said Ingmar.

Beorn looked at Beowulf: "Sigmund's a brave warrior, I admit, and as noble, as noble is—but... a 'Battle Lord'?"

"Hygelac trusted Sigmund enough to guard his queen," said

Beowulf. "He has a good head on his shoulders. If he's apt to error, I believe it'll be on the side of caution." Beowulf looked at Turin and Ingmar: "There's something I need you two to do. Take fresh horses, four of them, and ride to Land's End. Find Mikla, Captain of the coastguards. Mikla is loyal to our clan; he'll know who sent you. Tell him you require a ship and a trustworthy crew but say no more than that. If he presses you for your destination, say it's to do my bidding, and nothing more—do you understand?"

"Yes, Beowulf," said Turin.

"Go to Daneland," said Beowulf. "Once you've dropped anchor at Mörk Sand, ask for safe passage through Heorot Fort and an escort to Heorot Hall. Tell Hrothgar we need his Spear Danes. Tell him I'll be at Land's End, ten days hence."

Turin and Ingmar nodded and hurried away, intent on justifying Beowulf's trust.

That night, Beowulf and Elin sat in the Banquet Hall in front of the fire with Beorn. More moments passed in silence before Beorn stood and tugged on his beard.

"Who knows how long it will take the Danes to come," he said, "if they come at all."

"The Spear Danes will come," said Beowulf.

"You're that sure, are you?" said Beorn.

"You heard Beowulf," said Elin; "the Danes will come."

"Well," said Beorn, "since you both are sure help is forthcoming, I'm going to bed and dream of large women and blueberries."

Beorn started away; then stopped. Without looking back, he said, "Soon, Bear's Son, you'll be King of Geatland—whether you want to be or not."

Beowulf and Elin watched the Schaman leave the chamber. Elin held out her hand:

"Rest your mind, Beowulf," she said, "Come to bed."

Beowulf nodded. Elin's right, he told himself, there's nothing more to think. Too weary to ponder Beorn's cryptic pronouncement, Beowulf lifted Elin into his arms and carried her to bed.

63

BATTLE AT THE RIVER VATTERN

Accompanied by Sigmund and several warriors of the King's Guard, Heardred wandered through the subterranean vault beneath the Citadel that contained the wealth of Geatland. Most of that treasure accumulated during Hygelac's reign, thanks to Beowulf. After the Geats' victory over the Svear at Uppsala, Geatland prospered and its Longships, like those of the Danes, plied the Whale Road unchallenged.

Hygelac's son spotted Hrothgar's gifts to Beowulf—what Beowulf gave to Hygelac, upon returning from Daneland. Heardred wanted to arm and armor himself as befitting a new king. He took for himself a plumed helm of polished bronze in the likeness of a wolf's head. The helm once belonged to Hrothgar's older brother, Heorogar, long dead. Along with that splendid helm, Heardred took another prized heirloom, Heorogar's sword. He also took the polished chainmail shirt Heorogar once wore, and the crimson banner that had a horse's head center most, sewn with black thread. Heardred also knew of the war horses Beowulf returned from Daneland with and was resolved to ride the best of them when he led his army north against Onela.

Leaving one-hundred warriors of the King's Guard behind to defend his mother and the Citadel, Heardred rode from Falcon's Nest with three-hundred footmen, and one-hundred horse warriors. Alongside Heardred rode Sigmund, now Heardred's Battle Lord.

The sound of Heardred's banner flapping in the breeze delighted Heardred no end. His chest swelled with pride—pride for what he accomplished by outwitting Beowulf Waegmunding, and for being the youngest king to sit on the throne of Geatland.

Sigmund's mind rebelled at the thought of abandoning Falcon's Nest to march north with so few warriors against Onela. Still, he was as loyal a Thane as ever walked the earth and he felt duty-bound to obey his king. It didn't matter as to the rightness of it all. Sigmund was a Northman, reconciled to die in defense of his tribe regardless who sat on the throne. Against his Battle Lord's advice, Heardred stopped at midday and ordered his men to make camp. Heardred saw a look of concern come over Sigmund.

"You don't agree with the area?" said Heardred.

"No, my King, there's high ground south of the River Vattern. Here, we're exposed and vulnerable on three sides."

"If that's your sole objection," said Heardred, "send scouts ahead. I want to know where Onela's army is, lest we run into them unprepared."

"Very well, my King, as you command."

Sigmund sent scouts to the north and east while the Geats made camp and started cooking-fires.

That night Heardred summoned Sigmund and the Clan Chiefs to his pavilion to discuss tactics.

"Tell us, Sigmund," said Heardred; "what do you propose?"

"Just this, my King: First, we must assume we are fewer in number than the army Onela sends against us. Next, I suggest we take up a defensive position on this side of the river and fortify it against attack. Let Onela cross the Vattern. When he does our bowmen will let fly their arrows. Given the number of Svear we stand to kill, the odds should improve in our favor. Then we can counterattack."

"Very well," Heardred said; "your idea has merit. Anyone else wants to speak on the subject?"

"I would, my King," said Ragmund.

"What say you, Ragmund?"

"Sigmund's plan is a cautious plan, my King, and sound in all respects, except…"

"Except?" said Heardred.

"My spies tell me—"

"You mean... my spies?" said Heardred.

"Of course, my King," said Ragmund. "They say Onela has fewer men than we have, and his horse warriors are undisciplined."

"That's good news, Ragmund. What say you, Sigmund?"

"It is good news, my King if you believe it to be accurate."

"What do you mean?" said Heardred.

"Are you saying I'm lying?" said Ragmund.

"No," said Sigmund. "I'm suggesting our spies assertions may not be accurate."

"Very well," said Heardred, "What do you propose we do?"

"Push ahead tomorrow, my King," said Sigmund, "to the west bank of the River Vattern, and take-up a defensive position. If Onela has superior numbers, let him squander his advantage attacking us from across the river."

"Very well," said Heardred, "tomorrow, after we break fast, we'll march to the Vattern and see where matters stand—agreed, Ragmund?"

"Agreed, my King," said Ragmund, none too happy about it.

"Good," said Heardred. "Now I want the two of you to conclude peace!"

"If you'll excuse me, my King," said Sigmund, "I'll see to your army."

"With your permission, Great King," said Heardred, "I will return to the Citadel and console the Queen-Mother in your absence."

† † †

Relaxed and refreshed following his sauna, Onela plunged into the ice-cold waters of the river and dove underwater. Guardians of the Throne of Svearland, the Sveargaard lined the riverbank to rescue the Usurper from the fast-flowing current should he flounder. Onela's bulbous head burst to the surface; he coughed and spat water.

"Rope," he said, "throw me a line, you idiots!"

As their king began to float downstream, arms and legs flailing against the current, the Sveargarrd, all one-hundred of them, entered the water to rescue their rotund king and they did.

Onela was waterlogged and in an ill humor when he returned to his pavilion in West Fall's' Forest where the bulk of his army remained hidden. It was his plan to allow Heardred to arrive at River Vattern unchallenged, under the false belief he outnumbered Onela's army. It was, of course, a ruse; one that Ragmund had assured him would work, given what he knew of Heardred's propensity to let others do his thinking for him in matters other than fornicating.

† † †

It was mid-morning when Heardred's army arrived at the west bank of the river. Heardred convinced himself they'd reached there first, well ahead of Onela. Sigmund sent a small patrol across the river to search for signs of the Svear army. When they failed to return by midday, Sigmund conveyed his fears to his King.

"The riders I sent to locate Onela's army should have returned by now, my King."

"Meaning what?" said Ragmund.

"Meaning that Onela's army is across the river, hidden in West Falls' Forest. I beg you, my King—let us defend this side of the river and force the Usurper to cross the Vattern."

"That would be folly, my King," said Ragmund. "To stop now is to lose the initiative. If Onela would rather make a match of it in the forest, be it so! In the open, or in wooded terrain, we enjoy better numbers than Onela, or so our spies report!"

"And just who are these spies you speak of?" Sigmund said. "Why do I not know their names?"

"For their protection, I dare not reveal them," said Ragmund.

"Enough," said Heardred. "I've made up my mind. While we have the initiative, we'll press on, and take the fight to Onela! Understood?"

"If that's your wish, my King," said Sigmund.

"It is! You and Prince Eadgils will take half my horsemen. Attack Onela's left flank. Prince Eanmund and I will lead the rest of our riders against the Usurper's right. My brother-in-law, Eofor, will lead our footmen across the river, straight at Onela's center."

"What if we cross the Vattern and his army's not there my King?" said Eofor.

"If Onela's not there," said Heardred, "we'll find him elsewhere."

† † †

Led by Eofor, Chief of Clan Knupp, Heardred's warriors set out with grim determination on foot.

They were midway across the river when Onela's bowmen rushed forward from inside the tree line. The Svear had massed on their side of the river. They let loose hundreds of arrows when the Geats were in the river, up to their waists in water.

"Like spearing fish in a barrel," said Onela, from a place of concealment astride his warhorse.

As Heardred urged his horse forward alongside Prince Eanmund, he saw the slaughter underway in the river. Sigmund also saw what was taking place.

"On me," said Sigmund, "On me!"

"What are your orders?" said Prince Eadgils.

"Have at them so our footmen can fall back and regroup," said Sigmund.

Eadgils shouted to the fifty horsemen accompanying him. The Geat riders wheeled about and charged the ranks of the Svear who continued to let fly their arrows and spears at the Geats trapped in the water. The Geat horsemen, led by Sigmund and Eadgils, scattered the Svear in large numbers and forced them to flee for the safety of the forest. This tactic allowed Sigmund to cover the Geat's retreat to the west bank.

Elsewhere to the north, three-hundred Wylfing riders led by Onela himself set upon Heardred and Prince Eanmund and the fifty riders with them. Weohstan Waegmunding rode with the Svear and made straight for Prince Eanmund. Eanmund saw Weohstan come at him with his sword raised and fear overcame him. Eanmund tried to escape, but Weohstan thrust his sword through Eanmund's armor, and out his belly.

Heardred saw Prince Eanmund topple from his saddle and land face-down in the water. The current carried Eanmund's corpse away from the fighting. Seeing his men fall around him, Heardred retreated. He dug his heels into his horse's flanks just as an arrow brought that war horse down.

Thrown from his saddle, into the water, Heardred struggled against the current and was able to reach a sandbar in the middle of the river. Unable to make good his escape, Heardred watched, dumbfounded, as Sigmund led a good many Geats on foot and horse across the river, away from the battle to safety. While covering his men's retreat, Sigmund saw Prince Eadgils slump forward in his saddle, wounded.

† † †

Onela dismounted on the sandbar where several of his warriors held Heardred prisoner.

"I yield," said Heardred, cowering on both knees. "My people will pay gold to ransom me."

"Ransom?" said Onela. "There'll be no ransom for you. Crows will pick out your eyes and strip the flesh from your bones."

"I beg you," said Heardred, "don't kill me. I'm a king, like you!"

"You're a blubbering fool," said Onela, "and nothing like me." Onela turned to his Battle Lord, a Clan Chief named Bork. "Put him face down and hold him steady!"

Lord Bork gestured to warriors standing near. Obedient to Onela's order, they threw Heardred face down. They stood on his arms and legs, pinning him. Onela's warriors pulled Heardred's chainmail shirt up over his head, and then cut his linen undershirt up the middle, exposing his naked back. Onela's men then pulled Heardred's pants down over his boots, to his ankles. Onela released his man-muscle and penetrated Heardred. Heardred screamed. When Onela had spent himself, he hoisted his britches, cinched his belt, and knelt astride Heardred's hips. Heardred moaned, so great was the pain he experienced.

"I beg you, Great King," said Heardred. "Show me mercy!"

Onela said nothing. Using a knife borrowed from his Battle Lord, the Svear King started a cut at the base of Heardred's neck to the left of the spine, and while Heardred screamed, Onela cut through flesh and muscle. He used his hands to rip Heardred's flesh apart on either side of the cut. Onela thrust his right hand past Heardred's rib cage until he was able to purchase a firm hold on a lung. Using all his strength, Onela tore that air-sack free from Heardred's body. Heardred was no longer screaming when Onela got to his feet. He held that bloody organ over his head for his men to see and rejoice in their King's victory.

Sigmund watched what was taking place on the sandbar. Nearby, a Geat surgeon bound Prince Eadgils' wounds. The retreat to Falcon's Nest was already underway and those Geats who survived the battle knew there was no time to spare. Sigmund went to Eadgils and helped him on his horse.

"Ride!," said Sigmund. "Tell Beowulf what happened here. Perhaps one day you can make right the wrongs you've done him."

64

DIRE TIDINGS

While Beowulf kept watch, a score of Freemen dug a ditch that would bring water to the fields of rye and barley. Within the palisade, six warriors patrolled the wall-walk.

Inside the main lodge, Elin and several women sat at looms and wove baskets of thread into clothing.

Over the crest of a hill, a quarter-league west of Vindinstedt, a warrior rode at a gallop toward the farm. Upon seeing the rider, Beowulf shouted to his men to put down their picks and spades. As the lone horseman neared, Beowulf rode out to meet him. The rider halted his horse opposite Beowulf and removed his helm. It was Prince Eadgils. Beowulf had never seen the Svear prince before nor did Eadgils bear a shield identifying his clan or tribe. Beowulf did see that the young warrior had two wounds: a deep cut on his shield-arm, just above the elbow, and a gash midway on his right thigh. Bandages covered both cuts but hadn't stopped the bleeding.

"Who are you?" said Beowulf. "What's your business here?"

"I'm Eadgils, son of Ohthere; my business is with Beowulf Waegmunding." Eadgils was exhausted and lightheaded from losing blood.

"I ask you again—what's your business here?" said Beowulf.

"That's for Prince Beowulf to hear," said Eadgils. "If this is his farm, I pray you... take me to him."

Eadgils' eyes closed; his helm fell from his hand to the ground. He slumped forward in his saddle, unconscious.

When Eadgils' eyes next opened it was a day after his arrival at Vindinstedt Farm. As he regained his senses, he realized he was flat on his back on a bed of straw. It would take Eadgils a moment before he realized he was in a milking barn. His ears alerted him to a peculiar sound that kept repeating with a vigorous flourish—a squish-squish-squishing sound.

Pushing himself into a sitting position, Eadgils craned his head around in time to see a blushing milkmaid avert her eyes. Eadgils took notice of his cloak; someone had draped it over him like a blanket. The milkmaid ran giggling from the barn clutching a pail to her bosom. It would take Eadgils time to realize that, under his cloak, he was naked as a baby bird. Moreover, there were fresh, aromatic bandages wrapped around his wounds—the handiwork of an Annan Dere---a Schaman he would soon meet.

As his head cleared, Eadgils managed to get to his feet but could not yet rest his full weight on his wounded leg. Two attractive, but unsmiling young women entered the barn—Greta and Brigitte, household servants who took care of the day-to-day matters in Beowulf's lodge. Greta, the older of the two women, was Ingmar's sister. In her arms, she carried Eadgils' leather breeches, cleaned and sewn where a Svear axe had cut into his leg. She also held his wide leather belt with its silver buckle, along with his boots and a shirt. It was one of Ingmar's shirts. Brigitte was Ingmar's wife and a winter younger than Greta. She held a wicker basket containing a pot of porridge, smoked sausage, a loaf of bread, honey-butter and a clay flagon of ale. Around their waists, both women wore matching leather belts, and each carried a knife with a walrus tusk handle.

"Once you've eaten and dressed," said Greta, "Prince Beowulf invites you to his lodge. We'll take you there."

"That's kind of you, my ladies," said Eadgils; "but tell me—if a fellow needed to empty his bladder, where might he do it and not cause a fuss?"

"Cast your water where you like, Svearlander," said Greta, "but if it's the other you need to do, outside the barn, you'll find an outhouse—provided you know how to use one."

More amused by Greta's earnestness than offended by her tone, Eadgils said, "Just because I'm a Svearlander doesn't mean I go about on all fours dropping turds where I please."

Greta frowned. Brigitte put a hand over her mouth to stifle her laughter.

"In any event, I'm glad to have my breeches back, cleaned and mended, and I'm grateful for the food you bring. My first thought upon seeing you both was that you came as emissaries of the goddess, Frigga—two beautiful Valkyries intent on delivering me to the blessed Hall of Valhalla."

Greta was unimpressed by Eadgils' flirtations. When she tossed him his clothes, he dropped his cloak to catch them, and catch them he did, without dropping a single item. It was more than Eadgils' quick reflexes that brought a blush to Brigitte's cheeks. Eadgils was not going to dwell on the why or wherefore of it; he was hungry, so he sat and began eating. Eadgils ate with the gusto of a man who could not be sure he would outlive the morning. As he savored each mouthful, the women stood nearby watching. Once Eadgils had eaten, dressed and relieved himself, Greta and Brigitte escorted him from the barn.

Inside the Main Lodge, Eadgils found Beowulf and Beorn in the Banquet Hall. They were sitting in front of the fire, talking in hushed voices when Eadgils entered with Greta and Brigitte.

"That will be all, ladies," said Beowulf.

Greta and Brigitte left.

"Come closer, Svearlander," said Beorn; "I want to see how your wounds are doing."

"Is it you I have to thank for bringing me back to the land of the living?" said Eadgils.

"No," said the Schaman, "the gods took pity on you. Apart from your limp, you walk well enough, and your balance seems normal. What about your arm—any pain there?"

"Very little, my Lord," said Eadgils; "it troubles me not."

"I'm no Lord," said the Schaman. "I answer to Beorn. In any event, it pleases me to see you're feeling better than when you arrived."

Eadgils looked at Beowulf: "Are you Beowulf, Chief of Clan Waegmunding, Prince of Geatland?"

"And if I was?"

"Then I bring a message for you—from Sigmund, Battle Lord to King Heardred."

"Let's hear it then," said Beowulf; "for I'm the one you seek."

"Heardred is dead."

A moment passed in silence.

"What of Geatland's army?" said Beorn.

"Almost all dead," said Eadgils. "Those who got away retreated to Falcon's Nest. Sigmund ordered me to bring you news of the battle. He said if I reached Vindinstedt alive, I should pledge my loyalty; that is if you didn't kill me first."

Beorn laughed: "He's not lying."

"I know," said Beowulf and he looked at Eadgils: "How many warriors does Sigmund have to defend Falcon's Nest?"

"I don't know," said Eadgils. "He said he would muster every man and boy strong enough to wield a weapon."

At that moment, Elin entered the Banquet Hall. Beowulf and Beorn got to their feet.

Turning to see Elin appear, Prince Eadgils bowed.

"My Lady," said Eadgils.

"Beorn was right," said Elin, smiling, "he vouched you'd outlive your wounds."

"Heardred's dead, my love," said Beowulf, "So, too, is Eadgils' brother, Eanmund, along with Eofor Knupp, and the bulk of Geatland's army."

Elin's face grew pale:

"What of Queen Hygd's daughter, Ingrid, and her grandchild, Princess Adela?"

All eyes turned to Eadgils: "I believe they're safe for now, my Lady, in the Citadel at Falcon's Nest."

"Sit, Eadgils," said Beowulf, "tell us about the battle."

"Sigmund recommended positioning your army on the high ground," said Eadgils, "and then wait for Onela to cross the River Vattern. Had Onela's army done so, they'd be vulnerable to your bowmen. Heardred wouldn't listen. No sooner did the Geats begin to cross the river, Onela's army came out of the tree line. It wasn't just Svear. The Wylfings supplied Onela with horse warriors—three times our number. The whole weight of Onela's army, together with the Wylfing horsemen attacked the center of Heardred's army. The Geats retreated in disarray, into the river. Onela found Heardred on his knees, begging for his life, and killed him most cruelly. Your cousin, Weohstan, slew my brother."

Eadgils' voice was void of rancor. "My brother died a warrior's death—in battle. It was a glorious death. I bear Weohstan Waegmunding no grudge."

"Weohstan is an honorable man," said Beowulf. "He knew of Heardred's treachery against Hygelac; he thought you and your brother were part of it. Serving Onela was a ruse thought-up by Hygelac to explain Weohstan's presence in Uppsala. With Heardred dead, I've no doubt Weohstan will return here."

Elin stood. "If you'll excuse me, I'll retire and leave you men to your business."

Beorn stood and hugged Elin close.

"Rest well, child."

Eadgils stood and bowed as Elin left the chamber. Beowulf placed another log on the fire and looked at Eadgils:

"Where do you place Onela's army?"

"Last I know they were this side of River Vattern getting fat on the land."

"And the Wylfing horsemen?" said Beowulf.

"For now," said Eadgils, "they stick to Onela like cheese glue."

"Onela intends to lay siege to Falcon's Nest," said Beorn, "to get Hygelac's gold."

"I agree," said Beowulf. "But as long as Onela and the Wylfings anticipate no further opposition, they'll likely time getting there, to fatten their bellies."

"Crows picking-over a carcass," said Beorn.

"Yes," said Beowulf.

"What are your orders?" said Beorn.

"You and Prince Eadgils will remain here while I'm gone."

"Gone?" said Eadgils.

"Yes," said Beowulf. "I mean to go north and see for myself what numbers Onela brings against Falcon's Nest."

Beorn knew Beowulf would be riding south—not north, and that his destination would remain their secret.

"Well, then," said Beorn, "now that that's settled, let's have something to drink. All this talk has parched my throat."

† † †

That night, as Beowulf rested in bed with Elin, he stared at the shadows cast by the fire upon the ceiling of their bedchamber.

"What troubles you, husband?" she said.

Beowulf swung his legs over the side of the bed.

"Geatland has no king."

"You should be king, my love. Hrethel's blood flows in your veins. Besides, what hope does Hygd have to keep her throne?"

"I never wanted to become king."

"Geatland needs a king, Beowulf, not a queen, even as good and decent a queen as Hygd. When Hygd is gone, what chance does her daughter or granddaughter have of holding onto power? No need for you to say it, my love; we both know they've no chance at all, not without your protection."

"What are you saying, Elin?"

"What you already know. There are two thrones at Falcon's Nest. The Geats need a king, and a king needs a queen."

Elin got on her knees behind Beowulf and draped her arms over his shoulders.

"Listen, my love, for it's meant to be—Fate has ordained you to become King of Geatland. Now, at the time of Geatland's greatest peril."

"Crowns are fleeting things of metal," said Beowulf. "You, Elin, will always be my queen."

Beowulf turned so he could look into Elin's face.

"I'll love you and no other, Elin," he said.

Beowulf watched Elin pull her nightshirt over her head.

"Prove it," said Elin; "Kiss me hard and long, O' Lord of Lords!"

65

A PLAN TAKES SHAPE

Ten days passed since Turin and Ingmar rode south to Land's End. Beorn had left days before for the north. While Elin slept, Beowulf rode Storm Bringer away from the palisade. Eadgils stood on the wall-walk near the Main Gate and watched Beowulf ride toward Vindinstedt Forest. Beowulf would circle, and then continue south when he was certain no one followed.

Beowulf changed direction before midday. As soon as he reached the coast, he followed the shoreline south until he arrived at Land's End.

There, on the bluffs overlooking the sea, Beowulf found Mikla, Captain of the Coast Guard, with several of his men huddled together, warming their backsides in front of a cooking-fire. Ever watchful for Longships raiding Geatland's coast, Mikla and his men stared out to sea, but the thing that greeted their eyes was a fog bank; it stretched like an impenetrable gray wall over the ocean.

"We've been expecting you, my Prince," said Mikla.

Beowulf dismounted and handed the reins to a coast guard standing near.

"See that my horse is wiped-down, fed and watered. I rode him long and hard."

"At once, my Prince," the guard said.

Beowulf turned to Mikla: "What did my foster brother, Turin tell you?"

"He said his comings and goings was no one's business, but yours."

"And no one knows of his being here?"

"No one, save for us," said Mikla.

Beowulf looked skyward, and he prayed:

Once more, Great Odin, I beseech you; burn away the mist that hides the All Mother's face. Give the Spear Danes a clear sky so they can land their ships.

Beowulf turned, faced out to sea. He peered into the fog.

"We haven't seen the sun for two days, my Prince," said Mikla.

"Quiet!" said Beowulf. "Did you hear that?"

"No; not even the sound of a seabird has reached my ears all morning," said Mikla.

"Quickly now," said Beowulf, "Give me your horn!"

Mikla removed a ram's horn from his belt.

Beowulf went to the edge of the bluff. With the fog swirling around him, he blew the horn three times.

A moment later, from out at sea, came the sound of seventy rams' horns trumpeting a reply.

Aboard the Longships, Turin, Ingmar, and a thousand Spear Danes waited to disembark. In the moments that followed, the fog began to depart, revealing the sun and a clear blue sky. Again Beowulf lifted the horn to his lips and blew. Again the Danes replied in kind. Mikla and the Coast Guards were astonished; until Beowulf's arrival, they'd spent the entire morning trying to stay warm, oblivious to the fact the Danes had dropped anchor no more than two-hundred yards off their shore.

"Praise to Odin," said Beowulf. He unsheathed Naegling and stepped to the edge of the cliff.

A great cheer went up from the Danes at the sight of Beowulf atop the bluff, sunlight flashing off Naegling.

The Spear Danes revered that Prince of Geatland ever since he befriended their king and tribe by killing Grendel and the she-demon. Eager were they, to wet their swords with Svear blood. All the more eager had they become, knowing they'd be fighting alongside the bear's son.

When Turin and Ingmar leapt from King Hrothgar's battle craft, onto the beach, Beowulf and Mikla were there to greet them.

Hrothgar's emissaries, Unferth and Ulthur, followed those two young Geats onto Geatland's shore.

"Hail, Lords of Daneland," said Beowulf.

"Greetings from King Hrothgar," said Unferth.

"We bring you an army," said Ulthur. A broad grin spread across his face.

"We also brought your Longships," said Unferth; "left on the shore of Frisland. While the Frisians were holding funeral games in Day Raven's honor, we stole your ships from under their noses."

"For which Geatland will always be grateful, my Lords," said Beowulf.

Unferth and Ulthur walked with Beowulf to a place sheltered from the wind where they could discuss strategy and no ears, but theirs could partake.

"The news from the north is dire," said Beowulf. "Heardred is dead, as is the Svear prince, Eanmund. The Geats who survived the battle have retreated south to Falcon's Nest. Sigmund, Captain of Hygelac's Guard, sees to the defense of the city. To our advantage, Onela will most likely take his time getting there."

"Then time is on our side," said Unferth.

"Perhaps," said Beowulf; "but that doesn't mean we've time to lose."

"Order us," said Ulthur, "for Hrothgar would have it so."

"I'm humbled to have his trust, my Lords—and yours."

"What would you have the Spear Danes do?" said Unferth.

† † †

Vexed that Ragmund had sent for him in the midst of organizing the city's defenses, Sigmund entered the Throne Room. He went to the Throne where Queen Hygd sat. Hygd's widowed daughter, Ingrid, in the full bloom of her sixteenth winter, sat on the king's throne nursing her daughter, Adela. Ragmund stood before the dais, and was chagrined to see the Throne Room doubling as a nursery; nevertheless, he was careful to hide his displeasure. If all went as planned, it would be Ragmund, the crippled Angle, and former slave, who would rule over Geatland. That his kingship would be at Onela's behest was a secondary matter.

Sigmund bowed to Hygd and Princess Ingrid.

"You sent for me, my Queen?"

"Yes, Sigmund," said Hygd. "How goes the preparation of the city's defenses?"

"It goes as best it can, my Queen. With more men, we could do more, but our defenses are stout, and we've gathered food and provisions enough to withstand a month-long siege."

"Preposterous!" said Ragmund. "Apart from the one-hundred warriors of the Queen's Guard, you've no more than four-hundred men to place at the Main Gate and along the outer wall-walk. No fewer than eight-hundred warriors should stand there since that is Falcon's Nest first line of defense. What's more, half of the warriors you have are old men, and boys, farmers, shepherds, and who knows what else."

"They're Geatfolk," said Sigmund, "willing to give their lives in defense of their queen and Falcon's Nest. They'll fight when the time comes! If the Svear breaches our outer defenses, we'll withdraw to the Citadel. Gods willing, we can hold them off long enough for Prince Beowulf to return with reinforcements."

"Gods willing," said Hygd.

"Reinforcements?" said Ragmund. "What reinforcements? Onela destroyed our army at the River Vattern. Where in all of Geatland is Beowulf going to find reinforcements? For all we know, he, too, is dead!"

"I don't believe Prince Beowulf is dead," said Sigmund. "Who knows, perhaps he'll find reinforcements outside Geatland."

"Do you think it possible, Sigmund?" said the queen, eager to hear something she could wish upon in the loneliness of her bedchamber.

"Yes, my Queen," said Sigmund; "of this one thing I'm certain: Beowulf Waegmunding will come."

"Are you so sure," said Ragmund, "that you'd risk the lives of the Queen, her daughter, and granddaughter?"

"Beowulf will come," said Sigmund.

"How dare you give the Queen false hope! Our best course of action is to go to Onela and sue for peace. Give him enough gold, and he'll go away."

"Eager were you, Ragmund, to see King Heardred go to war against the Svear, and eager are you now to surrender Falcon's Nest without a fight."

"How dare you!" said Ragmund. "I've risked life and limb in defense of Falcon's Nest, and you accuse me of treason!"

"No, Ragmund, I accuse you of being eager to surrender."

"Enough," said Hygd. "I'll not have the two Lords I look to for reasoned, deliberate advice, arguing among themselves."

"Your pardon, my Queen," said Sigmund.

"Forgive me, gracious Queen," said Ragmund; he glared at Sigmund.

“Sigmund, return to your duties,” said Hygd.

Sigmund bowed and left the Throne Room. With each step Sigmund took, the more apparent it became to him—Ragmund warranted close watching.

† † †

Elin awoke to the sound of a horse entering the Palisade. She wrapped a shawl around her and left her bedchamber.

Hearing the Main Gate open, Greta and Brigitte dressed and went straight away to Beowulf’s lodge. Hastening to the Banquet Hall, they set out hot mulled wine, sausage and bread for Elin and Weohstan as they sat before the fire, talking in low voices.

“Handscio’s death in Daneland did honor to our clan,” said Weohstan. “I’m comforted he died alongside his cousin.”

“Handscio’s death wounded Beowulf to his core,” said Elin, “though he won’t speak of it—not to Beorn, or to me.”

“I bear Beowulf no ill will. By Odin’s eye, I look at him as though he was my son.”

“It gladdens my heart to hear you say that,” said Elin.

“Tell me,” said Weohstan; “does Turin know why I came to be in Onela’s camp?”

“No,” said Elin, “he doesn’t. He struggles against thinking what others believe—that you sold your sword to the Usurper.”

“And you say Turin’s in Daneland?”

“Yes,” said Elin, “with Ingmar, but if fortune favors us, they’ve returned to Geatland by now.”

“Gods willing,” said Weohstan.

“Will you remain here with us Weohstan, now that you’re home?” said Elin.

“I wish I could, Lady Elin, but I fear Onela’s army is further south than where I last saw it.”

“You’ll have to be careful,” said Elin. “When Onela finds you gone, he’ll declare you a spy and mark you for death. As goes the saying: you’re between a rock and a hard place.”

“You’re right,” said Weohstan.” As for Onela, I regret I lacked an opportunity to kill him!”

“When must you leave?”

"At first light, Lady Elin," said Weohstan.

Elin got to her feet: "I should check on Eadgils' wounds."

"Prince Eadgils? Here?" said Weohstan.

"Yes," said Elin. "He came to us wounded, seeking sanctuary. By the way, he bears you no grudge for the death of his brother."

"Just the same," said Weohstan, "I think I'll sleep with my knife under my pillow tonight."

† † †

With both hands, King Onela cupped the fullness of his young wife's breasts and squeezed. Onela had dark eyes—pig's' eyes, and he searched Astrid's face for signs of deception.

"Will your brother meddle in my dispute with the Geats," he said.

"Why should he, husband?" said Half-Dane's daughter. She winced from the pressure Onela's hands exerted on her most tender parts:

Drunken pig—I deserve better than you. I disavow the day I became your wife. If Hrothgar knew how you shame his sister he'd have your head for a footstool!

"Good," said Onela, releasing his grip on Astrid's breasts. "Tomorrow I return to Geatland, to rejoin my army."

Onela drained the mead in his drinking horn in several long gulps and belched. Overcome with drink; he drifted into a dreamless sleep. Astrid removed herself from their bed.

She stood over Onela and waited until he began to snore. When his jaws went slack and his lips parted, Astrid gathered a mouthful of spit and let it drop into his mouth.

† † †

"What are your orders, my Prince?" said Mikla. "What would you have the Coast Guards do?"

"I want you to maintain vigil here, Mikla. Send some of your men north to every farm and village. Let the word go out: 'Beowulf Waegmunding is coming!' Tell those who can fight to join me at Vindinstedt Farm—understood?"

“Yes, my Prince,” said Mikla; “But I’d rather be riding at your side.”

“I know old friend,” said Beowulf, “but I need you here. Keep your eyes peeled. If trouble comes, find me.”

Turin and Ulthur rode on either side of Beowulf as he led the three-hundred Spear Danes north. The sunlight flashed off the tips of their spears and was visible for three leagues in every direction. As seen from a distance, the riders appeared like a silver ribbon that snaked its way over Geatland’s verdant countryside. Beowulf had waited until midday before setting out from Land’s End, giving Mikla’s Coast Guards a head start to do his bidding.

Before sunset, Beowulf and the horse warriors reached the outskirts of Vindinstedt Farm. Smiles appeared on their faces when stretched out before them; they saw hundreds of Geatfolk gathered before the Main Gate. It was a ragtag army of country folk, peasants, and tradesmen—Freemen all, armed with the tools that defined their lives: pitchforks, hammers, axes, and pikes.

Upon seeing Beowulf, those hundreds waiting before the Palisade erupted with cheering. The sound brought Elin and Eadgils to the wall-walk. Brigitte and Greta, too, quit their chores and ran to join the others. They rejoiced with gladdened hearts at the sight of Ingmar returning.

The ones not there to savor the moment were Weohstan and Beorn. Weohstan being somewhere north of West Fall’s Forest while the Schaman’s whereabouts remained a mystery—a mystery to all save Beowulf.

It was nightfall when Onela reached the Svear encampment. His army had made camp south of the River Vattern, along with the Wylfing horse warriors. Bork, Onela’s Battle Lord, greeted his king inside Onela’s pavilion. The Svear King shouted for food and mead; then he ate and drank enough to satisfy the appetites of two large men before he turned his attention to matters of war.

"Where's my spy?" said Onela. "Where's Weohstan Waegmunding?"

The mead was working its will on the Svear King; besides, the journey from Uppsala had left him exhausted.

"He's not in camp, my King," said Bork.

"Not here?" said Onela. "Where is he?"

"He left after you departed for Uppsala, my King. He didn't say for where."

"That was days ago!" said Onela.

"Yes, my King," said Bork.

"I want him found! Take as many men as you need. My gut tells me there's a rat among us, plotting to steal my cheese."

"Yes, my King; but where are we to look? Shouldn't we concern ourselves, instead, with the march on Falcon's Nest?"

"Marching on Falcon's Nest is my concern! Yours is to get Weohstan Waegmunding! Bring him to me, Bork! Cast a wide net and meet me at Falcon's Nest in three days."

"Do you think Weohstan betrayed you, my King? He fought with us at River Vattern."

"Aye, he fought with us. But how many Geats did you see him kill?"

"I saw him kill Prince Eanmund."

"Exactly," said Onela. "Weohstan drenched his blade with Eanmund's blood, but who else did he kill?"

"I'll take two-hundred of the Wylfing horse warriors, my King. Their mounts are fleeter than ours."

"Do it," said Onela; "but find Weohstan Waegmunding! If he refuses, bring me his head in a basket!"

† † †

For the rest of the day, Beowulf went among the Geats and made sure they had food and drink. Later, that night, he addressed the throng outside the Main Gate.

"I bid you welcome," said Beowulf, in a clear, firm voice. "My heart soars to see so many Freemen willing to risk so much—Geats and Danes alike. You have my gratitude—all of you!"

The Geats and Danes cheered, for they knew Beowulf meant

every word, and they were prepared to die for him.

"Tomorrow," said Beowulf, "at first light, we march north toward Falcon's Nest. I will lead the Spear Danes who stand among you: men who have come far and risked everything to help us. The rest of you must follow on foot as best as you can, with one objective—to support the defense of Falcon's Nest. Will you do that?"

Again, Geats and Danes cheered.

"Tonight, we feast!" said Beowulf. "Eat well! Then get some sleep. You'll need it! For us, there can be no turning back."

† † †

That night, Beowulf and Elin hosted Ulthur in their lodge. Outside, Danes and Geatfolk mingled regardless of station, pledging friendship, all the while knowing that some, perhaps many, would die in the coming battle. That terrible knowledge, however, was insufficient to quash the sound of laughter.

"Gods willing," said Ulthur, "we'll defeat Onela's army."

"Gods willing, we will," said Beowulf.

"What then," said Ulthur, "once we've overthrown Onela, who will rule in Svearland?"

"The answer is behind you," said Beowulf.

They looked toward the entrance to the Banquet Hall.

"You sent for me?" said Eadgils.

"Yes," said Beowulf, "come and join us."

† † †

Resting his head on his saddle, and using his cloak for a blanket, Weohstan stretched-out on the ground. His horse, Graybold, was tethered nearby. Weohstan dare not make a fire since he knew the smell of smoke would carry a considerable distance. Before he closed his eyes, Weohstan gazed a long time into the night sky at the myriad stars sparkling above. He thanked the gods for the wife he once had, and the son she bore him, though Handscio was no more.

† † †

For the longest time, Beowulf and Elin held each and listened to the crackling of the fire.

"I love you more than life itself," said Beowulf.

"Promise me," said Elin, "that you'll come back. That's all I ask, my love. Just come back to me."

"I will, Elin," he said. "I swear it."

† † †

In the twilight preceding dawn, Beowulf left Vindinstedt Farm at the head of three-hundred horse warriors. Ulthur rode at Beowulf's side. So, too, rode Turin. Behind the horse-warriors marched Geats on foot, four hundreds of them led by Eadgils astride a war-horse. Leading footmen was little to Eadgil's liking since he wanted to be at Beowulf's side. As for those who remained at Vindinstedt Farm, they were old men, and boys, unsuited to go to war, and six warriors, all battle-tested, chosen by Beowulf to defend the farm in his absence.

† † †

Weohstan awoke at dawn. With the first morning light, he resumed riding northeast by east, toward the River Vattern in search of Onela's army. In his mind's eye, Weohstan drew a line as the crow flies between Falcon's Nest and where he last left the Svear army. Weohstan rode in the direction of Falcon's Nest until he was satisfied the Svear were nowhere close to the city.

Weohstan knew Geatland's flat lands, vales, and forests better than most of Hygelac's spies, except Beowulf. Stopping to rest his horse, Weohstan dismounted and walked about searching the ground.

There were no fresh tracks, no flattened grass, no wheel ruts from ox-driven carts, or indications of siege engines; no signs whatsoever, of an army on the move.

No matter, he thought; *the Svear must still be east of here.*

While Gray Bold rested and grazed on the emerald green grass of Geatland, Weohstan sat and partook of the blue berries, smoked salmon and rye crackers Elin packed for him to take on his journey. As he sat there beneath a cloudless blue sky, Weohstan thought of Handscio. In his heart, he knew he would never cease mourning the loss of his first-born son.

Weohstan felt a trembling. Out of the distance, a familiar sound reached his ears, one he had heard many times before in battle—the thunder of horses' hooves churning the earth. Weohstan got to his feet. He urged Gray Bold to the top of the closest ridge. From there he could see horse warriors—two-hundred or more a half-league away, riding abreast. They were sweeping the land in a long line like the blade of an immense scythe. Weohstan's gut told him they were Wylfings. If so, Onela and his army would not be far behind.

† † †

Chief of Svearland's most powerful clan, and now Onela's Battle Lord, Bork was the first to spot the lone rider on the ridge. He recognized the dapple-gray war horse and knew it belonged to Weohstan Waegmunding.

"There!" said Bork. "On the ridge!"

The Wylfing warriors dug their heels into their horse's' sides.

Weohstan turned Gray Bold about and started south. "Come, Gray Bold," said Weohstan, "time to stretch your legs!"

Rested, fed and watered, Gray Bold needed no urging and started away at a brisk pace.

† † †

Knut iron jaw's daughters hid. Fearful the soldiers would see, ravish and kill them, Ansa, Arla and Alva crouched behind a large clump of bushes on the side of a hill. They watched in silence as the Geat warriors appeared on foot in a column that stretched a quarter-league or more. On horseback, Eadgils was first to pass the girls' hiding place. Ansa, Arla, and Alva recognized Prince Eadgils, whom they thought peculiar for his not wanting to have his way with them while staying at their father's stronghold.

The day before, the sisters found themselves hiding from a large number of riders. A warrior they recognized, along with the black stallion he rode, led the horsemen. The three were too frightened to whisper his name. Unending toil on their father's farm, plus frequent beatings, had brutalized the girls in mind and body. Their hands were calloused, and they had the ability to withstand hardship, the sort that would buckle the knees of young boys.

Hatred consumed Ansa, Arla, and Alva. Hatred not just for their father, but hatred for all men.

Haraldr was dying. No brew, no potion known to Eydís could save him. Something was eating him from the inside where her eyes couldn't see; nor dared she cut him open to find the demon gnawing her father's innards.

"No Matter, my Daughter," said Haraldr. "I'm ready to die, but I've one last thing to do. Then, my debt to Ecgtheow Waegmunding will be paid—in full."

"Ecgtheow is dead, Father. He wouldn't ask it of you, nor would Prince Beowulf."

"Perhaps," said Haraldr. "But it's called for."

66

TWISTS & TURNS OF FATE

Elin was sitting at her loom when a tall bearded warrior named Gunner entered the weaving room. Elin stopped what she was doing.

"Yes, Gunner; what is it?"

"Three girls at the Main Gate, my Lady, begging for food and water."

Accompanied by Gunner, Elin went to the Main Gate and ordered it opened.

"Beowulf ordered the gate remain shut, my Lady," said Gunner.

"I'll not have it said I turned away three starving waifs, Gunner. Open the gate."

Gunner turned to two warriors standing at the entry-way and nodded. Elin proceeded past the gate and saw before her three desperate children, their faces and bare feet stained with dirt, their hair matted and tangled and their shifts in rags. The sisters' pinched faces were pale from weariness and hunger.

"Welcome to Vindinstedt farm," said Elin. "I'm Elin, wife to Beowulf Waegmunding. Come—we'll find you something to eat. You'll be safe here."

Ansa, the oldest, stepped forward. "You're wife to the bear's son?"

"Yes," said Elin.

She smiled at each of the girls, "I am."

Weohstan did not need to look back to know the Wylfings were gaining on him. Regarding brute strength, Wylfing warhorses were not as powerful as Gray Bold. The Wylfings bred their horses from different stock, different bloodlines than those of the Svear and Geats. Wylfing warhorses could go further without rest than the horses of other tribes, save for those bred in Frisland.

If Weohstan enjoyed an advantage over the two-hundred Wylfings pursuing him, it was his superior knowledge of the land. The westernmost edge of West fall's Forest was a league distant. If Weohstan could reach the forest, he stood a good chance of eluding the Wylfings. Still, he knew better than to bet his life on an "if."

It was then that he heard the sound of rolling thunder, the harbinger of an impending storm. He glanced upward fearing lightning would follow but saw a cloudless blue sky. Weohstan urged Gray Bold on faster toward a ridge three-hundred paces away.

Once Bork and the Wylfing riders sighted their prey they reformed, from a line riding abreast of each other, to a thundering herd without order or shape that convulsed the ground. They heard nothing except for the noise of their horses' hooves; otherwise, they would have heard their doom approaching. Bork and his Wylfing riders were no more than fifty paces behind Weohstan when Beowulf appeared over the top of the ridge.

Beowulf and three-hundred Spear Danes swept the length of the ridge at a gallop with sunlight flashing off the tips of their spears.

Weohstan pulled on the reins to keep Gray Bold from colliding with Beowulf's stallion.

"Die well, Cousin!" said Beowulf over the din.

Weohstan laughed for joy and shouted back.

"Die well, young Prince!"

The shrill strain of rams' horns sounding the alarm reached Sigmund's ears in the depths of the armory. He hurried from there to the highest part of the Citadel. Standing on the wall-walk, he looked east.

Thc warriors undcr Sigmund's command were proceeding to their assigned positions on the ramparts.

A smaller reserve force made up of the Queen's Guard took positions on the eastern wall-walk alongside their Battle Lord. No more than three leagues away, dazzling flashes of sunlight reflected off several-thousand spear tips announcing the arrival of

Onela's army.

Since the battle at the River Vattern Onela's army had swelled to three-thousand warriors on foot: bowmen, spearmen and those bearing swords and axes. Then there was the vaunted Sveargaard, numbering one-hundred warriors on horseback. Onela's army comprised every Svear warrior his lackeys could muster, not just from Uppsala, but also from every clan and village in Svearland. Not all these warriors flocked to Onela's banner with glad hearts but did so under pain of death.

As Sigmund looked past the environs of the city, Queen Hygd and Ragmund joined him on the eastern wall-walk. Together they looked toward the far horizon, at the approaching menace. For several moments no one spoke.

"When will they arrive?" said Hygd, her voice steady.

"Soon, my Queen," said Sigmund. "It's a matter of a half-day before their horse warriors arrive; then their men on foot, followed by their baggage train, and siege engines, if they have them. By nightfall, they'll pitch their tents and light cooking-fires."

"And while the Svear are celebrating their victory to come, what do you propose we do?" said Ragmund.

Not bothering to answer, Sigmund looked at Hygd:

"Tomorrow, my Queen, Onela will demand you surrender the city."

"And when I refuse?" said Hygd.

"They'll storm Falcon's Nest," said Ragmund; "just as sure as we're standing here now, great Queen."

"With your permission, my Queen," said Sigmund, "I'll order the women and children along with the old and the infirm brought into the Citadel. They'll be safer here."

"Safer," said Ragmund; "because you know you can't keep Onela outside the city."

"Your orders, my Queen?" said Sigmund, ignoring Ragmund.

"Do it, Sigmund," said Hygd. "Bring them all into the Citadel."

† † †

Elin found Greta and Brigitte baking bread in the kitchen, what they would distribute to the widows and children that lived under

Beowulf's protection.

"What of the three sisters?" Elin said. "Have you seen to their needs?"

"We have, my Lady," said Greta. "They've been fed, bathed, brushed and curried, and wear the garments and footwear you provided."

Elin laughed: "You speak of them as though they're war ponies, Greta."

"War horses are cleaner than those three, my Lady," said Greta. "It took dousing their hair in boiling water to rid them of lice."

"And war ponies are not secretive, and always whispering, my Lady," said Brigitte.

"They've been through much, ladies. They've earned the right to be wary of strangers and strange surroundings. Where are they now?"

"We gave them each a blanket and the Svear Prince's quarters to sleep in."

"In the milking barn?" said Elin.

Greta and Brigitte nodded.

When Elin entered the milking barn, she found the sisters sitting close together on blankets spread over fresh straw speaking in hushed voices. They stopped talking as Elin approached with a baked loaf of bread and honey butter.

"I brought you something to nibble on later," said Elin, smiling.

Ansa got to her feet and nudged Arla and Alva to do the same.

"Thank you, my Lady," said Ansa, "for everything."

"You're welcome," said Elin. "How are you called?"

Beginning with Ansa, each girl introduced herself.

"Well, Ansa, Arla, and Alva, what of your mother and father—they must be worried sick about you?"

Arla and Alva looked to Ansa to respond.

"We're from a small village north of here, my Lady. Our mother and father are dead; killed by soldiers who raided our village. My sisters and I got away because we were tending sheep when the soldiers came. We fled south, traveling at night."

"You poor children, I'm so sorry for your loss," said Elin. "You're welcome to stay here as long as you like. Tomorrow we'll find you suitable quarters."

"Please, my Lady," said Ansa; "we like it where we are, and

we'll work hard for our keep."

Elin smiled. "We can talk about that later. Enjoy your bread and honey."

† † †

Beowulf looked on as a score of Wylfing riders fled the battlefield. Of the two-hundred riders under Bork's command, those twenty Wylfings had survived and away they went, fast as their horses could carry them.

"Do you want us to give chase?" said Ulthur.

"No, Lord Ulthur," said Beowulf. "Rest your men and horses."

The action had been short-lived and intense. Bork was unprepared for the three-hundred spear Danes that came over the ridge and was the first to die at the hand of Beowulf.

The Danes buried fifteen of their fallen comrades in the rich earth of Geatland and piled stones there to mark the spot. They collected the riderless horses in one place, stripped the dead Wylfings of their armor and weapons and left that war gear stacked on the ground.

While the Danes busied themselves with these tasks, Weohstan took Turin aside.

"Ecgtheow taught you well," said Weohstan. "I couldn't be more proud of you, were you, my son. You fought bravely."

"Thank you, Lord Weohstan."

† † †

It was sunset when Onela eased his vast body into the steaming water that filled the copper basin in his pavilion. He sighed as the mint-scented water washed over him. The march to Falcon's Nest left Onela weary and his joints sore. Now that his army was camped less than half a league from the Main Gate of Falcon's Nest, Onela could relax. The one loose thread in Onela's mental tapestry, he did not have Weohstan's head in a basket. "Mead!" said the Usurper; "Bring me mead—and a woman! One that's clean."

† † †

As the sun began to set behind him, Sigmund looked east from the wall-walk. What he saw in the distance sent a shiver down his spine. The campfires of the Svear were more than he could count. Stretching a half-league, from north to south, the fires of Onela's army lit-up the encroaching darkness.

There are more now by far than we faced at the River Vattern. Where are you, Beowulf?

† † †

It was well after sunset when Beowulf and the Spear Danes made camp and lit fires. They would eat what food they brought in their saddlebags, then bed down. While Ulthur visited among his men, Beowulf sat before the fire with Weohstan, Turin, and Ingmar. Weohstan added a stick to the flames and spoke:

"There's something you need to know, Beowulf. Heardred isn't alone in his betrayal. There's another, just as close to the queen."

"Ragmund," said Beowulf.

"Yes," said Weohstan; "how did you know?"

"I didn't know for certain, but for a long time, I suspected as much. Now you've confirmed my suspicions."

"What are you going to do?" said Turin.

"Sleep," said Beowulf. "We'll settle with Ragmund soon enough."

Later as Beowulf stretched-out beside the fire he thought of Elin and their unborn child.

As he drifted into what would be a fitful sleep, Elin appeared before him. She was standing atop the wall-walk near the Main Gate of Vindinstedt Farm, waiting for Beowulf to return. In his dream, Beowulf could hear her calling him but before he could answer, or take Elin into his arms, a shadow, dark and terrible took shape behind her. It was Death, showing himself just as he had at Otters'Bay and Heorot Hall.

Beowulf sat up with a loud gasp. He felt a shiver travel along his spine. As Beowulf looked around, in the dim firelight, he could see the forms of his companions where they slept. Getting to his feet, Beowulf placed a log on the fire and looked into the star-filled sky.

Odin, he prayed, if you think us worthy, grant the Geatfolk victory tomorrow.

† † †

The fire heating the bedchamber died down to a pile of embers and cast but little light when Elin cried-out in her sleep. Awakened from her nightmare, Elin threw back the covers and swung her legs over the side of the bed. Perspiration soaked Elin's nightshirt, beads of sweat gathered on her forehead. Not bothering to knock, Brigitte and Greta rushed into Elin's chamber and went to her bedside.

Greta was first to speak: "My lady, are you alright? We heard you scream."

"A bad dream is all," said Elin. "Go back to bed, both of you; I'll be fine."

"Are you sure, my Lady?" said Brigitte, pulling her shawl around her shoulders. "Your nightshirt is soaked through."

"At least let us help you change, my Lady," said Greta.

Elin nodded: "Very well, ladies; find me a day-shift."

"Day-shift, my Lady, it's not even dawn yet?"

"I can't sleep," said Elin. "I may as well get up."

† † †

It was still dark when Beowulf shook his cousin awake: "Get up, Weohstan; it's time to go."

Beowulf went to Turin and Ingmar while Ulthur mustered the Spear Danes. There would be no lingering; they would make no cooking-fires. There was armor to put on, horses to feed and saddle, and leagues yet to ride. Beowulf and the Danes following him would break fast while riding, sharing with each other dried meats, cheese, and hard biscuits as they rode toward Falcon's Nest.

After dawn, Sigmund joined the four-hundred men and boys he assigned to the wall-walk that surrounded the earthworks. From his position in the watchtower above the Main Gate, Sigmund strained to see through the fog. Although a thick mist obscured the Svear encampment, he could hear sounds of axes chopping wood as Onela's army prepared their breakfast. The Svear and the mercenaries with them would begin the battle with full bellies, small recompense perhaps for mounting a full frontal assault on a well-defended position. Nevertheless, Onela had also promised his warriors silver, along with whatever spoils they could gather once the city fell, and that was to their liking.

To assail the earthworks that surrounded the city, the Svear needed to negotiate a broad ditch that ran the length of the perimeter. Sharpened stakes lined the ditch, and into it, the defenders poured pitch, the pitch they would set afire when the Svear attacked.

The one other way into the city was over a narrow stone causeway that spanned the ditch and stopped at the city gate.

To their advantage, the Geats occupied the high ground and benefited from the considerable protection the earthworks afforded. The Geats, too, would fight with full bellies, but it gave them no cause to celebrate that cold morning. Like the men around him, Sigmund reconciled himself to the fact he would be dead before nightfall.

† † †

Prince Eadgils rejoiced at the sight of the horses and the cache of weapons and armor stacked on the ground in the midst of the dead Wylfings. Always alert to the prospects of an easy meal, crows numbering in the hundreds had gathered to feast on the carcasses. They were ahead of the other scavengers that would soon arrive.

"Gather 'round," said Eadgils. "Those of you who can ride, take a horse from the herd. Pray you enjoy a better day than the Wylfing who owned it. Those of us with horses will ride ahead. I ask the rest of you proud Geatfolk to join the fray, fast as you can."

† † †

The fog disappeared, and the sun was overhead when Onela opened his eyes. As his blurred vision adjusted to the dim light inside his pavilion, he saw his Clan Chiefs gathered before him, thirty in all.

"What are you doing here," said Onela. He swung his legs over the side of his portable goose-feather bed.

A Svear Clan Chief named Eogla stepped forward. "We're awaiting your orders, my King."

Onela positioned a chamber pot between his thighs and commenced draining his bladder.

"Where's Bork? Why's he not here?"

"Bork hasn't returned, my King," Eogla said.

"Then you'll act in his stead," said Onela.

"I'm honored, my King."

"Of course you are! Now get out, all of you! Come back when you have a plan of attack!"

† † †

Ansa, Arla, and Alva sat in the meadow. Around them, sheep grazed on an abundance of sweet-grass.

"I like it here," said Alva, the youngest of the sisters. "I don't understand why you both want to leave so soon."

"Don't be stupid," said the middle sister, Arla. "Did you forget whose farm this is?"

"Our father's killer," said Alva. "I haven't forgotten."

"Stop arguing," said Ansa. "Sooner or later the bear's son will return, along with the hairy old demon that travels with him. If they find us here, I don't think they're going to be merciful."

"Oh," said Alva. "But... where will we go?"

"I don't know," said Ansa, "somewhere… soon."

"Even if we decided on a place," said Arla; "we have no food, no weapons, and no horses to get us there."

"We can take what we need from the Main Lodge," said Ansa, "and once we're outside the palisade, we can steal a horse."

"But Elin's body-stewards keep a close watch on us," said Arla.

"Yes," said Alva. "What about Greta and Brigitte?"

"What matters them," said Ansa. "We're not prisoners here. We have Lady Elin's permission to go about our business wherever we like."

"Every time those two look down their noses at me, I want to gouge their eyes out," said Arla.

"I know. I hate Greta, and the other one also," said Alva.

The three sat in silence, pondering their situation. Ansa erupted with laughter.

"What's so funny?" said Arla.

"Yes, Ansa, tell us," said Alva.

"I was picturing Greta and Brigitte without their noses."

Arla and Alva laughed.

"Or their ears!" said Alva.

The sisters laughed so hard their bellies shook. They rolled onto their backs and lay on the grass.

"Or their fingers," said Arla.

"And toes," said Alva.

Ansa stopped laughing. "I'd chop them into little pieces and feed them to the hogs."

Arla and Alva stopped laughing. Knut Iron Jaw's daughters lie in silence together, shoulder to shoulder, holding hands.

It was then an old woman appeared. Bent over and shriveled with age, the creases and wrinkles on her face spoke of an untold number of winters, and many hardships. To steady herself she leaned upon a shepherd's staff.

"Hello, children," said the old woman.

The girls scrambled to their feet.

"Who are you?" said Ansa. "This land belongs to Clan Waegmunding. They don't look kindly on trespassers."

"Clan Waegmunding be damned, child. They are liars, murderers, and thieves—all of them. Besides, all of Midgard, including the oceans, belongs to the All Mother—and no one else. Now listen well, for these are dark and dire times, and I came here to warn you."

"Who are you?" said Ansa. "And where have you come from?"

"Who I am is of no importance; but I have come from far, far away."

"I've never heard of Far, Far-Away," said Alva.
"It's not a place, stupid," said Alma.
"Don't call me stupid," said Alva.
"Quiet—both of you," said Ansa. "Tell us, grandmother. What is it you want to warn us about?"

† † †

Eogla and the Svear Clan Chiefs walked the perimeter of the three-sided fortifications facing them. They were careful to stay beyond the range of the Geat bowmen who were all too eager to end the life of any attacker they could reach with their arrows. Aware the Svear Chieftains were studying the city's defenses, Sigmund strode upon the wall-walk, encouraging his men. He wasted no time placing each one of his four-hundred warriors where he determined each man or boy could best defend the earthworks.

Eogla and the Svear Chieftains debated among themselves until they had formulated a plan of attack and presented it to Onela. That done, at Onela's behest Eogla proceeded to the city gate bareheaded under his upraised shield, for such was the custom when approaching an enemy to talk.

Looking down from the watchtower, Sigmund confronted the Svear chieftain standing on the causeway below.

"Tell your master the answer's, 'No'!"

Without having uttered a word, Eogla returned to Onela's pavilion.

"They won't surrender the city, my King."

"Who leads them?" said Onela.

"I don't know his name, but I recognize him from the battle at the River Vattern. The Geats who got away owe their lives to his quick thinking."

"Hmm," said Onela; "I know the warrior about whom you speak. He had his wits about him, for sure. Very well, Eogla, begin the attack."

Overlooking the city that had grown around it, Geat kings built the Citadel upon a sheer wall of rock five-hundred feet above the water. As a practical matter, the Svear could attack the city from the east. That was where the founders of Falcon's Nest built the City Gate.

In consultation with the other chieftains, Eogla chose to attack all three landlocked sides of the city; but not before they brought forward one of their two siege engines to menace the City Gate.

The siege tower moved forward at a turtle's pace over the wagon road leading to the causeway. Covered by wet animal hides, the tower stood fifteen hands higher than the log railing that protected the defenders inside the watchtower. In theory, the Svear would push the tower against the gate, then lower a platform that would allow them to leap down on the defenders in the watchtower. What the Svear would not know when they leapt—Sigmund and six Geat warriors would be there to greet them: four bowmen and two warriors wielding axes.

Ragmund had served his new master well, providing Onela with an accurate blueprint of the city's defenses. Thanks to Ragmund, Onela's carpenters knew how wide to build the tower and how high above the ground the tower should stand. Ragmund gave them the plans long before the Svear put that massive structure to the test, assailing the city where Geat kings had ruled for three-hundred winters.

In as loud a voice as he could summon, Sigmund addressed his men from his position inside the watchtower:

"You fight today for Geatland and your wives and children! Let your arrows fly without pity, for the Svear will show you none. If they breach the gate, fall back to the Citadel. Fight for every lodge, barn, and outbuilding! Make them pay for every step they take. Above all, die well, and remember—you're Thunder-Geats!"

A tremendous shout issued from the defenders, so great was their resolve to die that day. The bowmen in the watchtower dipped their arrows in pitch and lit them on fire.

Little by little, foot by foot, the tower continued to move closer to the causeway. The arrows of the Geats' didn't fail to reach the tower when it came into range, but the wet hides, like a second skin, prevented the siege tower from burning. To be sure, the spearhead of the attack was the tower, behind which, struggling, to move it along, were fifty warriors with push-poles.

No sooner had the front wheels of the tower rolled onto the causeway, then the shrill sound of a hundred rams' horns trumpeted the order—"*Attack*!"

Fifteen hundreds of Onela's warriors charged the earthworks surrounding the city. It was a bitter cup from which to drink. Regarding sheer numbers, the Svear, along with Onela's mercenaries, were six for every Geat defender.

As the first wave of Svear encountered the stake-laden ditch with their ladders their attack sputtered to a crawl. The fortified ditch slowed but didn't stop the attackers. Geat bowmen had scored many kills before the first ladder attained the earthworks.

Still, the Svear pressed forward. Sigmund tossed a torch into the ditch, setting the pitch on fire. Scores more of Onela's warriors died a painful death; others retreated a safe distance until the flames died down and the fuel fanning the fire burned out.

The sloping earthworks that formed the city's first line of defense were forty-hands high on all three sides. The wall-walk was broad enough that Geat warriors could stand three-deep if need be. Svear bowmen were also scoring kills because the Geat defenders did not shrink back as they loosed arrows, rocks, and spears on the attackers. Many Geats fell in that first assault, but not a single Svearlander set foot on the wall-walk.

The impact of the siege tower coming to a full stop at the city gate rocked Sigmund and the others in the watchtower. From the top of that tower a platform dropped. The spiked lip of the platform bit down on top of the protective rail of the watchtower and held the platform stationary. The first Svear warrior appeared —a tall, broad shouldered Clan Chief named Gunther Gustafson. A Geat arrow struck that brave Chieftain in one eye, and he fell to the ground. Two more Svearlanders rushed from the tower onto the platform. Geat arrows felled them also, just as they did the next two Svearlanders and the next two until no more rushed forward and a lull ensued. More Svear would have to climb the ladder into the tower since it could accommodate a mere handful of warriors at a time. Sigmund looked at the bowmen with him, noting their dwindling supply of arrows.

"Make your arrows count!" he said.

Their expressions grim, the bowmen nodded. More Svear came

across the platform, and like those, before them, they rushed forward without shields, since shields were too cumbersome and unwieldy in the tight confines of the siege tower. Just as before, the arrows of the Geats killed those brave Svearlanders.
From a place of safety in the rear, Onela watched warrior, after warrior, topple from the platform, growing the pile of dead on either side of the causeway. The Svear King became furious; he looked at Eogla:

"Send more men!" he said.

Eogla ordered six-hundred men forward, two-hundred from the east, two-hundred from the north and two-hundred from the south.

More of the attackers entered the tower and poured onto the platform, and the arrows of the Geats killed them, but more of Onela's men kept coming until the bowmen had exhausted their arrows. Casting aside their bows the Geat bowmen took up axes and waited. Their wait was not a long one. Soon another group of Svear rushed across the platform. With no arrows to stop them the Geats in the watchtower braced for close-quarter combat.

As the Svear leapt into the watchtower, Sigmund and the defenders struck at them with axe and sword, creating in that restricted space a pile of the dead that made the fighting more difficult and desperate. The Svear forced Sigmund and the Geats to flee to a fallback position on the earthworks. Sigmund looked around—the Svear and the mercenaries with them were close to overrunning the defenders.

"Fall back to the Great Square!" said Sigmund. "Fall back to the Common Area!"

Sigmund and less than two-hundred Geats, those who could still walk, withdrew from the earthworks and headed to the Common Area—a large, vacant square in the center of the city where Geatfolk gathered during festivals and executions.

Once the attackers controlled the earthworks, they milled about, savoring their victory by torturing and killing any wounded Geat they happened on. The Svear cleared the watchtower of the bodies piled there. Because the tower could not fit through the gate and had already served its purpose, Eogla ordered it pushed from the causeway and rolled to one side.

Ragmund had told the Svear what their spies already knew: they would need something else to assail the massive door of the

Citadel—a battering ram which the Svear built a month earlier according to Ragmund's precise specifications.

From her place on the wall-walk, Queen Hygd, accompanied by Ragmund and two of her guards looked toward the Common Area. They saw Sigmund and the last of his men form themselves into a shield wall in preparation for the onslaught to come. Hygd saw the Svear spilling into the city, and she trembled.

"My Queen," said Sigmund's younger brother, Eosin, shouting from the western wall-walk: "You need to see this!"

† † †

Onela paced back and forth inside his pavilion. In the camp with him was the Sveargarrd, his Guard of one-hundred warriors. There was also a reserve force of eight-hundred warriors on foot. Eogla entered the pavilion and bowed.

"It's about time," said Onela, "What news?"

"Their outer defenses have fallen, my King. The city's yours!"

"I don't want the bloody city!" said Onela. "I want Hygelac's gold inside the Citadel!"

"Our warriors are at the Citadel door even as we speak, my King."

"How many have we lost?"

"A thousand of our warriors are dead or wounded, my King."

"The price of victory I suppose," said Onela. "Rest, Eogla. Join me for a horn of mead."

"Thank you, my King, but I prefer to keep a clear head."

"If that's how you feel—go!" said Onela. "Return to the fighting!"

Eogla bowed and departed. Onela summoned the Captain of the Sveargarrd, a Clan Chief named Ule.

"Are there any women in camp?"

"There are many my King. Shall I send for one?"

"Two," said Onela; "and make sure they're clean—and pleasing to my eye!"

Followed by Ragmund and her guards, Queen Hygd walked the length of the wall-walk to where Eosin was standing.

Her heart quickened a beat at the sight of seventy Longships dropping anchor in the harbor. Ragmund's stomach tightened and turned sour at what he saw. Hygd shouted with joy and turned her smiling face toward his: "All's not lost, Lord Ragmund—see?"

"Yes, my Queen," said Ragmund, about to choke.

"Someone must tell Sigmund," said Eosin. "Permit me the honor, my Queen."

Hygd drew a full breath and took hold of her emotions.

"Yes, Eosin, go. Deliver Sigmund the excellent news."

As Eosin hurried away, Hygd looked upon the battle craft below with their dragon prows and colorful sails and the hundreds of Danes about to set foot on the shore of Geatland.

"I praise the gods," said Hygd. "My prayers are answered."

The sound of Ragmund vomiting interrupted Hygd's elation. Though nothing was thrown-up, Ragmund was pale, and he needed to steady himself against the wall. The fear Ragmund felt held him captive by the throat, and his lips quivered.

"Are you feeling alright, Ragmund?" said Hygd; "You don't look well at all."

† † †

Ragmund knew every path and shortcut in the city. He would be careful to avoid the Geats in the Common Area. Ragmund waited in the shadows of a metalsmith's workshop. From there he had an unobstructed view of the commotion in the Great Square; he need wait for an opportune moment to make his move toward the Svear lines. For the time being the Svear were content to loot the deserted lodges, shops and mead halls throughout the city while their chiefs lashed and exhorted them to push on to the Citadel. In the meantime, Eosin found Sigmund among the defenders gathered in the Great Square.

"Eosin—why aren't you with our queen?" said Sigmund. "I told you not to leave her side."

"Queen Hygd sends me here with the greatest good news, Brother. Even as I speak, the Danes are in the harbor!"

"The Spear Danes—here?" said Sigmund.

"Yes."

"The gods favor us," said Sigmund. He turned to his men: "Brothers, listen! The Danes have come to our aid. Everyone—fall back to the Citadel!"

Ragmund saw Sigmund and his men withdraw and he scurried from the shadows. He held empty hands high above his head lest the Svear mistakes him for a combatant and kill him on the spot. After everything he had risked, Ragmund was intent on delivering himself alive to the first Svear warrior he encountered.

Sigmund and the men with him entered the Citadel. When the last defender was inside, the Gate Wardens shut and barred that mighty door and returned to their positions on the wall-walk. The Citadel was a crowded place, what with the inhabitants of the city taking refuge inside, along with those who'd sworn to defend them.

Sigmund turned to his brother.

"Take charge of these men, Eosin. Place them on the eastern wall-walk and see that they get food and drink. They fought hard, and they deserve some comfort."

"I'll see it done," said Eosin, "but what of you, brother?"

"I go to meet the Spear Danes. Die well, Brother."

"And you, Brother," said Eosin. "Die well!"

67

THE SUN TURNS CRIMSON

Sigmund saw Unferth on the dock with several Danish chieftains. Behind them hundreds of Spear Danes waited, restless to disembark. Beckoned by Unferth, the Danes gathered their shields and spears and began to leave their Longships.

They assembled on the narrow strip of land between the cliff and the water that formed a wide path leading north and south.

"You're a welcome sight, my Lord," said Sigmund as he approached Unferth. "My queen bids you welcome."

"Greetings, Sigmund! What news?"

"The Svear have breached the city. Those of us left have taken positions on the wall-walk of the Citadel."

"Then we'd best get at it," said Unferth. "Beowulf said there's a path that will take us south of the city, unseen by the Svear."

"Yes," said Sigmund. "There is such a path. I'll guide you myself, but aren't your men in need of rest?"

"Rest?" said Unferth. "We've enjoyed fair winds and full sails since morning. We've been sitting on our arses all day!"

† † †

While Sigmund was greeting the Danes, the Svear pushed a battering ram within bowshot of the Citadel door. An iron tip, cast in the shape of a fist, would do the battering. The Svear made the body of the ram from a centuries-old pine tree, and great was its length, girth, and the force it exerted when swung. Planks covered with wet hides protected the machine, and the warriors pushing it, from a rain of fire.

The attackers, those not operating the massive siege engine, hung back since they lacked ladders long enough to assail the walls. For the one-thousand Svear gathered before the Citadel, the way to victory lie beyond the High Door. They cheered as the battering ram smashed, over and over, against that entrance, shaking it on its hinges; yet the Great Door held. From the wall-walk, the Geats hurled rocks, arrows, and flaming pitch on the siege engine. By sheer luck, the Geats managed to kill some of the operators, but the battering ram itself went unharmed. The sound of beams cracking with each new fracture wore on the nerves of the defenders.

Eosin and fifty handpicked warriors made a shield wall behind the door, clogging the passageway that led into the bowels of the Citadel. Those fifty Geats, young and old, exchanged grim looks. As the men around him, Eosin knew the time for words had passed —fell deeds lie ahead.

† † †

Ule, Captain of the Sveargarrd, stood outside Onela's pavilion. Warriors approached escorting a Geat whom Ule recognized as one of Onela's spies. The Svear had bound Ragmund's hands with rope.

"This Geat claims he's an Angle, and someone important," said one of the warriors; "he says he bears urgent news for our king."

"I'll vouch for him," said Ule.

"Take me to Onela," said Ragmund. "The news I bring can't wait."

"He's busy right now," said Ule.

"Busy?" said Ragmund. "There are hundreds, maybe a thousand Spear Danes massing on the plain south of the city, and you tell me your king is... 'busy?'!"

The curtain masking the entrance to Onela's tent parted. Out ran two women clutching their garments. Wearing his breeches, and nothing else, Onela's face was flush with anger.

"Spear Danes," said Onela, "Here? Where?"

"Yes," said Ragmund. "Here, just south of us."

Ule cut the bindings from Ragmund's wrists.

"Hundreds, maybe a thousand," said Ragmund.

The blood drained from Onela's face; his mouth fell open.

† † †

On the lush green plain south of Falcon's Nest, the Spear Danes formed their ranks into seven squares of one-hundred warriors each. The tents of the Svear encampment were visible in the distance, a half-league away.

"What would you have us do, Sigmund?" said Unferth. "You know the terrain and what awaits us."

"Attack the Svear encampment," said Sigmund; "where Onela waits with his reserve force. That way he cannot use them to assail the Citadel once the Svear breach the Great Door."

"Very well," said Unferth.

They clasped forearms. "Die well, Unferth."

"And you, Sigmund—die well!"

Eogla watched from a place of safety as the battering ram continued to pound the High Door. Behind him, a thousand warriors waited to wet their swords with the blood of the Geat defenders.

There was a tremendous cracking sound. The ram had completed its task breaking the beam that barred the way inside. The sundered door collapsed inward at an awkward angle—awkward for the Svear because the width of the entry was now less than before; which made it impossible for more than a few warriors to enter at the same time.

The men operating the siege engine were exhausted. Eogla knew this, and he ordered fifty more warriors to take their place and drag the ram to one side. When the Svear moved the battering ram out of the way, Eogla gave the order; his warriors rushed forward. Many brave Svearfell to the arrows of the Geats; much more made it to the shattered door.

Eosin felt himself shaking in anticipation of engaging the first Svear to enter the Citadel.

Let them come, for they will know it is I, Eosin, son of Gundur, who greets them!

A tall, black-bearded Svear named Uell stepped past the broken door. Eosin crouched low as Uell's sword sliced the air over his head. At the same time, Eosin struck sideways beneath Uell's shield severing the Clan Chief's leg at the knee. With an overhead blow, Eosin's sword cleaved Uell's helm, splitting his head to his chin. More Svear appeared like ants to a honey keg. It wasn't long before Geats and Svear alike were standing on the dead and dying to fight one another.

While his ears filled with the screams and desperate shouts from the men around him, Eosin's lungs strained for air and he felt his muscles tiring. Again and again, he struck with his sword, denying life to the men who sought his. Eosin would have killed more but for a wounded Gifth mercenary who drove his knife into Eosin's liver. Eosin's last thought was of his mother; then his knees buckled. He crumpled to the ground and darkness fell upon him.

So loud was the din of battle, Eogla did not hear the three-hundred rams' horns blowing from the north, nor did he see fifteen-hundred Brondings coming against him led by King Breca, accompanied by the Schaman, Beorn.

The Brondings poured through the city gate and came up behind Eogla's force. Great was the slaughter, for the Brondings had caught the Svear unaware. Sigmund found himself opposite Eogla and fierce was their combat until Sigmund drove a spear through Eogla's chest, killing him.

The defenders of the Citadel pushed forward with renewed fury over the bodies in the passageway. They forced the Svear back while Brondings and Geats surrounded the attackers in the Great Square.

After that, it wasn't long before Onela's warriors threw down their swords and lifted their arms to surrender; however, the Geats and Brondings were in no mood to take prisoners that day; nor did they.

† † †

In Onela's camp the Svear reserves made a shield wall four men deep along the northern edge of their encampment. Looking south, they faced the Danes led by Unferth, who was now no more than a hundred paces distant. The Svear reserves had little desire to engage the Danes and had no confidence in their king—what they had aplenty, was dread over the army they saw approaching.

Onela paced in his pavilion, racking his mind for a plan but none was forthcoming. So great was the fear that gripped him, his mouth was too dry to summon spit. He drained a horn of mead and reached for his helm. The Svear King started to secure the straps of his helm in place when he felt the ground trembling. He saw the tent poles inside his splendid pavilion quiver. At the same time, a loud rumbling sound reached Onela's ears. The Captain of the Sveargarrd rushed inside.

"My King," said Ule, "the bear's son's upon us!"

It was as Ule said. Beowulf had come against them from behind, with Ulthur and three-hundred horse warriors.

"What are your orders, my King?" said Ule.

Onela looked around; his face became a portrait of utter disbelief.

"Muster the Sveargarrd!" he said.

While the battle raged along the southern side of the Svear encampment, Onela and the Sveargaard fled east at a gallop.

† † †

Prince Eadgils glanced at the sun and reckoned the time. It was midday. Falcon's Nest was five leagues distant. Eadgils looked side to side at the Geats riding with him: a few were veteran warriors, the others were farmers and tradesmen—risking all in defense of their land and families.

Eadgils felt a pang of shame, for it was his tribe, the tribe of his ancestors, that threatened the lives and freedom of the men riding with him. As their horses cantered north, Eadgils and the Geat riders entered the neck of a narrow valley.

Eadgils signaled a halt. The Geat riders fanned-out in a line to the left and right and brought their horses to a stop. They also saw what Eadgils saw—a column of riders approaching, and they saw a banner—Onela's banner.

"Brave men of Geatland," said Eadgils. "Arm yourselves against the Usurper!"

When Onela saw the Geats on horses, he broke into a sweat, for now, Geats blocked his retreat to Uppsala.

"Look, my King," said Ule. He pointed to a single warrior approaching them unarmed. The man stopped midway between the two groups of riders and removed his helm.

Onela's eyes grew wide when he beheld it was Eadgils who faced him.

"Yes, Uncle," said Eadgils, so that all might hear: "It's me—Eadgils, son of Ohthere, brother of Eanmund."

Onela sat on his horse, speechless.

"There's no cause for further bloodshed," said Eadgils. "The battle for Falcon's Nest has turned against you, or you wouldn't be retreating. Let's settle our feud by a trial of combat—you against me, on foot. If you win, you and Ule may continue to Uppsala unopposed by the riders with me. You have my word on it! What say you?"

"I say I'm going to carve your heart out, boy," said Onela, swinging himself from his saddle to the ground with a thud.

Eadgils put his helm on and dismounted. He drew his sword and waited. Onela strode forward, sword in hand, shield raised. Eadgils' youth and stamina favored him, but regarding brute strength Onela was the stronger.

When he closed the distance separating them, Onela struck first with a powerful overhead blow that cut deep into Eadgils' shield and knocked him backward.

Recovering his balance, Prince Eadgils stepped forward. Onela struck, splintering Eadgil's shield. Eadgils continued to deflect Onela's rain of blows with his sword.

Exhausted by his exertions, Onela stepped back and tossed his shield to the ground. Panting, he pulled his helm off and cast it aside. His face turned beet red; he drenched himself in sweat.

Eadgils removed his helm and dropped it to the ground. Eadgils took several deep breaths and advanced. Striking high and low, Eadgils moved in a circle.

"Stand still and fight me," said Onela.

Onela could feel his strength draining and his legs close to buckling.

Eadgils said nothing. He continued circling and striking blows in quick succession. It wasn't long before Eadgils saw an opening. He drove the point of his sword through Onela's armor, into his liver, and out his back.

When Onela staggered to his knees coughing blood, Eadgils leaned close:

"I kill you for my dead brother. I kill you for the families you've destroyed. Most of all, Uncle, I kill you for me!"

Eadgils grabbed Onela by his hair and held him steady while he drove his sword up to the hilt between Onela's ribs. When Eadgils released his grip, Onela's lifeless body collapsed backward.

As Eadgils' sword came free, loud shouting erupted from the Geats.

Eadgils saw Ule hurl Onela's banner to the ground. Ule dismounted and walked toward Eadgils with his shield held flat above his head as a sign of submission. Ule stopped several paces away from where Eadgils waited.

"Lower your shield, Ule," said Eadgils; "You're not my enemy. You're free to leave—you and your men."

"We're Sveargaard, my Lord—now that you are king, we ride with you!"

68

THE BUTCHER'S BILL

It was late afternoon when the Geats on foot found Onela's corpse. Crows had picked-out his eyes and cheeks. They protested with choruses of cawing when the Geats interrupted their dinner.

"Look well, brothers," said a Freeman, "for the war must surely be over!"

The Geats crowded around Onela's corpse, but they were confused since none had ever seen a Svear King before that day.

"How can you be sure the war's over?" said another Geatlander.

"Because the bloated corpse you see before you is Onela, the Usurper, once King of Svearland."

"Then it must be true," said yet another Geatlander; "without their king, the war must be over!"

The Geats shouted and clapped one another on the back.

"Several of you should return to Vindinstedt and tell Lady Elin of Geatland's victory," said Eadgils. "The rest of us will continue to Falcon's Nest. The fighting may be over, brothers, but there'll be dead to bury."

Before the Geats continued to Falcon's Nest they stripped Onela of his battle gear, and undergarments, and tore the Usurper's banner into small patches of cloth to take home as souvenirs, fragments of cloth that would later attest to the part they played in the Great War.

† † †

The sun had dropped low in the sky by the time King Breca and the Schaman reached what remained of the Svear encampment. The Danes were milling about, laughing and singing. Beorn and Breca found Beowulf in Onela's pavilion.

"A sight you are, my friends," said Beowulf.

"And you, Bear's Son," said Breca. He looked around the tent:

“Where’s Prince Eadgils?”

“Svearland needs its king,” said Beowulf. “Eadgils left for Uppsala with the Sveargarrd and those of Onela’s army who surrendered after the Usurper fled. Unferth sent Ulthur and fifty Spear Danes to retrieve Hrothgar’s sister. They’ll see Astrid safely home to Daneland.”

The curtain over the entrance to the pavilion parted, and two Danes entered with Ragmund in their grip. Ragmund stared at the floor, unable to meet the stares that greeted him.

“We found him cowering beneath a pile of dead Svearlanders,” said one of the warriors.

“That’s no Svearlander you found,” said Weohstan; “he's a traitor who conspired against his king for the Usurper’s gold and the promise of a crown.”

Ragmund fell to his knees: “Mercy, Prince Beowulf.”

“This man is an Angle,” said Beowulf. “Honor him as Angles honor a traitor.”

Thus, in the Angle tradition, Ragmund’s limbs were tied to four horses that walked in different directions until they pulled the traitor, screaming all the while, apart.

† † †

Beowulf and the others bathed and cleaned their armor before leaving for the Citadel. Queen Hygd had invited King Breca and the chieftains of the three tribes—Geats, Danes and Brondings to a celebration feast. Meanwhile, the town folk and the Geats who arrived late began the unpleasant but necessary task of burying the dead.

A table and benches for the Danish and Bronding Chieftains occupied a place of honor. Hygd entered the Mead Hall accompanied by her daughter, and all in attendance rose as one and bowed to that gentle queen. Sigmund and four warriors followed. They carried a chest containing over three-thousand gold rings: one for every Danish and Bronding warrior, and for the families of those Danes and Brondings who died in Geatland’s defense.

“I come to thank the Spear Danes and Sea Brondings,” said Hygd. “You risked everything that Geatland might remain free.

Unferth, King Breca, the gold I bring, I bring not as payment, for I know you ask none. These rings are a token of a widowed queen's heartfelt gratitude—that, and that, alone."

"And we accept them as such, great Queen," said Unferth and Breca, speaking as one voice.

Hygd looked at her daughter. From the folds of her garments, Princess Ingrid held out the Crown of Kings, recast and made whole once more. Hygd took it from Ingrid's hands and turned to Beowulf.

"For three-hundred winters Geatland's kings have worn this simple band of braided gold and silver. Geatland needs a king, a forthright king, known and loved by his people, not a widow better suited to be a grandmother. That king is you, Beowulf Waegmunding. Come forward—and accept the Crown of Geatland."

"I don't know what to say, my Queen," said Beowulf.

"Then just come forward, for that is the last command I'll ever give. My daughter and I are tired. We will retire to our chambers while you and these worthy warriors celebrate."

The Hall remained silent as Beowulf stood in front of Hygd with head bowed.

Hygd spoke loud and clear: "You, who gather here, bear witness now to Geatland's king—Beowulf, Son of Liv and Ecgtheow."

Standing on her tiptoes, Hygd placed Geatland's Crown on Beowulf's head. Hygd kissed Beowulf on the cheek; then, with her daughter, Hygd departed. Every Geat Chieftain got in line, one behind the other, that each might bend a knee to Beowulf as a sign of fealty. When the last man had passed through the line, Beowulf addressed them all:

"You honor me with your presence, my Lords. Now let us feast and celebrate our victory. We are Spear Danes, Sea Brondings and Thunder-Geats joined in battle as we are in peace—shield brothers all."

Beowulf raised his arm and saluted the warriors assembled before him.

A great shout issued from the chieftains: "Bear's Son!"

Servants brought roasted meats and steaming loaves of bread into the Hall while others poured mead. Geats, Brondings, and Danes lifted drinking horns to honor their fallen comrades by calling-out their names. Sigmund's brother, Eosin, was one of many names cited that night. When the remembrances concluded, the heaviness in the Hall lifted. Soon laughter and good cheer prevailed.

It was after midnight when word of Geatland's victory reached Vindinstedt Farm. Great was Elin's joy, although the two Freemen who returned with the news could not provide any details regarding Beowulf himself.

Wondering if Beowulf would come back to her, Elin's mind raced from one dark place to the next. While Brigitte braided Elin's hair in preparation for bed, Elin rested her hands on her belly and felt the life within.

"Beowulf will return," she said to the life inside her. "He promised us he would.

† † †

Ansa, Arla, and Alva plotted the departure with great detail. They, too, heard the news of Geatland's victory and were convinced the old woman who warned them that day in the meadow was right—that Beowulf would return and murder them after he had ravaged them over and over before skinning them alive and roasting their hearts for his dinner.

A single candle confronted the conspiratorial darkness inside the milking barn. The sisters were of one mind: they would leave in the morning just before dawn. They would make use of the twilight to gather what they needed for their journey; then escape by way of a rope over the stake wall, but at a place removed from the Main Gate where Gunner and his men kept a sharp watch.

"I sent two messengers to Vindinstedt," said Beorn. "Soon, news that you are King will reach Elin."

"Thank you, old friend," said Beowulf. "Turin, Ingmar—tomorrow you'll return to the farm, and handle matters there in my absence."

"Yes, my King," said Turin.

"Weohstan, take twenty of our best men and go with them. I want you to escort Lady Elin to Falcon's Nest. She's Queen of Geatland now, and should be here, at my side."

"Yes, my King," said Weohstan; "I'll bring her."

"What of Hygd, her daughter and granddaughter?" said Sigmund.

"Hygd will want to return to her father's farm," said Beowulf; "I entrust their safety to you, Sigmund."

"Yes, my King."

"Beorn, for the next few days, I want you here with me. After the Danes depart and the dead are underground, Geatland will need a new direction going forward, and for that, I want your advice."

"Very well, Bear's Son," said the Schaman; "I mean—my King."

A smile came to Beowulf's lips: "All of you! Listen! I'm the same man now, as before I became your king. When we're alone among ourselves, call me 'Beowulf,' or 'Bear's Son,' and don't be shy about doing so."

† † †

Elin tossed and turned in bed while Greta and Brigitte slept on each side of her. In her dream Elin saw Beowulf engulfed in fire, wielding his sword against some horrific beast that towered above him, breathing flames.

Elin shook herself awake and gasped. The sight of Greta and Brigitte comforted her. Elin got up, put her slippers on and draped a shawl over her shoulders. She went to the fireplace, placed a log on a heap of glowing embers and stayed there a moment watching until the wood caught fire. Looking into the flames they reminded Elin of her nightmare, and she averted her eyes. Taking a candle to light her way, Elin left the bedchamber.

At the bottom of the stairs, she heard a rattling sound. Holding the candle out before her, Elin walked to the cooking chamber.

There she saw the silhouette of a girl she thought was Ansa. When Elin reached out, Ansa spun around. She thrust the blade of a carving knife deep as it would go into Elin's belly.
Disbelief froze on her face, Elin dropped the candle and fell to her knees. Her eyes began to close, and blood dripped from her mouth. Ansa placed her hand on Elin's forehead and smoothed her hair back.

"There, there," said Ansa. "The pain will soon be over."

"Why?" said Elin. "Why?"

Her face drained of its color, Elin's eyes rolled back, and she crumpled to the floor. A shimmering light enveloped Ansa, but it wasn't Ansa who stood there. It was Loki, the Deceiver—Hel's father.

"I'm sorry, gentle Lady" Loki said, "but after all, a promise is a promise."

Those were the last words Elin heard.

It was after sunrise when Greta and Brigitte discovered Elin's lifeless body. Their screams brought Gunner and several warriors to Beowulf's lodge. Gunner's heart stopped at the sight of Elin, cold and dead on the floor. Greta and Brigitte were sobbing.

Gunner shook them. "Who did this?" he said.
Greta and Brigitte looked at each other and shook their heads for they didn't know. Greta's mind raced to a conclusion:

"The sisters," she said; "the three sisters who sleep in the barn —ask them!"

Gunner proceeded to the milking barn but found the sisters gone.

When Weohstan and the others arrived, it was midday. Gunner greeted them. As best he could he told what had happened. Weohstan and Turin ran to Elin's chamber. Inside they found her on her bed in her finest gown. Around her neck, she wore the amber necklace Beowulf gave her the night they wed in Bronding Land.

Greta and Brigitte were brushing Elin's hair when Weohstan and Turin entered.

"Leave us," said Weohstan to the women.

When the room had cleared, Weohstan sat on the side of the bed and buried his face in his hands. Turin knelt on the floor. He took one of Elin's hands, pressed it between his own, and wept.

"Come, Turin," said Weohstan. "Elin's killers are out there, and we're going to find them."

Turin wiped the tears from his eyes and followed Weohstan outside. Weohstan addressed the others who were waiting on their horses near the well.

"The monsters who murdered Lady Elin—I want them found!"

Gunner led them to where his search had ended earlier that morning at a fast-flowing stream. There, the telltale tracks of the three sisters vanished.

"We'll go east," said Weohstan, and east, they went, through terrain dense with trees and bracken.

They beat the bushes until they heard a loud noise coming from not far off—the sound of voices: men's voices, shouting and laughing. Weohstan signaled for the others to halt. Turin and Ingmar dismounted and crept forward on hands and knees to see what was occurring. They came to the edge of a clearing and concealed themselves behind the rotting trunk of a fallen sycamore tree. In the midst of the clearing, they saw a score of Wylfing horsemen, survivors of the encounter with Beowulf and the Spear Danes the day before.

The Wylfings had tethered their horses and made camp for the night.

The source of the Wylfings' amusement was Ansa, Arla, and Alva. The sisters had stumbled into the Wylfing camp while fleeing from Vindinstedt Farm and the Wylfings had satisfied their lusty appetites throughout the morning. Turin and Ingmar returned to where Weohstan and the others waited and told them what they saw.

"Their legs will be weak and their strength spent," said

Weohstan.

He gave the order for the Geats to creep forward on foot. When the Geats had encircled the clearing, Weohstan gave a shout, and they descended on the Wylfings from every direction. It was just as Weohstan predicted; the Wylfings were weak from their recent exertions. They rushed to arm themselves, but it was too late; the Geats prevailed. Blanketing the grass in the clearing was Wylfing blood.

During the fighting, Ansa, Arla, and Alva huddled together in the center of the clearing. Naked, eyes wide with fear, the sisters whimpered as the Geat warriors gathered around and stared at them with cold, merciless eyes.

Turin looked at Weohstan. "Shall I do it?"

"No," said Weohstan.

Turin stepped back as Weohstan advanced with his sword in hand: "Which one of you killed Beowulf Waegmunding's wife?"

Ansa sobbed and clasped Weohstan around his knees: "We swear by all the gods, Lord Waegmunding, we didn't kill Lady Elin! I took what we needed for our trip and left. But that was before the sun rose or the cock crowed."

Weohstan lifted his sword overhead.

"Truly, great Lord," said Ansa, "we left the farm soon after nightfall and had been walking ever since. I swear it!"

Weohstan checked his swing and stepped back.

"Let's take them to Falcon's Nest," said Turin. "Beowulf will deal with them."

"No," said Weohstan to his men; "I won't have the blood of children on the hands of our king, nor would Elin want it."

Weohstan turned to the warriors watching him:

"Leave them blankets and food. We finish this business now, here!"

† † †

Weohstan rode to Falcon's Nest with a heavy heart and went straight away to the Throne Room.

He found Beowulf and Beorn holding council with the new Clan Chiefs who'd been chosen to replace those who had died with

Hygelac in Frisland. When Beowulf saw Weohstan and the grim expression on his face he felt a chill pass through him. Beowulf's mind reeled. He knew at his core—Elin was gone, and there was no getting her back.

"Elin's dead, my King," said Weohstan.

Beowulf left the throne and stepped from the dais. Weohstan bowed as Beowulf stopped in front of him.

"How?" said Beowulf.

"Murdered, my King, along with the child inside her," said Weohstan.

"Who—who killed her?"

"Possibly three children she gave shelter to," Weohstan said; "but something tells me they didn't do it."

"The girls must be Knut iron jaw's whelps, my King," said Beorn. "But... like Weohstan, I don't believe it was them. I sense a higher power at work here—such malice as can't be found in Midgard."

"Are you saying a god is responsible for this?" said Beowulf.

"Perhaps more than one, my King," said the Schaman.

The blood drained from Beowulf's face:

"The three girls—where are they now?" said Beowulf.

"I left them in Vindinstedt Forest, my King," said Weohstan. "Alive."

Beowulf's jaws tightened. Blood drained from his clenched fists. A moment passed; then his eyes softened, and his body relaxed. Beowulf looked at Sigmund.

"Sigmund, you will be in charge of the Citadel while I'm gone."

"Yes, my King."

Weohstan and the Schaman followed Beowulf from the Throne Room to the stables. Together they rode in silence away from Falcon's Nest toward Vindinstedt Farm.

69

EYDÍS

Haraldr had never been to Värg Slött, the Wylfing fortress from which the Iron Wolf once ruled, but he recognized the Wylfing's young King at once—it was the look of disdain etched on his face toward all who served him, the same look as his father once wore.

Adalfuns sat slumped against the back of the throne, drunk. He started drinking and hadn't stopped after news of Onela's defeat arrived the day before. The feeling of gloom in the Throne Room was palpable. Haraldr thought that if he reached out, he could grab a fistful of the poisonous air that hung around the head of the Wylfings' King.

In his arms, Haraldr struggled with the weight of an iron-banded chest. It made the sound of coins jingling when, with knees bent, he dropped it on the floor in front of the dais.

"My Counsellor tells me you're Haraldr, the Harii Chief who paid my father tribute to smuggle chattels into Frihamm. Is that so?"

Adalfuns slurred his words, but Haraldr understood.

Yes. That would be true, Great King," said Haraldr. "And I'm here to do so again."

"Hah!" said Adalfuns. He drained his mead cup and belched. "I thought you Harii had all departed for Germania."

"Yes, Great King. We've returned to our ancestral home and will remain there if the gods are willing, but we want to reestablish ties with Frihamm; which you, great king, control, now that Onela is dead and his nephew on the throne at Uppsala."

"Ah," said Adulfuns. "So you know about that?"

"Yes," said Haraldr. "bad news spreads quickly."

"So! How much have you got in the chest?" said Adulfuns. He tossed his mead cup aside.

"The same as before Great King," said Haraldr. "Only more."

"Very well, then," said Adalfuns. "Let's see it."

"May the Captain of your Guard strike me dead if I disappoint you, Great King."

Unamused, Balog, Captain of Adulfuns' Body Guard, scowled at the Harii Chief and drew his forefinger side-to-side, cut-throat style. Haraldr met Balog's death-stare and smiled.

"Well," said Adalfuns, "get on with it."

Haraldr opened the chest and lifted back the top. In less time than it took Adalfuns to call out or for Balog to draw his sword, Haraldr removed a throwing knife from the chest and hurled it. The point of the blade struck Adalfuns in the throat with such force the blade continued out the back of his neck and stuck in the Wylfing's Throne.

In an instant, Balog made good his threat. Haraldr lay dying in a pool of his blood, face down on the floor. As darkness overcame him, his last thought was of his daughter and grandson.

† † †

Eydís sat on the grass beneath a blue spruce tree while her son, Ikin, rested his head on her lap.

"Tell me again about my father," said Ikin.

"Well," said Eydís, "he was tall, like your Grandfather and, like your Grandpoppa, he was a mighty warrior who was both feared and honored."

"Is it true the Wylfings called him 'Widow Maker'?" said Ikin.

"Yes, my son. It's true.

"Why?" said Ikin.

"It's complicated," said Eydís. She smoothed Ikin's chestnut colored hair back away from his brow.

"Tell me, Mother. Did they name him that because he killed so many Wylfings?"

"Yes."

"Why?"

Eydís waited a moment before answering.

"Your father took revenge on the Wylfings because they killed someone close to him—someone, he loved very, very much."

"Was it the woman who bore my half-brother. The king of the Thunder-Geats Grandfather calls the Bear's Son?"

"Yes. King Beowulf is your half-brother."

"I want to meet Beowulf one day," said Ikin.

"Gods willing, perhaps you will."

A Clan Chief whom Eydís recognized approached the tree beneath which they were resting. Out of respect, Eydís and Ikin stood.

"I'm sorry, Eydís," said the man, "but you have to leave—you and Ikin."

The man speaking was Gundur, a Cimbrii clan Chief speaking on behalf of the women who composed the Council of Elders that represented the three tribes: Harii, Cimbrii, and Teutons.

"Why," asked Eydis. She held her son close to her as she spoke.

"By now, all the Wylfing clans will know it was Haraldr who murdered their king."

"So?" said Eydís.

"The Elders fear the Wylfings will seek revenge on our people," said Gundur.

"What proof do the Elders have?"

"They haven't any evidence, Eydís," said Gundur. "As I said: it is what the Elders fear may happen."

"Then they are frightened old women—all of them!" said Eydís.

Gundur shrugged but said nothing.

"What if I refuse to leave the village?" said Eydís.

"Refuse, and you and your son will be taken to Värg Slött in chains and turned over to whoever rules Öster Götaland."

Are my father's brothers of like mind with the Elders?" said Eydís.

Gundur nodded and hung his head.

"Then, be it so, and 'Good riddance!' I say," said Eydís. "Good riddance to the Elders, my uncles, and my tribe. From this day forward I'm no longer Harii! And neither is my son!"

Eydís started away.

"Eydís," said Gundur.

She turned and faced him. He held out a leather coin purse.

"Your uncles want you to have this. There's silver wedges and some gold coins inside. Here. Take it."

Eydís spat on the ground at Gundur's feet.

"Please," he said. "Take it, if only for the sake of your son."

Biting down on her rage, Eydís snatched the coin purse from Gundur's hand.

Beowulf, Weohstan, and Beorn rode long and hard through the night and arrived at the Farm after sunrise. Turin was there to greet them, though no one spoke. After they dismounted and grooms led the horses away, Beowulf turned to Weohstan and Turin.

"Have our men build a pyre," he said.

Beowulf went alone to his bedchamber. Illuminated by candlelight, he found Brigitte and Greta sitting beside the bed, attending Elin in death as they had in life. Their eyes were red and swollen, for neither had slept nor had they ceased weeping. Seeing Beowulf, they got to their feet, bowed and left the room.

Beowulf sat on the edge of the bed and looked at Elin's lifeless body. He took hold of one of her hands. It felt cold to his touch.

"Forgive me, Elin," said Beowulf. "I should have been here for you."

Through much of the morning, Beowulf sat motionless beside Elin. In his mind, he revisited as many moments as he could recollect, moments that composed their brief life together; then, knowing it was time, he gathered Elin into his arms and carried her to a pyre in the center of the palisade.

Beowulf set the pyre on fire, stepped back and joined the others to watch it burn. They stood there past midday while the flames did their work. Behind them, the Freemen and their families had gathered. The women sang traditional laments, dear to Geatfolk and Brondings alike, and many a warrior wept, so great was their love and devotion to the wife of their Lord, now king.

Beowulf turned to Beorn and Weohstan.

"After I've gathered Elin's ashes, I'm taking them away from here."

"Where will you go?" said Beorn.

"North," said Beowulf, "perhaps to the lake in the clouds.

The Schaman nodded.

"What are we to do in your absence?" said Weohstan.

"I'm appointing you, along with Beorn and Sigmund, to rule in my absence."

"When will you return?" said Turin.

"When I'm ready," Beowulf said. "I want you to run the farm in my absence, Turin. That would be something our father would give his blessing to."

"Thank you for your trust, my King," said Turin.

Beowulf removed the Crown of Geatland from his head and handed it to Beorn.

"Keep this safe," Beowulf said to the shaman.

† † †

Traveling at night, and sleeping by day, Eydís, and her son made their way to the coast of Germania. Thinking they were safe for the time-being and that neither her people nor Wylfings had pursued them, they continued walking west until they came to a small settlement at the mouth of a river where she saw several Longships at anchor.

Seeing men loading and unloading wares off the ships, Eydís hesitated. She thought about going into the woods, around the trading post, until she saw several women fetching water from a well. Seeing she would not be the only woman there, Eydís approached them. When the three women saw Eydís and the boy with her, their eyes widened with fear.

They shook their heads side-to-side as if trying to shout: "Be gone!' It was then Eydís saw the women's ankles were chained together. Terror on their faces was the last thing Eydís saw.

† † †

When Eydís awoke, the back of her head pounded against her skull, and someone had bound her with chains. She looked around, but in the darkness that greeted her eyes, she knew not where she was. She reached out hoping to find her son beside her, but all she felt was the straw on which she sat. The stench of urine and feces was gut-wrenching. Outside, from a place not far off, Eydís could hear the loud banter and raucous laughter of men—a hundred, or more.

She called out: “Ikin?”

Nothing. Only silence.

“Ikin?” Eydís said again.

“Quiet!” said a woman close to her through the darkness. She sounded neither young nor old but desperate, and she spoke in a hiss intended as a whisper. “If they hear us talking they’ll punish us.”

Using the same hushed voice as the woman, “Who?” said Eydís. “Who will punish us?”

“The Saxon slave traders,” said another voice, also a woman’s.

“How many are you?” said Eydís.

“Thirteen,” said a third woman’s voice; “Counting you.”

“When I came here I had my son with me,” said.

“We know,” said the first voice. “We tried to warn you away, but it was too late.”

“Do you know where they took him?” said Eydís.

Silence.

“Please,” said Eydís, “if you know where he is, please—tell me!”

“Your son is with the other men the Saxons captured,” said another woman. “We’re all to be sold.”

At that moment a flap that covered an entrance was lifted back allowing sunlight to enter, and illuminating a large, circular tent supported by poles and covered with cow hides stitched together.

A bald, bearded dwarf entered the tent. In one hand, the dwarf held a coiled whip made of braided leather. Several festering sores adorned the crown of slaver's head.

“By the gods, it stinks in here,” said the dwarf in a high-pitched voice.

He let the whip unravel to the ground; then, with a flick of his hand, snapped it. The hiss and crack the whip made as it sliced through the air caused many of the women to cry out.

Pleased by the terror he aroused, the dwarf laughed and slapped his knees before cracking the whip a second time.

“Out!” said the dwarf. “Everyone! Outside!”

Thirteen women, including Eydís, exited from the tent in single file. As they stepped outside, they had to shield their eyes from the brightness of the sun until their eyes adjusted to the light.

“Strip!” said the dwarf. “Now! All of you! Refuse, and I’ll rip the skin from your bones with this leather snake!"

Again the dwarf snapped his whip.

"And who's going to buy us after you've whipped us to shreds?" said Eydís.

"What's that, you bitch?" said the dwarf. "Do you dare defy me?"

"Yes," said Eydís.

A tall, muscular warrior, with long blond hair that flowed down his back from beneath his conical bronze helm, walked up behind the dwarf and stopped.

"She's right, Andur," said the warrior. "They're no good as chattels if they're cut and bleeding when we try to sell them. If you're in the mood to kill another woman, you're going to have to pay for her—in advance, just as before."

"Smell them for yourself!" said the dwarf. "The captives need to take off their rags and wash with water and vinegar."

"My name is Jules," said the warrior. "The cut-throat with the whip is Andur. He's an ugly little thing, isn't he?"

The veins on the dwarf's forehead bulged, and his cheeks flushed crimson.

"But here's a piece of truth for you all to bite on," said Jules, "he's every bit as ugly on the outside—as I am on the inside. I'll cut your throats and put you out of your misery if that's what you want."

A woman no more than fifteen winters young stepped forward.

"It's what I want," said the girl.

Astonished by what he heard, the Saxon looked the girl up and down. Wash the dirt from her face; brush her tangled hair and put a clean shift on her and a blind man could see she was a natural beauty. The Saxon took a deep breath, shook his head and sighed.

"Such a waste," he said.

In the time he takes to blink twice, he drew his knife and slashed the girl's throat beneath her chin.

The girl crumpled to the ground. Eydís and the other women looked away so as not to see her trying to gulp breaths of air while her life spilled out and stained the grass red.

"Now, then," said the Saxon, "those of you who want to live will do as we tell you: so strip off your garments and wash. There are sponges and water mixed with vinegar in the barrels behind me. The choice is yours, my lovelies. Live. Or, die."

† † †

Naked and bound like the women, the male captives were prodded by the slavers' spears and hardwood canes into the same fenced-in enclosure. Eydís saw her son straight away. He stood alone, teeth chattering and body shaking from head to foot.

"Ikin!" said Eydís.

She hurried to his side. Kneeling, she held him close. His eyes were red and swollen and glazed over. In an instant, Eydís realized her son had been drugged, along with the other males to make them docile and disinclined to escape.

"What did they do to you?" said Eydís.

Ikin said nothing, nor did he make any indication of having recognized his mother.

Before Eydís could say another word, two Saxon slavers ripped the boy from her arms. They dragged him out of the enclosure, up steps to an auction block, in front of which stood men of all stripes from many different tribes throughout Germania and beyond.

When Eydís tried to push her way through the throng of captives to follow her son, a slave-dealer with a staff struck her behind the knees. The blow toppled Eydís to the ground. While several of the women tried to comfort her, Eydís screamed her son's name until her voice gave out and she couldn't speak at all.

The auctioneer was a Saxon, bigger around the belly than his legs were long.

"We'll get things started with the best of the lot," said the auctioneer. "Look at this lad—young and supple he is and never enjoyed. Who'll start the bidding at ten gold rings?"

"You say no one's enjoyed the boy," said an Angle at the front of the crowd.

"That's right," said the auctioneer. "See for yourself, Carolinus, —the blush in the boy's cheeks."

"Those aren't the cheeks I want to see," said the Angle, causing a ripple of laughter from the crowd.

"Before I shell-out ten gold rings, I want proof he's a virgin!"

said a Frisian.

"That's right," said a one-eyed Syrian slave trader from Accra. "Give us proof."

The slave trader's name was Fynegeld. The ship he commanded was the Red Crow, identifiable by its crimson sail and a crow with wings spread and black as black can be, centered on the sail.

As the crowd shouted their agreement, the auctioneer frowned. He turned Ikin around, so the boy's back was to the men.

"Bend him over," said the auctioneer to the dwarf.

The dwarf struck Ikin a blow that knocked the air out of the boy, doubling him over.

"Now keep him like that," said the auctioneer.

The dwarf grabbed Ikin's head in an arm-lock and held him bent over, so Ikin's forehead almost touched his knees.

Without hesitating, the auctioneer rammed his thumb up the boy's shite-hole. Whatever drug the Saxon slavers gave Ikin, it couldn't silence the ear-splitting, terrible scream that issued from his core.

Watching from the enclosure, Eydís collapsed to her knees and sobbed.

"Proof enough?" said the auctioneer.

"Yes," said Fynegeld. "I'll give you twenty gold rings."

"Will anyone bid more?" said the auctioneer. "Will anyone give me twenty-one?"

His question hovered over the crowd. Silence.

"Twenty, once? Twenty, twice? Twenty, thrice? Very well—Done! Sold to Fynegeld for twenty gold rings."

Lifting herself off the ground, Eydís watched the trader's bodyguards lead Ikin away with a rope. The loose end formed a noose around Ikin's neck the way a farmer might lead a lamb from its mother to slaughter.

† † †

Eydís waited until midday to be auctioned and sold for five gold rings and another ten wedges of silver. It was the Saxon, Jules, who bought her and two other women. When the auction concluded, and there were no more captives to sell, Jules and each of his men, twenty in all, raped the women at least once. When their lust was satiated, Jules grabbed hold of Eydís's hair and pulled her to the bank of the river.

"Wash right there," he said, "where I can see you. Then we'll see about finding you something to wear."

Eydís limped bow-legged into the river. Although it pained her, she sat on a flat rock submerged in the water. While she massaged her legs, the fast-flowing water washed away the dried blood from her thighs and private places, along with the fluids from the men.

"Do you know why I shared you with my men?" said Jules.

She made no reply. Jules tossed a pebble at Eydís that struck the back of her head.

"No," said Eydís. Her voice was hoarse, akin to a whisper.

Jules struck her with a second pebble: "No, my Lord," he said.

"No, my Lord," said Eydís.

"I shared you with them because sharing what I have keeps those dogs loyal. But there's another reason I let them sheath their swords in you."

"Please tell me, my Lord," said Eydís.

She was willing to play the Saxon's game if it would save her from more pain.

"Much better," said Jules. "I let them take you so you'd know you're nothing special. You're a chattel. A thing for me to use as I please. That's all. Understand me, woman?"

Eydís looked over her shoulder at the Saxon: "Of course, my Lord."

"Good," said Jules. "Can you cook?"

"Yes, my Lord. With the right ingredients and the right herbs, like those growing all around us, and along the riverbank, I could prepare a meal befitting a king, Lord Kommander. I could make enough for your men as well."

"Oh, really?" said Jules. "A meal fit for a king, you say." The notion piqued his interest.

"Yes, my Lord. Really."

For a woman such as Eydís, the rest would be child's play.

She waited until Jules, and his men could do nothing more than snore and fart like pigs as they slept. The herbs, roots, and mushrooms she added to the roasted rabbit stew had induced a dreamless sleep among her captors; added to which, the Saxons were already drunk on mead and ale by the time the women served them dinner.

It bothered Eydís that she hadn't warned the women about the stew before Jules allowed them to partake of it. Now, they, too, slept. Doing what she'd done in secret was the only way Eydís could be certain no one betrayed her.

Eydís rolled Jules off of her without making a sound. She was, after all, a Harii, and taught, as were all Harii children, to survive in strange surroundings using stealth.

Not bothering to put on the shift Jules had thrown at her—his "gift" to her, he called it, Eydís searched until she found his knife.

Eydís took her time: she hummed a song that was one of Ecgtheow's favorites while she sat by the campfire sharpening the blade. Focusing on honing the edge of the Saxon's knife kept Eydís's mind off Ikin. But that lasted only so long.

† † †

Beginning with Jules, Eydís cut the testicles off every Saxon and did so without waking them. It took her into the twilight that preceded dawn the following day. When she had finished and was able to see, she saw the Saxon blood that covered her.

Eydís bathed in the cold, rushing water of the river until the sun shone over the surrounding hills.

Eydís found an assortment of women's clothes in a cargo chest. She found a shift her size, a coat made from elk hides, and boots lined with rabbit fur. From among the dead, she took a bow, a quiver of arrows, a sack of provisions, Jules' knife and other supplies.

Eydís looked at the remaining three women, still asleep.

"May the gods be with you," said Eydís.

The sun felt good on her back as she walked west.

70

DAYS OF DARKNESS

It was late afternoon when Beowulf left the farm with Elin's ashes. He rode straight away to the place he and Elin loved most. Beowulf removed his helm, tied it to the saddle and stroked Storm Bringer's neck.

"*Return to the farm, old friend. I'll be staying here a while.*"

Storm Bringer nuzzled Beowulf's face and left. There at the hot spring by the waterfall, Beowulf cast Elin's ashes to the wind. From there he hiked to the cave he once shared with Lüma where her bones remained.

Entering that place, he felt the damp, cool air against his face. He sat with his back against one side of the cave where he and his fur mother once slept. He stared into the darkness. It wasn't long before Beowulf saw Death sitting across from him.

"I knew you'd come," said Beowulf.

"I'm never far from you, Bear's Son. Besides, you look like you could use some company."

"I'm tired of killing," said Beowulf. "Just the thought of it sickens me."

"It's what you do best, Bear's son. It's your fate. Like your father, you were born to it."

"You're wrong," said Beowulf. He closed his eyes. "I'm tired of serving you... and I'm weary of talking."

"Makes no difference," said Death, "I can abide silence."

† † †

When Storm Bringer reached Vindinstedt Farm, Gunner brought the stallion inside the Palisade and summoned Turin. Turin searched the saddle but saw no traces of blood. He took that as a sign Beowulf was neither dead nor in harm's way. Searching through the saddlebags, Turin looked toward Vindinstedt Forest in the distance.

"You're out there somewhere, aren't you, my brother, my king!"

For twenty-nine days and nights, Beowulf sat with Death in the darkness of the cave. He ate nothing and drank but few drops of water that trickled down the inside of the cave from an aperture in the rock.

On the thirtieth day Elin appeared before his eyes as in a dream:

"Now's not your time, Beowulf. Geatland needs you—your people need you. Leave this place of death. Live!"

"Elin," said Beowulf, but she disappeared like morning mist with the arrival of the sun.

"I'm through sitting here with you," said Beowulf, but Death had already departed.

Weak from not having eaten in thirty days, and unsteady on his feet, Beowulf stumbled outside, into the light of day, not knowing his hair and beard had turned bright white. A light rain was falling.

Beowulf tried to walk, but his eyes rebelled against the light. At first blinded by the glare of the sun, Beowulf slipped on a moss covered rock. As he fell backward, his head struck the hard ground and darkness overtook him.

† † †

The next morning, when Beowulf regained consciousness, he knew neither where he was nor who he was. He pushed himself up and felt a dull ache between his temples. Reaching one hand to the back of his head, he felt a large lump, painful to the touch. When Beowulf took his hand away and looked, there was dried blood on his fingertips. Aware that eyes were on him, Beowulf looked to the side and saw wolves, twelve or more.

Adalwolf stepped close to Beowulf. "*You've changed, Bear's Son. Your fur is white as bleached bone; still, I know it's you.*"

"*I'm sorry, Wolf Lord,*" Beowulf said, "*I don't recognize you, but I understand your words.*"

"*Because you speak the language of the Forest Folk, Bear's Son. You learned it as a cub. I am Adalwolf, leader of the pack you see before you.*"

"*Forgive me, hunters of the night, and you, Lord Adalwolf, for I don't know where or who I am.*"

"*Something beyond my reckoning afflicts you, Bear's Son, but we're here for you should you need us.*"

That said, Adalwolf and the Gray Brethren left, and though Beowulf couldn't see them, he sensed one or more wolves watching him.

Adalwolf called me, 'Bear's Son'—and what was that about my living here as a child? What's happened to me, and why was I not afraid in the company of wolves?

Those questions danced like Lightning Bugs through the dark corners of Beowulf's mind. He staggered to the water beneath the waterfall, removed his linen undershirt and knelt by the edge of the pool. Beowulf studied his reflection.

Despite numerous scars that marked his upper body he looked like a warrior in his prime; except now his hair and beard were white.

Who are you? Beowulf said to his reflection. What are you?

Consumed with hunger, Beowulf put aside his unanswered questions, stripped, and eased himself into the pool and sank underwater. When he surfaced, he held a wiggling trout between his teeth. Beowulf climbed out of the pool and without delay bit into the fish. In a short time, he consumed many—all but the heads, guts, tails, and bones.

When Beowulf had eaten his fill, he dressed and went to the hot spring where he found a sheathed sword and a shirt of chainmail on the ground; it's hand-forged iron rings colored with rust. There was also a knife sheathed to a wide leather belt, and he saw a spear.

"I don't know who I am, but I know I'm no thief."

Feeling his strength return, Beowulf left that battle gear on the ground and walked away from the hot spring—due east.

While Sigmund remained at Falcon's Nest, Weohstan and Beorn arrived at Vindinstedt Farm with the King's Guard, all one-hundred of them.

Turin and Ingmar greeted Weohstan and Beorn as they rode past the Main Gate. When they had settled around the table in the Banquet Hall, Weohstan was first to speak:

"What news of Beowulf?" he said.

"Nothing," said Turin.

"Your message said Storm Bringer returned to the farm with Beowulf's helm," said the Schaman.

"Yes," said Turin, "and in one of the saddlebags was the urn that carried Elin's ashes to Falcon's Nest; all of which tells me Beowulf is probably alive--not dead."

Weohstan spoke up: "And you know this is true because?"

"It's what I think Beowulf meant to tell us," said Turin, "when he sent Storm Bringer home."

"Tomorrow," said Weohstan, "we'll beat the bushes bare until we find him."

"Something tells me he's not in his right mind," said Beorn, "though I confess, I can no longer say what his right mind is."

Beowulf traveled east in his boots and leather breeches without knowing why or even where he was going. As he felt his strength return it delighted him to leap from rock to rock along the riverbank. The bear's son followed the river as it snaked east. When the sun on his skin became too much, he dove into the river. He laughed as the white water rapids whisked him downstream over falls and through canyons.

Beowulf arrived at a bend in the river where the water became calm. He pulled himself onto a rock and rested there conversing with turtles and dragonflies until he felt like moving on. When and wherever Beowulf encountered one of the Forest Folk, he greeted it in the Silent Tongue before resuming his journey.

Beowulf didn't know where he was, where he was going or where the river might take him; nor did he care. He felt light, carefree, a part of everything under the sun, moon, and stars, free from all woe and suffering.

Weohstan, Beorn, and Turin halted their horses at the edge of the forest and faced the warriors accompanying them.

"Listen to me," said Beorn, "all of you! The creatures of Vindinstedt Forest know where Beowulf is; therefore, do no harm to them. Look for signs of Beowulf's presence; look for his tracks, search for anything that suggests he was here, but above all—do no harm to the Forest Folk!"

"Any questions?" said Weohstan.

A moment passed. No one spoke.

"Very well then," said Turin; "let's find our king!"

When Turin came upon Beowulf's battle gear at the hot spring, he blew on his ram's horn and waited for the others to join him. When Beorn, Weohstan and the men with them arrived at the hot spring, looks of disbelief crept into their faces.

"By the gods," said Weohstan, "why would he leave his battle gear behind—in the wilderness of all places?"

"Because he knows he doesn't need it," said Turin.

"Or perhaps," said Beorn, then he stopped himself.

"Say it, Beorn—perhaps what?" said Weohstan.

"Maybe he doesn't know who he is."

"What are you saying!" said Weohstan.

"Beowulf may be out of his head—and if he survives, he survives by his instincts alone."

"As the bear's son, you mean," said Turin.

"Yes," said Beorn, "as the bear's son."

"Unless," said Weohstan, "our king is dead!"

"No, Weohstan," said Beorn. "Trust me—if Beowulf were dead I'd feel it in my bones."

† † †

Throughout the remainder of the summer, the Geats searched for Beowulf. At the end of the growing season, Weohstan called off the search. He and Beorn returned to Falcon's Nest to placate the young new Clan Chiefs who clamored for answers as to King Beowulf's whereabouts.

† † †

After conferring with Sigmund, Weohstan and Beorn decided the best course of action was to lie; hence, words went out from the Citadel that Beowulf was in Brondingland and would return when it suited him and not a day earlier.

Turin returned to Vindinstedt Farm to manage the harvest, although his heart wasn't in it.

71

A QUEENDOM FOR THE TAKING

Two more summers came and went and, still, Beowulf remained gone. That autumn, Mikla, Captain of the Coastguards at Land's End, entered the Throne Room where Beorn, Sigmund, and Weohstan were seated at a table once used by Ragmund when transcribing King Hrethel' edicts. They had been conferring about matters at hand, but most of all the chaos in Wylfing Land, following the assassination of King Adalfuns.

That Mikla entered in haste, almost out of breath, was enough for the three to end their deliberations.

"Mikla," said Weohstan. "What is it that brings you here?"

"Yes," said Sigmund, "Catch your breath and tell us the news you bear?"

"Calamity has befallen the Spear Danes, My Lords."

"Tell us," said the Schaman.

"There are others with me, my Lords, who can tell it better. They're waiting in the Banquet Hall."

"Who?" said Weohstan.

"Queen Wealtheow, her daughter, Freawaru, and son, Prince Hrothmund."

"What?" said Sigmund. "The Harbor Master said nothing of their ship's arrival."

"They arrived at Land's End, my Lords, in a knarr laden with cargo. They disembarked in secrecy," said Mikla, "accompanied by Lord Ulthur."

"Escort them in at once," said the Schaman.

Mikla looked at Sigmund and Weohstan for confirmation.

"You heard Magister Beorn, Mikla. Do it!"

Mikla bowed. "My pardon, Magister Beorn. Yes, my Lords. At once."

"I always thought it a mistake not to have spies in Daneland after Ecgtheow returned," said Weohstan.

"Too late for looking backward, my Lords," said the Schaman.

Beorn, Weohstan, and Sigmund stood to receive their visitors.

Time had not diminished Queen Wealtheow's or her daughter, Freawaru's, outward beauty; yet on this day their eyes were red and swollen from the salt spray they endured during the crossing from Mork Sand to Land's End; but, and more than that, their eyes expressed great sadness.

Lord Ulthur and Prince Hrothmund stood in the middle, between the two women, their faces were grim. Behind, escorting them inside the Throne Room were twelve of Beowulf's Personal Guard, the Kungens Vakter.

With a wave of his hand, Sigmund, Captain of the Guards, dismissed the Kungens Vakter to resume their stations outside the Throne Room.

"Welcome to Falcon's Nest and the Citadel, great Queens," said Sigmund. "And you, Prince Hrothmund and you, Lord Ulthur—our heartfelt welcome to you all."

Prince Hrothmund and Lord Ulthur saluted their hosts with a hand placed over their hearts as they bowed.

"Thank you, Lord Sigmund," said Queen Wealtheow. "We remember when you came to Daneland with King Beowulf on behalf of my people and my late husband."

Weohstan and Sigmund exchanged looks that mirrored their surprise upon hearing of Hrothgar's passing. The Schaman's expression remained fixed as if he had known of this event already.

"If I may, my Queen," said Lord Ulthur to Wealtheow.

Wealtheow fought back her tears and nodded.

"Poison killed King Hrothgar in Germania, or so we believe; assassinated by his nephew, Hrothulf, son of Herogarated, the same night our King was celebrating his victory over the Heathobards and the return of Freawaru."

"And the Heathobard's King—Ingeld?" said Weohstan.

"Dead," said Ulthur, "by King Hrothgar's hand as Prince Hrothulf looked on. But there is much more to tell, my Lords, and I ask that you hear me out."

"Of course," said Sigmund and Weohstan in one voice.

"Upon our army's return to Daneland, along with Princess Freawaru and her father's ashes, Hrothulf declared himself King of Daneland and murdered Prince Hrethric, Hrothgar's rightful heir. Queen Wealtheow and her children fled in the misty twilight preceding dawn. Hrothulf has offered gold in exchange for their deaths so that none may contest his Kingship over Zealand."

"And what of King Hrothgar's younger brother, Prince Halga?" said Sigmund. "Surely he must have opposed Hrothulf's treachery?"

"On information given him by Hrothulf," said Ulthur, Prince Halga died pursuing the Heathobard Clan Chief responsible for poisoning his brother. The Heathobard said Hrothulf ordered it, in exchange for letting the Heathobard escape after the battle."

"Is Lord Unferth of the same mind, as to Hrothulf's part in all this?" said Sigmund.

"Sadly, Lord Unferth died valiantly along with Lord Wulfgar in the battle. But they acquitted themselves well, and sent many a Heathobard to Hell."

"Queen Wealtheow, Queen Freawaru, and you, Prince Hrothmund," said Weohstan, with a sweep of his hand toward the Schaman, "this is Magister Beorn, our king's most trusted friend, and adviser."

The Schaman bowed. The Danes did likewise.

"You are widely known, Magister Beorn," said Wealtheow, "both in Zealand, and across the Whale Road."

The Schaman was about to speak but stopped himself. He looked at Weohstan and Sigmund.

"By all means, Magister Beorn, speak your mind," said Weohstan.

"The usurper, Hrothulf, is dead, killed by his brother-in-law, Heroweard. Heroweard remained loyal to Queen Wealtheow. But he, too, has been killed—by a friend of Hrothulf's during an attack on Heorot. Warriors loyal to Hrothulf have burned that once great Hall to the ground. It pains me to tell you this, gentle Queen, the Scylding Dynasty of your father and his father's father is no more."

"How can you possibly know this, Magister Beorn?" said Wealtheow. "We left Daneland no more than fifteen days ago."

Tears flowed from Freawaru's and Hrothmund's eyes.

"I saw it in a vision," said the Schaman, "and asked Kungörn, Lord of the Sky Folk, to confirm what he could of the past goings-on in Zealand. Believe it, gentle Queen. All I have told you is true."

If it is sanctuary you seek, you shall have it, great Queen," said Weohstan.

Weohstan looked at Sigmund and the Schaman. "Agreed?"

Both the Beorn and Sigmund nodded.

"For now, great Queen," said Sigmund, "It might be best if you stay here at the Citadel until some new course of action presents itself."

"Thank you, my Lords," said Wealtheow.

"I suggest our guests be shown to quarters to rest," said Weohstan. "You, too, Lord Ulthur."

"Thank you, my Lords. For my part, I must return to Daneland to see what remains of our fleet and to rally those Clan Chiefs and warriors who may still be loyal to Queen Wealtheow and Prince Hrothmund."

"Very well," said Ulthur.

Tears ran down Wealtheow's cheeks. Her son, Hrothmund, placed an arm around his mother to steady her as Sigmund ushered them away.

"Lord Ulthur," said the Schaman, "a moment before you take your leave."

† † †

After Sigmund had returned, and all four men took seats at the Scribe's Table, servants entered with four cups, a small corked keg of cold dark beer, a large round of cheese, sliced meats and fresh, baked bread.

"What is it, Magister Beorn?" said Ulthur.

"Just this—Would your people consider resettling?" said the Schaman.

"Resettling?" said Ulthur. "To where?"

"Here," said the Schaman. "to a place here in Geatland."

So surprised was he by what he was hearing, Sigmund spit a mouthful of beer.

"What?" said Sigmund. He wiped beer off his chin. "Are you serious, Magister Beorn?"

"Truly, Beorn, that is something only Beowulf can grant," said Weohstan.

"But Beowulf's not here," said the Schaman," And who among us knows when he'll return?"

"No one," said Sigmund.

"True," said the Schaman. "No one. And did he not leave it to we three—to rule in his absence?"

"Yes," answered Weohstan. "He did."

"But the problem remains," said Ulthur, "where in Geatland might Spear Danes loyal to Prince Hrothmund settle, and still be welcomed by your people?"

"Skane," said the Schaman. "Do you know the place?"

"I know the place well," said Ulthur. "It lies just east of Lands End. A peninsula claimed by Storm Geats and Wylfings, alike; but settled by neither."

"Precisely," said the Schaman. "As your spies have no doubt told you, there's a sheltered cove there; which could easily accommodate a small fleet of ships, if need be. On the heights above the cove are rocks sufficient to build a watch tower, or Keep and, further inland, along the peninsula are forests where wood can be gotten to build lodges and fortify a sizable village. Fresh water is abundant from many small rivers that pour into the great Vanir River; which eventually empties into the sea. In Skane, there is also flatland with rich, dark soil for planting crops, and pasture land for horses, sheep, and oxen."

"And who would govern the Spear Danes," said Ulthur, "You, Magister Beorn? Or the three of you? Or would it be King Beowulf, should he ever return to Geatland? Who would we Spear Danes in exile look to, for permission to live in Skane?"

"Calm yourself, Lord Ulthur," said Weohstan. "I think I see where Magister Beorn is going with this."

"Well, then, by all means, tell me," said Ulthur. "For the idea leaves me dumbfounded."

"What if," said Weohstan, "Prince Hrothmund ruled Skane, as Regent for his mother, Queen Wealtheow."

"And why shouldn't Queen Wealtheow rule Skane?"

"Hah!" said Sigmund. "By all the gods, now I see where this is going!"

"Then tell me, Lord Sigmund," said Ulthur. "Before any more of this splendid beer goes to my head and has me seeing double."

"What Magister Beorn offers is a place. What Lord Weohstan suggests is a Spear Dane who, by right of succession, could rule there. The question then becomes—what of your Queen—yes?"

"Yes," said Ulthur, "What of my Queen, and Princess Freawaru?"

"Queen Wealtheow is royal born—and a Wylfing," said the Schaman, "and without someone on the throne at Varg Slott, Öster Gotaland will remain divided and in chaos."

"And how do we convince the Wylfing Clan Chiefs to accept Wealtheow as their Queen?"

"We make them an offer they can't refuse," said the Schaman.

† † †

Led by Sigmund and Weohstan, a fleet of sixty Longships carrying over two-thousand Storm Geats sailed by day to Land's End. Then, waiting until darkness fell, the Storm Geats sailed east through the night, then north, through the early morning fog.

At dawn, ten ships carrying four-hundred battle-hardened Storm Geats led by Sigmund sailed into the Fjord where Frihamm lie nestled.

Overcoming the Night Watch at the waterfront, and Sigmund took command of Frihamm before its inhabitants discovered the Storm Geats' presence in their streets.

Meanwhile, the remainder of the Geat's fleet, some fifty ships in all, sailed into the bay that housed the Wylfing fleet—the few ships that Adalfuns possessed, and set them on fire. The few Wylfings occupying Värg Slött watched the Geats disembark from their Longships.

Sigmund sent an emissary to the Main Gate of the fortress with a single demand—that whoever was in charge surrender. Seeing no point defending Värg Slött against such a superior force, the self-appointed Gate Warden of Värg Slött, a Wylfing chief named Helig, turned over the fortress.

After securing Värg Slött, Sigmund escorted Queen Wealtheow to the Throne Room. The Geats sent riders throughout the towns and villages surrounding Värg Slött proclaiming the return of Princess Wealtheow, daughter of the Iron Wolf and rightful Queen of the Wylfings and Spear Danes, along with her daughter, Freawaru, once Queen of the Heathobards.

Not long after that day, Wylfing Clan Chiefs accepted Wealtheow's invitation to convene in neutral Frihamm to discuss the future of their tribe. Although none were pleased by the intervention of the Storm Geats, the Wylfings welcomed the prospect of peace, now that they had a practiced Queen of Wylfing blood to rule Öster Götaland.

† † †

Wealtheow showed no emotion as she and Freawaru entered the Throne Room of her father, and her brother before her. Wealtheow walked directly to the Throne and stopped. She stared long and hard at the blood-stained throne where Adalfuns met his doom at the hand of the Harii Chief, Haraldr.

Wealtheow chose a Wylfing Clan Chief named Tokson to be her confidante and chief adviser concerning matters of war and peace. A fearless warrior and respected Clan Chief, Wealtheow looked to Tokson for another compelling reason; he and the Thunder-Geat, Lord Sigmund, were distant cousins dating far back to a time when Storm Geats and Wylfings lived as one great tribe.

"Come closer, daughter," said Wealtheow to Freawaru. "I want you to feel this."

Wealtheow and her daughter stood on the dais. Wealtheow ran her fingers over the blood stains on the back of the throne where Haraldr's knife entered Adalfun's throat and continued through his neck. The blood had run down the backrest, onto the seat, where it pooled and later hardened.

Wealtheow pointed to the blood-stained throne.

"Touch it, daughter, and learn by what you see and feel."

"I'll have the throne cleaned immediately, my Queen." said Tokson.

"No," said Wealtheow. "Leave the throne as it is, Lord Tokson. I never want to forget at what cost a throne is won and lost."

† † †

With peace established throughout Götaland, Beowulf's Regents: Beorn, Weohstan and Sigmund focused their attention on helping the Spear Danes, those who remained loyal to dead King Hrothgar's remaining son, and heir: Prince Hrothmund.

While Queen Wealtheow set about the immense task of reorganizing the Wylfing Tribe, Prince Hrothmund remained with the Schaman. Under Beorn's tutelage, Prince Hrothmund learned the mechanics of governing a decimated people. No small task, considering the Spear Danes who followed Lord Ulthur out of Daneland were dispirited and needed a firm hand to inspire and rally them toward the future, no matter what that future might be.

When Lord Ulthur returned from the last of many secretive trips to Daneland, he brought with him no fewer than forty Longships, and three times as many knarrs carrying supplies and the families of the two-thousand warriors who made the trip with him to Skane.

Though accepting of living in exile, it was the hope of every Spear Dane, every man, woman and child, that, one day, gods willing, they'd return west, to their fatherland.

70

A KING REBORN

Ignoring the rain that dampened their leather jerkins, Robbyn and the Twins crept through the forest, their bows fitted with arrows dipped in poison and held at the ready. The tracks they followed throughout the morning troubled them and more than once they thought of turning back. Unlike anything they had ever seen, these tracks were a mix of booted feet and bear tracks side by side: at least one adult bear and a cub.

Just a week before the three had stalked, trapped and killed a male bear in a glen fed by a stream not far from their lodge. The hunt came after they found one of their cattle with its throat torn out. Alongside the carcass were the unmistakable tracks of a bear, evidence as to the identity of the cattle killer. Their spirits rose when the rain stopped, and sunlight broke through the clouds.

"Let's go home," said Yanus.

At seventeen, three winters younger than their sister, Yanus was the gentlest of the Twins, Dolph the more impulsive.

"I agree with Yanus," said Dolph; "let's go home while it's light enough to see."

"Just a little further, brothers," said Robbyn, "until we learn the meaning of these tracks. Remember—this is our land!"

Much to the Twins' dismay, Robbyn pressed on until they heard water rushing over rocks. The three crept their way toward the sound of a fast-flowing stream. They were unprepared for what their eyes beheld.

There, in the center of a clearing, was a man, naked from the waist up. He was tall, sun burnt and muscular as if forged from iron. His arms and chest wore many scars, but what unnerved Robbyn and the Twins, this stranger was in the company of a bear and her cub. While the bears fished the stream, the stranger watched. The sight of the man and creatures commingling was unsettling enough, but what also disturbed the three was the wild tangle of white hair hanging past the stranger's waist, and his chest-length beard. It was white like his hair and made the man's age impossible to reckon. Robbyn and her brothers exchanged looks that mirrored each other's bewilderment.

"He must be a forest spirit!" said Robbyn.

"Or a demon!" said Dolph, under his breath.

"Let's get away from here," said Yanus. "Now!"

Wolves, twelve of them, led by Adalwolf, surrounded the three on all sides and offered no means of escape. They had trailed the young woman and her brothers from the vale where their village was.

"Put your bows on the ground," said Robbyn to her brothers. "There's magic here stronger than our arrows."

"What," said Dolph, "are you out of your mind?"

"Dolph's right," said Yanus. "Unarmed we've no chance."

Beowulf turned and faced the three. "Come closer," he said; "they won't harm you."

Following Robbyn's lead, the Twins placed their bows and quivers of arrows on the ground and stepped forward while the wolves formed circled them. Although some of the Gray Brethren flared their nostrils and bared their fangs, the wolves remained quiet. Beowulf fixed his eyes on Robbyn. Unable to withstand the intensity of his look, she stared at the ground.

"Why do you turn away, girl?" said Beowulf.

When Robbyn didn't respond, Dolph spoke: "Forgive our sister, she's unaccustomed to speaking to half-naked men in the company of wolves and bears."

"What are you hunting?" said Beowulf.

"We weren't," said Yanus. "We were following your tracks, for they made no sense alongside those of a bear and her cub."

Beowulf laughed: "Really?"

"Yes, O Spirit of the Forest," said Robbyn, still looking at her feet.

Beowulf winced: "Spirit of the Forest?"

"If not a spirit, what are you?" said Dolph.

"If you don't mind our asking," said Yanus.

A moment passed in silence.

"My brothers mean no insult," said Robbyn, daring to look at Beowulf. "We live near this forest and sometimes seek refuge here. My name is Robbyn. These are my brothers, Dolph and Yanus."

Beowulf looked them over: "I can't answer your question since I don't know who I am, or from where I come. I do know that I'm at home among the Forest Folk, and will suffer no harm to them. Do you understand?"

"Yes," said Robbyn; "we understand. But if we cannot hunt, how are we to live?"

"You have cattle, goats, and sheep?" said Beowulf.

"Yes, but they are few," said Robbyn.

"Then you must make love to the land," said Beowulf.

"What?" said Robbyn.

"You must learn how to farm," said Beowulf.

"We're Wylfings," said Dolph.

"We're warriors," said Yanus.

Beowulf thought for a moment. "If that means you don't know how to farm, I'll teach you."

"Farming is for Gifths, Geats, and Hugas," said Dolph, raising his voice.

Adalwolf's fur stood, and he made a low, growling sound.

"What my brother means," said Robbyn; "is that our tribe are renowned as warriors—and in times of peace, herdsmen; not tillers of the soil."

Robbyn and her brothers noticed the wolves were no longer sitting; nor was the she bear. They were on all fours staring at Robbyn and the Twins.

"But with someone to show us how," said Robbyn, "we can learn to farm." She cast a stern look at Dolph and Yanus: "Can't we, brothers?"

Dolph and Yanus looked at each other; then looked again at the wolves and the bear.

"Yes," said the brothers, "we can learn to farm!"

"Good," said Beowulf. "In the spring, I'll show you what you need to do. But before I come, you must acquire seeds: rye, barley, and seeds for vegetables. Can you do that before spring?"

Robbyn looked at her brothers:

"Yes," she said. "We know of a village where we can trade for seeds."

"Good!" said Beowulf. "Until then you may fish—take what you need, and such fowl as you find in the grasslands. But do no harm to the creatures in the forest—understood?"

"Yes," said Robbyn. "We understand."

That night, after they finished supper, Robbyn and her brothers sat before the hearth. As they warmed their hands and feet by the fire, it was a long while before anyone spoke. Throughout the remainder of the night, each time they heard a wolf howling in the distance, shivers raced along their spines.

"He won't last through the winter," said Dolph, fortified by his third mug of beer.

"That's right," said Yanus; "we'll be free of the old fool by spring."

† † †

The following morning, while her brothers slept-off the beer they'd consumed, Robbyn returned to the forest and the clearing by the stream. The stranger was gone, nor were any creatures noticeable. Still, from the shadows, Robbyn felt eyes upon her. In her hands, she held a woolen cloak, a man's leather jerkin, deerskin breeches, and a well-sewn linen shirt with leather patches on the elbows. A tall man like the stranger, they were once her father's best clothes.

Robbyn found a prominent rock near the stream and placed the garments there, along with a striking-flint for making fire; then she left and went back the way she came.

When Robbyn arrived at her family's farmhouse, she found a honeycomb wrapped in broad leaves left on the doorstep.

† † †

Throughout the autumn Turin busied himself seeing to the affairs of the farm. When winter came, there was little to do beyond staying warm and seeing to the welfare of the livestock. Turin knew of Beowulf's promise to the wolves, and he made sure the Gray Brethren did not go hungry when the snow fell, and the sun retreated.

Long cold nights of winter wore on Turin's nerves. Many days and nights the servants could hear him pacing the floor of his bedchamber, talking to himself.

† † †

When winter departed, it came as no surprise to anyone that Turin left the farm after the spring's Eve celebration.

"After all this time, what makes you think you'll find him?" said Beorn, who had come from Falcon's Nest to officiate the event.

"Because I don't believe he's dead," said Turin, "just lost."

"Beowulf… lost?" said the Schaman, "Bah!"

"You said it yourself, Beorn—Beowulf may not be in his right mind!"

"I was grasping for answers," said the Schaman.

"And now I'm the one grasping," said Turin, checking the anger he felt over the Schaman's tone.

Beorn kept silent and watched Turin tie the last saddlebag on the back of a pack-horse. It hung alongside a sack Beorn had placed there earlier without Turin seeing. When Turin finished, he mounted his horse and without looking back led Storm Bringer and the pack-horse east, away from Vindinstedt Farm.

Beorn walked past the Main Gate and watched Turin depart.

Praise the gods! He's finally going back for another look!

Grinning, the Schaman walked to Beowulf's lodge to flirt with Greta. Beorn did this in hopes of getting her to drink a mug of mead with him later. Not even Beorn, despite his considerable age, was immune to the demands of Idun of the Golden Apples, goddess of the spring.

The Twins were keeping watch over their small herd of cattle when something in the distance caught Yanus' eye. Dolph looked toward the tree line that marked the eastern edge of the forest. A thousand paces away, the woods were visible through the mist and drizzle.

They saw Beowulf walking in their direction. From their lodge, Robbyn stepped outside. She also looked to see who was approaching. Leaving their cattle to graze, the brothers returned to their dwelling and joined Robbyn.

"Go inside, Yanus," said Dolph. "Fetch our bows!"

"Do no such thing!" said Robbyn. Her eyes flashed: "Be still—or by the gods I'll crown you both with father's cudgel!"

The clothing that Robbyn left at the clearing the previous autumn fit the stranger well, or so she thought.

Beowulf walked to within ten paces of the porch and stopped. Looking around, he noticed the abandoned lodges, workshops and barns.

"Where are the others?" said Beowulf.

"Dead," said Dolph.

"But you stayed on, the three of you," said Beowulf.

"Yes," said Robbyn. "This was our father's land. We buried them here—our mother, father, an aunt, uncle and six cousins."

"The blood of our clan waters this earth, old man," said Dolph.

"We won't dishonor our ancestors' memory by leaving," said Yanus.

"Quiet, both of you!" said Robbyn. She turned and looked at Beowulf: "I'm sorry; my brothers mean no insult, but this is our land, and we won't abandon it."

"Have you a plowshare?" said Beowulf.

71

THE FOREST FOR THE TREES

"We told you, old man," said Yanus. "We Wylfings are warriors—not farmers. We've no need of a plowshare!"

"Does the metalsmith's furnace work?" said Beowulf.

"It did once," said Robbyn. "Perhaps it still does."

Beowulf looked Robbyn up-and-down. "I'll need one-third your weight in iron."

Robbyn looked at her brothers: "The swords and armor we keep hidden—get them!"

"What!" said Dolph; "They belonged to father and Uncle Oran!"

"Please, brothers," said Robbyn; "just do as he asks."

"And I'll need fuel for the furnace," said Beowulf.

"My brothers and I will help you," said Robbyn; "but what should we call you?"

"What's wrong with 'Old Man'?" said Dolph, grinning.

Yanus laughed. Robbyn flashed her brothers another angry look.

"Forgive my brothers," said Robbyn; "Until your arrival, they thought themselves Lords of this vale."

Stung, Dolph, and Yanus looked away. Robbyn studied the stranger's face, what she could see of it. The tangle of hair past Beowulf's shoulders and the wild, unkempt beard that reached to his chest concealed his features apart from his eyes and nose. Robbyn turned to her brothers: "There's work to do!"

† † †

Robbyn watched Yanus and Dolph carry swords, spears and two shirts of chainmail armor into the workshop; that done, she helped her brothers gather fuel for the furnace. There was plenty of wood available from the abandoned Wylfing lodges. As the three carried armloads of planks to the workshop they saw a fire burning in the furnace, and the stranger stripped to his boots and breeches, setting out hammers and tongs. While her brothers fetched wood, Robbyn watched Beowulf move from one spot to the next. His waist-long hair and beard courted sparks and flames that leapt from the furnace. Robbyn shook her head in disbelief and left.

A short while later she returned holding a pair of shears. She also had her father's razor along with a mug of blackberry paste.

"You'll set yourself on fire," said Robbyn. "Can't you smell your beard burning?"

Beowulf stopped what he was doing and looked at his beard, noting where the flames had singed it.

"It stinks, doesn't it," said Beowulf, holding his beard up before his eyes, smelling it.

"Allow me," said Robbyn. She held the shears out in front of him.

Beowulf placed the metalsmith's tongs on the anvil. "Be it so," he said.

Robbyn led Beowulf outside. "Sit!"

Beowulf sat on a tree stump outside the workshop and said nothing as Robbyn tied his hair back away from his face. She turned her attention to Beowulf's facial hair. Using the shears, she trimmed his beard close, and when she saw the scar on his face, it made her shudder.

"Is something wrong?" he said.

"No," she said. "Hold still."

As her brothers came and went from the workshop with armloads of wood, they stole furtive looks at what their sister was doing. It made them nervous to think what might happen should Robbyn nick the stranger with their father's razor. Neither Dolph nor Yanus would mind had Robbyn slit his throat.

"Something about him looks familiar," said Dolph, "but I don't know what it is."

"I do," said Yanus; "he's wearing Poppa's best shirt and breeches!"

Outside the workshop, the sun competed with the fog. Little by little, the mist lifted, and sunlight shone on an all but deserted village.

While Robbyn spread blackberry paste on his face, Beowulf closed his eyes, sniffed the air and smiled.

"Blackberry," he said, "my favorite."

"Good," said Robbyn; "now hold still!"

With measured strokes, Robbyn shaved Beowulf's face smooth. Although her expression remained impassive from start to finish, Robbyn was surprised at what she saw:

"By all the gods!" she said when done, "there's a handsome face under all that brush."

Beowulf ran his hands over his face and felt the smoothness of his cheeks. He looked at her a moment, then smiled. "Thank you."

"You're welcome, Bright Eyes," she said and left.

Listening to the whole time from just inside the workshop, the brothers tried to look busy when Beowulf entered.

"I'll need one of you to help with the bellows," said Beowulf; "while the other fuels the fire."

The brothers exchanged looks:

"Very well, Bright Eyes," said Dolph; and he chuckled. "We'll help you."

Beowulf cast the Twins a stern look.

"What!" said Dolph, in as innocent a voice as he could muster, "It's what Robbyn calls you."

"You're not her," said Beowulf. "Think of something else to call me. Now remove your father's sword from among the others and keep it for his namesake. You've brought more than enough iron for me to work with."

The brothers did as Beowulf said and they continued to watch in silence as he took their uncle's sword into his hands.

"This is a splendid sword," said Beowulf, lifting the sword overhead.

"It was our Uncle's," said Yanus.

With dizzying speed, Beowulf whirled the sword over his head and side-to-side. The brothers were dumbstruck. They exchanged a look of awe for the swordplay they were witnessing. Beowulf placed the blade on the underside of the anvil and bent the sword up until the tip of the blade met the pommel. No more a sword, Beowulf tossed that piece of twisted iron into the firebox initiating its rebirth. Beowulf removed the tips of two spears, tossed them into the firebox, then he stood between the Twins. Together they watched in silence as the heat from the fire transformed the metal into a molten mass.

"Who are the bandits that afflict you?" said Beowulf, while he pumped the bellows to bring more heat to bear.

"What can you tell me about them?"

"Most are Ostergoths," said Dolph. "Others are Hugas and Gifths—all are outcasts, renegades no tribe will abide.

"Each spring they come to claim part of our herd," said Yanus. "If they knew or suspected our sister's presence they would've taken her too. As matters stand, they leave us with a breeding bull and just enough stock to replenish the herd."

"So why not put an end to it?" said Beowulf.

"Because we're three; they are many," said Robbyn, standing at the entrance to the workshop.

In her hands, Robbyn held a water bag, a loaf of bread and a large wedge of goat's' milk cheese.

"The bandits number seventy or more," she said.

She placed the water bag and provisions on a table. Without saying another word, Robbyn turned to leave.

"Thank you," said Beowulf.

"For nothing," said Robbyn.

Beowulf waited until Robbyn was well away before looking at the Twins.

"Your sister's wrong about that," he said; "food is more than nothing—it's life itself."

† † †

The ten Clan Chiefs stood shoulder to shoulder in front of Weohstan, Beorn, and Sigmund. Their beardless faces, their ill-fitting armor, and rose-colored cheeks caught Beorn's attention.

Beorn guessed the age of the oldest, whose name was Baolin, to be no more than twenty winters. Eofor's nephew, Baolin, now ruled Clan Knupp.

"We think it long overdue, my Lords," said Baolin. "Geatland must have a king! One whom the people know is on the throne! Our tribe deserves a king whose bones are not moldering in some unknown part of Vindinstedt Forest."

"Any suggestions as to whom this king should be, Lord Baolin?" said Beorn.

"Any one of us here, Magister Beorn, is capable of ruling Geatland," said Baolin. "As you know, my uncle Eofor fathered a child with Hygelac's daughter. The blood of Clan Knupp is of their daughter, Princess Adela, just as mine; therefore—"

"Therefore," said Beorn, cutting Baolin short, "you feel you have a legitimate claim to the throne?"

"Well, yes," said Baolin, "I do! And these chieftains are of like mind."

"Really," said Weohstan, trying to control his temper, "with the full unconditional support of the clans?"

"Of course," said Baolin.

"And you're of one mind about this?" said Beorn.

Baolin looked at the Chieftains; they nodded in the affirmative.

"We are," said Baolin.

"Then," said Weohstan, "we see no reason not to call you out for what you are: traitors—every damn one of you!"

"Traitors?" said Baolin, dumbfounded.

"Yes," said Weohstan, "traitors to your rightful king and traitors to your tribe."

"Who are you to call us, traitors?" said Baolin.

"I'm Weohstan Waegmunding!" he said. "But answer me this—all of you: Who among you fought with Hygelac in Frisland? Step forward if you did."

None of the ten approached.

"That's right; not one of you fought in Frisland! None survived the slaughter that day save for Beowulf, your rightful king! Moreover, who among you, defended Falcon's Nest against the Usurper, Onela? Step forward if you fought with us that glorious day!"

None of the ten moved a muscle.

"That's right," said Weohstan, "not one of you fought! Also, Baolin Knupp, unless I'm misinformed, you've yet to piss your breeches in combat; yet you think you're fit to be King of Geatland! How by all the gods did you arrive at that conclusion?"

Humbled and fearful for his life, Baolin slunk back with the Chieftains. All were too ashamed to look the three in the face.

"Lord Sigmund," said Weohstan.

Sigmund stepped forward with his sword drawn.

"You don't mean to kill us!" said Baolin. "We're unarmed!"

"If it was up to me, and me, alone—I'd kill you on the spot," said Weohstan. "However, because I'm but one of Beowulf's regents, I leave your fate to Magister Beorn and Lord Sigmund. What say you, Magister Beorn; what say you, Lord Sigmund? What do we do with these traitors?"

"I'll defer to Magister Beorn," said Sigmund, "since the Magister's wisdom is legendary."

"Very well, Magister Beorn," said Weohstan; "It's up to you alone to decide the fate of these little rat bastards!"

Beorn rocked back and forth on his heels while he scratched his belly and tugged on his beard:

"Hanging would be too quick for the likes of them," said Beorn. "Nor will I lop their heads off with my axe; that, too, would be too kind. I'm thinking something exotic is called for, perhaps something Roman, or Angle, like the death of the traitor Ragmund. Yes—I might have them pulled apart by four horses trotting off in four directions. It's a rare sight the way the limbs stretch until the skin tears at the hips and shoulders and the bones pop from their sockets. On second thought, we could stake them naked to the ground in the Great Square, and smear them with honey; then let the ants eat their way inside their heads. Not just any ants, mind you—but Cannibal Ants from the deepest dark hole in West Falls Forest."

Sigmund leaned close to Weohstan's ear. In a whisper, he said, "Cannibal ants?"

"Never heard of them," said Weohstan.

"Seeing them devoured that way," said Beorn; "should amuse the people for quite some time and while the ants are taking their due, crows will come to peck out their eyes and rats will come in the night to gnaw on their innards."

One of the Chieftains fainted, another vomited. The ten dropped to their knees, raised their hands and begged for mercy.

"But that, too," continued Beorn; "would be a quick and easy death. Lest I fail to choose wisely, we'll keep you alive in the bowels of the Citadel until our king returns. I'll leave it to the bear's son to determine your fate. Until then, you'll pay for your food and keep by working in the stables, kitchen, and sewers—anywhere work needs doing. Guards—take these traitors below. Then send their men-at-arms back the way they came. Tell them to spread the word: there is one King of Geatland, and his name is Beowulf Waegmunding!"

Beorn turned around. With his back to the young Clan Chiefs, he winked at Weohstan and Sigmund who did their utmost not to laugh.

† † †

After thirty days traveling east, Turin no longer recognized the forest. At midday, an impenetrable fog settled over the ground in front of him and made the way ahead uncertain. He decided to make camp beside a stream where there was an abundance of sweet-grass. It makes no sense risking the safety of the horses riding blind in this mist.

Seeing first to the needs of the animals, Turin removed his battle gear and gathered wood for a fire.

He set off with his bow and quiver of arrows in-search of dinner. Turin walked along the stream bank. Through mist that swirled above the surface of the water, Turin saw much fat fish worth skewering with his arrows. It wasn't long before he returned to his campsite with two, foot-long water Lords to roast. Turin searched through his saddlebags for the leather pouch containing the cooking herbs Beorn gave him. What he found first, at the very bottom of one bag, left him breathless. In his hand, wrapped in cheesecloth, was the Crown of Geatland. A smile came to Turin's lips: Beorn!

The same instant Turin's fingers took hold of the herb pouch; he heard a sound coming from a league or more away. The sound was familiar, distinct and unmistakable: a metalsmith's hammer striking iron on an anvil, with slow, purposeful cadence. There are others about, but who—and how many? Turin looked at his campfire and saw which way the smoke blew.

"Whoever it is they're upwind and won't know I'm here."

Turin ate with gusto: There's more to these herbs than I ever imagined. Turin chuckled. Around him, the trees transformed into strange, colorful shapes that swayed and danced in the breeze. The rustling leaves and branches were as pleasing a song as he'd ever heard. Done eating and feeling light-headed, Turin stretched out on the grass. He used a saddle blanket to lie on and his cloak over him to keep the dampness at-bay. It was spring. Moody, fog-bound days were as much the rule as they were the exception. Indeed, for every day of uninterrupted sunshine, there were three days of storm clouds, gale-force winds, and driving rain. Turin closed his eyes and listened to the repetitive sound of the metalsmith's hammer.

As Turin daydreamed, he recalled the pride he felt delivering Beowulf's message to Hrothgar, King of the Danes in Heorot Hall. Standing in Hrothgar's Throne Room, he knew he was close to where Weohstan's son, Handscio had died, and where Beowulf bested the monster, Grendel. Turin recalled the thrill of going into battle alongside his foster father and Beowulf; but then, into his mind came the uninvited faces of every warrior he had killed; each with the same look in his eyes, each with the same unanswerable question on his lips: "*Why us, Turin? Why not you?*"

† † †

Turin heard the sound of the horses neighing and the stamping of hooves, and he felt a weight on his throat impeding his ability to breathe. It was no dream. Turin opened his eyes and struggled to rise which increased the force choking him. More shocking to Turin was the realization that the face looking down at him belonged to a beautiful young woman, and the pressure on his throat was her boot. Adding to that first impression the woman held a bow; drawn and ready to let loose an obsidian-tipped arrow at his chest.

Robbyn looked into Turin's face: "What are you doing here? Are you one of Ingvar's spies?"

Unable to speak, Turin gasped something inaudible.

"All right," said Robbyn, "I'm going to take my foot away and let you up—but keep your hands above your head or by the gods I'll put this arrow through your heart—understand?"

Turin nodded.

Robbyn removed her boot from his throat and stepped back while Turin gasped for air.

"Hands over your head," said Robbyn.

Turin did as instructed; he held his hands above his head and pushed himself into a sitting position.

"I ask you again," said Robbyn; "who are you and what are you doing here?"

"My name is Turin. I came this way in search of someone. Who are you?"

"My name is Robbyn. The land you trespass on is mine!"

"Well," said Turin, "I didn't know I was trespassing."

"Who is it you search for?" said Robbin.

Turin took a moment; then said: "A friend, my best friend. I fear he's lost and doesn't know his way home."

"Home?" said Robbyn.

"Far to the west," said Turin. "May I lower my arms now? They're getting tired."

"Go ahead," said Robbyn; "but don't think I won't kill you if you give me cause."

"I swear I won't," Turin said, with a broad grin on his face.

"Are you mocking me?" said Robbyn.

"On my honor—no!" said Turin.

"Then why are you grinning? I'm the one holding the bow; I'm the one pointing an arrow at your chest!"

"You won't believe me," said Turin.

"Try me," she said.

"Very well," he said. "I believe it has to do with something I ate: mushrooms and herbs a Schaman gave me to flavor my food."

A look of disbelief spread across Robbyn's face. All at once she lowered her bow and laughed. Turin noticed the tension on her bowstring go slack and he thanked the gods for it.

"Can you walk?" said Robbyn.

"More or less," said Turin, still in the throes of Beorn's herbs and unable to keep from grinning.

"Get up," said Robbyn, "get up! Someone wants to meet you."

"Yes, of course, but first tell me," said Turin.

"Tell you what?"

"How did you find me in this fog?"

"I had help," Robbyn said.

"Help?" said Turin.

"Him!" said Robbyn, pointing.

Turin looked to where Robbyn pointed and saw the large gray shape of a wolf approaching through the fog.

It was Adalwolf.

"He'll guide us to my village," said Robbyn.

"How can you be sure?"

"Because the one who wants to meet you told me he would."

"What about my horses and gear?"

"No harm will come to the horses or your battle gear."

72

INTRODUCTIONS ALL AROUND

Turin followed Adalwolf through the fog. Robbyn walked a cautious distance behind, with her bow slung over her shoulder. After walking a short distance, the fog lifted and Turin saw what appeared to be an abandoned village. The sound of the metalsmith's hammer came from a workshop straight ahead. The wolf leader turned and trotted back into the fog the way he came. Turin turned and faced Robbyn.

"At least tell me who it is who wants to meet me," said Turin.

"I can't," said Robbyn.

"What do you mean: you 'can't'?"

"I mean I can't because he doesn't know his name," said Robbyn, perturbed that a stranger, and a handsome one at that, would ask questions for which she had no answers.

"Wait here!" she said.

While Turin stood idle, Robbyn entered the workshop. Turin looked around and noticed that the other lodges of the village were indeed deserted and in varying states of disrepair. Off to one side, Turin saw a wooden plow lacking a plowshare and moldboard to complete it.

Robbyn emerged from the workshop with Dolph and Yanus behind her. With sullen looks on their faces, the brothers looked Turin up-and-down. Thinking it prudent to start a conversation, Turin flicked his head in the direction of the plow.

"That's a good looking plow," he said. It was as bold a lie as he could remember telling.

"It's rough around the edges, but it'll do," said Beowulf, stepping from the workshop. As Turin and Beowulf stared at each other, in a heartbeat Turin apprehended something wrong—there was not even a glimmer of recognition. Beowulf didn't recognize his foster brother and Thane. Unsettled by the sight of Beowulf's snow-white hair, Turin held his tongue and rejoiced—his search for his king had at last ended.

"He says his name is Turin," said Robbyn.

"And the name of your tribe?" said Beowulf.

Turin did not reply.

"Answer him!" said Dolph, "or my brother and I will give you a thrashing!"

One of Turin's eyebrows rose of its own accord; he didn't know whether to laugh or remain resigned to the antics of the youthful buffoons in front of him.

"I'm my Tribe," said Turin.

"The Tribe of One," said Beowulf.

"Yes," replied Turin. "A tribe of one."

"He's got the stones of a bull, doesn't he," said Dolph.

"Enough for two bulls," said Yanus.

"I've enough between my legs to face the two of you!" said Turin.

Beowulf laughed: "Well spoken, Turin—Tribe of One."

Turin turned to Robbyn:

"The metalsmith is not from here but who are you three—now that you know who I am."

"I'll tell you who we are, stranger," said Dolph, and he stepped forward with his hands made into fists.

Beowulf yanked Dolph back by the shoulder.

"Careful, boy," said Beowulf; "Tribe of One could kill you before you knew you were dead."

Skeptical as they were of Beowulf's unexpected warning, Dolph and Yanus stepped back.

"You already know my name," said Robbyn. "These two trouble-makers are my brothers, Dolph and Yanus. We're Wylfings, all that's left of our clan. This place is our village, such as it is."

Turin said nothing.

"So, Turin, Tribe of One, what brings you here?" said Beowulf.

Turin stood up straight: Do you not recognize me, my King? It's me, Turin—your foster brother! I've been searching for you! Tell me this is a dream!

"I came this way in search of a friend," said Turin. "I believe he's lost through no fault of his own, and I mean to find him."

"He must be a good friend," said Beowulf, "for you to come so far in search of him."

"He's more than a friend," said Turin; "he's my shield brother."

There was a prolonged moment of silence until Beowulf stepped close to Turin and whispered: "Can you make love to the land?"

"Say, what?" said Turin.

"What do you know about farming?" said Beowulf.

Turin hesitated. He looked at Robbyn and her brothers. They were staring at him, waiting to hear his response.

"Actually," said Turin; "I know very little." It was another lie, and he took no pleasure telling it.

"You're not alone there," said Dolph with a snicker.

"You're welcome to stay here," said Beowulf.

This time it was Robbyn and her brothers whom Beowulf took by surprise.

"This is our village, Bright Eyes," said Robbyn, "not yours! It's for my brothers and me to say who stays or goes! Besides, why should we trust this 'tribe of one'?"

"Because I think you trust me and I trust him," said Beowulf; "but perhaps the better question is, can he trust the three of you?"

"Why shouldn't he trust us?" said Dolph, offended by the question.

"We're trustworthy," said Yanus.

"Shut-up, Yanus," said Dolph.

"Both of you shut-up," said Robbyn. She faced Beowulf and Turin: "I speak for our clan—not them!"

"Then tell us," said Beowulf; "why should Tribe of One trust you? On the other hand, why should you trust me, or me trust you? Trust is a powerful thing, my four young friends."

Robbyn threw her hands into the air, exasperated.

"All right, enough!" she said. "He can stay, but I'll have my eyes on both of you—do you understand?"

"I understand," said Turin.

"Good, so do I," said Beowulf, "then it's settled."

"Tell me, metalsmith," said Turin, "what am I to call you?"

"I don't know," said Beowulf; "you'll have to think of something."

"Anything except 'Bright Eyes," said Robbyn; "that's what I call him."

"And you best not call him, 'Old Man,'" said Dolph; he winked at Yanus.

"Until some other name presents itself," said Turin, "I'll call you 'Metalsmith.'"

"Very well," said Beowulf, "Metalsmith, it is."

Turin looked at Robbyn and smiled. Robbyn frowned, muttered something no one could understand, turned on her heel and stormed off in the direction of her lodge.

While Beowulf continued to work in the workshop, Turin returned to his campsite, gathered his gear and the horses and returned to the village. Robbyn was there to meet him.

She took Turin to a lodge; one she said was suitable for him and "Bright Eyes." It was not by accident, however, that from her front door Robbyn would have an unfettered view of the lodge housing the two strangers.

Turin saw to the horses comfort then settled into the dwelling. In one corner of the abandoned lodge, he placed his and Beowulf's battle gear and covered it with a ground cloth. He found a broom and began sweeping the floor. Robbyn returned with candles, food, and drink. The Twins came with her, each carrying an armload of wood which they placed near the hearth.

"Thank you," said Turin as they departed. "I'm grateful to all of you."

Robbyn and her brothers nodded and left for their lodge. When Beowulf entered, he was pleased to find a fire burning.

"I'm hungry," said Beowulf. "Let's eat."

"Very well," said Turin.

Turin spread his saddle blankets on the floor in front of the hearth where they sat and ate in silence.

"So, Metalsmith," said Turin; "you're going to teach these Wylfings to farm."

"Yes," said Beowulf. "Do you have a problem with that?"

"No, it's just that Wylfings are herdsmen—not farmers."

"Yes," said Beowulf, "marvelous, isn't it."

"The girl told me you could speak with the creatures of the forest."

"Yes," said Beowulf.

"So can my friend—the friend I search for," said Turin.

"Tell me more about him."

"First," said Turin, "I'm not a tribe of one. I lied about that."

"Lied," said Beowulf. "Why?"

"Because I'm a Spear Dane, who was adopted by a Väster Geat, and both tribes are enemies of the Wylfings. The girl and her brothers would kill me in a heartbeat if they knew. My friend is my shield brother—but he's also my king, and my tribe has been too long without him!"

"What if you don't find him?" said Beowulf. "What will you do?"

"Oh, I'll find him," said Turin. "I believe he's closer than either of us knows. As sure as a storm follows me here, I sense it's a matter of time before I find him."

"On that hopeful note," said Beowulf, "I'll bid you good sleep, Turin, the Spear Dane, become a Väster Geat."

† † †

For the next seven days, from morning twilight to sundown, Beowulf stayed busy in the workshop. He made an array of farm tools for the Wylfings. When not assisting Beowulf, Turin continued to improve the condition of their lodge. When not doing that, he would fish and hunt pheasants to help feed the burgeoning village of five souls.

Making sure Turin was nowhere near, Robbyn went to see Beowulf. She found him outside the workshop attaching the plowshare and moldboard to the plow.

"May I speak with you?"

"Of course," said Beowulf. "What's on your mind—beside Turin?"

"What!" said Robbyn; "He's the last thing on my mind!"

Beowulf laughed. "Then I was wrong, and you mustn't believe anything I say—not ever!"

A moment passed before Robbyn could bring herself to look Beowulf straight in the eye.

"I lied, Bright Eyes; it's as you say, and it bothers me to admit it."

"Why should it bother you? He's a man, headstrong to be sure, but not so different from your brothers. You're a woman, and probably no different than the women he's accustomed to."

"That," said Robbyn "would be any woman who didn't threaten to loose an arrow at him as I did! A few days ago I didn't know he existed. I don't know what manner of man he is or why I'm attracted to him. But you talk about him as if you know him well."

"Around me Turin is unguarded," said Beowulf; "he trusts me, and that makes him easy to speak to."

"What," said Robbyn, "does he not trust me? I agreed to let him stay with us."

"Perhaps it's your beauty."

"By all the gods!" said Robbyn. "Men fight battles, face death daily, yet cower inwardly at the sight of a girl's face?"

Beowulf shrugged. "This much I know beyond all doubt: you're both headstrong beyond measure. Were it not so he wouldn't have made it this far in search of his friend; nor would you have stayed in this place as long as you have, afflicted by bandits; while raising two idiot brothers. What else is there to know, that time will not disclose?"

After a long moment, Robbyn answered: "I suppose you're right, Bright Eyes."

"Good," said Beowulf. "And now I need to speak with your bull."

"Speak? About what?" she said.

"About being harnessed to this plow."

† † †

After selecting a promising section of land contiguous to the stream, Beowulf urged the Wylfings' bull forward. The bull came from a long line of breeding bulls with a distinguished pedigree that stretched back countless generations. Still, this Prince of Green Pastures did not perform as Beowulf would have liked—far from it. The bull zigzagged left and right, and the plowshare did little more than scratch the All-Mother's skin. Try as they might—not to, Robbyn and the others laughed until their stomachs hurt.

Beowulf stopped and looked at his four critics: "Whichever one of you thinks you can do better is welcome to try."

"I warrant I can plow a straighter furrow than you, Metalsmith," said Turin.

"Very well, Tribe of One," said Beowulf, "start wherever you like."

Turin looked at Robbyn's brothers: "I need your help."

"What do you want us to do?" said Dolph.

"Bring me the most fertile cow you have, and put a rope around her neck."

"That's all—just that?" said Yanus.

"Yes."

The brothers soon returned leading a cow by a rope.

Turin went to where Beowulf was waiting. He grasped the handle in one hand, and the leather straps attached to the yolk, in his other hand.

Turin looked at Robbyn: "Will you help?"

"What do you want me to do?"

"Not fair," said Beowulf. "I had no help!"

Turin laughed. "Look and learn, Metalsmith," he said; then he turned to Robbyn.

"I want you to lead the cow in a straight line ahead of the bull—will you do that?"

"What!" said Robbyn, "You want me to walk with the cow ahead of you?"

"Yes," said Turin, "that's all."

Robbyn's hands tightened into fists. She cast a scathing look at the four men.

"Men are pigs—all of you! And that goes for the bull as well!"

"Ready when you are," Turin said, in as pleasant a voice as he could affect.

"Bah!" said Robbyn. She took hold of the rope and led the cow forward.

No sooner had the cow presented her backside to the bull the bull acquired an earnest interest in plowing

"Now, brother bull," said Turin, "let's show these Wylfings how to plow a field!"

Turin snapped the reins. The bull set off in tedious pursuit of the cow. The furrows that Turin made throughout the remainder of the morning ran deep and straight.

Walking behind Turin, Beowulf cast seeds into the furrows while Dolph and Yanus followed. Working with the spades

Beowulf that Beowulf had forged, the brothers covered the seeds with dirt.

When it came time to break fast, Beowulf and Turin remained with the plow while Robbyn and her brothers returned to their lodge to talk among themselves. Beowulf and Turin looked at the horizon where storm clouds were gathering.

"I told you, Metalsmith, a storm has followed me here."

73

TOWER STRUCK BY LIGHTNING

After spending the day tilling soil, it was near sunset when Beowulf and Turin finished supper. While Beowulf added wood to the cooking-fire, Turin stood in the doorway of their lodge. Two weeks had come and gone, and Turin was hard-pressed coping with Beowulf's condition; that, and the likelihood they would not leave the village anytime soon. Turin lifted his eyes and looked west in the direction of Geatland. The sun dropped low on the horizon turning clouds pink, gray and gold in the distance.

"You seem restless," said Beowulf, drinking beer in front of the fire; "As if your head is here and your heart is elsewhere."

Without turning around, Turin said: "That's the long and short of it, Metalsmith. I fear for my people without their king, and I worry for my king, without his people."

"Perhaps you fear too much, Turin," said Beowulf. "What will be, will be—even if it never happens. I can tell you this much: rain or sun, tomorrow I'll finish plowing.

"And then?" said Turin.

"I'll go back to the forest," said Beowulf.

Turin was about to speak when he saw Robbyn step outside her lodge. She wore a cloak of deepest blue with the hood thrown back, and a clean white shift, with a slender leather belt, draped around her waist. Her chestnut-colored hair was untied and hung past her waist. Robbyn and Turin nodded to one another across the distance that separated their lodges; then she, too, turned and looked west at sunset.

"What are you waiting for?" said Beowulf, standing behind Turin. He leaned close to Turin's ear: "Go talk to her. She's waiting for you!"

"How do you know she's waiting for me?" Turin said.

"For the first time since I've been here, she's dressed like a woman! Now, go—while it's still light outside. Go!"

With his elbow, Beowulf nudged Turin away from his fixed position in the doorway. Turin cast a disapproving look back before he continued to where Robbyn was standing, eyes fixed on the sunset.

"Beautiful, is it not," said Turin.

"Yes," said Robbyn; "Does it remind you of home when you look west?"

"I never thought about it like that; but, yes, I suppose it does."

"Is there a woman waiting for you there?" she said.

"No," said Turin.

"Too bad for her," said Robbyn.

Turin laughed. "She's no doubt the better for it—whoever she is."

"Why would she be the better for it?" said Robbyn; "Is it because you think you've nothing to offer?"

As Turin looked into Robbyn's eyes, he felt himself drawing close to her; it excited him—at the same time, he felt cautious.:

Turin smiled. "Is that an offer?"

Robbyn moved close to him. In her eyes, Turin could make out the colors of the sunset. She put her lips against his and kissed him.Turin took Robbyn in his arms and kissed her long and hard.

"I sent Dolph and Yanus to stay in the barn until morning," said Robbyn. "Come inside, and we can pretend."

"Pretend?" said Turin, holding Robbyn in his embrace.

"That I'm your woman, and you're my man."

Turin searched Robbyn's eyes. He lifted her into his arms and carried her inside the lodge where a fire burned, and candles welcomed them.

From his vantage point, Beowulf smiled and stepped back from the doorway into the shadows. It was when the door to Robbyn's lodge closed that Beowulf did the same.

He opened a keg of beer, one he chilled earlier in the ice-cold waters of the stream. Beowulf sat in front of the fire and sipped that cold dark brew. As he stared into the flames, in his mind's eye, Beowulf saw the face of a beautiful young woman with honey-colored hair, smiling at him. He strained his mind to see her, but wood-smoke obscured her face. The more Beowulf struggled to bring her image into focus the more she receded from view until the picture of her vanished. Feeling an emptiness come upon him,

Beowulf went to the corral to enjoy the company of the horses.

Beowulf entered the corral and doled out a handful of oats to the pack horse, mare, and the black stallion. The stallion forsook the handful of oats in favor of nuzzling Beowulf's face. When the black warhorse neighed, Beowulf laughed and stroked the horse's neck.

"*What's your name, Beautiful One?" Beowulf said.*

"*Storm Bringer*," said the stallion, using the Silent Tongue; *"it's the name you gave me when I was a colt, barely able to stand. Your father, Ecgtheow, gave me to you. Don't you remember the battles we fought, warriors you vanquished, places we've gone and the things we've seen—can you not recall our adventures together, Bear's Son*?"

"*Bear's Son is the name the Forest Folk call me*, said Beowulf, *and though they tell me the story behind the name, I remember nothing. I'm sorry, but I remember little, apart from walking for a long, long time. Walking without knowing why or where I was going, just to arrive here. But if you're mine, Storm Bringer, and I believe you are, how is it that the young warrior brought you here*?"

"*The Manling, Turin, is your foster brother, Bear's Son. He fought alongside your father and carried your banner into battle at the place the Manlings call Falcon's Nest. He's served you faithfully. Never did he lose hope of finding you, but there's something more you must know.*"

"*Tell me,*" said Beowulf.

"*You had a wife.*"

"*Wife—I have a wife? Do you know her?"*

"Your wife is dead, Bear's Son."

The sun dropped below the horizon taking with it the last of the light. Night arrived on the heels of that Great Star and blanketed the land with darkness. Beowulf touched his brow to Storm Bringer's forehead: "We'll speak again, my friend," said Beowulf.

"I will be here waiting for you, Bear's Son," said the stallion.

As Beowulf started away, Storm Bringer called to him:

"*Beware Bear's Son—a storm is coming.*"

Beowulf stopped and looked at the stallion:

"*I know.*"

Beowulf returned to the lodge and put more wood on the fire. *I had a wife* Beowulf told himself. He tossed log after log into the flames. *Is it her face I sometimes see in the flames of the fire? And Turin, my foster brother? By all the gods, why can't I remember what happened to me, or who I am?*

Beowulf lit the candles Robbyn had placed throughout the lodge. His eyes took notice of something in one corner. He lit a torch and went to where Turin stacked the gear he had brought and left covered beneath a ground cloth. Beowulf lifted the cloth away.

The torchlight reflected off two polished helms and chainmail shirts. Alongside that battle gear were three swords in tooled leather scabbards. As he looked over those two, noble blades, they seemed to beckon to him from some unreachable place in his mind.

Beowulf reached down and drew one of the swords—Naegling, from its scabbard. He looked at the blade. Turin kept it sharpened to perfection. Holding the torch in his left hand, Beowulf swung Naegling over his head and side to side.

Moving to the beat of unseen drums, Beowulf began to dance in front of the fire and slice the air, dismembering phantoms that leapt at him from the shadows until sweat began to fall from his forehead. Beowulf stopped. He placed Naegling in its scabbard and covered the gear with the cloth. Beowulf returned the torch to the holder on the wall and then sat in front of the hearth.

One of those helms and one, maybe two of the swords are mine, he told himself; I'm no beginner, but what good is it knowing this when I can't remember who I am? Why didn't Turin confide he was searching for me?

While Beowulf sat tormented by his thoughts, the sound of rain falling on the roof of the lodge brought him back to the moment. He tossed a log on the fire and lie before the hearth, warmed by the flames, and calmed by the sound of rain beating on the roof.

Spent and exhausted after a dance of a different sort, Turin and Robbyn were content to hold one another close in the candlelight. With eyes open, they listened to thunder rumbling in the distance, and the almost deafening sound the rain made as it pelted the roof of Robbyn's lodge.

The wind howled through the night, long after Turin and Robbyn fell asleep in a lovers' embrace.

† † †

It was twilight and still raining when Turin left Robbyn's side and dressed. He stood in the open doorway and looked around. Through the rain, Turin saw Beowulf plowing the last of the land the Wylfings had agreed to set aside for that purpose. He was naked from the waist up, and his long wet hair was soaked and clung to his back and shoulders in thick matted strands. Slung crosswise over his back was Beowulf's two swords: Naegling and Widow Maker.

"Turin, are you there?" It was Robbyn calling to him from her bed.

"I'm here," said Turin; "in the doorway watching the storm." Turin closed the door and returned to her side.

"Are you hungry?" she said. "I can make us something to eat?"

"No," said Turin; "go back to sleep. I'll return soon; we can break fast then."

Turin kissed Robbyn; then he put on his cloak. He pulled the hood over his head before stepping outside. Lightning streaked a jagged path across the sky, followed by a peal of thunder that shook the ground where Turin stood.

Robbyn threw back the goose-down comforter and sat with her legs over the edge of her bed. How am I supposed to sleep she wondered?

While Robbyn roused herself from the comfort of her bed, the bed she had never shared with a man until now, outside, in the field, Turin slogged through the mud until he stood in the path of the bull, halting it in its tracks.

"By the gods, Metalsmith—what are you doing?" said Turin; "Come inside, out of the rain!"

At the sight of Turin in front of him, blocking his way, Beowulf's eyes flashed:

"Call me by my real name!" said Beowulf; "You've known it all along; yet you didn't tell me!"

Turin struggled to find his tongue.

"I tried to tell you any number of times," said Turin, shouting over the sound of the rain.

Lightning slashed the sky, closer than before, and thunder

followed on its heels.

"Look around you, Beowulf; where we're standing! This place is a Wylfing village! Think what would have come of it had I let on who you are."

"Are you both mad!" said Robbyn from the porch outside her lodge. Once again she wore boots, breeches, and a long-sleeve linen shirt.

"Did you not see the sky fire overhead? Are you deaf to the thunder? Come back inside, you fools!" Robbyn started toward them.

"Tell her!" said Beowulf, and he caught sight of Dolph and Yanus stepping from the barn to see what caused the shouting and commotion.

"Tell them all who I am! It doesn't matter anymore if it ever did—I am who I am, whatever it portends!"

"He's gone mad!" said Robbyn, "come away, Turin!"

Turin remained rooted in place, not knowing what to do.

Attracted by the iron strapped to his back, lightning struck Beowulf. His knees buckled, and he fell face-forward onto the ground.

Terrorized by the lightning and thunder the bull lurched ahead dragging the plow behind. The brothers led the bull back to the relative safety of the barn.

Turin removed the swords from Beowulf's back and tossed them to one side. He turned Beowulf over. Beowulf's eyes were open but there was no sign of life in them, and he gave no indication he was breathing.

Turin placed his ear near Beowulf's mouth and listened for breath—nothing. He put an ear on Beowulf's chest and listened for a heartbeat. There was none. Turin took hold of Beowulf by the shoulders and shook him.

"I didn't come all this way to lose you now!" Turin said. "I'll not let you die! Do you hear me, Bear's Son? I'll not let you leave this way! Wake up, damn you! This death is not warrior's death!"

Turin raised his fist and brought it down full force seven times against Beowulf's chest.

Beowulf gasped; his heart began beating, and air rushed into his lungs. Without looking at Robbyn, Turin lifted Beowulf into his arms and struggled through the mud to their lodge.

He kicked the door open and carried Beowulf to the hearth where a small fire still burned. Putting Beowulf down, Turin added more kindling and logs to the flames. He removed his cloak and placed it over Beowulf as a blanket. Turin took one of Beowulf's hands into his own; it was cold. Beowulf's eyes had closed, but his breathing came easy, and Turin counted that a blessing.

While Turin searched his mind for a remedy, Beowulf's swords crashed upon the floor. Turin saw Robbyn glaring at him. Like him, the storm had soaked her garments.

"Whose blades are these?" said Robbyn, "and why was he wearing them? Why was he outside plowing and why, by all the gods, did you call him, Bear's Son?"

"Last night he said he'd finish the plowing, no matter what. He wanted to return to the forest. As for the swords, I brought them—the metalsmith saw them among my gear and took a fancy to them."

Ashamed of himself for the lies that escaped his lips, Turin looked away from her.

"Bright Eyes a metalsmith?" said Robbyn; "And you a 'Tribe of One'? He's no metalsmith, and you're no tribe of one! What else are you lying about, Turin—if that's your name!"

Turin assumed his full height: "I'm called Turin, the adopted son of Ecgtheow Waegmunding. The man you see there is Ecgtheow's first-born, Beowulf. My foster brother."

"Ecgtheow Waegmunding?" said Robbyn. A look of shock came over her face.

"The same Ecgtheow Waegmunding who murdered Prince Heatholaf, a warrior beloved by his people—my people!"

"Yes," said Turin. "Had I told you when you took me as your prisoner you would've loosed an arrow in me straight away—would you not?"

"Yes," she said. "More like two or three arrows and by all the gods I would have found a way to kill him also—wolves or no wolves!"

"Beowulf wandered here because he's out of his right mind. I came here in search of him. Now that I've found him we'll leave. I ask that you allow him to get better before we depart."

"Why should we? This is a Wylfing village!" said Robbyn.

"Why do you keep shouting?" said Turin, "I'm right here in

front of you!"

"Because I'm angry," said Robbyn.

Robbyn's brothers entered the lodge.

"What's going on?" said Dolph.

"Is the metalsmith dead?" said Yanus.

"No," said Robbyn; "he's not, and he's no metalsmith! He's a Thunder-Geat! His name is Beowulf Waegmunding, who our father and uncle called the 'Widow-Maker'! He was one of Hygelac's assassins, just like his father was for King Hrethel, and now the bear's son is King of Geatland."

"The bear's son!" said Dolph and Yanus.

The Twins stepped on each other in their haste to step back a safe distance from where Beowulf lay unconscious. There was no disguising their fear as they looked upon Beowulf's face, fixated by his facial scar illuminated in the firelight.

"I've asked Robbyn," said Turin to the brothers; "and now I'll ask you two: allow me more time here. When my king is well enough to ride, I'll take him away. Until then, I promise you: I'll keep to myself and will not trouble or—"

"Or what?" said Robbyn, "Kill us in our sleep?"

"Had I wanted to kill you I would have done it long ago," said Turin. "As soon as my king can ride his horse we'll trouble you no more. Until then I ask for peace between us."

"Peace," said Robbyn, "between Wylfings and Geats?" She looked to one side and spat on the floor.

"That is what I think of your peace, Geatlander!"

Robbyn turned on her heel and started for the door.

"Dolph, Yanus!" she said; "Come away from this place—the air here is rank with deception!"

The brothers followed their sister from the lodge. Turin went to the doorway and watched as they departed. Even after the Wylfings went inside, Turin continued to watch.

Dolph stepped outside holding his bow. Behind him stepped Robbyn. She struck Dolph on the back of his head. He yelped as Robbyn took him by the scruff of his neck and pulled him inside their lodge. Yanus stepped outside. He cast Turin no harsh look, no insulting gesture; rather, there was an expression of great disappointment on his face. Turin closed the door and returned to Beowulf's side.

74

THE CLARION'S CALL

Turin strapped Beowulf to Storm Bringer then led all three horses across the wet ground to the barn. Above them, lightning flashed, and thunder bellowed. Turin cared little if Robbyn and the Twins saw him. He was a Geat warrior and a Waegmunding—*to Helheim with Wylfings* he told himself. He could defend the barn with its one entrance better than the lodge. Besides, from the barn, Turin enjoyed a better view of the village. A would-be attacker would have to cross an empty field a hundred paces across.

Turin carried Beowulf to a corner of the barn where Dolph and Yanus had slept on pallets cushioned with long grass. Turin placed Beowulf there; then he put his sword, spear, and bow close to his pallet where he could get to them.

When done fortifying the barn, Turin fed the horses. Afterward, he set about cooking a stew, enough to last several days.

† † †

Robbyn's boots were drying beside the fire. Her eyes were red and swollen. Dolph and Yanus sat at the table with slouched shoulders and sullen expressions. For what seemed a long time, the Twins waited, helpless but to listen to their sister alone in her bedroom, sobbing.

When she emerged, Robbyn poured them each a hot drink made from herbs flavored with honey; the same honey Beowulf gave them. Robbyn joined her brothers at the table. She folded her cold hands around the cup, enjoying the warmth it provided.

"What are we going to do?" said Dolph.

"Yes," said Yanus; "What are we to do?"

"Do? We do nothing," said Robbyn. "We go about our business as though there's no one here but us. The Thunder-Geats will leave, and life will go back to what it was before they came. Then, all we'll have to worry about is—"

"King Ingvar," said the Twins, in unison.

"While you were changing your clothes," said Dolph, "Yanus and I saw Turin take the bear's son and horses into the barn."

"There's nothing in the barn we need," said Robbyn.

The three sipped the hot brew and breathed its aroma. After a period of silence, Robbyn said, "When the storm quits, and the ground dries out, I'll hunt for something delicious! How does that sound?"

"It sounds crazy," said Dolph. "The bear's son warned us against hunting in the forest, remember?"

"I remember," said Yanus.

"The bear's son is nothing more than a living corpse now," said Robbyn, "he can't stop us from feeding ourselves, nor can his kinsman; besides, I'm sick of eating fish and pheasant. I'm going to kill a boar or a deer, and we're going to eat red meat until we burst."

† † †

Robbyn waited one day after the rain quit before donning a fleece-lined waistcoat, a head-cover, and her best pair of sealskin breeches and boots, in case the rain returned. She carried a knife, her bow and a full quiver of arrows. As she left her lodge, Robbyn looked to where her brothers were keeping their eyes on the cattle. Like their sister, Dolph and Yanus kept their bows close at hand.

Leaving the environs of the village behind, Robbyn entered the woods in the hope of finding a wild pig to kill, gut and return with, just as she had promised. It was the first time Robbyn visited the forest since the previous autumn when she and her brothers first encountered the bear's son. It galled her that this slayer of her people was now in her barn, protected by the first man she knew she could love and together grow old. Robbyn heard a rustling of leaves. She crouched behind a bush and fitted her bowstring with an arrow. From behind her came a low, menacing growl. Robbyn relaxed the tension on her bow and looked around.

Behind her was the wolf Lord whom the bear's son called, Adalwolf. Robbyn stood and lowered her bow to her side. Unafraid, but with great respect, she looked into Adalwolf's gold-flecked eyes.

"I don't know if you can understand my words, Gray Lord," said Robbyn, "but my brothers and I have tired of eating fish and fowl. I come here searching for boar or deer. If I've offended you with my trespass, I ask forgiveness, and permission to depart. If you understand what I'm saying, also know that sky fire struck the bear's son during the storm. He lies in a barn in my village, neither alive nor dead. His foster kinsman, Turin, watches over him. That's all I have to say."

The wolf looked at her a moment longer before disappearing into the woods. Robbyn breathed a sigh of relief and started for the village empty handed.

† † †

Yanus was first to see seventy riders enter the valley from the northeast along with half their number in captives: men, women, and children roped together and driven before the riders like sheep.

"King Ingvar is coming!" said Yanus.

"What do we do?" said Dolph.

"I don't know."

"Well… think of something!"

"You think of something!" said Yanus.

"What would Robbyn do?"

"She'd tell us not to piss ourselves!" said Yanus.

"That's not it! That's not all she'd say," said Dolph.

"No!" said Yanus; "she'd tell us to be brave."

"What else?"

Yanus gave the matter some thought: "She'd tell us to leave the cattle here and sneak back to the lodge."

"Then what," said Dolph.

Yanus thought some more: "She'd tell us to bar the doors and windows and wait."

"Wait?" said Dolph. "Wait for what?"

The leader of the bandits was a one-eyed, one-eared white-bearded Ostergoth known as King Ingvar—not because he was a real king because he wasn't, but Ingvar believed he was and ruled over his band as such. Ingvar did this by way of a simple creed: "Do as I say, or Die!"

Long in the tooth, Ingvar's age had not tempered his proclivity for cruelty. His son, Hakan, was reputed to be as cruel as his father, perhaps even more so. After the last village had failed to provide the bandits with the requisite tribute, Hakan ordered every man, woman, and child gutted. Their innards he ordered collected and left in a pile except for the livers which the bandits roasted for dinner at the end of the day. It was a warning to the people of other villages lest they think of holding back what Ingvar demanded from them.

The bandits headed southwest accumulating captives from one defenseless village after another. Those men, women, and children who survived the journey to the coast, Ingvar intended to sell to slavers in Jutland and Germania. As the bandits neared the Wylfing village, Ingvar ordered Hakan to remind him of the particulars.

"The village is empty," said Hakan to his father, "except for the two idiots."

"Ah, yes," said Ingvar, "the Wylfing twins. Tell me again why we didn't kill them the last time we came through."

"Because they make sure we have cattle to feed on until we reach the coast and because they make you laugh."

"Very well, post riders ahead and tell the idiots King Ingvar is coming!"

"I'll go myself," said Hakan.

† † †

In the barn, Turin heard the sound of horses approaching the village. After dousing the cooking-fire with water, he looked through a crack between boards and saw three horsemen riding toward the village, all of them armed.

Turin sensed it was a scouting patrol and part of the bandit band that afflicted Robbyn and her brothers. He watched as the riders stopped their horses in front of Robbyn's lodge. One rider, in particular, commanded Turin's attention, it was the bandit sitting tallest in the saddle. That same man called to the Twins.

"Come out, come out, wherever you are! Your friend Hakan is back! Can you hear me, lads? Don't be afraid."

Hakan looked at the two warriors who accompanied him: "Search the lodge!"

The two bandits dismounted, looked inside the lodge and soon emerged. One of the two, a Gifth renegade named Brolin, held an embroidered shift which he handed to Hakan.

"I don't remember one of the idiots wearing that," said Brolin.

Hakan frowned: "Neither do I," he said. He held the garment under his nose and breathed. "Nor do I remember them smelling this good! I want you two to search the other lodges. I'll search the barn."

Hakan draped Robbyn's shift around his neck.

Turin continued to watch as two of the brigands searched the lodges on foot. The tall one rode his horse over the planted ground straight toward the barn.

Careful not to make noise, Turin removed the cross beam that held the barn door shut. He would make it easy for the bandit to enter. As he watched the bandit approach, out of the corner of his eye, Turin saw Robbyn enter the village from the west. Robbyn also had seen the three thieves, and she moved in the direction of her lodge. At the same time, east of the barn, Turin saw Dolph and Yanus playing cat-and-mouse with the two bandits Hakan sent to search the other lodges. Turin retrieved his sword and waited in the shadows.

"Hello in there," called Hakan, "it's me, your old friend Hakan —you're not hiding from me are you, lads?"

Hakan waited. When no response came from inside, he dismounted, drew his sword and pushed the barn door open. Hakan stepped forward. As he did, Turin stepped from the shadows, pulled the bandit inside and struck Hakan alongside the head with the hilt of his sword. As Hakan collapsed to his knees, his sword fell from his hand.

"Call out, and you're a dead man," said Turin.

"Don't kill me," said Hakan, "my father's King Ingvar, Ruler of the Northlands. He'll let you live if you let me go unharmed."

"Are you that important to him?" said Turin. "Ostergoths are famous for eating their offspring."

"Only if they're born deformed," said Hakan, "and it's our dogs that eat them—unless, of course, food is scarce."

"I'll try to remember that," said Turin.

He slammed his hilt a second time against the side of Hakan's head, knocking him unconscious.

Turin closed the barn door and barred it shut. He lost no time tying Hakan's hands and feet; then he stuffed a rag into the bandit's mouth. Turin returned to the front of the barn.

He could no longer see the twins but what he did see caused the hair on the back of his neck to stand. Robbyn was stalking the two bandits as they went from one lodge to the next. She loosed two arrows in quick succession that found their targets in the bandits' backs. That was when the twins reappeared, scampering from their hiding place. Turin watched as Robbyn and her brothers convened at their lodge; they entered and closed the door behind.

Inside their lodge, Robbyn hugged her brothers.

"You did well. Now hide yourselves in the forest. Wait there until Ingvar and his men have left—do you understand? No matter what you hear or see you're not to return until they're gone."

At the back of their minds, Dolph and Yanus didn't like what they were hearing, but they nodded their agreement with their sister's wishes.

"What about you?" they said; "What are you going to do?"

"I'm not sure yet," said Robbyn. "I'll think of something, but I won't be able to think of anything—unless I know you're both safe. Understand?"

Again the brothers nodded.

The bandit king climbed down out of his saddle by stepping on the back of one of his men. He grasped the hands of two more bandits who waited on either side to steady Ingvar's legs as he plopped to the ground.

Ingvar's saddle sores were seeping again, and they smelled. He was tired and in a foul mood after riding since sunup.

"Where's my son?" said Ingvar. "Where's Prince Hakan?"

A renegade named Arngol, an outcast from the Hetware Tribe, and one of Hakan's familiars, approached:

"Prince Hakan hasn't returned, my King."

Ingvar gave the matter his consideration. "We'll wait," he said.

Ingvar took several long gulps from a water bag. The bandit king then undid his belt and dropped his breeches to his ankles. He bent over, and with the help of two men to steady him, waited as the bandits' surgeon lanced his boils.

The would-be healer poured beer over the wounds to rinse out the pus. King Ingvar hoisted his breeches, and Arngol helped him fasten his belt.

"Get me on my horse!" said Ingvar. "Now, you worthless sons of crows!"

† † †

The bandits entered the village from the northeast and came upon the bodies of the two men who accompanied Hakan earlier. The thieves shouted Hakan's name, but the bandit prince didn't answer. Encountering no opposition, Ingvar led his men to Robbyn's lodge.

"You, there. Inside. Know it is I, King Ingvar who rules this land! Release my son—or die!"

"You can swallow your tongue, for all I care," said Robbyn from behind a shuttered window. "I've got Prince Hakan by the balls. I won't give him up without a trade!"

"Show him to me, girl! That way I'll know you're telling me straight."

"To Helheim with you, old man," said Robbyn; "I'll do no such thing!"

"Take care what you say, girl," said Arngol; "You're talking to King Ingvar, exalted Ruler of the Northland."

"Yes, yes, yes," said Robbyn; "of course he is. And I'm Robbyn, Goddess of the Moon!"

"You know my men could storm your lodge," said Ingvar, "cut

your throat and have their way with you! Do you want that for yourself, girl?"

"Send your dung-eaters against me, old man, but before they break the threshold of this lodge, I'll cut Hakan's manhood off, shove it in his mouth and slit his throat for good measure! Is that what you want O King of murderers, rapists, and thieves!"

A long moment passed while the Exalted Ruler of the North considered his options:

"What do you want, girl, in exchange for letting my son go? Maybe a new shift, embroidered with gold thread? Perhaps earrings made from silver, and amber? Or an ivory comb, made from whales' teeth? Or a silver broach? Anything you like, just tell me what you want!"

"I want the lives of my brothers and me in exchange for Hakan's!" said Robbyn. "I want you to let us leave here. You can have this village of ghosts for all I care!"

"And just when you seem so intent on staying," said Ingvar. "What a pity."

"What are you talking about, old man?" said Robbyn.

"I'm old, but I'm not blind, girl. Someone has plowed the field behind me. You're trying to farm, aren't you? And you a Wylfing of all things!"

"You're as bad at guessing, old man, as you are at king'ing," said Robbyn.

Ingvar turned to Arngol: "Bring the captives up here; place them where the girl can see!"

"At once, Great King!" said Arngol. He dug his heels into his horse's ribs and galloped off.

"There's something I want you to see, girl," said Ingvar.

Arngol soon returned with the captives under guard. He herded them into the open so Robbyn could watch.

"Until Hakan is released," said Ingvar, "I'll kill one of these slaves every time you say, 'No'—do you understand?"

"For every man, woman or child you kill, old man, I'll remove something of your son's, beginning with his toes—do you understand me, you gelded old pig?"

"You wouldn't dare harm my son," said Ingvar.

Behind Ingvar and his band of thieves came the shrill blast of a ram's horn.

A short distance outside the barn, Turin sat atop his horse, dressed in battle gear. Again, and again, Turin sounded the horn.

† † †

Occupying a place of shadows between the living and the dead, the far-reaching sound of Turin's horn penetrated some unfathomable part of Beowulf's brain. As the horn blasts continued, clouds of darkness in Beowulf's head dissolved, evaporated by the uncorrupted force of memory, and he heard Elin's voice call him:

"*Awaken, Beowulf! Awaken Bear's Son! Enemies threaten*!"

Beowulf's eyes opened wide.

† † †

"Hear me, dung eater," Turin said. "I, Turin, foster brother to Beowulf Waegmunding, hold your son prisoner in the barn. If you want him back, let the girl and her brothers go!"

"You know what angers me most, Geatlander," said Ingvar, "it's not that you and the girl are both terrible liars; it's because you have no respect for your elders!"

"Oh, we do," said Turin, "those deserving of it!"

"Tell me, Geatlander," said Ingvar; "how it is that you and the Wylfing woman are together in this? Why hasn't one of you killed the other?"

"To hear why would disappoint you," said Turin.

"The Geatlander tells it well," said Robbyn; "besides, it's no business of yours, you ancient fornicator of sheep!"

Several of Ingvar's men snickered; others laughed aloud. Ingvar silenced them with a look.

"I'm beginning to think my son is dead," said Ingvar, looking in Robbyn's direction. "Therefore, before I kill you both, I'll have my men set torches to this valley and put every living thing to the sword."

"That... you will not do!" said a voice that carried with it the force of thunder.

All eyes turned to see from whom the words issued.

Turin and Robbyn saw Beowulf approach on the back of Storm Bringer. Trailing behind walked Hakan, with a rope binding his hands. Beowulf fastened the loose end of the rope to his saddle. Beowulf wore breeches and boots but no armor. Without his helm, long white hair fanned down his back and danced in the wind.

"That's my son you hold prisoner," said Ingvar.

"I won't keep him prisoner for long," said Beowulf.

"Who are you?" said the bandit king.

"I'll tell you who he is," said Turin. "He's Beowulf Waegmunding, King of Geatland, whom some call the bear's son!"

"You lie," said Ingvar. "Beowulf Waegmunding is dead!"

"Perhaps he is," said Beowulf; "but the bear's son is very much alive!"

"Very well—if you are the bear's son," said Ingvar, "let's negotiate."

"You're a king of dung-beetles, worms and carrion birds," said Robbyn. "Why would the King of the Thunder-Geats negotiate with you?"

Ignoring the insult, Ingvar pointed to where the bandits positioned the group of captives.

"I propose a trade, Bear's Son," said Ingvar. "I'll trade the lives of these slaves, along with your own, and those of your ill-mannered friends in exchange for Prince Hakan. What say you? As you can see, my men outnumber you twenty to one."

When Beowulf made no reply, Turin laughed and drew his sword.

75

THE ONCE AND FUTURE KING

"See this field," said Beowulf; "It's been plowed and planted. All it lacks is the All Mother's blessing."

"That means nothing to me," said Ingvar.

Beowulf urged Storm Bringer to the center of the field. With a slight tug of the rope, he brought Hakan to his knees.

"Besides, what has that to do with my son?" said Ingvar.

"Everything," said Beowulf. He drew Naegling and severed Hakan's head from his shoulders. Beowulf let the rope fall from his hand; then he unsheathed Widow Maker.

"At them!" said Ingvar, unleashing lungs filled with rage.

The bandits were not keen on charging, not after witnessing what had befallen Hakan.

"Kill them!" said Ingvar. "Kill them, you sons of crows!"

Turin rode to Beowulf's side. That was when the wolves, badgers, forest cats and bears arrived, a hundred or more. Behind them came the Twins.

Robbyn stepped out of her lodge, raised her bow and loosed an arrow. It struck the bandit king in the throat and toppled Ingvar from his horse.

Turin and Beowulf rode toward Robbyn, killing as they went. The Forest Folk brought down many a bandit before those still alive elected to flee.

As a handful of bandits rode east, back the way they came, they found themselves pursued by the Gray Brethren.

As a silence descended over the village, Robbyn embraced her brothers. Beowulf and Turin rode to where the captives huddled together in the field.

"Cut their bindings," said Beowulf.

"At once, my King!" said Turin.

Turin dismounted and began to cut the bindings from the wrists of the captives. Robbyn appeared at his side.

"Let me help."

† † †

After Robbyn's brothers and the former captives had dragged the last dead bandit to the edge of the forest, to leave as food for the Forest Folk, a joyous celebration commenced.

The twins slaughtered a cow for roasting and opened many kegs of beer. Likewise, men and boys gathered wood for a great bonfire and the people celebrated long into the night, but Beowulf was not among them.

The bear's son combed and groomed his warhorse and listened to Storm Bringer's account of all that transpired at Vindinstedt Farm during his absence.

While Dolph and Yanus basked in the gratitude lavished on them by the former captives, Turin and Robbyn sat alone beside the stream where they first encountered one another. They stared at the stars, and delighted in the fact they were alive, and together.

† † †

Around mid-morning, the next day, Turin and Robbyn found Beowulf in the barn saddling Storm Bringer.

"I understand," said Beowulf, "if you want to stay here."

"No, my King, I'm coming with you," said Turin.

Beowulf stopped what he was doing, turned and faced Turin and Robbyn: "Are you sure?"

"I'm sure, my King," said Turin, "because Robbyn has consented to leave with me if you allow it."

Beowulf smiled at them both: "You've grown wise, Brother. Nothing would please me more than seeing you two together."

Robbyn stepped forward and hugged Beowulf.

"You're not the ogre I thought you were. I will forever thank the gods for bringing we three together."

"Be it so!" said Beowulf, "but what of your brothers? What will the Twins do without you? Tell them they're welcome to come with us."

"We'll make do for once without Robbyn," said Dolph, as he and Yanus entered the barn.

"We've spoken with the people you freed," said Yanus, "and

we've invited them to stay and help us bring the village back to life."

"Is that so?" said Beowulf.

"It is, Great King," said Dolph; "they were farmers and tradesmen and will be again; there's even a metalsmith among them."

"We're going to be a village again," said Yanus, "not a Wylfing village, but a village for everyone willing to work to make it their home."

"Then, be it so," said Beowulf. "I only ask that you do no harm to the creatures of the forest, and see that there's food for the Forest Folk in the winter, lest their young go hungry."

"It will be as you say," said Yanus.

Beowulf looked at Turin and Robbyn: "It's time to leave."

Turin reached into one of his saddlebags and removed the Crown of Geatland.

"The Crown of Geatland, my King," said Turin. "It's time you wore it once more."

† † †

They rode west until they reached Vindinstedt Farm. Freemen had seen them coming and the word of Beowulf's return spread. Beorn was also there to greet them, for he had foreseen Beowulf's return in a vision.

"Welcome back," said Beorn.

The Schaman chose his words with care, knowing there was no place Beowulf could call home: not the Citadel, not Vindinstedt Farm, not Lüma's cave, nor even the Schaman's old lodge with its sturdy walls at the Lake in the Clouds.

"Thank you, my friend," said Beowulf.

Beowulf and Beorn hugged. Immense and numerous were the feelings that passed between them.

Beorn turned to Turin and held him close.

"You did well," said Beorn. He looked at Robbyn and smiled. "Is this beauty your bride to be?"

"It is," said Turin. "Robbyn, this is Beorn. Don't mind his blue beard or the smell of wood smoke. He's ferocious in battle, but around a beautiful face, he's meek as can be."

Robbyn didn't hesitate. She stepped forward and hugged the Schaman.

"I love your beard and the smell of wood smoke," she said.

"Ha!" said Beorn. "I like this woman!"

"I don't see Lord Weohstan," said Turin. "Is he at Falcon's Nest?"

"Lord Weohstan is dead, Turin," said the Schaman. "He died in his sleep last winter. We stayed up late into the night talking and reminiscing. He was smiling, Turin, and in good spirits when he retired for the night. You mustn't be sad over the way he died."

"How so?" said Turin. "He deserved a warrior's death—in battle."

"When Greta and Brigitte found him the next morning, he was holding his sword with both hands folded over the hilt where it rested on his chest. He knew he was going to die. Rest assured Turin, if there is any justice in Asgard, Weohstan Waegmunding has a place in Valhalla with his son, Handscio."

"We will miss him greatly," said Beowulf, "but he would want us to rejoice and celebrate the life he lived, and we shall. Besides, Weohstan would tell us we have a wedding to plan—would he not?"

† † †

Once wed, Turin and Robbyn stayed behind to manage the affairs of the farm. Beowulf and Beorn departed for Falcon's Nest.

News that Beowulf was alive and on his way back to Falcon's Nest preceded his arrival. The city was overflowing with Geatfolk —those who inhabited Falcon's Nest the year around, and those who came from near and far to celebrate their king's return.

Accompanied by the Schaman, Beowulf rode into the city, and the people gathered in the Great Square. They cheered and shouted: "Bear's Son!"

From the eastern wall-walk of the Citadel, Sigmund saw Beorn and his king approach through the throng of Geatfolk. Masking his astonishment over the sight of Beowulf's white hair, Sigmund led the Guard outside the Citadel to make a path for the Bear's Son's return.

† † †

The following summer, on the night of the Solstice, Beorn dined with Beowulf. They ate alone, just as they had every night since Beowulf's return to Falcon's Nest.

Finished eating, Beorn pushed his chair back from the table, belched and then wiped his mouth with the end of his beard.

"I'll be leaving tomorrow," said the Schaman, "at sunrise."

"What?" said Beowulf. "Why? For where?"

"I've been here too long, Bear's Son. All Götaland is at peace, thanks to you. The Thunder-Geats are flourishing. The Whale Road remains open for trade. Even the least among the tribes have prospered in the absence of war. As for where I'm going…" Beorn hesitated. "I'll know it when I get there."

A moment passed in silence.

"Will I see you again?" said Beowulf.

Beorn smiled.

"If Fate wills it."

† † †

Dawn the next day, Beowulf and Beorn rode out the Main Gate onto the causeway. They halted their horses and looked at one another.

"Die well, my friend," said Beowulf.

"Die well, Bear's Son."

Beowulf waited on the causeway and watched as Beorn urged his horse away. Beowulf shielded his eyes as the sun began its ascent.

The Bear's Son continued to watch Beorn ride off until that fiery orb cleared the tops of the hills, blinding Beowulf with its brilliance, and concealing the Schaman from view.

76

A QUEST FOR THE OFFERING

Several moons following Beorn's departure, Sigmund found his King in the stables brushing and currying Storm Bringer after having taken the stallion for a morning ride.

"What is it, Sigmund?"

"An Outlander, Beowulf—she seeks an audience."

"She?"

"A woman dressed in rags and need of a bath. She carries herself like a warrior and with a noble bearing."

"Hmm. Did you tell this woman I hear petitions on the first Thor's Day after every New Moon?"

"I did, Beowulf. She said she hasn't come to ask you for anything. She says she has something to tell you—face to face."

"An Outlander, you say?"

"To hear her speak—yes. From Germania."

"Well, old friend, since we've nothing pressing that needs doing, let's hear what she has to say."

† † †

Beowulf entered the Throne Room accompanied by Sigmund. As they walked toward the dais, Beowulf saw a tall, slender woman with hair past her waist, standing to one side. She had about her the bearing of someone who'd endured great hardship. Nine warriors from Beowulf's Personal Guard, the Kungens Vakter escorted her.

Flicking his head toward the guards, Beowulf cast Sigmund a questioning look.

"Since your return, our spies abroad report more threats against your life, my King. I thought it prudent to—"

Beowulf silenced Sigmund with a wave of his hand.

"Your spies are to be commended, Lord Sigmund, but send the

Kungens Vakter away. I don't think this woman means me harm."

Sigmund signaled to the Kungens Vakter to resume their stations outside the entrance to the Throne Room. That done, Beowulf took his seat on Geatland's throne. He motioned to the woman to approach. She came forward, stopped a respectful distance from the dais and bowed. As she looked up, she met Beowulf's penetrating gaze without reservation.

"Do you find the color of my hair strange?" he said.

"No, Great King," said Eydís. "You are young, it is true, but you are not like any other man in Midgard

A long moment had passed before Beowulf spoke: "You requested an audience."

"Yes, Great King," said the woman.

"Who are you?" said Beowulf.

"My name is Eydís, daughter of Haraldr, once chief of the Harii."

"I've heard it said your father slew Adulfuns, the Wylfings' king?"

"Yes," said Eydís. "As payment for the service, Ecgtheow rendered my tribe years ago."

"Ah! I thought Haraldr's part in Adalfuns' death was only a rumor."

"Is no idle talk, Great King," said Eydís. "Haraldr knew he was dying and wanted to pay our tribe's debt to your father while yet he lived."

"Did you know Ecgtheow Waegmunding?" said Beowulf.

"Yes," said Eydís.

"Tell me more, daughter of Haraldr."

"Your father came to our village from Frihamm. He was near death and hunted by the Dark Queen. When he was better, he left. But he returned—with the Black Ship. Ecgtheow made it possible for our tribe—what remained of us, to reunite with our sister tribes, the Cimbrii, and Teutons, and reclaim our homeland from the Franks."

"And you say it was my father—the man known as the 'widow maker,' who did this?"

"No, Beowulf. I mean the man I loved—Ecgtheow Waegmunding—did this."

Beowulf stood and stepped down from the dais. He went to

Eydís.

"Then know that you're welcome here, Lady Eydís," said Beowulf.

He smiled at Eydís and embraced her. Beowulf turned toward Sigmund: "This woman is my honored guest. See to it she's looked after, Sigmund. Understood?"

"Of course, my King," said Sigmund.

Beowulf looked at Eydís: "Tonight, after you've had time to rest, we'll talk."

† † †

Present at supper that night were Beowulf, Eydís, and Sigmund. Bathed, with her hair washed and brushed, Eydís resembled the beautiful Eydís of old, except for a profound look in her eyes that hinted of madness. She wore an embroidered shift; one of Robbyn's, for when Robin and Turin visited the Citadel.

Instructed by Sigmund earlier, the servants made but little noise when bringing food and drink to the Banquet Hall.

Beowulf raised his drinking cup toward Eydís: "Here," said Beowulf, "Let's drink to the memory of the warriors who sired us —Ecgtheow and Haraldr."

They drank.

Eydís laughed. "*I can feel you are listening to my thoughts, Bear's Son,*" she said in the Silent Tongue.

"*I knew you had 'the gift.' I could feel you doing the same to me before you entered the Throne Room.*" said Beowulf: *"So, Eydís, daughter of Haraldr. Tell me: Why are you here*?"

† † †

For nine days and nights, Beowulf and Eydís plied the Whale Road aboard the Black Ship. With them were forty-two warriors— all handpicked by Beowulf from among the of the Kungens Vakter, two warriors to man the tiller, the other forty to row when necessary.

The rest of the Kungens Vakter would remain with Sigmund at the Citadel; since it was into Sigmund's steady hands the bear's son placed the Crown of Geatland for safe keeping during his absence.

† † †

It was just after sunrise, their tenth day at sea when Beowulf saw the coast of Jutland west of the Avenger's position; he also spied a huge crow, emblazoned on the crimson sail of a ship coming toward them.

Beowulf looked back toward the mast where Eydís sat preparing hot soup and roasted turnips over a brazier—breakfast for Beowulf's men as they sat on their benches rowing, awaiting their King's next command. With the Avenger's black sail furled, and with the sun behind them, Beowulf knew there was little chance the lookouts aboard the slave trader's ship had yet seen them. Downwind of the slave trader's ship, Beowulf could smell the food they were cooking for their breakfast.

"Eydís," said Beowulf in the Silent Tongue. "Look—in the distance, straight ahead."

"The Red Crow?" said Eydís.

Beowulf nodded. "Yes—the Red Crow."

Without being told, Eydís doused the cooking fire in the brazier and threw the soup and roasted turnips overboard.

"I think the warriors of the Kungens Vakter are angry I tossed their breakfast overboard," said Eydís.

Beowulf laughed. "Good! I want that bloody bunch of killers angry. The angrier, the better!"

† † †

With the sun in their eyes, the slavers had no time to prepare. When the Avenger was abreast of the Red Crow some of Beowulf's men hurled grappling hooks—the hooks bit into the wooden side of the slaver's ship to keep the two vessels from drifting apart. The remainder of the Kungens Vakter, along with Eydís, loosed arrows at the men aboard the slaver's ship, killing or wounding them all save for one.

Beowulf watched this Harii woman who once loved his father

go amongst the slave-traders, cutting their throats where they lie.

Several of the Kungens Vakter threw back a tarp and found the slave trader, Fynegeld, cowering there. With him was Eydís's son, Ikin.

Ikin's eyes were glazed; he was drugged and dressed in silks befitting a Syrian courtesan. His face was painted in a manner befitting a girl trained for one thing only—to please the man who owned her.

Eydís approached Fynegeld. Two of the Kungens Vakter held the slave trader by the arms. When Fynegeld saw the wild-eyed woman warrior and the blood dripping from the long curved blade of the knife she wielded, his eyes grew large. Urine flowed down one of his legs and pooled on the deck.

Eydís looked at Beowulf:

"He's yours to do with as you will," said Beowulf.

Eydís turned to the Kungens Vakter restraining the slave trader:

"Strip him," said Eydís. "Then turn him around, so I don't have to look at the face of this pig."

The two Kungens Vakter looked at their king. Beowulf nodded. The warriors laughed and tore the embroidered silk robes from Fynegeld's body.

"Now bend him over," said Eydís, "and hold him that way."

"No! I beg you," said the slave trader. "By all the gods, don't do this."

The warriors held the trembling Syrian doubled over.

"This is for my son," said Eydís.

She thrust the point of the knife blade into the slave trader's shite-hole, and while Fynegeld screamed, Eydís pushed the knife further inside, until it vanished from sight. The slave trader's body had convulsed several times before he crumpled to the deck—dead.

"What you did was just and called for," said Beowulf, still using the Silent Tongue.

Eydís stood in front of her son. The boy gave no indication that he recognized his mother.

"I will always love you, precious boy," said Eydís.

Eydís turned Ikin, so he faced away from her; then reached around and sliced his throat. Eydís lowered Ikin's body to the deck while blood spurted from his neck over her arms. Then he lay still.

Eydís turned to Beowulf, and in the Silent Tongue said: *"I couldn't let my son live with the shame he would feel knowing what he'd become. I couldn't live with such shame. Could you, Bear's Son?"*

"*No*," said Beowulf.

"*Thank you, son of Ecgtheow,*" said Eydís. "*May the gods watch over you, always.*"

Beowulf nodded. "*And you,*" he said.

Before Beowulf could stop her, Eydís placed the edge of the knife on the inside of her elbow and sliced deep into her flesh, all the way to her wrist, opening the artery. She was smiling as Beowulf helped her into a sitting position.

Eydís held her son in her arms and swayed back and forth as if rocking him to sleep. A moment later, Eydís, too, lay dead.

The warrior Beowulf had put in charge of the Kungens Vakter aboard the Avenger came forward:

"Your orders, my King?"

Beowulf continued to look at Eydís and her son: "Throw the slave trader and the bodies of his men overboard. Let the Sea Folk dispose of them. We'll make this ship Lady Eydís's pyre, for her and her son."

After the Thunder-Geats had tossed the Syrian's corpse and those of his men overboard, Beowulf's crew got back aboard the Avenger. Using olive oil to accelerate the burning, Beowulf put a torch to the Red Crow before rejoining his men.

While the Avenger sped over the waves for home, Beowulf watched the Red Crow burn until it slipped beneath the waves.

77

EBB & FLOW

Geatland flourished. Peace reigned. Tribes accustomed to war no longer contemplated Geatland's destruction, or so it seemed, not with the bear's son on the throne. In Frisland, warriors did talk of wresting control of the Whale Road from the Geats, but it was just that—talk! The Frisians lacked the stomach to face Day Raven's killer. Over time their fear of Beowulf had woven its way into the collective memory of their tribe, so much so that Frisian parents told their children the bear's son would return on full moon nights to eat them if they misbehaved.

† † †

King Octha of Kent studied the seven large chests overflowing with gold—gold the Emissary from the Emperor in the east ordered placed at Octha's feet, one chest for each of the rulers of the Seven Anglo-Saxon Kingdoms located on the Tin Isles: "Tell your exalted Emperor, he'll have his ships, and men to go with them," said Octha.

† † †

In the absence of strife, life at the Citadel grew stale for the bear's son. Beowulf often went to Vindinstedt Farm. It was there with Turin, Robbyn, and their children that Beowulf's heart was most at peace. Beowulf, Turin, and Elin had grown older together and time forged a bond between them that nothing but death could sunder. Robbyn and Turin brought six children into the world: four sons and two daughters. Of those six, three lived to have children of their own.

† † †

Late in life though it was, Weohstan's second wife, Isolde, had borne Weohstan, a son he named Wiglaf. Isolde died soon after giving birth, and after Weohstan's passing, it was Turin and Robbyn who raised Wiglaf while Beowulf trained him to be a warrior. In time, Wiglaf became as skilled as his father once was with spear, sword, and axe. It was to Wiglaf whom Beowulf looked to be his eyes and ears and the enforcer of his will throughout Geatland.

† † †

Early spring. Heavy snow fall in the mountains of Svearland that winter continued to melt, long after the spring solstice. The runoff from the snowmelt swelled the major rivers in the north; so, too, their tributaries in the south. Geatland's rivers were full and overflowed their banks even as the water from these mighty rivers rushed to the sea.

† † †

Wiglaf Waegmunding exhausted two horses to bring his king the news he received while attending to matters at Land's End. When Wiglaf entered the Throne Room, he was pale, out of breath.

"Take a moment to breathe, Cousin," said Beowulf, "then speak."

"Our spies in the Tin Isles say the Seven Kingdoms are building a mighty fleet of battle craft."

"How many ships?"

"All totaled: seven-hundred."

"By the gods," said Sigmund, choking on his words. "Is it known what the Seven Kingdoms are planning?"

"They plan to invade us," said Beowulf.

"Yes, my King," said Wiglaf. "Their plan is to recruit the Jutes, pacify Zealand, then come here—to Götaland."

Sigmund turned to Beowulf. "I'll send word to the Clan Chiefs to assemble their men-at-arms at once, my King."

"First let's hear what else our spies have learned."

"Each of the Seven Kingdoms," said Wiglaf, "is sending a hundred new ships, bought and paid for with gold from the Roman Emperor, Justinian."

"Roman bastard!" said Sigmund. "Justinian wants the North under his dominion, and he's using those Anglo Saxon dogs to do his bidding."

"You're right, Sigmund," said Beowulf, "Justinian wants to control all of the Westernesse, but he also wants revenge for what my father did."

"Anastasius was Emperor then," said Sigmund. "You've done Justinian no wrong."

"True, but my father humiliated the Roman Empire when he assassinated Gaius Aurelius, Master of the Gold Ship."

"But that was long ago—yes?" said Wiglaf.

"Yes," said Beowulf. "It was."

"So, why to take revenge now?" said Sigmund.

"Killing a man is one thing," said Beowulf. "And swift 'Blood Payment' is required. But wounding the pride of an empire? That cannot be allowed to stand. It makes Justinian appear weak."

Silence crowded the Throne Room. Beowulf left the dais.

"At last count," said Beowulf, "we had over one-hundred battle craft—yes?"

"One-hundred and ten worthy Longships, my King," said Sigmund, "not counting the Avenger."

"Hmm," said Beowulf. "I suppose they'll have to do."

Wiglaf and Sigmund exchanged looks mirroring their dismay: "What can one-hundred-and-eleven ships do against seven times that number?" said Sigmund.

"I was making a joke," said Beowulf. "Prince Hrothmund has forty battle craft in the Bay of Skane, where the River Vanir empties. Add to that two-hundred sturdy vessels King Breca possesses."

"But will Breca risk his fleet—for us?" said Sigmund.

"If the Seven Kingdoms conquer Götaland," said Beowulf, they will turn north for Brondingland, then take all of the Norwegan. Tell me, Wiglaf, do we know who'll lead this mighty fleet against us?"

"Only gossip," said Wiglaf. "One rumor has it that King Octha's oldest son, Prince Britannius, will lead the Angles and Saxons against us."

"I've heard of him, my King," said Wiglaf. "Britannius is said to an able Kommander and fierce in battle."

"True," said Sigmund. "I've heard Britannius is fearless in battle. But I also hear he's a clumsy, hot-head who prefers boys over women."

"When preparing for war," said Beowulf, "gossip isn't worth spit. Lord Sigmund knows this well. As for Prince Britannius, perhaps the truth lies somewhere in the middle."

"What are your orders, Beowulf?" said Sigmund.

"Have the Stable Master saddle Storm Bringer. He needs to stretch his legs, and I need to feel the wind on my face."

"And, me?" said Wiglaf.

"Get a good night's sleep, Wiglaf; tomorrow you're going to travel east."

Wiglaf bowed and left the Throne Room.

"And me, my King?" said Sigmund.

"Send riders to alert the Clan Chiefs; tell them to gather their warriors here; tell them to bring with them every master carpenter and metalsmith in Götaland. Then I want you to sail north."

"North?"

"Yes. To Brondingland! Deliver a message to King Breca. When you've done that, return to Land's End. I'll join you after I've seen to things in Skane."

† † †

Prince Hrothmund, son of Hrothgar and Wealtheow, hesitated before speaking.

"Is there something about my King's instructions you don't understand, Prince Hrothmund?" said Wiglaf.

"No, Lord Wiglaf. I know what King Beowulf wants me to do; although, I don't understand the why or wherefore of it."

"What else?" said Wiglaf.

"Where," said Hrothmund, "will I find the men necessary to complete this task in time? I've less than fifteen-hundred able bodied men—warriors, to be sure, but the rest of my people are women and children."

"Calm yourself, Prince Hrothmund. You'll have the help you need. They're on their way here now."

"But who'll oversee the work, Lord Wiglaf? I know nothing about building such things."

Wiglaf smiled. "Beowulf will come to Skane sooner than you know, great Prince. And when I return, we'll see this thing through together—yes?"

"Does my mother know anything about this?" said Hrothmund.

"She will, Prince Hrothmund, the day after tomorrow."

† † †

Queen Wealtheow listened as Wiglaf finished relaying Beowulf's message, word for word.

"After you've rested, tell your king his confidence in me honors me."

Wiglaf bowed and left the Throne Room.

"What would you have me do, Queen Mother?" said Freawaru, now Queen of Frihamm.

"You heard what Beowulf expects from us. Return to Frihamm immediately, Daughter. And tell no one a word of what you heard here today. Understand?"

"Yes, Queen-Mother. I understand."

† † †

"They're coming," said Andur, son of Guntur. They' gathering their ships in Londinium, on the great river that leads to the Whale Road."

Mikla's cousin, Andur, was Sigmund's choice to be Beowulf's eyes and ears on the Tin Isles, home to the Seven Kingdoms.

"How many, Andur?" said Sigmund. "We need to know how many."

"Just as we first heard, my Lord, seven-hundred new battle craft, each capable of carrying thirty men at the oars: two steering the tiller, and eight archers. But there's more, Lord Sigmund."

"Let's hear it."

"The Emperor, Justinian, sent his Gold Ship under the command of his greatest Legatus, Quintus Mandrocus, to lead them. And Artur, King of the Jutes, has allied his tribe with the Angles and Saxons for a share of the spoils and to keep his throne."

"How many ships have they?" said Sigmund.

"Ninety battle craft. Smaller than ours, but all battle worthy."

Sigmund stared down at the floor and shook his head. Andur heard Sigmund mutter something he couldn't make out.

"My Lord?" said Andur.

Sigmund looked at Andur. "Have you an idea as to when the Angles and Saxons will set out for Götaland?"

"With good weather, the Roman and Britannius will lead their ships east with the next full moon, my Lord. Once they reach Jutland, Artur's fleet will join them."

"You've done well, Andur," said Sigmund.

"Thank you, my Lord. What would you have me do now?"

"Disguise yourself as a sell-sword, a pirate even. And sail to Jutland. Offer your services to King Artur. As soon as you see the Angles and Saxons approaching Oigenthal, bring word to our Coast Guards in Land's End. They'll send riders to Falcon's Nest and Skane."

"Yes, Lord Sigmund. I'll leave at once."

Andur saluted with his fist over his heart and started away.

"Andur," said Sigmund.

Andur stopped. ""My Lord?"

"I'll let Beowulf know how well you've served our people."

Andur's chest swelled. "Thank you, my Lord."

† † †

Octha, Saxon King of Kent, sat beneath the open-air pavilion with the kings of Essex, Northumbria, Sussex, East Anglia, Mercia, and Wessex.

Behind Octha, stood his oldest son, Britannius. Also present was Emperor Justinian's greatest General, Legatus, Quintus Mandrocus.

"Good to be with you again, my Lords," said Octha. "And we are honored to have among us Emperor Justinian's greatest Legatus, Quintus Mandrocus, Kommandar of the Gold Ship. I see that everyone brought what was due—one-hundred stout battle craft. This gathering of Longships, my Lords, is the greatest fleet and army ever seen in the north. And I am honored, that we are all in agreement—that my son, Prince Britannius, should act as Battle Lord for the Seven Kingdoms. But enough from me—I'll let Prince Britannius reveal his battle plan."

† † †

"First," said Beowulf, "I believe Britannius will lead their fleet, along with the Gold Ship, from Londinium, downriver to the Whale Road. They'll sail east across the Great Channel to the coast of Belgica where they'll turn north. Once they reach the Nord Sea, the Angles and Saxons will turn east and sail to Oigenthal, where Jutland's King Artur has his Keep and battle craft. Once the Jutes have joined them, Britannius will sail to Mork Sand and destroy whatever vessels they find so the Danes can't use them against him. From Mork Sand, they'll travel to Land's End. Once they control Land's End, they'll sail north to Falcon's Nest, expecting to trap our fleet in the Fjord of Kuurin."

"How can you be sure that's Britannius's plan?" said Prince Hrothmund.

"Because it's what I would do," said Beowulf.

"Will there be no help from the Spear Danes in Zealand, my King?" said Turin.

"In Zealand, no, brother," said Beowulf. "They're too busy feuding among themselves. We've only those Danes who followed Prince Hrothmund to Skane to help us."

"But how will we know when the enemy's coming?" said Prince Hrothmund.

"I have a man in Jutland," said Sigmund. "He'll bring word to us once he spies the Angle Saxon fleet. In the event he's found out, our King has tasked me with placing several of our fastest ships far west of Land's End and off the coast of Zealand. As soon as the sails of the enemy fleet are sighted, one of our ships will bring word to Land's End. A second will sail to Skane, and a third to Falcon's Nest and the Citadel."

"You've done well, Sigmund."

"Thank you, my King.

"We may have an additional advantage, my Lords," said Beowulf. "The Roman Legatus, Quintus Mandrocus may not be inclined to take orders from King Octha's son, and I expect the same holds true with Prince Britannius. Neither are likely to defer to the other; that said, the likelihood they will argue over a plan of attack may work in our favor."

Beowulf scanned the faces of the men grouped around him.

"Any more questions, my Lords?" said Beowulf.

Sigmund, Prince Hrothmund, and the Clan Chiefs exchanged looks but said nothing.

"Good!" said Beowulf. "Now comes the hardest part."

"My King?" said the Danish prince, Hrothmund.

"Waiting," said Beowulf.

† † †

"Have you any questions, great Kings," said Prince Britannius.

"Yes," said Mangus, King of Sussex. "I have a question."

"Yes, My Lord," said Britannius.

"How many ships have the Thunder-Geats?"

"Not enough, I assure you," said Britannius.

There was a round of laughter from some of the others. Mangus, however, was in no mood to laugh and Britannius could see as much.

"Forgive me, King Mangus," said Britannius. "At last count, the Thunder-Geats had a hundred battle craft. Perhaps a few more than that. It's hard to know."

Don't your spies in Götaland know, Prince Britannius?" said Mangus.

"My spies have not returned, King Magnus. But one-hundred, even two-hundred ships, is no match for what we are bringing to defeat the bear's son."

"Are any of the other tribes in Götaland allied with the Thunder-Geats?" said Alfr, King of Mercia.

"Other tribes?" said Britannius.

"Yes," said Alfr, "like the Wylfings, or the Svear?"

"The Wylfings are ruled by a woman who is firmly under Beowulf's thumb. She has too few ships to be a threat to us. As for the Svear, King Eadgils won't want to risk his throne in a war he knows he can't profit from."

"What about the Sea Brondings?" said Charl, King of Northumbria. "How do we know Breca won't join forces with the Thunder-Geats, just as he has in times past."

"Again, my Lords," said Britannius, "Breca is no fool. Like Eadgils in Svearland, neither tribe wants any part of a war they can't win."

"It's the bear's son we're going up against, Prince Britannius. We should be cautious—yes?" said Alfr, King of Mercia. "We should know what we'll be facing."

"It matters not," said Britannius. "On the water, Beowulf's strength won't matter."

"Great kings," said the Roman Legatus, Quintus Mandrocus. "I have listened carefully to Prince Britannius's plan, and I think it a good one."

"But—?" said Britannius, annoyed by the very presence of the Roman Legatus.

"I propose an alternative strategy, one that will eliminate the necessity of waging a prolonged campaign on land and sea to subdue the entire region."

"And what strategy would that be?" said Octha.

We should split our fleet, Great Kings. Once we have taken Land's End, I propose sending half our ships north to take the Citadel and Falcon's Nest. We do this while the remainder of our fleet continues east to Frihamm, and from there, north to Värg Slött. Once we have defeated the Wylfings, we can march on the Svear at Uppsala. Attacking Götaland from the east and west will prevent the Wylfings and Svear from coming to the Thunder-Geats' aid at Falcon's Nest."

"What say you to that, my son?" said Octha, King of Kent.

"While Legatus Mandrocus's plan has merit, my King," said Britannius, "I do not think it wise to split our forces. By staying together, we present a force no army or fleet can withstand, Beowulf, or no Beowulf. But our chances of success lessen to the extent we diminish our numbers for the assault on the Citadel—and, that, my Lords, is the prize we seek. When the Citadel falls, all Götaland will be ours, Svearland, too."

"No," said the Roman.

"What, Legatus Mandrocus," said Octha. "do you object to?"

"Let me remind you all, Great Kings, and you, Prince Britannius—it is the Emperor Justinian, the Lion of the East, who commissioned this undertaking and has appointed me, his greatest general, undefeated on the battlefield to speak in his stead. The strategy I have outlined is the strategy the Emperor himself conceived. The plan I set forth is the one he wants you to follow."

"Your Emperor, Legatus Mandrocus, would be well advised to let Angles and Saxons determine the strategy to be employed," said Britannius. "Emperor Justinian's gold bought our ships, it's true, but we know the waters from Britannia to Götaland well. And, remember, Legatus Mandrocus, it is our blood spilled in the battle to come—not yours, or the Eastern Roman Empires.

"Enough," said King Octha, "I will leave it to you, Legatus Mandrocus, and Prince Britannius, to work out a compromise. In any event, you will set sail tomorrow. I do not want to delay Emperor Justinian's victory, and although he has paid handsomely for it, the spoils of his victory will be ours—Angles, Saxons, and Jutes. It is only fair."

Queen Wealtheow stood as King Eadgils entered her Throne Room. Eadgils had visited Wealtheow not long after she became Queen of Öster Götaland. He was also fond of Wealtheow's daughter, Freawaru, whom he often visited in Frihamm, and did so with Wealtheow's blessing.

"Thank you for coming, King Eadgils. I was afraid—"

"Be not afraid, great Queen—I'm here."

"And your ships?" said Wealtheow.

"On their way."

"I Thank the gods," said Wealtheow.

"Thank the bear's son," said Eadgils, "I owe Beowulf everything, including my life."

"As do I," said Wealtheow. "As do I. Sit with me, King Eadgils, for there's much Beowulf would have me tell you."

Beowulf and Wiglaf stood on high ground with Prince Hrothmund and looked toward the River Vanir in the distance. There was a silver sheen upon the surface of the fast-moving water as it flowed toward the Bay of Skane and the open sea beyond.

On both sides of the river, the Spear-Danes cleared large tracts of forest. Only the stumps of what was once centuries old spruce and pine trees remained. The air was thick with the smell of fresh cut wood.

"How many have we?" said Beowulf.

Wiglaf deferred to Prince Hrothmund with a nod.

"At present count, we have over two-hundred, Great King," said Prince Hrothmund.

"Do your warriors know what I expect of them?"

"They do, Great King," said Prince Hrothmund. "Day and night Wiglaf has been drilling them. I assure you—they're ready."

† † †

The journey to Jutland had been long and arduous. Thirteen ships belonging to King Mangus of Sussex, along with their entire crews, were lost beneath the waves in the Nord Sea when a squall descended on the Angle Saxon Fleet traveling north from Belgica.

Prince Britannius was in a foul mood when Artur, King of Jutland, greeted him and the Roman Legatus at Oigenthal.

After Britannius and the Roman had bathed, rested and eaten their fill, Artur turned to one of his guards.

"Bring in the Geatlander."

Andur was dragged naked in chains to the Mead Hall and thrown to the floor. His body was a mass of cuts and bruises and where his eyes had been, dark, empty sockets remained.

"Who is he?" said Britannius.

"A spy, my prince," said Artur. "My Coast Guards caught him preparing to return to Götaland just as the Gold Ship and your ships were sighted offshore."

"What did he tell you?" said Britannius.

"Nothing, my Prince."

Britannius cast his eyes up and down noting the Geat's

vacant eye sockets and cuts and bruises all over the young man's body. "All that, and he told you nothing?"

"He can't speak, my Prince," said Artur.

"Why?" said the Roman.

"He bit off his tongue before my men could subdue him."

"It matters little," said Quintus Mandrocus. "Once the Geats see what's coming toward them, they'll scatter like sparrows in the face of a gale."

"Let us hope so," said King Artur. "And where, Prince Britannius, do you want me and my fleet?"

"There has been a change of plans," said Britannius.

He cast a hard glance at the Roman General.

"Your fleet, King Artur, and one hundred ships from the Seven Kingdoms will sail to the Fjord of Kuurin and block the Geats' ships from escaping to the Whale Road."

"But—" said Artur, a look of consternation on his face.

"What?" said Britannius. "Does it not please you to be the vanguard of the attack, my Lord?"

King Artur scanned the faces of the Clan Chiefs gathered in the Hall. He saw them waiting to hear how he'd answer. He looked at Britannius:

"We Jutes will be honored to lead the attack on Falcon's Nest, Prince Britannius."

"Then be it so," said Britannius. "After I have taken Land's End, I will send five-thousand men north by land to lay siege to Falcon's Nest."

"And," said the Roman, "while King Artur's fleet and the ships accompanying him sail to the Fjord of Kuurin, I will take the Gold Ship east. Prince Britannius will follow with the remaining fleet—five-hundred ships."

Britannius said nothing. There was no disguising the look of contempt on his face—contempt for this Roman Legatus who carried about him the smell of peppermint oil and sweaT made all the more unbearable by Quintus Mandrocus's arrogance.

Beowulf faced his Clan Chiefs, together with Turin, Sigmund, and Wiglaf. Outside, where they gathered, flames from the fire pit danced high into the air, licking the darkness.

"My friends," said Beowulf. "Once again we will be outnumbered. But being outnumbered is something we're accustomed to, and unless Britannius's spies have slipped through our nets, the Angles and Jutes will not expect to find us waiting for them at Land's End. When the air clears, the first ship Prince Britannius and the Roman Legatus see will be the Black Ship.

"My warriors are eager, my King," said Lord Baolin, the same Clan Chief chastised by the shaman, Beorn, during Beowulf's long absence; "Eager to know where you will position us?"

"You, Lord Baolin, will take your ships north of Land's End, in plain sight of the Angle Saxon fleet when it arrives. I expect the Angles and Jutes to send ships to meet you in battle. But you are not to permit that to happen."

"My King?" said Baolin. "I don't understand."

"However many ships Britannius sends, do not make contact. Instead, turn north and make haste up the coast. I want to lure as many of the Angle Saxon ships away from Land's End as possible."

"And then what?" said Baolin.

"Make for Otters'Bay and beach your ships. If the Angles and Saxons attempt a landing, greet them with arrows and fire before they reach the shore. You'll find kegs of the pitch we use for burning, and a hundred bowmen from nearby villages, waiting for you there. Hold out as long as possible. If no help arrives, retire overland to Falcon's Nest and defend the city. Understand?"

"Yes," my King," said Baolin.

"Sigmund?" said Beowulf. "Anything to add?"

"Our Coast Guards have alerted our people living on the coast from Land's End to Falcon's Nest. The aged, infirm, and the women and children are being escorted to Falcon's Nest even as we speak."

"Good," said Beowulf. "Die well, my Lords. Now go.

Join your men."

"Die well," said the Clan Chiefs as with one voice.

When the others had left, Beowulf turned to Turin, Wiglaf, and Sigmund.

"Listen well, my friends," said Beowulf. "for here is what you must do."

† † †

Aboard his Longship, Leif tilted his head back to let the water from the goatskin splash over his face; his eyes stung from ocean spray and from straining to see through the darkness for what might be their doom—racing over the waves toward them. Cold as the water was, Leif felt refreshed but also tired; he had spent the last night until almost morning standing lookout. Soon, someone would take his place keeping watch. Leif yawned and pulled his cape tight around his shoulders.

† † †

In the twilight that precedes the dawn, Leif saw them. Lights flickering on the far horizon from south to north; the torches of almost a thousand ships coming toward them from the west.

"Wake up, brothers!" said Leif.

He went to each man, rousing him from sleep.

"They're coming! Raise the anchor, hoist sail, and take up oars. Back to Land's End with all speed!"

78

THE GOLD & BLACK

Legatus Quintus Mandrocus was in his cabin enjoying his mid-morning meal when the Gold Ship's Kommandar, an Athenian named Phostos Agamedes, knocked on the door of the Legatus's cabin.

"Come!" said QuintusMandrocus.

One thing the Legatus detested was being interrupted when he was eating, sleeping or fornicating, in that order.

Phostos Agamedes entered and saluted.

"You know I don't like to be interrupted, Kommandar; not when I'm eating."

"Were this not most urgent, Legatus Mandrocos, I wouldn't disturb you."

"Well," said the Legatus; "get on with it."

"We've sighted what may be the Black Ship."

"You don't seem convinced, Kommandar," said the Legatus. "Either it is, or it isn't the Black Ship. How many battle craft accompany it?"

"None, Legatus," said the Athenian.

"Are you trifling with me, Kommander?"

"Not at all, Legatus Mandrocus," said the Athenian. "There are sixty or more vessels spread out behind the Black Ship, but they are all knarrs."

"knarrs, you say?"

"Yes, Legatus—every one of them."

"That's absurd," said the Legatus. "The bear's son dares to oppose me with only the Black Ship and three-score merchant vessels?"

"It would appear so, Legatus Mandrocus."

"Very well, Kommandar. "I'll come above and have a look for myself."

† † †

Turin's excitement was more than he could contain.

"Look at that, my King—the Gold Ship! And so far out ahead of the pack."

"Even though the wind and current fight against it," said Beowulf, "the Gold Ship has three-hundred men rowing. But more than that, it's pride, my brother; pride compels this Roman Legatus to lead the Angles, Saxons, and Jutes here. He thinks there's an easy victory in the offering and he wants the lion's share for his Emperor."

"Your orders?" said Turin.

"Tell the Tillermen to turn us about."

† † †

Aboard his battle craft, Prince Britannius had his signal man wave a red pennant signifying: "proceed with caution," toward the Gold Ship.

"The Gold Ship isn't responding, my Prince," said Eegan, a slender, beardless Clan Chief with a boyish face. Eegan was Britannius's' most trusted adviser, in addition to being his lover.

"Greedy bastard, that Roman," said Britannius. "He wants the glory of defeating the bear's son for himself and no one else."

"Shall I have the signal repeated?" said Eegan.

"No, Eegan," said Britannius. "Let Hel have the Roman if she wants him. He means nothing to the Seven Kingdoms."

† † †

The knarrs were without crews; their anchors dropped over the sides and their sails furled. Using rope, the Thunder-Geats bound each knarr to the knarr on either side of it. They were all separated by a hundred feet of ocean, changes in wind and current notwithstanding.

On Beowulf's command, arrows wrapped with cloth rags soaked in lamp oil were lit on fire and loosed toward each knarr as the Black Ship passed, one knarr after another until all were ablaze.

Rather than the cargos they were accustomed to, each knarr carried a mound of straw and grease-wood soaked for several days with tallow, pine sap, whale oil, and pitch.

As the contents of the knarrs erupted into flames, black smoke billowed upward creating a dark cloud over the Whale Road. The coal-black smoke hung about the ocean surface like a thick wall, and it rose into the sky, turning the sun into a blood-red orb.

The Black Ship disappeared from view as the knarrs themselves began to burn, adding to the cloud of smoke blanketing the sea and rising skyward.

Soon, the ropes that bound the knarrs together also caught fire and came undone.

Before long, the current pushed the fiery, unleashed knarrs west toward the fast-approaching Gold Ship and the Angles, Saxons, and Jutes who followed with the wind in their faces, slowing them down.

† † †

The Roman Legatus, Quintus Mandrocus, and the Gold Ship's Kommandar, Phostos Agamedes, stared at the sea-borne inferno about to envelop them.

"Your orders, Legatus Mandrocus?" said the Greek Kommandar.

"Sail straight through, of course. The Gold Ship's iron ram can sink any ship it makes contact with, and those knarrs are nothing, Kommandar; or, don't you agree?"

"Those knarrs, Legatus, could set us afire if even one becomes impaled on our oars. Besides that, if we maintain our present course we'll soon be in the thick of that dark cloud stretched out before us. We'll be blind, Legatus."

"Only blind for as long as it takes to pass through, Kommandar. Go below. Tell your overseers to lash the backs of the oarsmen. I want more speed from them."

Kommandar Agamedes hated this Roman Legatus, and it made

no matter to the Athenian that Legatus Mandrocus had the Emperor's favor after winning a series of land battles; but, here, on the Whale Road: This fool of a general knows nothing about waging war on the water, or the Athenian told himself.

"What are you waiting for?" said the Legatus. "Go below and do as I've ordered."

Kommandar Agamedes saluted and left for the bowels of the Gold Ship where three-hundred young men and boys chained to the oars.

Whipped into submission, these slaves aboard the Gold Ship knew their only escape from the chains that held them captive was to die when they could no longer work the oars. Rare was the man kept below the Gold Ship's decks who lived into old age. No. Death and death alone could release these oarsmen from their bondage.

Below the Gold Ship's main deck were three more. The first provided the Gold's Ship's Kommandar with spacious living quarters, quarters now taken over by the Legatus, Quintus Mandrocus, forcing Kommandar Agamedes to bunk among his officers of lesser rank, and the warriors under their command; all of whom were now assembled on the Main Deck in readiness for battle. The two, bottom-most were home to three-hundred slaves, water bearers and a dozen replacements, all chained at their stations. These wretches were already exhausted by the furious pace they'd suffered to maintain from the Tin Isles and their reward for it—rotten food and lashing from their overseers.

The Athenian Kommandar went from the third deck to the fourth and shouted so all would hear.

"Cease rowing, and pulls the oars in now!"

When an overseer on the Third Deck hesitated to obey, the Athenian drew his sword and brought it down on top of the man's head, cleaving his skull and brain. Agamedes looked at the other overseers.

"Any of you sons of whores object—speak now!"

The overseers remained silent.

"Good," said the Athenian. "Now coil your whips and help the water bearers give the oarsmen water."

"But they're only slaves, Kommandar," said an overseer.

"They're men, damn you! If you hope to live through this day, it'll be on their backs and the strength of their arms that we live to see the morrow."

The overseers had only to look at their former comrade face-down between the rowing-benches where his brains and blood had spilled. They coiled their whips and began helping the water-bearers ladle water to the men at the oars.

Kommandar Agamedes gave the same orders on the Fourth Deck before returning to the area near the tiller where Legatus Mandrocus observed what he could through the smoke while holding a perfumed silk cloth over his nose and mouth.

The Legatus lowered the cloth from his face.

"Why, by the one true God, Kommandar, are we not moving?" said the Legatus.

"Because to do so now, your excellency will only invite disaster. Better to wait for the knarrs to pass. As the knarrs drift past us, so, in time, will the smoke lift."

† † †

With the wind and the current pushing the smoke and the burning knarrs closer to his fleet's position, Prince Britannius ordered his signalmen to flag the other Kommandars.

"Signal the Jutes' King to turn his ships north and swing around the knarrs and smoke. Signal Kommandar Deorwine of Sussex to do the same. When Artur and Deorwine confirm receiving my order, signal the other Kommandars: Eastmund of Mercia, Osweald of Northumbria, Aelfstan of Essex and Cyneweard of East Anglia, to follow my lead."

Britannius looked at the two Tillermen who steered his battle craft, men he trusted.

"Hard right, cousins!" said Britannius. "Take us south! When we're clear of the knarrs, we'll set a course north-east for Land's End!"

† † †

You dare disobey me, Kommandar?" said the Legatus. "I am the Emperor's emissary—or have you forgotten?"

"No," said the Athenian. "But our Emperor made me Kommandar of his Gold Ship. Implicit in the Emperor's trust is knowing I'll suffer no harm to it or my men by being imprudent or reckless. What you have ordered, Legatus Mandrocus is exactly that."

The Athenian Kommandar looked behind at the fleet led by Britannius that was breaking formation—one-hundred and eighty ships turning due north, to avoid the smoke and burning knarrs; while the bulk of the fleet, just under six-hundred battle craft, tacked to the south for the same reason.

"See that?" said the Athenian Kommandar with a wave of his hand. "Prince Britannius sees what's coming and has changed course to put his ships out of danger. If we wait here, the knarrs will eventually pass us by; at which time we can continue east."

"You impudent, Athenian dog!" said the Legatus.

Quintus Mandrocus raised his General's Baton and was about to bring it down on the Athenian when Agamedes caught hold of the Legatus's wrist, stopping the baton a mere few inches from his face. The Athenian was by far the stronger man and held the Legatus's wrist with a vice-like grip.

"How dare you touch a Roman Legatus, " said Quintus Mandrocus.

"Fool," said Agamedes. "Your stupidity will get us all killed."

No sooner had he spoke when he brought his dagger upward under the Legatus's chin, burying the blade deep.

Quintus Mandrocus's eyes bulged with surprise, and as Agamedes withdrew the knife, blood bubbled forth, and the Legatus sank to his knees, unable to speak or stem the flow of blood choking him.

Kommandar Agamedes turned to two of his warriors standing near.

"Throw this piece of garbage over the side. Let the fish suffer his presence; I will not."

As the body of Legatus Quintus Mandrocus dropped overboard, the Athenian shouted to his Master of Arms, another Greek, from southern Macedonia.

"Aristides!"

The Master of Arms hurried forward:

"Kommandar?"

"Furl our sails and alert the fire brigade. Stand ready should the Gold Ship catch fire."

"At once, Kommandar."

† † †

Because of its immense size, the leviathan that was the Gold Ship lay dead in the water; while smoke from the burning knarrs passed over and around it, turning day into night.

From his position on the dais near the tillermen, Kommandar Agamedes splashed water over his face to wash the soot off his face and soothe the burn he felt in his eyes.

As Agamedes dried his face he heard a series of screams from the direction of the prow; below which, the Gold Ship's iron ram protruded. What he couldn't see was the cause of the commotion.

Then came the sound of warriors shouting at one another in a confused fashion, accompanied by the hissing of arrows too numerous to count through the smoke-filled air. The screams and yelling continued; so, too, the hiss of arrows accompanied by the sound of swords clashing, and axes splintering shields.

† † †

When the last of the knarrs and the clouds of smoke pouring off them passed, the air grew clear—clear enough that the Athenian Kommandar's mouth dropped open when he saw the dead bodies of half his warriors on the Main Deck.

Facing the Athenian, he saw black clad warriors whose upper bodies and faces were painted black. They numbered close to sixty, most of whom knelt on the deck, armed with bows, ready to let loose more obsidian-tipped arrows at the warriors huddled together in front of their Kommandar.

The remaining warriors of the Gold Ship looked dazed and afraid, like sheep with nowhere to run, surrounded by a pack of bloodthirsty wolves.

A tall, broad-shouldered black-painted warrior stepped forward:

"I am Beowulf Waegmunding, King Of Geatland. There is no reason to continue this slaughter. The Gold Ship is mine. Do you agree?"

Kommandar Agamedes surveyed the carnage on the deck in front of him, and he took notice of the frightened faces of his warriors, who trembled before none other than the bear's son, himself.

"I agree. The Emperor's Ship is yours. I ask nothing for myself, only that you show mercy to my men, and the oarsmen chained below."

"And you are?" said Beowulf.

"Agamedes—Kommandar of the Gold Ship."

"Where is the Emperor's Battle Lord? I want him brought before me."

"By my hand, Legatus Quintus Mandrocus is dead, and his corpse thrown to the fishes."

"Then you've saved me the trouble of doing it myself," said Beowulf. "You have a choice, Kommandar; but you'll have to decide quickly. I can set the Gold Ship on fire; in which case, all aboard can attempt to swim to shore and likely drown. Or, you can serve me, and Queen Wealtheow of Frihamm, in our commercial undertakings—here, in the Northlands. But first, you will unchain the men below and restore their freedom. Those former slaves who want to remain on the Gold Ship deserve compensation—understood?"

"I am humbled by your generosity, Great King. But I cannot accept. I pledged loyalty to the Emperor Justinian. Only death can release me from that oath."

Beowulf nodded: "I understand."

The Athenian smiled and nodded. He stepped off the dais.

"With your permission?"

Beowulf nodded. Without hesitation, the Athenian threw himself over the side, into the cold, briny sea.

"Drop your weapons on the deck," Beowulf said to the Gold Ship's warriors. "Or die where you stand."

The Roman Emperor's men did as they were told and disarmed.

Beowulf turned to Turin: "Take ten men. Go below and unchain the oarsmen. Tell them they are free, and see that they have access to food and water."

"And the overseers?" said Turin.

"Let the oarsmen decide."

Turin grinned and nodded.

"What about these," said Turin; "those we haven't killed?"

Aristides, the Athenian Kommandar's Second-in-Command, stepped forward.

"Great King," said Aristides, "I am Kommandar Agamedes Second-in-Command; or rather, I was—until now. And, like Agamedes, I, too, am Greek by birth, and I value my freedom over all else. Let us fight with you against the Angles, Saxons, and Jutes."

"And your Emperor?" said Beowulf. "What about him? Did you not pledge your honor to serve him, like your Kommandar?"

"No, Great King," said Aristides. "I did not. Nor did the warriors you see before you. We are conscripts from different lands and have no great love for Justinian or the Eastern Roman Empire!"

Aristides looked at the men of the Gold Ship:

"The bear's son offers us the chance to live and fight as free men—what say you?"

The warriors of the Gold Ship dropped to one knee and shouted:

"Bear's son!" over and over until Beowulf raised his hand, calling for silence.

"Then be it so—today you will be Thunder-Geats! Now rise, and take back your weapons."

Turin reappeared on the Main Deck and looked around at what was taking place.

"This is Aristemedes. He had pledged his loyalty, his and the warriors under his command, to Geatland."

Beowulf stood eye to eye with Aristides. "You will be Second-in-Command to my brother, Turin."

"Gladly," said Aristides.

Beowulf looked at both men.

"Wait here until the Angles and Saxons main fleet is well ahead; then come with all haste and strike them from behind."

"And what if—?" said Turin.

"If things go badly for us," said Beowulf, "beach this gilded beast anywhere you can and set it afire. Understood?"

Both Turin and Aristemedes nodded.

"Die well," said Beowulf

† † †

Beowulf and his black-clad warriors, the Kungens Vakter, returned to the Black Ship by way of the ropes that were attached to the grappling hooks with which they boarded the Gold Ship using the smoke as cover.

Sigmund was there aboard the Black Ship to greet them.

"I see it went well, my King."

"Butcher's work," said Beowulf. He removed his helm and splashed fresh water over his face.

"And Turin?" said Sigmund.

"Sigmund will remain aboard with ten Kungens Vakter and the Gold Ship's Second-in-Command. They will join the fight when the time is right."

They were distracted by the sound of screams of men thrown over the side of the Gold Ship."

Sigmund gave Beowulf a questioning look.

"I told Turin to free the slaves below decks and to let them dispose of the overseers as they saw fit."

Sigmund nodded.

"What now, my King?" said Sigmund.

Beowulf looked north and saw the first of King Artur's fleet of Jute battle craft heading north. Soon they would encounter Lord Baolin's ships and perhaps give chase.

Beowulf turned and looked south, where Prince Britannius was reforming his fleet of almost six-hundred ships for an attack on Land's End.

† † †

With the wind against them and time of the essence, Beowulf ordered the sail furled while he took control of the Black Ship's tiller. Beowulf worked the tiller side-to-side like a fin speeding the Black Ship over the water.

Seeing their king exerting himself, giving the task his all, the Kungens Vakter rowed with renewed vigor, using all their combined strength. The Black Ship sped like a low-flying eagle over the surface of the water.

† † †

When the last of the smoke was well to the west, and behind him, Prince Britannius and his Second-in-Command, Lord Eegan, saw the Gold Ship at what appeared to be a standstill, with its sails furled and oars pulled in.

"What, by all the gods, is the Roman doing?" said Prince Britannius.

"It would appear the Emperor's Legatus is doing nothing, my Prince," said Lord Eegan.

"I can see that," said Britannius.

"Look there, my Prince!" said Eegan, pointing northeast from their position.

"Good eye, my friend," said Britannius. "I see it! The Black Ship! It has to be!"

"Your orders, my Prince?"

"No matter where the Black Ship goes, Eegan—we follow! Understood?"

† † †

King Artur of Jutland counted fifteen Geat battle craft close to the coast, just north of Land's End. These fifteen ships were coming straight toward Artur's eighty Longships and, behind those eighty, another eighty-seven battle craft from Sussex commanded by Lord Deorwine. Unlucky for Deorwine, it was his king, Magnus's ships, thirteen in all, that were lost in the Nord Sea when a storm descended on them and for a time dispersing the fleet.

For Prince, Britannius, having Deorwine accompany the Jutes was an easy decision, since Britannius had little confidence in Deorwine's ability to fight a battle on water. All Britannius expected of Deorwine, and the same for King Artur of Jutland, was for their ships to block the Fjord of Kuurin and prevent Beowulf's fleet from sailing south to attempt a sea defense of Land's End.

The Jutes' King turned to his Second-in-Command:

"Signal Kommandar Deorwine that we have sighted the Geats and are engaging."

† † †

Beowulf stood alone on the heights overlooking Land's End, just as he had so often in seasons past. The bear's son held his hands out to the sides, palms facing upward.

Wiglaf stopped a respectful distance behind Beowulf. He could see by his King's outstretched hands that Beowulf was offering prayers of supplication; but to who, or what, Wiglaf had no way of knowing. Mother. Father. You gave me life, and I have striven to bring honor and glory upon Clan Waegmunding.

This day, I will be tested again, as I've been so many times. But I swear, by Lüma the bear who raised me, and Beorn, the All Mother's servant who looked after me and taught me what I needed to know about who I was, and what I'd become. I will die to save Geatland and our people.

Mighty Thor, Hammer-Bearer and Thunder-Bringer, you who gave me my strength, I swear I'll not dishonor you. And you, Frigga, Great Goddess, I give praise to thee, for honoring my mother's prayer so very long ago....

It wasn't long before Beowulf lowered his hands and turned to face Wiglaf.

"All is in readiness, my King," said Wiglaf. "With your permission, I'll return to the Bay of Skane."

Beowulf nodded: "Die well, cousin."

"Die well, my King."

79

RED SKY AT MORNING

Lord Baolin felt his heart pounding against his chest. His lips felt dry, and he ran his tongue back and forth across them. His Second-in-Command hastened to Baolin's side:

"Your orders?"

"Let them close the distance, Sigurd, before we turn north. If we turn now, they may not take the bait."

"Either way it sounds risky, my Lord."

"It is risky, Sigurd; but I don't want it said we failed our King or clan."

† † †

A mile southwest of Land's End, the Black Ship was joined by twenty sleek battle craft, each ship carrying sixty Spear Danes: forty-four men at the oars, two men at the tiller, eleven archers, a Signalman, the warrior in charge and his Second-in-Command.

Indeed, these twenty battle craft accounted for half the ships Lord Ulthur, loyal to the House of Hrothgar, brought with him after fleeing Daneland for the sanctuary he and Prince Hrothmund were given in Skane, thanks to Beorn, Sigmund, and Weohstan, when they served as regents during Beowulf's absence.

Led by Lord Ulthur, the Spear Danes formed their ships into a column behind the Black Ship. They furled their sails as Beowulf ordered, shipped-oars, and waited.

† † †

As the Black Ship closed the distance between it and the Spear Danes, Beowulf turned the Black ship around; until it, too, faced the massive fleet of Angle and Saxon ships, their blue and gray sails stretching as far as the bear's son's, far-ranging eyes could see.

"Furl the sail," said Beowulf. "Cease rowing."

† † †

"Have you ever seen such arrogance, Eegan?" said Prince Britannius. "Not only does this Geatlander dare to face me with a score of ships, but they're also furling their sails and sitting there—waiting for us."

"They may be all Beowulf has to defend Land's End with, my Prince, which means the rest of his ships he probably anchored in the Fjord of Kuurin that leads to Falcon's Nest."

"I think you're right, Eegan," said Britannius. "Well, my friend, the time has come. Let's have at them. Let's see how well the bear's son's strength serves him on water—before I drown the whole lot of them."

† † †

The bear's son turned over the tiller to two of the Kungens Vakter and walked forward to the prow of the ship. He looked back at Sigmund.

"Stand ready, Lord Sigmund, to furl the sail and release the oars.

"Yes, my King."

"Signal Lord Ulthur and the Spear Danes to be ready to do the same."

"Yes, my King," said Sigmund. "You've only to give the word."

Beowulf walked between the rows of benches and addressed his warriors.

"You, my brothers, are Kungens Vakter—the best of the best, known and feared throughout the Northlands. On your shoulders rests a great weight, for it is up to us to shoulder the burden of protecting our homeland, the land of our fathers, and their father's fathers before them, for five-hundred winters. Fear nothing, and die well, my brothers!"

The Kungens Vakter rose from their benches and stood as one.

Each man stamped a foot on the deck, in unison, and together shouted: "Bear's Son!" over and over, in as loud a voice as their lungs and throats could muster.

† † †

The sound of the Kungens Vakter as they shouted "bear's son" over and over, carried across the choppy, wind-driven waves and penetrated the ears of the Angles and Saxons.

"Great Odin's beard," said Eegan. "He means to defend Land's End, my Prince. Why else would Beowulf be waiting there in column formation?"

"I can see that, Eegan. Well, let's oblige him. I'm eager to get this farce over and done. Tonight, we'll be celebrating in Geatland, my friend. I intend to put an apple in the bear's son's mouth and roast him over a spit for my dinner. Have the men row faster."

† † †

North of Land's End, Lord Baolin rubbed his hands together to warm them.

"Now, Sigurd, now!" said Lord Baolin. "Have the tillermen turn about and make for Otters'Bay. Signal our ships to follow!"

"At once, my Lord."

Baolin's craft signaled the other fourteen Longships, and all did as Lord Baolin commanded, and did so in a well-ordered fashion.

The race for Otters'Bay was on!

† † †

"By all the gods, I knew it," said Artur, King of Jutland. "These Geats have no stomach for a fight."

"Surely, my King, they must realize they're hopelessly outnumbered and are taking the word of our arrival back to Falcon's Nest."

"Perhaps, my friend. Perhaps. Signal our other ships to increase speed. We're going to chase these rabbits all the way to Norwegan if need be!"

† † †

Beowulf was standing alone looking west when Sigmund approached.

"Soon, my King, we'll be in the range of the Angles' and Saxon's arrows."

Beowulf said nothing. He continued staring west toward the distant shoreline.

"My King?" said Sigmund.

"Now," said Beowulf. "Now's the time, my friend. Raise sail and drops oars. And signal Lord Ulthur and his Spear Danes to do the same. We're going into battle."

A smile came into Sigmund's face: "With pleasure, my King—with pleasure!"

† † †

"Do you see that, Eegan?" said Prince Britannius.

"Yes, my Prince," said Eegan. "The Geats and Danes are raising sail and dropping oars."

"No," said Britannius. "Not that. There!"

Prince Britannius raised a hand and pointed northwest toward land.

"That!" said Britannius.

"Clouds, my Prince. Perhaps a storm approaches?"

"Perhaps, Eegan; but when have you seen clouds moving like that?"

"Not since the storm over the Nord Sea, my Prince, when thirteen of Kommandar Deorwine's ships sank."

"By the gods, Eegan—look again! Those aren't clouds," said Britannius.

† † †

They arrived, not in thousands—but in hundreds of thousands: eagles, falcons, crows, ospreys, kites, ravens and seagulls, gannets and cormorants.

The Eagle Lord, Kungorn, and several of his kind circled the

Black Ship and the battle craft of the Spear-Danes, protecting them from the onslaught of raptors and scavengers that followed.

The Skyfolk passed over Beowulf and the Spear-Danes. In one high shrieking mass, they descended on the ships of the Angles and Saxons.

The birds swooped down causing many a terrified Angle and Saxon warrior to soil his britches. The enemies of Geatland raised their shields or flailed the air to keep the birds from clawing at their faces, their arms, hands, and eyes. Warriors ceased rowing to protect themselves; even the Tillermen let go of the tillers to crouch and cover their heads.

On their ship, Prince Britannius and Lord Eegan were no exception—they crouched and swung their fists to keep the birds away.

† † †

Standing with Lord Sigmund near the prow of the Black Ship, Beowulf watched the nearest formations of Angle and Saxon ships become undone and, in complete disarray, veer off-course and collide.

The ships furthest back had a choice: to turn around and sail away, or continue forward and risk colliding with the fast-forming tangle of ships ahead of them.

Beowulf looked skyward where Kunghorn was circling.

"Thank you, great Lord," said Beowulf. "If my people are victorious this day, it will be because of you and the Skyfolk, Lord Kunghorn."

"Never, Bear's Son," said Kunghorn, "have we Skyfolk had an opportunity to visit our wrath on Manlings in battle. On behalf of the Skyfolk, it is I, Kunghorn, who should thank you. Good hunting, Bear's Son!"

"Good hunting, Kunghorn."

As the Black Ship came abreast of the closest enemy Longship, Beowulf shouted to his archers: "Take care your arrows strike no Skyfolk!"

The Kungens Vakter loosed flaming arrows at the sails and hulls of every Saxon and Angle Longship they passed. Behind the Black Ship, Lord Ulthur and his twenty battle craft did the same.

As scores of the Angle and Saxon ships caught fire and their crews leapt overboard, the birds moved on to other vessels and continued as they had been doing—causing fear, panic, and confusion among the Manlings aboard.

Those Angles and Saxons who sought to avoid death by fire would not have survived for long, not in the frigid water; but now predators of the Whale Road arrived, attracted by the commotion on the surface of their world.

The screams of men flailing about in the water died away, as hags bit into them and dragged them below. Soon, there appeared a bloody slick on the surface, cut through by black, triangular fins too numerous to count.

† † †

Kommandar Aelfstan, leading the King of Essex's one-hundred ships was at the very back—the last formation of the Seven Kingdoms' fleet of ships that was, as yet, untouched by the dense, swirling dark cloud that blotted out the sun.

Aelfstan turned to his Second-in-Command: "Signal the captains of our ships to turn about and sail west."

Yes, Kommandar," said his Second-in-Command. "But... for where?"

"I don't know," said Aelfstan. "Just give the order. I need time to think."

† † †

Commanding the ships from Northumbria, Kommandar Osweald was alerted by some of his men who saw Aelfstan, the Angle Kommandar behind them turn and change course due west toward Daneland.

Osweald was a shrewd and practical Kommandar. He had witnessed the disaster that fell upon Prince Britannius and the other

Angle-Saxon Kommandars at the forefront: Lords Eastmund of Mercia, Dunstan of Wessex, and Cyneweard of East Anglia. No longer were their ships in tight battle formation; they were spread out in all directions; some on fire; some sinking after having collided with other ships—all were in disarray.

By the gods, Aelfstan's got it right Osweald thought. I won't risk my ships either—not for that boastful fool leading us!

Osweald shouted to his Second-in-Command: "Signal our ships to turn around and sail west."

"For where Kommandar?" said Osweald's Second-in-Command.

"Anywhere! Anywhere, but here!"

† † †

For the Angles and Saxons, the attack upon them from the sky seemed unending. As more of their ships caught fire, the smoke rising into the air became dense, unbreathable.

The smoke, however, proved an unexpected ally for the men from the Tin Isles; since it was the smoke from the burning ships that forced the birds to withdraw from the battle, for the clean air over land.

Beowulf saw the birds departing. Kunghorn, the Eagle Lord, was last to quit the area:

"Good hunting, Bear's Son," said Kunghorn.

Beowulf waved farewell. "I will forever be grateful, Great Lord. Good hunting!"

Beowulf shouted to his Tillermen: "Turn us around and make for Land's End!"

† † †

Prince Britannius's ship had not caught fire, although hundreds of birds clawing at the wet woolen sail ripped and tore holes in it; still, the sail was not so damaged as to be useless.

Britannius looked at the scratches on his hands and his blood that was dripping on the deck. His chainmail shirt had kept talons from clawing his torso, but one of his cheeks was scratched and bleeding. He removed his helm and saw it covered with bird shite; so, too, was much of the deck. His men had been able to kill several seagulls and a kite, but that was all, and they, too, were spotted helm-to-boots with bird droppings.

Prince Britannius grabbed hold of the arm of a warrior standing near. The man's face; his arms and hands, were scratched and bled and he appeared dazed.

"Here!" said Britannius to the warrior. He thrust his helm into the warrior's hands. "Clean the shite off my helm. And take care you get no blood on it."

Appearing bewildered, the warrior stared at his Prince's helm.

"Clean it with what, my Prince?"

"With your tongue, if need be, you idiot. But get it clean!"

"Yes, my Prince," said the warrior. He returned to his bench and with his cape began to clean Britannius's helm.

"Your orders, my Prince?" said Eegan.

"Britannius surveyed the damage done to his once great fleet of ships. Forty ships from Kent were burning. Another thirty ships furnished by the King of Mercia were also on fire, including the ship of Lord Eastmund, the Mercian Kommandar. Eastman had been fortunate enough to be plucked from the ocean's grasp before he drowned or the hags got to him.

Britannius looked to the northeast and saw Beowulf and all his ships far ahead, departing for Land's End.

Britannius screamed his loudest: "I'm coming for you, Bear's Son! You hear me? I, Britannius, Prince of Kent, am coming to kill you!"

Britannius was not so far away that he couldn't see the tall figure at the stern of the Black Ship beckoning Britannius to follow.

Britannius screamed again; this time it was the rage that spewed from his throat. He grabbed hold of Eegan by the shoulders and shouted into Eegan's face, peppering his companion with spittle.

"Signal the other ships to form columns. We're going after them!"

"Yes, my Prince," said Eegan, his voice trembling. "But have you not looked west—behind us."

Britannius turned and looked west and saw the ships of Essex and Northumbria departing west by southwest toward Daneland.

Britannius could not contain the fury that erupted from his core.

"Cowards!" said Britannius. "You—Aelfstan! And you—Osweald! Cowards! Both of you!"

Eegan placed a comforting hand on Britannius's shoulder: "They're too far away, my Prince," said Eegan. "They cannot hear you."

Britannius spun around and backhanded his friend, confidante, and lover across the mouth, splitting Eegan's lower lip such that it bled.

In his Prince's eyes, Eegan saw unspeakable fury that blood and blood, alone, could pacify.

† † †

When Lord Baolin's ships reached Otters'Bay, the tide was low. Baolin ordered the captains of all fifteen ships to align themselves end to end, one behind the next, across the mouth of the bay in waist-deep water where they would rope themselves together creating a shield wall. Baolin then gave the order to furl sails, ship oars and drop anchors.

On the shore to greet them were over a hundred bowmen standing at the water's edge, cheering the arrival of Baolin and his Longships with no fewer than seven-hundred-and-fifty warriors aboard.

"Your orders, Lord Baolin?" said Sigurd, Baolin's Second-in-Command.

"Go ashore, Sigurd, tell whoever's in command that if the Angles and Saxons swallow the bait, we'll hold them enemy at bay if we can, before we retreat to shore. It's Beowulf's wish that we delay the Angles and Saxons from reaching the Fjord of Kuurin as long as we're able. Take some men, and bring back as much whale oil as you can."

"Is it your plan to set our ships on fire"" said Sigurd.

"If we must—yes!" said Baolin.

Beowulf and the Black Ship continued northwest toward Land's End but at a much slower pace than Lord Ulthur's twenty battle craft—that was the plan.

The bear's son could sense the Prince of Kent's fury and Beowulf wanted to tease him—to play with his mind the way a feral, tavern cat makes a tasty toy out of a much larger rat before biting through its neck, severing the main artery and draining it of its blood.

"You think to toy with me?" said Britannius, standing at the prow of his longship. He shouted across the water with as much force as his lungs could muster.

"That would be too easy," said Beowulf, allowing the wind to usher his words across the distance that separated the Black ship from Britannius's vessel.

"You are too soft, Prince Britannius. You are not worthy to fight me man to man," said Beowulf. "Besides—what kind of warrior takes his lover into battle with him?"

Britannius's face turned pale white, and his lips twitched. He turned to the men at the oars.

"Row faster, damn you! Faster!"

† † †

Artur, King of Jutland, was taken by surprise. So, too, was the Kommandar of the ships from Sussex, sailing behind the Jutes, when he saw the Geats had ceased their flight and had formed a shield wall across the entrance to a small bay.

Excited beyond measure, Artur turned to his Second-in-Command and shouted: "Now we have them! Signal all ships to attack! Attack! Attack! Attack!"

† † †

The Bowmen on the shore divided their number into two groups and took up positions on both sides of the cove. From there they could rain their arrows down upon any of the enemy attempting to flank Lord Baolin's shield wall by land.

The warriors on the ships cheered to see their tribesman put themselves into harm's way along the rocky shoreline.

† † †

It wasn't the Longships stretched across the entrance to the cove that posed the greatest tactical challenge to the Jutes and Saxons. The mouth leading into Otters'Bay would accommodate no more than twenty or twenty-five ships, at most. To assail the Geats' shield wall meant that three-score of the Jutes' battle craft and Kommandar Deorwine's fleet of eighty-seven ships would have to remain idle offshore; useless, that is, unless they dropped anchor along the coast and attacked the Geats by land.

There was no question in Kommandar Deorwine's mind; there was no glory remaining idle; he would order an attack by land. With over four thousand warriors aboard his eighty-seven ships, he knew the Geats would either flee or die along the shore.

† † †

The Jute King's ship spearheaded the attack on the Longships aligned against him.

At great risk to themselves, the bowmen on the shore let loose arrows set on fire at the sails of Artur' ships from as far away as sixty yards.

As some sails were struck and began to burn, Artus exhorted his captains to ram the Geats' shield wall with force sufficient to smash a way through.

From the shield wall, Lord Baolin's warriors traded arrows with their attackers, but still, the Jutes came on. In but a few moments King Artur's ships closed the distance and struck the Geats' shield wall.

As his warriors attempted to board the ships of their enemy, the Geat warriors met the men from Jutland with spears, battle-axes, and swords.

While the Jutes fought to break the Geats' shield wall, more Jute ships followed and formed columns, each battle craft tied to the one in front of it. That way, they created bridges by which reinforcements worked their way forward and joined the fray.

The Kommandar from Sussex, Deorwine, saw the opportunity to encircle the Geats by dividing his fleet. Half he ordered north of the cove, where his warriors could beach their ships and go ashore without fear of the bowmen on the north side of the entry into Otters'Bay. The other half of his fleet he would lead himself to a place just south of the cove and disembark. Deorwine knew it would not take long before his warriors surrounded the Geats.

As the dead began to pile up on the decks of the Geatlanders' ships, Lord Baolin gave the order to withdraw to the beach. As those Geats who remained alive leapt into the water and waded toward the shore, the bowmen on both sides of the entry into Otters'Bay shot fire arrows onto the Geats' ships. The decks were soaked with whale's oil and erupted into flames that spread from ship to ship until all fifteen battle craft became a wall of fire, setting scores of Jutes on fire and forcing others to fall back to their ships or leap into the water to keep from burning.

It wasn't long before the bowmen saw their enemies come ashore south and north of Otters'Bay. It was then that the bowmen left their dead behind and carried their wounded with them to where Lord Baolin was rallying his warriors on the beach. Baolin knew it would not be long before the inferno across the mouth of the Cove burned out and allowed the Jutes to come forward.

"Your orders, my Lord?" said Sigurd; himself cut and bleeding like all the Geats who defended the shield wall and survived to regroup ashore.

80

THE BAY OF SKANE

The Black Ship continued east, past Land's End. Beowulf looked over his shoulder: Britannius, Prince of Kent, was closest, accompanied by three-hundred and thirty battle worthy longships; however, the chaos wrought by the Skyfolk and the quick strike by Beowulf and the Spear-Danes had left almost two-thirds of the Prince of Kent's warriors exhausted and demoralized.

"Perhaps your men need time to rest and catch their breath," said Beowulf. He repeated over and over, loud enough so that Britannius and his warriors would hear the mockery in Beowulf's tone.

No matter how Britannius treated him, Eegan remained loyal to his Prince. Where many a man would sulk over being mistreated the way Britannius mistreated Eegan, it was not in Eegan's character to hold a grudge against the man he'd loved from the time they were boys.

"Shall we look for a place to put ashore and attack Land's End my Prince?" said Eegan.

"Not until I've got Beowulf's head in a box to take back to Kent," said Britannius.

"But we're over three-hundred ships to his one, my Prince. Perhaps it would be prudent to take only our ships with us, in pursuit of the bear's son; while the ships from Wessex and East Anglia search for somewhere suitable to disembark for the attack on Land's End."

"No!" said Britannius. "After seeing Osweald and Aelfstan turn and run for home, I won't have Dunstan and Cyneweard doing the same. No, Eegan. The fleet goes where I go—and I'm going after the bear's son, even if that means to the end of the Whale Road and back!"

Turin stood on the upraised deck where the Tillermen guided the Gold Ship and watched, as did everyone aboard, the two-hundred longships passing by in the near distance. The only sounds to be heard were the sounds of the Angles' and Saxons' oars dipping in-and-out of the water as their ships continued west by southwest.

"Listen to me—all of you!" said Wiglaf. You who were slaves, chained to the oars, are now free. You have the word of my king, Beowulf Waegmunding, on that. You have seen for yourselves Angles and Saxons quitting this fight. Now is the time to aid my king. We will attack the Angles and Saxons from behind. You who were once warriors of the Eastern Roman Emperor; you, too, are free men. Now that freedom must be secured. Oarsmen, return to your oars. You warriors who have pledged your loyalty to my king, prepare for battle!"

Thunderous cheering followed from the five-hundred men who crewed the Gold Ship.

† † †

The sound of men cheering aboard the Gold Ship stretched across the water to reach the Angles and Saxons departing for the west.

Aboard his ship, the Kommandar of the ships from Northumbria, Osweald, spit his contempt for Emperor Justinian and those aboard the Gold Ship.

Osweald leaned over the side of his ship and shouted with all his breath: "Tell your emperor he can shag himself, for he'll not be getting his ships back. They belong to the King of Northumbria now!"

Aboard his vessel, Kommandar Aelfstan of Essex also heard the sound of cheering from the Gold Ship. Disheartened by electing to withdraw from the battle and, upon hearing cheering from the Gold Ship as his ships passed by, Aelfstan looked at his feet and muttered "Bollocks!"

When the Black Ship sailed into the Bay of Skane Lord Ulthur and the Spear Danes were there—not with twenty battle craft as before, but with all forty of their longships. Many of the Spear-Danes aboard these ships were none other than the Järngardet, or "Iron Guard," who once served Prince Hrothmund's father, King Hrothgar, as his Body Guard. Ulthur had formed the ships close to the shoreline in a crescent shape that matched the contour of the bay.

Beowulf ordered the Black Ship turned around and positioned in the center of the crescent, less than thirty-yards ahead of the Spear-Danes and the shoreline.

Beowulf looked at Sigmund and smiled: "Just like old times—yes?"

Sigmund smiled: "Yes, my King—like times of old. Especially the waiting."

Beowulf laughed. "It won't be long. Britannius is out of his head with rage by now and right on my heels. Die well, my friend."

"Die well, my King."

† † †

At Otters'Bay Lord Baolin, his warriors and the bowmen were of one mind: they would stay and fight rather than retreat north toward Falcon's nest. Their King had asked them to give him as much time as they could, and if it meant their death doing so; then be it so.

The Thunder Geats numbered just under nine-hundred men and formed themselves into a three-sided shield wall, three men deep, with archers inner-most.

Preparing offshore to attack them were no fewer than six-thousand Angles and Jutlanders.

† † †

Prince Britannius could have danced out of sheer joy when he saw the Black Ship so close at hand and the small number of ships accompanying the bear's son.

"Give the order, Eegan," said Britannius. "Signal the attack!"
"All our ships, my Prince?"
Britannius glared at Eegan: "Yes, by Odin's all-seeing eye—do it!"

The signal was given to the ships closest in line and relayed to the battle craft furthest from the bay.

† † †

When no fewer than two-hundred Angle-Saxon ships entered the Bay of Skane, and Prince Britannius's battle craft was no further than fifty yards from the Black Ship, Beowulf looked at Sigmund and nodded.

From his belt, Sigmund removed a red pennant and hurried to the stern.

† † †

From the heights, five-hundred feet above the bay, Wiglaf could see everything taking place below. Beside him was Prince Hrothmund, Hrothgar's only living son and rightful heir to the throne of Daneland. Also there, watching, was Wealtheow, become rightful Queen of the Wylfings, and her daughter, Freawaru, made Queen of Frihamm.

"Look there, Wiglaf," said Hrothmund. "The signal!"

Wiglaf smiled. He also saw the red pennant waving in the wind from Sigmund's outstretched hand from where he stood near the Black Ship's tiller.

Wiglaf filled his lungs with air and shouted so all those on the heights surrounding the Bay of Skane would hear: "Now!" said Wiglaf. "Loose!"

From over two-hundred catapults, rocks that weighed as much as a man rained down on the Bay of Skane and the Angle-Saxon ships that were crowded together below.

† † †

Prince Britannius could not believe what he was witnessing: rocks the size of full-grown pigs raining on his fleet from the heights overlooking the bay.

The Prince of Kent looked side to side and behind him. It was the same no matter where he gazed—the catapults battered his fleet worse than any storm could do in as short time.

Britannius was about to tell Eegan to signal their ships to retreat when a rock tore Eegan apart as it passed over the deck and landed in the water taking Eegan's upper body with it.

Britannius stared at the lower half of Eagan's body in front of him, and the entrails splattered over the side of the ship.

† † †

The Jutes were first to reach the three-sided shield wall where the Geats led by Lord Baolin had resolved to make a final stand. No matter how many Jute warriors were brought down by the arrows of the Geats, more and more Jute warriors rushed the shield wall thirsty for blood and vengeance.

Fierce was the fighting taking place. The Geats fought with the desperation of men who realized they would die and it hardened them to kill as many of their foes as they might so that their courage would earn them a seat for all time in the Great Mead Hall of Valhalla in Asgard.

† † †

The warriors in charge of each of the Angle and Saxon longships; that is, of those battle craft that remained intact and afloat, sought a means to escape the bay and the crushing force of the rocks that pelted them without end from the heights above.

The Angles and Saxons still trapped inside the bay tried to turn about and make good their escape. As they did, ships collided with one another, further jamming the bay with so much crushed wood tangled with ropes and collapsed sails that any but the best of seamen would be hard-pressed to navigate around such wreckage and the Angle-Saxon warriors struggling in the water. Men drowned crushed beneath the hulls of escaping longships, for none dared stop long enough to pull survivors from the water.

Britannius had no sooner noticed the sky ceased raining rocks on the Bay of Skane when he saw the Black Ship coming straight for him.

Britannius's ship remained isolated in the forefront, but for the sinking Angle-Saxon ships beside and behind it.

"Ship oars," said Britannius to his warriors. "Prepare to be rammed!"

His warriors shipped-oars and took up their shields. To a man, they braced themselves to be rammed by the Black Ship. Behind and to the sides of the Black Ship, the forty battle craft of the Spear Danes were also now on the attack and did so with speed tempered by caution lest they also strike wreckage already choking the Bay.

† † †

The Jutes, reinforced by hundreds of Kommandar Deorwine's warriors who waded ashore north and south of Otters' Bay, had Baolin and his men surrounded on all three sides of the Geats' shield wall.

The Geats' ground was thick with bodies piled on each other—bodies of friend and foe alike. Knowing they, too, would die, Baolin and his men fought on with renewed fury.

Then, when lesser men would have fallen on their swords or dropped to their knees and begged for their lives, there came the sound of two-hundred rams' horn trumpeting offshore just north of the Bay.

It was Breca—King of the Sea Brondings and two hundred battle craft with ten-thousand Bronding warriors aboard!

† † †

No sooner had the Black Ship struck Britannius's flagship, the Kungen's Vakter threw grappling hooks aboard, binding the two battle craft together.

Britannius drew his sword: "To the front! All of you!"

As the warriors from Kent moved toward the front of their ship expecting scores of Geats to board, only one man appeared—

Beowulf, the bear's son.

Beowulf leapt from the prow of the Black Ship to the deck of Britannius's vessel. He carried his father's sword, Widow Maker, and Naegling, the Sword of Kings.

Britannius's men stumbled over one another in their haste to back away from the tall, broad-shouldered black-clad warrior they knew could only be Beowulf, King of the Geats.

When they could back up no further, Britannius shouted: "Wh are you retreating? You are fifty—he is one!"

Beowulf scanned the frightened faces of the warriors facing him:

"Those of you who want to live, throw down your weapons and jump overboard—now!"

Beowulf flicked his head first to his left, then to his right. To a man, Britannius's warriors dropped their weapons and jumped overboard leaving only Prince Britannius to face the bear's son.

Beowulf walked toward the stern where Britannius was standing. The Prince of Kent took a shield from the deck and strode toward Beowulf.

They met near the mast, Britannius struck first—two quick overhead blows. Beowulf blocked each, in turn, first using one blade, then the other.

Again Britanius swung his sword, this time side-to-side, but each time Beowulf parried. After blocking several more sword-thrusts Beowulf brought Widow Maker straight overhead, cleaving Britannius's shield in two.

Britannius tossed what remained of his shattered oak shield to the ground. Gripping his sword with two hands, he swung a mighty blow overhead. Beowulf blocked Britannius's blade inches away from his helm.

Naegling proved the better steel that day, for the Prince of Kent's sword broke in half. With the better part of his blade at his feet and the shard useless, Britannius tossed what remained of his weapon into the water.

"Will you accept my surrender?" said Prince Britannius, son of Octha, King of Kent.

"No," replied Beowulf.

That said, Beowulf brought the blades of both swords crosswise like shears. The head of the Prince of Kent landed at Beowulf's feet.

Beowulf stepped back as Britannius's headless body collapsed to its knees, blood spewing from the trunk as it fell forward, twitched several times; then remained still.

Including the Angle-Saxon ships that escaped from the Bay of Skane and the battle craft that had not yet entered, there were no more than a hundred and eighty seaworthy longships in total. They were all that remained of the Seven Kingdoms Battle Fleet except for the two-hundred ships from Northumbria and Essex that departed from the battle early on and were now taking on provisions and fresh water at the Danish port of Mörk Sand for the return journey home.

With the Prince of Kent dead, there was no one to take charge. The captains of the few ships from Kent that were left afloat, along with the Kommandars of the ships from Wessex and East Anglia, too the initiative and gave such orders intended to save their ships. Kommandar Eastmund leading the ships from Mercia died when three rocks struck his ship; one landed on top of his head. The other two rocks smashed holes through the wooden planks of the hull, sinking the ship.

The Angle and Saxon Captains made no attempt to regroup and attack the Bay; they had but one imperative--survive! With survival in mind, the Angles and Saxons turned their ships west for the Tin Isles.

Too late to make good their escape, the Angles and Saxons found the Gold Ship coming at them. With its iron, saw-toothed ram jutting out from below the waterline some twenty-feet, and rowed by free men who'd give their all to maintain their newfound freedom, the Gold Ship rammed the much smaller battle craft of the enemy. Sinking one ship after another, the warriors on the Main Deck of the Gold Ship loosed arrows by the hundreds, down on the Angle-Saxon warriors trying to row their ships to safety.

The possibility of escaping to someplace safe evaporated like mist beneath the midday sun when out of the east, came the Flagship of King Eadgils leading two-hundred Svear battle craft accompanied by forty Wylfing Longships—Queen Wealtheow's contribution to the defense of Götaland.

† † †

Ten days after the War of the Seven Kingdoms ended with the loss of five-hundred and eighty Angle, Saxon and Jute battle craft, the Geats placed the headless body of the former Prince of Kent into a wooden box filled with salt and smuggled Britannius's remains into the Tin Isles.

From the coast, the body was taken by spies in Beowulf's employ to the Kingdom of Kent.

Disguised as peasants, these spies transported the corpse by way of an ox cart piled high with straw. They unloaded the box in the middle of the night outside the Keep where Britannius's father, King Octha, sat on the throne.

The box was discovered at sunrise the following morning. When King Octha learned that the box contained the decaying remains of his oldest son, heir to the throne of Kent, minus his head, Octha retired to his chamber, grief-stricken.

King Octha died in his bed, three days later.

In addition to the combined loss of five-hundred-and-eighty-ships, just under twenty-nine thousand Saxons, Angles, and Jutes, in the fullness of manhood died.

Beowulf, King of Geatland, was in no mood to show mercy; nor was Breca, King of the Brondings, or Eadgils, King of Svearland.

Wealtheow, the Wylfing Queen, remained silent on the matter of taking prisoners; she knew it was a choice best deferred to the men who had done the fighting.

† † †

In Constantinople, Justinian, Emperor of the Eastern Roman Empire, felt obliged to listen; although in no mood to hear bad news.

"What have you learned?" said Justinian to his Spy Master, Haji Babba.

"The news from the North lands is dire, my Emperor," said Haji Babba.

"When has news from the north lands ever been pleasing since the time of Anastasius?" said the Emperor.

His Spy Master shrugged.

"Very well, Haji Babba," said Justinian, "get on with it. Let me hear the news, dire as you say it is."

"The Seven Kingdoms were defeated by a combined force of Geats, Wylfings, Svear and Sea Brondings. They annihilated our entire fleet, but for two-hundred ships that retreated, and returned to the Tin Isles."

"What of my Gold?"

"Lost, my Emperor, to the Thunder-Geats."

"Beowulf has my Gold Ship—is that what you're saying?"

"Actually, no, my Emperor. King Beowulf made a gift of the Gold Ship to Queen Wealtheow's daughter, Freawaru, now Queen of Frihamm.

"He, what?"

"It was a gift, my Emperor, on the occasion of Queen Freawaru's wedding to Eadgils, King of Svearland."

Justinian turned to the Captain of his Guard.

"Have we anyone in our dungeons, Captain?" Justinian said.

"Yes, my Emperor," said the Captain. "Our cages are nearly full."

"Empty them," said Justinian. "I want everyone released."

"Once we release the prisoners—what then, my Emperor?"

"Cut off their heads, of course."

81

FIRE & IRON

Upon returning from the wedding of King Eadgils to Freawaru, Queen of Frihamm, Beowulf traveled to Vindenstedt Farm to rest.

One night after supper, Beowulf, Wiglaf, Turin, and Robbyn sat together at the banquet table and drank ale in front of the hearth. For a while no one spoke; rather, they listened to the hissing and crackling of the logs and enjoyed the warmth of the fire.

Over time both Turin and Robbyn noticed a change in Beowulf. They sensed a darkness encroaching on their friend and king. Robbyn broke the silence:

"Remember, Beowulf, when I called you, Bright Eyes?"

Beowulf looked at Robbyn and smiled. "As if it was yesterday. And if I recall rightly, Turin called himself a 'tribe of one.'"

Wiglaf laughed. "Truly?"

"It's true," said Robbyn, "he did."

"I had to," said Turin, "or Robbyn would have shot me full of arrows."

"No," said Wiglaf.

"Yes," said Robbyn, "I would have."

Robbyn leaned close and kissed Turin.

"Tell us, Beowulf," said Wiglaf, "what you see ahead for Geatland—for our people?"

Beowulf thought about the question.

"When I'm dead, Geatland's enemies will come. The Franks, Frisians, Hetware, and others; they will all be eager for revenge and the chance to take our land and wealth. The Merovingian Kingdom is ascending; one day, they, too, will look in Geatland's direction. Beware Wiglaf, when the time comes you must assume the throne and act swiftly, Turin will advise you. Mobilize the clans, prepare for war. Seek the help of our old friends the Brondings, Harii, Wylfings, and Spear Danes. Together we bested our foes in the past. Perhaps, together, you can do so again."

Silence overtook them. Beowulf stared into the fire.

"I'm tired," said Beowulf. "I need to rest."

Turin, Robbyn, and Wiglaf stood and watched Beowulf trudge upstairs to his room, the one he and Elin once shared.

"He looks tired, more than I've ever seen him look," said Robbyn. Tears welled in her eyes, "and so alone."

Turin nodded: "You're right on both counts, sweet wife."

† † †

The following day, when it came time to celebrate spring's Eve, Beowulf gave thanks to the gods and invoked their blessing and protection. Now Chief of Clan Waegmunding, it was Wiglaf who spilled his blood on the ground as an offering to the All Mother.
After Turin and Wiglaf lit the bonfire the celebration and feasting commenced. It had become Beowulf's custom to go alone on foot to the forest. There at the hot spring near the waterfall, he spoke to the Forest Folk who came to visit. At those times he learned their concerns and did what he could to make their lives better; even more so during the rigors of winter when food was scarce. Vindinstedt Forest was a sanctuary for the Forest Folk. Beowulf would not have it otherwise.
The next day, accompanied by Wiglaf, Beowulf departed for Falcon's Nest. Robbyn and Turin had accustomed themselves to their king's dark moods long ago; that, and the brevity of his visits.

† † †

That autumn in northwest Geatland, Coast Guards intercepted a wayfarer clothed in rags. He was running for his life and clutching a silver cup to his chest. Seeing the rags the man wore and the magnificent chalice in his hands, the Border Guards judged him a thief. They bound the wretch, put him on a horse and rode toward Falcon's Nest.

† † †

Beowulf dismissed the sentries on duty that he might stand alone on the western wall-walk overlooking the harbor and the Fjord of Kuurin.

The gods have been good to me Beowulf told himself. *In my time I've seen distant places, bested monsters on land and sea and defeated entire armies. Even now no man in all Midgard would dare stand against me. Great kings and queens honor me; yet, it is with the Forest Folk I'm most at home.Now, so many of those I loved are gone, and so few remain.*

"*Those many you think are gone are with you still, Bear's Son. You have only to evoke their memory; then, listen, and you will hear their words no matter where you are. You will feel them spoken on the wind, as they caress your skin. You will hear them in the soft murmuring of autumn leaves scattered by breezes across the ground. And in the sound of waves, lapping on the shore. As I said, you've only to think of us, and we will hear you."*

The voice Beowulf heard was familiar and close:

"*Beorn? Is that you?*"

"*Yes, Bear's Son—it's me.*"

"*Where are you, Beorn?"*

"Here—beside you."

"Then why can't I see you, old friend?"

"There are worlds within worlds within worlds, Bear's Son; worlds that coexist; separated by only the thinnest of veils. It takes a way of seeing without using your eyes, and the ability to hear without listening, to move from one such world to the next. One day you will do as I am doing now."

"I have questions, Beorn; questions only you can answer."

"Yet, here you are, about to hurl yourself from the wall-walk and end your life—is that not so, Bear's Son?"

"I was considering it."

"I'll take that as a 'yes,'Bear's Son. Any death other than to die in battle would be most unbecoming for you, Beowulf, son of Liv and Ecgtheow, King of Geatland."

"I know, Beorn; but how am I to die in battle when I cannot be defeated?"

"My King?" said Wiglaf as he approached. "There's something you will want to see."

† † †

The Border Guards had turned the supposed thief over to the Kungens Vakter who then took the wretch to Wiglaf and delivered the chalice into his hands. When Beowulf entered the Throne Room, he saw the cup resting on the seat of his throne.

"Where did you come upon this?" Beowulf said to the thief.

"I found it in a cave north of here, Great King, where the River Tern empties into the Whale Road. I fell through the floor of a barrow into a cave. Through no fault of my own, I landed on a treasure trove."

The Chieftains in attendance laughed. Wiglaf silenced them with a look. The next moment there came the sound of rams' horns —sounding the alarm.

"Bring him," said Beowulf.

Wiglaf placed the chalice on Beowulf's throne; then grasped the thief by the arm and neck. They followed Beowulf out of the Throne Room to the eastern wall-walk overlooking the city. What their eyes beheld was not comprehensible—not at first glance.

A winged dragon, a Fired Drake twice the length of a Longship circled the Citadel. Wiglaf mustered every Bowman and the warriors of the King's Guard; they crowded the wall-walk with their weapons ready.

Beowulf turned to the thief: "What do you know about this—speak!"

"The worm was asleep within the cave, Great King," said the thief. "I awakened it while climbing over the treasure mound."

"You stole from a Barrow Worm?"

"I didn't think of it as stealing, Great King."

No sooner had the thief stopped talking, the dragon dove toward the Citadel and spat fire. Beowulf and Wiglaf crouched behind the wall. Flames passed over them but struck the thief. He screamed and fell burning from the wall-walk.

The arrows that found their target bounced off the dragon's bright green scales as it flew over the city spitting fire bolts. Several wooden lodges exploded in flames, and the ensuing fire spread to other structures. The terrified Geatfolk abandoned their homes and fled with all they could carry to the Citadel, and the relative safety its walls of stone afforded.

Beowulf looked on, helpless but to watch as the dragon

continued its rampage. Then, with half the city on fire, the dragon turned north and flew toward its barrow while laying waste to the countryside.

"We need to save what we can before the entire city burns," said Beowulf.

Wiglaf hurried away to mobilize the fire brigade. Long into the day and night the Geats fought fires and managed to save part of the city. The damage done to Falcon's Nest was extensive and left hundreds of men, women, and children homeless.

Beowulf stood for a long time on the wall-walk watching the conflagration before he left for the Armory. There, Beowulf gathered the blades of twenty swords and twenty axes.

"Melt these blades," said Beowulf to the Master Metalsmith in charge.

"Yes, my King," he said.

"Fashion a shield of iron as thick as your thumb is long," said Beowulf. "Make it my height and half-again the width of my shoulders. Give it an iron boss and a cutout on the right side sufficient to rest my spear. Pad the grip well with fleece and give the shield a padded ledge where I can rest my forearm."

"Yes, my King—We'll start at once!"

The metalsmith and his assistants worked throughout the remainder of the day and into the night fashioning that iron shield. When they finished the shield, it required the strength of four large men to carry it to the Throne Room where Beowulf and Wiglaf waited. Ten Clan Chiefs were also present—the grandsons of the chiefs Beorn imprisoned those many summers before when they were no more than boys in men's armor. These ten, including Baolin, who distinguished himself at Otters' Bay during the War of the Seven Kingdoms, stepped forward at the same time.

"We want to accompany you north, my King," said Baolin. "We will help you slay the worm."

Beowulf studied their faces: "Will you, now?" he said before turning his back.

Beowulf went to where the metalsmith waited. Beowulf took hold of the grip and lifted the shield off the floor. He tested it for balance and nodded his approval. Beowulf was indeed old, but his strength remained considerable:

"We leave at dawn," he said.

Storm Bringer had long passed. It was a stallion sired by one of Storm Bringer's many sons, whom Beowulf went to the stables to visit.

"*Hail, Wind Chaser*," said Beowulf. "*Tomorrow, we go north into battle.*"

"*I will not fail you, Bear's Son*."

† † †

That night, as he slept, Beowulf dreamed of Elin, just as he had every night since her passing. He no longer tried to hold her, for he knew it was a dream; still, it soothed his troubled mind to see Elin's eyes and smiling face.

At dawn, Beowulf, Wiglaf, and the ten Chieftains rode north from Falcon's Nest. As they left the Citadel and passed through the city, they looked at the charred ruins of what the dragon had wrought. Beowulf was keen for vengeance; it showed in his face, for his resolve to kill the beast had hardened there like the scar he bore from his first battle in the Valley of Shadows.

The riders stopped to rest their horses by a brook. While their horses grazed on sweet grass, Beowulf and the others broke fast. As they ate, they did so in silence; since no one knew what words to summon.

Finally, when they finished eating, Beowulf spoke:

"I don't expect any of you to face the worm—that's for me to do. Besides, your Linden shields will be no protection against its fire."

"Still, my King," said Baolin, "it is right we be at your side in the battle to come."

"You say that now," said Beowulf, "but mark my words, Lord Baolin—you'll think differently when the worm shows itself."

† † †

It was midday when Beowulf and the others reached the River Tern. They followed it west until they came to where the Tern's clear waters emptied into the sea. They saw the barrow about which the thief spoke. It was on high ground overlooking the ocean, and they saw the entrance to a cave. Vines had concealed the entrance for centuries, but the dragon had torn the vines away when, in its wrath, it exited from the barrow in pursuit of the thief.

"*Wait here, Wind Chaser,*" said Beowulf.

They had brought an extra horse to carry the iron shield. Beowulf went to the pack horse and lifted the shield from the horse's back.

"*You've borne a heavy weight for me, my friend; you have my thanks.*"

The horse neighed and went to join Wind Chaser.

Beowulf looked at Wiglaf and the ten.

"No need to follow until the worm shows itself."

Beowulf took hold of his spear and iron shield and waded into the river. The water reached his waist. For a fleeting moment, Beowulf's thoughts returned to the pool beneath the waterfall where he and Elin once swam and made love.

It didn't take him long to cross the Tern. When he reached the other side, he looked at the others on the far bank. When Beowulf raised his spear high, Wiglaf and the ten saluted their king.

"Die well!" they said as one voice.

Beowulf walked to within fifty paces of the entrance to the cave and rested his shield on the ground.

"Great Worm—I'm here to do battle with you! Come and face me. It is I, Beowulf, the bear's son, King of the Thunder-Geats, who invites you to fight!"

† † †

Deep within the cavern beneath the barrow, the Fire Drake raised the thick eyelids of its bulbous eyes lifted, revealing a cold, centuries' old malice therein.

Who is this Manling—this Beowulf the bear's son who beckons me away from this place; this place where I've slept a thousand winters and more? Did the Manlings not learn from my wrath? Must I revisit them and leave none alive? Does this upstart not know it is Xanadaeth, the Destroyer, who guards this treasure hoard? Xanadaeth, begotten by Nunniad, the Man Slayer, begotten by Quimma, of the Eternal Fire, born of Zeipoa, the Victorious, born of Baytialth, the Dark One, begotten by Zizzad, Lord of Fire, born to Unolth, Fate Bringer and Froarunder, Destroyer of Men. Winters beyond reckoning have I guarded the wealth of old Troy, the city of Priam, far across the Whale Road. I brought low the Thracians who came to this land of my ancestors and took their wealth. The thief who awakened me is dead, as are many of those who gave him sanctuary, and their city is in ruins, for great is my wrath. Now there is one who dares to face me in the open. What puny, stupid creatures these Manlings are.

"Hear me, Beowulf the bear's son, for it is I, Xanadaeth, the Destroyer you've awakened. I am coming for you Manling. Prepare to die a slow, painful death."

"Come!" said Beowulf. *"Come you lazy worm. I am tired of waiting for the clumsy beast that you are!"*

† † †

From deep within the cave came a fierce roar. The earth trembled with each ponderous step the dragon took on its way outside. Terrible in aspect, the dragon's scaled body filled the mouth of the cave.

When the creature emerged, it stopped and stretched its wings wide to the sides. Xanadaeth moved on four fat legs; its tail thick with cartilage. From its head down its spine was a row of ivory spikes. Red with rage, the dragon's bulbous eyes fixed on Beowulf; then it roared and spat fire at Geatland's King.

Beowulf stood behind his shield. It deflected the flames over and around him. He poised his spear on the cutout of the shield and strode forward.

The dragon spewed more bolts of flame, but did no harm; except Beowulf could feel the iron getting warm against his arm. When the dragon rose on its back legs, Beowulf hurled Death Stalker with all his might. The spear pierced deep into the dragon's side.

For the first time in a thousand winters, Xanadaeth felt pain. The monster lurched and spat fire. This time Beowulf greeted it with Naegling, the Sword of Kings.

Across the river, Beowulf's thanes sat upon their horses and watched—all of them unable to voice to their fear.

"My Lords," said Wiglaf; "I can't wait here; not while our

king's in peril. I beg you—ride with me to his aid."

"Beowulf told us the choice was ours," said Baolin, "and I, for one, won't disobey my king."

"Nor I," said another.

Wiglaf looked each of the ten in the face. To a man, they averted their eyes.

"Then live with your shame," said Wiglaf.

Wiglaf charged toward the river. At the last moment, he stopped. Paralyzed with fear, he turned his horse around and started back toward the others: *Why* he asked himself. *Are you so afraid to die, that you will not aid your kinsman and king*?

Wiglaf urged his horse a second time toward the river, and again he stopped. *My King is alone and no match for the beast. Why, Wiglaf? Why do you hesitate? Are you not the son of Weohstan Waegmunding?*

Wiglaf shouted his battle cry a third time and this time crossed the Tern with his spear poised to hurl. When he was in striking distance, he gripped the shaft and threw it with all his strength. It passed over Beowulf and struck the dragon on the forehead. That best of iron spikes bounced off the creature and landed on the ground at Beowulf's feet.

Beowulf turned and saw his cousin approach.

"Go back!" said Beowulf; "Go back!"

Enraged, Xanadaeth spat a jet of flame at Wiglaf, which sent that brave warrior from his saddle to the ground with his shield on fire. Scorched and maddened with fear, Wiglaf's horse raced back to the river. Wiglaf threw his shield to the ground and hastened toward Beowulf. Beowulf stepped backward to close the distance between them.

"Get behind me," he said.

Wiglaf drew his sword and stepped behind Beowulf while flames engulfed them both.

Every time the dragon lunged, Beowulf struck with Naegling. No longer warm, the iron shield became hot and Beowulf's arm tired from the weight it bore. He rested the shield on the ground and sank to his knees. A great weariness, far more than fatigue, revealed itself in Beowulf's eyes.

"Our best chance is to move closer," said Beowulf, "and get under it."

"I'm with you, my King."

Lifting his shield Beowulf stood and advanced. Xanadaeth lurched forward. This time it got its mouth around the top of Beowulf's shield. To Beowulf's great surprise, the worm wrested that iron shield from Beowulf's grip and lifted the shield high into the air.

"Now, Wiglaf—now!" said Beowulf.

They rushed forward and plunged their swords again and again into the dragon's chest.

The dragon spat the shield from its mouth. It roared and seized Beowulf between its jaws and bit down. Foot-long fangs pierced Beowulf's best armor, front, and back.

Beowulf screamed as the worm's poison-laden teeth tore into his body searing flesh, tearing cartilage, and crushing bone. The dragon lifted Beowulf high into the air and shook him side-to-side in the same way a Sabre Cat would a rabbit.

Wiglaf stepped forward and drove his sword up to the hilt in the dragon's chest, piercing its heart. Xanadaeth released Beowulf and bellowed. Before its legs buckled, the Fire Drake spewed the last bolt of flame skyward.

Beowulf landed on his back; blood bubbled from his many wounds. Wiglaf knelt beside his broken, bloodied king. He removed Beowulf's helm. Beowulf opened his eyes and smiled.

"You did well, son of Weohstan. You killed it."

"No, my King. It was the two of us who sent the worm to Helheim."

Seeing the severity of Beowulf's wounds a chill settled on Wiglaf's heart; his eyes began to moisten.

"I'm thirsty, Wiglaf. Bring me water from the Tern."

"Yes, my King."

Wiglaf wiped his eyes dry with the back of his wrist and hurried away.

Summoning all his strength, Beowulf got to his feet and staggered toward the entrance to the cave. Once there, an eerie blue light showed him the way forward through the darkness.

The ten Chieftains crossed the stream and went to where Wiglaf was filling Beowulf's helm with water. There was no mistaking the look of disdain on Wiglaf's face when he set eyes on them.

"Don't rebuke us with that look," said Baolin. "We, too, love our king, and came here freely."

Wiglaf looked at them a moment: "Is that what you want me to tell our King—that you came with him 'freely'?"

Ashamed, the ten looked away.

When Wiglaf returned to where he left Beowulf, he found him gone.

† † †

Beowulf came to where the tunnel emptied into a vast cavern. There, Beowulf saw mounds of gold, silver and precious gems; which, even in the dim light of the cavern, sparkled. Beowulf lurched toward a pile of treasure and collapsed on his back. Propped by gold and silver, Beowulf looked around. Was then he saw Death step toward him from the shadows.

"I've been waiting for you, Bear's Son."

"I knew I'd find you here," said Beowulf. Blood trickled past his lips.

"Then you know why I've come."

"Yes," said Beowulf.

He could feel the life force ebbing from his torn, bloodied body,

"There will never be another like you, Bear's Son—you are the last."

"The last?" said Beowulf, not understanding.

"Yes," said Death, "like the Fire Drake outside, and Grendel and his Dam in Daneland, and like the trolls you killed in Finn's Land —you were all bigger than life, the last of your kind. Now, Midgard belongs to humankind, alone, thanks to you. Our work together is finished, Bear's Son."

† † †

"Beowulf!" said Wiglaf.

He saw Beowulf on a mound of treasure and rushed to his side. Wiglaf cradled Beowulf's head and gave him water.

"Did you see him?" said Beowulf.

Wiglaf looked side-to-side but saw nothing apart from the treasure trove.

"Who, my King? I see no one here but us."
"No matter," said Beowulf.
Beowulf smiled at Wiglaf and drew a final breath.
"Die well."
"Die well, my King."
As Beowulf's eyes began to close, Elin appeared above him. She smiled and held out her hand:
"*Come, my love.*"

† † †

Wiglaf took Beowulf's body to Falcon's Nest, to a place outside the city that overlooked the Whale Road. There, the Geatfolk built a pyre using wood gathered from Vindinstedt Forest. After Robbyn had washed Beowulf's wounds, with Turin's assistance, Wiglaf placed his king's body on a stretcher. Together, they lifted it on top of the pyre.

At sunset, Wiglaf set the wood ablaze and stepped back. A cloud of smoke billowed high into the sky while the King's Guard walked their horses in a circle, around the pyre. They did this to keep the heartbroken Geatfolk away from the flames and out of danger. Throughout the night, Robbyn and the women sang a lament; while Wiglaf, Turin and the Thunder-Geats beat upon their shields and lifted their spears in a final salute to their king.

The Geatfolk kept vigil long into the night until the flames did their work and darkness began to wane with the coming dawn.

† † †

At sunrise, Wiglaf saddled Wind Chaser. He filled a leather pouch with some of Beowulf's cremains. The rest the Geatfolk consigned to a barrow on a cliff that overlooked the Whale Road. That done, Wiglaf rode alone to Vindinstedt Forest. He knew the perfect place to cast the ashes—at a hot spring near a waterfall.

The End

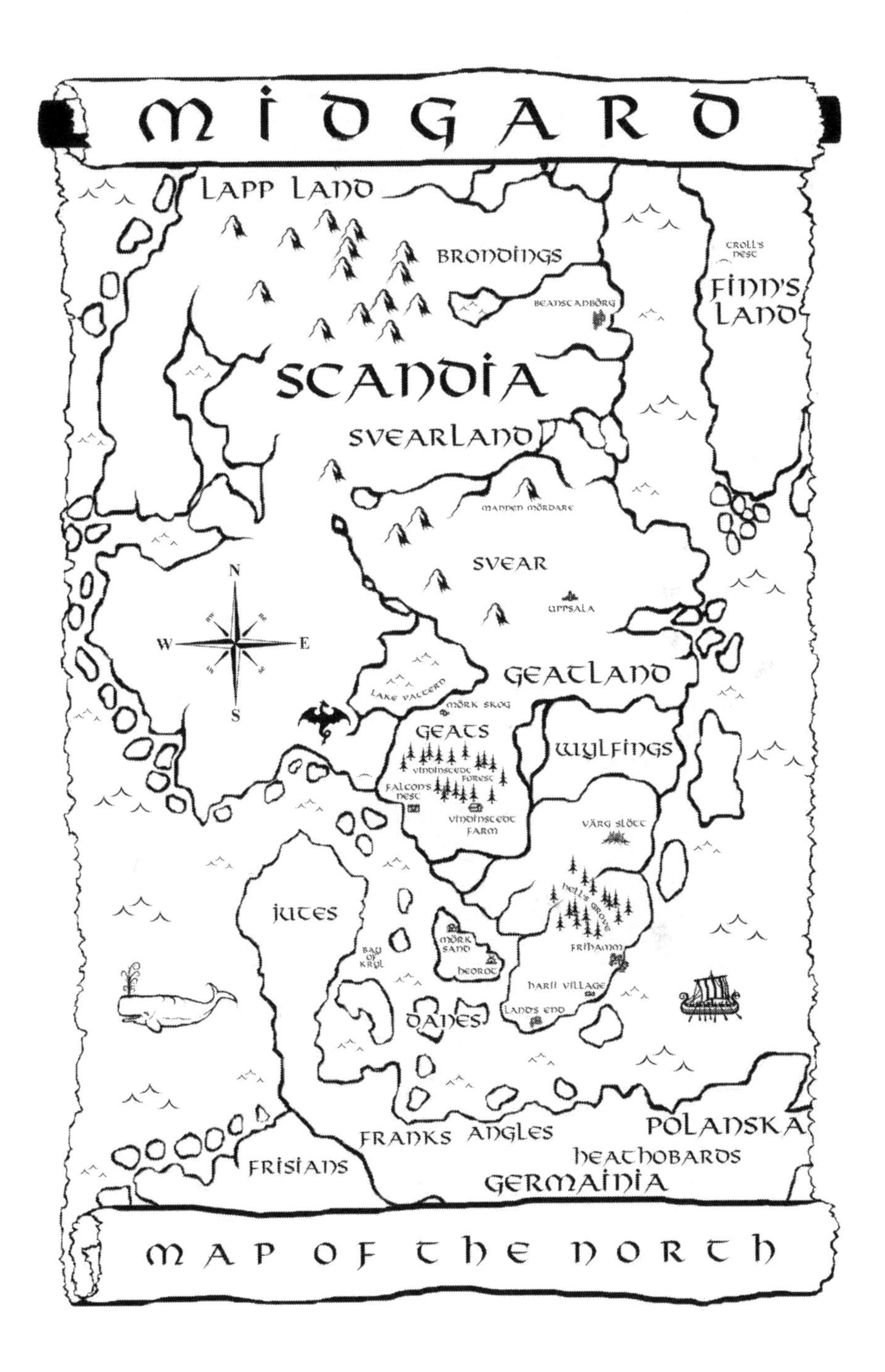
MIDGARD
LAPP LAND
BRONDINGS
TROLL'S NEST
FINN'S LAND
BEANSTANBÖRG
SCANDIA
SVEARLAND
MANNEN MÖRDARE
SVEAR
UPPSALA
N
W
E
S
GEATLAND
LAKE VATTERN
MÖRK SKOG
GEATS
WYLFINGS
VINDINSTEDT FOREST
FALCON'S NEST
VINDINSTEDT FARM
VÄRG SLÖTT
HELL'S GROVE
JUTES
BAY OF KRYL
MÖRK SAND
HEOROT
FRIHAMN
HARN VILLAGE
LANDS END
DANES
POLANSKA
FRANKS
ANGLES
HEATHOBARDS
FRISIANS
GERMAINIA
MAP OF THE NORTH

A Glossary of Names

Adalfuns (Adal-funs): Wylfing King Amunwolf's first-born son and Kommandar of his fleet of Longships.

Adalwolf (A-dal-wolf): Wolf pack leader of the Grey Brethren.

Aeschere (Es-sheer): Trusted friend and adviser to Hrothgar, King of the Spear Danes.

All Mother: Earth, the giver of life including Nature, the All Mother's handmaiden.

Amunwolf (Ah-mun-wolf): King of the Wylfing tribe. Father of Adalfuns and Wealtheow.

Andé Herré: Swedish for Spiritual Healer and-or a Schaman.

Artur (R-tur): King of Jutes who joins the Angles and Saxons to attack Götaland.

Baolin (Bay-o-lin): A Geat Clan Chief who distinguished himself during the War of the Seven Kingdoms.

Beanstan (Bane-stan): King of the Sea Brondings, and father of Prince Breca.

Berenson (Bare-n-son): Kommandar of Hrothgar's fleet of Longships.

Beowulf (Bay-o-wulf): Son of Ecgtheow and Liv of Clan Waegmunding.

Borg: A Svear Clan Chief and King Onela's Battle Lord.

Breca (Breh-cah): Son of King Beanstan. Later King of the Sea Brondings.

Britannius: Son of the King of Kent, Britannius leads an attack on Götaland in the War of the Seven Kingdoms.

Brondings (Brawn-dings): The ruling tribe in Norwegan (Norway).

Citadel: The stone fortress and seat of power for the kings of the Storm Geats.

Day Raven: Battle Lord and king of the Frisians.

Death Stalker: The name of Beowulf's spear.

Dolph (Rhymes with golf): Wylfing brother of Robbyn and Yanus' twin.

Eadgils (Aid-gills): Younger brother of Eanmund, a Prince of Svearland.

Eanmund (Ee-n-mund): Svear King Othere's first-born son. Onela's nephew and rival.

Ecgtheow (Edge-thee-ow) Waegmunding: Liv's husband, Beowulf's father and Chief of Clan Waegmunding.

Einer (Ee-ner): Bother to Ecgtheow Waegmunding.

Elifr (El-ee-fur): Brother to Ecgtheow Waegmunding.

Elin (Ee-linn): Bronding niece of King Beanstan, and Prince Breca's cousin.

Falcon's Nest: The Capital of the Storm Geats.

Frigga (Frig-guh): Far-sighted Warrior-Goddess of magic and wisdom. Odin's wife.

Frihamm (Free-Ham): Free Port for trade, ruled over by Modryth, the Dark Queen.

Frisia (Free-zee-uh): A land across the Whale Road, south of Götaland.

Geats (Gates): Beowulf's tribe in Väster (western) Geatland (Southern Sweden).

Germanicus (Ger-man-ee-cuss): Captain of Queen Modryth's Bodyguard.

Grendel (Gren-dell): A powerful flesh-eating creature from the Abyss.

Grendel's Dam: Grendel's mother. Come from their subterranean world to Midgard.

Freawaru (Free-uh-war-ooh): Daughter of King Hrothgar and Queen Wealtheow.

Frigga: (Frig-guh): Wife of Odin and warrior-goddess of magic, Wisdom, and Far-sightedness.

Freya: Goddess of beauty, love, and fertility.

Frihamm (Free-ham): Port-O-Call for trade and commerce and Modryth's Queendom.
Haethcyn (Hayth-sin): King Hrethel's second-born son.

Hag: Swedish for "shark."

Handscio (Hand-c-o): Beowulf's cousin and childhood friend.

Haraldr (Har-all-door): Chief of the Harii. Father of Éydis.

Harii (Harr-ee): A tribe from Germania who became smugglers in Götaland.

Hathus (Hath-us): An Ostrogoth bounty hunter and assassin.

Heardred (Heard-red): Hygelac's first-born son.

Heatholaf (Hee-tho-laff): Wylfing Prince, and bastard son of the Iron Wolf.

Hel (Hell): Loki's daughter, Judge of the Dead and Queen of the Underworld.

Helheim (Hell-hyme): One of the Nine Worlds where the souls of the dead travel to for judgment.

Heorot (Hare-ought): The gold-gilded Capital (Hall) of Hrothgar, King of the Danes.

Herebeald (Here-be-ald): King Hrethel's first-born son.

Hrethel (Ree-thull): King of the Storm Geats.

Hrothmund (Ree-thrick): Oldest son of King Hrothgar and Queen Wealtheow.

Hrothmund (Rowth-mund): Youngest son of King Hrothgar and Queen Wealtheow.

Hrothulf (Rowth-ulf): Hrothgar's nephew, son of Hrothgar's older brother Herogar.

Hygd (Hi-gud): Hygelac's wife, later his Queen.

Hygelac (Hi-geh-lack): King Hrethel's youngest son.

Ingvar (Ing-varr): A slave trading bandit and self-proclaimed King of the North.

Järngardet (Jarn-gar-dett) The Iron Guard, Body Guard to the House of Hrothgar.
knarr (Kuh-narr): Smaller, slower and wider than Longships. Because of their sturdiness, knarrs hauled cargo across the Whale Road.

Knut "Iron Jaw" Eriksson (Kuh-noot): Chief of the Clan Eriksson.

Kungens Vakter: Handpicked warriors serving as bodyguards to the Geat King(s).

Land's End: A Port-O-Call for trade & commerce, at the southern tip of Geatland.

Liv (leave): King Hrethel's only daughter. Married Ecgtheow Waegmunding.

Loki (Low-key): Hel's father. A god and shape-shifter, also known as Loki, The Deceiver, Mischief Maker.

Lüma (Loom-uh): A she bear who adopts Beowulf as a child.

Mikla (Mick-la): Son of Trygve who became King Hygelac's Chief of Coastguards at Land's End.

Modryth (Moh-drith): Amunwolf's consort, Queen of Frihamm and mother of Prince Heatholaf.

Naegling (Nay-gling): The "Sword of Kings" held, in turn, by kings of the Storm Geats.

Odin (O-dinn): The All Father and One-eyed Chief of the Gods of Asgard.

Ondska (Owned-ska)

Onela (Own-e-la): the Usurper. Brother of Othere, once King of Svearland.

Ragmund (Rag-mund): King Hrethel's adviser in matters of commerce and diplomacy.

Rain Dancer: Ecgtheow's stallion and war horse.

Robbyn (Rob-in): A Wylfing woman-warrior.

Sanning: (Also known as Truth) The name of Beorn's legendary, dual-bladed, battle-axe.

Seven Kingdoms: Seven Angle-Saxon kingdoms in the Tin Isles: Kent, Essex, Sussex, Mercia, Northumbria, East Anglia and Wessex.

Storm Bringer: Beowulf's first stallion and war horse.

Svear (Svere): The largest, most powerful tribe in Scandia.

Sveargaard: The vaunted, one-hundred warrior bodyguard to the Svear King.

Swamp Dog: A dog of enormous proportion bred to hunt and kill men.

Tand: (Tooth) The name Beowulf gave his knife.

Thor: God of war, Hammer Bearer, and lightning-bringer.

Trolloggs (Trawl-logs): Giant, one-eyed creatures Beowulf encounters in Finn's Land.

Trygve (Tryg-vay): Chief of Coast Guards at Land's End. Father of Mikla.

Turin: One of Ecgtheow's adopted sons, and Beowulf's foster-brother.

Unferth (Un-furth): One of King Hrothgar's trusted advisers and spies.

Uppsala (Oop-sall-ah): The Capital of Svearland and King's seat of power.

Ulthur (Ool-thur): Hrothgar's ambassador-at-large and spy.

Val: Swedish for a whale.

Värg Slött (Varg-sloat): The Capital and fortress stronghold of the Wylfing Kings.

Valhalla (Val-Hal-la): The Mead Hall where courageous warriors who died in battle are allowed to remain.

Vit Haj: Swedish for White Shark.

Waegmunding (Vag-mund-ing): The most powerful clan in Western Geatland.

Wealtheow (Veel-thee-ow): Daughter of the Iron Wolf. Later became the wife of King Hrothgar.

Weohstan (Vay-o-stan): Handscio's father and a cousin to Ecgtheow & Beowulf.

Whale Road: The sea.

Widow Maker: The name of Ecgtheow Waegmunding's sword.

Wiglaf (Vig-laff): Weohstan Waegmunding's second-born son.

Wylfings (Villf-ings): A powerful tribe occupying Öster Geatland.

Xanadaeth, the Destroyer (Zan-a-death): The dragon Beowulf fights late in life.

Yanus (Yann-us): Wylfing brother of Robbyn, and Dolph's twin.

Ydrasil (Ee-draw-sill): The Great Tree that binds the Nine Worlds to the Cosmos.

Yngvarr (Yung-varr): King Amunwolf's Battle-Lord.

BIBLIOGRAPHY

Anthonio Ackkermans, *Wilderness Survival* (wildernesssurvival.com)
Rob Bicevskis, *Wilderness Survival* (ibid.)
Bing Images, *Map of Ancient Sweden* (Internet)
Allen "Bow" Beauchamp, *Wilderness Survival.*
Richard Hall, *The World of the Vikings* (New York, 2007)
Seamus Heaney, *Beowulf* (Faber & Faber 1999)
Mark Hicks, *How to Make a Homemade (and deadly) bow* (Field & Stream Magazine)
Lisa Mercer, *Viking Celebrations in Sweden* (Article: Demand Media)
Mary MacGregor, *Stories of the Vikings* (The Baldwin Project)
Peter Moc, *Wilderness Survival.*
Viking Answer Lady, *VikingAnswerLady.com*
Wikipedia, *Norse Mythology*
Wikipedia, *Sword Making*

ABOUT THE AUTHOR

The progeny of a young Irish dancer from County Clare and an American Naval Commander—Poet, novelist, and recovering lawyer, Jon Christopher lives on the road with his fur children, Misty &Bay.

Made in the USA
Lexington, KY
14 November 2019